Sandra Belloni by George Meredith

Originally published as **EMILIA IN ENGLAND**

George Meredith, OM, was born in Portsmouth, England on February 12th, 1828, a son and grandson of naval outfitters. His mother died when he was only five.

As a fourteen year old teenager he was sent to a Moravian School in Neuwied, Germany, staying there for two years.

After reading law he was articled as a solicitor, but quickly abandoned that career path for journalism and poetry. He collaborated with Edward Gryffydh Peacock, son of Thomas Love Peacock in publishing a privately circulated literary magazine, the Monthly Observer.

At age twenty-one he married Mary Ellen Nicolls, Edward Peacock's beautiful widowed sister, and mother of a child, on August 8th, 1849. Mary Ellen was twenty-eight. The marriage produced one child; Arthur (1853–1890).

Meredith collected his early writings, all previously published in periodicals, in an 1851 volume, Poems.

In 1856 he posed as the model for The Death of Chatterton, a well-known picture by the English Pre-Raphaelite painter Henry Wallis, which romantised the teenage Chatterton's demise.

Although Meredith received some publicity for this his wife received rather more attention from Wallis because of it. Mary Ellen ran off with Wallis in 1858, shortly before giving birth to a child that all assumed to be Wallis. Tragically she died three years later.

From that dreadful experience emerged a collection of sonnets entitled Modern Love in 1862 together with much of his first major novel; The Ordeal of Richard Feverel.

Meredith married Marie Vulliamy on September 20th, 1864 and they settled in Surrey. Together they had two children; William (born in 1865) and Mariette (born in 1874).

He continued writing novels and poetry, often inspired by nature. He had a keen understanding of comedy and his Essay on Comedy (1877) remains a reference work in the history of comic theory.

In The Egoist, published in 1879, he applies some of his theories of comedy in one of his most thoughtful and enduring novels.

During most of his career, he had difficulty crossing over from critical acclamation to popular success. It was only in 1885 that his first genuine commercial success appeared; Diana of the Crossways.

An artist's life throughout the ages, when not subsidised by a patron, is often difficult. Meredith found it no different. With an unreliable income stream he sought to bolster that with a job as a publisher's reader.

The company that gave him this lifeline was Chapman & Hall (an eminent publishing house who could include Charles Dickens, William Makepeace Thackeray, Elizabeth Barrett Browning and Anthony Trollope on their roster). His advice to the company was very well received and made him influential in the world of letters.

To this influence he was able to add a circle of friends that included William and Dante Gabriel Rossetti, Algernon Charles Swinburne, Cotter Morison, Leslie Stephen, Robert Louis Stevenson, George Gissing and J. M. Barrie.

In 1868 Meredith was introduced to Thomas Hardy. Hardy had submitted his first novel, The Poor Man and the Lady. Meredith felt the book was too bitter a satire on the rich and told Hardy to put it aside as it was likely it would be savaged by reviewers and destroy his nascent career. Meredith had received the same reaction with The Ordeal of Richard Feverel. Although it had brought him success it was judged so shocking that Mudie's circulating library cancelled an order of 300 copies.

But these years, creatively, were very prolific and successful for Meredith. Novels and poems flowed from his pen including everything from The Adventures of Harry Richmond to Diana of the Crossways and many poetry volumes include The Lark Ascending (which later inspired the Vaughan Williams music)

In 1886, tragedy struck the Meredith household when his second wife, Marie Vulliamy, died of cancer.

Whilst his personal life was producing horrendous scars he was receiving many accolades. Oscar Wilde was a fan. In The Decay of Lying, (originally published in the January 1889 issue of The Nineteenth Century) he says of Meredith "Ah, Meredith! Who can define him? His style is chaos illumined by flashes of lightning".

In 1891 Meredith was even the subject of homage when Sir Arthur Conan Doyle in his Sherlock Holmes short story The Boscombe Valley Mystery, (published in the popular Strand magazine) when Sherlock Holmes turns to Watson during case discussions and says "And now let us talk about George Meredith, if you please, and we shall leave all minor matters until tomorrow."

Before his death, Meredith was honoured from many quarters: he succeeded Lord Tennyson as president of the Society of Authors; in 1905 he was appointed to the Order of Merit by King Edward VII.

George Meredith, aged 81, died at his home in Box Hill, Surrey on May 18th, 1909. He is buried in the cemetery at Dorking, Surrey.

Index of contents

CHAPTER I

THE POLES PRELUDE

We are to make acquaintance with some serious damsels, as this English generation knows them, and at a season verging upon May. The ladies of Brookfield, Arabella, Cornelia, and Adela Pole, daughters of a flourishing City-of-London merchant, had been told of a singular thing: that in the neighbouring fir-wood a voice was to be heard by night, so wonderfully sweet and richly toned, that it required their strong sense to correct strange imaginings concerning it. Adela was herself the chief witness to its unearthly sweetness, and her testimony was confirmed by Edward Buxley, whose ear had likewise taken in the notes, though not on the same night, as the pair publicly proved by dates. Both declared that the voice belonged to an opera-singer or a spirit. The ladies of Brookfield, declining the alternative, perceived that this was a surprise furnished for their amusement by the latest celebrity of their circle, Mr. Pericles, their father's business ally and fellow-speculator; Mr. Pericles, the Greek, the man who held millions of money as dust compared to a human voice. Fortified by this exquisite supposition, their strong sense at once dismissed with scorn the idea of anything unearthly, however divine, being heard at night, in the nineteenth century, within sixteen miles of London City. They agreed that Mr. Pericles had hired some charming cantatrice to draw them into the woods and delightfully bewilder them. It was to be expected of his princely nature, they said. The Tinleys, of Bloxholme, worshipped him for his wealth; the ladies of Brookfield assured their friends that the fact of his being a money-maker was redeemed in their sight by his devotion to music. Music was now the Art in the ascendant at Brookfield. The ladies (for it is as well to know at once that they were not of that poor order of women who yield their admiration to a thing for its abstract virtue only)—the ladies were scaling society by the help of the Arts. To this laudable end sacrifices were now made to Euterpe to assist them. As mere daughters of a merchant, they were compelled to make their house not simply attractive, but enticing; and, seeing that they liked music, it seemed a very agreeable device. The Tinleys of Bloxholme still kept to dancing, and had effectually driven away Mr. Pericles from their gatherings. For Mr. Pericles said: "If that they will go 'so,' I will be amused." He presented a top-like triangular appearance for one staggering second. The Tinleys did not go 'so' at all, and consequently they lost the satirical man, and were called 'the ballet-dancers' by Adela which thorny scoff her sisters permitted to pass about for a single day, and no more. The Tinleys were their match at epithets, and any low contention of this kind obscured for them the social summit they hoped to attain; the dream whereof was their prime nourishment.

That the Tinleys really were their match, they acknowledged, upon the admission of the despicable nature of the game. The Tinleys had winged a dreadful shaft at them; not in itself to be dreaded, but that it struck a weak point; it was a common shot that exploded a magazine; and for a time it quite upset their social policy, causing them to act like simple young ladies who feel things and resent them. The ladies of Brookfield had let it be known that, in their privacy together, they were Pole, Polar, and North Pole. Pole, Polar, and North Pole were designations of the three shades of distance which they could convey in a bow: a form of salute they cherished as peculiarly their own; being a method they had invented to rebuke the intrusiveness of the outer world, and hold away all strangers until approved worthy. Even friends had occasionally to submit to it in a softened form. Arabella, the eldest, and Adela, the youngest, alternated Pole and Polar; but North Pole was shared by Cornelia with none. She was the fairest of the three; a nobly-built person; her eyes not vacant of tenderness when she put off her armour. In her war-panoply before unhappy strangers, she was a Britomart. They bowed to an iceberg, which replied to them with the freezing indifference of the floating colossus, when the Winter sun despatches a feeble greeting messenger-beam from his miserable Arctic wallet. The simile must be accepted in its might, for no lesser one will express the scornfulness toward men displayed by this strikingly well-favoured, formal lady, whose heart of hearts demanded for her as spouse, a lord, a philosopher, and a Christian, in one: and he must be a member of Parliament. Hence her isolated air.

Now, when the ladies of Brookfield heard that their Pole, Polar, and North Pole, the splendid image of themselves, had been transformed by the Tinleys, and defiled by them to Pole, Polony, and Maypole, they should have laughed contemptuously; but the terrible nerve of ridicule quivered in witness against them, and was not to be stilled. They could not understand why so coarse a thing should affect them. It stuck in their flesh. It gave them the idea that they saw their features hideous, but real, in a magnifying mirror.

There was therefore a feud between the Tinleys and the Poles; and when Mr. Pericles entirely gave up the former, the latter rewarded him by spreading abroad every possible kind interpretation of his atrocious bad manners. He was a Greek, of Parisian gilding, whose Parisian hat flew off at a moment's notice, and whose savage snarl was heard at the slightest vexation. His talk of renowned prime-donne by their Christian names, and the way that he would catalogue emperors, statesmen, and noblemen known to him, with familiar indifference, as things below the musical Art, gave a distinguishing tone to Brookfield, from which his French accentuation of our tongue did not detract.

Mr. Pericles grimaced bitterly at any claim to excellence being set up for the mysterious voice in the woods. Tapping one forefinger on the uplifted point of the other, he observed that to sing abroad in the night air of an English Spring month was conclusive of imbecility; and that no imbecile sang at all. Because, to sing, involved the highest accomplishment of which the human spirit could boast. Did the ladies see? he asked. They thought they saw that he carried on a deception admirably. In return, they inquired whether he would come with them and hunt the voice, saying that they would catch it for him. "I shall catch a cold for myself," said Mr. Pericles, from the elevation of a shrug, feeling that he was doomed to go forth. He acted reluctance so well that the ladies affected a pretty imperiousness; and when at last he consented to join the party, they thanked him with a nicely simulated warmth, believing that they had pleased him thoroughly.

Their brother Wilfrid was at Brookfield. Six months earlier he had returned from India, an invalided cornet of light cavalry, with a reputation for military dash and the prospect of a medal. Then he was their heroic brother he was now their guard. They love him tenderly, and admired him when it was necessary; but they had exhausted their own sensations concerning his deeds of arms, and fancied that he had served their purpose. And besides, valour is not an intellectual quality, they said. They were ladies so aspiring, these daughters of the merchant Samuel Bolton Pole, that, if Napoleon had been their brother, their imaginations would have overtopped him after his six months' inaction in the Tuileries. They would by that time have made a stepping-stone of the emperor. 'Mounting' was the title given to this proceeding. They went on perpetually mounting. It is still a good way from the head of the tallest of men to the stars; so they had their work before them; but, as they observed, they were young. To be brief, they were very ambitious damsels, aiming at they knew not exactly what, save that it was something so wide that it had not a name, and so high in the air that no one could see it. They knew assuredly that their circle did not please them. So, therefore, they were constantly extending and refining it: extending it perhaps for the purpose of refining it. Their susceptibilities demanded that they should escape from a city circle. Having no mother, they ruled their father's house and him, and were at least commanders of whatsoever forces they could summon for the task.

It may be seen that they were sentimentalists. That is to say, they supposed that they enjoyed exclusive possession of the Nice Feelings, and exclusively comprehended the Fine Shades. Whereof more will be said; but in the meantime it will explain their propensity to mount; it will account for their irritation at the material obstructions surrounding them; and possibly the philosopher will now have his eye on the source of that extraordinary sense of superiority to mankind which was the crown of their complacent brows. Eclipsed as they may be in the gross appreciation of the world by other people, who excel in this and that accomplishment, persons that nourish Nice Feelings and are intimate with the Fine Shades carry their own test of intrinsic value.

Nor let the philosopher venture hastily to despise them as pipers to dilettante life. Such persons come to us in the order of civilization. In their way they help to civilize us. Sentimentalists are a perfectly natural growth of a fat soil. Wealthy communities must engender them. If with attentive minds we mark the origin of classes, we shall discern that the Nice Feelings and the Fine Shades play a principal part in our human development and social history. I dare not say that civilized man is to be studied with the eye of a naturalist; but my vulgar meaning might almost be twisted to convey: that our sentimentalists are a variety owing their existence to a certain prolonged term of comfortable feeding. The pig, it will be retorted, passes likewise through this training. He does. But in him it is not combined with an indigestion of high German romances. Here is so notable a difference, that he cannot possibly be said to be of the family. And I maintain it against him, who have nevertheless listened attentively to the eulogies pronounced by the vendors of prize bacon.

After thus stating to you the vast pretensions of the ladies of Brookfield, it would be unfair to sketch their portraits. Nothing but comedy bordering on burlesque could issue from the contrast, though they graced a drawing-room or a pew, and had properly elegant habits and taste in dress, and were all fair to the sight. Moreover, Adela had not long quitted school. Outwardly they were not unlike other young ladies with wits alert. They were at the commencement of their labours on this night of the expedition when they were fated to meet something greatly confusing them.

CHAPTER II

Half of a rosy mounting full moon was on the verge of the East as the ladies, with attendant cavaliers, passed, humming softly, through the garden-gates. Arabella had, by right of birth, made claim to Mr. Pericles: not without an unwontedly fretful remonstrance from Cornelia, who said, "My dear, you must allow that I have some talent for drawing men out."

And Arabella replied: "Certainly, dear, you have; and I think I have some too."

The gentle altercation lasted half-an-hour, but they got no farther than this. Mr. Pericles was either hopeless of protecting himself from such shrewd assailants, or indifferent to their attacks, for all his defensive measures were against the cold. He was muffled in a superbly mounted bearskin, which came up so closely about his ears that Arabella had to repeat to him all her questions, and as it were force a way for her voice through the hide. This was provoking, since it not only stemmed the natural flow of conversation, but prevented her imagination from decorating the reminiscence of it subsequently (which was her profound secret pleasure), besides letting in the outer world upon her. Take it as an axiom, when you utter a sentimentalism, that more than one pair of ears makes a cynical critic. A sentimentalism requires secresy. I can enjoy it, and shall treat it respectfully if you will confide it to me alone; but I and my friends must laugh at it outright.

"Does there not seem a soul in the moonlight?" for instance. Arabella, after a rapturous glance at the rosy orb, put it to Mr. Pericles, in subdued impressive tones. She had to repeat her phrase; Mr. Pericles then echoing, with provoking monotony of tone, "Sol?"—whereupon "Soul!" was reiterated, somewhat sharply: and Mr. Pericles, peering over the collar of the bear, with half an eye, continued the sentence, in the manner of one sent thereby farther from its meaning: "Ze moonlight?" Despairing and exasperated, Arabella commenced afresh: "I said, there seems a soul in it"; and Mr. Pericles assented bluntly: "In ze light!"—which sounded so little satisfactory that Arabella explained, "I mean the aspect;" and having said three times distinctly what she meant, in answer to a terrific glare from the unsubmerged whites of the eyes of Mr. Pericles, this was his comment, almost roared forth:

"Sol! you say so-whole—in ze moonlight—Luna? Hein? Ze aspect is of Sol!—Yez."

And Mr. Pericles sank into his bear again, while Wilfrid Pole, who was swinging his long cavalry legs to rearward, shouted; and Mr. Sumner, a rising young barrister, walking beside Cornelia, smiled a smile of extreme rigidity. Arabella was punished for claiming rights of birth. She heard the murmuring course of the dialogue between Cornelia and Mr. Sumner, sufficiently clear to tell her it was not fictitious and was well sustained, while her heart was kept thirsting for the key to it. In advance were Adela and Edward Buxley, who was only a rich alderman's only son, but had the virtue of an extraordinary power of drawing caricatures, and was therefore useful in exaggerating the features of disagreeable people, and showing how odious they were: besides endearing pleasant ones exhibiting how comic they could be. Gossips averred that before Mr. Pole had been worried by his daughters into giving that mighty sum for Brookfield, Arabella had accepted Edward as her suitor; but for some reason or other he had apparently fallen from his high estate. To tell the truth, Arabella conceived that he had simply obeyed her wishes, while he knew he was naughtily following his own; and Adela, without introspection at all, was making her virgin effort at the caricaturing of our sex in his person: an art for which she promised well.

Out of the long black shadows of the solitary trees of the park, and through low yellow moonlight, they passed suddenly into the muffed ways of the wood. Mr. Pericles was ineffably provoking. He had come for gallantry's sake, and was not to be rallied, and would echo every question in a roar, and there was no drawing of the man out at all. He knocked against branches, and tripped over stumps, and ejaculated with energy; but though he gave no heed or help to his fair associate, she thought not the worse of him, so heroic can women be toward any creature that will permit himself to be clothed by a mystery. At times the party hung still, fancying the voice aloft, and then, after listening to the unrelieved stillness, they laughed, and trod the stiff dry ferns and soft mosses once more. At last they came to a decided halt, when the proposition to return caused Adela to come up to Mr. Pericles and say to him, "Now, you must confess! You have prohibited her from singing to-night so that we may continue to be mystified. I call this quite shameful of you!"

And even as Mr. Pericles was protesting that he was the most mystified of the company, his neck lengthened, and his head went round, and his ear was turned to the sky, while he breathed an elaborate "Ah!" And sure enough that was the voice of the woods, cleaving the night air, not distant. A sleepy fire of early moonlight hung through the dusky fir-branches. The voice had the woods to itself, and seemed to fill them and soar over them, it was so full and rich, so light and sweet. And now, to add to the marvel, they heard a harp accompaniment, the strings being faintly touched, but with firm fingers. A woman's voice: on that could be no dispute. Tell me, what opens heaven more flamingly to heart and mind, than the voice of a woman, pouring clear accordant notes to the blue night sky, that grows light blue to the moon? There was no flourish in her singing. All the notes were firm, and rounded, and sovereignly distinct. She seemed to have caught the ear of Night, and sang confident of her charm. It was a grand old Italian air, requiring severity of tone and power. Now into great mournful hollows the voice sank steadfastly. One soft sweep of the strings succeeded a deep final note, and the hearers breathed freely.

"Stradella!" said the Greek, folding his arms.

The ladies were too deeply impressed to pursue their play with him. Real emotions at once set aside the semi-credence they had given to their own suggestions.

"Hush! she will sing again," whispered Adela. "It is the most delicious contralto." Murmurs of objection to the voice being characterized at all by any technical word, or even for a human quality, were heard.

"Let me find zis woman!" cried the prose enthusiast Mr. Pericles, imperiously, with his bearskin thrown back on his shoulders, and forth they stepped, following him.

In the middle of the wood there was a sandy mound, rising half the height of the lesser firs, bounded by a green-grown vallum, where once an old woman, hopelessly a witch, had squatted, and defied the authorities to make her budge: nor could they accomplish the task before her witch-soul had taken wing in the form of a black night-bird, often to be heard jarring above the spot. Lank dry weeds and nettles, and great lumps of green and gray moss, now stood on the poor old creature's place of habitation, and the moon, slanting through the fir-clumps, was scattered on the blossoms of twisted orchard-trees, gone wild again. Amid this desolation, a dwarfed pine, whose roots were partially bared as they grasped the broken bank that was its perch, threw far out a cedar-like hand. In the shadow of it sat the fair singer. A musing touch of her harp-strings drew the intruders to the charmed circle, though they could discern nothing save the glimmer of the instrument and one set of fingers caressing it. How she viewed their rather impertinent advance toward her, till they had ranged in a half-circle nearer and nearer, could not be guessed. She did not seem abashed in any way, for, having preluded, she threw herself into another song.

The charm was now more human, though scarcely less powerful. This was a different song from the last: it was not the sculptured music of the old school, but had the richness and fulness of passionate blood that marks the modern Italian, where there is much dallying with beauty in the thick of sweet anguish. Here, at a certain passage of the song, she gathered herself up and pitched a nervous note, so shrewdly triumphing, that, as her voice sank to rest, her hearers could not restrain a deep murmur of admiration.

Then came an awkward moment. The ladies did not wish to go, and they were not justified in stopping. They were anxious to speak, and they could not choose the word to utter. Mr. Pericles relieved them by moving forward and doffing his hat, at the same time begging excuse for the rudeness they were guilty of.

The fair singer answered, with the quickness that showed a girl: "Oh, stay; do stay, if I please you!" A singular form of speech, it was thought by the ladies.

She added: "I feel that I sing better when I have people to listen to me."

"You find it more sympathetic, do you not?" remarked Cornelia.

"I don't know," responded the unknown, with a very honest smile. "I like it."

She was evidently uneducated. "A professional?" whispered Adela to Arabella. She wanted little invitation to exhibit her skill, at all events, for, at a word, the clear, bold, but finely nervous voice, was pealing to a brisker measure, that would have been joyous but for one fall it had, coming unexpectedly, without harshness, and winding up the song in a ringing melancholy.

After a few bars had been sung, Mr. Pericles was seen tapping his forehead perplexedly. The moment it ended, he cried out, in a tone of vexed apology for strange ignorance: "But I know not it? It is Italian yes, I swear it is Italian! But—who then? It is superbe! But I know not it!"

"It is mine," said the young person.

"Your music, miss?"

"I mean, I composed it."

"Permit me to say, Brava!"

The ladies instantly petitioned to have it sung to them again; and whether or not they thought more of it, or less, now that the authorship was known to them, they were louder in their applause, which seemed to make the little person very happy.

"You are sure it pleases you?" she exclaimed.

They were very sure it pleased them. Somehow the ladies were growing gracious toward her, from having previously felt too humble, it may be. She was girlish in her manner, and not imposing in her figure. She would be a sweet mystery to talk about, they thought: but she had ceased to be quite the same mystery to them.

"I would go on singing to you," she said; "I could sing all night long: but my people at the farm will not keep supper for me, when it's late, and I shall have to go hungry to bed, if I wait."

"Have you far to go?" ventured Adela.

"Only to Wilson's farm; about ten minutes' walk through the wood," she answered unhesitatingly.

Arabella wished to know whether she came frequently to this lovely spot.

"When it does not rain, every evening," was the reply.

"You feel that the place inspires you?" said Cornelia.

"I am obliged to come," she explained. "The good old dame at the farm is ill, and she says that music all day is enough for her, and I must come here, or I should get no chance of playing at all at night."

"But surely you feel an inspiration in the place, do you not?" Cornelia persisted.

She looked at this lady as if she had got a hard word given her to crack, and muttered: "I feel it quite warm here. And I do begin to love the place."

The stately Cornelia fell back a step.

The moon was now a silver ball on the edge of the circle of grey blue above the ring of firs, and by the light falling on the strange little person, as she stood out of the shadow to muffle up her harp, it could be seen that she was simply clad, and that her bonnet was not of the newest fashion. The sisters remarked a boot-lace hanging loose. The peculiar black lustre of her hair, and thickness of her long black eyebrows, struck them likewise. Her harp being now comfortably mantled, Cornet Wilfrid Pole, who had been watching her and balancing repeatedly on his forward foot, made a stride, and "really could not allow her to carry it herself," and begged her permission that he might assist her. "It's very heavy, you know," he added.

"Too heavy for me," she said, favouring him with a thankful smile. "I have some one who does that. Where is Jim?"

She called for Jim, and from the back of the sandy hillock, where he had been reclining, a broad-shouldered rustic came lurching round to them.

"Now, take my harp, if you please, and be as careful as possible of branches, and don't stumble." She uttered this as if she were giving Jim his evening lesson: and then with a sudden cry she laughed out: "Oh! but I haven't played you your tune, and you must have your tune!"

Forthwith she stript the harp half bare, and throwing a propitiatory bright glance at her audience on the other side of her, she commenced thrumming a kind of Giles Scroggins, native British, beer-begotten air, while Jim smeared his mouth and grinned, as one who sees his love dragged into public view, and is not the man to be ashamed of her, though he hopes you will hardly put him to the trial.

"This is his favourite tune, that he taught me," she emphasized to the company. "I play to him every night, for a finish; and then he takes care not to knock my poor harp to pieces and tumble about."

The gentlemen were amused by the Giles Scroggins air, which she had delivered with a sufficient sense of its lumping fun and leg-for-leg jollity, and they laughed and applauded; but the ladies were silent after the performance, until the moment came to thank her for the entertainment she had afforded them: and then they broke into gentle smiles, and trusted they might have the pleasure of hearing her another night.

"Oh! just as often and as much as you like," she said, and first held her hand to Arabella, next to Cornelia, and then to Adela. She seemed to be hesitating before the gentlemen, and when Wilfrid raised his hat, she was put to some confusion, and bowed rather awkwardly, and retired.

"Good night, miss!" called Mr. Pericles.

"Good night, sir!" she answered from a little distance, and they could see that she was there emboldened to drop a proper curtsey in accompaniment.

Then the ladies stood together and talked of her, not with absolute enthusiasm. For, "Was it not divine?" said Adela; and Cornelia asked her if she meant the last piece; and, "Oh, gracious! not that!" Adela exclaimed. And then it was discovered how their common observation had fastened on the boot-lace; and this vagrant article became the key to certain speculations on her condition and character.

"I wish I'd had a dozen bouquets, that's all!" cried Wilfrid, "she deserved them."

"Has she sentiment for what she sings? or is it only faculty?" Cornelia put it to Mr. Sumner.

That gentleman faintly defended the stranger for the intrusion of the bumpkin tune. "She did it so well!" he said.

"I complain that she did it too well," uttered Cornelia, whose use of emphasis customarily implied that the argument remained with her.

Talking in this manner, and leisurely marching homeward, they were startled to hear Mr. Pericles, who had wrapped himself impenetrably in the bear, burst from his cogitation suddenly to cry out, in his harshest foreign accent: "Yeaz!" And thereupon he threw open the folds, and laid out a forefinger, and delivered himself: "I am made my mind! I send her abroad to ze Academie for one, two, tree year. She shall be instructed as was not before. Zen a noise at La Scala. No—Paris! No—London! She shall astonish London fairst.—Yez! if I take a theatre! Yez! if I buy a newspaper! Yez! if I pay feefty-sossand pound!"

His singular outlandish vehemence, and the sweeping grandeur of a determination that lightly assumed the corruptibility of our Press, sent a smile circling among the ladies and gentlemen. The youth who had wished to throw the fair unknown a dozen bouquets, caught himself frowning at this brilliant prospect for her, which was to give him his opportunity.

CHAPTER III

The next morning there were many "tra-las" and "tum-te-turns" over the family breakfast-table; a constant humming and crying, "I have it"; and after two or three bars, baffled pauses and confusion of mind. Mr. Pericles was almost abusive at the impotent efforts of the sisters to revive in his memory that particular delicious melody, the composition of the fair singer herself. At last he grew so impatient as to arrest their opening notes, and even to interrupt their unmusical consultations, with "No: it is no use; it is no use: no, no, I say!" But instantly he would plunge his forehead into the palm of his hand, and rub it red, and work his eyebrows frightfully, until tender humanity led the sisters to resume. Adela's, "I'm sure it began low down—tum!" Cornelia's: "The key-note, I am positive, was B flat—ta!" and Arabella's putting of these two assertions together, and promise to combine them at the piano when breakfast was at an end, though it was Sunday morning, were exasperating to the exquisite lover of music. Mr. Pericles was really suffering torments. Do you know what it is to pursue the sylph, and touch her flying skirts, think you have caught her, and are sure of her—that she is yours, the rapturous evanescent darling! when some well-meaning earthly wretch interposes and trips you, and off she flies and leaves you floundering? A lovely melody nearly grasped and lost in this fashion, tries the temper. Apollo chasing Daphne could have been barely polite to the wood-nymphs in his path, and Mr. Pericles was rude to the daughters of his host. Smoothing his clean square chin and thick moustache hastily, with outspread thumb and fingers, he implored them to spare his nerves. Smiling rigidly, he trusted they would be merciful to a sensitive ear. Mr. Pole—who, as an Englishman, could not understand anyone being so serious in the pursuit of a tune—laughed, and asked questions, and almost drove Mr. Pericles mad. On a sudden the Greek's sallow visage lightened. "It is to you! it is to you!" he cried, stretching his finger at Wilfrid. The young officer, having apparently waited till he had finished with his knife and fork, was leaning his cheek on his fist, looking at nobody, and quietly humming a part of the air. Mr. Pericles complimented and thanked him.

"But you have ear for music extraordinaire!" he said.

Adela patted her brother fondly, remarking—"Yes, when his feelings are concerned."

"Will you repeat zat?" asked the Greek. "'To-to-ri:' hein? I lose it. 'To-to-ru:' bah! I lose it; 'To-ri:—to—ru—ri ro:' it is no use: I lose it."

Neither his persuasions, nor his sneer, "Because it is Sunday, perhaps!" would induce Wilfrid to be guilty of another attempt. The ladies tried sisterly cajoleries on him fruitlessly, until Mr. Pole, seeing the desperation of his guest, said: "Why not have her up here, toon and all, some week-day? Sunday birds won't suit us, you know. We've got a piano for her that's good enough for the first of 'em, if money means anything."

The ladies murmured meekly: "Yes, papa."

"I shall find her for you while you go to your charch," said Mr. Pericles. And here Wilfrid was seized with a yawn, and rose, and asked his eldest sister if she meant to attend the service that morning.

"Undoubtedly," she answered; and Mr. Pole took it up: "That's our discipline, my boy. Must set an example: do our duty. All the house goes to worship in the country."

"Why, in ze country?" queried Mr. Pericles.

"Because"—Cornelia came to the rescue of her sire; but her impetuosity was either unsupported by a reason, or she stooped to fit one to the comprehension of the interrogator: "Oh, because—do you know, we have very select music at our church?"

"We have a highly-paid organist," added Arabella.

"Recently elected," said Adela.

"Ah! mon Dieu!" Mr. Pericles ejaculated. "Some music sound well at afar—mellow, you say. I prefer your charch music mellow."

"Won't you come?" cried Wilfrid, with wonderful briskness.

"No. Mellow for me!"

The Greek's grinders flashed, and Wilfrid turned off from him sulkily. He saw in fancy the robber-Greek prowling about Wilson's farm, setting snares for the marvellous night-bird, and it was with more than his customary inattention to his sisters' refined conversation that he formed part of their male escort to the place of worship.

Mr. Pericles met the church-goers on their return in one of the green bowery lanes leading up to Brookfield. Cold as he was to English scenes and sentiments, his alien ideas were not unimpressed by the picture of those daintily-clad young women demurely stepping homeward, while the air held a revel of skylarks, and the scented hedgeways quickened with sunshine.

"You have missed a treat!" Arabella greeted him.

"A sermon?" said he.

The ladies would not tell him, until his complacent cynicism at the notion of his having missed a sermon, spurred them to reveal that the organ had been handled in a masterly manner; and that the voluntary played at the close of the service was most exquisite.

"Even papa was in raptures."

"Very good indeed," said Mr. Pole. "I'm no judge; but you might listen to that sort of playing after dinner."

Mr. Pericles seemed to think that was scarcely a critical period, but he merely grimaced, and inquired: "Did you see ze player?"

"Oh, no: they are hidden," Arabella explained to him, "behind a curtain."

"But, what!" shouted the impetuous Greek: "have you no curiosity? A woman! And zen, you saw not her?"

"No," remarked Cornelia, in the same aggravating sing-song voice of utter indifference: "we don't know whether it was not a man. Our usual organist is a man, I believe."

The eyes of the Greek whitened savagely, and he relapsed into frigid politeness.

Wilfrid was not present to point their apprehensions. He had loitered behind; but when he joined them in the house subsequently, he was cheerful, and had a look of triumph about him which made his sisters say, "So, you have been with the Copleys:" and he allowed them to suppose it, if they pleased; the Copleys being young ladies of position in the neighbourhood, of much higher standing than the Tinleys, who, though very wealthy, could not have given their brother such an air, the sisters imagined.

At lunch, Wilfrid remarked carelessly: "By the way, I met that little girl we saw last night."

"The singer! where?" asked his sisters, with one voice.

"Coming out of church."

"She goes to church, then!"

This exclamation showed the heathen they took her to be.

"Why, she played the organ," said Wilfrid.

"And how does she look by day? How does she dress?"

"Oh! very jolly little woman! Dresses quiet enough."

"She played the organ! It was she, then! An organist! Is there anything approaching to gentility in her appearance?"

"I—really I'm no judge," said Wilfrid. "You had better ask Laura Tinley. She was talking to her when I went up."

The sisters exchanged looks. Presently they stood together in consultation. Then they spoke with their aunt, Mrs. Lupin, and went to their papa. The rapacity of those Tinleys for anything extraordinary was known to them, but they would not have conceived that their own discovery, their own treasure, could have been caught up so quickly. If the Tinleys got possession of her, the defection of Mr. Pericles might be counted on, and the display of a phenomenon would be lost to them. They decided to go down to Wilson's farm that very day, and forestall their rivals by having her up to Brookfield. The idea of doing this had been in a corner of their minds all the morning: it seemed now the most sensible plan in the world. It was patronage, in its right sense. And they might be of great service to her, by giving a proper elevation and tone to her genius; while she might amuse them, and their guests, and be let off, in fact, as a firework for the nonce. Among the queenly cases of women who are designing to become the heads of a circle (if I may use the term), an accurate admeasurement of reciprocal advantages can scarcely be expected to rank; but the knowledge that an act, depending upon us for execution, is capable of benefiting both sides, will make the proceeding appear so unselfish, that its wisdom is overlooked as well as its motives. The sisters felt they were the patronesses of the little obscure genius whom they longed for to illumine their household, before they knew her name. Cornet Wilfrid Pole must have chuckled mightily to see them depart on their mission. These ladies, who managed everybody, had themselves been very cleverly managed. It is doubtful whether the scheme to surprise and delight Mr. Pericles would have actuated the step they took, but for the dread of seeing the rapacious Tinleys snatch up their lawful prey. The Tinleys were known to be quite capable of doing so. They had, on a particular occasion, made transparent overtures to a celebrity belonging to the Poles, whom they had first met at Brookfield: could never have hoped to have seen had they not met him at Brookfield; and girls who behaved in this way would do anything. The resolution was taken to steal a march on them; nor did it seem at all odd to people naturally so hospitable as the denizens of Brookfield, that the stranger of yesterday should be the guest of to-day. Kindness of heart, combined with a great scheme in the brain, easily put aside conventional rules.

"But we don't know her name," they said, when they had taken the advice of the gentlemen on what they had already decided to do: all excepting Mr. Pericles, for whom the surprise was in store.

"Belloni—Miss Belloni," said Wilfrid.

"Are you sure? How do you know—?"

"She told Laura Tinley."

Within five minutes of the receipt of this intelligence the ladies were on their way to Wilson's farm.

CHAPTER IV

EMILIA'S FIRST TRIAL IN PUBLIC

The circle which the ladies of Brookfield were designing to establish just now, was of this receipt:— Celebrities, London residents, and County notables, all in their severally due proportions, were to meet, mix, and revolve: the Celebrities to shine; the Metropolitans to act as satellites; the County ignoramuses to feel flattered in knowing that all stood forth for their amusement: they being the butts of the quick-witted Metropolitans, whom they despised, while the sons of renown were encouraged to be conscious of their magnanimous superiority over both sets, for whose entertainment they were ticketed.

This is a pudding indeed! And the contemplation of the skill and energy required to get together and compound such a Brookfield Pudding, well-nigh leads one to think the work that is done out of doors a very inferior business, and, as it were, mere gathering of fuel for the fire inside. It was known in the neighbourhood that the ladies were preparing one; and moreover that they had a new kind of plum; in other words, that they intended to exhibit a prodigy of genius, who would flow upon the world from Brookfield. To announce her with the invitations, rejecting the idea of a surprise in the assembly, had been necessary, because there was no other way of securing Lady Gosstre, who led the society of the district. The great lady gave her promise to attend: "though," as she said to Arabella, "you must know I abominate musical parties, and think them the most absurd of entertainments possible; but if you have anything to show, that's another matter."

Two or three chosen friends were invited down beforehand to inspect the strange girl, and say what they thought of her; for the ladies themselves were perplexed. They had found her to be commonplace: a creature without ideas and with a decided appetite. So when Tracy Runningbrook, who had also been a plum in his day, and was still a poet, said that she was exquisitely comic, they were induced to take the humorous view of the inexplicable side in the character of Miss Belloni, and tried to laugh at her eccentricities. Seeing that Mr. Pericles approved of her voice as a singer, and Tracy Runningbrook let pass her behaviour as a girl, they conceived that on the whole they were safe in sounding a trumpet loudly. These gentlemen were connoisseurs, each in his walk.

Concerning her position and parentage, nothing was known. She had met Adela's delicately-searching touches in that direction with a marked reserve. It was impossible to ask her point-blank, after probing her with a dozen suggestions, for the ingenuousness of an indifferent inquiry could not then be assumed, so that Adela was constantly baked and felt that she must some day be excessively 'fond with her,' which was annoying. The girl lit up at any sign of affection. A kind look gave Summer depths to her dark eyes. Otherwise she maintained a simple discretion and walked in her own path, content to look quietly pleased on everybody, as one who had plenty to think of and a voice in her ear.

Apparently she was not to be taught to understand 'limits': which must be explained as a sort of magnetic submissiveness to the variations of Polar caprice; so that she should move about with ease, be cheerful, friendly, and, at a signal, affectionate; still not failing to recognize the particular nooks where the family chalk had traced a line. As the day of exhibition approached, Adela thought she would give her a lesson in limits. She ventured to bestow a small caress on the girl, after a compliment; thinking that the compliment would be a check: but the compliment was passed, and the caress instantly replied to with two arms and a tender mouth. At which, Adela took fright and was glad to slip away.

At last the pudding flowed into the bag.

Emilia was posted by the ladies in a corner of the room. Receiving her assurance that she was not hungry, they felt satisfied that she wanted nothing. Wilfrid came up to her to console her for her loneliness, until Mr. Pericles had stationed himself at the back of her chair, and then Wilfrid nodded languidly and attended to his graver duties. Who would have imagined that she had hurt him? But she certainly looked with greater animation on Mr. Pericles; and when Tracy Runningbrook sat down by her, a perfect little carol of chatter sprang up between them. These two presented such a noticeable contrast, side by side, that the ladies had to send a message to separate them. She was perhaps a little the taller of the two; with smoothed hair that had the gloss of black briony leaves, and eyes like burning brands in a cave; while Tracy's hair was red as blown flame, with eyes of a grey-green hue, that may be seen glistening over wet sunset. People, who knew him, asked: "Who is she?" and it was not in the design of the ladies to have her noted just yet.

Lady Gosstre's exclamation on entering the room was presently heard. "Well! and where's our extraordinary genius? Pray, let me see her immediately."

Thereat Laura Tinley, with gross ill-breeding, rushed up to Arabella, who was receiving her ladyship, and touching her arm, as if privileges were permitted her, cried: "I'm dying to see her. Has she come?"

Arabella embraced the offensive girl in a hostess's smile, and talked flowingly to the great lady.

Laura Tinley was punished by being requested to lead off with a favourite song in a buzz. She acceded, quite aware of the honour intended, and sat at the piano, taming as much as possible her pantomime of one that would be audible. Lady Gosstre scanned the room, while Adela, following her ladyship's eyeglass, named the guests.

"You get together a quaint set of men," said Lady Gosstre.

"Women!" was on Adela's tongue's tip. She had really thought well of her men. Her heart sank.

"In the country!" she began.

"Yes, yes!" went my lady.

These were the lessons that made the ladies of Brookfield put a check upon youth's tendency to feel delightful satisfaction with its immediate work, and speedily conceive a discontented suspicion of anything whatsoever that served them.

Two other sacrifices were offered at the piano after Laura Tinley. Poor victims of ambition, they arranged their dresses, smiled at the leaves, and deliberately gave utterance to the dreadful nonsense of the laureates of our drawing-rooms. Mr. Pericles and Emilia exchanged scientific glances during the performance. She was merciless to indifferent music. Wilfrid saw the glances pass. So, now, when Emilia was beckoned to the piano, she passed by Wilfrid, and had a cold look in return for beaming eyes.

According to directions, Emilia sang a simple Neapolitan air. The singer was unknown, and was generally taken for another sacrifice.

"Come; that's rather pretty," Lady Gosstre hailed the close.

"It is of ze people—such as zat," assented Mr. Pericles.

Adela heard my lady ask for the singer's name. She made her way to her sisters. Adela was ordinarily the promoter, Cornelia the sifter, and Arabella the director, of schemes in this management. The ladies had a moment for counsel over a music-book, for Arabella was about to do duty at the piano. During a pause, Mr. Pole lifting his white waistcoat with the effort, sent a word abroad, loudly and heartily, regardless of its guardian aspirate, like a bold-faced hoyden flying from her chaperon. They had dreaded it. They loved their father, but declined to think his grammar parental. Hushing together, they agreed that it had been a false move to invite Lady Gosstre, who did not care a bit for music, until the success of their Genius was assured by persons who did. To suppose that she would recognize a Genius, failing a special introduction, was absurd. The ladies could turn upon aristocracy too, when it suited them.

Arabella had now to go through a quartett. The fever of ill-luck had seized the violin. He would not tune. Then his string broke; and while he was arranging it the footman came up to Arabella. Misfortunes, we know, are the most united family on earth. The news brought to her was that a lady of the name of Mrs. Chump was below. Holding her features rigidly bound, not to betray perturbation, Arabella confided the fact to Cornelia, who, with a similar mental and muscular compression, said instantly, "Manoeuvre her." Adela remarked, "If you tell her the company is grand, she will come, and her Irish once heard here will destroy us. The very name of Chump!"

Mrs. Chump was the wealthy Irish widow of an alderman, whose unaccountable bad taste in going to Ireland for a wife, yet filled the ladies with astonishment. She pretended to be in difficulties with her lawyers; for which reason she strove to be perpetually in consultation with her old flame and present trustee Mr. Pole. The ladies had fought against her in London, and since their installation at Brookfield they had announced to their father that she was not to be endured there. Mr. Pole had plaintively attempted to dilate on the virtues of Martha Chump. "In her place," said the ladies, and illustrated to him that amid a nosegay of flowers there was no fit room for an exuberant vegetable. The old man had sighed and seemed to surrender. One thing was certain: Mrs. Chump had never been seen at Brookfield. "She never shall be, save by the servants," said the ladies.

Emilia, not unmarked of Mr. Pericles, had gone over to Wilfrid once or twice, to ask him if haply he disapproved of anything she had done. Mr. Pericles shrugged, and went "Ah!" as who should say, "This must be stopped." Adela now came to her and caught her hand, showering sweet whispers on her, and bidding her go to her harp and do her best. "We love you; we all love you!" was her parting instigation.

The quartett was abandoned. Arabella had departed with a firm countenance to combat Mrs. Chump.

Emilia sat by her harp. The saloon was critically still; so still that Adela fancied she heard a faint Irish protest from the parlour. Wilfrid was perhaps the most critical auditor present: for he doubted whether she could renew that singular charm of her singing in the pale lighted woods. The first smooth contralto notes took him captive. He scarcely believed that this could be the raw girl whom his sisters delicately pitied.

A murmur of plaudits, the low thunder of gathering acclamation, went round. Lady Gosstre looked a satisfied, "This will do." Wilfrid saw Emilia's eyes appeal hopefully to Mr. Pericles. The connoisseur shrugged. A pain lodged visibly on her black eyebrows. She gripped her harp, and her eyelids appeared to quiver as she took the notes. Again, and still singing, she turned her head to him. The eyes of Mr. Pericles were white, as if upraised to intercede for her with the Powers of Harmony. Her voice grew unnerved. On a sudden she excited herself to pitch and give volume to that note which had been the enchantment of the night in the woods. It quavered. One might have thought her caught by the throat.

Emilia gazed at no one now. She rose, without a word or an apology, keeping her eyes down.

"Fiasco!" cruelly cried Mr. Pericles.

That was better to her than the silly kindness of the people who deemed it well to encourage her with applause. Emilia could not bear the clapping of hands, and fled.

CHAPTER V

EMILIA PLAYS ON THE CORNET

The night was warm under a slowly-floating moon. Full of compassion for the poor girl, who had moved him if she had failed in winning the assembly, Wilfrid stepped into the garden, where he expected to find her, and to be the first to pet and console her. Threading the scented shrubs, he came upon a turn in one of the alleys, from which point he had a view of her figure, as she stood near a Portugal laurel on the lawn. Mr. Pericles was by her side. Wilfrid's intention was to join them. A loud sob from Emilia checked his foot.

"You are cruel," he heard her say.

"If it is good, I tell it you; if it is bad; abominable, I tell it you, juste ze same," responded Mr. Pericles.

"The others did not think it very bad."

"Ah! bah!" Mr. Pericles cut her short.

Had they been talking of matters secret and too sweet, Wilfrid would have retired, like a man of honour. As it was, he continued to listen. The tears of his poor little friend, moreover, seemed to hold him there in the hope that he might afford some help.

"Yes; I do not care for the others," she resumed. "You praised me the night I first saw you."

"It is perhaps zat you can sing to z' moon," returned Mr. Pericles. "But, what! a singer, she must sing in a house. To-night it is warm, to-morrow it is cold. If you sing through a cold, what noise do we hear? It is a nose, not a voice. It is a trompet."

Emilia, with a whimpering firmness, replied: "You said I am lazy. I am not."

"Not lazy," Mr. Pericles assented.

"Do I care for praise from people who do not understand music? It is not true. I only like to please them."

"Be a street-organ," Mr. Pericles retorted.

"I must like to see them pleased when I sing," said Emilia desperately.

"And you like ze clap of ze hands. Yez. It is quite natural. Yess. You are a good child, it is clear. But, look. You are a voice uncultivated, sauvage. You go wrong: I hear you: and dese claps of zese noodels send you into squeaks and shrills, and false! false away you go. It is a gallop ze wrong way."

Here Mr. Pericles attempted the most horrible reproduction of Emilia's failure. She cried out as if she had been bitten.

"What am I to do?" she asked sadly.

"Not now," Mr. Pericles answered. "You live in London?—at where?"

"Must I tell you?"

"Certainly, you must tell me."

"But, I am not going there; I mean, not yet."

"You are going to sing to z' moon through z' nose. Yez. For how long?"

"These ladies have asked me to stay with them. They make me so happy. When I leave them—then!"

Emilia sighed.

"And zen?" quoth Mr. Pericles.

"Then, while my money lasts, I shall stay in the country."

"How much money?"

"How much money have I?" Emilia frankly and accurately summed up the condition of her treasury. "Four pounds and nineteen shillings."

"Hom! it is spent, and you go to your father again?"

"Yes."

"To ze old Belloni?"

"My father."

"No!" cried Mr. Pericles, upon Emilia's melancholy utterance. He bent to her ear and rapidly spoke, in an undertone, what seemed to be a vivid sketch of a new course of fortune for her. Emilia gave one joyful outcry; and now Wilfrid retreated, questioning within himself whether he should have remained so long. But, as he argued, if he was convinced that the rascally Greek fellow meant mischief to her, was he not bound to employ every stratagem to be her safeguard? The influence of Mr. Pericles already exercised over her was immense and mysterious. Within ten minutes she was singing triumphantly indoors. Wilfrid could hear that her voice was firm and assured. She was singing the song of the woods. He found to his surprise that his heart dropped under some burden, as if he had no longer force to sustain it.

By-and-by some of the members of the company issued forth. Carriages were heard on the gravel, and young men in couples, preparing to light the ensign of happy release from the ladies (or of indemnification for their absence, if you please), strolled about the grounds.

"Did you see that little passage between Laura Tinley and Bella Pole?" said one, and forthwith mimicked them: "Laura commencing:-'We must have her over to us.' 'I fear we have pre-engaged her.'—'Oh, but you, dear, will do us the favour to come, too?' 'I fear, dear, our immediate engagements will preclude the possibility.'—'Surely, dear Miss Pole, we may hope that you have not abandoned us?'—'That, my dear Miss Tinley, is out of the question.'—'May we not name a day?'—'If it depends upon us, frankly, we cannot bid you do so.'"

The other joined him in laughter, adding: "'Frankly' 's capital! What absurd creatures women are! How the deuce did you manage to remember it all?"

"My sister was at my elbow. She repeated it, word for word."

"Pon my honour, women are wonderful creatures!"

The two young men continued their remarks, with a sense of perfect consistency.

Lady Gosstre, as she was being conducted to her carriage, had pronounced aloud that Emilia was decidedly worth hearing.

"She's better worth knowing," said Tracy Runningbrook. "I see you are all bent on spoiling her. If you were to sit and talk with her, you would perceive that she's meant for more than to make a machine of her throat. What a throat it is! She has the most comical notion of things. I fancy I'm looking at the budding of my own brain. She's a born artist, but I'm afraid everybody's conspiring to ruin her."

"Surely," said Adela, "we shall not do that, if we encourage her in her Art."

"He means another kind of art," said Lady Gosstre. "The term 'artist,' applied to our sex, signifies 'Frenchwoman' with him. He does not allow us to be anything but women. As artists then we are largely privileged, I assure you."

"Are we placed under a professor to learn the art?" Adela inquired, pleased with the subject under such high patronage.

"Each new experience is your accomplished professor," said Tracy. "One I'll call Cleopatra a professor: she's but an illustrious example."

"Imp! you are corrupt." With which my lady tapped farewell on his shoulder. Leaning from the carriage window, she said: "I suppose I shall see you at Richford? Merthyr Powys is coming this week. And that reminds me: he would be the man to appreciate your 'born artist.' Bring her to me. We will have a dinner. I will despatch a formal invitation to-morrow. The season's bad out of town for getting decent people to meet you. I will do my best."

She bowed to Adela and Tracy. Mr. Pole, who had hovered around the unfamiliar dialogue to attend the great lady to the door, here came in for a recognition, and bowed obsequiously to the back of the carriage.

Arabella did not tell her sisters what weapons she had employed to effect the rout of Mrs. Chump. She gravely remarked that the woman had consented to go, and her sisters thanked her. They were mystified by Laura's non-recognition of Emilia, and only suspected Wilfrid so faintly that they were able to think they did not suspect him at all. On the whole, the evening had been a success. It justified the ladies in repeating a well-known Brookfield phrase: "We may be wrong in many things, but never in our judgement of the merits of any given person." In the case of Tracy Runningbrook, they had furnished a signal instance of their discernment. Him they had met at the house of a friend of the Tinleys (a Colonel's wife distantly connected with great houses). The Tinleys laughed at his flaming head and him, but the ladies of Brookfield had ears and eyes for a certain tone and style about him, before they learnt that he was of the blood of dukes, and would be a famous poet. When this was mentioned, after his departure, they had made him theirs, and the Tinleys had no chance. Through Tracy, they achieved their introduction to Lady Gosstre. And now they were to dine with her. They did not say that this was through Emilia. In fact, they felt a little that they had this evening been a sort of background to their prodigy: which was not in the design. Having observed, "She sang deliciously," they dismissed her, and referred to dresses, gaucheries of members of the company, pretensions here and there, Lady Gosstre's walk, the way to shuffle men and women, how to start themes for them to converse upon, and so forth. Not Juno and her Court surveying our mortal requirements in divine independence of fatigue, could have been more considerate for the shortcomings of humanity. And while they were legislating this and that for others, they still accepted hints for their own improvement, as those who have Perfection in view may do. Lady Gosstre's carriage of her shoulders, and general manner, were admitted to be worthy of study. "And did you notice when Laura Tinley interrupted her conversation with Tracy Runningbrook, how quietly she replied to the fact and nothing else, so that Laura had not another word?"—"And did you observe her deference to papa, as host?"—"And did you not see, on more than one occasion, with what consummate ease she would turn a current of dialogue when it had gone far enough?" They had all noticed, seen, and observed. They agreed that there was a quality beyond art, beyond genius, beyond any special cleverness; and that was, the great social quality of taking, as by nature, without assumption, a queenly position in a circle, and making harmony of all the instruments to be found in it. High praise of Lady Gosstre ensued. The ladies of Brookfield allowed themselves to bow to her with the greater humility, owing to the secret sense they nursed of overtopping her still in that ineffable Something which they alone possessed: a casket little people will be wise in not hurrying our Father Time to open for them, if they would continue to enjoy the jewel they suppose it to contain. Finally, these energetic young ladies said their prayers by the morning twitter of the birds, and went to their beds, less from a desire for rest than because custom demanded it.

Three days later Emilia was a resident in the house, receiving lessons in demeanour from Cornelia, and in horsemanship from Wilfrid. She expressed no gratitude for kindnesses or wonder at the change in her fortune, save that pleasure sat like an inextinguishable light on her face. A splendid new harp arrived one day, ticketed, "For Miss Emilia Belloni."

"He does not know I have a second Christian name," was her first remark, after an examination of the instrument.

"'He?'" quoth Adela. "May it not have been a lady's gift?"

Emilia clearly thought not.

"And to whom do you ascribe it?"

"Who sent it to me? Mr. Pericles, of course."

She touched the strings immediately, and sighed.

"Are you discontented with the tone, child?" asked Adela.

"No. I—I'll guess what it cost!"

Surely the ladies had reason to think her commonplace!

She explained herself better to Wilfrid, when he returned to Brookfield after a short absence. Showing the harp, "See what Mr. Pericles thinks me worth!" she said.

"Not more than that?" was his gallant rejoinder. "Does it suit you?"

"Yes; in every way."

This was all she said about it.

In the morning after breakfast, she sat at harp or piano, and then ran out to gather wild flowers and learn the names of trees and birds. On almost all occasions Wilfrid was her companion. He laughed at the little sisterly revelations the ladies confided concerning her too heartily for them to have any fear that she was other than a toy to him. Few women are aware with how much ease sentimental men can laugh outwardly at what is internal torment. They had apprised him of their wish to know what her origin was, and of her peculiar reserve on that topic: whereat he assured them that she would have no secrets from him. His conduct of affairs was so open that none could have supposed the gallant cornet entangled in a maze of sentiment. For, veritably, this girl was the last sort of girl to please his fancy; and he saw not a little of fair ladies: by virtue of his heroic antecedents, he was himself well seen of them. The gallant cornet adored delicacy and a gilded refinement. The female flower could not be too exquisitely cultivated to satisfy him. And here he was, running after a little unformed girl, who had no care to conceal the fact that she was an animal, nor any notion of the necessity for doing so! He had good reason to laugh when his sisters talked of her. It was not a pleasant note which came from the gallant cornet then. But, in the meadows, or kindly conducting Emilia's horse, he yielded pretty music. Emilia wore Arabella's riding-habit, Adela's hat, and Cornelia's gloves. Politic as the ladies of Brookfield were, they were full of natural kindness; and Wilfrid, albeit a diplomatist, was not yet mature enough to control and guide a very sentimental heart. There was an element of dim imagination in all the family: and it was this that consciously elevated them over the world in prospect, and made them unconsciously subject to what I must call the spell of the poetic power.

Wilfrid in his soul wished that Emilia should date from the day she had entered Brookfield. But at times it seemed to him that a knowledge of her antecedents might relieve him from his ridiculous perplexity of feeling. Besides though her voice struck emotion, she herself was unimpressionable. "Cold by nature," he said; looking at the unkindled fire. She shook hands like a boy. If her fingers were touched and retained, they continued to be fingers for as long as you pleased. Murmurs and whispers passed by her like the breeze. She appeared also to have no enthusiasm for her Art, so that not even there could Wilfrid find common ground. Italy, however, he discovered to be the subject that made her light up. Of Italy he would speak frequently, and with much simulated fervour.

"Mr. Pericles is going to take me there," said Emilia. "He told me to keep it secret. I have no secrets from my friends. I am to learn in the academy at Milan."

"Would you not rather let me take you?"

"Not quite." She shook her head. "No; because you do not understand music as he does. And are you as rich? I cost a great deal of money even for eating alone. But you will be glad when you hear me when I come back. Do you hear that nightingale? It must be a nightingale."

She listened. "What things he makes us feel!"

Bending her head, she walked on silently. Wilfrid, he knew not why, had got a sudden hunger for all the days of her life. He caught her hand and, drawing her to a garden seat, said: "Come; now tell me all about yourself before I knew you. Do you mind?"

"I'll tell you anything you want to hear," said Emilia.

He enjoined her to begin from the beginning.

"Everything about myself?" she asked.

"Everything. I have your permission to smoke?"

Emilia smiled. "I wish I had some Italian cigars to give you. My father sometimes has plenty given to him."

Wilfrid did not contemplate his havannah with less favour.

"Now," said Emilia, taking a last sniff of the flowers before surrendering her nostril to the invading smoke. She looked at the scene fronting her under a blue sky with slow flocks of clouds: "How I like this!" she exclaimed. "I almost forget that I long for Italy, here."

Beyond a plot of flowers, a gold-green meadow dipped to a ridge of gorse bordered by dark firs and the tips of greenest larches.

CHAPTER VI

EMILIA SUPPLIES THE KEY TO HERSELF AND CONTINUES HER PERFORMANCE ON THE CORNET

"My father is one of the most wonderful men in the whole world!"

Wilfrid lifted an eyelid.

"He is one of the first-violins at the Italian Opera!"

The gallant cornet's critical appreciation of this impressive announcement was expressed in a spiral ebullition of smoke from his mouth.

"He is such a proud man! And I don't wonder at that: he has reason to be proud."

Again Wilfrid lifted an eyelid, and there is no knowing but that ideas of a connection with foreign Counts, Cardinals, and Princes passed hopefully through him.

"Would you believe that he is really the own nephew of Andronizetti!"

"Deuce he is!" said Wilfrid, in a mist. "Which one?"

"The composer!"

Wilfrid emitted more smoke.

"Who composed—how I love him!—that lovely 'la, la, la, la,' and the 'te-de, ta-da, te-dio,' that pleases you, out of 'Il Maladetto.' And I am descended from him! Let me hope I shall not be unworthy of him. You will never tell it till people think as much of me, or nearly. My father says I shall never be so great, because I am half English. It's not my fault. My mother was English. But I feel that I am much more Italian than English. How I long for Italy—like a thing underground! My father did something against the Austrians, when he was a young man. Would not I have done it? I am sure I would—I don't know what. Whenever I think of Italy, night or day, pant-pant goes my heart. The name of Italy is my nightingale: I feel that somebody lives that I love, and is ill-treated shamefully, crying out to me for help. My father had to run away to save his life. He was fifteen days lying in the rice-fields to escape from the soldiers— which makes me hate a white coat. There was my father; and at night he used to steal out to one of the villages, where was a good, true woman—so they are, most, in Italy! She gave him food; maize-bread and wine, sometimes meat; sometimes a bottle of good wine. When my father thinks of it he cries, if there is gin smelling near him. At last my father had to stop there day and night. Then that good woman's daughter came to him to keep him from starving; she risked being stripped naked and beaten with rods, to keep my father from starving. When my father speaks of Sandra now, it makes my mother—she does not like it. I am named after her: Emilia Alessandra Belloni. 'Sandra' is short for it. She did not know why I was christened that, and will never call me anything but Emilia, though my father says Sandra, always. My father never speaks of that dear Sandra herself, except when he is tipsy. Once I used to wish him to be tipsy; for then I used to sit at my piano while he talked, and I made all his words go into music. One night I did it so well, my father jumped right up from his chair, shouting 'Italia!' and he caught his wig off his head, and threw it into the fire, and rushed out into the street quite bald, and people thought him mad.

"It was the beginning of all our misfortunes! My father was taken and locked up in a place as a tipsy man. That he has never forgiven the English for! It has made me and my mother miserable ever since. My mother is sure it is all since that night. Do you know, I remember, though I was so young, that I felt the music—oh! like a devil in my bosom? Perhaps it was, and it passed out of me into him. Do you think it was?"

Wilfrid answered: "Well, no! I shouldn't think you had anything to do with the devil." Indeed, he was beginning to think her one of the smallest of frocked female essences.

"I lost my piano through it," she went on. "I could not practise. I was the most miserable creature in all the world till I fell in love with my harp. My father would not play to get money. He sat in his chair, and only spoke to ask about meal-time, and we had no money for food, except by selling everything we had. Then my piano went. So then I said to my mother, I will advertize to give lessons, as other people do, and make money for us all, myself. So we paid money for a brass-plate, and our landlady's kind son put it up on the door for nothing, and we waited for pupils to come. I used to pray to the Virgin that she would blessedly send me pupils, for my poor mother's complaints were so shrill and out of tune it's impossible to tell you what I suffered. But by-and-by my father saw the brass-plate. He fell into one of his dreadful passions. We had to buy him another wig. His passions were so expensive: my mother used to say, 'There goes our poor dinner out of the window!' But, well! he went to get employment now. He can, always, when he pleases; for such a touch on the violin as my father has, you never heard. You feel yourself from top to toe, when my father plays. I feel as if I breathed music like air. One day came news from Italy, all in the newspaper, of my father's friends and old companions shot and murdered by the Austrians. He read it in the evening, after we had a quiet day. I thought he did not mind it much, for he read it out to us quite quietly; and then he made me sit on his knee and read it out. I cried with rage, and he called to me, 'Sandra! Peace!' and began walking up and down the room, while my mother got the bread and cheese and spread it on the table, for we were beginning to be richer. I saw my father take out his violin. He put it on the cloth and looked at it. Then he took it up, and laid his chin on it like a man full of love, and drew the bow across just once. He whirled away the bow, and knocked down our candle, and in the darkness I heard something snap and break with a hollow sound. When I could see, he had broken it, the neck from the body—the dear old violin! I could cry still. I—I was too late to save it. I saw it broken, and the empty belly, and the loose strings! It was murdering a spirit—that was! My father sat in a corner one whole week, moping like such an old man! I was nearly dead with my mother's voice. By-and-by we were all silent, for there was nothing to eat. So I said to my mother, 'I will earn money.' My mother cried. I proposed to take a lodging for myself, all by myself; go there in the morning and return at night, and give lessons, and get money for them. My landlady's good son gave me the brass-plate again. Emilia Alessandra Belloni! I was glad to see my name. I got two pupils very quickly one, an old lady, and one, a young one. The old lady—I mean, she was not grey—wanted a gentleman to marry her, and the landlady told me—I mean my pupil—it makes me laugh—asked him what he thought of her voice: for I had been singing. I earned a great deal of money: two pounds ten shillings a week. I could afford to pay for lessons myself, I thought. What an expense! I had to pay ten shillings for one lesson! Some have to pay twenty; but I would pay it to learn from the best masters;—and I had to make my father and mother live on potatoes, and myself too, of course. If you buy potatoes carefully, they are extremely cheap things to live upon, and make you forget your hunger more than anything else.

"I suppose," added Emilia, "you have never lived upon potatoes entirely? Oh, no!"

Wilfrid gave a quiet negative.

"But I was pining to learn, and was obliged to keep them low. I could pitch any notes, and I was clear but I was always ornamenting, and what I want is to be an accurate singer. My music-master was a German—not an Austrian—oh, no!—I'm sure he was not. At least, I don't think so, for I liked him. He was harsh with me, but sometimes he did stretch his fingers on my head, and turn it round, and say words that I pretended not to think of, though they sent me home burning. I began to compose, and this gentleman tore up the whole sheet in a rage, when I showed it him; but he gave me a dinner, and left off charging me ten shillings—only seven, and then five—and he gave me more time than he gave others. He also did something which I don't know yet whether I can thank him for. He made me know the music of the great German. I used to listen: I could not believe such music could come from a German. He followed me about, telling me I was his slave. For some time I could not sleep. I laughed at myself for composing. He was not an Austrian: but when he was alive he lived in Vienna, the capital of Austria. He ate Austrian bread, and why God gave him such a soul of music I never can think!—Well, by-and-by my father wanted to know what I did in the day, and why they never had anything but potatoes for dinner. My mother came to me, and I told her to say, I took walks. My father said I was an idle girl, and like my mother—who was a slave to work. People are often unjust! So my father said he would watch me. I had to cross the park to give a lesson to a lady who had a husband, and she wanted to sing to him to keep him at home in the evening. I used to pray he might not have much ear for music. One day a gentleman came behind me in the park. He showed me a handkerchief, and asked me if it was mine. I felt for my own and found it in my pocket. He was certain I had dropped it. He looked in the corners for the name, I told him my name—Emilia Alessandra Belloni. He found A.F.G. there. It was a beautiful cambric handkerchief, white and smooth. I told him it must be a gentleman's, as it was so large; but he said he had picked it up close by me, and he could not take it, and I must; and I was obliged to keep it, though I would much rather not. Near the end of the park he left me."

At this point Wilfrid roused up. "You met him the next day near the same place?" he remarked.

She turned to him with astonishment on her features. "How did you know that? How could you know?"

"Sort of thing that generally happens," said Wilfrid.

"Yes; he was there," Emilia slowly pursued, controlling her inclination to question further. "He had forgotten about the handkerchief, for when I saw him, I fancied he might have found the owner. We talked together. He told me he was in the Army, and I spoke of my father's playing and my singing. He was so fond of music that I promised him he should hear us both. He used to examine my hand, and said they were sensitive fingers for playing. I knew that. He had great hopes of me. He said he would give me a box at the Opera, now and then. I was mad with joy; and so delighted to have made a friend. I had never before made a rich friend. I sang to him in the park. His eyes looked beautiful with pleasure. I know I enchanted him."

"How old were you then?" inquired Wilfrid.

"Sixteen. I can sing better now, I know; but I had voice then, and he felt that I had. I forgot where we were, till people stood round us, and he hurried me away from them, and said I must sing to him in some quiet place. I promised to, and he promised he would have dinner for me at Richmond Hill, in the country, and he would bring friends to hear me."

"Go on," said Wilfrid, rather sharply.

She sighed. "I only saw him once after that. It was such a miserable day! It rained. It was Saturday. I did not expect to find him in the rain; but there he stood, exactly where he had given me the handkerchief. He smiled kindly, as I came up. I dislike gloomy people! His face was always fresh and nice. His moustache reminded me of Italy. I used to think of him under a great warm sky, with olives and vine-trees and mulberries like my father used to speak of. I could have flung my arms about his neck."

"Did you?" The cornet gave a strangled note.

"Oh, no!" said Emilia seriously. "But I told him how happy the thought of going into the country made me, and that it was almost like going to Italy. He told me he would take me to Italy, if I liked. I could have knelt at his feet. Unfortunately his friends could not come. Still, I was to go, and dine, and float on the water, plucking flowers. I determined to fancy myself in Venice, which is the place my husband must take me to, when I am married to him. I will give him my whole body and soul for his love, when I am there!"

Here the cornet was capable of articulate music for a moment, but it resolved itself into: "Well, well! Yes, go on!"

"I took his arm this time. It gave me my first timid feeling that I remember, and he laughed at me, and drove it quite away, telling me his name: Augustus Frederick what was it? Augustus Frederick—it began with G something. O me! have I really forgotten? Christian names are always easier to remember. A captain he was—a riding one; just like you. I think you are all kind!"

"Extremely," muttered the ironical cornet. "A.F.G.;—those are the initials on the handkerchief!"

"They are!" cried Emilia. "It must have been his own handkerchief!"

"You have achieved the discovery," quoth Wilfrid. "He dropped it there overnight, and found it just as you were passing in the morning."

"That must be impossible," said Emilia, and dismissed the subject forthwith, in a feminine power of resolve to be blind to it.

"I am afraid," she took up her narrative, "my father is sometimes really almost mad. He does such things! I had walked under this gentleman's umbrella to the bridge between the park and the gardens with the sheep, and beautiful flowers in beds. In an instant my father came up right in our faces. He caught hold of my left hand. I thought he wanted to shake it, for he imitates English ways at times, even with us at home, and shakes our hands when he comes in. But he swung me round. He stood looking angrily at this gentleman, and cried 'Yes! yes!' to every word he spoke. The gentleman bowed to me, and asked me to take his umbrella; but I was afraid to; and my father came to me,—oh, Madonna, think of what he did! I saw that his pockets were very big. He snatched out potatoes, and began throwing them as hard as he could throw them at the gentleman, and struck him with some of them. He threw nine large potatoes! I begged him to think of our dinner; but he cried 'Yes! it is our dinner we give to your head, vagabond!' in his English. I could not help running up to the gentleman to beg for his pardon. He told me not to cry, and put some potatoes he had been picking up all into my hand. They were muddy, but he wiped them first; and he said it was not the first time he had stood fire, and then said good-bye; and I slipped the potatoes into my pocket immediately, thankful that they were not wasted. My father pulled me away roughly from the laughing and staring people on the bridge. But I knew the potatoes were only bruised. Even three potatoes will prevent you from starving. They were very fine ones, for I always took care to buy them good. When I reached home—"

Wilfrid had risen, and was yawning with a desperate grimace. He bade her continue, and pitched back heavily into his seat.

"When I reached home and could be alone with my mother, she told me my father had been out watching me the day before, and that he had filled his pockets that morning. She thought he was going to walk out in the country and get people on the road to cook them for him. That is what he has done when he was miserable,—to make himself quite miserable, I think, for he loves streets best. Guess my surprise! My mother was making my head ache with her complaints, when, as I drew out the potatoes to show her we had some food, there was a purse at the bottom of my pocket,—a beautiful green purse! O that kind gentleman! He must have put it in my hand with the potatoes that my father flung at him! How I have cried to think that I may never sing to him my best to please him! My mother and I opened the purse eagerly. It had ten pounds in paper money, and five sovereigns, and silver,—I think four shillings. We determined to keep it a secret; and then we thought of the best way of spending it, and decided not to spend it all, but to keep some for when we wanted it dreadfully, and for a lesson or two for me now and then, and a music-score, and perhaps a good violin for my father, and new strings for him and me, and meat dinners now and then, and perhaps a day in the country: for that was always one of my dreams as I watched the clouds flying over London. They seemed to be always coming from happy places and going to happy places, never stopping where I was! I cannot be sorrowful long. You know that song of mine that you like so much—my own composing? It was a song about that kind gentleman. I got words to suit it as well as I could, from a penny paper, but they don't mean anything that I mean, and they are only words."

She did not appear to hear the gallant cornet's denial that he cared particularly for that song.

"What I meant was,—that gentleman speaks—I have fought for Italy; I am an English hero and have fought for Italy, because of an Italian child; but now I am wounded and a prisoner. When you shoot me, cruel Austrians, I shall hear her voice and think of nothing else, so you cannot hurt me."

Emilia turned spitefully on herself at this close. "How I spoil it! My words are always stupid, when I feel.—Well, now my mother and I were quite peaceful, and my father was better fed. One night he brought home a Jew gentleman, beautifully dressed, with diamonds all over him. He sparkled like the Christmas cakes in pastry-cooks' windows. I sang to him, and he made quite a noise about me. But the man made me so uncomfortable, touching my shoulders, and I could not bear his hands, even when he was praising me. I sang to him till the landlady made me leave off, because of the other lodgers who wanted to sleep. He came every evening; and then said I should sing at a concert. It turned out to be a public-house, and my father would not let me go; but I was sorry; for in public the man could not touch me as he did. It damped the voice!"

"I should like to know where that fellow lives," cried the cornet.

"I don't know, I'm sure," she said. "He lends money. Do you want any? I heard your sisters say something, one day. You can always have all that I have, you know."

A quick spirit of pity and honest kindness went through Wilfrid's veins and threatened to play the woman with his eyes, for a moment. He took her hand and pressed it. She put her lips to his fingers.

"Once," she continued, "when the Jew gentleman had left, I spoke to my father of his way with me, and then my father took me on his knee, and the things he told me of what that man felt for me made my mother come and tear me away to bed. I was obliged to submit to the Jew gentleman patting and touching me always. He used to crush my dreams afterwards! I know my voice was going. My father was so eager for me to please him, I did my best; but I felt dull, and used to sit and shake my head at my harp, crying; or else I felt like an angry animal, and could have torn the strings.

"Think how astonished I was when my mother came to me to say my father had money in his pockets!— one pound, seventeen shillings, she counted: and he had not been playing! Then he brought home a new violin, and he said to me, 'I shall go; I shall play; I am Orphee, and dinners shall rise!' I was glad, and kissed him; and he said, 'This is Sandra's gift to me,' showing the violin. I only knew what that meant two days afterwards. Is a girl not seventeen fit to be married?"

With this abrupt and singular question she had taken an indignant figure, and her eyes were fiery: so that Wilfrid thought her much fitter than a minute before.

"Married!" she exclaimed. "My mother told me about that. You do not belong to yourself: you are tied down. You are a slave, a drudge; mustn't dream, mustn't think! I hate it. By-and-by, I suppose it will happen. Not yet! And yet that man offered to take me to Italy. It was the Jew gentleman. He said I should make money, if he took me, and grow as rich as princesses. He brought a friend to hear me, another Jew gentleman; and he was delighted, and he met me near our door the very next morning, and offered me a ring with blue stones, and he proposed to marry me also, and take me to Italy, if I would give up his friend and choose him instead. This man did not touch me, and, do you know, for some time I really thought I almost, very nearly, might,—if it had not been for his face! It was impossible to go to Italy—yes, to go to heaven! through that face of his! That face of his was just like the pictures of dancing men with animals' hairy legs and hoofs in an old thick poetry book belonging to my mother. Just fancy a nose that seemed to be pecking at great fat red lips! He met me and pressed me to go continually, till all of a sudden up came the first Jew gentleman, and he cried out quite loud in the street that he was being robbed by the other; and they stood and made a noise in the street, and I ran away. But then I heard that my father had borrowed money from the one who came first, and that his violin came from that man; and my father told me the violin would be taken from him, and he would have to go to prison, if I did not marry that man. I went and cried in my mother's arms. I shall never forget her kindness; for though she could never see anybody crying without crying herself, she did not, and was quiet as a mouse, because she knew how her voice hurt me. There's a large print-shop in one of the great streets of London, with coloured views of Italy. I used to go there once, and stand there for I don't know how long, looking at them, and trying to get those Jew gentlemen—"

"Call them Jews—they're not gentlemen," interposed Wilfrid.

"Jews," she obeyed the dictate, "out of my mind. When I saw the views of Italy they danced and grinned up and down the pictures. Oh, horrible! There was no singing for me then. My music died. At last that oldish lady gave up her lessons, and said to me, 'You little rogue! you will do what I do, some day;' for she was going to be married to that young man who thought her voice so much improved; and she paid me three pounds, and gave me one pound more, and some ribbons and gloves. I went at once to my mother, and made her give me five pounds out of the gentleman's purse. I took my harp and music-scores. I did not know where I was going, but only that I could not stop. My mother cried: but she helped to pack my things. If she disobeys me I act my father, and tower over her, and frown, and make her mild. She was such a poor good slave to me that day! but I trusted her no farther than the door. There I kissed her, full of love, and reached the railway. They asked me where I was going, and named places to me: I did not know one. I shut my eyes, and prayed to be directed, and chose Hillford. In the train I was full of music in a moment. There I met farmer Wilson, of the farm near us—where your sisters found me; and he was kind, and asked me about myself; and I mentioned lodgings, and that I longed for woods and meadows. Just as we were getting out of the train, he said I was to come with him; and I did, very gladly. Then I met you; and I am here. All because I prayed to be directed—I do think that!"

Emilia clasped her hands, and looked pensively at the horizon sky, with a face of calm gratefulness.

The cornet was on his legs. "So!" he said. "And you never saw anything more of that fellow you kissed in the park?"

"Kissed?—that gentleman?" returned Emilia. "I have not kissed him. He did not want it. Men kiss us when we are happy, and we kiss them when they are unhappy."

Wilfrid was perhaps incompetent to test the truth of this profound aphoristic remark, delivered with the simplicity of natural conviction. The narrative had, to his thinking, quite released from him his temporary subjection to this little lady's sway. All that he felt for her personally now was pity. It speaks something for the strength of the sentiment with which he had first conceived her, that it was not pelted to death, and turned to infinite disgust, by her potatoes. For sentiment is a dainty, delicate thing, incapable of bearing much: revengeful, too, when it is outraged. Bruised and disfigured, it stood up still, and fought against them. They were very fine ones, as Emilia said, and they hit him hard. However, he pitied her, and that protected him like a shield. He told his sisters a tale of his own concerning the strange damsel, humorously enough to make them see that he enjoyed her presence as that of no common oddity.

CHAPTER VII

THREATS OF A CRISIS IN THE GOVERNMENT OF BROOKFIELD: AND OF THE VIRTUE RESIDENT IN A TAIL-COAT

While Emilia was giving Wilfrid her history in the garden, the ladies of Brookfield were holding consultation over a matter which was well calculated to perplex and irritate them excessively. Mr. Pole had received a curious short epistle from Mrs. Chump, informing him of the atrocious treatment she had met with at the hands of his daughter; and instead of reviewing the orthography, incoherence, and deliberate vulgarity of the said piece of writing with the contempt it deserved, he had taken the unwonted course of telling Arabella that she had done a thing she must necessarily repent of, or in any case make apology for. An Eastern Queen, thus addressed by her Minister of the treasury, could not have felt greater indignation. Arabella had never seen her father show such perturbation of mind. He spoke violently and imperiously. The apology was ordered to be despatched by that night's post, after having been submitted to his inspection. Mr. Pole had uttered mysterious phrases: "You don't know what you've been doing:—You think the ship'll go on sailing without wind: You'll drive the horse till he drops," and such like; together with mutterings. The words were of no import whatsoever to the ladies. They were writings on the wall; untranslateable. But, as when the earth quakes our noble edifices totter, their Palace of the Fine Shades and the Nice Feelings groaned and creaked, and for a moment they thought: "Where are we?" Very soon they concluded, that the speech Arabella had heard was due to their darling papa's defective education.

In the Council of Three, with reference to the letter of apology to Mrs. Chump, Adela proposed, if it pleased Arabella, to fight the battle of the Republic. She was young, and wished both to fight and to lead, as Arabella knew. She was checked. "It must be left to me," said Arabella.

"Of course you resist, dear?" Cornelia carelessly questioned.

"Assuredly I do."

"Better humiliation! better anything! better marriage! than to submit in such a case," cried Adela.

For, so united were the ladies of Brookfield, and so bent on their grand hazy object, that they looked upon married life unfavourably: and they had besides an idea that Wedlock, until 'late in life' (the age of thirty, say), was the burial alive of woman intellectual.

Toward midday the ladies put on their garden hats and went into the grounds together, for no particular purpose. Near the West copse they beheld Mr. Pole with Wilfrid and Emilia talking to a strange gentleman. Assuming a proper dignity, they advanced, when, to their horror, Emilia ran up to them crying: "This is Mr. Purcell Barrett, the gentleman who plays the organ at church. I met him in the woods before I knew you. I played for him the other Sunday, and I want you to know him."

She had hold of Arabella's hand and was drawing her on. There was no opportunity for retreat. Wilfrid looked as if he had already swallowed the dose. Almost precipitated into the arms of the ladies, Mr. Barrett bowed. He was a tolerably youthful man, as decently attired as old black cloth could help him to be. A sharp inspection satisfied the ladies that his hat and boots were inoffensive: whereupon they gave him the three shades of distance, tempered so as not to wound his susceptible poverty.

The superlative Polar degree appeared to invigorate Mr. Barrett. He devoted his remarks mainly to Cornelia, and cheerfully received her frozen monosyllables in exchange. The ladies talked of Organs and Art, Emilia and Opera. He knew this and that great organ, and all the operas; but he amazed the ladies by talking as if he knew great people likewise. This brought out Mr. Pole, who, since he had purchased Brookfield, had been extinguished by them and had not once thoroughly enjoyed his money's worth. A courtly poor man was a real pleasure to him.

Giving a semicircular sweep of his arm: "Here you see my little estate, sir," he said. "You've seen plenty bigger in Germany, and England too. We can't get more than this handful in our tight little island. Unless born to it, of course. Well! we must be grateful that all our nobility don't go to the dogs. We must preserve our great names. I speak against my own interest."

He lifted Adela's chin on his forefinger. She kept her eyes demurely downward, and then gazed at her sisters with gravity. These ladies took a view of Mr. Barrett. His features wore an admirable expression of simple interest. "Well, sir; suppose you dine with us to-day?" Mr. Pole bounced out. "Neighbours should be neighbourly."

This abrupt invitation was decorously accepted.

"Plain dinner, you know. Nothing like what you get at the tables of those Erzhogs, as you call 'em, over in Germany. Simple fare; sound wine! At all events, it won't hurt you. You'll come?"

Mr. Barrett bowed, murmuring thanks. This was the very man Mr. Pole wanted to have at his board occasionally: one who had known great people, and would be thankful for a dinner. He could depreciate himself as a mere wealthy British merchant imposingly before such a man. His daughters had completely cut him off from his cronies; and the sense of restriction, and compression, and that his own house was fast becoming alien territory to him, made him pounce upon the gentlemanly organist. His daughters wondered why he should, in the presence of this stranger, exaggerate his peculiar style of speech. But the worthy merchant's consciousness of his identity was vanishing under the iron social rule of the ladies. His perishing individuality prompted the inexplicable invitation, and the form of it.

After Mr. Barrett had departed, the ladies ventured to remonstrate with their papa. He at once replied by asking whether the letter to Mrs. Chump had been written; and hearing that it had not, he desired that Arabella should go into the house and compose it straightway. The ladies coloured. To Adela's astonishment, she found that Arabella had turned. Joining her, she said, "Dearest, what a moment you have lost! We could have stood firm, continually changing the theme from Chump to Barrett, Barrett to Chump, till papa's head would have twirled. He would have begun to think Mr. Barrett the Irish widow, and Mrs. Chump the organist."

Arabella rejoined: "Your wit misleads you, darling. I know what I am about. I decline a wordy contest. To approach to a quarrel, or, say dispute, with one's parent apropos of such a person, is something worse than evil policy, don't you think?"

So strongly did the sisters admire this delicate way of masking a piece of rank cowardice, that they forgave her. The craven feeling was common to them all, which made it still more difficult to forgive her.

"Of course, we resist?" said Cornelia.

"Undoubtedly."

"We retire and retire," Adela remarked. "We waste the royal forces. But, dear me, that makes us insurgents!"

She laughed, being slightly frivolous. Her elders had the proper sentimental worship of youth and its supposed quality of innocence, and caressed her.

At the ringing of the second dinner-bell, Mr. Pole ran to the foot of the stairs and shouted for Arabella, who returned no answer, and was late in her appearance at table. Grace concluded, Mr. Pole said, "Letter gone? I wanted to see it, you know."

"It was as well not, papa," Arabella replied.

Mr. Pole shook his head seriously. The ladies were thankful for the presence of Mr. Barrett. And lo! this man was in perfect evening uniform. He looked as gentlemanly a visitor as one might wish to see. There was no trace of the poor organist. Poverty seemed rather a gold-edge to his tail-coat than a rebuke to it; just as, contrariwise, great wealth is, to the imagination, really set off by a careless costume. One need not explain how the mind acts in such cases: the fact, as I have put it, is indisputable. And let the young men of our generation mark the present chapter, that they may know the virtue residing in a tail-coat, and cling to it, whether buffeted by the waves, or burnt out by the fire, of evil angry fortune. His tail-coat safe, the youthful Briton is always ready for any change in the mind of the moody Goddess. And it is an almost certain thing that, presuming her to have a damsel of condition in view for him as a compensation for the slaps he has received, he must lose her, he cannot enter a mutual path with her, if he shall have failed to retain this article of a black tail, his social passport. I mean of course that he retain respect for the article in question. Respect for it firmly seated in his mind, the tail may be said to be always handy. It is fortune's uniform in Britain: the candlestick, if I may dare to say so, to the candle; nor need any young islander despair of getting to himself her best gifts, while he has her uniform at command, as glossy as may be.

The ladies of Brookfield were really stormed by Mr. Barrett's elegant tail. When, the first glass of wine nodded over, Mr. Pole continued the discourse of the morning, with allusions to French cooks, and his cook, their sympathies were taken captive by Mr. Barrett's tact: the door to their sympathies having been opened to him as it were by his attire. They could not guess what necessity urged Mr. Pole to assert his locked-up self so vehemently; but it certainly made the stranger shine with a beautiful mild lustre. Their spirits partly succumbed to him by a process too lengthened to explain here. Indeed, I dare do no more than hint at these mysteries of feminine emotion. I beg you to believe that when we are dealing with that wonder, the human heart female, the part played by a tail-coat and a composed demeanour is not insignificant. No doubt the ladies of Brookfield would have rebutted the idea of a tail-coat influencing them in any way as monstrous. But why was it, when Mr. Pole again harped on his cook, in almost similar words, that they were drawn to meet the eyes of the stranger, on whom they printed one of the most fabulously faint fleeting looks imaginable, with a proportionately big meaning for him that might read it? It must have been that this uniform of a tail had laid a basis of equality for the hour, otherwise they never would have done so; nor would he have enjoyed the chance of showing them that he could respond to the remotest mystic indications, with a muffled adroitness equal to their own, and so encouraged them to commence a language leading to intimacy with a rapidity that may well appear magical to the uninitiated. In short, the man really had the language of the very elect of polite society. If you are not versed in this alphabet of mute intelligence, you are in the ranks with waiters and linen-drapers, and are, as far as ladies are concerned, tail-coated to no purpose.

Mr. Pole's fresh allusion to his cook: "I hope you don't think I keep a man! No; no; not in the country. Wouldn't do. Plays the deuce, you know. My opinion is, Mrs. Mallow's as clever as any man-cook going. I'd back her:" and Mr. Barrett's speech: "She is an excellent person!" delivered briefly, with no obtrusion of weariness, confirmed the triumph of the latter; a triumph all the greater, that he seemed unconscious of it. They leaped at one bound to the conclusion that there was a romance attached to him. Do not be startled. An attested tail-coat, clearly out of its element, must contain a story: that story must be interesting; until its secret is divulged, the subtle essence of it spreads an aureole around the tail. The ladies declared, in their subsequent midnight conference, that Mr. Barrett was fit for any society. They had visions of a great family reduced; of a proud son choosing to earn his bread honourably and humbly, by turning an exquisite taste to account. Many visions of him they had, and were pleased.

Patronage of those beneath, much more than the courting of those above them, delighted the ladies of Brookfield. They allowed Emilia to give Mr. Barrett invitations, and he became a frequent visitor; always neat, pathetically well-brushed, and a pleasanter pet than Emilia, because he never shocked their niceties. He was an excellent talker, and was very soon engaged in regular contests with the argumentative Cornelia. Their political views were not always the same, as Cornelia sometimes had read the paper before he arrived. Happily, on questions of religion, they coincided. Theories of education occupied them mainly. In these contests Mr. Barrett did not fail to acknowledge his errors, when convicted, and his acknowledgment was hearty and ample. She had many clear triumphs. Still, he could be positive; a very great charm in him. Women cannot repose on a man who is not positive; nor have they much gratification in confounding him. Wouldst thou, man, amorously inclining! attract to thee superior women, be positive. Be stupidly positive, rather than dubious at all. Face fearful questions with a vizor of brass. Array thyself in dogmas. Show thy decisive judgement on the side of established power, or thy enthusiasm in the rebel ranks, if it must be so; but be firm. Waver not. If women could tolerate waverings and weakness, and did not rush to the adoration of decision of mind, we should not behold them turning contemptuously from philosophers in their agony, to find refuge in the arms of smirking orthodoxy. I do not say that Mr. Barrett ventured to play the intelligent Cornelia like a fish; but such a fish was best secured by the method he adopted: that of giving her signal victory in trifles, while on vital matters he held his own.

Very pleasant evenings now passed at Brookfield, which were not at all disturbed by the wonder expressed from time to time by Mr. Pole, that he had not heard from Martha, meaning Mrs. Chump. "You have Emilia," the ladies said; this being equivalent to "She is one of that sort;" and Mr. Pole understood it so, and fastened Emilia in one arm, with "Now, a kiss, my dear, and then a toon." Emilia readily gave both. As often as he heard instances of her want of ladylike training, he would say, "Keep her here; we'll better her." Mr. Barrett assisted the ladies to see that there was more in Emilia than even Mr. Pericles had perceived. Her story had become partially known to them; and with two friendly dependents of the household, one a gentleman and the other a genius, they felt that they had really attained a certain eminence, which is a thing to be felt only when we have something under our feet. Flying about with a desperate grip on the extreme skirts of aristocracy, the ladies knew to be the elevation of dependency, not true eminence; and though they admired the kite, they by no means wished to form a part of its tail. They had brains. A circle was what they wanted, and they had not to learn that this is to be found or made only in the liberally-educated class, into the atmosphere of which they pressed like dungeoned plants. The parasite completes the animal, and a dependent assures us of our position. The ladies of Brookfield, therefore, let Emilia cling to them, remarking, that it seemed to be their papa's settled wish that she should reside among them for a time. Consequently, if the indulgence had ever to be regretted, they would not be to blame. In their hearts they were aware that it was Emilia who had obtained for them their first invitation to Lady Gosstre's. Gratitude was not a part of their policy, but when it assisted a recognition of material facts they did not repress it. "And if," they said, "we can succeed in polishing her and toning her, she may have something to thank us for, in the event of her ultimately making a name." That event being of course necessary for the development of so proper a sentiment. Thus the rides with Wilfrid continued, and the sweet quiet evenings when she sang.

CHAPTER VIII

IN WHICH A BIG DRUM SPEEDS THE MARCH OF EMILIA'S HISTORY

The windows of Brookfield were thrown open to the air of May, and bees wandered into the rooms, gold spots of sunshine danced along the floors. The garden-walks were dazzling, and the ladies went from flower-bed to flower-bed in broad garden hats that were, as an occasional light glance flung at a window-pane assured Adela, becoming. Sunshine had burst on them suddenly, and there was no hat to be found for Emilia, so Wilfrid placed his gold-laced foraging-cap on her head, and the ladies, after a moment's misgiving, allowed her to wear it, and turned to observe her now and then. There was never pertness in Emilia's look, which on the contrary was singularly large and calm when it reposed: perhaps her dramatic instinct prompted her half-jaunty manner of leaning against the sunny corner of the house where the Chinese honeysuckle climbed. She was talking to Wilfrid. Her laughter seemed careless and easy, and in keeping with the Southern litheness of her attitude.

"To suit the cap; it's all to suit the cap," said Adela, the keen of eye. Yet, critical as was this lady, she acknowledged that it was no mere acting effort to suit the cap.

The philosopher (I would keep him back if I could) bids us mark that the crown and flower of the nervous system, the head, is necessarily sensitive, and to that degree that whatsoever we place on it, does, for a certain period, change and shape us. Of course the instant we call up the forces of the brain, much of the impression departs but what remains is powerful, and fine-nerved. Woman is especially subject to it. A girl may put on her brother's boots, and they will not affect her spirit strongly; but as soon as she puts on her brother's hat, she gives him a manly nod. The same philosopher who fathers his dulness on me, asserts that the modern vice or fastness ['Trotting on the Epicene Border,' he has it) is bred by apparently harmless practices of this description. He offers to turn the current of a Republican's brain, by resting a coronet on his forehead for just five seconds.

Howsoever these things be, it was true that Emilia's feet presently crossed, and she was soon to be seen with her right elbow doubled against her head as she leaned to the wall, and the little left fist stuck at her belt. And I maintain that she had no sense at all of acting Spanish prince disguised as page. Nor had she an idea that she was making her friend Wilfrid's heart perform to her lightest words and actions, like any trained milk-white steed in a circus. Sunlight, as well as Wilfrid's braided cap, had some magical influence on her. He assured her that she looked a charming boy, and she said, "Do I?" just lifting her chin.

A gardener was shaving the lawn.

"Please, spare those daisies," cried Emilia. "Why do you cut away daisies?"

The gardener objected that he really must make the lawn smooth. Emilia called to Adela, who came, and hearing the case, said: "Now this is nice of you. I like you to love daisies and wish to protect them. They disfigure a lawn, you know." And Adela stooped, and picked one, and called it a pet name, and dropped it.

She returned to her sisters in the conservatory, and meeting Mr. Barren at the door, made the incident a topic. "You know how greatly our Emilia rejoices us when she shows sentiment, and our thirst is to direct her to appreciate Nature in its humility as well as its grandeur."

"One expects her to have all poetical feelings," said Mr. Barrett, while they walked forth to the lawn sloping to the tufted park grass.

Cornelia said: "You have read Mr. Runningbrook's story?"

"Yes."

But the man had not brought it back, and her name was in it, written with her own hand.

"Are you of my opinion in the matter?"

"In the matter of the style? I am and I am not. Your condemnation may be correct in itself; but you say, 'He coins words'; and he certainly forces the phrase here and there, I must admit. The point to be considered is, whether friction demands a perfectly smooth surface. Undoubtedly a scientific work does, and a philosophical treatise should. When we ask for facts simply, we feel the intrusion of a style. Of fiction it is part. In the one case the classical robe, in the other any mediaeval phantasy of clothing."

"Yes; true;" said Cornelia, hesitating over her argument. "Well, I must conclude that I am not imaginative."

"On the contrary, permit me to say that you are. But your imagination is unpractised, and asks to be fed with a spoon. We English are more imaginative than most nations."

"Then, why is it not manifested?"

"We are still fighting against the Puritan element, in literature as elsewhere."

"Your old bugbear, Mr. Barrett!"

"And more than this: our language is not rich in subtleties for prose. A writer who is not servile and has insight, must coin from his own mint. In poetry we are rich enough; but in prose also we owe everything to the licence our poets have taken in the teeth of critics. Shall I give you examples? It is not necessary. Our simplest prose style is nearer to poetry with us, for this reason, that the poets have made it. Read French poetry. With the first couplet the sails are full, and you have left the shores of prose far behind. Mr. Runningbrook coins words and risks expressions because an imaginative Englishman, pen in hand, is the cadet and vagabond of the family—an exploring adventurer; whereas to a Frenchman it all comes inherited like a well filled purse. The audacity of the French mind, and the French habit of quick social intercourse, have made them nationally far richer in language. Let me add, individually as much poorer. Read their stereotyped descriptions. They all say the same things. They have one big Gallic trumpet. Wonderfully eloquent: we feel that: but the person does not speak. And now, you will be surprised to learn that, notwithstanding what I have said, I should still side with Mr. Runningbrook's fair critic, rather than with him. The reason is, that the necessity to write as he does is so great that a strong barrier—a chevaux-de-frise of pen points—must be raised against every newly minted word and hazardous coiner, or we shall be inundated. If he can leap the barrier he and his goods must be admitted. So it has been with our greatest, so it must be with the rest of them, or we shall have a Transatlantic literature. By no means desirable, I think. Yet, see: when a piece of Transatlantic slang happens to be tellingly true— something coined from an absolute experience; from a fight with the elements—we cannot resist it: it invades us. In the same way poetic rashness of the right quality enriches the language. I would make it prove its quality."

Cornelia walked on gravely. His excuse for dilating on the theme, prompted her to say: "You give me new views": while all her reflections sounded from the depths: "And yet, the man who talks thus is a hired organ-player!"

This recurring thought, more than the cogency of the new views, kept her from combating certain fallacies in them which had struck her.

"Why do you not write yourself, Mr. Barrett?"

"I have not the habit."

"The habit!"

"I have not heard the call."

"Should it not come from within?"

"And how are we to know it?"

"If it calls to you loudly!"

"Then I know it to be vanity."

"But the wish to make a name is not vanity."

"The wish to conceal a name may exist."

Cornelia took one of those little sly glances at his features which print them on the brain. The melancholy of his words threw a somber hue about him, and she began to think with mournfulness of those firm thin lips fronting misfortune: those sunken blue eyes under its shadow.

They walked up to Mr. Pole, who was standing with Wilfrid and Emilia on the lawn; giving ear to a noise in the distance.

A big drum sounded on the confines of the Brookfield estate. Soon it was seen entering the precincts at one of the principal gates, followed by trombone, and horn, and fife. In the rear trooped a regiment of Sunday-garmented villagers, with a rambling tail of loose-minded boys and girls. Blue and yellow ribands dangled from broad beaver hats, and there were rosettes of the true-blue mingled with yellow at buttonholes; and there was fun on the line of march. Jokes plumped deep into the ribs, and were answered with intelligent vivacity in the shape of hearty thwacks, delivered wherever a surface was favourable: a mode of repartee worthy of general adoption, inasmuch as it can be passed on, and so with certainty made to strike your neighbour as forcibly as yourself: of which felicity of propagation verbal wit cannot always boast. In the line of procession, the hat of a member of the corps shot sheer into the sky from the compressed energy of his brain; for he and all his comrades vociferously denied having cast it up, and no other solution was possible. This mysterious incident may tell you that beer was thus early in the morning abroad. In fact, it was the procession day of a provincial Club-feast or celebration of the nuptials of Beef and Beer; whereof later you shall behold the illustrious offspring.

All the Brookfield household were now upon the lawn, awaiting the attack. Mr. Pole would have liked to impound the impouring host, drum and all, for the audacity of the trespass, and then to have fed them liberally, as a return for the compliment. Aware that he was being treated to the honours of a great man of the neighbourhood, he determined to take it cheerfully.

"Come; no laughing!" he said, directing a glance at the maids who were ranged behind their mistresses. "'Hem! we must look pleased: we mustn't mind their music, if they mean well."

Emilia, whose face was dismally screwed up at the nerve-searching discord, said: "Why do they try to play anything but a drum?"

"In the country, in the country;" Mr. Pole emphasized. "We put up with this kind of thing in the country. Different in town; but we—a—say nothing in the country. We must encourage respect for the gentry, in the country. One of the penalties of a country life. Not much harm in it. New duties in the country."

He continued to speak to himself. In proportion as he grew aware of the unnecessary nervous agitation into which the drum was throwing him, he assumed an air of repose, and said to Wilfrid: "Read the paper to-day?" and to Arabella, "Quiet family dinner, I suppose?"

"Yes, sir," he remarked to Mr. Barrett, as if resuming an old conversation: "I dare say, you've seen better marching in foreign parts. Right—left; right—left. Ha! ha! And not so bad, not so bad, I call it! with their right—left; right—left. Ha! ha! You've seen better. No need to tell me that. But, in England, we look to the meaning of things. We're a practical people. What's more, we're volunteers. Volunteers in everything. We can't make a regiment of ploughmen march like clock-work in a minute; and we don't want to. But, give me the choice; I'll back a body of volunteers any day."

"I would rather be backed by them, sir," said Mr. Barrett.

"Very good. I mean that. Honest intelligent industry backing rank and wealth! That makes a nation strong. Look at England!"

Mr. Barrett observed him stand out largely, as if filled by the spirit of the big drum.

That instrument now gave a final flourish and bang whereat Sound, as if knocked on the head, died languishingly.

And behold, a spokesman was seen in relief upon a background of grins, that were oddly intermixed with countenances of extraordinary solemnity.

The same commenced his propitiatory remarks by assuring the proprietor of Brookfield that he, the spokesman, and every man present, knew they had taken a liberty in coming upon Squire Pole's grounds without leave or warning. They knew likewise that Squire Pole excused them.

Chorus of shouts from the divining brethren.

Right glad they were to have such a gentleman as Squire Pole among them: and if nobody gave him a welcome last year, that was not the fault of the Yellow-and-Blues. Eh, my boys?

Groans and cheers.

Right sure was spokesman that Squire Pole was the friend of the poor man, and liked nothing better than to see him enjoy his holiday. As why shouldn't he enjoy his holiday now and then, and have a bit of relaxation as well as other men?

Acquiescent token on the part of the new dignitary, Squire Pole.

Spokesman was hereby encouraged to put it boldly, whether a man was not a man all the world over.

"For a' that!" was sung out by some rare bookworm to rearward: but no Scot being present, no frenzy followed the quotation.

It was announced that the Club had come to do homage to Squire Pole and ladies: the Junction Club of Ipley and Hillford. What did Junction mean? Junction meant Harmony. Harmonious they were, to be sure: so they joined to good purpose.

Mr. Barrett sought Emilia's eyes smilingly, but she was intent on the proceedings.

A cry of "Bundle o' sticks, Tom Breeks. Don't let slip 'bout bundle o' sticks," pulled spokesman up short. He turned hurriedly to say, "All right," and inflated his chest to do justice to the illustration of the faggots of Aesop: but Mr. Tom Breeks had either taken in too much air, or the ale that had hitherto successfully prompted him was antipathetic to the nice delicacy of an apologue; for now his arm began to work and his forehead had to be mopped, and he lashed the words "Union and Harmony" right and left, until, coming on a sentence that sounded in his ears like the close of his speech, he stared ahead, with a dim idea that he had missed a point. "Bundle o' sticks," lustily shouted, revived his apprehension; but the sole effect was to make him look on the ground and lift his hat on the point of a perplexed finger. He could not conceive how the bundle of sticks was to be brought in now; or what to say concerning them. Union and Harmony:—what more could be said? Mr. Tom Breeks tried a remonstrance with his backers. He declared to them that he had finished, and had brought in the Bundle. They replied that they had not heard it; that the Bundle was the foundation—sentiment of the Club; the first toast, after the Crown; and that he must go on until the Bundle had been brought in. Hereat, the unhappy man faced Squire Pole again. It was too abject a position for an Englishman to endure. Tom Breeks cast his hat to earth. "I'm dashed if I can bring in the bundle!"

There was no telling how conduct like this might have been received by the Yellow-and-Blues if Mr. Barrett had not spoken. "You mean everything when you say 'Union,' and you're quite right not to be tautological. You can't give such a blow with your fingers as you can with your fists, can you?"

Up went a score of fists. "We've the fists: we've the fists," was shouted.

Cornelia, smiling on Mr. Barrett, asked him why he had confused the poor people with the long word "tautological."

"I threw it as a bone," said he. "I think you will observe that they are already quieter. They are reflecting on what it signifies, and will by-and-by quarrel as to the spelling of it. At any rate it occupies them."

Cornelia laughed inwardly, and marked with pain that his own humour gave him no merriment.

At the subsiding of the echoes that coupled Squire Pole and the Junction Club together, Squire Pole replied. He wished them well. He was glad to see them, and sorry he had not ale enough on the premises to regale every man of them. Clubs were great institutions. One fist was stronger than a thousand fingers—"as my friend here said just now." Hereat the eyelids of Cornelia shed another queenly smile on the happy originator of the remark.

Squire Pole then descended to business. He named the amount of his donation. At this practical sign of his support, heaven heard the gratitude of the good fellows. The drum awoke from its torpor, and summoned its brethren of the band to give their various versions of the National Anthem.

"Can't they be stopped?" Emilia murmured, clenching her little hands.

The patriotic melody, delivered in sturdy democratic fashion, had to be endured. It died hard, but did come to an end, piecemeal. Tom Breeks then retired from the front, and became a unit once more. There were flourishes that indicated a termination of the proceedings, when another fellow was propelled in advance, and he, shuffling and ducking his head, to the cries of "Out wi' it, Jim!" and, "Where's your stomach?" came still further forward, and showed a most obsequious grin.

"Why, it's Jim!" exclaimed Emilia, on whom Jim's eyes were fastened. Stepping nearer, she said, "Do you want to speak to me?"

Jim had this to say: which, divested of his petition for pardon on the strength of his perfect knowledge that he took a liberty, was, that the young lady had promised, while staying at Wilson's farm, that she would sing to the Club-fellows on the night of their feast.

"I towl'd 'em they'd have a rare treat, miss," mumbled Jim, "and they're all right mad for 't, that they be—bain't ye, boys?"

That they were! with not a few of the gesticulations of madness too.

Emilia said: "I promised I would sing to them. I remember it quite well. Of course I will keep my promise."

A tumult of acclamation welcomed her words, and Jim looked immensely delighted.

She was informed by several voices that they were the Yellow-and-Blues, and not the Blues: that she must not go to the wrong set: and that their booth was on Ipley Common: and that they, the Junction Club, only would honour her rightly for the honour she was going to do them: all of which Emilia said she would bear in mind.

Jim then retired hastily, having done something that stout morning ale would alone have qualified him to perform. The drum, in the noble belief that it was leading, announced the return march, and with three cheers for Squire Pole, and a crowning one for the ladies, away trooped the procession.

CHAPTER IX

THE RIVAL CLUBS

Hardly had the last sound of the drum passed out of hearing, when the elastic thunder of a fresh one claimed attention. The truth being, that the Junction Club of Ipley and Hillford, whose colours were yellow and blue, was a seceder from the old-established Hillford Club, on which it had this day shamefully stolen a march by parading everywhere in the place of it, and disputing not only its pasture-grounds but its identity.

There is no instrument the sound of which proclaims such a vast internal satisfaction as the drum. I know not whether it be that the sense we have of the corpulency of this instrument predisposes us to imagine it supremely content: as when an alderman is heard snoring the world is assured that it listens to the voice of its own exceeding gratulation. A light heart in a fat body ravishes not only the world but the philosopher. If monotonous, the one note of the drum is very correct. Like the speaking of great Nature, what it means is implied by the measure. When the drum beats to the measure of a common human pulsation it has a conquering power: inspiring us neither to dance nor to trail the members, but to march as life does, regularly, and in hearty good order, and with a not exhaustive jollity. It is a sacred instrument.

Now the drum which is heard to play in this cheerful fashion, while at the same time we know that discomfiture is cruelly harrying it: that its inmost feelings are wounded, and that worse is in store for it, affects the contemplative mind with an inexpressibly grotesque commiseration. Do but listen to this one, which is the joint corporate voice of the men of Hillford. Outgeneraled, plundered, turned to ridicule, it thumps with unabated briskness. Here indeed might Sentimentalism shed a fertile tear!

Anticipating that it will eventually be hung up among our national symbols, I proceed. The drum of Hillford entered the Brookfield grounds as Ipley had done, and with a similar body of decorated Clubmen; sounding along until it faced the astonished proprietor, who held up his hand and requested to know the purpose of the visit. One sentence of explanation sufficed.

"What!" cried Mr. Pole, "do you think you can milk a cow twice in ten minutes?"

Several of the Hillford men acknowledged that it would be rather sharp work.

Their case was stated: whereupon Mr. Pole told them that he had just been 'milked,' and regretted it, but requested them to see that he could not possibly be equal to any second proceeding of the sort. On their turning to consult together, he advised them to bear it with fortitude. "All right, sir!" they said: and a voice from the ranks informed him that their word was 'Jolly.' Then a signal was given, and these indomitable fellows cheered the lord of Brookfield as lustily as if they had accomplished the feat of milking him twice in an hour. Their lively hurrahs set him blinking in extreme discomposure of spirit, and he was fumbling at his pocket, when the drum a little precipitately thumped: the ranks fell into order, and the departure was led by the tune of the 'King of the Cannibal islands:' a tune that is certain to create a chorus on the march. On this occasion, the line:—

"Oh! didn't you know you were done, sir?"

became general at the winding up of the tune. Boys with their elders frisked as they chimed it, casting an emphasis of infinite relish on the declaration 'done'; as if they delighted in applying it to Mr. Pole, though at their own expense.

Soon a verse grew up:—

"We march'd and call'd on Mister Pole,
Who hadn't a penny, upon his soul,
For Ipley came and took the whole,
And didn't you know you were done, sir!"

I need not point out to the sagacious that Hillford and not Mr. Pole had been 'done;' but this was the genius of the men who transferred the opprobrium to him. Nevertheless, though their manner of welcoming misfortune was such, I, knowing that there was not a deadlier animal than a 'done' Briton, have shudders for Ipley.

We relinquished the stream of an epic in turning away from these mighty drums.

Mr. Pole stood questioning all who surrounded him: "What could I do? I couldn't subscribe to both. They don't expect that of a lord, and I'm a commoner. If these fellows quarrel and split, are we to suffer for it? They can't agree, and want us to pay double fines. This is how they serve us."

Mr. Barrett, rather at a loss to account for his excitement, said, that it must be admitted they had borne the trick played upon them, with remarkable good humour.

"Yes, but," Mr. Pole fumed, "I don't. They put me in the wrong, between them. They make me uncomfortable. I've a good mind to withdraw my subscription to those rascals who came first, and have nothing to do with any of them. Then, you see, down I go for a niggardly fellow. That's the reputation I get. Nothing of this in London! you make your money, pay your rates, and nobody bothers a man."

"You should have done as our darling here did, papa," said Adela. "You should have hinted something that might be construed a promise or not, as we please to read it."

"If I promise I perform," returned Mr. Pole.

"Our Hillford people have cause for complaint," Mr. Barrett observed. And to Emilia: "You will hardly favour one party more than another, will you?"

"I am for that poor man Jim," said Emilia, "He carried my harp evening after evening, and would not even take sixpence for the trouble."

"Are you really going to sing there?"

"Didn't you hear? I promised."

"To-night?"

"Yes; certainly."

"Do you know what it is you have promised?"

"To sing."

Adela glided to her sisters near at hand, and these ladies presently hemmed Emilia in. They had a method of treating matters they did not countenance, as if nature had never conceived them, and such were the monstrous issue of diseased imaginations. It was hard for Emilia to hear that what she designed to do was "utterly out of the question and not to be for one moment thought of." She reiterated, with the same interpreting stress, that she had given her promise.

"Do you know, I praised you for putting them off so cleverly," said Adela in tones of gentle reproach that bewildered Emilia.

"Must we remind you, then, that you are bound by a previous promise?" Cornelia made a counter-demonstration with the word. "Have you not promised to dine with us at Lady Gosstre's to-night?"

"Oh, of course I shall keep that," replied Emilia. "I intend to. I will sing there, and then I will go and sing to those poor people, who never hear anything but dreadful music—not music at all, but something that seems to tear your flesh!"

"Never mind our flesh," said Adela pettishly: melodiously remonstrating the next instant: "I really thought you could not be in earnest."

"But," said Arabella, "can you find pleasure in wasting your voice and really great capabilities on such people?"

Emilia caught her up—"This poor man? But he loves music: he really knows the good from the bad. He never looks proud but when I sing to him."

The situation was one that Cornelia particularly enjoyed. Here was a low form of intellect to be instructed as to the precise meaning of a word, the nature of a pledge. "There can be no harm that I see, in your singing to this man," she commenced. "You can bid him come to one of the out-houses here, if you desire, and sing to him. In the evening, after his labour, will be the fit time. But, as your friends, we cannot permit you to demean yourself by going from our house to a public booth, where vulgar men are smoking and drinking beer. I wonder you have the courage to contemplate such an act! You have pledged your word. But if you had pledged your word, child, to swing upon that tree, suspended by your arms, for an hour, could you keep it? I think not; and to recognize an impossibility economizes time and is one of the virtues of a clear understanding. It is incompatible that you should dine with Lady Gosstre, and then run away to a drinking booth. Society will never tolerate one who is familiar with boors. If you are to succeed in life, as we, your friends, can conscientiously say that we most earnestly hope and trust you will do, you must be on good terms with Society. You must! You pledge your word to a piece of folly. Emancipate yourself from it as quickly as possible. Do you see? This is foolish: it, therefore, cannot be. Decide, as a sensible creature."

At the close of this harangue, Cornelia, who had stooped slightly to deliver it, regained her stately posture, beautified in Mr. Barrett's sight by the flush which an unwonted exercise in speech had thrown upon her cheeks.

Emilia stood blinking like one sensible of having been chidden in a strange tongue.

"Does it offend you—my going?" she faltered.

"Offend!—our concern is entirely for you," observed Cornelia.

The explanation drew out a happy sparkle from Emilia's eyes. She seized her hand, kissed it, and cried: "I do thank you. I know I promised, but indeed I am quite pleased to go!"

Mr. Barrett swung hurriedly round and walked some paces away with his head downward. The ladies remained in a tolerant attitude for a minute or so, silent. They then wheeled with one accord, and Emilia was left to herself.

CHAPTER X

THE LADIES OF BROOKFIELD AT SCHOOL

Richford was an easy drive from Brookfield, through lanes of elm and white hawthorn.

The ladies never acted so well as when they were in the presence of a fact which they acknowledged, but did not recognize. Albeit constrained to admit that this was the first occasion of their ever being on their way to the dinner-table of a person of quality, they could refuse to look the admission in the face. A peculiar lightness of heart beset them; for brooding ambition is richer in that first realizing step it takes, insignificant though it seem, than in any subsequent achievement. I fear to say that the hearts of the ladies boiled, because visages so sedate, and voices so monotonously indifferent, would witness decidedly against me. The common avoidance of any allusion to Richford testified to the direction of their thoughts; and the absence of a sign of exultation may be accepted as a proof of the magnitude of that happiness of which they might not exhibit a feature. The effort to repress it must have cost them horrible pain. Adela, the youngest of the three, transferred her inward joy to the cottage children, whose staring faces from garden porch and gate flashed by the carriage windows. "How delighted they look!" she exclaimed more than once, and informed her sisters that a country life was surely the next thing to Paradise. "Those children do look so happy!" Thus did the weak one cunningly relieve herself. Arabella occupied her mind by giving Emilia leading hints for conduct in the great house. "On the whole, though there is no harm in your praising particular dishes, as you do at home, it is better in society to say nothing on those subjects until your opinion is asked: and when you speak, it should be as one who passes the subject by. Appreciate flavours, but no dwelling on them! The degrees of an expression of approbation, naturally enough, vary with age. Did my instinct prompt me to the discussion of these themes, I should be allowed greater licence than you." And here Arabella was unable to resist a little bit of the indulgence Adela had taken: "You are sure to pass a most agreeable evening, and one that you will remember."

North Pole sat high above such petty consolation; seldom speaking, save just to show that her ideas ranged at liberty, and could be spontaneously sympathetic on selected topics.

Their ceremonious entrance to the state-room of Richford accomplished, the ladies received the greeting of the affable hostess; quietly perturbed, but not enough so to disorder their artistic contemplation of her open actions, choice of phrase, and by-play. Without communication or pre-arrangement, each knew that the other would not let slip the opportunity, and, after the first five minutes of languid general converse; they were mentally at work comparing notes with one another's imaginary conversations, while they said "Yes," and "Indeed," and "I think so," and appeared to belong to the world about them.

"Merthyr, I do you the honour to hand this young lady to your charge," said Lady Gosstre, putting on equal terms with Emilia a gentleman of perhaps five-and-thirty years; who reminded her of Mr. Barrett, but was unclouded by that look of firm sadness which characterized the poor organist. Mr. Powys was a travelled Welsh squire, Lady Gosstre's best talker, on whom, as Brookfield learnt to see, she could perfectly rely to preserve the child from any little drawing-room sins or dinner-table misadventures. This gentleman had made sacrifices for the cause of Italy, in money, and, it was said, in blood. He knew the country and loved the people. Brookfield remarked that there was just a foreign tinge in his manner; and that his smile, though social to a degree unknown to the run of English faces, did not give him all to you, and at a second glance seemed plainly to say that he reserved much.

Adela fell to the lot of a hussar-captain: a celebrated beauty, not too foolish. She thought it proper to punish him for his good looks till propitiated by his good temper.

Nobody at Brookfield could remember afterwards who took Arabella down to dinner; she declaring that she had forgotten. Her sisters, not unwilling to see insignificance banished to annihilation, said that it must have been nobody in person, and that he was a very useful guest when ladies were engaged. Cornelia had a different lot. She leaned on the right arm of the Member for Hillford, the statistical debate, Sir Twickenham Pryme, who had twice before, as he ventured to remind her, enjoyed the honour of conversing, if not of dining, with her. Nay, more, he revived their topics. "And I have come round to your way of thinking as regards hustings addresses," he said. "In nine cases out of ten—at least, nineteen-twentieths of the House will furnish instances—one can only, as you justly observed, appeal to the comprehension of the mob by pledging oneself either to their appetites or passions, and it is better plainly to state the case and put it to them in figures." Whether the Baronet knew what he was saying is one matter: he knew what he meant.

Wilfrid was cavalier to Lady Charlotte Chillingworth, of Stornley, about ten miles distant from Hillford; ninth daughter of a nobleman who passed current as the Poor Marquis; he having been ruined when almost a boy in Paris, by the late illustrious Lord Dartford. Her sisters had married captains in the army and navy, lawyers, and parsons, impartially. Lady Charlotte was nine-and-twenty years of age; with clear and telling stone-blue eyes, firm but not unsweet lips, slightly hollowed cheeks, and a jaw that certainly tended to be square. Her colour was healthy. Walking or standing her figure was firmly poised. Her chief attraction was a bell-toned laugh, fresh as a meadow spring. She had met Wilfrid once in the hunting-field, so they soon had common ground to run on.

Mr. Powys made Emilia happy by talking to her of Italy, in the intervals of table anecdotes.

"Why did you leave it?" she said.

"I found I had more shadows than the one allotted me by nature; and as I was accustomed to a black one, and not half a dozen white, I was fairly frightened out of the country."

"You mean, Austrians."

"I do."

"Do you hate them?"

"Not at all."

"Then, how can you love the Italians?"

"They themselves have taught me to do both; to love them and not to hate their enemies. Your Italians are the least vindictive of all races of men."

"Merthyr, Merthyr!" went Lady Gosstre; Lady Charlotte murmuring aloud: "And in the third chapter of the Book of Paradox you will find these words."

"We afford a practical example and forgive them, do we not?" Mr. Powys smiled at Emilia.

She looked round her, and reddened a little.

"So long as you do not write that Christian word with the point of a stiletto!" said Lady Charlotte.

"You are not mad about the Italians?" Wilfrid addressed her.

"Not mad about anything, I hope. If I am to choose, I prefer the Austrians. A very gentlemanly set of men! At least, so I find them always. Capital horsemen!"

"I will explain to you how it must be," said Mr. Powys to Emilia. "An artistic people cannot hate long. Hotly for the time, but the oppression gone, and even in the dream of its going, they are too human to be revengeful."

"Do we understand such very deep things?" said Lady Gosstre, who was near enough to hear clearly.

"Yes: for if I ask her whether she can hate when her mind is given to music, she knows that she cannot. She can love."

"Yet I think I have heard some Italian operatic spitfires, and of some!" said Lady Charlotte.

"What opinion do you pronounce in this controversy?" Cornelia made appeal to Sir Twickenham.

"There are multitudes of cases," he began: and took up another end of his statement: "It has been computed that five-and-twenty murders per month to a population...to a population of ninety thousand souls, is a fair reckoning in a Southern latitude."

"Then we must allow for the latitude?"

"I think so."

"And also for the space into which the ninety thousand souls are packed," quoth Tracy Runningbrook.

"Well! well!" went Sir Twickenham.

"The knife is the law to an Italian of the South," said Mr. Powys. "He distrusts any other, because he never gets it. Where law is established, or tolerably secure, the knife is not used. Duels are rare. There is too much bonhomie for the point of honour."

"I should like to believe that all men are as just to their mistresses," Lady Charlotte sighed, mock-earnestly.

Presently Emilia touched the arm of Mr. Powys. She looked agitated. "I want to be told the name of that gentleman." His eyes were led to rest on the handsome hussar-captain.

"Do you know him?"

"But his name!"

"Do me the favour to look at me. Captain Gambier."

"It is!"

Captain Gambier's face was resolutely kept in profile to her.

"I hear a rumour," said Lady Gosstre to Arabella, "that you think of bidding for the Besworth estate. Are you tired of Brookfield?"

"Not tired; but Brookfield is modern, and I confess that Besworth has won my heart."

"I shall congratulate myself on having you nearer neighbours. Have you many, or any rivals?"

"There is some talk of the Tinleys wishing to purchase it. I cannot see why."

"What people are they?" asked Lady Charlotte. "Do they hunt?"

"Oh, dear, no! They are to society what Dissenters are to religion. I can't describe them otherwise."

"They pass before me in that description," said Lady Gosstre.

"Besworth's an excellent centre for hunting," Lady Charlotte remarked to Wilfrid. "I've always had an affection for that place. The house is on gravel; the river has trout; there's a splendid sweep of grass for the horses to exercise. I think there must be sixteen spare beds. At all events, I know that number can be made up; so that if you're too poor to live much in London, you can always have your set about you."

The eyes of the fair economist sparkled as she dwelt on these particular advantages of Besworth.

Richford boasted a show of flowers that might tempt its guests to parade the grounds on balmy evenings. Wilfrid kept by the side of Lady Charlotte. She did not win his taste a bit. Had she been younger, less decided in tone, and without a title, it is very possible that she would have offended his native, secret, and dominating fastidiousness as much as did Emilia. Then, what made him subject at all to her influence, as he felt himself beginning to be? She supplied a deficiency in the youth. He was growing and uncertain: she was set and decisive. In his soul he adored the extreme refinement of woman; even up to the thin edge of inanity (which neighbours what the philosopher could tell him if he would, and would, if it were permitted to him). Nothing was too white, too saintly, or too misty, for his conception of abstract woman. But the practical wants of our nature guide us best. Conversation with Lady Charlotte seemed to strengthen and ripen him. He blushed with pleasure when she said: "I remember reading your name in the account of that last cavalry charge on the Dewan. You slew a chief, I think. That was creditable, for they are swordsmen. Cavalry in Europe can't win much honour—not individual honour, I mean. I suppose being part of a victorious machine is exhilarating. I confess I should not think much of wearing that sort of feather. It's right to do one's duty, comforting to trample down opposition, and agreeable to shed blood, but when you have matched yourself man to man, and beaten—why, then, I dub you knight."

Wilfrid bowed, half-laughing, in a luxurious abandonment to his sensations. Possibly because of their rule over him then, the change in him was so instant from flattered delight to vexed perplexity. Rounding one of the rhododendron banks, just as he lifted his head from that acknowledgment of the lady's commendation, he had sight of Emilia with her hand in the hand of Captain Gambier. What could it mean? what right had he to hold her hand? Even if he knew her, what right?

The words between Emilia and Captain Gambier were few.

"Why did I not look at you during dinner?" said he. "Was it not better to wait till we could meet?"

"Then you will walk with me and talk to me all the evening?"

"No: but I will try and come down here next week and meet you again."

"Are you going to-night?"

"Yes."

"To-night? To-night before it strikes a quarter to ten, I am going to leave here alone. If you would come with me! I want a companion. I know they will not hurt me, but I don't like being alone. I have given my promise to sing to some poor people. My friends say I must not go. I must go. I can't break a promise to poor people. And you have never heard me really sing my best. Come with me, and I will."

Captain Gambier required certain explanations. He saw that a companion and protection would be needed by his curious little friend, and as she was resolved not to break her word, he engaged to take her in the carriage that was to drive him to the station.

"You make me give up an appointment in town," he said.

"Ah, but you will hear me sing," returned Emilia. "We will drive to Brookfield and get my harp, and then to Ipley Common. I am to be sure you will be ready with the carriage at just a quarter to ten?"

The Captain gave her his assurance, and they separated; he to seek out Adela, she to wander about, the calmest of conspirators against the serenity of a household.

Meeting Wilfrid and Lady Charlotte, Emilia was asked by him, who it was she had quitted so abruptly.

"That is the gentleman I told you of. Now I know his name. It is Captain Gambier."

She was allowed to pass on.

"What is this she says?" Lady Charlotte asked.

"It appears...something about a meeting somewhere accidentally, in the park, in London, I think; I really don't know. She had forgotten his name."

Lady Charlotte spurred him with an interrogative "Yes?"

"She wanted to remember his name. That's all. He was kind to her."

"But, after all," remonstrated Lady Charlotte, "that's only a characteristic of young men, is it not? no special distinction. You are all kind to girls, to women, to anything!"

Captain Gambier and Adela crossed their path. He spoke a passing word, Lady Charlotte returned no answer, and was silent to her companion for some minutes. Then she said, "If you feel any responsibility about this little person, take my advice, and don't let her have appointments and meetings. They're bad in any case, and for a girl who has no brother—has she? no:—well then, you should make the best provision you can against the cowardice of men. Most men are cowards."

Emilia sang in the drawing-room. Brookfield knew perfectly why she looked indifferent to the plaudits, and was not dissatisfied at hearing Lady Gosstre say that she was a little below the mark. The kindly lady brought Emilia between herself and Mr. Powys, saying, "I don't intend to let you be the star of the evening and outshine us all." After which, conversation commenced, and Brookfield had reason to admire her ladyship's practised play upon the social instrument, surely the grandest of all, the chords being men and women. Consider what an accomplishment this is!

Albeit Brookfield knew itself a student at Richford, Adela was of too impatient a wit to refrain from little ventures toward independence, if not rivalry. "What we do," she uttered distinctively once or twice. Among other things she spoke of "our discovery," to attest her declaration that, to wakeful eyes, neither Hillford nor any other place on earth was dull. Cornelia flushed at hearing the name of Mr. Barrett pronounced publicly by her sister.

"An organist an accomplished man!" Lady Gosstre repeated Adela's words. "Well, I suppose it is possible, but it rather upsets one's notions, does it not?"

"Yes, but agreeably," said Adela, with boldness; and related how he had been introduced, and hinted that he was going to be patronized.

"The man cannot maintain himself on the income that sort of office brings him," Lady Gosstre observed.

"Oh, no," said Adela. "I fancy he does it simply for some sort of occupation. One cannot help imagining a disguise."

"Personally I confess to an objection to gentlemen in disguise," said Lady Gosstre. "Barrett!—do you know the man?"

She addressed Mr. Powys.

"There used to be good quartett evenings given by the Barretts of Bursey," he said. "Sir Justinian Barrett married a Miss Purcell, who subsequently preferred the musical accomplishments of a foreign professor of the Art."

"Purcell Barrett is his name," said Adela. "Our Emilia brought him to us. Where is she? But, where can she be?"

Adela rose.

"She pressed my hand just now," said Lady Gosstre.

"She was here when Captain Gambler quitted the room," Arabella remarked.

"Good heaven!"

The exclamation came from Adela.

"Oh, Lady Gosstre! I fear to tell you what I think she has done."

The scene of the rival Clubs was hurriedly related, together with the preposterous pledge given by Emilia, that she would sing at the Ipley Booth: "Among those dreadful men!"

"They will treat her respectfully," said Mr. Powys.

"Worship her, I should imagine, Merthyr," said Lady Gosstre. "For all that, she had better be away. Beer is not a respectful spirit."

"I trust you will pardon her," Arabella pleaded. "Everything that explanations of the impropriety of such a thing could do, we have done. We thought that at last we had convinced her. She is quite untamed."

Mr. Powys now asked where this place was that she had hurried to.

The unhappy ladies of Brookfield, quick as they were to read every sign surrounding them, were for the moment too completely thrown off their balance by Emilia's extraordinary exhibition of will, to see that no reflex of her shameful and hideous proceeding had really fallen upon them. Their exclamations were increasing, until Adela, who had been the noisiest, suddenly adopted Lady Gosstre's tone. "If she has gone, I suppose she must be simply fetched away."

"Do you see what has happened?" Lady Charlotte murmured to Wilfrid, between a phrase.

He stumbled over a little piece of gallantry.

"Excellent! But, say those things in French.—Your dark-eyed maid has eloped. She left the room five minutes after Captain Gambier."

Wilfrid sprang to his feet, looking eagerly to the corners of the room.

"Pardon me," he said, and moved up to Lady Gosstre. On the way he questioned himself why his heart should be beating at such a pace. Standing at her ladyship's feet, he could scarcely speak.

"Yes, Wilfrid; go after her," said Adela, divining his object.

"By all means go," added Lady Gosstre. "Now she is there, you may as well let her keep her promise; and then hurry her home. They will saddle you a horse down below, if you care to have one."

Wilfrid thanked her ladyship, and declined the horse. He was soon walking rapidly under a rough sky in the direction of Ipley, with no firm thought that he would find Emilia there.

BOOK II

CHAPTER XI

IN WHICH WE SEE THE MAGNANIMITY THAT IS IN BEER

At half-past nine of the clock on the evening of this memorable day, a body of five-and-twenty stout young fellows, prize-winners, wrestlers, boxers, and topers, of the Hillford Club, set forth on a march to Ipley Common.

Now, a foreigner, hearing of their destination and the provocation they had endured, would have supposed that they were bent upon deeds of vengeance; and it requires knowledge of our countrymen to take it as a fact that the idea and aim of the expedition were simply to furnish the offending Ipley boys a little music. Such were the idea and the aim. Hillford had nothing to do with consequences: no more than our England is responsible when she sails out among the empires and hemispheres, saying, 'buy' and 'sell,' and they clamour to be eaten up entire. Foreigners pertinaciously misunderstand us. They have the barbarous habit of judging by results. Let us know ourselves better. It is melancholy to contemplate the intrigues, and vile designs, and vengeances of other nations; and still more so, after we have written so many pages of intelligible history, to see them attributed to us. Will it never be perceived that we do not sow the thing that happens? The source of the flooding stream which drinks up those rich acres of low flat land is not more innocent than we. If, as does seem possible, we are in a sort of alliance with Destiny, we have signed no compact, and accomplish our work as solidly and merrily as a wood-hatchet in the hands of the woodman. This arrangement to give Ipley a little music, was projected as a return for the favours of the morning: nor have I in my time heard anything comparable to it in charity of sentiment, when I consider the detestable outrage Hillford suffered under.

The parading of the drum, the trombone, a horn, two whistles, and a fife, in front of Hillford booth, caught the fancy of the Clubmen, who roared out parting adjurations that the music was not to be spared; and that Tom Breeks was a musical fellow, with a fine empty pate, if any one of the instruments should fail perchance. They were to give Ipley plenty of music: for Ipley wanted to be taught harmony. Harmony was Ipley's weak point. "Gie 'em," said one jolly ruddy Hillford man, "gie 'em whack fol, lol!" And he smacked himself, and set toward an invisible partner. Nor, as recent renowned historians have proved, are observations of this nature beneath the dignity of chronicle. They vindicate, as they localize, the sincerity of Hillford.

Really, to be an islander full of ale, is to be the kindest creature on or off two legs. For that very reason, it may be, his wrath at bad blood is so easily aroused. In our hot moods we would desire things like unto ourselves, and object violently to whatsoever is unlike. And also we desire that the benefits we shed be appreciated. If Ipley understands neither our music nor our intent, haply we must hold a performance on the impenetrable sconce of Ipley.

At the hour named, the expedition, with many a promise that the music should be sweet, departed hilariously: Will Burdock, the left-handed cricketer and hard-hitter, being leader; with Peter Bartholomew, potboy, John Girling, miller's man, and Ned Thewk, gardener's assistant, for lieutenants. On the march, silence was proclaimed, and partially enforced, after two fights against authority. Near the sign of King William's Head, General Burdock called a halt, and betrayed irresolution with reference to the route to be adopted; but as none of his troop could at all share such a condition of mind in the neighbourhood of an inn, he was permitted to debate peacefully with his lieutenants, while the rest burst through the doors and hailed the landlord: a proceeding he was quickly induced to imitate. Thus, when the tail shows strongest decision of purpose, the head must follow.

An accurate oinometer, or method of determining what shall be the condition of the spirit of man according to the degrees of wine or beer in him, were surely of priceless service to us. For now must we, to be certain of our sanity and dignity, abstain, which is to clip, impoverish, imprison the soul: or else, taking wings of wine, we go aloft over capes, and islands, and seas, but are even as balloons that cannot make for any line, and are at the mercy of the winds—without a choice, save to come down by virtue of a collapse. Could we say to ourselves, in the great style, This is the point where desire to embrace humanity is merged in vindictiveness toward individuals: where radiant sweet temper culminates in tremendous wrath: where the treasures of anticipation, waxing riotous, arouse the memory of wrongs: in plain words, could we know positively, and from the hand of science, when we have had enough, we should stop. There is not a doubt that we should stop. It is so true we should stop, that, I am ready to say, ladies have no right to call us horrid names, and complain of us, till they have helped us to some such trustworthy scientific instrument as this which I have called for. In its absence, I am persuaded that the true natural oinometer is the hat. Were the hat always worn during potation; were ladies when they retire to place it on our heads, or, better still, chaplets of flowers; then, like the wise ancients, we should be able to tell to a nicety how far we had advanced in our dithyramb to the theme of fuddle and muddle. Unhappily the hat does not forewarn: it is simply indicative. I believe, nevertheless, that science might set to work upon it forthwith, and found a system. When you mark men drinking who wear their hats, and those hats are seen gradually beginning to hang on the backs of their heads, as from pegs, in the fashion of a fez, the bald projection of forehead looks jolly and frank: distrust that sign: the may-fly of the soul is then about to be gobbled up by the chub of the passions. A hat worn fez-fashion is a dangerous hat. A hat on the brows shows a man who can take more, but thinks he will go home instead, and does so, peaceably. That is his determination. He may look like Macduff, but he is a lamb. The vinous reverses the non-vinous passionate expression of the hat. If I am discredited, I appeal to history, which tells us that the hats of the Hillford five-and-twenty were all exceedingly hind-ward-set when the march was resumed. It followed that Peter Bartholomew, potboy, made irritable objections to that old joke which finished his name as though it were a cat calling, and the offence being repeated, he dealt an impartial swing of his stick at divers heads, and told them to take that, which they assured him they had done by sending him flying into a hedge. Peter, being reprimanded by his commanding officer, acknowledged a hot desire to try his mettle, and the latter responsible person had to be restrained from granting the wish he cherished by John Girling, whom he threw for his trouble and as Burdock was the soundest hitter, numbers cried out against Girling, revolting him with a sense of overwhelming injustice that could be appeased only by his prostrating two stout lads and squaring against a third, who came up from a cross-road. This one knocked him down with the gentleness of a fist that knows how Beer should be treated, and then sang out, in the voice of Wilfrid Pole: "Which is the nearest way to Ipley, you fellows?"

"Come along with us, sir, and we'll show you," said Burdock.

"Are you going there?"

"Well, that's pretty clear."

"Hillford men, are you?"

"We've left the women behind."

"I'm in a hurry, so, good night."

"And so are we in a hurry, sir. But, you're a gentleman, and we want to give them chaps at Ipley a little surprise, d'ye see, in the way of a dollop o' music: and if you won't go givin' 'em warning, you may trot; and that road'll take you."

"All right," said Wilfrid, now fairly divided between his jealousy of Gambier and anxiety for Emilia.

Could her artist nature, of which he had heard perplexing talk, excuse her and make her heart absolutely guiltless (what he called 'innocent'), in trusting herself to any man's honour? I regret to say that the dainty adorers of the sex are even thus grossly suspicious of all women when their sentiment is ever so triflingly offended.

Lights on Ipley Common were seen from a rise of the hilly road. The moon was climbing through drifts of torn black cloud. Hastening his pace, for a double reason now, Wilfrid had the booth within hearing, listened a moment; and then stood fast. His unconscious gasp of the words: "Thank God; there she is!" might have betrayed him to another.

She was sitting near one end of the booth, singing as Wilfrid had never yet heard her sing: her dark eyes flashing. Behind her stood Captain Gambier, keeping guard with all the composure of a gentleman-usher at a royal presentation. Along the tables, men and women were ranged facing her; open-mouthed, some of them but for the most part wearing a predetermined expression of applausive judgement, as who should say, "Queer, but good." They gave Emilia their faces, which was all she wanted! and silence, save for an intermingling soft snore, here and there, the elfin trumpet of silence. To tell truth, certain heads had bowed low to the majesty of beer, and were down on the table between sprawling doubled arms. No essay on the power of beer could exhibit it more convincingly than, the happy indifference with which they received admonishing blows from quart-pots, salutes from hot pipe-bowls, pricks from pipe-ends, on nose, and cheek, and pate; as if to vindicate for their beloved beverage a right to rank with that old classic drink wherewith the fairest of women vanquished human ills. The majority, however, had been snatched out of this bliss by the intrusion of their wives, who sat beside them like Consciences in petticoats; and it must be said that Emilia was in favour with the married men, for one reason, because she gave these broad-ribboned ladies a good excuse for allowing their lords to stop where they were so comfortable, a continually-extending five minutes longer.

Yet, though the words were foreign and the style of the song and the singer were strange, many of the older fellows' eyes twinkled, and their mouths pursed with a kind of half-protesting pleasure. All were reverent to the compliment paid them by Emilia's presence. The general expression was much like that seen when the popular ear is given to the national anthem. Wilfrid hung at the opening of the booth, a cynical spectator. For what on earth made her throw such energy, and glory of music, into a song before fellows like these? He laughed dolorously, "she hasn't a particle of any sense of ridicule," he said to himself. Forthwith her voice took hold of him, and led him as heroes of old were led unwillingly into enchanted woods. If she had been singing things holy, a hymn, a hallelujah, in this company, it struck him that somehow it would have seemed appropriate; not objectionable; at any rate, not ridiculous. Dr. Watts would have put a girdle about her; but a song of romance sung in this atmosphere of pipes and beer and boozy heads, chagrined Wilfrid in proportion as the softer half of him began to succumb to the deliciousness of her voice.

Emilia may have had some warning sense that admiration is only one ingredient of homage, that to make it fast and true affection must be won. Now, poor people, yokels, clods, cannot love what is incomprehensible to them. An idol must have their attributes: a king must show his face now and then: a song must appeal to their intelligence, to subdue them quite. This, as we know, is not the case in the higher circles. Emilia may have divined it: possibly from the very great respect with which her finale was greeted. Vigorous as the "Brayvos" were, they sounded abashed: they lacked abandonment. In fact, it was gratitude that applauded, and not enthusiasm. "Hillford don't hear stuff like that, do 'em?" which was the main verbal encomium passed, may be taken testificatorily as to this point.

"Dame! dame!" cried Emilia, finding her way quickly to one of the more decently-bonneted women; "am I not glad to see you here! Did I please you? And you, dear Farmer Wilson? I caught sight of you just as I was finishing. I remember the song you like, and I want to sing it. I know the tune, but the words! the words! what are the words? Humming won't do."

"Ah, now!" quoth Farmer Wilson, pointing out the end of his pipe, "that's what they'll swallow down; that's the song to make 'em kick. Sing that, miss. Furrin songs 's all right enough; but 'Ale it is my tipple, and England is my nation!' Let's have something plain and flat on the surface, miss."

Dame Wilson jogged her husband's arm, to make him remember that talking was his dangerous pastime, and sent abroad a petition for a song-book; and after a space a very doggy-eared book, resembling a poodle of that genus, was handed to her. Then uprose a shout for this song and that; but Emilia fixed upon the one she had in view, and walked back to her harp, with her head bent, perusing it attentively all the way. There, she gave the book to Captain Gambier, and begged him to hold it open before her, with a passing light of eyes likely to be rather disturbing to a jealous spectator. The Captain seized the book without wincing, and displayed a remarkable equanimity of countenance as he held it out, according to direction. No sooner had Emilia struck a prelude of the well-known air, than the interior of the booth was transfigured; legs began to move, elbows jerked upward, fingers filipped: the whole body of them were ready to duck and bow, dance, and do her bidding she had fairly caught their hearts. For, besides the pleasure they had in their own familiar tune, it was wonderful to them that Emilia should know what they knew. This was the marvel, this the inspiration. She smiled to see how true she had struck, and seemed to swim on the pleasure she excited. Once, as her voice dropped, she looked up at Captain Gambier, so very archly, with the curving line of her bare throat, that Wilfrid was dragged down from his cynical observatory, and made to feel as a common man among them all.

At the "thrum-thrum" on the harp-strings, which wound up the song, frenzied shouts were raised for a repetition. Emilia was perfectly willing to gratify them; Captain Gambier appeared to be remonstrating with her, but she put up her joined hands, mock-petitioningly, and he with great affability held out the book anew. Wilfrid was thinking of moving to her to take her forcibly away when she recommenced.

At the same instant—but who, knowing that a house of glass is about to be shattered, can refrain from admiring its glitter in the beams?—Ipley crooned a ready accompaniment: the sleepers had been awakened: the women and the men were alive, half-dancing, half-chorusing here a baby was tossed, and there an old fellow's elbow worked mutely, expressive of the rollicking gaiety within him: the whole length of the booth was in a pleasing simmer, ready to overboil with shouts humane and cheerful, while Emilia pitched her note and led; archly, and quite one with them all, and yet in a way that critical Wilfrid could not object to, so plainly did she sing to give happiness.

I cannot delay; but I request you, that are here privileged to soar aloft with the Muse, to fix your minds upon one point in this flight. Let not the heat and dust of the ensuing fray divert your attention from the magnanimity of Beer. It will be vindicated in the end but be worthy of your seat beside the Muse, who alone of us all can take one view of the inevitable two that perplex mortal judgements.

For, if Ipley had jumped jovially up, and met the Hillford alarum with laughter,—how then? Why, then I maintain that the magnanimity of Beer would have blazed effulgent on the spot: there would have been louder laughter and fraternal greetings. As it was, the fire on the altar of Wisdom was again kindled by Folly, and the steps to the altar were broken heads, after the antique fashion.

In dismay, Ipley started. The members of the Club stared. Emilia faltered in horror.

A moment her voice swam stemming the execrable concert, but it was overwhelmed. Wilfrid pressed forward to her. They could hear nothing but the din. The booth raged like an insurgent menagerie. Outside it sounded of brazen beasts, and beasts that whistled, beasts that boomed. A whirlwind huddled them, and at last a cry, "We've got a visit from Hillford," told a tale. At once the stoutest hearts pressed to the opening. "My harp!" Emilia made her voice reach Wilfrid's ear. Unprovided with weapons, Ipley parleyed. Hillford howled in reply. The trombone brayed an interminable note, that would have driven to madness quiescent cats by steaming kettles, and quick, like the springing pulse of battle, the drum thumped and thumped. Blood could not hear it and keep from boiling. The booth shook violently. Wilfrid and Gambier threw over half-a-dozen chairs, forms, and tables, to make a barrier for the protection of the women.

"Come," Wilfrid said to Emilia, "leave the harp, I will get you another. Come."

"No, no," she cried in her nervous fright.

"For God's sake, come!" he reiterated, she, stamping her foot, as to emphasize "No! no! no!"

"But I will buy you another harp;" he made audible to her through the hubbub.

"This one!" she gasped with her hand on it. "What will he think if he finds that I forsook it?"

Wilfrid knew her to allude to the unknown person who had given it to her.

"There—there," said he. "I sent it, and I can get you another. So, come. Be good, and come."

"It was you!"

Emilia looked at him. She seemed to have no senses for the uproar about her.

But now the outer barricade was broken through, and the rout pressed on the second line. Tom Breeks, the orator, and Jim, transformed from a lurching yokel to a lithe dog of battle, kept the retreat of Ipley, challenging any two of Hillford to settle the dispute. Captain Gambier attempted an authoritative parley, in the midst of which a Hillford man made a long arm and struck Emilia's harp, till the strings jarred loose and horrid. The noise would have been enough to irritate Wilfrid beyond endurance. When he saw the fellow continuing to strike the harp-frame while Emilia clutched it, in a feeble defence, against her bosom, he caught a thick stick from a neighbouring hand and knocked that Hillford man so clean to earth that Hillford murmured at the blow. Wilfrid then joined the front array.

"Half-a-dozen hits like that a-piece, sir," nodded Tom Breeks.

"There goes another!" Jim shouted.

"Not quite, my lad," interposed Ned Thewk, though Peter Bartholomew was reeling in confirmation.

His blow at Jim missed, but came sharply in the swing on Wilfrid's cheek-bone.

Maddened at the immediate vision of that feature swollen, purple, even as a plum with an assiduous fly on it, certifying to ripeness:—Says the philosopher, "We are never up to the mark of any position, if we are in a position beneath our own mark;" and it is true that no hero in conflict should think of his face, but Wilfrid was all the while protesting wrathfully against the folly of his having set foot in such a place:—Maddened, I say, Wilfrid, a keen swordman, cleared a space. John Girling fell to him: Ned Thewk fell to him, and the sconce of Will Burdock rang.

"A rascally absurd business!" said Gambier, letting his stick do the part of a damnatory verb on one of the enemy, while he added, "The drunken vagabonds!"

All the Hillford party were now in the booth. Ipley, meantime, was not sleeping. Farmer Wilson and a set of the Ipley men whom age had sagaciously instructed to prefer stratagem to force, had slipped outside, and were labouring as busily as their comrades within: stooping to the tent-pegs, sending emissaries to the tent-poles.

"Drunk!" roared Will Burdock. "Did you happen to say 'drunk?'" And looking all the while at Gambier, he, with infernal cunning, swung at Wilfrid's fated cheekbone. The latter rushed furiously into the press of them, and there was a charge from Ipley, and a lock, from which Wilfrid extricated himself to hurry off Emilia. He perceived that bad blood was boiling up.

"Forward!" cried Will Burdock, and Hillford in turn made a tide.

As they came on in numbers too great for Ipley to stand against, an obscuration fell over all. The fight paused. Then a sensation as of some fellows smoothing their polls and their cheeks, and leaning on their shoulders with obtrusive affection, inspirited them to lash about indiscriminately. Whoops and yells arose; then peals of laughter. Homage to the cleverness of Ipley was paid in hurrahs, the moment Hillford understood the stratagem by which its men of valour were lamed and imprisoned. The truth was, that the booth was down on them, and they were struggling entangled in an enormous bag of canvas.

Wilfrid drew Emilia from under the drooping folds of the tent. He was allowed, on inspection of features, to pass. The men of Hillford were captured one by one like wild geese, as with difficulty they emerged, roaring, rolling with laughter, all.

Yea; to such an extent did they laugh that they can scarce be said to have done less than make the joke of the foe their own. And this proves the great and amazing magnanimity of Beer.

CHAPTER XII

SHOWING HOW SENTIMENT AND PASSION TAKE THE DISEASE OF LOVE

A pillar of dim silver rain fronted the moon on the hills. Emilia walked hurriedly, with her head bent, like a penitent: now and then peeping up and breathing to the keen scent of the tender ferns. Wilfrid still grasped her hand, and led her across the common, away from the rout.

When the uproar behind them had sunk, he said "You'll get your feet wet. I'm sorry you should have to walk. How did you come here?"

She answered: "I forget."

"You must have come here in some conveyance. Did you walk?"

Again she answered: "I forget;" a little querulously; perhaps wilfully.

"Well!" he persisted: "You must have got your harp to this place by some means or other?"

"Yes, my harp!" a sob checked her voice.

Wilfrid tried to soothe her. "Never mind the harp. It's easily replaced."

"Not that one!" she moaned.

"We will get you another."

"I shall never love any but that."

"Perhaps we may hear good news of it to-morrow."

"No; for I felt it die in my hands. The third blow was the one that killed it. It's broken."

Wilfrid could not reproach her, and he had not any desire to preach. So, as no idea of having done amiss in coming to the booth to sing illumined her, and she yet knew that she was in some way guilty, she accused herself of disregard for that dear harp while it was brilliant and serviceable. "Now I remember what poor music I made of it! I touched it with cold fingers. The sound was thin, as if it had no heart. Tick-tick!—I fancy I touched it with a dead man's finger-nails."

She crossed her wrists tight at the clasp of her waist, and letting her chin fall on her throat, shook her body fretfully, much as a pettish little girl might do. Wilfrid grimaced. "Tick-tick" was not a pathetic elegy in his ears.

"The only thing is, not to think about it," said he. "It's only an instrument, after all."

"It's the second one I've seen killed like a living creature," replied Emilia.

They walked on silently, till Wilfrid remarked, that he wondered where Gambier was. She gave no heed to the name. The little quiet footing and the bowed head by his side, moved him to entreat her not to be unhappy. Her voice had another tone when she answered that she was not unhappy.

"No tears at all?" Wilfrid stooped to get a close view of her face. "I thought I saw one. If it's about the harp, look!—you shall go into that cottage where the light is, sit there, and wait for me, and I will bring you what remains of it. I dare say we can have it mended."

Emilia lifted her eyes. "I am not crying for the harp. If you go back I must go with you."

"That's out of the question. You must never be found in that sort of place again."

"Let us leave the harp," she murmured. "You cannot go without me. Let me sit here for a minute. Sit with me."

She pointed to a place beside herself on the fork of a dry log under flowering hawthorn. A pale shadowy blue centre of light among the clouds told where the moon was. Rain had ceased, and the refreshed earth smelt all of flowers, as if each breeze going by held a nosegay to their nostrils.

Wilfrid was sensible of a sudden marked change in her. His blood was quicker than his brain in feeling it. Her voice now, even in common speaking, had that vibrating richness which in her singing swept his nerves.

"If you cry, there must be a cause, you know," he said, for the sake of keeping the conversation in a safe channel.

"How brave you are!" was Emilia's sedate exclamation, in reply.

Her cheeks glowed, as if she had just uttered a great confession, but while the colour mounted to her eyes, they kept their affectionate intentness upon him without a quiver of the lids.

"Do you think me a coward?" she relieved him by asking sharply, like one whom the thought had turned into a darker path. "I am not. I hung my head while you were fighting, because, what could I do? I would not have left you. Girls can only say, 'I will perish with him.'"

"But," Wilfrid tried to laugh, "there was no necessity for that sort of devotion. What are you thinking of? It was half in good-humour, all through. Part of their fun!"

Clearly Emilia's conception of the recent fray was unchangeable.

"And the place for girls is at home; that's certain," he added.

"I should always like to be where..." Her voice flowed on with singular gravity to that stop.

Wilfrid's hand travelled mechanically to his pricking cheek-bone.

Was it possible that a love-scene was coming on as a pendant to that monstrously ridiculous affair of half-an-hour back? To know that she had sufficient sensibility was gratifying, and flattering that it aimed at him. She was really a darling little woman: only too absurd! Had she been on the point of saying that she would always like to be where he, Wilfrid, was? An odd touch of curiosity, peculiar to the languid emotions, made him ask her this: and to her soft "Yes," he continued briskly, and in the style of condescending fellowship: "Of course we're not going to part!"

"I wonder," said Emilia.

There she sat, evidently sounding right through the future with her young brain, to hear what Destiny might have to say.

The 'I wonder' rang sweetly in his head. It was as delicate a way of confessing, "I love you with all my soul," as could be imagined. Extremely refined young ladies could hardly have improved upon it, saving with the angelic shades of sentiment familiar to them.

Convinced that he had now heard enough for his vanity, Wilfrid returned emphatically to the tone of the world's highroad.

"By the way," he said, "you mustn't have any exaggerated idea of this night's work. Remember, also, I have to share the honours with Captain Gambier."

"I did not see him," said Emilia.

"Are you not cold?" he asked, for a diversion, though he had one of her hands.

She gave him the other.

He could not quit them abruptly: nor could he hold both without being drawn to her.

"What is it you say?" Wilfrid whispered: "men kiss us when we are happy. Is that right? and are you happy?"

She lifted a clear full face, to which he bent his mouth. Over the flowering hawthorn the moon stood like a windblown white rose of the heavens. The kiss was given and taken. Strange to tell, it was he who drew away from it almost bashfully, and with new feelings.

Quite unaware that he played the feminine part, Wilfrid alluded to her flight from Richford, with the instinct to sting his heart by a revival of his jealous sensations previously experienced, and so taste the luxury of present satisfaction.

"Why did you run away from me?" he said, semi-reproachfully.

"I promised."

"Would you not break a promise to stay with me?"

"Now I would!"

"You promised Captain Gambier?"

"No: those poor people."

"You are sorry that you went?"

No: she was happy.

"You have lost your harp by it," said Wilfrid.

"What do you think of me for not guessing—not knowing who sent it?" she returned. "I feel guilty of something all those days that I touched it, not thinking of you. Wicked, filthy little creature that I was! I despise ungrateful girls."

"I detest anything that has to do with gratitude," Wilfrid appended, "pray give me none. Why did you go away with Captain Gambier?"

"I was very fond of him," she replied unhesitatingly, but speaking as it were with numbed lips. "I wanted to tell him, to thank him and hold his hand. I told him of my promise. He spoke to me a moment in the garden, you know. He said he was leaving to go to London early, and would wait for me in the carriage: then we might talk. He did not wish to talk to me in the garden."

"And you went with him in the carriage, and told him you were so grateful?"

"Yes; but men do not like us to be grateful."

"So, he said he would do all sorts of things on condition that you were not grateful?"

"He said—yes: I forget: I do forget! How can I tell what he said?" Emilia added piteously. "I feel as if I had been emptied out of a sack!"

Wilfrid was pierced with laughter; and then the plainspoken simile gave him a chilling sensation while he was rising to the jealous pitch.

"Did he talk about taking you to Italy? Put your head into the sack, and think!"

"Yes," she answered blandly, an affirmative that caused him some astonishment, for he had struck at once to the farthest end of his suspicions.

"He feels as I do about the Italian Schools," said Emilia. "He wishes me to owe my learning to him. He says it will make him happy, and I thought so too." She threw in a "then."

Wilfrid looked moodily into the opposite hedge.

"Did he name the day for your going?" he asked presently, little anticipating another "Yes": but it came: and her rather faltering manner showed her to be conscious too that the word was getting to be a black one to him.

"Did you say you would go?"

"I did."

Question and answer crossed like two rapiers.

Wilfrid jumped up.

"The smell of this tree's detestable," he said, glancing at the shadowing hawthorn.

Emilia rose quietly, plucked a flower off the tree, and put it in her bosom.

Their way was down a green lane and across long meadow-paths dim in the moonlight. A nightingale was heard on this side and on that. Overhead they had a great space of sky with broken cloud full of the glory of the moon. The meadows dipped to a brook, slenderly spanned by a plank. Then there was an ascent through a cornfield to a copse. Rounding this they had sight of Brookfield. But while they were yet at the brook, Wilfrid said, "When is it you're going to Italy?"

In return he had an eager look, so that he was half-ashamed to add, "With Captain Gambier, I mean." He was suffering, and by being brutal he expected to draw balm on himself; nor was he deceived.

Emilia just then gave him her hand to be led over, and answered, as she neared him, "I am never to leave you."

"You never shall!" Wilfrid caught her in his arms, quite conquered by her, proud of her. He reflected with a loving rapture that her manner at that moment was equal to any lady's; and the phantom of her with her hand out, and her frank look, and trustful footing, while she spoke those words, kept on advancing to him all the way to Brookfield, at the same time that the sober reality murmured at his elbow.

Love, with his accustomed cunning, managed thus to lift her out of the mire and array her in his golden dress to idealize her, as we say. Reconciled for the hour were the contesting instincts in the nature of this youth the adoration of feminine refinement and the susceptibility to sensuous impressions. But Emilia walked with a hero: the dream of all her days! one, generous and gentle, as well as brave: who had fought for her, had thought of her tenderly, was with her now, having raised her to his level with a touch! How much might they not accomplish together: he with sword, she with harp? Through shadowy alleys in the clouds, Emilia saw the bright Italian plains opening out to her: the cities of marble, such as her imagination had fashioned them, porticos of stately palaces, and towers, and statues white among cypresses; and farther, minutely-radiant in the vista as a shining star, Venice of the sea. Fancy made the flying minutes hours. Now they marched with the regiments of Italy, under the folds of her free banner; now she sang to the victorious army, waving the banner over them; and now she floated in a gondola, and turning to him, the dear home of her heart, yet pale with the bleeding of his wound for Italy, said softly, in the tone that had power with him, "Only let me please you!"

"When? Where? What with?" came the blunt response from England, with electric speed, and Emilia fell from the clouds.

"I meant my singing; I thought of how I sang to you. Oh, happy time!" she exclaimed, to cut through the mist of vision in her mind.

"To me? down at the booth?" muttered Wilfrid, perplexed.

"Oh, no! I mean, just now—" and languid with the burden of so full a heart, she did not attempt to explain herself further, though he said, invitingly, "I thought I heard you humming?"

Then he was seized with a desire to have the force of her spirit upon him, for Brookfield was in view; and with the sight of Brookfield, the natural fascination waxed a shade fainter, and he feared it might be going. This (he was happily as ignorant as any other youth of the working of his machinery) prompted him to bid her sing before they parted. Emilia checked her steps at once to do as he desired. Her throat filled, but the voice quavered down again, like a fainting creature sick unto death. She made another effort and ended with a sorrowful look at his narrowly-watching eyes.

"I can't," she said; and, in fear of his anger, took his hand to beg forgiveness, while her eyelids drooped.

Wilfrid locked her fingers in a strong pressure, and walked on, silent as a man who has faced one of the veiled mysteries of life. It struck a full human blow on his heart, dragging him out of his sentimental pastures precipitately. He felt her fainting voice to be the intensest love-cry that could be uttered. The sound of it coursed through his blood, striking a rare illumination of sparks in his not commonly brilliant brain. In truth, that little episode showed an image of nature weak with the burden of new love. I do not charge the young cavalry officer with the power of perceiving images. He saw no more than that she could not sing because of what was in her heart toward him; but such a physical revelation was a divine love-confession, coming involuntarily from one whose lips had not formed the name of love; and Wilfrid felt it so deeply, that the exquisite flattery was almost lost, in a certain awed sense of his being in the presence of an absolute fact: a thing real, though it was much talked about, and visible, though it did not wear a hat or a petticoat.

It searched him thoroughly enough to keep him from any further pledges in that direction, propitious as the moment was, while the moon slipped over banks of marble into fields of blue, and all the midnight promised silence. They passed quickly through the laurel shrubs, and round the lawn. Lights were in the sleepless ladies' bed-room windows.

"Do I love her?" thought Wilfrid, as he was about to pull at the bell, and the thought that he should feel pain at being separated from her for half-a-dozen hours, persuaded him that he did. The self-restraint which withheld him from protesting that he did, confirmed it.

"To-morrow morning," he whispered.

"I shall be down by daylight," answered Emilia.

"You are in the shade—I cannot see you," said he.

The door opened as Emilia was moving out of the line of shadow.

CHAPTER XIII

CONTAINS A SHORT DISCOURSE ON PUPPETS

On the morrow Wilfrid was gone. No one had seen him go. Emilia, while she touched the keys of a muted piano softly in the morning quiet of the house, had heard the front-door close. At that hour one attributes every noise to the servants. She played on and waited patiently, till the housemaid expelled her into the dewy air.

The report from his bedchamber, telling the ladies of his absence, added that he had taken linen for a lengthened journey.

This curious retreat of my hero belongs to the order of things that are done 'None know why;' a curtain which drops conveniently upon either the bewilderment of the showman or the infirmities of the puppet.

I must own (though I need not be told what odium frowns on such a pretension to excess of cleverness) that I do know why. I know why, and, unfortunately for me, I have to tell what I know. If I do not tell, this narrative is so constituted that there will be no moral to it.

One who studies man in puppets (in which purpose lies the chief value of this amusing species), must think that we are degenerating rapidly. The puppet hero, for instance, is a changed being. We know what he was; but now he takes shelter in his wits. His organs affect his destiny. Careless of the fact that the hero's achievement is to conquer nature, he seems rather to boast of his subservience to her.

Still, up to this day, the fixture of a nose upon the puppet-hero's frontispiece has not been attempted. Some one does it at last. When the alternative came: "No nose to the hero, no moral to the tale;" could there be hesitation?

And I would warn our sentimentalists to admit the nose among the features proper to heroes, otherwise the race will become extinct. There is already an amount of dropping of the curtain that is positively wearisome, even to extremely refined persons, in order to save him from apparent misconduct. He will have to go altogether, unless we boldly figure him as other men. Manifestly the moment his career as a fairy prince was at end, he was on the high road to a nose. The beneficent Power that discriminated for him having vanished utterly, he was, like a bankrupt gentleman, obliged to do all the work for himself. This is nothing more than the tendency of the generations downward from the ideal.

The springs that moved Wilfrid upon the present occasion were simple. We will strip him of his heroic trappings for one fleeting instant, and show them.

Jumping briskly from a restless bed, his first act was to address his features to the looking-glass: and he saw surely the most glorious sight for a hero of the knightly age that could possibly have been offered. The battle of the previous night was written there in one eloquent big lump, which would have passed him current as hero from end to end of the land in the great days of old. These are the tea-table days. His preference was for the visage of Wilfrid Pole, which he saw not. At the aspect of the fearful mask, this young man stared, and then cursed; and then, by an odd transition, he was reminded, as by the force of a sudden gust, that Emilia's hair was redolent of pipe-smoke.

His remark was, "I can't be seen in this state." His thought (a dim reminiscence of poetical readings): "Ambrosial locks indeed!" A sad irony, which told that much gold-leaf had peeled away from her image in his heart.

Wilfrid was a gallant fellow, with good stuff in him. But, he was young. Ponder on that pregnant word, for you are about to see him grow. He was less a coxcomb than shamefaced and sentimental; and one may have these qualities, and be a coxcomb to boot, and yet be a gallant fellow. One may also be a gallant fellow, and harsh, exacting, double-dealing, and I know not what besides, in youth. The question asked by nature is, "Has he the heart to take and keep an impression?" For, if he has, circumstances will force him on and carve the figure of a brave man out of that mass of contradictions. In return for such benefits, he pays forfeit commonly of the dearest of the things prized by him in this terrestrial life. Whereat, albeit created man by her, he reproaches nature, and the sculptor, circumstance; forgetting that to make him man is their sole duty, and that what betrayed him was the difficulty thrown in their way by his quondam self—the pleasant boonfellow!

He forgets, in fact, that he was formerly led by his nose, and sacrificed his deeper feeling to a low disgust.

When the youth is called upon to look up, he can adore devoutly and ardently; but when it is his chance to look down on a fair head, he is, if not worse, a sentimental despot.

Wilfrid was young, and under the dominion of his senses; which can be, if the sentimentalists will believe me, as tyrannous and misleading when super-refined as when ultra-bestial. He made a good stout effort to resist the pipe-smoke. Emilia's voice, her growing beauty, her simplicity, her peculiar charms of feature, were all conjured up to combat the dismal images suggested by that fatal, dragging-down smell. It was vain. Horrible pipe-smoke pervaded the memory of her. It seemed to his offended dainty fancy that he could never dissociate her from smoking-booths and abominably bad tobacco; and, let us add (for this was part of the secret), that it never could dwell on her without the companionship of a hideous disfigured countenance, claiming to be Wilfrid Pole. He shuddered to think that he had virtually almost engaged himself to this girl. Or, had he? Was his honour bound? Distance appeared to answer the question favourably. There was safety in being distant from her. She possessed an incomprehensible attractiveness. She was at once powerful and pitiable: so that while he feared her, and was running from her spell, he said, from time to time, "Poor little thing!" and deeply hoped she would not be unhappy.

A showman once (a novice in his art, or ambitious beyond the mark), after a successful exhibition of his dolls, handed them to the company, with the observation, "satisfy yourselves, ladies and gentlemen." The latter, having satisfied themselves that the capacity of the lower limbs was extraordinary, returned them, disenchanted. That showman did ill. But I am not imitating him. I do not wait till after the performance, when it is too late to revive illusion. To avoid having to drop the curtain, I choose to explain an act on which the story hinges, while it is advancing: which is, in truth, an impulse of character. Instead of his being more of a puppet, this hero is less wooden than he was. Certainly I am much more in awe of him.

CHAPTER XIV

THE BESWORTH QUESTION

Mr. Pole was one of those men whose characters are read off at a glance. He was neat, insignificant, and nervously cheerful; with the eyes of a bird, that let you into no interior. His friends knew him thoroughly. His daughters were never in doubt about him. At the period of the purchase of Brookfield he had been excitable and feverish, but that was ascribed to the projected change in his habits, and the stern necessity for an occasional family intercommunication on the subject of money. He had a remarkable shyness of this theme, and reversed its general treatment; for he would pay, but would not talk of it. If it had to be discussed with the ladies, he puffed, and blinked, and looked so much like a culprit that, though they rather admired him for what seemed to them the germ of a sense delicate above his condition, they would have said of any man they had not known so perfectly, that he had painful reasons for wishing to avoid it. Now that they spoke to him of Besworth, assuring him that they were serious in their desire to change their residence, the fit of shyness was manifested, first in outrageous praise of Brookfield, which was speedily and inexplicably followed by a sort of implied assent to the proposition to depart from it. For Besworth displayed numerous advantages over Brookfield, and to contest one was to plunge headlong into the money question. He ventured to ask his daughters what good they expected from the change. They replied that it was simply this: that one might live fifty years at Brookfield and not get such a circle as in two might be established at Besworth. They were restricted. They had gathering friends, and no means of bringing them together. And the beauty of the site of Besworth made them enthusiastic.

"Well, but," said Mr. Pole: "what does it lead to? Is there nothing to come after?"

He explained: "You're girls, you know. You won't always stop with me. You may do just as well at Brookfield for yourselves, as over there."

The ladies blushed demurely.

"You forecast very kindly for us, papa," said Cornelia. "Our object is entirely different."

"I wish I could see it," he returned.

"But, you do see, papa, you do see," interposed Adela, "that a select life is preferable to that higgledy-piggledy city-square existence so many poor creatures are condemned to!"

"Select!" said Mr. Pole, thinking that he had hit upon a weakness in their argument; "how can it be select when you want to go to a place where you may have a crowd about you?"

"Selection can only be made from a crowd," remarked Arabella, with terrible placidity. "It is where we see few that we are at the mercy of kind fortune for our acquaintances."

"Don't you see, papa, that the difference between the aristocracy and the bourgeoisie is, that the former choose their sets, and the latter are obliged to take what comes to them?" said Adela.

This was the first domestic discussion upon Besworth. The visit to Richford had produced the usual effect on the ladies, who were now looking to other heights from that level. The ladies said: "We have only to press it with papa, and we shall quit this place." But at the second discussion they found that they had not advanced. The only change was in the emphasis that their father added to the interrogations already uttered. "What does it lead to? What's to come after? I see your object. But, am I to go into a new house for the sake of getting you out of it, and then be left there alone? It's against your interests, too. Never mind how. Leave that to a business man. If your brother had proposed it...but he's too reasonable."

The ladies, upon this hint, wrote to Wilfrid to obtain his concurrence and assistance. He laughed when he read the simple sentence: "We hope you will not fancy that we have any peculiar personal interest in view;" and replied to them that he was sure they had none: that he looked upon Besworth with favour, "and I may inform you," he pursued, "that your taste is heartily applauded by Lady Charlotte Chillingworth, she bids me tell you." The letter was dated from Stornley, the estate of the marquis, Lady Charlotte's father. Her ladyship's brother was a member of Wilfrid's Club. "He calls Besworth the most habitable place in the county, and promises to be there as many months out of the twelve as you like to have him. I agree with him that Stornley can't hold a candle to it. There are three residences in England that might be preferred to it, and, of those, two are ducal."

The letter was a piece of that easy diplomacy which comes from habit. The "of those, two are ducal," was masterly. It affected the imagination of Brookfield. "Which two?" And could Besworth be brought to rival them? Ultimately, it might be! The neighbourhood to London, too, gave it noble advantages. Rapid relays of guests, and a metropolitan reputation for country attractions, would distinguish Besworth above most English houses. A house where all the chief celebrities might be encountered: a house under suave feminine rule; a house, a home, to a chosen set, and a refreshing fountain to a widening circle!

"We have a dispute," they wrote playfully to Wilfrid "a dispute we wish you or Lady Charlotte to settle. I, Arabella, know nothing of trout. I, Cornelia, know nothing of river-beds. I, Adela, know nothing of engineering. But, we are persuaded, the latter, that the river running for a mile through Besworth grounds may be deepened: we are persuaded, the intermediate, that the attempt will damage the channel: we are persuaded, the first, that all the fish will go."

In reply, Wilfrid appeared to have taken them in earnest. "I rode over yesterday with Lady Charlotte," he said. "We think something might be done, without at all endangering the fish or spoiling the channel. At all events, the idea of making the mile of broad water serviceable for boats is too good to give up in a hurry. How about the dining-hall? I told Lady Charlotte you were sure to insist upon a balcony for musicians. She laughed. You will like her when you know her."

Thus the ladies of Brookfield were led on to be more serious concerning Besworth than they had thought of being, and began to feel that their honour was pledged to purchase this surpassing family seat. In a household where every want is supplied, and money as a topic utterly banished, it is not surprising that they should have had imperial views.

Adela was Wilfrid's favoured correspondent. She described to him gaily the struggle with their papa. "But, if you care for Besworth, you may calculate on it.—Or is it only for our sakes, as I sometimes think?—Besworth is won. Nothing but the cost of the place (to be considered you know!) could withhold it from us; and of that papa has not uttered a syllable, though he conjures up every possible objection to a change of abode, and will not (perhaps, poor dear, cannot) see what we intend doing in the world. Now, you know that rich men invariably make the question of the cost their first and loudest outcry. I know that to be the case. They call it their blood. Papa seems indifferent to this part of the affair. He does not even allude to it. Still, we do not progress. It is just possible that the Tinleys have an eye on beautiful Besworth. Their own place is bad enough, but good enough for them. Give them Besworth, and they will sit upon the neighbourhood. We shall be invaded by everything that is mean and low, and a great chance will be gone for us. I think I may say, for the county. The country? Our advice is, that you write to papa one of your cleverest letters. We know, darling, what you can do with the pen as well as the sword. Write word that you have written."

Wilfrid's reply stated that he considered it unadviseable that he should add his voice to the request, for the present.

The ladies submitted to this quietly until they heard from their father one evening at dinner that he had seen Wilfrid in the city.

"He doesn't waste his time like some young people I know," said Mr. Pole, with a wink.

"Papa; is it possible?" cried Adela.

"Everything's possible, my dear."

"Lady Charlotte?"

"There is a Lady Charlotte."

"Who would be Lady Charlotte still, whatever occurred!"

Mr. Pole laughed. "No, no. You get nothing out of me. All I say is, be practical. The sun isn't always shining."

He appeared to be elated with some secret good news.

"Have you been over to Besworth, the last two or three days?" he asked.

The ladies smiled radiantly, acknowledging Wilfrid's wonderful persuasive powers, in their hearts.

"No, papa; we have not been," said Adela. "We are always anxious to go, as I think you know."

The merchant chirped over his glass. "Well, well! There's a way."

"Straight?"

"Over a gate; ha, ha!"

His gaiety would have been perplexing, but for the allusion to Lady Charlotte.

The sisters, in their unfailing midnight consultation, persuaded one another that Wilfrid had become engaged to that lady. They wrote forthwith Fine Shades to him on the subject. His answer was Boeotian, and all about Besworth. "Press it now," he said, "if you really want it. The iron is hot. And above all things, let me beg you not to be inconsiderate to the squire, when he and I are doing all we can for you. I mean, we are bound to consider him, if there should happen to be anything he wishes us to do."

What could the word 'inconsiderate' imply? The ladies were unable to summon an idea to solve it. They were sure that no daughters could be more perfectly considerate and ready to sacrifice everything to their father. In the end, they deputed the volunteering Adela to sit with him in the library, and put the question of Besworth decisively, in the name of all. They, meantime, who had a contempt for sleep, waited aloft to hold debate over the result of the interview.

An hour after midnight, Adela came to them, looking pale and uncertain: her curls seeming to drip, and her blue eyes wandering about the room, as if she had seen a thing that kept her in a quiver between belief and doubt.

The two ladies drew near to her, expressing no verbal impatience, from which the habit of government and great views naturally saved them, but singularly curious.

Adela's first exclamation: "I wish I had not gone," alarmed them.

"Has any change come to papa?" breathed Arabella.

Cornelia smiled. "Do you not know him too well?"

An acute glance from Adela made her ask whether Besworth was to be surrendered.

"Oh, no! my dear. We may have Besworth."

"Then, surely!"

"But, there are conditions?" said Arabella.

"Yes. Wilfrid's enigma is explained. Bella, that woman has seen papa."

"What woman?"

"Mrs. Chump."

"She has our permission to see him in town, if that is any consolation to her."

"She has told him," continued Adela, "that no explanation, or whatever it may be, was received by her."

"Certainly not, if it was not sent."

"Papa," and Adela's voice trembled, "papa will not think of Besworth,—not a word of it!-until—until we consent to welcome that woman here as our guest."

Cornelia was the first to break the silence that followed this astounding intelligence. "Then," she said, "Besworth is not to be thought of. You told him so?"

Adela's head drooped. "Oh!" she cried, "what shall we do? We shall be a laughing-stock to the neighbourhood. The house will have to be locked up. We shall live like hermits worried by a demon. Her brogue! Do you remember it? It is not simply Irish. It's Irish steeped in brine. It's pickled Irish!"

She feigned the bursting into tears of real vexation.

"You speak," said Cornelia contemptuously, "as if we had very humbly bowed our heads to the infection."

"Papa making terms with us!" murmured Arabella.

"Pray, repeat his words."

Adela tossed her curls. "I will, as well as I can. I began by speaking of Besworth cheerfully; saying, that if he really had no strong affection for Brookfield, that would make him regret quitting it, we saw innumerable advantages in the change of residence proposed. Predilection,—not affection—that was what I said. He replied that Besworth was a large place, and I pointed out that therein lay one of its principal merits. I expected what would come. He alluded to the possibility of our changing our condition. You know that idea haunts him. I told him our opinion of the folly of the thing. I noticed that he grew red in the face, and I said that of course marriage was a thing ordained, but that we objected to being submerged in matrimony until we knew who and what we were. I confess he did not make a bad reply, of its kind. 'You're like a youngster playing truant that he may gain knowledge.' What do you think of it?"

"A smart piece of City-speech," was Arabella's remark: Cornelia placidly observing, "Vulgarity never contains more than a minimum of the truth."

"I said," Adela went on, "Think as you will, papa, we know we are right. He looked really angry. He said, that we have the absurdest ideas—you tell me to repeat his words—of any girls that ever existed; and then he put a question: listen: I give it without comment: 'I dare say, you all object to widows marrying again.' I kept myself quiet. 'Marrying again, papa! If they marry once they might as well marry a dozen times.' It was the best way to irritate him. I did not intend it; that is all I can say. He jumped from his chair, rubbed his hair, and almost ran up and down the library floor, telling me that I prevaricated. 'You object to a widow marrying at all—that's my question!' he cried out loud. Of course I contained my voice all the more. 'Distinctly, papa.' When I had spoken, I could scarcely help laughing. He went like a pony that is being broken in, crying, I don't know how many times, 'Why? What's your reason?' You may suppose, darlings, that I decline to enter upon explanation. If a person is dense upon a matter of pure sentiment, there is no ground between us: he has simply a sense wanting. 'What has all this to do with Besworth?' I asked. 'A great deal more than you fancy,' was his answer. He seemed to speak every word at me in capital letters. Then, as if a little ashamed, he sat down, and reached out his hand to mine, and I saw his eyes were moist. I drew my chair nearer to him. Now, whether I did right or wrong in this, I do not know I leave it entirely to your judgement. If you consider how I was placed, you will at all events excuse me. What I did was—you know, the very farthest suspicion one has of an extreme possibility one does not mind mentioning: I said 'Papa, if it should so happen that money is the objection to Besworth, we will not trouble you.' At this, I can only say that he behaved like an insane person. He denounced me as wilfully insulting him that I might avoid one subject."

"And what on earth can that be?" interposed Arabella.

"You may well ask. Could a genie have guessed that Mrs. Chump was at the bottom of it all? The conclusion of the dreadful discussion is this, that papa offers to take the purchase of Besworth into his consideration, if we, as I said before, will receive Mrs. Chump as our honoured guest. I am bound to say, poor dear old man, he spoke kindly, as he always does, and kissed me, and offered to give me anything I might want. I came from him stupefied. I have hardly got my senses about me yet."

The ladies caressed her, with grave looks; but neither of them showed a perturbation of spirit like that which distressed Adela.

"Wilfrid's meaning is now explained," said Cornelia. "He is in league with papa; or has given in his adhesion to papa's demands, at least. He is another example of the constant tendency in men to be what they call 'practical' at the expense of honour and sincerity."

"I hope not," said Arabella. "In any case, that need not depress you so seriously, darling."

She addressed Adela.

"Do you not see?" Adela cried, in response. "What! are you both blind to the real significance of papa's words? I could not have believed it! Or am I this time too acute? I pray to heaven it may be so!"

Both ladies desired her to be explicit; Arabella, eagerly; Cornelia with distrust.

"The question of a widow marrying! What is this woman, whom papa wishes to force on us as our guest? Why should he do that? Why should he evince anxiety with regard to our opinion of the decency of widows contemplating re-union? Remember previous words and hints when we lived in the city!"

"This at least you may spare us," said Cornelia, ruffling offended.

Adela smiled in tenderness for her beauty.

"But, it is important, if we are following a track, dear. Think over it."

"No!" cried Arabella. "It cannot be true. We might easily have guessed this, if we ever dreamed of impossibilities."

"In such cases, when appearances lean in one direction, set principles in the opposite balance," added Cornelia. "What Adela apprehends may seem to impend, but we know that papa is incapable of doing it. To know that, shuts the gates of suspicion. She has allowed herself to be troubled by a ghastly nightmare."

Adela believed in her own judgement too completely not to be sure that her sisters were, perhaps unknowingly, disguising a slowness of perception they were ashamed of, by thus partially accusing her of giddiness. She bit her lip.

"Very well; if you have no fears whatever, you need not abandon the idea of Besworth."

"I abandon nothing," said Arabella. "If I have to make a choice, I take that which is least objectionable. I am chagrined, most, at the idea that Wilfrid has been treacherous."

"Practical," Cornelia suggested. "You are not speaking of one of our sex."

Questions were then put to Adela, whether Mr. Pole had spoken in the manner of one who was prompted: whether he hesitated as he spoke: whether, in short, Wilfrid was seen behind his tongue. Adela resolved that Wilfrid should have one protectress.

"You are entirely mistaken in ascribing treachery to him," she said. "It is papa that is changed. You may suppose it to be without any reason, if you please. I would tell you to study him for yourselves, only I am convinced that these special private interviews are anything but good policy, and are strictly to be avoided, unless of course, as in the present instance, we have something directly to do."

Toward dawn the ladies had decreed that it was policy to be quite passive, and provoke no word of Mrs. Chump by making any allusion to Besworth, and by fencing with the mention of the place.

As they rarely failed to carry out any plan deliberately conceived by them, Mr. Pole was astonished to find that Besworth was altogether dropped. After certain scattered attempts to bring them upon Besworth, he shrugged, and resigned himself, but without looking happy.

Indeed he looked so dismal that the ladies began to think he had a great longing for Besworth. And yet he did not go there, or even praise it to the discredit of Brookfield! They were perplexed.

"Let me ask you how it is," said Cornelia to Mr. Barrett, "that a person whom we know—whose actions and motives are as plain to us as though discerned through a glass, should at times produce a completer mystification than any other creature? Or have you not observed it?"

"I have had better opportunities of observing it than most people," Mr. Barren replied, with one of his saddest amused smiles. "I have come to the conclusion that the person we know best is the one whom we never understand."

"You answer me with a paradox."

"Is it not the natural attendant on an assumption?"

"What assumption?"

"That you know a person thoroughly."

"May we not?"

"Do you, when you acknowledge this 'complete mystification'?"

"Yes." Cornelia smiled when she had said it. "And no."

Mr. Barrett, with his eyes on her, laughed softly. "Which is paradox at the fountain-head! But, when we say we know any one, we mean commonly that we are accustomed to his ways and habits of mind; or, that we can reckon on the predominant influence of his appetites. Sometimes we can tell which impulse is likely to be the most active, and which principle the least restraining. The only knowledge to be trusted is a grounded or scientific study of the springs that move him, side by side with his method of moving the springs. If you fail to do this, you have two classes under your eyes: you have sane and madman: and it will seem to you that the ranks of the latter are constantly being swollen in an extraordinary manner. The customary impression, as we get older, is that our friends are the maddest people in the world. You see, we have grown accustomed to them; and now, if they bewilder us, our judgement, in self-defence, is compelled to set them down lunatic."

Cornelia bowed her stately head with gentle approving laughter.

"They must go, or they despatch us thither," she said, while her fair face dimpled into serenity. The remark was of a lower nature than an intellectual discussion ordinarily drew from her: but could Mr. Barrett have read in her heart, he might have seen that his words were beginning to rob that organ of its native sobriety. So that when he spoke a cogent phrase, she was silenced, and became aware of a strange exultation in her blood that obscured grave thought. Cornelia attributed this display of mental weakness altogether to Mr. Barrett's mental force. The interposition of a fresh agency was undreamt of by the lady.

Meanwhile, it was evident that Mr. Pole was a victim to one of his fevers of shyness. He would thrum on the table, frowning; and then, as he met the look of one of the ladies, try to disguise the thought in his head with a forced laugh. Occasionally, he would turn toward them, as if he had just caught a lost idea that was peculiarly precious. The ladies drawing up to attend to the communication, had a most trivial matter imparted to them, and away he went. Several times he said to them "You don't make friends, as you ought;" and their repudiation of the charge made him repeat: "You don't make friends—home friends."

"The house can be as full as we care to have it, papa."

"Yes, acquaintances! All very well, but I mean friends—rich friends."

"We will think of it, papa," said Adela, "when we want money."

"It isn't that," he murmured.

Adela had written to Wilfrid a full account of her interview with her father. Wilfrid's reply was laconic. "If you cannot stand a week of the brogue, give up Besworth, by all means." He made no further allusion to the place. They engaged an opera-box, for the purpose of holding a consultation with him in town. He wrote evasively, but did not appear, and the ladies, with Emilia between them, listened to every foot-fall by the box-door, and were too much preoccupied to marvel that Emilia was just as inattentive to the music as they were. When the curtain dropped they noticed her dejection.

"What ails you?" they asked.

"Let us go out of London to-night," she whispered, and it was difficult to persuade her that she would see Brookfield again.

"Remember," said Adela, "it is you that run away from us, not we from you."

Soft chidings of this description were the only reproaches for her naughty conduct. She seemed contrite very still and timid, since that night of adventure. The ladies were glad to observe it, seeing that it lent her an air of refinement, and proved her sensible to correction.

At last Mr. Pole broke the silence. He had returned from business, humming and rubbing his hands, like one newly primed with a suggestion that was the key of a knotty problem. Observant Adela said: "Have you seen Wilfrid, papa?"

"Saw him in the morning," Mr. Pole replied carelessly.

Mr. Barrett was at the table.

"By the way, what do you think of our law of primogeniture?" Mr. Pole addressed him.

He replied with the usual allusion to a basis of aristocracy.

"Well, it's the English system," said Mr. Pole. "That's always in its favour at starting. I'm Englishman enough to think that. There ought to be an entail of every decent bit of property, eh?"

It was observed that Mr. Barrett reddened as he said, "I certainly think that a young man should not be subject to his father's caprice."

"Father's caprice! That isn't common. But, if you're founding a family, you must entail."

"We agree, sir, from my point of view, and from yours."

"Knits the family bond, don't you think? I mean, makes the trunk of the tree firm. It makes the girls poor, though!"

Mr. Barrett saw that he had some confused legal ideas in his head, and that possibly there were personal considerations in the background; so he let the subject pass.

When the guest had departed, Mr. Pole grew demonstrative in his paternal caresses. He folded Adela in one arm, and framed her chin in his fingers: marks of affection dear to her before she had outgrown them.

"So!" he said, "you've given up Besworth, have you?"

At the name, Arabella and Cornelia drew nearer to his chair.

"Given up Besworth, papa? It is not we who have given it up," said Adela.

"Yes, you have; and quite right too. You say, 'What's the use of it, for that's a sort of thing that always goes to the son.'"

"You suppose, papa, that we indulge in ulterior calculations?" came from Cornelia.

"Well, you see, my love!—no, I don't suppose it at all. But to buy a place and split it up after two or three years—I dare say they wouldn't insure me for more, that's nonsense. And it seems unfair to you, as you must think—"

"Darling papa! we are not selfish!" it rejoiced Adela to exclaim.

His face expressed a transparent simple-mindedness that won the confidence of the ladies and awakened their ideal of generosity.

"I know what you mean, papa," said Arabella. "But, we love Besworth; and if we may enjoy the place for the time that we are all together, I shall think it sufficient. I do not look beyond."

Her sisters echoed the sentiment, and sincerely. They were as little sordid as creatures could be. If deeply questioned, it would have been found that their notion of the position Providence had placed them in (in other words, their father's unmentioned wealth), permitted them to be as lavish as they pleased. Mr. Pole had endowed them with a temperament similar to his own; and he had educated it. In feminine earth it flourished wonderfully. Shy as himself, their shyness took other forms, and developed with warm youth. Not only did it shut them up from others (which is the first effect of this disease), but it tyrannized over them internally: so that there were subjects they had no power to bring their minds to consider. Money was in the list. The Besworth question, as at present considered, involved the money question. All of them felt that; father and children. It is not surprising, therefore, that they hurried over it as speedily as they could, and by a most comical exhibition of implied comprehension of meanings and motives.

"Of course, we're only in the opening stage of the business," said Mr. Pole. "There's nothing decided, you know. Lots of things got to be considered. You mean what you say, do you? Very well. And you want me to think of it? So I will. And look, my dears, you know that—" (here his voice grew husky, as was the case with it when touching a shy topic even beneath the veil; but they were above suspicion) "you know that—a—that we must all give way a little to the other, now and then. Nothing like being kind."

"Pray, have no fear, papa dear!" rang the clear voice of Arabella.

"Well, then, you're all for Besworth, even though it isn't exactly for your own interest? All right."

The ladies kissed him.

"We'll each stretch a point," he continued. "We shall get on better if we do. Much! You're a little hard on people who're not up to the mark. There's an end to that. Even your old father will like you better."

These last remarks were unintelligible to the withdrawing ladies.

On the morning that followed, Mr. Pole expressed a hope that his daughters intended to give him a good dinner that day; and he winked humorously and kindly by which they understood him to be addressing a sort of propitiation to them for the respect he paid to his appetite.

"Papa," said Adela, "I myself will speak to Cook."

She added, with a smile thrown to her sisters, without looking at them, "I dare say, she will know who I am."

Mr. Pole went down to his wine-cellar, and was there busy with bottles till the carriage came for him. A bason was fetched that he might wash off the dust and cobwebs in the passage. Having rubbed his hands briskly with soap, he dipped his head likewise, in an oblivious fit, and then turning round to the ladies, said, "What have I forgotten?" looking woebegone with his dripping vacant face. "Oh, ah! I remember now;" and he chuckled gladly.

He had just for one moment forgotten that he was acting, and a pang of apprehension had caught him when the water covered his face, to the effect that he must forfeit the natural artistic sequence of speech and conduct which disguised him so perfectly. Away he drove, nodding and waving his hand.

"Dear, simple, innocent old man!" was the pitiful thought in the bosoms of the ladies; and if it was accompanied by the mute exclamation, "How singular that we should descend from him!" it would not have been for the first time.

They passed one of their delightful quiet days, in which they paved the future with gold, and, if I may use so bold a figure, lifted parasols against the great sun that was to shine on them. Now they listened to Emilia, and now strolled in the garden; conversed on the social skill of Lady Gosstre, who was nevertheless narrow in her range; and on the capacities of mansions, on the secret of mixing people in society, and what to do with the women! A terrible problem, this latter one. Not terrible (to hostesses) at a mere rout or drum, or at a dance pure and simple, but terrible when you want good talk to circulate for then they are not, as a body, amused; and when they are not amused, you know, they are not inclined to be harmless; and in this state they are vipers; and where is society then? And yet you cannot do without them!—which is the revolting mystery. I need not say that I am not responsible for these critical remarks. Such tenderness to the sex comes only from its sisters.

So went a day rich in fair dreams to the ladies; and at the hour of their father's return they walked across the parvenu park, in a state of enthusiasm for Besworth, that threw some portion of its decorative light on the donor of Besworth. When his carriage was heard on the road, they stood fast, and greeted his appearance with a display of pocket-handkerchiefs in the breeze, a proceeding that should have astonished him, being novel; but seemed not to do so, for it was immediately responded to by the vigorous waving of a pair of pocket-handkerchiefs from the carriage-window! The ladies smiled at this piece of simplicity which prompted him to use both his hands, as if one would not have been enough. Complacently they continued waving. Then Adela looked at her sisters; Cornelia's hand dropped and Arabella, the last to wave, was the first to exclaim: "That must be a woman's arm!"

The carriage stopped at the gate, and it was one in the dress of a woman at least, and of the compass of a big woman, who descended by the aid of Mr. Pole. Safely alighted, she waved her pocket-handkerchief afresh. The ladies of Brookfield did not speak to one another; nor did they move their eyes from the object approaching. A simultaneous furtive extinction of three pocket-handkerchiefs might have been noticed. There was no further sign given.

CHAPTER XV

WILFRID'S EXHIBITION OF TREACHERY

A letter from Brookfield apprised Wilfrid that Mr. Pole had brought Mrs. Chump to the place as a visitor, and that she was now in the house. Formal as a circular, the idea of it appeared to be that the bare fact would tell him enough and inspire him with proper designs. No reply being sent, a second letter arrived, formal too, but pointing out his duty to succour his afflicted family, and furnishing a few tragic particulars. Thus he learnt, that while Mr. Pole was advancing toward the three grouped ladies, on the day of Mrs. Chump's arrival, he called Arabella by name, and Arabella went forward alone, and was engaged in conversation by Mrs. Chump. Mr. Pole left them to make his way to Adela and Cornelia. "Now, mind, I expect you to keep to your agreement," he said. Gradually they were led on to perceive that this simple-minded man had understood their recent talk of Besworth to signify a consent to the stipulation he had previously mentioned to Adela. "Perfect simplicity is as deceiving as the depth of cunning," Adela despairingly wrote, much to Wilfrid's amusement.

A third letter followed. It was of another tenor, and ran thus, in Adela's handwriting:

"My Darling Wilfrid,

"We have always known that some peculiar assistance would never be wanting in our extremity—aid, or comfort, or whatever you please to call it. At all events, something to show we are not neglected. That old notion of ours must be true. I shall say nothing of our sufferings in the house. They continue. Yesterday, papa came from town, looking important. He had up some of his best wine for dinner. All through the service his eyes were sparkling on Cornelia. I spare you a family picture, while there is this huge blot on it. Naughty brother! But, listen! your place is here, for many reasons, as you will be quick enough to see. After dinner, papa took Cornelia into the library alone, and they were together for ten minutes. She came out very pale. She had been proposed for by Sir Twickenham Pryme, our Member for the borough. I have always been sure that Cornelia was born for Parliament, and he will be lucky if he wins her. We know not yet, of course, what her decision will be. The incident is chiefly remarkable to us as a relief to what I need not recount to you. But I wish to say one thing, dear Wilfrid. You are gazetted to a lieutenancy, and we congratulate you: but what I have to say is apparently much more trifling, and it is, that—will you take it to heart?—it would do Arabella and myself infinite good if we saw a little more of our brother, and just a little less of a very gentlemanly organ-player phenomenon, who talks so exceedingly well. He is a very pleasant man, and appreciates our ideas, and so forth; but it is our duty to love our brother best, and think of him foremost, and we wish him to come and remind us of our duty.

"At our Cornelia's request, with our concurrence, papa is silent in the house as to the purport of the communication made by Sir T.P.

"By the way, are you at all conscious of a sound-like absurdity in a Christian name of three syllables preceding a surname of one? Sir Twickenham Pryme! Cornelia's pronunciation of the name first gave me the feeling. The 'Twickenham' seems to perform a sort of educated monkey kind of ridiculously decorous pirouette and entrechat before the 'Pryme.' I think that Cornelia feels it also. You seem to fancy elastic limbs bending to the measure of a solemn church-organ. Sir Timothy? But Sir Timothy does not jump with the same grave agility as Sir Twickenham! If she rejects him, it will be half attributable to this.

"My own brother! I expect no confidences, but a whisper warns me that you have not been to Stornley twice without experiencing the truth of our old discovery, that the Poles are magnetic? Why should we conceal it from ourselves, if it be so? I think it a folly, and fraught with danger, for people not to know their characteristics. If they attract, they should keep in a circle where they will have no reason to revolt at, or say, repent of what they attract. My argumentative sister does not coincide. If she did, she would lose her argument.

"Adieu! Such is my dulness, I doubt whether I have made my meaning clear.

"Your thrice affectionate

"Adela.

"P.S.—Lady Gosstre has just taken Emilia to Richford for a week. Papa starts for Bidport to-morrow."

This short and rather blunt exercise in Fine Shades was read impatiently by Wilfrid. "Why doesn't she write plain to the sense?" he asked, with the usual injustice of men, who demand a statement of facts, forgetting how few there are to feed the post; and that indication and suggestion are the only language for the multitude of facts unborn and possible. Twilight best shows to the eye what may be.

"I suppose I must go down there," he said to himself, keeping a meditative watch on the postscript, as if it possessed the capability of slipping away and deceiving him. "Does she mean that Cornelia sees too much of this man Barrett? or, what does she mean?" And now he saw meanings in the simple passages, and none at all in the intricate ones; and the double-meanings were monsters that ate one another up till nothing remained of them. In the end, however, he made a wrathful guess and came to a resolution, which brought him to the door of the house next day at noon. He took some pains in noting the exact spot where he had last seen Emilia half in moonlight, and then dismissed her image peremptorily. The house was apparently empty. Gainsford, the footman, gave information that he thought the ladies were upstairs, but did not volunteer to send a maid to them. He stood in deferential footman's attitude, with the aspect of a dog who would laugh if he could, but being a footman out of his natural element, cannot.

"Here's a specimen of the new plan of treating servants!" thought Wilfrid, turning away. "To act a farce for their benefit! That fellow will explode when he gets downstairs. I see how it is. This woman, Chump, is making them behave like schoolgirls."

He conceived the idea sharply, and forthwith, without any preparation, he was ready to treat these high-aspiring ladies like schoolgirls. Nor was there a lack of justification; for when they came down to his shouts in the passage, they hushed, and held a finger aloft, and looked altogether so unlike what they aimed at being, that Wilfrid's sense of mastery became almost contempt.

"I know perfectly what you have to tell me," he said. "Mrs. Chump is here, you have quarrelled with her, and she has shut her door, and you have shut yours. It's quite intelligible and full of dignity. I really can't smother my voice in consequence."

He laughed with unnecessary abandonment. The sensitive young women wanted no other schooling to recover themselves. In a moment they were seen leaning back and contemplating him amusedly, as if he had been the comic spectacle, and were laughing for a wager. There are few things so sour as the swallowing of one's own forced laugh. Wilfrid got it down, and commenced a lecture to fill the awkward pause. His sisters maintained the opera-stall posture of languid attention, contesting his phrases simply with their eyebrows, and smiling. He was no match for them while they chose to be silent: and indeed if the business of life were conducted in dumb show, women would beat men hollow. They posture admirably. In dumb show they are equally good for attack and defence. But this is not the case in speech. So, when Arabella explained that their hope was to see Mrs. Chump go that day, owing to the rigorous exclusion of all amusement and the outer world from the house, Wilfrid regained his superior footing and made his lecture tell. In the middle of it, there rang a cry from the doorway that astonished even him, it was so powerfully Irish.

"The lady you have called down is here," said Arabella's cold glance, in answer to his.

They sat with folded hands while Wilfrid turned to Mrs. Chump, who advanced, a shock of blue satin to the eye, crying, on a jump: "Is ut Mr. Wilfrud?"

"It's I, ma'am." Wilfrid bowed, and the censorious ladies could not deny that, his style was good, if his object was to be familiar. And if that was his object, he was paid for it. A great thick kiss was planted on his cheek, with the motto: "Harm to them that thinks ut."

Wilfrid bore the salute like a man who presumes that he is flattered.

"And it's you!" said Mrs. Chump. "I was just off. I'm packed, and bonnutted, and ready for a start; becas, my dear, where there's none but women, I don't think it natural to stop. You're splendid! How a little fella like Pole could go and be father to such a mighty big son, with your bit of moustache and your blue eyes! Are they blue or a bit of grey in 'em?" Mrs. Chump peered closely. "They're kill'n, let their colour be anyhow. And I that knew ye when ye were no bigger than my garter! Oh, sir! don't talk of ut; I'll be thinkin', of my coffin. Ye're glad to see me? Say, yes. Do!"

"Very glad," quoth Wilfrid.

"Upon your honour, now?"

"Upon my honour!"

"My dears" (Mrs. Chump turned to the ladies), "I'll stop; and just thank your brother for't, though you can't help being garls."

Reduced once more to demonstrate like schoolgirls by this woman, the ladies rose together, and were retiring, when Mrs. Chump swung round and caught Arabella's hand. "See heer," she motioned to Wilfrid. Arabella made a bitter effort to disengage herself. "See, now! It's jeal'sy of me, Mr. Wilfrud, becas I'm a widde and just an abom'nation to garls, poor darlin's! And twenty shindies per dime we've been havin', and me such a placable body, if ye'll onnly let m' explode. I'm all powder, avery bit! and might ha' been christened Saltpetre, if born a boy. She hasn't so much as a shot to kill a goose, says Chump, poor fella! But he went, anyway. I must kiss somebody when I talk of 'm. Mr. Wilfrud, I'll take the girls, and entitle myself to you."

Arabella was the first victim. Her remonstrance was inarticulate. Cornelia's "Madam!" was smothered. Adela behaved better, being more consciously under Wilfrid's eye; she prepared her pocket-handkerchief, received the salute, and deliberately effaced it.

"There!" said Mrs. Chump; "duty to begin with. And now for you, Mr. Wilfrud."

The ladies escaped. Their misery could not be conveyed to the mind. The woman was like a demon come among them. They felt chiefly degraded, not by her vulgarity, but by their inability to cope with it, and by the consequent sickening sense of animal inefficiency—the block that was put to all imaginative delight in the golden hazy future they figured for themselves, and which was their wine of life. An intellectual adversary they could have combated; this huge brogue-burring engine quite overwhelmed them. Wilfrid's worse than shameful behaviour was a common rallying-point; and yet, so absolutely critical were they by nature, their blame of him was held mentally in restraint by the superior ease of his manner as contrasted with their own lamentably silly awkwardness. Highly civilized natures do sometimes, and keen wits must always, feel dissatisfied when they are not on the laughing side: their dread of laughter is an instinctive respect for it.

Dinner brought them all together again. Wilfrid took his father's seat, facing his Aunt Lupin, and increased the distress of his sisters by his observance of every duty of a host to the dreadful intruder, whom he thus established among them. He was incomprehensible. His visit to Stornley had wrought in him a total change. He used to like being petted, and would regard everything as right that his sisters did, before he went there; and was a languid, long-legged, indifferent cavalier, representing men to them: things made to be managed, snubbed, admired, but always virtually subservient and in the background. Now, without perceptible gradation, his superiority was suddenly manifest; so that, irritated and apprehensive as they were, they could not, by the aid of any of their intricate mental machinery, look down on him. They tried to; they tried hard to think him despicable as well as treacherous. His style was too good. When he informed Mrs. Chump that he had hired a yacht for the season, and added, after enlarging on the merits of the vessel, "I am under your orders," his sisters were as creatures cut in twain—one half abominating his conduct, the other approving his style. The bow, the smile, were perfect. The ladies had to make an effort to recover their condemnatory judgement.

"Oh!" cried Mrs. Chump; "and if you've got a yacht, Mr. Wilfrud, won't ye have a great parcel o' the arr'stocracy on board?"

"You may spy a title by the aid of a telescope," said Wilfrid.

"And I'm to come, I am?"

"Are you not elected captain?"

"Oh, if ye've got lords and real ladies on board, I'll come, be sure of ut! I'll be as sick as a cat, I will. But, I'll come, if it's the rroon of my stomach. I'd say to Chump, 'Oh, if ye'd only been born a lord, or would just get yourself struck a knight on one o' your shoulders,—oh, Chump!' I'd say, 'it wouldn't be necessary to be rememberin' always the words of the cerr'mony about lovin' and honourin' and obeyin' of a little whistle of a fella like you.' Poor lad! he couldn't stop for his luck! Did ye ask me to take wine, Mr. Wilfrud? I'll be cryin', else, as a widde should, ye know!"

Frequent administrations of wine arrested the tears of Mrs. Chump, until it is possible that the fulness of many a checked flow caused her to redden and talk slightly at random. At the first mention of their father's name, the ladies went out from the room. It was foolish, for they might have watched the effect of certain vinous innuendoes addressed to Wilfrid's apprehensiveness; but they were weakened and humbled, and everything they did was foolish. From the fact that they offended their keen critical taste, moreover, they were targets to the shaft that wounds more fatally than all. No ridicule knocks the strength out of us so thoroughly as our own.

Whether or not he guessed their condition favourable for his plans, Wilfrid did not give them time to call back their scattered powers. At the hour of eleven he sent for Arabella to come to him in the library. The council upstairs permitted Arabella to go, on the understanding that she was prepared for hostilities, and ready to tear the mask from Wilfrid's face.

He commenced, without a shadow of circumlocution, and in a matter-of-fact way, as if all respect for the peculiar genius of the house of Pole had vanished: "I sent for you to talk a word or two about this woman, who, I see, troubles you a little. I'm sorry she's in the house."

"Indeed!" said Arabella.

"I'm sorry she's in the house, not for my sake, but for yours, since the proximity does not seem to... I needn't explain. It comes of your eternal consultations. You are the eldest. Why not act according to your judgement, which is generally sound? You listen to Adela, young as she is; or a look of Cornelia's leads you. The result is the sort of scene I saw this afternoon. I confess it has changed my opinion of you; it has, I grieve to say it. This woman is your father's guest; you can't hurt her so much as you hurt him, if you misbehave to her. You can't openly object to her and not cast a slur upon him. There is the whole case. He has insisted, and you must submit. You should have fought the battle before she came."

"She is here, owing to a miserable misconception," said Arabella.

"Ah! she is here, however. That is the essential, as your old governess Madame Timpan would have said."

"Nor can a protest against coarseness be sweepingly interpreted as a piece of unfilial behaviour," said Arabella.

"She is coarse," Wilfrid nodded his head. "There are some forms of coarseness which dowagers would call it coarseness to notice.

"Not if you find it locked up in the house with you—not if you suffer under a constant repulsion. Pray, do not use these phrases to me, Wilfrid. An accusation of coarseness cannot touch us."

"No, certainly," assented Wilfrid. "And you have a right to protest. I disapprove the form of your protest nothing more. A schoolgirl's...but you complain of the use of comparisons."

"I complain, Wilfrid, of your want of sympathy."

"That for two or three weeks you must hear a brogue at your elbow? The poor creature is not so bad; she is good-hearted. It's hard that you should have to bear with her for that time and receive nothing better than Besworth as your reward."

"Very; seeing that we endure the evil and decline the sop with it."

"How?"

"We have renounced Besworth."

"Have you! And did this renunciation make you all sit on the edge of your chairs, this afternoon, as if Edward Buxley had arranged you? You give up Besworth? I'm afraid it's too late."

"Oh, Wilfrid! can you be ignorant that something more is involved in the purchase of Besworth?"

Arabella gazed at him with distressful eagerness, as one who believes in the lingering of a vestige of candour.

"Do you mean that my father may wish to give this woman his name?" said Wilfrid coolly. "You have sense enough to know that if you make his home disagreeable, you are taking the right method to drive him into such a course. Ha! I don't think it's to be feared, unless you pursue these consultations. And let me say, for my part, we have gone too far about Besworth, and can't recede."

"I have given out everywhere that the place is ours. I did so almost at your instigation. Besworth was nothing to me till you cried it up. And now I won't detain you. I know I can rely on your sense, if you will rely on it. Good night, Bella."

As she was going a faint spark of courage revived Arabella's wits. Seeing that she was now ready to speak, he opened the door wide, and she kissed him and went forth, feeling driven.

But while Arabella was attempting to give a definite version of the interview to her sisters, a message came requesting Adela to descend. The ladies did not allow her to depart until two or three ingenuous exclamations from her made them share her curiosity.

"Ah?" Wilfrid caught her hand as she came in. "No, I don't intend to let it go. You may be a fine lady, but you're a rogue, you know, and a charming one, as I hear a friend of mine has been saying. Shall I call him out? Shall I fight him with pistols, or swords, and leave him bleeding on the ground, because he thinks you a pretty rogue?"

Adela struggled against the blandishment of this old familiar style of converse—part fun, part flattery—dismissed since the great idea had governed Brookfield.

"Please tell me what you called me down for, dear?"

"To give you a lesson in sitting on chairs. 'Adela, or the Puritan sister,' thus: you sit on the extremest edge, and your eyes peruse the ceiling; and..."

"Oh! will you ever forget that perfectly ridiculous scene?" Adela cried in anguish.

She was led by easy stages to talk of Besworth.

"Understand," said Wilfrid, "that I am indifferent about it. The idea sprang from you—I mean from my pretty sister Adela, who is President of the Council of Three. I hold that young woman responsible for all that they do. Am I wrong? Oh, very well. You suggested Besworth, at all events. And—if we quarrel, I shall cut off one of your curls."

"We never will quarrel, my darling," quoth Adela softly. "Unless—" she added.

Wilfrid kissed her forehead.

"Unless what?"

"Well, then, you must tell me who it is that talks of me in that objectionable manner; I do not like it."

"Shall I convey that intimation?"

"I choose to ask, simply that I may defend myself."

"I choose to keep him buried, then, simply to save his life."

Adela made a mouth, and Wilfrid went on: "By the way, I want you to know Lady Charlotte; you will take to one another. She likes you, already—says you want dash; but on that point there may be two opinions."

"If dash," said Adela, quite beguiled, "—that is, dash!—what does it mean? But, if Lady Charlotte means by dash—am I really wanting in it? I should define it, the quality of being openly natural without vulgarity; and surely...!"

"Then you two differ a little, and must meet and settle your dispute. You don't differ about Besworth: or, didn't. I never saw a woman so much in love with a place as she is."

"A place?" emphasized Adela.

"Don't be too arch. I comprehend. She won't take me minus Besworth, you may be sure."

"Did you, Wilfrid!—but you did not—offer yourself as owner of Besworth?"

Wilfrid kept his eyes slanting on the floor.

"Now I see why you should still wish it," continued Adela. "Perhaps you don't know the reason which makes it impossible, or I would say—Bacchus! it must be compassed. You remember your old schoolboy oath which you taught me? We used to swear always, by Bacchus!"

Adela laughed and blushed, like one who petitions pardon for this her utmost sin, that is not regretted as it should be.

"Mrs. Chump again, isn't it?" said Wilfrid. "Pole would be a preferable name. If she has the ambition, it elevates her. And it would be rather amusing to see the dear old boy in love."

Adela gave her under-lip a distressful bite.

"Why do you, Wilfrid—why treat such matters with levity?"

"Levity? I am the last to treat ninety thousand pounds with levity."

"Has she so much?" Adela glanced at him.

"She will be snapped up by some poor nobleman. If I take her down to the yacht, one of Lady Charlotte's brothers or uncles will bite; to a certainty."

"It would be an excellent idea to take her!" cried Adela.

"Excellent! and I'll do it, if you like."

"Could you bear the reflex of the woman?"

"Don't you know that I am not in the habit of sitting on the extreme edge...?"

Adela started, breathing piteously: "Wilfrid, dear! you want something of me—what is it?"

"Simply that you should behave civilly to your father's guest."

"I had a fear, dear; but I think too well of you to entertain it for a moment. If civility is to win Besworth for you, there is my hand."

"Be civil—that's all," said Wilfrid, pressing the hand given. "These consultations of yours and acting in concert—one tongue for three women—are a sort of missish, unripe nonsense, that one sees only in bourgeoise girls—eh? Give it up. Lady Charlotte hit on it at a glance."

"And I, my chameleon brother, will return her the compliment, some day," Adela said to herself, as she hurried back to her sisters, bearing a message for Cornelia. This lady required strong persuasion. A word from Adela: "He will think you have some good reason to deny him a private interview," sent her straight to the stairs.

Wilfrid was walking up and down, with his arms folded and his brows bent. Cornelia stood in the doorway.

"You desire to speak to me, Wilfrid? And in private?"

"I didn't wish to congratulate you publicly, that's all. I know it's rather against your taste. We'll shut the door, and sit down, if you don't mind. Yes, I congratulate you with all my heart," he said, placing a chair for Cornelia.

"May I ask, wherefore?"

"You don't think marriage a matter for congratulation?"

"Sometimes: as the case may be."

"Well, it's not marriage yet. I congratulate you on your offer."

"I thank you."

"You accept it, of course."

"I reject it, certainly."

After this preliminary passage, Wilfrid remained silent long enough for Cornelia to feel uneasy.

"I want you to congratulate me also," he recommenced. "We poor fellows don't have offers, you know. To be frank, I think Lady Charlotte Chillingworth will have me, if—She's awfully fond of Besworth, and I need not tell you that as she has position in the world, I ought to show something in return. When you wrote about Besworth, I knew it was as good as decided. I told her so and—Well, I fancy there's that sort of understanding between us. She will have me when... You know how the poorer members of the aristocracy are situated. Her father's a peer, and has a little influence. He might push me; but she is one of a large family; she has nothing. I am certain you will not judge of her as common people might. She does me a particular honour."

"Is she not much older than you, Wilfrid?" said Cornelia.

"Or, in other words," he added, "is she not a very mercenary person?"

"That, I did not even imply."

"Honestly, was it not in your head?"

"Now you put it so plainly, I do say, it strikes me disagreeably; I have heard of nothing like it."

"Do you think it unreasonable that I should marry into a noble family?"

"That is, assuredly, not my meaning."

"Nevertheless, you are, on the whole, in favour of beggarly alliances."

"No, Wilfrid."

"Why do you reject this offer that has been made to you?"

Cornelia flushed and trembled; the traitorous feint had thrown her off her guard. She said, faltering:

"Would you have me marry one I do not love?"

"Well, well!" He drew back. "You are going to do your best to stop the purchase of Besworth?"

"No; I am quiescent."

"Though I tell you how deeply it concerns me!"

"Wilfrid, my own brother!" (Cornelia flung herself before him, catching his hand,) "I wish you to be loved, first of all. Think of the horror of a loveless marriage, however gilded! Does a woman make stipulations ere she gives her hand? Does not love seek to give, to bestow? I wish you to marry well, but chiefly that you should be loved."

Wilfrid pressed her head in both his hands.

"I never saw you look so handsome," he said. "You've got back your old trick of blushing, too! Why do you tremble? By the way, you seem to have been learning a great deal about that business, lately?"

"What business?"

"Love."

A river of blood overflowed her fair cheeks.

"How long has this been?" his voice came to her.

There was no escape. She was at his knees, and must look up, or confess guilt.

"This?"

"Come, my dearest girl!" Wilfrid soothed her. "I can help you, and will, if you'll take advice. I've always known your heart was generous and tender, under that ice you wear so well. How long has this been going on?"

"Wilfrid!"

"You want plain speech?"

She wanted that still less.

"We'll call it 'this,'" he said. "I have heard of it, guessed it, and now see it. How far have you pledged yourself in 'this?'"

"How far?"

Wilfrid held silent. Finding that her echo was not accepted as an answer, she moaned his name lovingly. It touched his heart, where a great susceptibility to passion lay. As if the ghost of Emilia were about him, he kissed his sister's hand, and could not go on with his cruel interrogations.

His next question was dew of relief to her.

"Has your Emilia been quite happy, of late?"

"Oh, quite, dear! very. And sings with more fire."

"She's cheerful?"

"She does not romp. Her eyes are full and bright."

"She's satisfied with everything here?"

"How could she be otherwise?"

"Yes, yes! You weren't severe on her for that escapade—I mean, when she ran away from Lady Gosstre's?"

"We scarcely alluded to the subject, or permitted her to."

"Or permitted her to!" Wilfrid echoed, with a grimace. "And she's cheerful now?"

"Quite."

"I mean, she doesn't mope?"

"Why should she?"

Cornelia had been too hard-pressed to have suspicion the questions were an immense relief.

Wilfrid mused gloomily. Cornelia spoke further of Emilia, and her delight in the visits of Mr. Powys, who spent hours with her, like a man fascinated. She flowed on, little aware that she was fast restoring to Wilfrid all his judicial severity.

He said, at last: "I suppose there's no engagement existing?"

"Engagement?"

"You have not, what they call, plighted your troth to the man?"

Cornelia struggled for evasion. She recognized the fruitlessness of the effort, and abandoning it stood up.

"I am engaged to no one."

"Well, I should hope not," said Wilfrid. "An engagement might be broken."

"Not by me."

"It might, is all that I say. A romantic sentiment is tougher. Now, I have been straightforward with you: will you be with me? I shall not hurt the man, or wound his feelings."

He paused; but it was to find that no admission of the truth, save what oozed out in absence of speech, was to be expected. She seemed, after the fashion of women, to have got accustomed to the new atmosphere into which he had dragged her, without any conception of a forward movement.

"I see I must explain to you how we are situated," said Wilfrid. "We are in a serious plight. You should be civil to this woman for several reasons—for your father's sake and your own. She is very rich."

"Oh, Wilfrid!"

"Well, I find money well thought of everywhere."

"Has your late school been good for you?"

"This woman, I repeat, is rich, and we want money. Oh! not the ordinary notion of wanting money, but the more we have the more power we have. Our position depends on it."

"Yes, if we can be tempted to think so," flashed Cornelia.

"Our position depends on it. If you posture, and are poor, you provoke ridicule: and to think of scorning money, is a piece of folly no girls of condition are guilty of. Now, you know I am fond of you; so I'll tell you this: you have a chance; don't miss it. Something unpleasant is threatening; but you may escape it. It would be madness to throw such a chance away, and it is your duty to take advantage of it. What is there plainer? You are engaged to no one."

Cornelia came timidly close to him. "Pray, be explicit!"

"Well!—this offer."

"Yes; but what—there is something to escape from."

Wilfrid deliberately replied: "There is no doubt of the Pater's intentions with regard to Mrs. Chump."

"He means...?"

"He means to marry her."

"And you, Wilfrid?"

"Well, of course, he cuts me out. There—there! forgive me: but what can I do?"

"Do you conspire—Wilfrid, is it possible?—are you an accomplice in the degradation of our house?"

Cornelia had regained her courage, perforce of wrath. Wilfrid's singular grey eyes shot an odd look at her. He is to be excused for not perceiving the grandeur of the structure menaced; for it was invisible to all the world, though a real fabric.

"If Mrs. Chump were poor, I should think the Pater demented," he said. "As it is—! well, as it is, there's grist to the mill, wind to the organ. You must be aware" (and he leaned over to her with his most suspicious gentleness of tone) "you are aware that all organs must be fed; but you will make a terrible mistake if you suppose for a moment that the human organ requires the same sort of feeding as the one in Hillford Church."

"Good-night," said Cornelia, closing her lips, as if for good.

Wilfrid pressed her hand. As she was going, the springs of kindness in his heart caused him to say "Forgive me, if I seemed rough."

"Yes, dear Wilfrid; even brutality, rather than your exultation over the wreck of what was noble in you."

With which phrase Cornelia swept from the room.

CHAPTER XVI

HOW THE LADIES OF BROOKFIELD CAME TO THEIR RESOLVE

"Seen Wilfrid?" was Mr. Pole's first cheery call to his daughters, on his return. An answer on that head did not seem to be required by him, for he went on: "Ah the boy's improved. That place over there, Stornley, does him as much good as the Army did, as to setting him up, you know; common sense, and a ready way of speaking and thinking. He sees a thing now. Well, Martha, what do you,—eh? what's your opinion?"

Mrs. Chump was addressed. "Pole," she said, fanning her cheek with vehement languor, "don't ask me! my heart's gone to the young fella."

In pursuance of a determination to which the ladies of Brookfield had come, Adela, following her sprightly fancy, now gave the lead in affability toward Mrs. Chump.

"Has the conqueror run away with it to bury it?" she laughed.

"Och! won't he know what it is to be a widde!" cried Mrs. Chump. "A widde's heart takes aim and flies straight as a bullet; and the hearts o' you garls, they're like whiffs o' tobacca, curlin' and wrigglin' and not knowin' where they're goin'. Marry 'em, Pole! marry 'em!" Mrs. Chump gesticulated, with two dangling hands. "They're nice garls; but, lord! they naver see a man, and they're stuputly contented, and want to remain garls; and, don't ye see, it was naver meant to be? Says I to Mr. Wilfrud (and he agreed with me), ye might say, nice sour grapes, as well as nice garls, if the creatures think o' stoppin' where they are, and what they are. It's horrud; and, upon my honour, my heart aches for 'm!"

Mr. Pole threw an uneasy side-glance of inquisition at his daughters, to mark how they bore this unaccustomed language, and haply intercede between the unworthy woman and their judgement of her. But the ladies merely smiled. Placidly triumphant in its endurance, the smile said: "We decline even to feel such a martyrdom as this."

"Well, you know, Martha; I," he said, "I—no father could wish—eh? if you could manage to persuade them not to be so fond of me. They must think of their future, of course. They won't always have a home—a father, a father, I mean. God grant they may never want!—eh? the dinner; boh! let's in to dinner. Ma'am!"

He bowed an arm to Mrs. Chump, who took it, with a scared look at him: "Why, if ye haven't got a tear in your eye, Pole?"

"Nonsense, nonsense," quoth he, bowing another arm to Adela.

"Papa, I'm not to be winked at," said she, accepting convoy; and there was some laughter, all about nothing, as they went in to dinner.

The ladies were studiously forbearing in their treatment of Mrs. Chump. Women are wonderfully quick scholars under ridicule, though it half-kills them. Wilfrid's theory had impressed the superior grace of civility upon their minds, and, now that they practised it, they were pleased with the contrast they presented. Not the less were they maturing a serious resolve. The suspicion that their father had secret vile designs in relation to Mrs. Chump, they kept in the background. It was enough for them that she was to be a visitor, and would thus destroy the great circle they had projected. To accept her in the circle, they felt, was out of the question. Wilfrid's plain-speaking broke up the air-bubble, which they had so carefully blown, and in which they had embarked all their young hopes. They had as much as given one another a pledge that their home likewise should be broken up.

"Are you not almost too severe a student?" Mr. Barrett happened to say to Cornelia, the day after Wilfrid had worried her.

"Do I show the signs?" she replied.

"By no means. But last night, was it not your light that was not extinguished till morning?"

"We soon have morning now," said Cornelia; and her face was pale as the first hour of the dawn. "Are you not a late foot-farer, I may ask in return?"

"Mere restlessness. I have no appetite for study. I took the liberty to cross the park from the wood, and saw you—at least I guessed it your light, and then I met your brother."

"Yes? you met him?"

Mr. Barrett gestured an affirmative.

"And he—did he speak?"

"He nodded. He was in some haste."

"But, then, you did not go to bed at all that night? It is almost my turn to be lecturer, if I might expect to be listened to."

"Do you not know—or am I constitutionally different from others?" Mr. Barrett resumed: "I can't be alone in feeling that there are certain times and periods when what I would like to call poisonous influences are abroad, that touch my fate in the days to come. I know I am helpless. I can only wander up and down."

"That sounds like a creed of fatalism."

"It is not a creed; it is a matter of nerves. A creed has its 'kismet.' The nerves are wild horses."

"It is something to be fought against," said Cornelia admonishingly.

"Is it something to be distrusted?"

"I should say, yes."

"Then I was wrong?"

He stooped eagerly, in his temperate way, to catch sight of her answering face. Cornelia's quick cheeks took fire. She fenced with a question of two, and stood in a tremble, marvelling at his intuition. For possibly, at that moment when he stood watching her window-light (ah, poor heart!) she was half-pledging her word to her sisters (in a whirl of wrath at Wilfrid, herself, and the world), that she would take the lead in breaking up Brookfield.

An event occurred that hurried them on. They received a visit from their mother's brother, John Pierson, a Colonel of Uhlans, in the Imperial-Royal service. He had rarely been in communication with them; his visit was unexpected. His leave of absence from his quarters in Italy was not longer than a month, and he was on his way to Ireland, to settle family business; but he called, as he said, to make acquaintance with his nieces. The ladies soon discovered, in spite of his foreign-cut chin and pronounced military habit of speech and bearing, that he was at heart fervidly British. His age was about fifty: a man of great force of shoulder and potent length of arm, courteous and well-bred in manner, he was altogether what is called a model of a cavalry officer. Colonel Pierson paid very little attention to his brother-in-law, but the ladies were evidently much to his taste; and when he kissed Cornelia's hand, his eyes grew soft, as at a recollection.

"You are what your mother once promised to be," he said. To her he gave that mother's portrait, taking it solemnly from his breast-pocket, and attentively contemplating it before it left his hands. The ladies pressed him for a thousand details of their mama's youthful life; they found it a strange consolation to talk of her and image her like Cornelia. The foreign halo about the Colonel had an effect on them that was almost like what nobility produces; and by degrees they heated their minds to conceive that they were consenting to an outrage on that mother's memory, in countenancing Mrs. Chump's transparent ambition to take her place, as they did by staying in the house with the woman. The colonel's few expressive glances at Mrs. Chump, and Mrs. Chump's behaviour before the colonel, touched them with intense distaste for their present surly aspect of life. Civilized little people are moved to fulfil their destinies and to write their histories as much by distaste as by appetite. This fresh sentimental emotion, which led them to glorify their mother's image in their hearts, heightened and gave an acid edge to their distaste for the think they saw. Nor was it wonderful that Cornelia, said to be so like that mother, should think herself bound to accept the office of taking the initiative in a practical protest against the desecration of the name her mother had borne. At times, I see that sentiment approaches too near the Holy of earthly Holies for us to laugh at it; it has too much truth in it to be denounced—nay, if we are not alert and quick of wit, we shall be deceived by it, and wonder in the end, as the fool does, why heaven struck that final blow; concluding that it was but another whimsy of the Gods. The ladies prayed to their mother. They were indeed suffering vile torture. Ethereal eyes might pardon the unconscious jugglery which made their hearts cry out to her that the step they were about to take was to save her children from seeming to acquiesce in a dishonour to her memory. Some such words Adela's tongue did not shrink from; and as it is a common habit for us to give to the objects we mentally address just as much brain as is wanted for the occasion, she is not to be held singular.

Colonel Pierson promised to stay a week on his return from Ireland. "Will that person be here?" he designated Mrs. Chump; who, among other things, had reproached him for fighting with foreign steel and wearing any uniform but the red.

The ladies and Colonel Pierson were soon of one mind in relation to Mrs. Chump. Certain salient quiet remarks dropped by him were cherished after his departure; they were half-willing to think that he had been directed to come to them, bearer of a message from a heavenly world to urge them to action. They had need of a spiritual exaltation, to relieve them from the palpable depression caused by the weight of Mrs. Chump. They encouraged one another with exclamations on the oddness of a visit from their mother's brother, at such a time of tribulation, indecision, and general darkness.

Mrs. Chump remained on the field. When Adela begged her papa to tell her how long the lady was to stay, he replied: "Eh? By the way, I haven't asked her;" and retreated from this almost too obvious piece of simplicity, with, "I want you to know her: I want you to like her—want you to get to understand her. Won't talk about her going just yet."

If they could have seen a limit to that wholesale slaughter of the Nice Feelings, they might have summoned patience to avoid the desperate step to immediate relief: but they saw none. Their father's quaint kindness and Wilfrid's treachery had fixed her there, perhaps for good. The choice was, to let London come and see them dragged through the mire by the monstrous woman, or to seek new homes. London, they contended, could not further be put off, and would come, especially now that the season was dying. After all, their parting from one another was the bitterest thing to bear, and as each seemed content to endure it for the good of all, and as, properly considered, they did not bury their ambition by separating, they said farewell to the young delicious dawn of it. By means of Fine Shades it was understood that Brookfield was to be abandoned. Not one direct word was uttered. There were expressions of regret that the village children of Ipley would miss the supervizing eyes that had watched over them—perchance! at any rate, would lose them. All went on in the household as before, and would have continued so, but that they had a chief among them. This was Adela Pole, who found her powers with the occasion.

Adela thought decisively: "People never move unless they are pushed." And when you have got them to move ever so little, then propel; but by no means expect that a movement on their part means progression. Without propulsion nothing results. Adela saw what Cornelia meant to do. It was not to fly to Sir Twickenham, but to dismiss Mr. Barrett. Arabella consented to write to Edward Buxley, but would not speak of old days, and barely alluded to a misunderstanding; though if she loved one man, this was he. Adela was disengaged. She had moreover to do penance, for a wrong committed; and just as children will pinch themselves, pleased up to the verge of unendurable pain, so do sentimentalists find a keen relish in performing secret penance for self-accused offences. Thus they become righteous to their own hearts, and evade, as they hope, the public scourge. The wrong committed was (translated out of Fine Shades), that she had made love to her sister's lover. In the original tongue—she had innocently played with the sacred fire of a strange affection; a child in the temple!—Our penitent child took a keen pinching pleasure in dictating words for Arabella to employ toward Edward.

And then, recurring to her interview with Wilfrid, it struck her: "Suppose that, after all, Money!..." Yes, Mammon has acted Hymen before now. Nothing else explained Mrs. Chump; so she thought, in one clear glimpse. Inveterate sentimental habit smeared the picture with two exclamations—"Impossible!" and "Papa!" I desire it to be credited that these simple interjections absolutely obscured her judgement. Little people think either what they are made to think, or what they choose to think; and the education of girls is to make them believe that facts are their enemies-a naughty spying race, upon whom the dogs of Pudeur are to be loosed, if they surprise them without note of warning. Adela silenced her suspicion, easily enough; but this did not prevent her taking a measure to satisfy it. Petting her papa one evening, she suddenly asked him for ninety pounds.

"Ninety!" said Mr. Pole, taking a sharp breath. He was as composed as possible.

"Is that too much, papa, darling?"

"Not if you want it—not if you want it, of course not."

"You seemed astonished."

"The sum! it's an odd sum for a girl to want. Ten, twenty, fifty—a hundred; but you never hear of ninety, never! unless it's to pay a debt; and I have all the bills, or your aunt has them."

"Well, papa, if it excites you, I will do without it. It is for a charity, chiefly."

Mr. Pole fumbled in his pocket, muttering, "No money here—cheque-book in town. I'll give it you," he said aloud, "to-morrow morning—morrow morning, early."

"That will do, papa;" and Adela relieved him immediately by shooting far away from the topic.

The ladies retired early to their hall of council in the bedchamber of Arabella, and some time after midnight Cornelia went to her room; but she could not sleep. She affected, in her restlessness, to think that her spirits required an intellectual sedative, so she went down to the library for a book; where she skimmed many—a fashion that may be recommended, for assisting us to a sense of sovereign superiority to authors, and also of serene contempt for all mental difficulties. Fortified in this way, Cornelia took a Plutarch and an Encyclopaedia under her arm, to return to her room. But one volume fell, and as she stooped to recover it, her candle shared its fate. She had to find her way back in the dark. On the landing of the stairs, she fancied that she heard a step and a breath. The lady was of unshaken nerves. She moved on steadily, her hand stretched out a little before her. What it touched was long in travelling to her brain; but when her paralyzed heart beat again, she knew that her hand clasped another hand. Her nervous horror calmed as the feeling came to her of the palpable weakness of the hand.

"Who are you?" she asked. Some hoarse answer struck her ear. She asked again, making her voice distincter. The hand now returned her pressure with force. She could feel that the person, whoever it was, stood collecting strength to speak. Then the words came—

"What do you mean by imitating that woman's brogue?"

"Papa!" said Cornelia.

"Why do you talk Irish in the dark? There, goodnight. I've just come up from the library; my candle dropped. I shouldn't have been frightened, but you talked with such a twang."

"But I have just come from the library myself," said Cornelia.

"I mean from the dining-room," her father corrected himself hastily. "I can't sit in the library; shall have it altered—full of draughts. Don't you think so, my dear? Good-night. What's this in your arm? Books! Ah, you study! I can get a light for myself."

The dialogue was sustained in the hard-whispered tones prescribed by darkness. Cornelia kissed her father's forehead, and they parted.

At breakfast in the morning it was the habit of all the ladies to assemble, partly to countenance the decency of matin-prayers, and also to give the head of the household their dutiful society till business called him away. Adela, in earlier days, had maintained that early rising was not fashionable; but she soon grasped the idea that a great rivalry with Fashion, in minor matters (where the support of the satirist might be counted on), was the proper policy of Brookfield. Mrs. Chump was given to be extremely fashionable in her hours, and began her Brookfield career by coming downstairs at ten and eleven o'clock, when she found a desolate table, well stocked indeed, but without any of the exuberant smiles of nourishment which a morning repast should wear.

"You are a Protestant, ma'am, are you not?" Adela mildly questioned, after informing her that she missed family prayer by her late descent. Mrs. Chump assured her that she was a firm Protestant, and liked to see faces at the breakfast-table. The poor woman was reduced to submit to the rigour of the hour, coming down flustered, and endeavouring to look devout, while many uncertainties as to the condition of the hooks of her attire distracted her mind and fingers. On one occasion, Gainsford, the footman, had been seen with his eye on her; and while Mr. Pole read of sacred things, at a pace composed of slow march and amble, this unhappy man was heard struggling to keep under and extinguish a devil of laughter, by which his human weakness was shaken: He retired from the room with the speed of a voyager about to pay tribute on high seas. Mr. Pole cast a pregnant look at the servants' row as he closed the book; but the expression of his daughters' faces positively signified that no remark was to be made, and he contained himself. Later, the ladies told him that Gainsford had done no worse than any uneducated man would have been guilty of doing. Mrs. Chump had, it appeared, a mother's feeling for one flat curl on her rugged forehead, which was often fondly caressed by her, for the sake of ascertaining its fixity. Doubts of the precision of outline and general welfare of this curl, apparently, caused her to straighten her back and furtively raise her head, with an easy upward motion, as of a cork alighted in water, above the level of the looking-glass on her left hand—an action she repeated, with a solemn aspect, four times; at which point Gainsford gave way. The ladies accorded him every extenuation for the offence. They themselves, but for the heroism of exalted natures, must have succumbed to the gross temptation. "It is difficult, dear papa, to bring one's mind to religious thoughts in her company, even when she is quiescent," they said. Thus, by the prettiest exercise of charity that can be conceived, they pleaded for the man Gainsford, while they struck a blow at Mrs. Chump; and in performing one of the virtues laid down by religion, proved their enemy to be hostile to its influences.

Mrs. Chump was this morning very late. The office of morning reader was new to Mr. Pole, who had undertaken it, when first Squire of Brookfield, at the dictate of the ladies his daughters; so that, waiting with the book before him and his audience expectant, he lacked composure, spoke irritably in an under-breath of 'that woman,' and asked twice whether she was coming or not. At last the clump of her feet was heard approaching. Mr. Pole commenced reading the instant she opened the door. She stood there, with a face like a petrified Irish outcry. An imploring sound of "Pole! Pole!" issued from her. Then she caught up one hand to her mouth, and rolled her head, in evident anguish at the necessitated silence. A convulsion passed along the row of maids, two of whom dipped to their aprons; but the ladies gazed with a sad consciousness of wicked glee at the disgust she was exciting in the bosom of their father.

"Will you shut the door?" Mr. Pole sternly addressed Mrs. Chump, at the conclusion of the first prayer.

"Pole! ye know that money ye gave me in notes? I must speak, Pole!"

"Shut the door."

Mrs. Chump let go the door-handle with a moan. The door was closed by Gainsford, now one of the gravest of footmen. A chair was placed for her, and she sat down, desperately watching the reader for the fall of his voice. The period was singularly protracted. The ladies turned to one another, to question with an eyelid why it was that extra allowance was given that morning. Mr. Pole was in a third prayer, stumbling on and picking himself up, apparently unaware that he had passed the limit. This continued until the series of ejaculations which accompanied him waxed hotter—little muffled shrieks of: "Oh!—Deer—Oh, Lard!—When will he stop? Oh, mercy! Och! And me burrstin' to speak!—Oh! what'll I do? I can't keep 't in!—Pole! ye're kill'n me—Oh, deer! I'll be sayin' somethin' to vex the prophets presently. Pole!"

If it was a race that he ran with Mrs. Chump, Mr. Pole was beaten. He came to a sudden stop.

Mrs. Chump had become too deeply absorbed in her impatience to notice the change in his tone; and when he said, "Now then, to breakfast, quick!" she was pursuing her lamentable interjections. At sight of the servants trooping forth, she jumped up and ran to the door.

"Ye don't go.—Pole, they're all here. And I've been robbed, I have. Avery note I had from ye, Pole, all gone. And my purse left behind, like the skin of a thing. Lord forbid I accuse annybody; but when I get up, my first rush is to feel in my pocket. And, ask 'em!—If ye didn't keep me so poor, Pole, they'd know I'm a generous woman, but I cann't bear to be robbed. And pinmoney 's for spendin;' annybody'll tell you that. And I ask ye t' examine 'em, Pole; for last night I counted my notes, wantin' change, and I thought of a salmon I bought on the banks of the Suir to make a present to Chump, which was our onnly visit to Waterford together: for he naver went t' Ireland before or after—dyin' as he did! and it's not his ingrat'tude, with his talk of a Severrn salmon-to the deuce with 'm! that makes me soft-poor fella!—I didn't mean to the deuce;—but since he's gone, his widde's just unfit to bargain for a salmon at all, and averybody robs her, and she's kept poor, and hatud!—D'ye heer, Pole? I've lost my money, my money! and I will speak, and ye shann't interrupt me!"

During the delivery of this charge against the household, Mr. Pole had several times waved to the servants to begone; but as they had always the option to misunderstand authoritative gestures, they preferred remaining, and possibly he perceived that they might claim to do so under accusation.

"How can you bring this charge against the inmates of my house—eh? I guarantee the honesty of all who serve me. Martha! you must be mad, mad!—Money? why, you never have money; you waste it if you do."

"Not money, Pole? Oh! and why? Becas ye keep me low o' purpose, till I cringe like a slut o' the scullery, and cry out for halfpence. But, oh! that seventy-five pounds in notes!"

Mr. Pole shook his head, as one who deals with a gross delusion: "I remember nothing about it."

"Not about—?" Mrs. Chump dropped her chin. "Ye don't remember the givin' of me just that sum of seventy-five, in eight notes, Pole?"

"Eh? I daresay I have given you the amount, one time or other. Now, let's be quiet about it."

"Yesterday mornin', Pole! And the night I go to bed I count my money, and, says I, I'll not lock ut up, for I'll onnly be unlockin' again to-morrow; and doin' a thing and undoin' ut's a sign of a brain that's addled—like yours, Pole, if ye say ye didn't go to give me the notes."

Mr. Pole frowned at her sagaciously. "Must change your diet, Martha!"

"My dite? And what's my dite to do with my money?"

"Who went into Mrs. Chump's bedchamber this morning?" asked Mr. Pole generally.

A pretty little housemaid replied, with an indignant flush, that she was the person. Mrs. Chump acknowledged to being awake when the shutters were opened, and agreed that it was not possible her pockets could have been rifled then.

"So, you see, Martha, you're talking nonsense," said Mr. Pole. "Do you know the numbers of those notes?"

"The numbers at the sides, ye mean, Pole?"

"Ay, the numbers at the sides, if you like; the 21593, and so on?"

"The 21593! Oh! I can't remember such a lot as that, if ever I leave off repeatin' it."

"There! you see, you're not fit to have money in your possession, Martha. Everybody who has bank-notes looks at the numbers. You have a trick of fancying all sorts of sums in your pocket; and when you don't find them there, of course they're lost! Now, let's have some breakfast."

Arabella told the maids to go out. Mr. Pole turned to the breakfast-table, rubbing his hands. Seeing herself and her case abandoned, Mrs. Chump gave a deplorable shout. "Ye're crool! and young women that look on at a fellow-woman's mis'ry. Oh! how can ye do ut! But soft hearts can be the hardest. And all my seventy-five gone, gone! and no law out of annybody. And no frightenin' of 'em off from doin' the like another time! Oh, I will, I will have my money!"

"Tush! Come to breakfast, Martha," said Mr. Pole. "You shall have money, if you want it; you have only to ask. Now, will you promise to be quiet? and I'll give you this money—the amount you've been dreaming about last night. I'll fetch it. Now, let us have no scenes. Dry your eyes."

Mr. Pole went to his private room, and returned just as Mrs. Chump had got upon a succession of quieter sobs with each one of which she addressed a pathetic roll of her eyes to the utterly unsympathetic ladies respectively.

"There, Martha; there's exactly the sum for you—free gift. Say thank you, and eat a good breakfast to show your gratitude. Mind, you take this money on condition that you let the servants know you made a mistake."

Mrs. Chump sighed heavily, crumpling the notes, that the crisp sweet sound might solace her for the hard condition.

"And don't dream any more—not about money, I mean," said Mr. Pole.

"Oh! if I dream like that I'll be living double." Mrs. Chump put her hand to the notes, and called him kind, and pitied him for being the loser. The sight of a fresh sum in her possession intoxicated her. It was but feebly that she regretted the loss to her Samuel Bolton Pole. "Your memory's worth more than that!" she said as she filled her purse with the notes. "Anyhow, now I can treat somebody," and she threw a wink of promise at Adela. Adela's eyes took refuge with her papa, who leaned over to her, and said: "You won't mind waiting till you see me again? She's taken all I had." Adela nodded blankly, and the next moment, with an angry glance toward Mrs. Chump, "Papa," said she, "if you wish to see servants in the house on your return, you must yourself speak to them, and tell them that we, their master and mistresses, do not regard them as thieves." Out of this there came a quarrel as furious as the ladies would permit it to be. For Mrs. Chump, though willing to condone the offence for the sum she had received, stuck infamy upon the whole list of them. "The Celtic nature," murmured Cornelia. And the ladies maintained that their servants should be respected, at any cost. "You, ma'am," said Arabella, with a clear look peculiar to her when vindictive—"you may have a stain on your character, and you are not ruined by it. But these poor creatures..."

"Ye dare to compar' me—!"

"Contrast you, ma'am."

"It's just as imp'dent."

"I say, our servants, ma'am..."

"Oh! to the deuce with your 'ma'am;' I hate the word. It's like fittin' a cap on me. Ye want to make one a turbaned dow'ger, ye malicious young woman!"

"Those are personages that are, I believe, accepted in society!"

So the contest raged, Mrs. Chump being run clean through the soul twenty times, without touching the consciousness of that sensitive essence. Mr. Pole appeared to take the part of his daughters, and by-and-by Mrs. Chump, having failed to arouse Mrs. Lupin's involuntary laugh (which always consoled her in such cases), huffed out of the room. Then Mr. Pole, in an abruptly serious way, bashfully entreated the ladies to be civil to Martha, who had the best heart in the world. It sounded as if he were going to say more. After a pause, he added emphatically, "Do!" and went. He was many days absent: nor did he speak to Adela of the money she had asked for when he returned. Adela had not the courage to allude to it.

CHAPTER XVII

IN THE WOODS

Emilia sat in her old place under the dwarf pine. Mr. Powys had brought her back to Brookfield, where she heard that Wilfrid had been seen; and now her heart was in contest with an inexplicable puzzle: "He was here, and did not come to me!" Since that night when they had walked home from Ipley Green, she had not suffered a moment of longing. Her senses had lain as under a charm, with heart at anchor and a mind free to work. No one could have guessed that any human spell was on the girl. "Wherever he is, he thinks of me. I find him everywhere. He is safe, for I pray for him and have my arms about him. He will come." So she waited, as some grey lake lies, full and smooth, awaiting the star below the twilight. If she let her thoughts run on to the hour of their meeting, she had to shut her eyes and press at her heart; but as yet she was not out of tune for daily life, and she could imagine how that hour was to be strewn with new songs and hushed surprises. And 'thus' he would look: and 'thus.' "My hero!" breathed Emilia, shuddering a little. But now she was perplexed. Now that he had come and gone, she began to hunger bitterly for the sight of his face, and that which had hitherto nourished her grew a sickly phantom of delight. She wondered how she had forced herself to be patient, and what it was that she had found pleasure in.

None of the ladies were at home when Emilia returned. She went out to the woods, and sat, shadowed by the long bent branch; watching mechanically the slow rounding and yellowing of the beam of sunlight over the thick floor of moss, up against the fir-stems. The chaffinch and the linnet flitted off the grey orchard twigs, singing from new stations; and the bee seemed to come questioning the silence of the woods and droning disappointed away. The first excess of any sad feeling is half voluntary. Emilia could not help smiling, when she lifted her head out of a musing fit, to find that she had composed part of a minuet for the languid dancing motes in the shaft of golden light at her feet. "Can I remember it?" she thought, and forgot the incident with the effort.

Down at her right hand, bordering a water, stood a sallow, a dead tree, channelled inside with the brown trail of a goat-moth. Looking in this direction, she saw Cornelia advancing to the tree. When the lady had reached it, she drew a little book from her bosom, kissed it, and dropped it in the hollow. This done, she passed among the firs. Emilia had perceived that she was agitated: and with that strange instinct of hearts beginning to stir, which makes them divine at once where they will come upon the secret of their own sensations, she ran down to the tree and peered on tiptoe at the embedded volume. On a blank page stood pencilled: "This is the last fruit of the tree. Come not to gather more." There was no meaning for her in that sentimental chord but she must have got some glimpse of a meaning; for now, as in an agony, her lips fashioned the words: "If I forget his face I may as well die;" and she wandered on, striving more and more vainly to call up his features. The—"Does he think of me?" and— "What am I to him?"—such timorous little feather-play of feminine emotion she knew nothing of: in her heart was the strong flood of a passion.

She met Edward Buxley and Freshfield Sumner at a cross-path, on their way to Brookfield; and then Adela joined the party, which soon embraced Mr. Barrett, and subsequently Cornelia. All moved on in a humming leisure, chattering by fits. Mr. Sumner was delicately prepared to encounter Mrs. Chump, "whom," said Adela, "Edward himself finds it impossible to caricature;" and she affected to laugh at the woman.

"Happy the pencil that can reproduce!" Mr. Barrett exclaimed; and, meeting his smile, Cornelia said: "Do you know, my feeling is, and I cannot at all account for it, that if she were a Catholic she would not seem so gross?"

"Some of the poetry of that religion would descend upon her, possibly," returned Mr. Barrett.

"Do you mean," Freshfield said quickly, "that she would stand a fair chance of being sainted?"

Out of this arose some polite fencing between the two. Freshfield might have argued to advantage in a Court of law; but he was no match, on such topics and before such an audience, for a refined sentimentalist. More than once he betrayed a disposition to take refuge in his class (he being son to one of the puisne Judges). Cornelia speedily punished him, and to any correction from her he bowed his head.

Adela was this day gifted with an extraordinary insight. Emilia alone of the party was as a blot to her; but the others she saw through, as if they had been walking transparencies. She divined that Edward and Freshfield had both come, in concert, upon amorous business—that it was Freshfield's object to help Edward to a private interview with her, and, in return, Edward was to perform the same service for him with Cornelia. So that Mr. Barrett was shockingly in the way of both; and the perplexity of these stupid fellows—who would insist upon wondering why the man Barrett and the girl Emilia (musicians both: both as it were, vagrants) did not walk together and talk of quavers and minims—was extremely comic. Passing the withered tree, Mr. Barrett deserved thanks from Freshfield, if he did not obtain them; for he lingered, surrendering his place. And then Adela knew that the weight of Edward Buxley's remonstrative wrath had fallen on silent Emilia, to whom she clung fondly.

"I have had a letter," Edward murmured, in the voice that propitiates secrecy.

"A letter?" she cried loud; and off flew the man like a rabbit into his hole, the mask of him remaining.

Emilia presently found Mr. Barrett at her elbow. His hand clasped the book Cornelia had placed in the tree.

"It is hers," said Emilia.

He opened it and pointed to his initials. She looked in his face.

"Are you very ill?"

Adela turned round from Edward's neighbouring head. "Who is ill?"

Cornelia brought Freshfield to a stop: "Ill?"

Before them all, book in hand, Mr. Barrett had to give assurance that he was hearty, and to appear to think that his words were accepted, in spite of blanched jowl and reddened under-lid. Cornelia threw him one glance: his eyes closed under it. Adela found it necessary to address some such comforting exclamation as 'Goodness gracious!' to her observant spirit.

In the park-path, leading to the wood, Arabella was seen as they came out the young branches that fringed the firs. She hurried up.

"I have been looking for you. Papa has arrived with Sir Twickenham Pryme, who dines with us."

Adela unhesitatingly struck a blow.

"Lady Pryme, we make place for you."

And she crossed to Cornelia. Cornelia kept her eyes fixed on Adela's mouth, as one looks at a place whence a venomous reptile has darted out. Her eyelids shut, and she stood a white sculpture of pain, pitiable to see. Emilia took her hand, encouraging the tightening fingers with a responsive pressure. The group shuffled awkwardly together, though Adela did her best. She was very angry with Mr. Barrett for wearing that absurdly pale aspect. She was even angry with his miserable bankrupt face for mounting a muscular edition of the smile Cornelia had shown. "His feelings!" she cried internally; and the fact presented itself to her, that feelings were a luxury utterly unfit for poor men, who were to be accused of presumption for indulging in them.

"Now, I suppose you are happy?" she spoke low between Arabella and Edward.

The effect of these words was to colour violently two pair of cheeks. Arabella's behaviour did not quite satisfy the fair critic. Edward Buxley was simply caught in a trap: He had the folly to imagine that by laughing he released himself.

"Is not that the laugh of an engaged?" said Adela to Freshfield.

He replied: "That would have been my idea under other conditions," and looked meaningly.

She met the look with: "There are harsh conditions in life, are there not?" and left him sufficiently occupied by his own sensations.

"Mr. Barrett," she inquired (partly to assist the wretch out of his compromising depression, and also that the question represented a real matter of debate in her mind), "I want your opinion; will you give it me? Apropos of slang, why does it sit well on some people? It certainly does not vulgarize them. After all, in many cases, it is what they call 'racy idiom.' Perhaps our delicacy is strained?"

Now, it was Mr. Barrett's established manner to speak in a deliberately ready fashion upon the introduction of a new topic. Habit made him, on this occasion, respond instantly; but the opening of the gates displayed the confusion of ideas within and the rageing tumult.

He said: "In many cases. There are two sorts. If you could call it the language of nature! which anything... I beg your pardon, Slang! Polite society rightly excludes it, because...."

"Yes, yes," returned Adela; "but do we do rightly in submitting to the absolute tyranny?—I mean, I think, originality flies from us in consequence."

The pitiable mortal became a trifle more luminous: "The objection is to the repetition of risked phrases. A happy audacity of expression may pass. It is bad taste to repeat it, that is all. Then there is the slang of heavy boorishness, and the slang of impatient wit..."

"Is there any fine distinction between the extremes?" said Cornelia, in as clear a tone as she could summon.

"I think," observed Arabella, "that whatever shows staleness speedily is self-condemned; and that is the case with slang."

"And yet it's to avoid some feeling of the sort that people employ it," was Adela's remark; and the discussion of this theme dropped lifelessly, and they walked on as before.

Coming to a halt near the garden gate, Adela tapped Emilia's cheek, addressing her: "How demure she has become!"

"Ah!" went Arabella, "does she know papa has had a letter from Mr. Pericles, who wrote from Milan to say that he has made arrangements for her to enter the Academy there, and will come to fetch her in a few days?"

Emilia's wrists crossed below her neck, while she gave ear.

"To take me away?" she said.

The tragic attitude and outcry, with the mournful flash of her eyes, might have told Emilia's tale.

Adela unwillingly shielded her by interpreting the scene. "See! she must be a born actress. They always exaggerate in that style, so that you would really think she had a mighty passion for Brookfield."

"Or in it," suggested Freshfield.

"Or in it!" she laughed assentingly.

Mr. Pole was perceived entering the garden, rubbing his hands a little too obsequiously to some remark of the baronet's, as the critical ladies imagined. Sir Twickenham's arm spread out in a sweep; Mr. Pole's head nodded. After the ceremony of the salute, the ladies were informed of Sir Twickenham's observation: Sir Twickenham Pryme, a statistical member of Parliament, a well-preserved half-century in age, a gentleman in bearing, passably grey-headed, his whiskers brushed out neatly, as if he knew them individually and had the exact amount of them collectively at his fingers' ends: Sir Twickenham had said of Mr. Pole's infant park that if devoted to mangold-wurzel it would be productive and would pay: whereas now it was not ornamental and was waste.

"Sir Twickenham calculates," said Mr. Pole, "that we should have a crop of—eh?"

"The average?" Sir Twickenham asked, on the evident upward mounting of a sum in his brain. And then, with a relaxing look upon Cornelia: "Perhaps you might have fifteen, sixteen, perhaps for the first year; or, say—you see, the exact acreage is unknown to me. Say roughly, ten thousand sacks the first year."

"Of what?" inquired Cornelia.

"Mangold-wurzel," said the baronet.

She gazed about her. Mr. Barrett was gone.

"But, no doubt, you take no interest in such reckonings?" Sir Twickenham added.

"On the contrary, I take every interest in practical details."

Practical men believe this when they hear it from the lips of gentlewomen, and without philosophically analyzing the fact that it is because the practical quality possesses simply the fascination of a form of strength. Sir Twickenham pursued his details. Day closed on Brookfield blankly. Nevertheless, the ladies felt that the situation was now dignified by tragic feeling, and remembering keenly how they had been degraded of late, they had a sad enjoyment of the situation.

BOOK III

CHAPTER XVIII

RETURN OF THE SENTIMENTALIST INTO BONDAGE

Meantime Wilfrid was leading a town-life and occasionally visiting Stornley. He was certainly not in love with Lady Charlotte Chillingworth, but he was in harness to that lady. In love we have some idea whither we would go: in harness we are simply driven, and the destination may be anywhere. To be reduced to this condition (which will happen now and then in the case of very young men who are growing up to something, and is, if a momentary shame to them, rather a sign of promise than not) the gentle male need not be deeply fascinated. Lady Charlotte was not a fascinating person. She did not lay herself out to attract. Had she done so, she would have failed to catch Wilfrid, whose soul thirsted for poetical refinement and filmy delicacies in a woman. What she had, and what he knew that he wanted, and could only at intervals assume by acting as if he possessed it, was a victorious aplomb, which gave her a sort of gallant glory in his sight. He could act it well before his sisters, and here and there a damsel; and coming fresh from Lady Charlotte's school, he had recently done so with success, and had seen the ladies feel toward him, as he felt under his instructress in the art. Some nature, however, is required for every piece of art. Wilfrid knew that he had been brutal in his representation of the part, and the retrospect of his conduct at Brookfield did not satisfy his remorseless critical judgement. In consequence, when he again saw Lady Charlotte, his admiration of that one prized characteristic of hers paralyzed him. She looked, and moved, and spoke, as if the earth were her own. She was a note of true music, and he felt himself to be an indecisive chord; capable ultimately of a splendid performance, it might be, but at present crying out to be played upon. This is the condition of a man in harness, whom witlings may call what they will. He is subjugated: not won. In this state of subjugation he will joyfully sacrifice as much as a man in love. For, having no consolatory sense of happiness, such as encircles and makes a nest for lovers, he seeks to attain some stature, at least, by excesses of apparent devotion. Lady Charlotte believed herself beloved at last. She was about to strike thirty; and Rumour, stalking with a turban of cloud on her head,—enough that this shocking old celestial dowager, from condemnation had passed to pity of the dashing lady. Beloved at last! After a while there is no question of our loving; but we thirst for love, if we have not had it. The key of Lady Charlotte will come in the course of events. She was at the doubtful hour of her life, a warm-hearted woman, known to be so by few, generally consigned by devout-visaged Scandal (for who save the devout will dare to sit in the chair of judgement?) as a hopeless rebel against conventional laws; and worse than that, far worse,—though what, is not said.

At Stornley the following letter from Emilia hit its mark:—

Dear Mr. Wilfrid,

"It is time for me to see you. Come when you have read this letter. I cannot tell you how I am, because my heart feels beating in another body. Pray come; come now. Come on a swift horse. The thought of you galloping to me goes through me like a flame that hums. You will come, I know. It is time. If I write foolishly, do forgive me. I can only make sure of the spelling, and I cannot please you on paper, only when I see you."

The signature of 'Emilia Alessandra Belloni' was given with her wonted proud flourish.

Wilfrid stared at the writing. "What! all this time she has been thinking the same thing!" Her constancy did not swim before him in alluring colours. He regarded it as a species of folly. Disgust had left him. The pool of Memory would have had to be stirred to remind him of the pipe-smoke in her hair. "You are sure to please me when you see me?" he murmured. "You are very confident, young lady!" So much had her charm faded. And then he thought kindly of her, and that a meeting would not be good for her, and that she ought to go to Italy and follow her profession. "If she grows famous," whispered coxcombry, "why then oneself will take a little of the praises given to her." And that seemed eminently satisfactory. Men think in this way when you have loved them, ladies. All men? No; only the coxcombs; but it is to these that you give your fresh affection. They are, as it were, the band of the regiment of adorers, marching ahead, while we sober working soldiers follow to their music. "If she grows famous, why then I can bear in mind that her heart was once in my possession: and it may return to its old owner, perchance." Wilfrid indulged in a pleasant little dream of her singing at the Opera-house, and he, tied to a ferocious, detested wife, how softly and luxuriously would he then be sighing for the old time! It was partly good seed in his nature, and an apprehension of her force of soul, that kept him from a thought of evil to her. Passion does not inspire dark appetite. Dainty innocence does, I am told. Things are tested by the emotions they provoke. Wilfrid knew that there was no trifling with Emilia, so he put the letter by, commenting thus "she's right, she doesn't spell badly." Behind, which, to those who have caught the springs of his character, volumes may be seen.

He put the letter by. Two days later, at noon, the card of Captain Gambier was brought to him in the billiard-room,—on it was written: "Miss Belloni waits on horseback to see you." Wilfrid thought "Waits!" and the impossibility of escape gave him a notion of her power.

"So, you are letting that go on," said Lady Charlotte, when she heard that Emilia and the captain were in company.

"There is no fear for her whatever."

"There is always fear when a man gives every minute of his time to that kind of business," retorted her ladyship.

Wilfrid smiled the smile of the knowing. Rivalry with Gambier (and successful too!) did not make Emilia's admiration so tasteless. Some one cries out: "But, what a weak creature is this young man!" I reply, he was at a critical stage of his career. All of us are weak in the period of growth, and are of small worth before the hour of trial. This fellow had been fattening all his life on prosperity; the very best dish in the world; but it does not prove us. It fattens and strengthens us, just as the sun does. Adversity is the inspector of our constitutions; she simply tries our muscle and powers of endurance, and should be a periodical visitor. But, until she comes, no man is known. Wilfrid was not absolutely engaged to Lady

Charlotte (she had taken care of that), and being free, and feeling his heart beat in more lively fashion, he turned almost delightedly to the girl he could not escape from. As when the wriggling eel that has been prodded by the countryman's fork, finds that no amount of wriggling will release it, to it twists in a knot around the imprisoning prong. This simile says more than I mean it to say, but those who understand similes will know the measure due to them.

There sat Emilia on her horse. "Has Gambier been giving her lessons?" thought Wilfrid. She sat up, well-balanced; and, as he approached, began to lean gently forward to him. A greeting 'equal to any lady's,' there was no doubt. This was the point Emilia had to attain, in his severe contemplation. A born lady, on her assured level, stood a chance of becoming a Goddess; but ladyship was Emilia's highest mark. Such is the state of things to the sentimental fancy when girls are at a disadvantage. She smiled, and held out both hands. He gave her one, nodding kindly, but was too confused to be the light-hearted cavalier. Lady Charlotte walked up to her horse's side, after receiving Captain Gambier's salute, and said: "Come, catch hold of my hands and jump."

"No," replied Emilia; "I only came to see him."

"But you will see him, and me in the bargain, if you stay."

"I fancy she has given her word to return early," interposed Wilfrid.

"Then we'll ride back with her," said Lady Charlotte. "Give me five minutes. I'll order a horse out for you."

She smiled, and considerately removed the captain, by despatching him to the stables.

A quivering dimple of tenderness hung for a moment in Emilia's cheeks, as she looked upon Wilfrid. Then she said falteringly, "I think they wish to be as we do."

"Alone?" cried Wilfrid.

"Yes; that is why I brought him over. He will come anywhere with me."

"You must be mistaken."

"No; I know it."

"Did he tell you so?"

"No; Mr. Powys did."

"Told you that Lady Charlotte—"

"Yes. Not, is; but, was. And he used that word... there is no word like it,... he said 'her lover'—Oh! mine!" Emilia lifted her arms. Her voice from its deepest fall had risen to a cry.

Wilfrid caught her as she slipped from her saddle. His heart was in a tumult; stirred both ways: stirred with wrath and with love. He clasped her tightly.

"Am I?—am I?" he breathed.

"My lover!" Emilia murmured.

He was her slave again.

For, here was something absolutely his own. His own from the roots; from the first growth of sensation. Something with the bloom on it: to which no other finger could point and say: "There is my mark."

(And, ladies, if you will consent to be likened to a fruit, you must bear with these observations, and really deserve the stigma. If you will smile on men, because they adore you as vegetable products, take what ensues.)

Lady Charlotte did no more than double the time she had asked for. The party were soon at a quiet canter up the lanes; but entering a broad furzy common with bramble-plots and oak-shaws, the Amazon flew ahead. Emilia's eyes were so taken with her, that she failed to observe a tiny red-flowing runlet in the clay, with yellow-ridged banks almost baked to brick. Over it she was borne, but at the expense of a shaking that caused her to rely on her hold of the reins, ignorant of the notions of a horse outstripped. Wilfrid looked to see that the jump had been accomplished, and was satisfied. Gambier was pressing his hack to keep a respectable second.

Lady Charlotte spun round suddenly, crying, "Catch the mare!" and galloped back to Emilia, who was deposited on a bush of bramble. Dismounting promptly, the lady said: "My child, you're not hurt?"

"Not a bit." Emilia blinked.

"Not frightened?"

"Not a bit," was half whispered.

"That's brave. Now jump on your feet. Tell me why you rode over to us this morning. Quick. Don't hesitate."

"Because I want Wilfrid to see his sister Cornelia," came the answer, with the required absence of indecision.

Emilia ran straightway to meet Wilfrid approaching; and as both her hands, according to her fashion, were stretched out to him to assure him of her safety and take his clasp, forgetful of the instincts derived from riding-habits, her feet became entangled; she trod herself down, falling plump forward and looking foolish—perhaps for the first time in her life plainly feeling so.

"Up! little woman," said Lady Charlotte, supporting her elbow.

"Now, Sir Wilfrid, we part here; and don't spoil her courage, now she has had a spill, by any 'assiduous attentions' and precautions. She's sure to take as many as are needed. If Captain Gambler thinks I require an escort, he may offer."

The captain, taken by surprise, bowed, and flowed in ardent commonplace. Wilfrid did not look of a wholesome colour.

"Do you return?" he stammered; not without a certain aspect of righteous reproach.

"Yes. You will ride over to us again, probably, in a day or two? Captain Gambler will see me safe from the savage admirers that crowd this country, if I interpreted him rightly."

Emilia was lifted to her seat. Lady Charlotte sprang unassisted to hers. "Ta-ta!" she waved her fingers from her lips. The pairs then separated; one couple turning into green lanes, the other dipping to blue hills.

CHAPTER XIX

LIFE AT BROOKFIELD

Gossip of course was excited on the subject of the choice of a partner made by the member for the county. Cornelia placed her sisters in one of their most pleasing of difficulties. She had not as yet pledged her word. It was supposed that she considered it due to herself to withhold her word for a term. The rumour in the family was, that Sir Twickenham appreciated her hesitation, and desired that he might be intimately known before he was finally accepted. When the Tinleys called, they heard that Cornelia's acceptance of the baronet was doubtful. The Copleys, on the other hand, distinctly understood that she had decided in his favour. Owing to the amiable dissension between the Copleys and the Tinleys, each party called again; giving the ladies of Brookfield further opportunity for studying one of the levels from which they had risen. Arabella did almost all the fencing with Laura Tinley, contemptuously as a youth of station returned from college will turn and foil an ill-conditioned villager, whom formerly he has encountered on the green.

"Had they often met, previous to the... the proposal?" inquired Laura; and laughed: "I was going to say 'popping.'"

"Pray do not check yourself, if a phrase appears to suit you," returned Arabella.

"But it was in the neighbourhood, was it not?"

"They have met in the neighbourhood."

"At Richford?"

"Also at Richford."

"We thought it was sudden, dear; that's all."

"Why should it not be?"

"Perhaps the best things are, it is true."

"You congratulate us upon a benefit?"

"He is to be congratulated seriously. Naturally. When she decides, let me know early, I do entreat you, because... well, I am of a different opinion from some people, who talk of another attachment, or engagement, and I do not believe in it, and have said so."

Rising to depart, Laura Tinley resumed: "Most singular! You are aware, of course, that poor creature, our organist—I ought to say yours—who looked (it was Mr. Sumner I heard say it—such a good thing!) as if he had been a gentleman in another world, and was the ghost of one in this: really one of the cleverest things! but he is clever!—Barrett's his name: Barrett and some: musical name before it, like Handel. I mean one that we are used to. Well, the man has totally and unexpectedly thrown up his situation."

"His appointment," said Arabella. Permitting no surprise to be visible, she paused: "Yes. I don't think we shall give our consent to her filling the post."

Laura let it be seen that her adversary was here a sentence too quick for her.

"Ah! you mean your little Miss Belloni?"

"Was it not of her you were thinking?"

"When?" asked Laura, shamefully bewildered.

"When you alluded to Mr. Barrett's vacant place."

"Not at the moment."

"I thought you must be pointing to her advancement."

"I confess it was not in my mind."

"In what consisted the singularity, then?"

"The singularity?"

"You prefaced your remarks with the exclamation, 'Singular!'"

Laura showed that Arabella had passed her guard. She hastened to compliment her on her kindness to Emilia, and so sheathed her weapon for the time, having just enjoyed a casual inspection of Mrs. Chump entering the room, and heard the brogue an instant.

"Irish!" she whispered, smiling, with a sort of astonished discernment of the nationality, and swept through the doorway: thus conveying forcibly to Arabella her knowledge of what the ladies of Brookfield were enduring: a fine Parthian shot.

That Cornelia should hold a notable county man, a baronet and owner of great acres, in a state between acceptance and rejection, was considered high policy by the ladies, whom the idea of it elevated; and they encouraged her to pursue this course, without having a suspicion, shrewd as they were, that it was followed for any other object than the honour of the family. But Mr. Pole was in the utmost perplexity, and spoke of baronets as things almost holy, to be kneeled to, prayed for. He was profane. "I thought, papa," said Cornelia, "that women conferred the favour when they gave their hands!"

It was a new light to the plain merchant. "How should you say if a Prince came and asked for you?"

"Still that he asked a favour at my hands."

"Oh!" went Mr. Pole, in the voice of a man whose reason is outraged. The placidity of Cornelia's reply was not without its effect on him, nevertheless. He had always thought his girls extraordinary girls, and born to be distinguished. "Perhaps she has a lord in view," he concluded: it being his constant delusion to suppose that high towering female sense has always a practical aim at a material thing. He was no judge of the sex in its youth. "Just speak to her," he said to Wilfrid.

Wilfrid had heard from Emilia that there was a tragic background to this outward placidity; tears on the pillow at night and long vigils. Emilia had surprised her weeping, and though she obtained no confidences, the soft mood was so strong in the stately lady, that she consented to weep on while Emilia clasped her. Petitioning on her behalf to Wilfrid for aid, Emilia had told him the scene; and he, with a man's stupidity, alluded to it, not thinking what his knowledge of it revealed to a woman.

"Why do you vacillate, and keep us all in the dark as to what you mean?" he began.

"I am not prepared," said Cornelia; the voice of humility issuing from a monument.

"One of your oracular phrases! Are you prepared to be straightforward in your dealings?"

"I am prepared for any sacrifice, Wilfrid."

"The marrying of a man in his position is a sacrifice!"

"I cannot leave papa."

"And why not?"

"He is ill. He does not speak of it, but he is ill. His actions are strange. They are unaccountable."

"He has an old friend to reside in his house?"

"It is not that. I have noticed him. His mind...he requires watching."

"And how long is it since you made this discovery?"

"One sees clearer perhaps when one is not quite happy."

"Not happy! Then it's for him that you turn the night to tears?"

Cornelia closed her lips. She divined that her betrayer must be close in his confidence. She went shortly after to Emilia, whose secret at once stood out bare to a kindled suspicion. There was no fear that Cornelia would put her finger on it accusingly, or speak of it directly. She had the sentimentalist's profound respect for the name and notion of love. She addressed Emilia vaguely, bidding her keep guard on her emotions, and telling her there was one test of the truth of masculine protestations; this, Will he marry you? The which, if you are poor, is a passably infallible test. Emilia sucked this in thoughtfully. She heard that lovers were false. Why, then of course they were not like her lover! Cornelia finished what she deemed her duty, and departed, while Emilia thought: "I wonder whether he could be false to me;" and she gave herself shrewd half-delicious jarrings of pain, forcing herself to contemplate the impossible thing.

She was in this state when Mrs. Chump came across her, and with a slight pressure of a sovereign into her hand, said: "There, it's for you, little Belloni! and I see ye've been thinkin' me one o' the scrape-hards and close-fists. It's Pole who keeps me low, on purpose. And I'm a wretch if I haven't my purse full, so you see I'm all in the dark in the house, and don't know half so much as the sluts o' the kitchen. So, ye'll tell me, little Belloni, is Arr'bella goin' to marry Mr. Annybody? And is Cornelia goin' to marry Sir Tickleham? And whether Mr. Wilfrud's goin' to marry Lady Charlotte Chill'nworth? Becas, my dear, there's Arr'bella, who's sharp, she is, as a North-easter in January, (which Chump 'd cry out for, for the sake of his ships, poor fella—he kneelin' by 's bedside in a long nightgown and lookin' just twice what he was!) she has me like a nail to my vary words, and shows me that nothin' can happen betas o' what I've said. And Cornelia—if ye'll fancy a tall codfish on its tail: 'Mrs. Chump, I beg ye'll not go to believe annything of me.' So I says to her, 'Cornelia! my dear! do ye think, now, it's true that Chump went and marrud his cook, that ye treat me so? becas my father,' I tell her, 'he dealt in porrk in a large way, and I was a fine woman, full of the arr'stocracy, and Chump a little puffed-out bladder of a man.' So then she says: 'Mrs. Chump, I listen to no gossup: listen you to no gossup. 'And Mr. Wilfrud, my dear, he sends me on the flat o' my back, laughin'. And Ad'la she takes and turns me right about, so that I don't see the thing I'm askin' after; and there's nobody but you, little Belloni, to help me, and if ye do, ye shall know what the crumple of paper sounds like."

Mrs. Chump gave a sugary suck with her tongue. Emilia returned the money to her.

"Ye're foolush!" said Mrs. Chump. "A shut fist's good in fight and bad in friendship. Do ye know that? Open your hand."

"Excuse me," persisted Emilia.

"Pooh! take the money, or I'll say ye're in a conspiracy to make me blindman's-buff of the parrty. Take ut."

"I don't want it."

"Maybe, it's not enough?"

"I don't want any, ma'am."

"Ma'am, to the deuce with ye! I'll be callin' ye a forr'ner in a minute, I will."

Emilia walked away from a volley of terrific threats.

For some reason, unfathomed by her, she wanted to be alone with Wilfrid and put a question to him. No other, in sooth, than the infallible test. Not, mind you, that she wished to be married. But something she had heard (she had forgotten what it was) disturbed her, and that recent trifling with pain, in her excess of happiness, laid her open to it. Her heart was weaker, and fluttered, as if with a broken wing. She thought, "if I can be near him to lean against him for one full hour!" it would make her strong again. For, she found that if her heart was rising on a broad breath, suddenly, for no reason that she knew, it seemed to stop in its rise, break, and sink, like a wind-beaten billow. Once or twice, in a quick fear, she thought: "What is this? Is this a malady coming before death?" She walked out gloomily, thinking of the darkness of the world to Wilfrid, if she should die. She plucked flowers, and then reproached herself with plucking them. She tried to sing. "No, not till I have been with him alone;" she said, chiding her voice to silence. A shadow crossed her mind, as a Spring-mist dulls the glory of May. "Suppose all singing has gone from me—will he love wretched me?"

By-and-by she met him in the house. "Come out of doors to-night," she whispered.

Wilfrid's spirit of intrigue was never to be taken by surprise. "In the wood, under the pine, at nine," he replied.

"Not there," said Emilia, seeing this place mournfully dark from Cornelia's grief. "It is too still; say, where there's water falling. One can't be unhappy by noisy water."

Wilfrid considered, and named Wilming Weir. "And there we'll sit and you'll sing to me. I won't dine at home, so they won't susp-a-fancy anything.—Soh! and you want very much to be with me, my bird? What am I?" He bent his head.

"My lover."

He pressed her hand rapturously, half-doubting whether her pronunciation of the word had not a rather too confident twang.

Was it not delightful, he asked her, that they should be thus one to the other, and none know of it. She thought so too, and smiled happily, promising secrecy, at his request; for the sake of continuing so felicitous a life.

"You, you know, have an appointment with Captain Gambier, and, I with Lady Charlotte Chillingworth," said he. "How dare you make appointments with a captain of hussars?" and he bent her knuckles fondlingly.

Emilia smiled as before. He left her with a distinct impression that she did not comprehend that part of her lesson.

Wilfrid had just bled his father of a considerable sum of money; having assured him that he was the accepted suitor of Lady Charlotte Chillingworth, besides making himself pleasant in allusion to Mrs. Chump, so far as to cast some imputation on his sisters' judgement for not perceiving the virtues of the widow. The sum was improvidently large. Mr. Pole did not hear aright when he heard it named. Even at the repetition, he went: "Eh?" two or three times, vacantly. The amount was distinctly nailed to his ear:

whereupon he said, "Ah!—yes! you young fellows want money: must have it, I suppose. Up from the bowels of the earth Up from the—: you're sure they're not playing the fool with you, over there?"

Wilfrid understood the indication to Stornley. "I think you need have no fear of that, sir." And so his father thought, after an examination of the youth, who was of manly shape, and had a fresh, non-fatuous, air.

"Well, if that's all right..." sighed Mr. Pole. "Of course you'll always know that money's money. I wish your sisters wouldn't lose their time, as they do. Time's worth more than money. What sum?"

"I told you, sir, I wanted—there's the yacht, you know, and a lot of tradesmen's bills, which you don't like to see standing:-about—perhaps I had better name the round sum. Suppose you write down eight hundred. I shan't want more for some months. If you fancy it too much..."

Mr. Pole had lifted his head. But he spoke nothing. His lips and brows were rigid in apparent calculation. Wilfrid kept his position for a minute or so; and then, a little piqued, he moved about. He had inherited the antipathy to the discussion of the money question, and fretted to find it unnecessarily prolonged.

"Shall I come to you on this business another time, sir?"

"No, God bless my soul!" cried his father; "are you going to keep this hanging over me for ever? Eight hundred, you said." He mumbled: "salary of a chief clerk of twenty years' standing. Eight: twice four:—there you have it exactly."

"Will you send it me in a letter?" said Wilfrid, out of patience.

"I'll send it you in a letter," assented his father. Upon which Wilfrid changed his mind. "I can take a chair, though. I can easily wait for it now."

"Save trouble, if I send it. Eh?"

"Do you wish to see whether you can afford it, sir?"

"I wish to see you show more sense—with your confounded 'afford.' Have you any idea of bankers' books?—bankers' accounts?" Mr. Pole fished his cheque-book from a drawer and wrote Wilfrid's name and the sum, tore out the leaf and tossed it to him. "There, I've written to-day. Don't present it for a week." He rubbed his forehead hastily, touching here and there a paper to put it scrupulously in a line with the others. Wilfrid left him, and thought: "Kind old boy! Of course, he always means kindly, but I think I see a glimpse of avarice as a sort of a sign of age coming on. I hope he'll live long!"

Wilfrid was walking in the garden, imagining perhaps that he was thinking, as the swarming sensations of little people help them to imagine, when Cornelia ran hurriedly up to him and said: "Come with me to papa. He's ill: I fear he is going to have a fit."

"I left him sound and well, just now," said Wilfrid. "This is your mania."

"I found him gasping in his chair not two minutes after you quitted him. Dearest, he is in a dangerous state!"

Wilfrid stept back to his father, and was saluted with a ready "Well?" as he entered; but the mask had slipped from half of the old man's face, and for the first time in his life Wilfrid perceived that he had become an old man.

"Well, sir, you sent for me?" he said.

"Girls always try to persuade you you're ill—that's all," returned Mr. Pole. His voice was subdued; but turning to Cornelia, he fired up: "It's preposterous to tell a man who carries on a business like mine, you've observed for a long while that he's queer!—There, my dear child, I know that you mean well. I shall look all right the day you're married."

This allusion, and the sudden kindness, drew a storm of tears to Cornelia's eyelids.

"Papa! if you will but tell me what it is!" she moaned.

A nervous frenzy seemed to take possession of him. He ordered her out of the room.

She was gone, but his arm was still stretched out, and his expression of irritated command did not subside.

Wilfrid took his arm and put it gently down on the chair, saying: "You're not quite the thing to-day, sir."

"Are you a fool as well?" Mr. Pole retorted. "What do you know of, to make me ill? I live a regular life. I eat and drink just as you all do; and if I have a headache, I'm stunned with a whole family screaming as hard as they can that I'm going to die. Damned hard! I say, sir, it's—" He fell into a feebleness.

"A little glass of brandy, I think," Wilfrid suggested; and when Mr. Pole had gathered his mind he assented, begging his son particularly to take precautions to prevent any one from entering the room until he had tasted the reviving liquor.

CHAPTER XX

BY WILMING WEIR

A half-circle of high-banked greensward, studded with old park-trees, hung round the roar of the water; distant enough from the white-twisting fall to be mirrored on a smooth-heaved surface, while its out-pushing brushwood below drooped under burdens of drowned reed-flags that caught the foam. Keen scent of hay, crossing the dark air, met Emilia as she entered the river-meadow. A little more, and she saw the white weir-piles shining, and the grey roller just beginning to glisten to the moon. Eastward on her left, behind a cedar, the moon had cast off a thick cloud, and shone through the cedar-bars with a yellowish hazy softness, making rosy gold of the first passion of the tide, which, writhing and straining on through many lights, grew wide upon the wonderful velvet darkness underlying the wooded banks. With the full force of a young soul that leaps from beauty seen to unimagined beauty, Emilia stood and watched the picture. Then she sat down, hushed, awaiting her lover.

Wilfrid, as it chanced, was ten minutes late. She did not hear his voice till he had sunk on his knee by her side.

"What a reverie!" he said half jealously. "Isn't it lovely here?"

Emilia pressed his hand, but without turning her face to him, as her habit was. He took it for shyness, and encouraged her with soft exclamations and expansive tenderness.

"I wish I had not come here!" she murmured.

"Tell me why?" He folded his arm about her waist.

"Why did you let me wait?" said she.

Wilfrid drew out his watch; blamed the accident that had detained him, and remarked that there were not many minutes to witness against him.

She appeared to throw off her moodiness. "You are here at last. Let me hold your hand, and think, and be quite silent."

"You shall hold my hand, and think, and be quite silent, my own girl! if you will tell me what's on your mind."

Emilia thought it enough to look in his face, smiling.

"Has any one annoyed you?" he cried out.

"No one."

"Then receive the command of your lord, that you kiss him."

"I will kiss him," said Emilia; and did so.

The salute might have appeased an imperious lord, but was not so satisfactory to an exacting lover. He perceived, however, that, whether as lover or as lord, he must wait for her now, owing to her having waited for him: so, he sat by her, permitting his hand to be softly squeezed, and trying to get at least in the track of her ideas, while her ear was turned to the weir, and her eyes were on the glowing edges of the cedar-tree.

Finally, on one of many deep breaths, she said: "It's over. Why were you late? But, never mind now. Never let it be long again when I am expecting you. It's then I feel so much at his mercy. I mean, if I am where I hear falling water; sometimes thunder."

Wilfrid masked his complete mystification with a caressing smile; not without a growing respect for the only person who could make him experience the pangs of conscious silliness. You see, he was not a coxcomb.

"That German!" Emilia enlightened him.

"Your old music-master?"

"I wish it, I wish it! I should soon be free from him. Don't you know that dreadful man I told you about, who's like a black angel to me, because there is no music like his? and he's a German! I told you how I first dreamed about him, and then regularly every night, after talking with my father about Italy and his black-yellow Tedeschi, this man came over my pillow and made me call him Master, Master. And he is. He seems as if he were the master of my soul, mocking me, making me worship him in spite of my hate. I came here, thinking only of you. I heard the water like a great symphony. I fell into dreaming of my music. That's when I am at his mercy. There's no one like him. I must detest music to get free from him. How can I? He is like the God of music."

Wilfrid now remembered certain of her allusions to this rival, who had hitherto touched him very little. Perhaps it was partly the lovely scene that lifted him to a spiritual jealousy, partly his susceptibility to a sentimental exaggeration, and partly the mysterious new charm in Emilia's manner, that was as a bordering lustre, showing how the full orb was rising behind her.

"His name?" Wilfrid asked for.

Emilia's lips broke to the second letter of the alphabet; but she cut short the word. "Why should you hear it? And now that you are here, you drive him away. And the best is," she laughed, "I am sure you will not remember any of his pieces. I wish I could not—not that it's the memory; but he seems all round me, up in the air, and when the trees move all together...you chase him away, my lover!"

It was like a break in music, the way that Emilia suddenly closed her sentence; coming with a shock of flattering surprise upon Wilfrid.

Then she pursued: "My English lover! I am like Italy, in chains to that German, and you...but no, no, no! It's not quite a likeness, for my German is not a brute. I have seen his picture in shop-windows: the wind seemed in his hair, and he seemed to hear with his eyes: his forehead frowning so. Look at me, and see. So!"

Emilia pressed up the hair from her temples and bent her brows.

"It does not increase your beauty," said Wilfrid.

"There's the difference!" Emilia sighed mildly. "He sees angels, cherubs, and fairies, and imps, and devils; or he hears them: they come before him from far off, in music. They do to me, now and then. Only now and then, when my head's on fire.—My lover!"

Wilfrid pressed his mouth to the sweet instrument. She took his kiss fully, and gave her own frankly, in return. Then, sighing a very little, she said: "Do not kiss me much."

"Why not?"

"No!"

"But, look at me."

"I will look at you. Only take my hand. See the moon is getting whiter. The water there is like a pool of snakes, and then they struggle out, and roll over and over, and stream on lengthwise. I can see their long flat heads, and their eyes: almost their skins. No, my lover! do not kiss me. I lose my peace."

Wilfrid was not willing to relinquish his advantage, and the tender deep tone of the remonstrance was most musical and catching. What if he pulled her to earth from that rival of his in her soul? She would then be wholly his own. His lover's sentiment had grown rageingly jealous of the lordly German. But Emilia said, "I have you on my heart more when I touch your hand only, and think. If you kiss me, I go into a cloud, and lose your face in my mind."

"Yes, yes;" replied Wilfrid, pleased to sustain the argument for the sake of its fruitful promises. "But you must submit to be kissed, my darling. You will have to."

She gazed inquiringly.

"When you are married, I mean."

"When will you marry me?" she said.

The heir-apparent of the house of Pole blinked probably at that moment more foolishly than most mortal men have done. Taming his astonishment to represent a smile, he remarked: "When? are you thinking about it already?"

She answered, in a quiet voice that conveyed the fact forcibly, "Yes."

"But you're too young yet; and you're going to Italy, to learn in the schools. You wouldn't take a husband there with you, would you? What would the poor devil do?"

"But you are not too young," said she.

Wilfrid supposed not.

"Could you not go to my Italy with me?"

"Impossible! What! as a dangling husband?" Wilfrid laughed scornfully.

"They would love you too," she said. "They are such loving people. Oh, come! Consent to come, my lover! I must learn. If I do not, you will despise me. How can I bring anything to lay at your feet, my dear! my dear! if I do not?"

"Impossible!" Wilfrid reiterated, as one who had found moorings in the word.

"Then I will give up Italy!"

He had not previously acted hypocrite with this amazing girl. Nevertheless, it became difficult not to do so. He could scarcely believe that he had on a sudden, and by strange agency, slipped into an earnest situation. Emilia's attitude and tone awakened him to see it. Her hands were clenched straight down from the shoulders: all that she conceived herself to be renouncing for his sake was expressed in her face.

"Would you, really?" he murmured.

"I will!"

"And be English altogether?"

"Be yours!"

"Mine?"

"Yes; from this time."

Now stirred his better nature: though not before had he sceptically touched her lips and found them cold, as if the fire had been taken out of them by what they had uttered. He felt that it was no animal love, but the force of a soul drawn to him; and, forgetting the hypocritical foundation he had laid, he said: "How proud I shall be of you!"

"I shall go with you to battle," returned Emilia.

"My little darling! You won't care to see those black fellows killed, will you?"

Emilia shuddered. "No; poor things! Why do you hurt them? Kill wicked people, tyrant white-coats! And we will not talk of killing now. Proud of me? If I can make you!"

"You sigh so heavily!"

"Something makes me feel like a little beggar."

"When I tell you I love you?"

"Yes; but I only feel rich when I am giving; and I seem to have nothing to give now:—now that I have lost Italy!"

"But you give me your love, don't you?"

"All of it. But I seem to give it to you in tatters it's like a beggar; like a day without any sun."

"Do you think I shall have that idea when I hear you sing to me, and know that this little leaping fountain of music here is mine?"

Dim rays of a thought led Emilia to remark, "Must not men keel to women? I mean, if they are to love them for ever?"

Wilfrid smiled gallantly: "I will kneel to you, if it pleases you."

"Not now. You should have done so, once, I dreamed only once, just for a moment, in Italy; when all were crying out to me that I had caught their hearts. I fancied standing out like a bright thing in a dark crowd, and then saying 'I am his!' pointing to you, and folding my arms, waiting for you to take me."

The lover's imagination fired at the picture, and immediately he told a lover's lie; for the emotion excited by the thought of her glory coloured deliciously that image of her abnegation of all to him. He said: "I would rather have you as you are."

Emilia leaned to him more, and the pair fixed their eyes on the moon, that had now topped the cedar, and was pure silver: silver on the grass, on the leafage, on the waters. And in the West, facing it, was an arch of twilight and tremulous rose; as if a spirit hung there over the shrouded sun.

"At least," thought Wilfrid, "heaven, and the beauty of the world, approve my choice." And he looked up, fancying that he had a courage almost serene to meet his kindred with Emilia on his arm.

She felt his arm dreamily stressing its clasp about her, and said: "Now I know you love me. And you shall take me as I am. I need not be so poor after all. My dear! my dear! I cannot see beyond you."

"Is that your misery?" said he.

"My delight! my pleasure! One can live a life anywhere. And how can I belong to Italy, if I am yours? Do you know, when we were silent just now, I was thinking that water was the history of the world flowing out before me, all mixed up of kings and queens, and warriors with armour, and shouting armies; battles and numbers of mixed people; and great red sunsets, with women kneeling under them. Do you know those long low sunsets? I love them. They look like blood spilt for love. The noise of the water, and the moist green smell, gave me hundreds of pictures that seemed to hug me. I thought—what could stir music in me more than this? and, am I not just as rich if I stay here with my lover, instead of flying to strange countries, that I shall not care for now? So, you shall take me as I am. I do not feel poor any longer."

With that she gave him both her hands.

"Yes," said Wilfrid.

As if struck by the ridicule of so feeble a note, falling upon her passionate speech, he followed it up with the "yes!" of a man; adding: "Whatever you are, you are my dear girl; my own love; mine!"

Having said it, he was screwed up to feel it as nearly as possible, such virtue is there in uttered words.

Then he set about resolutely studying to appreciate her in the new character she had assumed to him. It is barely to be supposed that he should understand what in her love for him she sacrificed in giving up Italy, as she phrased it. He had some little notion of the sacrifice; but, as he did not demand any sacrifice of the sort, and as this involved a question perplexing, irritating, absurd, he did not regard it very favourably. As mistress of his fancy, her prospective musical triumphs were the crown of gold hanging over her. As wife of his bosom, they were not to be thought of. But the wife of his bosom must take her place by virtue of some wondrous charm. What was it that Emilia could show, if not music? Beautiful eyebrows: thick rare eyebrows, no doubt couched upon her full eyes, they were a marvel: and her eyes were a marvel. She had a sweet mouth, too, though the upper lip did not boast the aristocratic conventional curve of adorable pride, or the under lip a pretty droop to a petty rounded chin. Her face was like the aftersunset across a rose-garden, with the wings of an eagle poised outspread on the light. Some such coloured, vague, magnified impression Wilfrid took of her. Still, it was not quite enough to make him scorn contempt, should it whisper: nor even quite enough to combat successfully the image of elegant dames in their chosen attitudes—the queenly moments when perhaps they enter an assembly, or pour out tea with an exquisite exhibition of arm, or recline upon a couch, commanding homage of the world of little men. What else had this girl to count upon to make her exclusive? A devoted heart; she had a loyal heart, and perfect frankness: a mind impressible, intelligent, and fresh. She gave promise of fair companionship at all seasons. She could put a spell upon him, moreover. By that power of hers, never wilfully exercised, she came, in spite of the effect left on him by her early awkwardnesses and 'animalities,' nearer to his idea of superhuman nature than anything he knew of. But how would she be regarded when the announcement of Mrs. Wilfrid Pole brought scrutinizing eyes and gossiping mouths to bear on her?

It mattered nothing. He kissed her, and the vision of the critical world faded to a blank. Whatever she was, he was her prime luminary, so he determined to think that he cast light upon a precious, an unrivalled land.

"You are my own, are you not, Emilia?"

"Yes; I am," she answered.

"That water seems to say 'for ever,'" he murmured; and Emilia's fingers pressed upon his.

Of marriage there was no further word. Her heart was evidently quite at ease; and that it should be so without chaining him to a date, was Wilfrid's peculiar desire. He could pledge himself to eternity, but shrank from being bound to eleven o'clock on the morrow morning.

So, now, the soft Summer hours flew like white doves from off the mounting moon, and the lovers turned to go, all being still: even the noise of the waters still to their ears, as life that is muffled in sleep. They saw the cedar grey-edged under the moon: and Night, that clung like a bat beneath its ancient open palms. The bordering sward about the falls shone silvery. In its shadow was a swan. These scenes are but beckoning hands to the hearts of lovers, waving them on to that Eden which they claim: but when the hour has fled, they know it; and by the palpitating light in it they know that it holds the best of them.

CHAPTER XXI

RETURN OF MR. PERICLES

At this season Mr. Pericles reappeared. He had been, he said, through "Paris, Turin, Milano, Veniss, and by Trieste over the Summering to Vienna on a tour for a voice." And in no part of the Continent, his vehement declaration assured the ladies, had he found a single one. It was one universal croak—ahi! And Mr. Pericles could, affirm that Purgatory would have no pains for him after the torments he had recently endured. "Zey are frogs if zey are not geese," said Mr. Pericles. "I give up. Opera is dead. Hein? for a time;" and he smiled almost graciously, adding: "Where is she?" For Emilia was not present.

The ladies now perceived a greatness of mind in the Greek's devotion to music, and in his non-mercenary travels to assist managers of Opera by discovering genius. His scheme for Emilia fired them with delight. They were about to lay down all the material arrangements at once, but Mrs. Chump, who had heard that there was a new man in the house, now entered the room, prepared to conquer him. As thus, after a short form of introduction: "D'ye do, sir! and ye're Mr. Paricles. Oh! but ye're a Sultan, they say. Not in morr'ls, sir. And vary pleasant to wander on the Cont'nent with a lot o' lacqueys at your heels. It's what a bachelor can do. But I ask ye, sir, is ut fair, ye think, to the poor garls that has to stop at home?"

Hereat the ladies of Brookfield, thus miserably indicated, drew upon their self-command that sprang from the high sense of martyrdom.

Mr. Pericles did not reply to Mrs. Chump at all. He turned to Adela, saying aloud: "What is zis person?"

It might have pleased them to hear any slight put publicly on Mrs. Chump in the first resistance to the woman, but in the present stage their pride defended her. "Our friend," was the reply with which Arabella rebuked his rudeness; and her sister approved her. "We can avoid showing that we are weak in our own opinion, whatsoever degrades us," they had said during a consultation. Simultaneously they felt that Mr. Pericles being simply a millionaire and not In Society, being also a middle-class foreigner (a Greek whose fathers ran with naked heels and long lank hair on the shores of the Aegean), before such a man they might venture to identify this their guest with themselves an undoubted duty, in any case, but not always to be done; at least, not with grace and personal satisfaction. Therefore, the "our friend" dispersed a common gratulatory glow. Very small points, my masters; but how are coral-islands built?

Mrs. Chump fanned her cheek, in complete ignorance of the offence and defence. Chump, deceased, in amorous mood, had praised her management of the fan once, when breath was in him: "'Martha,' says he, winkin' a sort of 'mavourneen' at me, ye know—'Martha! with a fan in your hand, if ye're not a black-eyed beauty of a Spaniard, ye little devil of Seville!' says he." This she had occasionally confided to the ladies. The marital eulogy had touched her, and she was not a woman of coldly-flowing blood, she had an excuse for the constant employment of the fan.

"And well, Mr. Paricles! have ye got nothin' to tell us about foreign countesses and their slips? Because, we can listen, sir, garls or not. Sure, if they understand ye, ye teach 'em nothin'; and if they don't understand ye, where's the harm done? D'ye see, sir? It's clear in favour of talkin'."

Mr. Pericles administered consolation to his moustache by twisting it into long waxy points. "I do not know; I do not know," he put her away with, from time to time. In the end Mrs. Chump leaned over to Arabella. "Don't have 'm, my dear," she murmured.

"You mean—?" quoth Arabella.

"Here's the driest stick that aver stood without sap."

Arabella flushed when she took the implication that she was looking on the man as a husband. Adela heard the remarks, and flushed likewise. Mrs. Chump eyed them both. "It's for the money o' the man," she soliloquized aloud, as her fashion was. Adela jumped up, and with an easy sprightly posture of her fair, commonly studious person, and natural run of notes "Oh!" she cried, "I begin to feel what it is to be like a live fish on the fire, frying, frying, frying! and if he can keep his Christian sentiments under this infliction, what a wonderful hero he must be! What a hot day!"

She moved swiftly to the door, and flung it open. A sight met her eyes at which she lost her self-possession. She started back, uttering a soft cry.

"Ah! aha! oh!" went the bitter ironic drawl of Mr. Pericles, whose sharp glance had caught the scene as well.

Emilia came forward with a face like sunset. Diplomacy, under the form of Wilfrid Pole, kicked its heels behind, and said a word or two in a tone of false cheerfulness.

"Oh! so!" Mr. Pericles frowned, while Emilia held her hand out to him. "Yeas! You are quite well? H'm! You are burnt like a bean—hein? I shall ask you what you have been doing, by and by."

Happily for decency, Mrs. Chump had not participated in the fact presented by ocular demonstration. She turned about comfortably to greet Wilfrid, uttering the inspired remark: "Ye look red from a sly kiss!"

"For one?" said he, sharpening his blunted wits on this dull instrument.

The ladies talked down their talk. Then Wilfrid and Mr. Pericles interchanged quasi bows.

"Oh, if he doesn't show his upper teeth like an angry cat, or a leopard I've seen!" cried Mrs. Chump in Adela's ear, designating Mr. Pericles. "Does he know Mr. Wilfrud's in the British army, and a new lieuten't, gazetted and all?"

Mr. Pericles certainly did not look pleasantly upon Wilfrid: Emilia received his unconcealed wrath and spite.

"Go and sing a note!" he said.

"At the piano?" Emilia quietly asked.

"At piano, harp, what you will—it is ze voice I want."

Emilia pitched her note high from a full chest and with glad bright eyes, which her fair critics thought just one degree brazen, after the revelation in the doorway.

Mr. Pericles listened; wearing an aching expression, as if he were sending one eye to look up into his brain for a judgement disputed in that sovereign seat.

Still she held on, and then gave a tremulous, rich, contralto note.

"Oh! the human voice!" cried Adela, overcome by the transition of tones.

"Like going from the nightingale to the nightjar," said Arabella.

Mrs. Chump remarked: "Ye'll not find a more susceptible woman to musuc than me."

Wilfrid looked away. Pride coursed through his veins in a torrent.

When the voice was still, Mr. Pericles remained in a pondering posture.

"You go to play fool with zat voice in Milano, you are flogged," he cried terribly, shaking his forefinger.

Wilfrid faced round in wrath, but Mr. Pericles would not meet his challenge, continuing: "You hear? you hear?—so!" and Mr. Pericles brought the palms of his hands in collision.

"Marcy, man!" Mrs. Chump leaped from her chair; "d'ye mean that those horrud forr'ners'll smack a full-grown young woman?—Don't go to 'm, my dear. Now, take my 'dvice, little Belloni, and don't go. It isn't the sting o' the smack, ye know—"

"Shall I sing anything to you?" Emilia addressed Mr. Pericles. The latter shrugged to express indifference. Nevertheless she sang. She had never sung better. Mr. Pericles clutched his chin in one hand, elbow on knee. The ladies sighed to think of the loss of homage occasioned by the fact of so few being present to hear her. Wilfrid knew himself the fountain of it all, and stood fountain-like, in a shower of secret adulation: a really happy fellow. This: that his beloved should be the centre of eyes, and pronounced exquisite by general approbation, besides subjecting him to a personal spell: this was what he wanted. It was mournful to think that Circumstance had not at the same time created the girl of noble birth, or with an instinct for spiritual elegance. But the world is imperfect.

Presently he became aware that she was understood to be singing pointedly to him: upon which he dismissed the council of his sensations, and began to diplomatize cleverly. Leaning over to Adela, he whispered:

"Pericles wants her to go to Italy. My belief is, that she won't."

"And why?" returned Adela, archly reproachful.

"Well, we've been spoiling her a little, perhaps. I mean, we men, of course. But, I really don't think that I'm chiefly to blame. You won't allow Captain Gambier to be in fault, I know."

"Why not?" said Adela.

"Well, if you will, then he is the principal offender."

Adela acted disbelief; but, unprepared for her brother's perfectly feminine audacity of dissimulation, she thought: "He can't be in earnest about the girl," and was led to fancy that Gambier might, and to determine to see whether it was so.

By this manoeuvre, Wilfrid prepared for himself a defender when the charge was brought against him.

Mr. Pericles was thunderstruck on hearing Emilia refuse to go to Italy. A scene of tragic denunciation on the one hand, and stubborn decision on the other, ensued.

"I shall not mind zis" (he spoke of Love and the awakening of the female heart) "not when you are trained. It is good, zen, and you have fire from it. But, now! little fool, I say, it is too airly—too airly! How shall you learn—eh? with your brain upon a man? And your voice, little fool, a thing of caprice, zat comes and goes as he will, not you will. Hein? like a barrel-organ, which he turns ze handle.—Mon Dieu! Why did I leave her?" Mr. Pericles struck his brow with his wrist, clutching at the long thin slice of hair that did greasy duty for the departed crop on his poll. "Did I not know it was a woman? And so you are, what you say, in lofe."

Emilia replied: "I have not said so," with exasperating coolness.

"You have your eye on a man. And I know him, zat man! When he is tired of you—whiff, away you go, a puff of smoke! And you zat I should make a Queen of Opera! A Queen? You shall have more rule zan twenty Queens—forty! See" (Mr. Pericles made his hand go like an aspen-leaf from his uplifted wrist); "So you shall set ze hearts of sossands! To dream of you, to adore you! and flowers, flowers everywhere, on your head, at your feet. You choose your lofer from ze world. A husband, if it is your taste. Bose, if you please. Zen, I say, you shall, you shall lofe a man. Let him tease and sting—ah! it will be magnifique: Aha! ze voice will sharpen, go deep; yeas! to be a tale of blood. Lofe till you could stab yourself:—Brava! But now? Little fool, I say!"

Emilia believed that she was verily forfeiting an empire. Her face wore a soft look of delight. This renunciation of a splendid destiny for Wilfrid's sake, seemed to make her worthier of him, and as Mr. Pericles unrolled the list of her rejected treasures, her bosom heaved without a regret.

"Ha!" Mr. Pericles flung away from her: "go and be a little gutter-girl!"

The musical connoisseur drew on his own disappointment alone for eloquence. Had he been thinking of her, he might have touched cunningly on her love for Italy. Music was the passion of the man; and a millionaire's passion is something that can make a stir. He knew that in Emilia he had discovered a pearl of song rarely to be found, and his object was to polish and perfect her at all cost: perhaps, as a secondary and far removed consideration, to point to her as a thing belonging to him, for which Emperors might envy him. The thought of losing her drove him into fits of rage. He took the ladies one by one, and treated them each to a horrible scene of gesticulation and outraged English. H accused their brother of conduct which they were obliged to throw (by a process of their own) into the region of Fine Shades, before they dared venture to comprehend him. Gross facts in relationship with the voice, this grievous "machine, not man,"—as they said—stated to them, harshly, impetuously. The ladies felt that he had bored their ears with hot iron pins. Adela tried laughter as a defence from his suggestion against Wilfrid, but had shortly afterwards to fly from the fearful anatomist. She served her brother thoroughly in the Council of Three; so that Mr. Pericles was led by them to trust that there had; been mere fooling in his absence, and that the emotions he looked to as the triumphant reserve in Emilia's bosom, to be aroused at some crisis when she was before the world, slumbered still. She, on her part, contrasting her own burning sensations with this quaint, innocent devotion to Art and passion for music, felt in a manner guilty; and whenever he stormed with additional violence, she became suppliant, and seemed to bend and have regrets. Mr. Pericles would then say, with mollified irritability: "You will come to Italy to-morrow?—Ze day after?—not at all?" The last was given with a roar, for lack of her immediate response. Emilia would find a tear on her eyelids at times. Surround herself as she might with her illusions, she had no resting-place in Wilfrid's heart, and knew it. She knew it as the young know that they are to die on a future day, without feeling the sadness of it, but with a dimly prevalent idea that this life is therefore incomplete. And again her blood, as with a wave of rich emotion, washed out the blank spot. She thought: "What can he want but my love?" And thus she satisfied her own hungry questioning by seeming to supply an answer to his.

The ladies of Brookfield by no means encouraged Emilia to refuse the generous offer of Mr. Pericles. They thought, too, that she might—might she? Oh! certainly she might go to Italy under his protection. "Would you let one of your blood?" asked Wilfrid brutally. With some cunning he led them to admit that Emilia's parents should rightly be consulted in such a case.

One day Mr. Pericles said to the ladies: "I shall give a fete: a party monstre. In ze air: on grass. I beg you to invite friends of yours."

Before the excogitation of this splendid resolve, he had been observed to wear for some period a conspiratorial aspect. When it was delivered, and Arabella had undertaken the management of the "party monstre"—(which was to be on Besworth Lawn, and, as it was not their own party, could be conducted with a sort of quasi-contemptuous superiority to incongruous gatherings)—this being settled, the forehead of Mr. Pericles cleared and he ceased to persecute Emilia.

"I am not one that is wopped," he said significantly; nodding to his English hearers, as if this piece of shrewd acquaintance with the expressive mysteries of their language placed them upon equal terms.

It was really 'a providential thing' (as devout people phrase it) that Laura Tinley and Mabel Copley should call shortly after this, and invite the ladies to a proposed picnic of theirs on Besworth Lawn. On Besworth Lawn, of all places! and they used the word 'picnic.'

"A word suggestive of gnawed drumstick and ginger-beer bottles." Adela quoted some scapegoat of her acquaintance, as her way was when she wished to be pungent without incurring the cold sisterly eye of reproof for a vulgarism.

Both Laura and Mabel, when they heard of the mighty entertainment fixed for Besworth Lawn by Mr. Pericles, looked down. They were invited, and looked up. There was the usual amount of fencing with the combative Laura, who gave ground at all points, and as she was separating, said (so sweetly!) "Of course you have heard of the arrest of your—what does one call him?—friend?—or a French word?"

"You mean?" quoth Arabella.

"That poor, neatly brushed, nice creature whom you patronized—who played the organ!" she jerked to Arabella's dubious eyes.

"And he?" Arabella smiled, complacently.

"Then perhaps you may know that all is arranged for him?" said Laura, interpreting by the look more than the word, after a habit of women.

"Indeed, to tell you the truth, I know nothing," said Arabella.

"Really?" Laura turned sharply to Cornelia, who met her eyes and did not exhibit one weak dimple.

The story was, that Mr. Chips, the Bookseller of Hillford, objected to the departure of Mr. Barrett, until Mr. Barrett had paid the bill of Mr. Chips: and had signified his objection in the form of a writ. "When, if you know anything of law," said Laura, "you will see why he remains. For, a writ once served, you are a prisoner. That is, I believe, if it's above twenty pounds. And Mr. Chips' bill against Mr. Barrett was, I have heard, twenty-three pounds and odd shillings. Could anything be more preposterous? And Mr. Chips deserves to lose his money!"

Ah! to soar out of such a set as this, of which Laura Tinley is a sample, are not some trifling acts of inhumanity and practices in the art of 'cutting' permissible? So the ladies had often asked of the Unseen in their onward course, if they did not pointedly put the question now. Surely they had no desire to give pain, but the nature that endowed them with a delicate taste, inspired them to defend it. They listened gravely to Laura, who related that not only English books, but foreign (repeated and emphasized), had been supplied by Mr. Chips to Mr. Barrett.

They were in the library, and Laura's eyes rested on certain yellow and blue covers of books certainly not designed for the reading of Mr. Pole.

"I think you must be wrong as to Mr. Barrett's position," said Adela.

"No, dear; not at all," Laura was quick to reply. "Unless you know anything. He has stated that he awaits money remittances. He has, in fact, overrun the constable, and my brother Albert says, the constable is very likely to overrun ham, in consequence. Only a joke! But an organist with, at the highest computation—poor absurd thing!—fifty-five pounds per annum: additional for singing lessons, it is true,—but an organist with a bookseller's bill of twenty-three pounds! Consider!"

"Foreign books, too!" interjected Adela.

"Not so particularly improving to his morals, either!" added Laura.

"You are severe upon the greater part of the human race," said Arabella.

"So are the preachers, dear," returned Laura.

"The men of our religion justify you?" asked Arabella.

"Let me see;—where were we?" Laura retreated in an affected mystification.

"You had reached the enlightened belief that books written by any but English hands were necessarily destructive of men's innocence," said Arabella; and her sisters thrilled at the neatness of the stroke, for the moment, while they forgot the ignoble object it transfixed. Laura was sufficiently foiled by it to be unable to return to the Chips-Barrett theme. Throughout the interview Cornelia had maintained a triumphant posture, superior to Arabella's skill in fencing, seeing that it exposed no weak point of the defence by making an attack, and concealed especially the confession implied by a relish for the conflict. Her sisters considerately left her to recover herself, after this mighty exercise of silence.

CHAPTER XXII

Cornelia sat with a clenched hand. "You are rich and he is poor," was the keynote of her thoughts, repeated from minute to minute. "And it is gold gives you the right in the world's eye to despise him!" she apostrophized the vanished Laura, clothing gold with all the baseness of that person. Now, when one really hates gold, one is at war with one's fellows. The tide sets that way. There is no compromise: to hate it is to try to stem the flood. It happens that this is one of the temptations of the sentimentalist, who should reflect, but does not, that the fine feelers by which the iniquities of gold are so keenly discerned, are a growth due to it, nevertheless. Those 'fine feelers,' or antennae of the senses, come of sweet ease; that is synonymous with gold in our island-latitude. The sentimentalists are represented by them among the civilized species. It is they that sensitively touch and reject, touch and select; whereby the laws of the polite world are ultimately regulated, and civilization continually advanced, sometimes ridiculously. The sentimentalists are ahead of us, not by weight of brain, but through delicacy of nerve, and, like all creatures in the front, they are open to be victims. I pray you to observe again the shrinking life that afflicts the adventurous horns of the snail, for example. Such are the sentimentalists to us—the fat body of mankind. We owe them much, and though they scorn us, let us pity them.

Especially when they are young they deserve pity, for they suffer cruelly. I for my part prefer to see boys and girls led into the ways of life by nature; but I admit that in many cases, in most cases, our good mother has not (occupied as her hands must be) made them perfectly presentable; by which fact I am warned to have tolerance for the finer beings who labour under these excessive sensual subtleties. I perceive their uses. And they are right good comedy; for which I may say that I almost love them. Man is the laughing animal: and at the end of an infinite search, the philosopher finds himself clinging to laughter as the best of human fruit, purely human, and sane, and comforting. So let us be cordially thankful to those who furnish matter for sound embracing laughter.

Cornelia detested gold—entirely on general grounds and for abstract reasons. Not a word of Mr. Barrett was shaped, even in fancy; but she interjected to herself, with meditative eye and mouth: "The saints were poor!" (the saints of whom he had read, translating from that old Latin book) "St. Francis! how divine was his life!" and so forth, until the figure of Mr. Penniless Barrett walked out in her imagination clad in saintly garments, superior not only to his creditor, Mr. Chips, but to all who bought or sold.

"I have been false," she said; implying the "to him." Seeing him on that radiant height above her, she thought "How could I have fallen so!" It was impossible for her mind to recover the delusion which had prompted her signing herself to bondage—pledging her hand to a man she did not love. Could it have been that she was guilty of the immense folly, simply to escape from that piece of coarse earth, Mrs. Chump? Cornelia smiled sadly, saying: "Oh, no! I should not have committed a wickedness for so miserable an object." Despairing for a solution of the puzzle, she cried out, "I was mad!", and with a gasp of horror saw herself madly signing her name to perdition.

"I was mad!" is a comfortable cloak to our sins in the past. Mournful to think that we have been bereft of reason; but the fit is over, and we are not in Bedlam!

Cornelia next wrestled with the pride of Mr. Barrett. Why had he not come to her once after reading the line pencilled in the book? Was it that he would make her his debtor in everything? He could have reproached her justly; why had he held aloof? She thirsted to be scourged by him, to hang her head ashamed under his glance, and hug the bitter pain he dealt her. Revolving how the worst man on earth would have behaved to a girl partially in his power (hands had been permitted to be pressed, and the gateways of the eyes had stood open: all but vows had been interchanged), she came to regard Mr. Barrett as the best man on the earth. That she alone saw it, did not depreciate the value of her knowledge. A goal gloriously illumined blazed on her from the distance. "Too late!" she put a curb on the hot courses in her brain, and they being checked, turned all at once to tears and came in a flood. How indignant would the fair sentimentalist have been at a whisper of her caring for the thing before it was too late!

Cornelia now daily trod the red pathways under the firs, and really imagined herself to be surprised, even vexed, when she met Mr. Barrett there at last. Emilia was by his side, near a drooping birch. She beckoned to Cornelia, whose North Pole armour was doing its best to keep down a thumping heart.

"We are taking our last walk in the old wood," said, Mr. Barrett, admirably collected. "That is, I must speak for myself."

"You leave early?" Cornelia felt her throat rattle hideously.

"In two days, I expect—I hope," said he.

"Why does he hope?" thought Cornelia, wounded, until a vision of the detaining Chips struck her with pity and remorse.

She turned to Emilia. "Our dear child is also going to leave us."

"I?" cried Emilia, fierily out of languor.

"Does not your Italy claim you?"

"I am nothing to Italy any more. Have I not said so? I love England now."

Cornelia smiled complacently. "Let us hope your heart is capacious enough to love both."

"Then your theory is" (Mr. Barrett addressed Cornelia in the winning old style), "that the love of one thing enlarges the heart for another?"

"Should it not?" She admired his cruel self-possession pitiably, as she contrasted her own husky tones with it.

Emilia looked from one to the other, fancying that they must have her case somewhere in prospect, since none could be unconscious of the vehement struggle going on in her bosom; but they went farther and farther off from her comprehension, and seemed to speak of bloodless matters. "And yet he is her lover," she thought. "When they meet they talk across a river, and he knows she is going to another man, and does not gripe her wrist and drag her away!" The sense that she had no kinship with such flesh shut her mouth faster than Wilfrid's injunctions (which were ordinarily conveyed in too subtle a manner for her to feel their meaning enough to find them binding). Cornelia, for a mask to her emotions, gave Emilia a gentle, albeit high-worded lecture on the artist's duty toward Art, quoting favourite passages from Mr. Barrett's favourite Art-critic. And her fashion of dropping her voice as she declaimed the more dictatorial sentences (to imply, one might guess, by a show of personal humility that she would have you to know her preaching was vicarious; that she stood humbly in the pulpit, and was but a vessel for the delivery of the burden of the oracle), all this was beautiful to him who could see it. I cannot think it was wholesome for him; nor that Cornelia was unaware of a naughty wish to glitter temporarily in the eyes of the man who made her feel humble. The sorcery she sent through his blood communicated itself to hers. When she had done, Emilia, convincedly vanquished by big words, said, "I cannot talk," and turned heavily from them without bestowing a smile upon either.

Cornelia believed that the girl would turn back as abruptly as she had retreated; and it was not until Emilia was out of sight that she remembered the impropriety of being alone with Mr. Barrett. The Pitfall of Sentiment yawned visible, but this lady's strength had been too little tried for her to lack absolute faith in it. So, out of deep silences, the two leapt to speech and immediately subsided to the depths again: as on a sultry summer's day fishes flash their tails in the sunlight and leave a solitary circle widening on the water.

Then Cornelia knew what was coming. In set phrase, and as one who performs a duty frigidly pleasant, he congratulated her on her rumored union. One hand was in his buttoned coat; the other hung elegantly loose: not a feature betrayed emotion. He might have spoken it in a ballroom. To Cornelia, who exulted in self-compression, after the Roman method, it was more dangerous than a tremulous tone.

"You know me too well to say this, Mr. Barrett."

The words would come. She preserved her steadfast air, when they had escaped, to conceal her shame. Seeing thus much, he took it to mean that it was a time for plain-speaking. To what end, he did not ask.

"You have not to be told that I desire your happiness above all earthly things," he said: and the lady shrank back, and made an effort to recover her footing. Had he not been so careful to obliterate any badge of the Squire of low degree, at his elbows, cuffs, collar, kneecap, and head-piece, she might have achieved it with better success. For cynicism (the younger brother of sentiment and inheritor of the family property) is always on the watch to deal fatal blows through such vital parts as the hat or the H's, or indeed any sign of inferior estate. But Mr. Barrett was armed at all points by a consummate education and a most serviceable clothesbrush.

"You know how I love this neighbourhood!" said she.

"And I! above all that I have known!"

They left the pathway and walked on mosses—soft yellow beds, run over with grey lichen, and plots of emerald in the midst.

"You will not fall off with your reading?" he recommenced.

She answered "Yes," meaning "No"; and corrected the error languidly, thinking one of the weighty monosyllables as good as the other: for what was reading to her now?

"It would be ten thousand pities if you were to do as so many women do, when... when they make these great changes," he continued.

"Of what avail is the improvement of the mind?" she said, and followed his stumble over the "when," and dropped on it.

"Of what avail! Is marriage to stop your intellectual growth?"

"Without sympathy," she faltered, and was shocked at what she said; but it seemed a necessity.

"You must learn to conquer the need for it."

Alas! his admonition only made her feel the need more cravingly.

"Promise me one thing," he said. "You will not fall into the rut? Let me keep the ideal you have given me. For the sake of heaven, do not cloud for me the one bright image I hold! Let me know always that you are growing, and that the pure, noble intelligence which distinguishes you advances, and will not be subdued."

Cornelia smiled faintly. "You have judged me too generously, Mr. Barrett."

"Too little so! might I tell you!" He stopped short, and she felt the silence like a great wave sweeping over her.

They were nearing the lake, with the stump of the pollard-willow in sight, and toward it they went.

"I shall take the consolation of knowing that I shall hear of you, some day," she said, having recourse to a look of cheerfulness.

He knew her to allude to certain hopes of fame. "I am getting wiser, I fear—too wise for ambition!"

"That is a fallacy, a sophism."

He pointed to the hollow tree. "Is there promise of fruit from that?"

"You...you are young, Mr. Barrett."

"And on a young, forehead it may be written, 'Come not to gather more.'"

Cornelia put her hand out: "Oh, Mr. Barrett! unsay it!" The nakedness of her spirit stood forth in a stinging tear. "The words were cruel."

"But, if they live, and are?"

"I feel that you must misjudge me. When I wrote them...you cannot know! The misery of our domestic life was so bitter! And yet, I have no excuse, none! I can only ask for pity."

"And if you are wretched, must not I be? You pluck from me my last support. This, I petitioned Providence to hear from you—that you would be happy! I can have no comfort but in that."

"Happy!" Cornelia murmured the word musically, as if to suck an irony from the sweetness of the sound. "Are we made for happiness?"

Mr. Barrett quoted the favourite sage, concluding: "But a brilliant home and high social duties bring consolation. I do acknowledge that an eminent station will not only be graced by you, but that you give the impression of being born to occupy it. It is your destiny."

"A miserable destiny!"

It pleased Cornelia to become the wilful child who quarrels with its tutor's teachings, upon this point.

Then Mr. Barrett said quickly: "Your heart is not in this union?"

"Can you ask? I have done my duty."

"Have you, indeed!"

His tone was severe in the deliberation of its accents.

Was it her duty to live an incomplete life? He gave her a definition of personal duty, and shadowed out all her own ideas on the subject; seeming thus to speak terrible, unanswerable truth.

As one who changes the theme, he said: "I have forborne to revert to myself in our interviews; they were too divine for that. You will always remember that I have forborne much."

"Yes!" She was willing at the instant to confess how much.

"And if I speak now, I shall not be misinterpreted?"

"You never would have been, by me."

"Cornelia!"

Though she knew what was behind the door, this flinging of it open with her name startled the lady; and if he had faltered, it would not have been well for him. But, plainly, he claimed the right to call her by her Christian name. She admitted it; and thenceforward they were equals.

It was an odd story that he told of himself. She could not have repeated it to make it comprehensible. She drank at every sentence, getting no more from it than the gratification of her thirst. His father, at least, was a man of title, a baronet. What was meant by estates not entailed? What wild freak of fate put this noble young man in the power of an eccentric parent, who now caressed him, now made him an outcast? She heard of the sum that was his, coming from his dead mother to support him just one hundred pounds annual! Was ever fate so mournful?

Practically, she understood that if Mr. Barrett would write to his father, pledging himself to conform to his mysterious despotic will in something, he would be pardoned and reinstated.

He concluded: "Hitherto I have preferred poverty. You have taught me at what a cost! Is it too late?"

The fall of his voice, with the repetition of her name, seemed as if awakening her, but not in a land of reason.

"Why...why!" she whispered.

"Beloved?"

"Why did you not tell me this before?"

"Do you upbraid me?"

"Oh, no! Oh, never!" she felt his hand taking hers gently. "My friend," she said, half in self-defence; and they, who had never kissed as lovers, kissed under the plea of friendship.

CHAPTER XXIII

WILFRID DIPLOMATIZES

All Wilfrid's diplomacy was now brought into play to baffle Mr. Pericles, inspire Emilia with the spirit of secresy, and carry on his engagement to two women to their common satisfaction. Adela, whose penetration he dreaded most, he had removed by a flattering invitation to Stornley; and that Emilia might be occupied during his absences, and Mr. Pericles thrown on a false scent, he persuaded Tracy Runningbrook to come to Brookfield, and write libretti for Emilia's operas. The two would sit down together for an hour, drawing wonderful precocious noses upon juvenile visages, when Emilia would sigh and say: "I can't work!"—Tracy adding, with resignation: "I never can!" At first Mr. Pericles dogged them assiduously. After a little while he shrugged, remarking: "It is a nonsense."

They were, however, perfectly serious about the production of an opera, Tracy furnishing verse to Emilia's music. He wrote with extraordinary rapidity, but clung to graphic phrases, that were not always supple enough for nuptials with modulated notes. Then Emilia had to hit his sense of humour by giving the words as they came in the run of the song. "You make me crow, or I croak," she said.

"The woman follows the man, and music fits to verse," cried Tracy. "Music's the vine, verse the tree."

Emilia meditated. "Not if they grow up together," she suggested, and broke into a smile at his rapture of amusement; which was succeeded by a dark perplexity, worthy of the present aspect of Mr. Pericles.

"That's what has upset us," he said. "We have been trying to 'grow up together,' like first-cousins, and nature forbids the banns. To-morrow you shall have half a libretto. And then, really, my child, you must adapt yourself to the words."

"I will," Emilia promised; "only, not if they're like iron to the teeth."

"My belief is," said Tracy savagely, "that music's a fashion, and as delusive a growth as Cobbett's potatoes, which will go back to the deadly nightshade, just as music will go back to the tom-tom."

"What have you called out when I sang to you!" Emilia reproached him for this irreverent nonsense.

"Oh! it was you and not the music," he returned half-cajolingly, while he beat the tom-tom on air.

"Hark here!" cried Emilia. She recited a verse. "Doesn't that sound dead? Now hark!" She sang the verse, and looked confidently for Tracy's verdict at the close.

"What a girl that is!" He went about the house, raving of her to everybody, with sundry Gallic interjections; until Mrs. Chump said: "'Deed, sir, ye don't seem to have much idea of a woman's feelin's."

Tracy produced in a night two sketches of libretti for Emilia to choose from—the Roman Clelia being one, and Camillus the other. Tracy praised either impartially, and was indifferent between them, he told her. Clelia offered the better theme for passionate song, but there was a winning political object and rebuff to be given to Radicalism in Camillus. "Think of Rome!" he said.

Emilia gave the vote for Camillus, beginning forthwith to hum, with visions of a long roll of swarthy cavalry, headed by a clear-eyed young chief, sunlight perching on his helm.

"Yes; but you don't think of the situations in Clelia, and what I can do with her," snapped Tracy. "I see a song there that would light up all London. Unfortunately, the sentiment's dead Radical. It wouldn't so much matter if we were certain to do Camillus as well; because one would act as a counterpoise to the other, you know. Well, follow your own fancy. Camillus is strictly classical. I treat opera there as Alfieri conceived tragedy. Clelia is modern style. Cast the die for Camillus, and let's take horse. Only, we lose the love-business—exactly where I show my strength. Clelia in the camp of the king: dactyllic chorus-accompaniment, while she, in heavy voluptuous anapaests, confesses her love for the enemy of her country. Remember, this is our romantic opera, where we do what we like with History, and make up our minds for asses telling us to go home and read our 'student's Rome.' Then that scene where she and the king dance the dactyls, and the anapaests go to the chorus. Sublime! Let's go into the woods and begin. We might give the first song or two to-night. In composition, mind, always strike out your great scene, and work from it—don't work up to it, or you've lost fire when you reach the point. That's my method."

They ran into the woods, skipping like schoolboy and schoolgirl. On hearing that Camillus would not be permitted to love other than his ungrateful country, Emilia's conception of the Roman lord grew pale, and a controversy ensued-she maintaining that a great hero must love a woman; he declaring that a great hero might love a dozen, but that it was beneath the dignity of this drama to allow of a rival to Rome in Camillus's love.

"He will not do for music," said Emilia firmly, and was immoveable. In despair, Tracy proposed attaching a lanky barbarian daughter to Brennus, whose deeds of arms should provoke the admiration of the Roman.

"And so we relinquish Alfieri for Florian! There's a sentimental burlesque at once!" the youth ejaculated, in gloom. "I chose this subject entirely to give you Rome for a theme."

Emilia took his hand. "I do thank you. If Brennus has a daughter, why not let her be half Roman?"

Tracy fired out: "she's a bony woman, with a brawny development; mammoth haunches, strong of the skeleton; cheek-bones, flat-forward, as a fish 's rotting on a beach; long scissor lips-nippers to any wretched rose of a kiss! a pugilist's nose to the nostrils of a phoca; and eyes!—don't you see them?—luminaries of pestilence; blotted yellow, like a tallow candle shining through a horny lantern."

At this horrible forced-poetic portrait, Emilia cried in pain: "You hate her suddenly!"

"I loathe the creature—pah!" went Tracy.

"Why do you make her so hideous?" Emilia complained. "I feel myself hating her too. Look at me. Am I such a thing as that?"

"You!" Tracy was melted in a trice, and gave the motion of hugging, as a commentary on his private opinion.

"Can you also be sure that Camillus can love nothing but his country? Would one love stop the other?" she persisted, gazing with an air of steady anxiety for the answer.

"There isn't a doubt about it," said Tracy.

Emilia caught her face in her hands, and exclaimed in a stifling voice: "It's true! it's true!"

Tracy saw that her figure was shaken with sobs—unmistakeable, hard, sorrowful convulsions.

"Confound historical facts that make her cry!" he murmured to himself, in a fury at the Roman fables. "It's no use comforting her with Niebuhr now. She's got a live Camillus in her brain, and there he'll stick." Tracy began to mutter the emphatic D.; quite cognizant of her case, as he supposed. This intensity of human emotion about a dry faggot of history by no means surprised him; and he was as tender to the grief of his darling little friend as if he had known the conflict that tore her in two. Subsequently he related the incident, in a tone of tender delight, to Wilfrid, whom it smote. "Am I a brute?" asked the latter of the Intelligences in the seat of his consciousness, and they for the moment gravely affirmed it. I have observed that when young men obtain this mental confirmation of their suspicions, they wax less reluctant to act as brutes than when the doubt restrained them.

He reasoned thus: "I can bring my mind to the idea of losing her, if it must be so." (Hear, hear! from the unanimous internal Parliament.) "But I can't make her miserable (cheers)—I can't go and break her heart" (loud cheers, drowning a faint dissentient hum).—The scene, of which Tracy had told him, gave Wilfrid a kind of dread of the girl. If that was her state of feeling upon a distant subject, how would it be when he applied the knife. Simply, impossible to use the knife at all! Wield it thou, O Circumstance, babe-munching Chronos, whosoever thou art, that jarrest our poor human music effectually from hour to hour!

Colonel Pierson paid his promised visit, on his way back to his quarters at Verona. His stay was shortened by rumours of anticipated troubles in Italy. One day at table he chanced to observe, speaking of the Milanese, that they required another lesson, and that it would save the shedding of blood if, annually, the chief men of the city took a flogging for the community (senseless arrogance that sensible, and even kindly, men will sometimes be tempted to utter, and prompted to act on, in that deteriorating state of a perpetual repressive force).—Emilia looked at him till she caught his eye: "I hope I shall never meet you there," she said.

The colonel coloured, and drew his finger along each curve of his moustache. The table was silent. Colonel Pierson was a gentleman, but a false position and the irritating topic deprived him of proper self-command.

"What would you do?" he said, not gallantly.

Emilia would have been glad to have been allowed to subside, but the tone stung her.

"I could not do much; I am a woman," said she.

Whereto the colonel: "It's only the women who do anything over there."

"And that is why you flog them!"

The colonel, seeing himself surrounded by ladies, lost the right guidance of his wits, at this point, reddened, and was saved by an Irish outcry of horror from some unpleasant and possibly unmanly retort. "Mr. Paricles said exactly the same. Oh, sir! do ye wear an officer's uniform to go about behavin' in that shockin' way to poor helpless females?"

This was the first time Mrs. Chump had ever been found of service at the Brookfield dining-table. Colonel Pierson joined the current smile, and the matter passed.

He was affectionate with Wilfrid, and invited him to Verona, with the assurance that his (the Austrian) school of cavalry was the best in the world. "You beat us in pace and weight; but you can't skirmish, you can't manage squadrons, and you know nothing of outpost duty," said the colonel. Wilfrid promised to visit him some day: a fact he denied to Emilia, when she charged him with it. Her brain seemed to be set on fire by the presence of an Austrian officer. The miserable belief that she had abandoned her country pressing on her remorsefully, she lost appetite, briskness of eye, and the soft reddish-brown ripe blood-hue that made her cheeks sweet to contemplate. She looked worn, small, wretched: her very walk indicated self-contempt. Wilfrid was keen to see the change for which others might have accused a temporary headache. Now that she appeared under this blight, it seemed easier to give her up; and his magnanimity being thus encouraged (I am not hard on him—remember the constitution of love, in which a heart un-aroused is pure selfishness, and a heart aroused heroic generosity; they being one heart to outer life)—his magnanimity, I say, being under this favourable sun, he said to himself that there should be an end of double-dealing; and, possibly consoled by feeling a martyr, he persuaded himself to act the gentle ruffian. To which end, he was again absent from Brookfield, for a space, and bitterly missed.

Emilia, for the last two Sundays, had taken Mr. Barrett's place at the organ. She was playing the prelude to one of the evening hymns, when the lover, whose features she dreaded to be once more forgetting, appeared in the curtained enclosure. A stoppage in the tune, and a prolonged squeal of the instrument, gave the congregation below matter to speculate upon. Wilfrid put up his finger and sat reverently down, while Emilia plunged tremblingly at the note that was howling its life away. And as she managed to swim into the stream of the sacred melody again, her head was turned toward her lover under a new sensation; and the first words she murmured were, "We have never been in church together, before."

"Not in the evening," he whispered, likewise impressed.

"No," said Emilia softly; flattered by his greater accuracy.

If Wilfrid could have been sure that he would be perfect master of that sentimental crew known to him under the denomination of his feelings, the place he selected for their parting interview might be held creditable to this young officer's acknowledged strategical ability. It was a place where any fervid appeals were impossible; where he could contemplate her, listen to her, be near her, alone with her, having nothing to dread from tears, supplications, or passion, as a consequence of the short indulgence of his tenderness. But he had failed to reckon on the chances that he himself might prove weak and be betrayed by the crew for whose comfort he was always providing; and now, as she sat there, her face being sideways to him, the flush of delight faint on her cheek, and her eyelids half raised to the gilded pipes, while full and sonorous harmony rolled out from her touch, it seemed the very chorus of the heavens that she commanded, and a subtle misty glory descended upon her forehead, which he was long in perceiving to be cast from a moisture on his eyelids.

When the sermon commenced, Emilia quitted the organ and took his hand. In very low whispers, they spoke:

"I have wanted to see you so!"

"You see me now, little woman."

"On Friday week next I am to go away."

"Nonsense! You shall not."

"Your sisters say, yes! Mr. Pericles has got my father's consent, they say, to take me to Italy."

"Do you think of going?"

Emilia gazed at her nerveless hands lying in her lap.

"You shall not go!" he breathed imperiously in her ear.

"Then you will marry me quite soon?" And Emilia looked as if she would be smiling April, at a word.

"My dear girl!" he had an air of caressing remonstrance.

"Because," she continued, "if my father finds me out, I must go to Italy, or go to that life of torment in London—seeing those Jew-people—horrible!—or others and the thought of it is like being under the earth, tasting bitter gravel! I could almost bear it before you kissed me, my lover! It would kill me now. Say! say! Tell me we shall be together. I shudder all day and night, and feel frozen hands catching at me. I faint—my heart falls deep down, in the dark…I think I know what dying is now!"

She stopped on a tearless sob; and, at her fingers' ends, Wilfrid felt the quivering of her frame.

"My darling!" he interjected. He wished to explain the situation to her, as he then conceived it. But he had, in his calculation, failed also to count on a peculiar nervous fretfulness, that the necessity to reiterate an explanation in whispers must superinduce. So, when Emilia looked vacant of the intelligence imparted to her, he began anew, and emphatically; and ere he was half through it, Mr. Marter, from the pulpit underneath, sent forth a significant reprimand to the conscience of a particular culprit of his congregation, in the form of a solemn cough. Emilia had to remain unenlightened, and she proceeded to build on her previous assumption; doing the whispering easily and sweetly; in the prettiest way from her tongue's tip, with her chin lifted up; and sending the vowels on a prolonged hushed breath, that seemed to print them on the hearing far more distinctly than a volume of sound. Wilfrid fell back on monosyllables. He could not bring his mouth to utter flinty negatives, so it appeared that he assented; and then his better nature abused him for deluding her. He grew utterly ashamed of his aimless selfish double-dealing. "Can it be?" he questioned his own mind, and listened greedily to any mental confirmations of surpassing excellence in her, that the world might possibly acknowledge. Having, with great zeal, created a set of circumstances, he cursed them heartily, after the fashion of little people. He grew resigned to abandon Lady Charlotte, and to give his name to this subduing girl; but a comfortable quieting sensation came over him, at the thought that his filial duty stood in the way. His father, he knew, was anxious for him to marry into a noble family—incomprehensibly anxious to have the affair settled; and, as two or three scenes rose in his mind, Wilfrid perceived that the obstacle to his present fancy was his father.

As clearly as he could, with the dread of the preacher's admonishing cough before him, Wilfrid stated the case to Emilia; saying that he loved her with his whole heart; but that the truth was, his father was not in a condition of health to bear contradiction to his wishes, and would, he was sure, be absolutely opposed to their union. He brought on himself another reprimand from Mr. Marter, in seeking to propitiate Emilia's reason to comprehend the position rightly; and could add little more to the fact he had spoken, than that his father had other views, which it would require time to combat.

Emilia listened attentively, replying with a flying glance to the squeeze of his hand. He was astonished to see her so little disconcerted. But now the gradual fall of Mr. Marter's voice gave them warning.

"My lover?" breathed Emilia, hurriedly and eagerly; questioning with eye and tone.

"My darling!" returned Wilfrid.

She sat down to the organ with a smile. He was careful to retreat before the conclusion of the service; somewhat chagrined by his success. That smile of hers was inexplicable to him.

CHAPTER XXIV

EMILIA MAKES A MOVE

Mr. Pole was closeted in his City counting-house with Mr. Pericles, before a heap of papers and newly-opened foreign letters; to one of which, bearing a Russian stamp, he referred fretfully at times, as if to verify a monstrous fact. Any one could have seen that he was not in a condition to transact business. His face was unnaturally patched with colour, and his grey-tinged hair hung tumbled over his forehead like waves blown by a changeing wind. Still, he maintained his habitual effort to look collected, and defeat the scrutiny of the sallow-eyed fellow opposite; who quietly glanced, now and then, from the nervous feet to the nervous fingers, and nodded to himself a sardonic outlandish nod.

"Now, listen to me," said Mr. Pericles. "We shall not burst out about zis Riga man. He is a villain,—very well. Say it. He is a villain,—say so. And stop. Because" (and up went the Greek's forefinger), "we must not have a scandal, in ze fairst place. We do not want pity, in ze second. Saird, we must seem to trust him, in spite. I say, yeas! What is pity to us of commerce? It is contempt. We trust him on, and we lose what he pocket—a sossand. We burst on him, and we lose twenty, serty, forty; and we lose reputation."

"I'd have every villain hanged," cried Mr. Pole. "The scoundrel! I'd hang him with his own hemp. He talks of a factory burnt, and dares to joke about tallow! and in a business letter! and when he is telling one of a loss of money to that amount!"

"Not bad, ze joke," grinned Mr. Pericles. "It is a lesson of coolness. We learn it. But mind! he say, 'possible loss.' It is not positif. Hein! ze man is trying us. So! shall we burst out and make him desperate? We are in his hand at Riga, you see?"

"I see this," said Mr. Pole, "that he's a confounded rascal, and I'll know whether the law can't reach him."

"Ha! ze law!" Mr. Pericles sneered. "So you are, you. English. Always, ze law! But, we are men—we are not machine. Law for a machine, not a man! We punish him, perhaps. Well; he is punished. He is imprisoned—forty monz. We pay for him a sossand pound a monz. He is flogged—forty lashes. We pay for him a sossand pound a lash. You can afford zat? It is a luxury like anozer. It is not for me."

"How long are we to trust the villain?" said Mr. Pole. "If we trust him at all, mind! I don't say I do, or will."

"Ze money is locked up for a year, my friend. So soon we get it, so soon he goes, from ze toe off." Mr. Pericles' shining toe's-tip performed an agile circuit, and he smoothed his square clean jaw and venomous moustache reflectively. "Not now," he resumed. "While he hold us in his hand, we will not drive him to ze devil, or we go too, I believe, or part of ze way. But now, we say, zat money is frozen in ze Nord. We will make it in Australie, and in Greek waters. I have exposed to you my plan."

"Yes," said Mr. Pole, "and I've told you I've no pretensions to be a capitalist. We have no less than three ventures out, already."

"It is like you English! When you have ze world to milk, you go to one point and stick. It fails, and you fail. What is zat word?"—Mr. Pericles tapped his brow—"pluck,—you want pluck. It is your decadence. Greek, and Russian, and Yankee, all zey beat you. For, it is pluck. You make a pin's head, not a pin. It is in brain and heart you do fail. You have only your position,—an island, and ships, and some favour. You are no match in pluck. We beat you. And we live for pleasure, while you groan and sweat—mon Dieu! it is slavery."

Mr. Pericles twinkled his white eyes over the blinking merchant, and rose from his chair, humming a bit of opera, and announcing, casually, that a certain prima-donna had obtained a divorce from her husband.

"But," he added suddenly, "I say to you, if you cannot afford to speculate, run away from it as ze fire. Run away from it, and hold up your coat-tail. Jump ditches, and do not stop till you are safe home— hein? you say 'cosy?' I hear my landlady. Run till you are safe cosy. But if you are a man wis a head and a pocket, zen you know that 'speculate' means a dozen ventures. So, you come clear. Or, it is ruin. It is ruin, I say: you have been playing."

"An Englishman," returned Mr. Pole, disgusted at the shrugs he had witnessed—"an Englishman's as good as any of you. Look at us—look at our history—look at our wealth. By Jingo! But we like plain-dealing and common sense; and as to afford, what do you mean?"

"No, no," Mr. Pericles petitioned with uplifted hand; "my English is bad. It is—ah! bad. You shall look it over—my plan. It will strike your sense. Next week I go to Italy. I take ze little Belloni. You will manage all. I have in you, my friend, perfec' confidence. An Englishman, he is honest. An Englishman and a Greek conjoined, zey beat ze world! It is true, ma foi. For zat, I seek you, and not a countryman. A Frenchman?—oh, no! A German?—not a bit! A Russian?—never! A Yankee?—save me! I am a Greek—I take an Englishman."

"Well, well, you must leave me to think it over," said Mr. Pole, pleasantly smoothed down. "As to honesty, that's a matter of course with us: that's the mere footing we go upon. We don't plume ourselves upon what's general, here. There is, I regret to say, a difference between us and other nations. I believe it's partly their religion. They swindle us, and pay their priests for absolution with our money. If you're a double-dyed sinner, you can easily get yourself whitewashed over there. Confound them! When that fellow sent no remittance last month, I told you I suspected him. Who was, the shrewdest then? As for pluck, I never failed in that yet. But, I will see a thing clear. The man who speculates blindfold, is a fowl who walks into market to be plucked. Between being plucked, and having pluck, you'll see a distinction when you know the language better; but you must make use of your head, or the chances are you won't be much of a difference,—eh? I'll think over your scheme. I'm not a man to hesitate, if the calculations are sound. I'll look at the papers here."

"My friend, you will decide before zat I go to Italy." said Mr. Pericles, and presently took his leave.

When he was gone, Mr. Pole turned his chair to the table, and made an attempt to inspect one of the papers deliberately. Having untied it, he retied it with care, put it aside, marked 'immediate,' and read the letter from Riga anew. This he tore into shreds, with animadversions on the quality of the rags that had produced it, and opened the important paper once more. He got to the end of a sentence or two, when his fingers moved about for the letter; and then his mind conceived a necessity for turning to the directory, for which he rang the bell. The great red book was brought into his room by a youthful clerk, who waited by, while his master, unaware of his presence, tracked a name with his forefinger. It stopped at Pole, Samuel Bolton; and a lurking smile was on the merchant's face as he read the name: a smile of curious meaning, neither fresh nor sad; the meditative smile of one who looks upon an afflicted creature from whom he is aloof. After a lengthened contemplation of this name, he said, with a sigh, "Poor Chump! I wonder whether he's here, too." A search for the defunct proved that he was out of date. Mr. Pole thrust his hand to the bell that he might behold poor Chump in an old directory that would call up the blotted years.

"I am here, sir," said his clerk, who had been holding deferential watch at a few steps from the table.

"What do you do here then, sir, all this time?"

"I waited, sir, because—"

"You waste and dawdle away twenty or thirty minutes, when you ought to be doing your work. What do you mean?" Mr. Pole stood up and took an angry stride.

The young man could scarcely believe his master was not stooping to jest with him. He said: "For that matter, sir, it can't be a minute that I have been wasting."

"I called you in half an hour ago," returned Mr. Pole, fumbling at his watch-fob.

"It must have been somebody else, sir."

"Did you bring in this directory? Look at it! This?"

"This is the book that I brought in, sir."

"How long since?"

"I think, not a minute and a half, sir."

Mr. Pole gazed at him, and coughed slowly. "I could have sworn..." he murmured, and commenced blinking.

"I suppose I must be a little queer," he pursued; and instantly his right hand struck out, quivering. The young clerk grasped it, and drew him to a chair.

"Tush," said his master, working his feverish fingers across his forehead. "Want of food. I don't eat like you young fellows. Fetch me a glass of wine and a biscuit. Good wine, mind. Port. Or, no; you can't trust tavern Port:—brandy. Get it yourself, don't rely on the porter. And bring it yourself, you understand the importance? What is your name?"

"Braintop," replied the youth, with the modesty of one whose name has been too frequently subjected to puns.

"I think I never heard so singular a name in my life," Mr. Pole ejaculated seriously. "Braintop! It'll always make me think of brandy. What are you waiting for now?"

"I took the liberty of waiting before, to say that a lady wished to see you, sir."

Mr. Pole started from his chair. "A foreign lady?"

"She may be foreign. She speaks English, sir, and her name, I think, was foreign. I've forgotten it, I fear."

"It's the wife of that fellow from Riga!" cried the merchant. "Show her in. Show her in, immediately. I suspected this. She's in London, I know. I'm equal to her: show her in. When you fetch the Braintop and biscuit, call me to the door. You understand."

The youth affected meekly to enjoy this fiery significance given to his name, and said that he understood, without any doubt. He retired, and in a few moments ushered in Emilia Belloni.

Mr. Pole was in the middle of the room, wearing a countenance of marked severity, and watchful to maintain it in his opening bow; but when he perceived his little Brookfield guest standing timidly in the doorway, his eyebrows lifted, and his hands spread out; and "Well, to be sure!" he cried; while Emilia hurried up to him. She had to assure him that everything was right at home, and was next called upon to state what had brought her to town; but his continued exclamation of "Bless my soul!" reprieved her reply, and she sat in a chair panting quickly.

Mr. Pole spoke tenderly of refreshments; wine and cake, or biscuits.

"I cannot eat or drink," said Emilia.

"Why, what's come to you, my dear?" returned Mr. Pole in unaffected wonder.

"I am not hungry."

"You generally are, at home, about this time—eh?"

Emilia sighed, and feigned the sad note to be a breath of fatigue.

"Well, and why are you here, my dear?" Mr. Pole was beginning to step to the right and the left of her uneasily.

"I have come—" she paused, with a curious quick speculating look between her eyes; "I have come to see you."

"See me, my dear? You saw me this morning."

"Yes; I wanted to see you alone."

Emilia was having the first conflict with her simplicity; out of which it was not to issue clear, as in the foregone days. She was thinking of the character of the man she spoke to, studying him, that she might win him to succour the object she had in view. It was a quality going, and a quality coming; nor will we, if you please, lament a law of growth.

"Why, you can see me alone, any day, my dear," said Mr. Pole; "for many a day, I hope."

"You are more alone to me here. I cannot speak at Brookfield. Oh!"—and Emilia had to still her heart's throbbing—"you do not want me to go to Italy, do you?"

"Want you to go? Not a bit. There is some talk of it, isn't there? I don't want you to go. Don't you want to go."

"No! no!" said Emilia, with decisive fervour.

"Don't want to go?"

"No: to stay! I want to stay!"

"Eh? to stay?"

"To stay with you! Never to leave England, at least! I want to give up all that I may stay."

"All?" repeated Mr. Pole, evidently marvelling as to what that sounding box might contain; and still more, perplexed to hear Emilia's vehement—"Yes! all!" as if there were that in the mighty abnegation to make a reasonable listener doubtful.

"No. I really don't want you to go," he said. "In fact," and the merchant's hospitable nature was at war with something in his mind, "I like you, my dear; I like to have you about me. You're cheerful; you're agreeable; I like your smile; your voice, too. You're a very pleasant companion. Only, you know, we may break up our house. If the girls get married, I must live somewhere in lodgings, and I couldn't very well ask you to cook for me."

"I can cook a little," Emilia smiled. "I went into the kitchen, till Adela objected."

"Yes, but it wouldn't do, you know," pursued Mr. Pole, with the seriousness of a man thrown out of his line of argument. "You can cook, eh? Got an idea of it? I always said you were a useful little woman. Do have a biscuit and some wine:—No? well, where was I?—That confounded boy. Brainty-top, top! that's it Braintop. Was I talking of him, my dear? Oh no! about your getting married. For if you can cook, why not? Get a husband and then you won't got to Italy. You ought to get one. Some young fellows don't look for money."

"I shall make money come, in time," said Emilia; in the leaping ardour of whose eyes might be seen that what she had journeyed to speak was hot within her. "I know I shall be worth having. I shall win a name, I think—I do hope it!"

"Well, so Pericles says. He's got a great notion of you. Perhaps he means it himself. He's rich. Rash, I admit. But, as the chances go, he's tremendously rich. He may mean it."

"What?" asked Emilia.

"Marry you, you know."

"Ah, what a torture!"

In that heat of her feelings she realized the horror of the words to her, with an intensity that made them seem to quiver like an arrow in her breast.

"You don't like him?" said Mr. Pole.

"Not love him! not love him!"

"Yes, yes, but that comes after marriage. Often the case. Look here: don't you go against your interests. You mustn't be flighty. If Pericles speaks to you, have him. Clap your hands. Dozens of girls would, that I know."

"But, oh!" interposed Emilia; "if he married me he would kiss me!"

Mr. Pole coughed and blinked. "Well!" he remarked, as one gravely cogitating; and with the native delicacy of a Briton turned it off in a playful, "So shall I now," adding, "though I ain't your husband."

He stooped his head. Emilia put her hands on his shoulders, and submitted her face to him.

"There!" went Mr. Pole: "'pon my honour, it does me good:—better than medicine! But you mustn't give that dose to everybody, my dear. You don't, of course. All right, all right—I'm quite satisfied. I was only thinking of you going to Italy, among those foreign rascals, who've no more respect for a girl than they have for a monkey—their brother. A set of swindlers! I took you for the wife of one when you came in, at first. And now, business is business. Let's get it over. What have you come about? Glad to see you—understand that."

Emilia lifted her eyes to his.

"You know I love you, sir."

"I'm sure you're a grateful little woman."

She rose: "Oh! how can I speak it!"

An idea that his daughters had possibly sent her to herald one of the renowned physicians of London, concerning whom he was perpetually being plagued by them, or to lead him to one, flashed through Mr. Pole. He was not in a state to weigh the absolute value of such a suspicion, but it seemed probable; it explained an extraordinary proceeding; and, having conceived, his wrath took it up as a fact, and fought with it.

"Stop! If that's what you've come for, we'll bring matters to a crisis. You fancy me ill, don't you, my dear?"

"You do not look well, sir."

Emilia's unhesitating reply confirmed his suspicion.

"I am well. I am, I say! And now, understand that, if that's your business, I won't go to the fellow, and I won't see him here. They'll make me out mad, next. He shall never have a guinea from me while I live. No, nor when I die. Not a farthing! Sit down, my dear, and wait for the biscuits. I wish to heaven they'd come. There's brandy coming, too. Where's Braintop?"

He took out his handkerchief to wipe his forehead, and jerked it like a bell-rope.

Emilia, in a singular bewilderment, sat eyeing a beam of sombre city sunlight on the dusty carpet. She could only suppose that the offending "he" was Wilfrid; but, why he should be so, she could not guess: and how to plead for him, divided her mind.

"Don't blame him; be angry with me, if you are angry," she began softly. "I know he thinks of you anxiously. I know he would do nothing to hurt you. No one is so kind as he is. Would you deprive him of money, because he offends you?"

"Deprive him of money," repeated Mr. Pole, with ungrudging accentuation. "Well, I've heard about women, but I never knew one so anxious for a doctor to get his fee as you are."

Emilia wonderingly fixed her sight on him an instant, and, quite unillumined, resumed: "Blame me, sir. But, I know you will be too kind. Oh! I love him. So, I must love you, and I would not give you pain. It is true he loves me. You will not see him, because he loves me?"

"The doctor?" muttered Mr. Pole. "The doctor?" he almost bellowed; and got sharp up from his chair, and looked at himself in the glass, blinking rapidly; and then turned to inspect Emilia.

Emilia drew him to her side again.

"Go on," he said; and there became visible in his face a frightful effort to comprehend her, and get to the sense of her words.

And why it was so frightful as to be tragic, you will know presently.

He thought of the arrival of Braintop, freighted with brandy, as the only light in the mist, and breathing heavily from his nose, almost snorting the air he took in from a widened mouth, he sat and tried to listen to her words as well as for Braintop's feet.

Emilia was growing too conscious of her halting eloquence, as the imminence of her happiness or misery hung balancing in doubtful scales before her.

"Oh! he loves me, and I love him," she gasped, and wondered why words should be failing her. "See us together, sir, and hear us. We will make you well."

The exclamation "Good Lord!" groaned out in a tone as from the lower pits of despair, cut her short.

Tearfully she murmured: "You will not see us, sir?"

"Together?" bawled the merchant.

"Yes, I mean together."

"If you're not mad, I am." And he jumped on his legs and walked to the farther corner of the room. "Which of us is it?" His features twitched in horribly comic fashion. "What do you mean? I can't understand a word. My brain must have gone;" throwing his hand over his forehead. "I've feared so for the last four months. Good God! a lunatic asylum! and the business torn like a piece of old rag! I know that fellow at Riga's dancing like a cannibal, and there—there 'll be articles in the papers.—Here, girl! come up to the light. Come here, I say."

Emilia walked up to him.

"You don't look mad. I dare say everybody else understands you. Do they?"

The sad-flushed pallor of his face provoked Emilia to say: "You ought to have the doctor here immediately. Let me bring him, sir."

A gleam as of a lantern through his oppressive mental fog calmed the awful irritability of his nerves somewhat.

"You've got him outside?"

"No, sir."

The merchant's eagerness faded out. He put his hand to her shoulder, and went along to a chair, sinking into it, and closing his eyelids. So they remained, Emilia at his right hand. She watched him breathing with a weak open mouth, and thought more of the doctor now than of Wilfrid.

CHAPTER XXV

A FARCE WITHIN A FARCE

Braintop's knock at the door had been unheeded for some minutes. At last Emilia let him in. The brandy and biscuits were placed on a table, and Emilia resumed her watch by Mr. Pole. She saw that his lips moved, after a space, and putting her ear down, understood that he desired not to see any one who might come for an interview with him: nor were the clerks to be admitted. The latter direction was given in precise terms. Emilia repeated the orders outside. On her return, the merchant's eyes were open.

"My forehead feels damp," he said; "and I'm not hot at all. Just take hold of my hands. They're like wet crumpets. I wonder what makes me so stiff. A man mustn't sit at business too long at a time. Sure to make people think he's ill. What was that about a doctor? I seem to remember. I won't see one."

Emilia had filled a glass with brandy. She brought it nearer to his hand, while he was speaking. At the touch of the glass, his fingers went round it slowly, and he raised it to his mouth. The liquor revived him. He breathed "ah!" several times, and grimaced, blinking, as if seeking to arouse a proper brightness in his eyes. Then, he held out his empty glass to her, and she filled it, and he sipped deliberately, saying: "I'm warm inside. I keep on perspiring so cold. Can't make it out. Look at my finger-ends, my dear. They're whitish, aren't they?"

Emilia took the hand he presented, and chafed it, and put it against her bosom, half under one arm. The action appeared to give some warmth to his heart, for he petted her, in return.

A third time he held out the glass, and remarked that this stuff was better than medicine.

"You women!" he sneered, as at a reminiscence of their faith in drugs.

"My legs are weak, though!" He had risen and tested the fact. "Very shaky. I wonder what makes 'em—I don't take much exercise." Pondering on this problem, he pursued: "It's the stomach. I'm as empty as an egg-shell. Odd, I've got no appetite. But, my spirits are up. I begin to feel myself again. I'll eat by-and-by, my dear. And, I say; I'll tell you what:—I'll take you to the theatre to-night. I want to laugh. A man's all right when he's laughing. I wish it was Christmas. Don't you like to see the old pantaloon tumbled over, my boy?—my girl, I mean. I did, when I was a boy. My father took me. I went in the pit. I can smell oranges, when I think of it. I remember, we supped on German sausage; or ham—one or the other. Those were happy old days!"

He shook his head at them across the misty gulf.

"Perhaps there's a good farce going on now. If so, we'll go. Girls ought to learn to laugh as well as boys. I'll ring for Braintop."

He rang the bell, and bade Emilia be careful to remind him that he wanted Braintop's address; for Braintop was useful.

It appeared that there were farces at several of the theatres. Braintop rattled them out, their plot and fun and the merits of the actors, with delightful volubility, as one whose happy subject had been finally discovered. He was forthwith commissioned to start immediately and take a stage-box at one of the places of entertainment, where two great rivals of the Doctor genus promised to laugh dull care out of the spirit of man triumphantly, and at the description of whose drolleries any one with faith might be half cured. The youth gave his address on paper to Emilia.

"Make haste, sir," said Mr. Pole. "And, stop. You shall go, yourself; go to the pit, and have a supper, and I'll pay for it. When you've ordered the box—do you know the Bedford Hotel? Go there, and see Mrs. Chickley, and tell her I am coming to dine and sleep, and shall bring one of my daughters. Dinner, sittingroom, and two bed-rooms, mind. And tell Mrs. Chickley we've got no carpet-bag, and must come upon her wardrobe. All clear to you? Dinner at half-past five going to theatre."

Braintop bowed comprehendingly.

"Now, that fellow goes off chirping," said Mr. Pole to Emilia. "It's just the thing I used to wish to happen to me, when I was his age—my master to call me in and say 'There! go and be jolly.' I dare say the rascal'll order a champagne supper. Poor young chap! let his heart be merry. Ha! ha! heigho!—Too much business is bad for man and boy. I feel better already, if it weren't for my legs. My feet are so cold. Don't you think I'm pretty talkative, my dear?"

"I am glad to hear you talk," said Emilia, striving to look less perplexed than she felt.

He asked her slyly why she had come to London; and she begged that she might speak of it by-and-by; whereat Mr. Pole declared that he intended to laugh them all out of that nonsense. "And what did you say about being in love with him? A doctor in good practice—but you needn't commence by killing me if you do go and marry the fellow. Eh? what is it?"

Emilia was too much entangled herself to attempt to extricate him; and apparently his wish to be enlightened passed away, for he was the next instant searching among his papers for the letter from Riga. Not finding it, he put on his hat.

"Must give up business to-day. Can't do business with a petticoat in the room. I wish the Lord Mayor'd stop them all at Temple Bar. Now we'll go out, and I'll show you a bit of the City."

He offered her his arm, and she noticed that in walking through the office, he was erect, and the few words he spoke were delivered in the peremptory elastic tone of a vigorous man.

"My girls," he said to her in an undertone, "never come here. Well! we don't expect ladies, you know. Different spheres in this world. They mean to be tip-top in society; and quite right too. My dear, I think we'll ride. Do you mind being seen in a cab?"

He asked her hesitatingly: and when Emilia said, "Oh, no! let us ride," he seemed relieved. "I can't see the harm in a cab. Different tastes, in this world. My girls—but, thank the Lord! they've got carriages."

For an hour the merchant and Emilia drove about the City. He showed her all the great buildings, and dilated on the fabulous piles of wealth they represented, taking evident pleasure in her exclamations of astonishment.

"Yes, yes; they may despise us City fellows. I say, 'Come and see,' that's all! Now, look up that court. Do you see three dusty windows on the second floor? That man there could buy up any ten princes in Europe—excepting one or two Austrians or Russians. He wears a coat just like mine."

"Does he?" said Emilia, involuntarily examining the one by her side.

"We don't show our gold-linings, in the City, my dear."

"But, you are rich, too."

"Oh! I—as far as that goes. Don't talk about me. I'm—I'm still cold in the feet. Now, look at that corner house. Three months ago that man was one of our most respected City merchants. Now he's a bankrupt, and can't show his head. It was all rotten. A medlar! He tampered with documents; betrayed trusts. What do you think of him?"

"What was it he did?" asked Emilia.

Mr. Pole explained, and excused him; then he explained, and abused him.

"He hadn't a family, my dear. Where did the money go? He's called a rascal now, poor devil! Business brings awful temptations. You think, this'll save me! You catch hold of it and it snaps. That'll save me; but you're too heavy, and the roots give way, and down you go lower and lower. Lower and lower! The gates of hell must be very low down if one of our bankrupts don't reach 'em." He spoke this in a deep underbreath. "Let's get out of the City. There's no air. Look at that cloud. It's about over Brookfield, I should say."

"Dear Brookfield!" echoed Emilia, feeling her heart fly forth to sing like a skylark under the cloud.

"And they're not satisfied with it," murmured Mr. Pole, with a voice of unwonted bitterness.

At the hotel, he was received very cordially by Mrs. Chickley, and Simon, the old waiter.

"You look as young as ever, ma'am," Mr. Pole complimented her cheerfully, while he stamped his feet on the floor, and put forward Emilia as one of his girls; but immediately took the landlady aside, to tell her that she was "merely a charge—a ward—something of that sort;" admitting, gladly enough, that she was a very nice young lady. "She's a genius, ma'am, in music:—going to do wonders. She's not one of them." And Mr. Pole informed Mrs. Chickley that when they came to town, they usually slept in one or other of the great squares. He, for his part, preferred old quarters: comfort versus grandeur.

Simon had soon dressed the dinner-table. By the time dinner was ready, Mr. Pole had sunk into such a condition of drowsiness, that it was hard to make him see why he should be aroused, and when he sat down, fronting Emilia, his eyes were glazed, and he complained that she was scarcely visible.

"Some of your old yellow seal, Simon. That's what I want. I haven't got better at home."

The contents of this old yellow seal formed the chief part of the merchant's meal. Emilia was induced to drink two full glasses.

"Doesn't that make your feet warm, my dear?" said Mr. Pole.

"It makes me want to talk," Emilia confessed.

"Ah! we shall have some fun to-night. 'To-the-rutte-ta-to!' If you could only sing, 'Begone dull care!' I like glees: good, honest, English, manly singing for me! Nothing like glees and madrigals, to my mind. With chops and baked potatoes, and a glass of good stout, they beat all other music."

Emilia sang softly to him.

When she had finished, Mr. Pole applauded her mildly.

"Your music, my dear?"

"My music: Mr. Runningbrook's words. But only look. He will not change a word, and some of the words are so curious, they make me lift my chin and pout. It's all in my throat. I feel as if I had to do it on tiptoe. Mr. Runningbrook wrote the song in ten minutes."

"He can afford to—comes of a family," said Mr. Pole, and struck up a bit of "Celia's Arbour," which wandered into "The Soldier Tired," as he came bendingly, both sets of fingers filliping, toward Emilia, with one of those ancient glee—suspensions, "Taia—haia—haia—haia," etc., which were meant for jolly fellows who could bear anything.

"Eh?" went Mr. Pole, to elicit approbation in return.

Emilia smoothed the wrinkles of her face, and smiled.

"There's nothing like Port," said Mr. Pole. "Get little Runningbrook to write a song: 'There's nothing like Port.' You put the music. I'll sing it."

"You will," cried Emilia.

"Yes, upon my honour! now my feet are warmer, I by Jingo! what's that?" and again he wore that strange calculating look, as if he were being internally sounded, and guessed at his probable depth. "What a twitch! Something wrong with my stomach. But a fellow must be all right when his spirits are up. We'll be off as quick as we can. Taia—haihaia—hum. If the farce is bad, it's my last night of theatre-going."

The delight at being in a theatre kept Emilia dumb when she gazed on the glittering lights. After an inspection of the house, Mr. Pole kindly remarked: "You must marry and get out of this. This'd never do. All very well in the boxes: but on the stage—oh, no! I shouldn't like you to be there. If my girls don't approve of the doctor, they shall look out somebody for you. I shouldn't like you to be painted, and rigged out; and have to squall in this sort of place. Stage won't do for you. No, no!"

Emilia replied that she had given up the stage; and looked mournfully at the drop-scene, as at a lost kingdom, scarcely repressing her tears.

The orchestra tuned and played a light overture. She followed up the windings of the drop-scene valley, meeting her lover somewhere beneath the castle-ruin, where the river narrowed and the trees intertwined. On from dream to dream the music carried her, and dull fell the first words of the farce. Mr. Pole said, "Now, then!" and began to chuckle. As the farce proceeded, he grew more serious, repeating to Emilia, quite anxiously: "I wonder whether that boy Braintop's enjoying it." Emilia glanced among the sea of heads, and finally eliminated the head of Braintop, who was respectfully devoting his gaze to the box she occupied. When Mr. Pole had been assisted to discover him likewise, his attention alternated between Braintop and the stage, and he expressed annoyance from time to time at the extreme composure of Braintop's countenance. "Why don't the fellow laugh? Does he think he's listening to a sermon?" Poor Braintop, on his part, sat in mortal fear lest his admiration of Emilia was perceived. Divided? between this alarming suspicion, and a doubt that the hair on his forehead was not properly regulated, he became uneasy and fitful in his deportment. His imagination plagued him with a sense of guilt, which his master's watchfulness of him increased. He took an opportunity to furtively to eye himself in a pocket-mirror, and was subsequently haunted by an additional dread that Emilia might have discovered the instrument; and set him down as a vain foolish dog. When he saw her laugh he was sure of it. Instead of responding to Mr. Pole's encouragement, he assumed a taciturn aspect worthy of a youthful anchorite, and continued to be the spectator of a scene to which his soul was dead.

"I believe that fellow's thinking of nothing but his supper," said Mr. Pole.

"I dare say he dined early in the day," returned Emilia, remembering how hungry she used to be in the evenings of the potatoe-days.

"Yes, but he might laugh, all the same." And Mr. Pole gave Emilia the sound advice: "Mind you never marry a fellow who can't laugh."

Braintop saw Emilia smile. Then, in an instant, her face changed its expression to one of wonder and alarm, and her hands clasped together tightly. What on earth was the matter with her? His agitated fancy, centred in himself, now decided that some manifestation of most shocking absurdity had settled on his forehead, or his hair, for he was certain of his neck-tie. Braintop had recourse to his pocket-mirror once more. It afforded him a rapid interchange of glances with a face which he at all events could distinguish from the mass, though we need not.

The youth was in the act of conveying the instrument to its retreat, when conscience sent his eyes toward Emilia, who, to his horror, beckoned to him, and touched Mr. Pole, entreating him to do the same. Mr. Pole gesticulated imperiously, whereat Braintop rose, and requested his neighbour to keep his seat for ten minutes, as he was going into that particular box; and "If I don't come back in ten minutes, I shall stop there," said Braintop, a little grandly, through the confusion of his ideas, as he guessed at the possible reasons for the summons.

Emilia had seen her father in the orchestra. There he sat, under the leader, sullenly fiddling the prelude to the second play, like a man ashamed, and one of the beaten in this world. Flight had been her first thought. She had cause to dread him. The more she lived and the dawning knowledge of what it is to be a woman in the world grew with her, the more she shrank from his guidance, and from reliance on him. Not that she conceived him designedly base; but he outraged her now conscious delicacy, and what she had to endure as a girl seemed unbearable to her now. Besides, she felt a secret shuddering at nameless things, which made her sick of the thought of returning to him and his Jew friends. But, alas! he looked so miserable—a child of harmony among the sons of discord! He kept his head down, fiddling like a machine. The old potatoe-days became pathetically edged with dead light to Emilia. She could not be cruel. "When I am safe," she laid stress on the word in her mind, to awaken blessed images, "I will see him often, and make him happy; but I will let him know that all is well with me now, and that I love him always."

So she said to Mr. Pole, "I know one of those in the orchestra. May I write a word to him on a piece of paper before we go? I wish to."

Mr. Pole reflected, and seeing her earnest in her desire to do this, replied: "Well, yes; if you must—the girls are not here."

Emilia borrowed his pencil-case, and wrote:—

"Sandra is well, and always loves her caro papa, and is improving, and will see him soon. Her heart is full of love for him and for her mama; and if they leave their lodgings they are to leave word where they go. Sandra never forgets Italy, and reads the papers. She has a copy of the score of an unknown opera by our Andronizetti, and studies it, and anatomy, English, French, and pure Italian, and can ride a horse. She has made rich friends, who love her. It will not be long, and you will see her."

The hasty scrawl concluded with numerous little caressing exclamations in Italian diminutives. This done, Emilia thought: "But he will look up and see me!" She resolved not to send it till they were about to quit the theatre. Consequently, Braintop, on his arrival, was told to sit down. "You don't look cheerful in the pit," said Mr. Pole. "You're above it?—eh? You're all alike in that. None of you do what your dads did. Up-up-up! You may get too high, eh?—Gallery?" and Mr. Pole winked knowingly and laughed.

Braintop, thus elevated, tried his best to talk to Emilia, who sat half fascinated with the fear of seeing her father lift his eyes and recognize her suddenly. She sat boldly in the front, as before; not being a young woman to hide her head where there was danger, and having perhaps a certain amount of the fatalism which is often youth's philosophy in the affairs of life. "If this is to be, can I avert it?"

Mr. Pole began to nod at the actors, heavily. He said to Emilia, "If there is any fun going on, give me a nudge." Emilia kept her eyes on her father in the orchestra, full of pity for his deplorable wig, in which she read his later domestic history, and sad tales of the family dinners.

"Do you see one of those"—she pointed him out to Braintop; "he is next to the leader, with his back to us. Are you sure? I want you to give him this note before he goes; when we go. Will you do it? I shall always be thankful to you."

Considering what Braintop was ready to do that he might be remembered for a day and no more, the request was so very moderate as to be painful to him.

"You will leave him when you have given it into his hand. You are not to answer any questions," said Emilia.

With a reassuring glance at the musician's wig, Braintop bent his head.

"Do see," she pursued, "how differently he bows from the other men, though it is only dance music. Oh, how his ears are torn by that violoncello! He wants to shriek:—he bears it!"

She threw a piteous glance across the agitated instruments, and Braintop was led to inquire: "Is he anything particular?"

"He can bring out notes that are more like honey—if you can fancy a thread of honey drawn through your heart as if it would never end! He is Italian."

Braintop modestly surveyed her hair and brows and cheeks, and taking the print of her eyes on his brain to dream over, smelt at a relationship with the wry black wig, which cast a halo about it.

The musicians laid down their instruments, and trooped out, one by one. Emilia perceived a man brush against her father's elbow. Her father flicked at his offended elbow with the opposite hand, and sat crumpled up till all had passed him: then went out alone. That little action of disgust showed her that he had not lost spirit, albeit condemned to serve amongst an inferior race, promoters of discord.

Just as the third play was opening, some commotion was seen in the pit, rising from near Braintop's vacated seat; and presently a thing that shone flashing to the lights, came on from hand to hand, each hand signalling subsequently toward Mr. Pole's box. It approached. Braintop's eyes were in waiting on Emilia, who looked sadly at the empty orchestra. A gentleman in the stalls, a head beneath her, bowed, and holding up a singular article, gravely said that he had been requested to pass it. She touched Mr. Pole's shoulder. "Eh? anything funny?" said he, and glanced around. He was in time to see Braintop lean hurriedly over the box, and snatch his pocket-mirror from the gentleman's hand. "Ha! ha!" he laughed, as if a comic gleam had illumined him. A portion of the pit and stalls laughed too. Emilia smiled merrily. "What was it?" said she; and perceiving many faces beneath her red among handkerchiefs, she was eager to see the thing that the unhappy Braintop had speedily secreted.

"Come, sir, let's see it!" quoth Mr. Pole, itching for a fresh laugh; and in spite of Braintop's protest, and in defiance of his burning blush, he compelled the wretched youth to draw it forth, and be manifestly convicted of vanity.

A shout of laughter burst from Mr. Pole. "No wonder these young sparks cut us all out. Lord, what cunning dogs they are! They ain't satisfied with seeing themselves in their boots, but they—ha! ha! By George! We've got the best fun in our box. I say, Braintop! you ought to have two, my boy. Then you'd see how you looked behind. Ha-ha-hah! Never enjoyed an evening so much in my life! A looking-glass for their pockets! ha! ha!—hooh!"

Luckily the farce demanded laughter, or those parts of the pit which had not known Braintop would have been indignant. Mr. Pole became more and more possessed by the fun, as the contrast of Braintop's abject humiliation with this glaring testimony to his conceit tickled him. He laughed till he complained of hunger. Emilia, though she thought it natural that Braintop should carry a pocket-mirror if he pleased, laughed from sympathy; until Braintop, reduced to the verge of forbearance, stood up and remarked that, to perform the mission entrusted to him, he must depart immediately. Mr. Pole was loth to let him go, but finally commending him to a good supper, he sighed, and declared himself a new man.

"Oh! what a jolly laugh! The very thing I wanted! It's worth hundreds to me. I was queer before: no doubt about that!"

Again the ebbing convulsion of laughter seized him. "I feel as clear as day," he said; and immediately asked Emilia whether she thought he would have strength to get down to the cab. She took his hand, trying to assist him from the seat. He rose, and staggered an instant. "A sort of reddish cloud," he murmured, feeling over his forehead. "Ha! I know what it is. I want a chop. A chop and a song. But, I couldn't take you, and I like you by me. Good little woman!" He patted Emilia's shoulder, preparatory to leaning on it with considerable weight, and so descended to the cab, chuckling ever and anon at the reminiscence of Braintop.

There was a disturbance in the street. A man with a foreign accent was shouting by the door of a neighbouring public-house, that he would not yield his hold of the collar of a struggling gentleman, till the villain had surrendered his child, whom he scandalously concealed from her parents. A scuffle ensued, and the foreign voice was heard again:

"Wat! wat you have de shame, you have de pluck, ah! to tell me you know not where she is, and you bring me a letter? Ho!—you have de cheeks to tell me!"

This highly effective pluralizing of their peculiar slang, brought a roar of applause from the crowd of Britons.

"Only a street row," said Mr. Pole, to calm Emilia.

"Will he be hurt?" she cried.

"I see a couple of policemen handy," said Mr. Pole, and Emilia cowered down and clung to his hand as they drove from the place.

BOOK IV

CHAPTER XXVI

SUGGESTS THAT THE COMIC MASK HAS SOME KINSHIP WITH A SKULL

It was midnight. Mr. Pole had appeased his imagination with a chop, and was trying to revive the memory of his old after-theatre night carouses by listening to a song which Emilia sang to him, while he sipped at a smoking mixture, and beat time on the table, rejoiced that he was warm from head to foot at last.

"That's a pretty song, my dear," he said. "A very pretty song. It does for an old fellow; and so did my supper: light and wholesome. I'm an old fellow; I ought to know I've got a grown-up son and grown-up daughters. I shall be a grandpa, soon, I dare say. It's not the thing for me to go about hearing glees. I had an idea of it. I'm better here. All I want is to see my children happy, married and settled, and comfortable!"

Emilia stole up to him, and dropped on one knee: "You love them?"

"I do. I love my girls and my boy. And my brandy-and-water, do you mean to say, you rogue?"

"And me?" Emilia looked up at him beseechingly.

"Yes, and you. I do. I haven't known you long, my dear, but I shall be glad to do what I can for you. You shall make my house your home as long as you live; and if I say, make haste and get married, it's only just this: girls ought to marry young, and not be in an uncertain position."

"Am I worth having?"

"To be sure you are! I should think so. You haven't got a penny; but, then, you're not for spending one. And"—Mr. Pole nodded to right and left like a man who silenced a host of invisible logicians, urging this and that—"you're a pleasant companion, thrifty, pretty, musical: by Jingo! what more do they want? They'll have their song and chop at home."

"Yes; but suppose it depends upon their fathers?"

"Well, if their fathers will be fools, my dear, I can't help 'em. We needn't take 'em in a lump: how about the doctor? I'll see him to-morrow morning, and hear what he has to say. Shall I?"

Mr. Pole winked shrewdly.

"You will not make my heart break?" Emilia's voice sounded one low chord as she neared the thing she had to say.

"Bless her soul!" the old merchant patted her; "I'm not the sort of man for that."

"Nor his?"

"His?" Mr. Pole's nerves became uneasy in a minute, at the scent of a mystification. He dashed his handkerchief over his forehead, repeating: "His? Break a man's heart! I? What's the meaning of that? For God's sake, don't bother me!"

Emilia was still kneeling before him, eyeing him with a shadowed steadfast air.

"I say his, because his heart is in mine. He has any pain that hurts me."

"He may be tremendously in love," observed Mr. Pole; "but he seems a deuced soft sort of a doctor! What's his name?"

"I love Wilfrid."

The merchant appeared to be giving ear to her, long after the words had been uttered, while there was silence in the room.

"Wilfrid? my son?" he cried with a start.

"He is my lover."

"Damned rascal!" Mr. Pole jumped from his chair. "Going and playing with an unprotected girl. I can pardon a young man's folly, but this is infamous. My dear child," he turned to Emilia, "if you've got any notion about my son Wilfrid, you must root it up as quick as you can. If he's been behaving like a villain, leave him to me. I detest, I hate, I loathe, I would kick, a young man who deceives a girl. Even if he's my son!—more's the reason!"

Mr. Pole was walking up and down the room, fuming as he spoke. Emilia tried to hold his hand, as he was passing, but he said: "There, my child! I'm very sorry for you, and I'm damned angry with him. Let me go."

"Can you, can you be angry with him for loving me?"

"Deceiving you," returned Mr. Pole; "that's what it is. And I tell you, I'd rather fifty times the fellow had deceived me. Anything rather than that he should take advantage of a girl."

"Wilfrid loves me and would die for me," said Emilia.

"Now, let me tell you the fact," Mr. Pole came to a halt, fronting her. "My son Wilfrid Pole may be in love, as he says, here and there, but he is engaged to be married to a lady of title. I have his word—his oath. He got near a thousand pounds out of my pocket the other day on that understanding. I don't speak about the money, but—now—it's a lump—others would have made a nice row about it—but is he a liar? Is he a seducing, idling, vagabond dog? Is he a contemptible scoundrel?"

"He is my lover," said Emilia.

She stood without changing a feature; as in a darkness, holding to the one thing she was sure of. Then, with a sudden track of light in her brain: "I know the mistake," she said. "Pardon him. He feared to offend you, because you are his father, and he thought I might not quite please you. For, he loves me.

He has loved me from the first moment he saw me. He cannot be engaged to another. I could bring him from any woman's side. I have only to say to myself—he must come to me. For he loves me! It is not a thing to doubt."

Mr. Pole turned and recommenced his pacing with hasty steps. All the indications of a nervous tempest were on him. Interjecting half-formed phrases, and now and then staring at Emilia, as at an incomprehensible object, he worked at his hair till it lent him the look of one in horror at an apparition.

"The fellow's going to marry Lady Charlotte Chillingworth, I tell you. He has asked my permission. The infernal scamp! he knew it pleased me. He bled me of a thousand pounds only the other day. I tell you, he's going to marry Lady Charlotte Chillingworth."

Emilia received this statement with a most perplexing smile. She shook her head. "He cannot."

"Cannot? I say he shall, and must, and in a couple of months, too!"

The gravely sceptical smile on Emilia's face changed to a blank pallor.

"Then, you make him, sir—you?"

"He'll be a beggar, if he don't."

"You will keep him without money?"

Mr. Pole felt that he gazed on strange deeps in that girl's face. Her voice had the wire-like hum of a rising wind. There was no menace in her eyes: the lashes of them drooped almost tenderly, and the lips were but softly closed. The heaving of the bosom, though weighty, was regular: the hands hung straight down, and were open. She looked harmless; but his physical apprehensiveness was sharpened by his nervous condition, and he read power in her: the capacity to concentrate all animal and mental vigour into one feeling—this being the power of the soul.

So she stood, breathing quietly, steadily eyeing him.

"No, no;" went on Mr. Pole. "Come, come. We'll sit down, and see, and talk—see what can be done. You know I always meant kindly by you."

"Oh, yes!" Emilia musically murmured, and it cost her nothing to smile again.

"Now, tell me how this began." Mr. Pole settled himself comfortably to listen, all irritation having apparently left him, under the influence of the dominant nature. "You need not be ashamed to talk it over to me."

"I am not ashamed," Emilia led off, and told her tale simply, with here and there one of her peculiar illustrations. She had not thought of love till it came to life suddenly, she said; and then all the world looked different. The relation of Wilfrid's bravery in fighting for her, varied for a single instant the low monotony of her voice. At the close of the confession, Mr. Pole wore an aspect of distress. This creature's utter unlikeness to the girls he was accustomed to, corroborated his personal view of the case, that Wilfrid certainly could not have been serious, and that she was deluded. But he pitied her, for he had sufficient imagination to prevent him from despising what he did not altogether comprehend. So, to fortify the damsel, he gave her a lecture: first, on young men—their selfish inconsiderateness, their weakness, the wanton lives they led, their trick of lying for any sugar-plum, and how they laughed at their dupes. Secondly, as to the conduct consequently to be prescribed to girls, who were weaker, frailer, by disposition more confiding, and who must believe nothing but what they heard their elders say.

Emilia gave patient heed to the lecture.

"But I am safe," she remarked, when he had finished; "for my lover is not as those young men are."

To speak at all, and arrange his ideas, was a vexation to the poor merchant. He was here like an irritable traveller, who knocks at a gate, which makes as if it opens, without letting him in. Emilia's naive confidence he read as stupidity. It brought on a fresh access of the nervous fever lurking in him, and he cried, jumping from his seat: "Well, you can't have him, and there's an end. You must give up—confound! why! do you expect to have everything you want at starting? There, my child—but, upon my honour! a man loses his temper at having to talk for an hour or so, and no result. You must go to bed; and—do you say your prayers? Well! that's one way of getting out of it—pray that you may forget all about what's not good for you. Why, you're almost like a young man, when you set your mind on a thing. Bad! won't do! Say your prayers regularly. And, please, pour me out a mouthful of brandy. My hand trembles—I don't know what's the matter with it;—just like those rushes on the Thames I used to see when out fishing. No wind, and yet there they shake away. I wish it was daylight on the old river now! It's night, and no mistake. I feel as if I had a fellow twirling a stick over my head. The rascal's been at it for the last month. There, stop where you are, my dear. Don't begin to dance!"

He pressed at his misty eyes, half under the impression that she was taking a succession of dazzling leaps in air. Terror of an impending blow, which he associated with Emilia's voice, made him entreat her to be silent. After a space, he breathed a long breath of relief, saying: "No, no; you're firm enough on your feet. I don't think I ever saw you dance. My girls have given it up. What led me to think...but, let's to bed, and say our prayers. I want a kiss."

Emilia kissed him on the forehead. The symptoms of illness were strange to her, and passed unheeded. She was too full of her own burning passion to take evidence from her sight. The sun of her world was threatened with extinction. She felt herself already a wanderer in a land of tombs, where none could say whether morning had come or gone. Intensely she looked her misery in the face; and it was as a voice that said, "No sun: never sun any more," to her. But a blue-hued moon slipped from among the clouds, and hung in the black outstretched fingers of the tree of darkness, fronting troubled waters. "This is thy light for ever! thou shalt live in thy dream." So, as in a prison-house, did her soul now recall the blissful hours by Wilming Weir. She sickened but an instant. The blood in her veins was too strong a tide for her to crouch in that imagined corpse-like universe which alternates with an irradiated Eden in the brain of the passionate young.

"Why should I lose him!" The dry sob choked her.

She struggled with the emotion in her throat, and Mr. Pole, who had previously dreaded supplication and appeals for pity, caressed her. Instantly the flood poured out.

"You are not cruel. I knew it. I should have died, if you had come between us. Oh, Wilfrid's father, I love you!—I have never had a very angry word on my mouth. Think! think! if you had made me curse you. For, I could! You would have stopped my life, and Wilfrid's. What would our last thoughts have been? We could not have forgiven you. Take up dead birds killed by frost. You cry: Cruel winter! murdering cold! But I knew better. You are Wilfrid's father, whom I can kneel to. My lover's father! my own father! my friend next to heaven! Oh! bless my love, for him. You have only to know what my love for him is! The thought of losing him goes like perishing cold through my bones;—my heart jerks, as if it had to pull up my body from the grave every time it beats...."

"God in heaven!" cried the horrified merchant, on whose susceptible nerves these images wrought with such a force that he absolutely had dread of her. He gasped, and felt at his heart, and then at his pulse; rubbed the moisture from his forehead, and throwing a fixedly wild look on her eyes, he jumped up and left her kneeling.

His caress had implied mercy to Emilia: for she could not reconcile it with the rejection of the petition of her soul. She was now a little bewildered to see him trotting the room, frowning and blinking, and feeling at one wrist, at momentary pauses, all his words being: "Let's be quiet. Let's be good. Let's go to bed, and say our prayers;" mingled with short ejaculations.

"I may say," she intercepted him, "I may tell my dear lover that you bless us both, and that we are to live. Oh, speak! sir! let me hear you!"

"Let's go to bed," iterated Mr. Pole. "Come, candles! do light them. In God's name! light candles. And let's be off and say our prayers."

"You consent, sir?"

"What's that your heart does?" Mr. Pole stopped to enquire; adding: "There, don't tell me. You've played the devil with mine. Who'd ever have made me believe that I should feel more at ease running up and down the room, than seated in my arm-chair! Among the wonders of the world, that!"

Emilia put up her lips to kiss him, as he passed her. There was something deliciously soothing and haven-like to him in the aspect of her calmness.

"Now, you'll be a good girl," said he, when he had taken her salute.

"And you," she rejoined, "will be happier!"

His voice dropped. "If you go on like this, you've done for me!"

But she could make no guess at any tragic meaning in his words. "My father—let me call you so!"

"Will you see that you can't have him?" he stamped the syllables into her ears: and, with a notion of there being a foreign element about her, repeated:—"No!—not have him!—not yours!—somebody else's!"

This was clear enough.

"Only you can separate us," said Emilia, with a brow levelled intently.

"Well, and I—" Mr. Pole was pursuing in the gusty energy of his previous explanation. His eyes met Emilia's, gravely widening. "I—I'm very sorry," he broke down: "upon my soul, I am!"

The old man went to the mantel-piece and leaned his elbow before the glass.

Emilia's bosom began to rise again.

She was startled to hear him laugh. A slight melancholy little burst; and then a louder one, followed by a full-toned laughter that fell short and showed the heart was not in it.

"That boy Braintop! What fun it was!" he said, looking all the while into the glass. "Why can't we live in peace, and without bother! Is your candle alight, my dear?"

Emilia now thought that he was practising evasion.

"I will light it," she said.

Mr. Pole gave a wearied sigh. His head being still turned to the glass, he listened with a shrouded face for her movements: saying, "Good night; good night; I'll light my own. There's a dear!"

A shouting was in his ears, which seemed to syllable distinctly: "If she goes at once, I'm safe."

The sight of pain at all was intolerable to him; but he had a prophetic physical warning now that to witness pain inflicted by himself would be more than he could endure.

Emilia breathed a low, "Good night."

"Good night, my love—all right to-morrow!" he replied briskly; and remorse touching his kind heart as the music of her 'good night' penetrated to it by thrilling avenues, he added injudiciously: "Don't fret. We'll see what we can do. Soon make matters comfortable."

"I love you, and I know you will not stab me," she answered.

"No; certainly not," said Mr. Pole, still keeping his back to her.

Struck with a sudden anticipating fear of having to go through this scene on the morrow, he continued: "No misunderstands, mind! Wilfrid's done with."

There was a silence. He trusted she might be gone. Turning round, he faced her; the light of the candle throwing her pale visage into ghostly relief.

"Where is sleep for you if you part us?"

Mr. Pole flung up his arms. "I insist upon your going to bed. Why shouldn't I sleep? Child's folly!"

Though he spoke so, his brain was in strings to his timorous ticking nerves; and he thought that it would be well to propitiate her and get her to utter some words that would not haunt his pillow.

"My dear girl! it's not my doing. I like you. I wish you well and happy. Very fond of you;—blame circumstances, not me." Then he murmured: "Are black spots on the eyelids a bad sign? I see big flakes of soot falling in a dark room."

Emilia's mated look fleeted. "You come between us, sir, because I have no money?"

"I tell you it's the boy's only chance to make his hit now." Mr. Pole stamped his foot angrily.

"And you make my Cornelia marry, though she loves another, as Wilfrid loves me, and if they do not obey you they are to be beggars! Is it you who can pray? Can you ever have good dreams? I saved my father from the sin, by leaving him. He wished to sell me. But my poor father had no money at all, and I can pardon him. Money was a bright thing to him: like other things to us. Mr. Pole! What will any one say for you!"

The unhappy merchant had made vehement efforts to perplex his hearing, that her words might be empty and not future dragons round his couch. He was looking forward to a night of sleep as a cure for the evil sensations besetting him—his only chance. The chance was going; and with the knowledge that it was unjustly torn from him—this one gleam of clear reason in his brain undimmed by the irritable storm which plucked him down—he cried out, to clear himself:—

"They are beggars, both, and all, if they don't marry before two months are out. I'm a beggar then. I'm ruined. I shan't have a penny. I'm in a workhouse. They are in good homes. They are safe, and thank their old father. Now, then; now. Shall I sleep?"

Emilia caught his staggering arm. The glazed light of his eyes went out. He sank into a chair; white as if life had issued with the secret of his life. Wonderful varying expressions had marked his features and the tones of his voice, while he was uttering that sharp, succinct confession; so that, strange as it sounded, every sentence fixed itself on her with incontrovertible force, and the meaning of the whole flashed through her mind. It struck her too awfully for speech. She held fast to his nerveless hand, and kneeling before him, listened for his long reluctant breathing.

The 'Shall I sleep?' seemed answered.

CHAPTER XXVII

SMALL LIFE AT BROOKFIELD

For days after the foregoing scene, Brookfield was unconscious of what had befallen it. Wilfrid was trying his yacht, the ladies were preparing for the great pleasure-gathering on Besworth lawn, and shaping astute designs to exclude the presence of Mrs. Chump, for which they partly condemned themselves; but, as they said, "Only hear her!" The excitable woman was swelling from conjecture to certainty on a continuous public cry of, "'Pon my hon'r!—d'ye think little Belloni's gone and marrud Pole?"

Emilia's supposed flight had deeply grieved the ladies, when alarm and suspicion had subsided. Fear of some wretched male baseness on the part of their brother was happily diverted by a letter, wherein he desired them to come to him speedily. They attributed her conduct to dread of Mr. Pericles. That fervid devotee of Euterpe received the tidings with an obnoxious outburst, which made them seriously ask themselves (individually and in secret) whether he was not a moneyed brute, and nothing more. Nor could they satisfactorily answer the question. He raved: "You let her go. Ha! what creatures you are— hein? But you find not anozer in fifty years, I say; and here you stop, and forty hours pass by, and not a sing in motion. What blood you have! It is water—not blood. Such a voice, a verve, a style, an eye, a devil, zat girl! and all drawn up and out before ze time by a man: she is spoilt!"

He exhibited an anguish that they were not able to commiserate. Certain expressions falling from him led them to guess that he had set some plot in motion, which Emilia's flight had arrested; but his tragic outcries were all on the higher ground of the loss to Art. They were glad to see him go from the house. Soon he returned to demand Wilfrid's address. Arabella wrote it out for him with rebuking composure. Then he insisted upon having Captain Gambier's, whom he described as "ce nonchalant dandy."

"Him you will have a better opportunity of seeing by waiting here," said Adela; and the captain came before Mr. Pericles had retreated. "Ce nonchalant" was not quite true to his title, when he heard that Emilia had flown. He did not say much, but iterated "Gone!" with an elegant frown, adding, "She must come back, you know!" and was evidently more than commonly puzzled and vexed, pursuing the strain in a way that satisfied Mr. Pericles more thoroughly than Adela.

"She shall come back as soon as she has a collar," growled Mr. Pericles, meaning captivity.

"If she'd only come back with her own maiden name," interjected Mrs. Chump, "I'll give her a character; but, upon my hon'r—d'ye think ut possible, now...?"

Arabella talked over her, and rescued her father's name.

The noisy sympathy and wild speculations of the Tinleys and Copleys had to be endured. On the whole, the feeling toward Emilia was kind, and the hope that she would come to no harm was fervently expressed by all the ladies; frequently enough, also, to show the opinion that it might easily happen. On such points Mrs. Chump never failed to bring the conversation to a block. Supported as they were by Captain Gambier, Edward Buxley, Freshfield Sumner, and more than once by Sir Twickenham (whom Freshfield, launching angry shafts, now called the semi-betrothed, the statistical cripple, and other strong things that show a developing genius for street-cries and hustings—epithets in every member of the lists of the great Rejected, or of the jilted who can affect to be philosophical), notwithstanding these aids, the ladies of Brookfield were crushed by Mrs. Chump. Her main offence was, that she revived for them so much of themselves that they had buried. "Oh! the unutterably sordid City life!" It hung about her like a smell of London smoke. As a mere animal, they passed her by, and had almost come to a state of mind to pass her off. It was the phantom, or rather the embodiment of their First Circle, that they hated in the woman. She took heroes from the journals read by servant-maids; she thought highly of the Court of Aldermen; she went on public knees to the aristocracy; she was proud, in fact, of all City appetites. What, though none saw the peculiar sting? They felt it; and one virtue in possessing an 'ideal' is that, lodging in you as it does, it insists upon the interior being furnished by your personal satisfaction, and not by the blindness or stupidity of the outer world. Thus, in one direction, an ideal precludes humbug. The ladies might desire to cloak facts, but they had no pleasure in deception. They had the feminine power of extinguishing things disagreeable, so long as nature or the fates did them no violence. When these forces sent an emissary to confound them, as was clearly the case with Mrs. Chump, they fought. The dreadful creature insisted upon shows of maudlin affection that could not be accorded to her, so that she existed in a condition of preternatural sensitiveness. Among ladies pretending to dignity of life, the horror of acrid complaints alternating with public offers of love from a gross woman, may be pictured in the mind's eye. The absence of Mr. Pole and Wilfrid, which caused Mrs. Chump to chafe at the restraint imposed by the presence of males to whom she might not speak endearingly, and deprived the ladies of proper counsel, and what good may be at times in masculine authority, led to one fierce battle, wherein the great shot was fired on both sides. Mrs. Chump was requested to leave the house: she declined. Interrogated as to whether she remained as an enemy, knowing herself to be so looked upon, she said that she remained to save them from the dangers they invited. Those dangers she named, observing that Mrs. Lupin, their aunt, might know them, but was as liable to be sent to sleep by a fellow with a bag of jokes as a watchdog to be quieted by a bone. The allusion here was to Mrs. Lupin's painful, partially inexcusable, incurable sense of humour, especially when a gleam of it led to the prohibited passages of life. The poor lady was afflicted so keenly that, in instances where one of her sex and position in the social scale is bound to perish rather than let even the shadow of a laugh appear, or any sign of fleshly perception or sympathy peep out, she was seen to be mutely, shockingly, penitentially convulsed: a degrading sight. And albeit repeatedly remonstrated with, she, upon such occasions, invariably turned imploring glances—a sort of frowning entreaty—to the ladies, or to any of her sex present. "Did you not see that? Oh! can you resist it?" she seemed to gasp, as she made those fruitless efforts to drag them to her conscious level. "Sink thou, if thou wilt," was the phrase indicated to her. She had once thought her propensity innocent enough, and enjoyable. Her nieces had almost cured her, by sitting on her, until Mrs. Chump came to make her worst than ever. It is to be feared that Mrs. Chump was beginning to abuse her power over the little colourless lady. We cannot, when we find ourselves possessed of the gift of sending a creature into convulsions, avoid exercising it. Mrs. Lupin was one of the victims of the modern feminine 'ideal.' She was in mind merely a woman; devout and charitable, as her nieces admitted; but radically—what? They did not like to think, or to say, what;—repugnant, seemed to be the word. A woman who consented to perceive the double-meaning, who acknowledged its suggestions of a violation of decency laughable, and who could not restrain laughter, was, in their judgement, righteously a victim. After signal efforts to lift her up, the verdict was that their Aunt Lupin did no credit to her sex. If we conceive a timorous little body of finely-strung nerves, inclined to be gay, and shrewdly apprehensive, but depending for her opinion of herself upon those about her, we shall see that Mrs. Lupin's life was one of sorrow and scourges in the atmosphere of the 'ideal.' Never did nun of the cloister fight such a fight with the flesh, as this poor little woman, that she might not give offence to the Tribunal of the Nice Feelings which leads us to ask, "Is sentimentalism in our modern days taking the place of monasticism to mortify our poor humanity?" The sufferings of the Three of Brookfield under Mrs. Chump was not comparable to Mrs. Lupin's. The good little woman's soul withered at the self-contempt to which her nieces helped her daily. Laughter, far from expanding her heart and invigorating her frame, was a thing that she felt herself to be nourishing as a traitor in her bosom: and the worst was, that it came upon her like a reckless intoxication at times, possessing her as a devil might; and justifying itself, too, and daring to say, "Am I not Nature?" Mrs. Lupin shrank from the remembrance of those moments.

In another age, the scenes between Mrs. Lupin and Mrs. Chump, greatly significant for humanity as they are, will be given without offence on one side or martyrdom on the other. At present, and before our sentimentalists are a concrete, it would be profitless rashness to depict them. When the great shots were fired off (Mrs. Chump being requested to depart, and refusing) Mrs. Lupin fluttered between the belligerents, doing her best to be a medium for the restoration of peace. In repeating Mrs. Chump's remarks, which were rendered purposely strong with Irish spice by that woman, she choked; and when she conveyed to Mrs. Chump the counter-remarks of the ladies, she provoked utterances that almost killed her. A sadder life is not to be imagined. The perpetual irritation of a desire to indulge in her mortal weakness, and listening to the sleepless conscience that kept watch over it; her certainty that it would be better for her to laugh right out, and yet her incapacity to contest the justice of her nieces' rebuke; her struggle to resist Mrs. Chump, which ended in a sensation of secret shameful liking for her—all these warring influences within were seen in her behaviour.

"I have always said," observed Cornelia, "that she labours under a disease." What is more, she had always told Mrs. Lupin as much, and her sisters had echoed her. Three to one in such a case is a severe trial to the reason of solitary one. And Mrs. Lupin's case was peculiar, inasmuch as the more she yielded to Chump-temptation and eased her heart of its load of laughter, the more her heart cried out against her and subscribed to the scorn of her nieces. Mrs. Chump acted a demon's part; she thirsted for Mrs. Lupin that she might worry her. Hitherto she had not known that anything peculiar lodged in her tongue, and with no other person did she think of using it to produce a desired effect; but now the scenes in Brookfield became hideous to the ladies, and not wanting in their trials to the facial muscles of the gentlemen. A significant sign of what the ladies were enduring was, that they ceased to speak of it in their consultations. It is a blank period in the career of young creatures when a fretting wretchedness forces them out of their dreams to action; and it is then that they will do things that, seen from the outside (i.e. in the conduct of others), they would hold to be monstrous, all but impossible. Or how could Cornelia persuade herself, as she certainly persuaded Sir Twickenham and the world about her, that she had a contemplative pleasure in his society? Arabella drew nearer to Edward Buxley, whom she had not treated well, and who, as she might have guessed, had turned his thoughts toward Adela; though clearly without encouragement. Adela indeed said openly to her sisters, with a Gallic ejaculation, "Edward follows me, do you know; and he has adopted a sort of Sicilian-vespers look whenever he meets me with Captain Gambier. I could forgive him if he would draw out a dagger and be quite theatrical; but, behold, we meet, and my bourgeois grunts and stammers, and seems to beg us to believe that he means nothing whatever by his behaviour. Can you convey to his City-intelligence that he is just a trifle ill-bred?"

Now, Arabella had always seen Edward as a thing that was her own, which accounts for the treatment to which, he had been subjected. A quick spur of jealousy—a new sensation—was the origin of her leaning toward Edward; and the plea of saving Adela from annoyance excused and covered it. He, for his part, scarcely concealed his irritation, until a little scented twisted note was put in his hand, which said, "You are as anxious as I can be about our sweet lost Emilia! We believe ourselves to be on her traces." This gave him wonderful comfort. It put Adela in a beautiful fresh light as a devoted benefactress and delicious intriguante. He threw off some of his most telling caricatures at this period. Adela had divined that Captain Gambier suspected his cousin Merthyr Powys of abstracting Emilia, that he might shield her from Mr. Pericles. The Captain confessed it, calmly blushing, and that he was in communication with Miss Georgiana Ford, Mr. Powys's half-sister; about whom Adela was curious, until the Captain ejaculated, "A saint!"—whereat she was satisfied, knowing by instinct that the preference is for sinners. Their meetings usually referred to Emilia; and it was astonishing how willingly the Captain would talk of her. Adela repeated to herself, "This is our mask," and thus she made it the Captain's; for it must be said that the conquering Captain had never felt so full of pity to any girl or woman to whom he fancied he had done damage, as to Emilia. He enjoyed a most thorough belief that she was growing up to perplex him with her love, and he had not consequently attempted to precipitate the measure; but her flight had prematurely perplexed him. In grave debate with the ends of his moustache for a term, he concluded by accusing Merthyr Powys; and with a little feeling of spite not unknown to masculine dignity, he wrote to Merthyr's half-sister—"merely to inquire, being aware that whatever he does you have been consulted on, and the friends of this Miss Belloni are distressed by her absence."

The ladies of Brookfield were accustomed to their father's occasional unpremeditated absences, and neither of them had felt an apprehension which she could not dismiss, until one morning Mr. Powys sent up his card to Arabella, requesting permission to speak with her alone.

CHAPTER XXVIII

GEORGIANA FORD

Georgiana Ford would have had little claim among the fair saints to be accepted by them as one of their order. Her reputation for coldness was derived from the fact of her having stood a siege from Captain Gambier. But she loved a creature of earth too well to put up a hand for saintly honours. The passion of her life centred in devotion to her half-brother. Those who had studied her said, perhaps with a touch of malignity, that her religious instinct had its source in a desire to gain some place of intercession for him. Merthyr had leaned upon it too often to doubt the strength of it, whatever its purity might be. She, when barely more than a child (a girl of sixteen), had followed him over the then luckless Italian fields— sacrificing as much for a cause that she held to be trivial, as he in the ardour of his half-fanatical worship. Her theory was: "These Italians are in bondage, and since heaven permits it, there has been guilt. By endurance they are strengthened, by suffering chastened; so let them endure and suffer." She would cleave to this view with many variations of pity. Merthyr's experience was tolerant to the weaker vessel's young delight in power, which makes her sometimes, though sweet and merciful by nature, enunciate Hebraic severities oracularly. He smiled, and was never weary of pointing out practical refutations. Whereat she said, "Will a thousand instances change the principle?" When the brain, and especially the fine brain of a woman, first begins to act for itself, the work is of heavy labour; she finds herself plunging abroad on infinite seas, and runs speedily into the anchorage of dogmas, obfuscatory saws, and what she calls principles. Here she is safe; but if her thinking was not originally the mere action of lively blood upon that battery of intelligence, she will by-and-by reflect that it is not well for a live thing to be tied to a dead, and that long clinging to safety confesses too much. Merthyr waited for Georgians patiently. On all other points they were heart-in-heart. It was her pride to say that she loved him with no sense of jealousy, and prayed that he might find a woman, in plain words, worthy of him. This woman had not been found; she confessed that she had never seen her.

Georgians received Captain Gambier's communication in Monmouth. Merthyr had now and then written of a Miss Belloni; but he had seemed to refer to a sort of child, and Georgians had looked on her as another Italian pensioner. She was decisive. The moment she awoke to feel herself brooding over the thought of this girl, she started to join Merthyr. Solitude is pasturage for a suspicion. On her way she grew persuaded that her object was bad, and stopped; until the thought came, 'If he is in a dilemma, who shall help him save his sister?' And, with spiritually streaming eyes at a vision of companionship broken (but whether by his taking another adviser, or by Miss Belloni, she did not ask), Georgiana continued her journey.

At the door of Lady Gosstre's town-house she hesitated, and said in her mind, "What am I doing? and what earthliness has come into my love for him?"

Or, turning to the cry, "Will he want me?" stung herself. Conscious that there was some poison in her love, but clinging to it not less, she entered the house, and was soon in Merthyr's arms.

"Why have you come up?" he asked.

"Were you thinking of coming to me quickly?" she murmured in reply.

He did not say yes, but that he had business in London. Nor did he say what.

Georgiana let him go.

"How miserable is such a weakness! Is this my love?" she thought again.

Then she went to her bedroom, and knelt, and prayed her Saviour's pardon for loving a human thing too well. But, if the rays of her mind were dimmed, her heart beat too forcibly for this complacent self-deceit. "No; not too well! I cannot love him too well. I am selfish. When I say that, it is myself I am loving. To love him thrice as dearly as I do would bring me nearer to God. Love I mean, not idolatry— another form of selfishness."

She prayed to be guided out of the path of snares.

"CAN YOU PRAY? CAN YOU PUT AWAY ALL PROPS OF SELF? THIS IS TRUE WORSHIP, UNTO WHATSOEVER POWER YOU KNEEL."

This passage out of a favourite book of sentences had virtue to help her now in putting away the 'props of self.' It helped her for the time. She could not foresee the contest that was commencing for her.

"LOVE THAT SHRIEKS AT A MORTAL WOUND, AND BLEEDS HUMANLY, WHAT IS HE BUT A PAGAN GOD, WITH THE PASSIONS OF A PAGAN GOD?"

"Yes," thought Georgiana, meditating, "as different from the Christian love as a brute from a man!"

She felt that the revolution of the idea of love in her mind (all that consoled her) was becoming a temptation. Quick in her impulses, she dismissed it. "I am like a girl!" she said scornfully. "Like a woman" would not have flattered her. Like what did she strive to be? The picture of another self was before her—a creature calmly strong, unruffled, and a refuge to her beloved. It was a steady light through every wind that blew, save when the heart narrowed; and then it waxed feeble, and the life in her was hungry for she knew not what.

Georgiana's struggle was to make her great passion eat up all the others. Sure of the intensity and thoroughness of her love for Merthyr, she would forecast for herself tasks in his service impossible save to one sensually dead and therefore spiritually sexless. "My love is pure," she would say; as if that were the talisman which rendered it superhuman. She was under the delusion that lovers' love was a reprehensible egoism. Her heart had never had place for it; and thus her nature was unconsummated, and the torment of a haunting insufficiency accompanied her sweetest hours, ready to mislead her in all but very clearest actions.

She saw, or she divined, much of this struggle; but the vision of it was fitful, not consecutive. It frightened and harassed without illuminating her. Now, upon Merthyr's return, she was moved by it just enough to take his hand and say:—

"We are the same?"

"What can change us?" he replied.

"Or who?" and as she smiled up to him, she was ashamed of her smile.

"Yes, who!" he interjected, by this time quite enlightened. All subtle feelings are discerned by Welsh eyes when untroubled by any mental agitation. Brother and sister were Welsh, and I may observe that there is human nature and Welsh nature.

"Forgive me," she said; "I have been disturbed about you."

Perceiving that it would be well to save her from any spiritual twists and turns that she might reach what she desired to know, he spoke out fully: "I have not written to you about Miss Belloni lately. I think it must be seven or eight days since I had a letter from her—you shall see it—looking as if it had been written in the dark. She gave the address of a London hotel. I went to her, and her story was that she had come to town to get Mr. Pole's consent to her marriage with his son; and that when she succeeded in making herself understood by him, the old man fell, smitten with paralysis, crying out that he was ruined, and his children beggars."

"Ah!" said Georgiana; "then this son is engaged to her?"

"She calls him her lover."

"Openly?"

"Have I not told you? 'naked and unashamed.'"

"Of course that has attracted my Merthyr!" Georgians drew to him tenderly, breathing as one who has a burden off her heart.

"But why did she write to you?" the question started up.

For this reason: it appears that Mr. Pole showed such nervous irritation at the idea of his family knowing the state he was in, that the doctor attending him exacted a promise from her not to communicate with one of them. She was alone, in great perplexity, and did what I had requested her to do. She did me the honour to apply to me for any help it was in my power to give.

Georgiana stood eyeing the ground sideways. "What is she like?"

"You shall see to-morrow, if you will come with me."

"Dark, or fair?"

Merthyr turned her face to the light, laughing softly. Georgiana coloured, with dropped eyelids.

She raised her eyes under their load of shame. "I will come gladly," she said.

"Early to-morrow, then," rejoined Merthyr.

On the morrow, as they were driving to the hotel, Georgians wanted to know whether he called 'this Miss Belloni' by her Christian name—a question so needless that her over-conscious heart drummed with gratitude when she saw that he purposely spared her from one meaning look. In this mutual knowledge, mutual help, in minute as in great things, as well as in the recognition of a common nobility of mind, the love of the two was fortified.

Emilia had not been left by Mr. Powys without the protection of a woman's society in her singular position. Lady Charlotte's natural prompt kindness required no spur from her friend that she should go and brace up the spirits of a little woman, whom she pitied doubly for loving a man who was deceiving her, and not loving one who was good for her. She went frequently to Emilia, and sat with her in the sombre hotel drawing-room. Still, frank as she was and blunt as she affected to be, she could not bring her tongue to speak of Wilfrid. If she had fancied any sensitive shuddering from the name and the subject to exist, she would have struck boldly, being capable of cruelty and, where she was permitted to see a weakness, rather fond of striking deep. A belief in the existence of Emilia's courage touched her to compassion. One day, however, she said, "What is it you take to in Merthyr Powys?" and this brought on plain speaking.

Emilia could give no reason; and it is a peculiarity of people who ask such questions that they think a want of directness in the answer suspicious.

Lady Charlotte said gravely, "Come, come!"

"What do you mean?" asked Emilia. "I like so many things in him."

"You don't like one thing chiefly?"

"I like—what do I like?—his kindness."

"His kindness!" This was the sort of reply to make the lady implacable. She seldom read others shrewdly, and could not know, that near her, Emilia thought of Wilfrid in a way that made the vault of her brain seem to echo with jarred chords. "His kindness! What a picture is the 'grateful girl!' I have seen rows of white-capped charity children giving a bob and a sniffle as the parson went down the ranks promising buns. Well! his kindness! You are right in appreciating as much as you can see. I'll tell you why I like him;—because he is a gentleman. And you haven't got an idea how rare that animal is. Dear me! Should I be plainer to you if I called him a Christian gentleman? It's the cant of a detestable school, my child. It means just this—but why should I disturb your future faith in it? The professors mainly profess to be 'a comfort to young women,' and I suppose you will meet your comfort, and worship them with the 'growing mind;' and I must confess that they bait it rather cunningly; nothing else would bite. They catch almost all the raw boys who have anything in them. But for me, Merthyr himself would have been caught long ago. There's no absolute harm in them, only that they're a sentimental compromise. I deny their honesty; and if it's flatly proved, I deny their intelligence. Well! this you can't understand."

"I have not understood you at all," said Emilia.

"No? It's the tongue that's the natural traitor to a woman, and takes longer runs with every added year. I suppose you know that Mr. Powys wishes to send you to Italy?"

"I do," said Emilia.

"When are you going?"

"I am not going?"

"Why?"

Emilia's bosom rose. She cried "Dear lady!" on the fall of it, and was scarce audible—adding, "Do you love Wilfrid?"

"Well, you have brought me to the point quickly," Lady Charlotte remarked. "I don't commonly beat the bush long myself. Love him! You might as well ask me my age. The indiscretion would be equal, and the result the same. Love! I have a proper fear of the word. When two play at love they spoil the game. It's enough that he says he loves me."

Emilia looked relieved. "Poor lady!" she sighed.

"Poor!" Lady Charlotte echoed, with curious eyes fixed on the puzzle beside her.

"Tell me you will not believe him," Emilia continued. "He is mine; I shall never give him up. It is useless for you or any one else to love him. I know what love is now. Stop while you can. I can be sorry for you, but I will not let him go from me. He is my lover."

Emilia closed her lips abruptly. She produced more effect than was visible. Lady Charlotte drew out a letter, saying, "Perhaps this will satisfy you."

"Nothing!" cried Emilia, jumping to her feet.

"Read it—read it; and, for heaven's sake, ma fille sauvage, don't think I'm here to fight for the man! He is not Orpheus; and our modern education teaches us that it's we who are to be run after. Will you read it?"

"No."

"Will you read it to please me?"

Emilia changed from a look of quiet opposition to gentleness of feature. "Why will it please you if I read that he has flattered you? I never lie about what I feel; I think men do." Her voice sank.

"You won't allow yourself to imagine, then, that he has spoken false to you?"

"Tell me," retorted Emilia, "are you sure in your heart—as sure as it beats each time—that he loves you? You are not."

"It seems that we are dignifying my gentleman remarkably," said Lady Charlotte. "When two women fight for a man, that is almost a meal for his vanity. Now, listen. I am not, as they phrase it, in love. I am an experienced person—what is called a woman of the world. I should not make a marriage unless I had come to the conclusion that I could help my husband, or he me. Do me the favour to read this letter."

Emilia took it and opened it slowly. It was a letter in the tone of the gallant paying homage with some fervour. Emilia searched every sentence for the one word. That being absent, she handed back the letter, her eyes lingering on the signature.

"Do you see what he says?" asked Lady Charlotte; "that I can be a right hand to him, as I believe I can."

"He writes like a friend." Emilia uttered this as when we have a contrast in the mind.

"You excuse him for writing to me in that style?"

"Yes; he may write to any woman like that."

"He has latitude! You really fancy that's the sort of letter a friend would write?"

"That is how Mr. Powys would write to me," said Emilia. Lady Charlotte laughed. "My unhappy Merthyr!"

"Only if I could be a great deal older," Emilia hastened to add; and Lady Charlotte slightly frowned, but rubbed it out with a smile.

Rising, the lady said: "I have spoken to you upon equal terms; and remember, very few women would have done what I have done. You are cared for by Merthyr Powys, and that's enough. It would do you no harm to fix your eyes upon him. You won't get him; but it would do you no harm. He has a heart, as they call it; whatever it is, it's as strong as a cable. He is a knight of the antique. He is specially guarded, however. Well, he insists that you are his friend; so you are mine, and that is why I have come to you and spoken to you. You will be silent about it, I need not say. No one but yourself is aware that Lieutenant Pole does me the honour to liken me to the good old gentleman who accompanied Telemachus in his voyages, and chooses me from among the handmaidens of earth. On this head you will promise to be silent."

Lady Charlotte held forth her hand. Emilia would not take it before she had replied, "I knew this before you came," and then she pressed the extended fingers.

Lady Charlotte drew her close. "Has Wilfrid taken you into his confidence so far?"

Emilia explained that she had heard it from his father.

The lady's face lit up as from a sting of anger. "Very well—very well," she said; and, presently, "You are right when you speak of the power of lying in men. Observe—Wilfrid told me that not one living creature knew there was question of an engagement between us. What would you do in my case?"

Emilia replied, "Forgive him; and I should think no more of it."

"Yes. It would be right; and, presuming him to have the vice, I could be of immense service to him, if at least he does not lie habitually. But this is a description of treachery, you know."

"Oh!" cried Emilia, "what kind of treachery is that, if he only will keep his heart open for me to give all mine to it!"

She stood clutching her hands in the half-sobbing ecstasy which signalises a spiritual exaltation built on disquiet. She had shown small emotion hitherto. The sight of it was like the sight of a mighty hostile power to Lady Charlotte—a power that moved her—that challenged, and irritated, and subdued her. For she saw there something that she had not; and being of a nature leaning to great-mindedness, though not of the first rank, she could not meanly mask her own deficiency by despising it. To do this is the secret evil by which souls of men and women stop their growth.

Lady Charlotte decided now to say good-bye. Her parting was friendly—the form of it consisting of a nod, an extension of the hand, and a kind word or two.

When alone, Emilia wondered why she kept taking long breaths, and tried to correct herself: but the heart laboured. Yet she seemed to have no thought in her mind; she had no active sensation of pity or startled self-love. She went to smooth Mr. Pole's pillow, as to a place of forgetfulness. The querulous tyrannies of the invalid relieved her; but the heavy lifting of her chest returned the moment she was alone. She mentioned it to the doctor, who prescribed for liver, informing her that the said organ conducted one of the most important functions of her bodily system.

Emilia listened to the lecturer, and promised to take his medicine, trusting to be perfectly quieted by the nauseous draught; but when Mr. Powys came, she rushed up to him, and fell with a cry upon his breast, murmuring broken words that Georgiana might fairly interpret as her suspicions directed. Nor had she ever seen Merthyr look as he did when their eyes next met.

CHAPTER XXIX

FIRST SCOURGING OF THE FINE SHADES

The card of Mr. Powys found Arabella alone in the house. Mrs. Lupin was among village school-children; Mrs. Chump had gone to London to see whether anything was known of Mr. Pole at his office, where she fell upon the youth Braintop, and made him her own for the day. Adela was out in the woods, contemplating nature; and Cornelia was supposed to be walking whither her stately fancy drew her.

"Will you take long solitary walks unprotected?" she was asked.

"I have a parasol," she replied; and could hear, miles distant, the domestic comments being made on her innocence; and the story it would be—"She thinks of no possible danger but from the sun."

A little forcing of her innocence now was necessary as an opiate for her conscience. She was doing what her conscience could only pardon on the plea of her extreme innocence. The sisters, and the fashion at Brookfield, permitted the assumption, and exaggerated it willingly. It chanced, however, that Adela had reason to feel discontented. It was a breach of implied contract, she thought, that Cornelia should, as she did only yesterday, tell her that she had seen Edward Buxley in the woods, and that she was of opinion that the air of the woods was bad for her. Not to see would have been the sisterly obligation, in Adela's idea—especially when seeing embraced things that no loving sister should believe.

Bear in mind that we are sentimentalists. The eye is our servant, not our master; and—so are the senses generally. We are not bound to accept more than we choose from them. Thus we obtain delicacy; and thus, as you will perceive, our civilization, by the aid of the sentimentalists, has achieved an effective varnish. There, certainly, to the vulgar, mind a tail is visible. The outrageous philosopher declares vehemently that no beast of the field or the forest would own such a tail. (His meaning is, that he discerns the sign of the animal slinking under the garb of the stately polished creature. I have all the difficulty in the world to keep him back and let me pursue my course.) These philosophers are a bad-mannered body. Either in opposition, or in the support of them, I maintain simply that the blinking sentimentalist helps to make civilization what it is, and civilization has a great deal of merit.

"Did you not leave your parasol behind you at Ipley?" said Adela, as she met Cornelia in the afternoon.

Cornelia coloured. Her pride supported her, and she violated fine shades painfully in her response: "Mr. Barrett left me there. Is that your meaning?"

Adela was too much shocked to note the courageousness of the reply. "Well! if all we do is to come into broad daylight!" was her horrified mental ejaculation.

The veil of life was about to be lifted for these ladies. They found Arabella in her room, crying like an unchastened school-girl; and their first idea was one of intense condemnation—fresh offences on the part of Mrs. Chump being conjectured. Little by little Arabella sobbed out what she had heard that day from Mr. Powys.

After the first stupor Adela proposed to go to her father instantly, and then suggested that they should all go. She continued talking in random suggestions, and with singular heat, as if she conceived that the sensibility of her sisters required to be aroused. By moving and acting, it seemed to her that the prospect of a vast misery might be expunged, and that she might escape from showing any likeness to Arabella's shamefully-discoloured face. It was impossible for her to realize grief in her own bosom. She walked the room in a nervous tremour, shedding a note of sympathy to one sister and to the other. At last Arabella got fuller command of her voice. When she had related that her father's positive wish, furthered by the doctor's special injunction to obey it scrupulously, was that they were not to go to him in London, and not to breathe a word of his illness, but to remain at Brookfield entertaining friends, Adela stamped her foot, saying that it was more than human nature could bear.

"If we go," said Arabella, "the London doctor assured Mr. Powys that he would not answer for papa's life."

"But, good heavens! are we papa's enemies? And why may Mr. Powys see him if we, his daughters, cannot? Tell me how Mr. Powys met him and knew of it! Tell me—I am bewildered. I feel that we are cheated in some way. Oh! tell me something clear."

Arabella said calmingly: "Emilia is with papa. She wrote to Mr. Powys. Whether she did rightly or not we have not now to inquire. I believe that she thought it right."

"Entertain friends!" interjected Adela. "But papa cannot possibly mean that we are to go through—to—the fete on Besworth Lawn, Bella! It's in two days from this dreadful day."

"Papa has mentioned it to Mr. Powys; he desires us not to postpone it. We..." Arabella's voice broke piteously.

"Oh! but this is torture!" cried Adela, with a deplorable vision of the looking-glass rising before her, as she felt the tears sting her eyelids. "This cannot be! No father would...not loving us as dear papa does! To be quiet! to sit and be gay! to flaunt at a fete! Oh, mercy! mercy! Tell me—he left us quite well—no one could have guessed. I remember he looked at me from the carriage window. Tell me—it must be some moral shock—what do you attribute it to? Wilfrid cannot be the guilty one. We have been only too compliant to papa's wishes about that woman. Tell me what you think it can be!"

A voice said, "Money!"

Which of the sisters had spoken Adela did not know. It was bitter enough that one could be brought to utter the thing, even if her ideas were so base as to suspect it. The tears now came dancing over her under-lids like triumphing imps. "Money!" echoed through her again and again. Curiously, too, she had no occasion to ask how it was that money might be supposed to have operated on her father's health. Unable to realize to herself the image of her father lying ill and suffering, but just sufficiently touched by what she could conceive of his situation, the bare whisper of money came like a foul insult to overwhelm her in floods of liquid self-love. She wept with that last anguish of a woman who is compelled to weep, but is incapable of finding any enjoyment in her tears. Cornelia and Arabella caught her hands; she was the youngest, and had been their pet. It gratified them that Adela should show a deep and keen feeling. Adela did not check herself from a demonstration that enabled her to look broadly, as it were, on her own tenderness of heart. Following many outbursts, she asked, "And the illness—what is it? not its cause—itself!"

A voice said, "Paralysis!"

Adela's tears stopped. She gazed on both faces, trying with open mouth to form the word.

CHAPTER XXX

OF THE DOUBLE-MAN IN US, AND THE GREAT FIGHT WHEN THESE ARE FULL-GROWN

Flying from port to port to effect an exchange of stewards (the endless occupation of a yacht proprietor), Wilfrid had no tidings from Brookfield. The night before the gathering on Besworth Lawn he went to London and dined at his Club—a place where youths may drink largely of the milk of this world's wisdom. Wilfrid's romantic sentiment was always corrected by an hour at his Club. After dinner he strolled to a not perfectly regulated theatre, in company with a brother officer; and when they had done duty before the scenes for a space of time, they lounged behind to disenchant themselves, in obedience to that precocious cynicism which is the young man's extra-Luxury. The first figure that caught Wilfrid's attention there was Mr. Pericles, in a white overcoat, stretched along a sofa—his eyelids being down, though his eyes were evidently vigilant beneath. A titter of ladies present told of some recent interesting commotion.

"Only a row between that rich Greek fellow who gave the supper, and Marion," a vivacious dame explained to Wilfrid. "She's in one of her jealous fits; she'd be jealous if her poodle-dog went on its hind-legs to anybody else."

"Poodle, by Jove!" said Wilfrid. "Pericles himself looks like an elongated poodle shaved up to his moustache. Look at him. And he plays the tyrant, does he?"

"Oh! she stands that. Some of those absurd women like it, I think. She's fussing about another girl."

"You wouldn't?"

"What man's worth it?"

"But, would you?"

"It depends upon the 'him,' monsieur."

"Depends upon his being very handsome!"

"And good."

"And rich?"

"No!" the lady fired up. "There you don't know us."

The colloquy became almost tender, until she said, "Isn't this gassy, and stifling? I confess I do like a carriage, and Richmond on a Sunday. And then, with two daughters, you know! But what I complain of is her folly in being in love, or something like it, with a rich fellow."

"Love the poor devil—manage the rich, you mean."

"Yes, of course; that makes them both happy."

"It's a method of being charitable to two."

A rather fleshy fairy now entered, and walked straight up to the looking-glass to examine her paint—pronouncedly turning her back to the sofa, where Mr. Pericles still lay at provoking full length. Her panting was ominous of a further explosion.

"Innocent child!" in the mockery of a foreign accent, commenced it; while Wilfrid thought how unjustly and coldly critically he had accused his little Emilia of vulgarity, now that he had this feminine display of it swarming about him.

"Innocent child, indeed! Be as deaf as you like, you shall hear. And sofas are not made for men's dirty boots, in this country. I believe they're all pigs abroad—the men; and the women—cats! Oh! don't open your eyes—don't speak, pray. You're certain I must go when the bell rings. You're waiting for that, you unmanly dog!"

"A pig," Mr. Pericles here ventured to remind her, murmuring as one in a dream.

"A peeg!" she retorted mildly, somewhat mollified by her apparent success. But Mr. Pericles had relapsed into his exasperating composure. The breath of a deliberate and undeserved peacefulness continued to be drawn in by his nostrils.

At the accustomed warning there was an ostentatious rustle of retiring dresses; whereat Mr. Pericles chose to proclaim himself awake. The astute fairy-fury immediately stepped before him.

"Now you can't go on pretending sleep. You shall hear, and everybody shall hear. You know you're a villain! You're a wolf seeking..."

Mr. Pericles waved his hand, and she was caught by the wrist and told that the scene awaited her.

"Let them wait!" she shouted, and, sharpening her cry as she was dragged off, "Dare to take that girl to Italy! I know what that means, with you. An Englishman might mean right—but you! You think you've been dealing with a fool! Why, I can stop this in a minute, and I will. It's you're the fool! Why, I know her father: he plays in the orchestra. I know her name—Belloni!"

Up sprang the Greek like a galvanized corpse; while two violent jerks from the man hauling her out rattled the laugh of triumph which burst from her. At the same time Wilfrid strove forward, with the frown of one still bent listening, and he and Pericles were face to face. The eyebrows of the latter shot up in a lively arch. He made a motion toward the ceremony of 'shake-hands;' but, perceiving no correspondent overture, grinned, "It is warm—ha?"

"You feel the heat? Step outside a minute," said Wilfrid.

"Oh, no!" Mr. Pericles looked pleasantly sagacious. "Ze draught—a cold."

"Will you come?" pursued Wilfrid.

"Many sanks!"

Wilfrid's hand was rising. At this juncture his brother officer slipped out some languid words in his ear, indicative of his astonishment that he should be championing a termagant, and horror at the idea of such a thing being publicly imagined, tamed Wilfrid quickly. He recovered himself with his usual cleverness. Seeing the signs of hostility vanish, Mr. Pericles said, "You are on a search for your father? You have found him? Hom! I should say a maladie of nerfs will come to him. A pin fall—he start! A storm at night—he is out dancing among his ships of venture! Not a bid of corage!—which is bad. If you shall find Mr. Pole for to-morrow on ze lawn, vary glad."

With a smile compounded of sniffing dog and Parisian obsequiousness, Mr. Pericles passed, thinking "He has not got her:" for such was his deduction if he saw that a man could flush for a woman's name.

Wilfrid stood like a machine with a thousand wheels in revolt. Sensations pricked at ideas, and immediately left them to account for their existence as they best could. The ideas committed suicide without a second's consideration. He felt the great gurgling sea in which they were drowned heave and throb. Then came a fresh set, that poised better on the slack-rope of his understanding. By degrees, a buried dread in his brain threw off its shroud. The thought that there was something wrong with his father stood clearly over him, to be swallowed at once in the less tangible belief that a harm had come to Emilia—not was coming, but had come. Passion thinks wilfully when it thinks at all. That night he lay in a deep anguish, revolving the means by which he might help and protect her. There seemed no way open, save by making her his own; and did he belong to himself? What bound him to Lady Charlotte? She was not lovely or loving. He had not even kissed her hand; yet she held him in a chain.

The two men composing most of us at the outset of actual life began their deadly wrestle within him, both having become awakened. If they wait for circumstance, that steady fire will fuse them into one, who is commonly a person of some strength; but throttling is the custom between them, and we are used to see men of murdered halves. These men have what they fought for: they are unaware of any guilt that may be charged against them, though they know that they do not embrace Life; and so it is that we have vague discontent too universal. Change, O Lawgiver! the length of our minority, and let it not end till this battle is thoroughly fought out in approving daylight. The period of our duality should be one as irresponsible in your eyes as that of our infancy. Is he we call a young man an individual—who is a pair of alternately kicking scales? Is he educated, when he dreams not that he is divided? He has drunk Latin like a vital air, and can quote what he remembers of Homer; but how has he been fortified for this tremendous conflict of opening manhood, which is to our life here what is the landing of a soul to the life to come?

Meantime, it is a bad business when the double-man goes about kneeling at the feet of more than one lady. Society (to give that institution its due) permits him to seek partial invulnerability by dipping himself in a dirty Styx, which corrects, as we hear said, the adolescent tendency to folly. Wilfrid's sentiment had served him (well or ill as it may be), by keeping him from a headlong plunge in the protecting river; and his folly was unchastened. He did not even contemplate an escape from the net at Emilia's expense. The idea came. The idea will come to a young man in such a difficulty. "My mistress! My glorious stolen fruit! My dark angel of love!" He deserves a little credit for seeing that Emilia never could be his mistress, in the debased sense of the term. Union with her meant life-long union, he knew. Ultimate mental subjection he may also have seen in it, unconsciously. For, hazy thoughts of that nature may mix with the belief that an alliance with her degrades us, in this curious hotch-potch of emotions known to the world as youthful man. A wife superior to her husband makes him ridiculous wilfully, if the wretch is to be laughed at; but a mistress thus ill-matched cannot fail to cast the absurdest light on her monstrous dwarf-custodian. Wilfrid had the sagacity to perceive, and the keen apprehension of ridicule to shrink from, the picture. Besides, he was beginning to love Emilia. His struggle now was to pluck his passion from his heart; and such was already his plight that he saw no other way of attempting it than by taking horse and riding furiously in the direction of Besworth.

CHAPTER XXXI

BESWORTH LAWN

"I am curious to see what you will make of this gathering. I can cook a small company myself. It requires the powers of a giantess to mix a body of people in the open air; and all that is said of commanders of armies shall be said of you, if you succeed."

This was Lady Gosstre's encouragement to the fair presidents of the fete on Besworth Lawn. There had been a time when they would have cried out internally: "We will do it, fail who may." That fallow hour was over. Their sole thought was to get through the day. A little feverish impulse of rivalry with her great pattern may have moved Arabella; but the pressure of grief and dread, and the contrast between her actions and feelings, forcibly restrained a vain display. As a consequence, she did her duty better, and won applause from the great lady's moveable court on eminences of the ground.

"These girls are clever," she said to Lady Charlotte. "They don't bustle too much. They don't make too distinct a difference of tone with the different sets. I shall propose Miss Pole as secretary to our Pin and Needle Relief Society."

"Do," was the reply. "There is also the Polish Dance Committee; and, if she has any energy left, she might be treasurer to the Ladies' General Revolution Ball."

"That is an association with which I am not acquainted," said Lady Gosstre, directing her eye-glass on the field. "Here comes young Pole. He's gallant, they tell me, and handsome: he studies us too obviously. That's a mistake to be corrected, Charlotte. One doesn't like to see a pair of eyes measuring us against a preconception quelconque. Now, there is our Ionian Am...but you have corrected me, Merthyr:—host, if you please. But, see! What is the man doing? Is he smitten with madness?"

Mr. Pericles had made a furious dash at the band in the centre of the lawn, scattered their music, and knocked over the stands. When his gesticulations had been observed for some moments, Freshfield Sumner said: "He has the look of a plucked hen, who remembers that she once clapped wings, and tries to recover the practice."

"Very good," said Lady Gosstre. She was not one who could be unkind to the professional wit. "And the music-leaves go for feathers. What has the band done to displease him? I thought the playing was good."

"The instruments appear to have received a dismissal," said Lady Charlotte. "I suppose this is a clearing of the stage for coming alarums and excursions. Behold! the 'female element' is agitated. There are— can you reckon at this distance, Merthyr?—twelve, fourteen of my sex entreating him in the best tragic fashion. Can he continue stern?"

"They seem to be as violent as the women who tore up Orpheus," said Lady Gosstre.

Tracy Runningbrook shrieked, in a paroxysm, "Splendid!" from his couch on the sward, and immediately ran off with the idea, bodily.

"Have I stumbled anywhere?" Lady Gosstre leaned to Mr. Powys.

He replied with a satiric sententiousness that told Lady Gosstre what she wanted to know.

"This is the isolated case where a little knowledge is truly dangerous," said Lady Gosstre. "I prohibit girls from any allusion to the classics until they have taken their degree and are warranted not to open the wrong doors. On the whole, don't you think, Merthyr, it's better for women to avoid that pool?"

"And accept what the noble creature chooses to bring to us in buckets," added Lady Charlotte. "What is your opinion, Georgey? I forget: Merthyr has thought you worthy of instruction."

"Merthyr taught me in camp," said Georgians, looking at her brother—her face showing peace and that confirmed calm delight habitual to it. "We found that there are times in war when you can do nothing, and you are feverish to be employed. Then, if you can bring your mind to study, you are sure to learn quickly. I liked nothing better than Latin Grammar."

"Studying Latin Grammar to the tune of great guns must be a new sensation," Freshfield Sumner observed.

"The pleasure is in getting rid of all sensation," said she. "I mean you command it without at all crushing your excitement. You cannot feel a fuller happiness than when you look back on those hours: at least, I speak for myself."

"So," said Lady Gosstre, "Georgey did not waste her time after all, Charlotte."

What the latter thought was: "She could not handle a sword or fire a pistol. Would I have consented to be mere camp-baggage?" Yet no woman admired Georgiana Ford so much. Disappointment vitiated many of Lady Charlotte's first impulses; and not until strong antagonism had thrown her upon her generosity could she do justice to the finer natures about her. There was full life in her veins; and she was hearing the thirty fatal bells that should be music to a woman, if melancholy music; and she had not lived. Time, that sounded in her ears, as it kindled no past, spoke of no future. She was in unceasing rivalry with all of her sex who had a passion, or a fixed affection, or even an employment. A sense that she was wronged by her fate haunted this lady. Rivalry on behalf of a man she would have held mean— she would have plucked it from her bosom at once. She was simply envious of those who in the face of death could say, "I have lived." Pride, and the absence of any power of self-inspection, kept her blind to her disease. No recollection gave her boy save of the hours in the hunting-field. There she led gallantly; but it was not because of leading that she exulted. There the quick blood struck on her brain like wine, and she seemed for a time to have some one among the crowns of life. An object—who cared how small?—was ahead: a poor old fox trying to save his brush; and Charlotte would have it if the master of cunning did not beat her. "It's my natural thirst for blood," she said. She did not laugh as she thought now and then that the old red brush dragging over grey dews toward a yellow yolk in the curdled winter-morning sky, was the single thing that could make her heart throb.

Brookfield was supported in its trial by the discomfiture of the Tinleys. These girls, with their brother, had evidently plotted to 'draw out' Mrs. Chump. They had asked concerning her, severally; and hearing that she had not returned from town, had each shown a blank face, or had been doubtful of the next syllable. Of Wilfrid, Emilia, and Mr. Pole, question and answer were interchanged. "Wilfrid will come in a few minutes. Miss Belloni, you know, is preparing for Italy. Papa? Papa, I really do fear will not be able to join us." Such was Brookfield's concerted form of reply. The use of it, together with the gaiety of dancing blood, gave Adela (who believed that she ought to be weeping, and could have wept easily) strange twitches of what I would ask permission to call the juvenile 'shrug-philosophy.' As thus: 'What creatures we are, but life is so!' And again, 'Is not merriment dreadful when a duty!' She was as miserable as she could be but not knowing that youth furnished a plea available, the girl was ashamed of being cheerful at all. Edward Burley's sketch of Mr. Pericles scattering his band, sent her into muffled screams of laughter; for which she did internal penance so bitter that, for her to be able to go on at all, the shrug-philosophy was positively necessary; Mr. Pericles himself saw the sketch, and remarked critically, "It is zat I have more hair:" following which, he tapped the signal for an overture to commence, and at the first stroke took a run, with his elbows clapping exactly as the shrewd hand of Edward had drawn him.

"See him—zat fellow," Mr. Pericles said to Laura Tinley, pointing to the leader. "See him pose a maestro! zat leads zis tintamarre. He is a hum-a-bug!"

Laura did the vocal caricaturing, when she had gathered plenty of matter of this kind. Altogether, as host, Mr. Pericles accomplished his duty in furnishing amusement.

Late in the afternoon, Sir Twickenham Pryme and Wilfrid arrived in company. The baronet went straight to Cornelia. Wilfrid beckoned to Adela, from whom he heard of his father's illness at the hotel in town, and the conditions imposed on them. He nodded, said lightly, "Where's Emilia?" and nodded again to the answer, "With papa," and then stopped as he was walking off to one of the groups. "After all, it won't do for us to listen to the whims of an invalid. I'm going back. You needn't say you've seen me."

"We have the doctor's most imperative injunction, dearest," pleaded Adela, deceived for a moment. "Papa's illness is mental chiefly. He is able to rise and will be here very soon, if he is not in any way crossed. For heaven's sake, command yourself as we have done—painfully indeed! Besides, you have been seen."

"Has she—?" Wilfrid began; and toned an additional carelessness. "She writes, of course?"

"No, not once; and we are angry with her. It looks like ingratitude, or stupidity. She can write."

"People might say that we are not behaving well," returned Wilfrid, repeating that he must go to town. But now Edward Burley came running with a message from the aristocratic heights, and thither Wilfrid walked captive—saying in Adela's ear, "Don't be angry with her."

Adela thought, very justly, "I shall, if you've been making a fool of her, naughty boy!"

Wilfrid saluted the ladies, and made his bow of introduction to Georgiana Ford, at whom he looked twice, to confirm an impression that she was the perfect contrast to Emilia; and for this reason he chose not to look at her again. Lady Charlotte dropped him a quick recognition.

If Brookfield could have thrown the burden from its mind, the day was one to feel a pride in. Three Circles were present, and Brookfield denominated two that it had passed through, and patronized all—from Lady Gosstre (aristocracy) to the Tinley set (lucre), and from these to the representative Sumner girls (cultivated poverty). There were also intellectual, scientific, and Art circles to deal with; music, pleasant to hear, albeit condemned by Mr. Pericles; agreeable chatter, courtly flirtation and homage, and no dread of the defection of the letter H from their family.

"I feel more and more convinced," said Adela, meeting Arabella, "that we can have really no cause for alarm; otherwise papa would not have been cruel to his children." Arabella kindly reserved her opinion. "So let us try and be happy," continued Adela, determining to be encouraged by silence. With that she went on tiptoe gracefully and blew a kiss to her sister's lips. Running to Captain Gambier, she said, "Do you really enjoy this?"

"Charming," replied the ever-affable gentleman. "If I might only venture to say what makes it so infinitely!"

Much to her immediate chagrin at missing a direct compliment, which would have had to be parried, and might have led to 'vistas,' the too sprightly young lady found herself running on: "It's as nice as sin, without the knowledge that you are sinning."

"Oh! do you think that part of it disagreeable?" said the captain.

"I think the heat terrific:" she retrieved her ground.

"Coquet et coquette," muttered Lady Charlotte, observing them from a distance; and wondered whether her sex might be strongly represented in this encounter.

It was not in the best taste, nor was it perhaps good policy (if I may quote the Tinley set), for the ladies of Brookfield to subscribe openly to the right of certain people present to be exclusive. Arabella would have answered: "Lady Gosstre and her party cannot associate with you to your mutual pleasure and profit; and do you therefore blame her for not attempting what would fail ludicrously?" With herself, as she was not sorry to show, Lady Gosstre could associate. Cornelia had given up work to become a part of the Court. Adela made flying excursions over the lawn. Laura Tinley had the field below and Mr. Pericles to herself. That anxious gentleman consulted his watch from time to time, as if he expected the birth of an event.

Lady Gosstre grew presently aware that there was more acrimony in Freshfield Sumner's replies to Sir Twickenham (whom he had seduced into a political argument) than the professional wit need employ; and as Mr. Powys's talk was getting so attractive that the Court had become crowded, she gave a hint to Georgiana and Lady Charlotte, prompt lieutenants, whose retirement broke the circle.

"I never shall understand how it was done," Adela said subsequently. It is hoped that everybody sees the importance of understanding such points.

She happened to be standing alone when a messenger came up to her and placed a letter in her hand, addressed to her sister Cornelia. Adela walked slowly up to the heights. She knew Mr. Barrett's handwriting. "Good heavens!"—her thought may be translated out of Fine Shades—"does C. really in her heart feel so blind to our situation that she can go on playing still?" When she reached the group it was to hear Mr. Powys speaking of Mr. Barrett. Cornelia was very pale, and stood wretchedly in contrast among the faces. Adela beckoned her to step aside. "Here is a letter," she said: "there's no postmark. What has been the talk of that man?"

"Do you mean of Mr. Barrett?" Cornelia replied:—"that his father was a baronet, and a madman, who has just disinherited him."

"Just?" cried Adela. She thought of the title. Cornelia had passed on. A bizarre story of Mr. Barrett's father was related to Adela by Sir Twickenham. She grappled it with her sense, and so got nothing out of it. "Disinherited him because he wrote to his father, who was dying, to say that he had gained a livelihood by playing the organ! He had a hatred of music? It's incomprehensible! You know, Sir Twickenham, the interest we take in Mr. Barrett." The masked anguish of Cornelia's voice hung in her ears. She felt that it was now possible Cornelia might throw over the rich for the penniless baronet, and absolutely for an instant she thought nakedly, "The former ought not to be lost to the family." Thick clouds obscured the vision. Lady Gosstre had once told her that the point of Sir Twickenham's private character was his susceptibility to ridicule. Her ladyship had at the same time complimented his discernment in conjunction with Cornelia. "Yes," Adela now thought; "but if my sister shows that she is not so wise as she looks!" Cornelia's figure disappeared under the foliage bordering Besworth Lawn.

As usual, Arabella had all the practical labour—a fact that was noticed from the observant heights. "One sees mere de famille written on that young woman," was the eulogy she won from Lady Gosstre. How much would the great dame have marvelled to behold the ambition beneath the bustling surface! Arabella was feverish, and Freshfield Sumner reported brilliant things uttered by her. He became after a time her attendant, aide, and occasional wit-foil. They had some sharp exchanges: and he could not but reflect on the pleasure her keen zest of appreciation gave him compared with Cornelia's grave smile, which had often kindled in him profane doubts of the positive brightness, or rapidity of her intelligence.

"Besworth at sunset! What a glorious picture to have living before you every day!" said Lady Charlotte to her companion.

Wilfrid flushed. She read his look; and said, when they were out of hearing, "What a place for old people to sit here near the end of life! The idea of it makes one almost forgive the necessity for getting old— doesn't it? Tracy Runningbrook might make a poem about silver heads and sunset—something, you know! Very easy cantering then—no hunting! I suppose one wouldn't have even a desire to go fast—a sort of cock-horse, just as we began with. The stables, let me tell you, are too near the scullery. One is bound to devise measures for the protection of the morals of the household."

While she was speaking, Wilfrid's thoughts ran: "My time has come to strike for liberty."

This too she perceived, and was prepared for him.

He said: "Lady Charlotte, I feel that I must tell you...I fear that I have been calculating rather more hopefully..." Here the pitfall of sentiment yawned before him on a sudden. "I mean" (he struggled to avoid it, but was at the brink in the next sentence) "—I mean, dear lady, that I had hopes...Besworth pleased you... to offer you this..."

"With yourself?" she relieved him. A different manner in a protesting male would have charmed her better. She excused him, knowing what stood in his way.

"That I scarcely dared to hope," said Wilfrid, bewildered to see the loose chain he had striven to cast off gather tightly round him.

"You do hope it?"

"I have."

"You have hoped that I..." (she was not insolent by nature, and corrected the form) "—to marry me?"

"Yes, Lady Charlotte, I—I had that hope...if I could have offered this place—Besworth. I find that my father will never buy it; I have misunderstood him."

He fixed his eyes on her, expecting a cool, or an ironical, rejoinder to end the colloquy;—after which, fair freedom! She answered, "We may do very well without it."

Wilfrid was not equal to a start and the trick of rapturous astonishment. He heard the words like the shooting of dungeon-bolts, thinking, "Oh, heaven! if at the first I had only told the woman I do not love her!" But that sentimental lead had ruined him. And, on second thoughts, how could he have spoken thus to the point, when they had never previously dealt in anything save sentimental implications? The folly was in his speaking at all. The game was now in Lady Charlotte's hands.

Adela, in another part of the field, had released herself by a consummate use of the same weapon Wilfrid had so clumsily handled. Her object was to put an end to the absurd and compromising sighs of Edward Buxley; and she did so with the amiable contempt of a pupil dismissing a first instructor in an art "We saw from the beginning it could not be, Edward." The enamoured caricaturist vainly protested that he had not seen it from the beginning, and did not now. He recalled to her that she had said he was 'her first.' She admitted the truth, with eyes dwelling on him, until a ringlet got displaced. Her first. To be that, sentimental man would perish in the fires. To have been that will sometimes console him, even when he has lived to see what a thing he was who caught the budding fancy. The unhappy caricaturist groaned between triumph as a leader, and anguish at the prospect of a possible host of successors. King in that pure bosom, the thought would come—King of a mighty line, mayhap! And sentimental man, awakened to this disastrous view of things, endures shrewder pangs of rivalry in the contemplation of his usurping posterity than if, as do they, he looked forward to a tricked, perfumed, pommaded whipster, pirouetting like any Pierrot—the enviable image of the one who realized her first dream, and to whom specially missioned angels first opened the golden gates of her heart.

"I have learnt to see, Edward, that you do not honour me with a love you have diverted from one worthier than I am;" and in answer to the question whether, though having to abjure her love, she loved him: "No, no; it is my Arabella I love. I love, I will love, no one but her"—with sundry caressing ejaculations that spring a thirst for kisses, and a tender 'putting of the case,' now and then.

So much for Adela's part in the conflict. Edward was unaware that the secret of her mastering him was, that she was now talking common-sense in the tone of sentiment. He, on the contrary, talked sentiment in the tone of common-sense. Of course he was beaten: and O, you young lovers, when you hear the dear lips setting what you call the world's harsh language to this music, know that an hour has struck for you! It is a fatal sound to hear. Edward believed that his pleading had produced an effect when he saw Miss Adela's bosom rise as with a weight on it. The burden of her thoughts was—"How big and heavy Edward's eyes look when he is not amusing!" To get rid of him she said, as with an impassioned coldness, "Go." Her figure, repeating this under closed eyelids, was mysterious, potent. When he exclaimed, "Then I will go," her eyelids lifted wide: she shut them instantly, showing at the same time a slight tightening-in of the upper lip. You beheld a creature tied to the stake of Duty.

But she was exceedingly youthful, and had not reckoned upon man's being a live machine, possessing impulses of his own. A violent seizure of her waist, and enough of kisses to make up the sum popularly known as a 'shower,' stopped her performance. She struggled, and muttered passionately to be released. "We are seen," she hazarded. At the repetition, Edward, accustomed to dread the warning, let her go and fled. Turning hurriedly about, Adela found that she had spoken truth unawares, and never wished so much that she had lied. Sir Twickenham Pryme came forward to her, with his usual stiff courtly step.

"If you could have been a little—a little earlier," she murmured, with an unflurried face, laying a trembling hand in his; and thus shielded herself from a suspicion.

"Could I know that I was wanted?" He pressed her hand.

"I only know that I wish I had not left your side," said she—adding, "Though you must have thought me what, if I were a man, you Members of Parliament would call 'a bore,' for asking perpetual questions."

"Nay, an apposite interrogation is the guarantee of a proper interest in the subject," said the baronet.

Cornelia was very soon reverted to.

"Her intellect is contemplative," said Adela, exhibiting marvellous mental composure. "She would lose her unerring judgement in active life. She cannot weigh things in her mind rapidly. She is safe if her course of action is clear."

Sir Twickenham reserved his opinion of the truth of this. "I wonder whether she can forgive those who offend or insult her, easily?"

A singular pleasure warmed Adela's veins. Her cheeks kindling, she replied, giving him her full face. "No; if they are worthy of punishment. But—" and now he watched a downcast profile—"one must have some forgiveness for fools."

"Indeed, you speak like charity out of the windows of wisdom," said the baronet.

"Do you not require in Parliament to be tolerant at times?" Adela pursued.

He admitted it, and to her outcry of "Oh, that noble public life!" smiled deprecatingly—"My dear young lady, if you only knew the burden it brings!"

"It brings its burden," said Adela, correcting, with a most proper instinct, another enthusiastic burst. "At the same time the honour is above the load. Am I talking too romantically? You are at least occupied."

"Nine-tenths of us to no very good purpose," the baronet appended.

She rejoined: "If it were but a fraction, the good done would survive."

"And be more honourable to do, perhaps," he ejaculated. "The consolation should be great."

"And is somehow small," said she; and they laughed softly.

At this stage, Adela was 'an exceedingly interesting young person' in Sir Twickenham's mental register. He tried her on politics and sociology. She kept her ears open, and followed his lead carefully—venturing here and there to indicate an opinion, and suggesting dissent in a pained interrogation. Finally, "I confess," she said, "I understand much less than I am willing to think; and so I console myself with the thought that, after all, the drawing-room, and the... the kitchen?—well, an educated 'female' must serve her term there, if she would be anything better than a mere ornament, even in the highest walks of life—I mean the household is our sphere. From that we mount to companionship—if we can."

Amazement of Sir Twickenham, on finding his own thought printed, as it were, on the air before him by these pretty lips!

The conversation progressed, until Adela, by chance, turned her eyes up a cross pathway and perceived her sister Cornelia standing with Mr. Barrett under a beech. The man certainly held one of her hands pressed to his heart; and her attitude struck a doubt whether his other hand was disengaged or her waist free. Adela walked nervously on without looking at the baronet; she knew by his voice presently that his eyes had also witnessed the sight. "Two in a day," she thought; "what will he imagine us to be!" The baronet was thinking: "For your sister exposed, you display more agitation than for yourself insulted."

Adela found Arabella in so fresh a mood that she was sure good news had been heard. It proved that Mrs. Chump had sent a few lines in a letter carried by Braintop, to this effect: "My dears all! I found your father on his back in bed, and he discharged me out of the room; and the sight of me put him on his legs, and you will soon see him. Be civil to Mr. Braintop, who is a faithful young man, of great merit, and show your gratitude to—Martha Chump."

Braintop confirmed the words of the letter: and then Adela said—"You will do us the favour to stay and amuse yourself here. To-night there will be a bed at Brookfield."

"What will he do?" Arabella whispered.

"Associate with the Tinleys," returned Adela.

In accordance with the sentiment here half concealed, Brookfield soon showed that it had risen from the hour of depression when it had simply done its duty. Arabella formed an opposition-Court to the one in which she had studied; but Mr. Pericles defeated her by constantly sending to her for advice concerning the economies of the feast. Nevertheless, she exhibited good pretensions to social queendom, both personal and practical; and if Freshfield Sumner, instead of his crisp waspish comments on people and things, had seconded her by keeping up a two-minutes' flow of talk from time to time, she might have thought that Lady Gosstre was only luckier than herself—not better endowed.

Below, the Tinleys and their set surrounded Mr. Pericles—prompting him, as was seen, to send up continual messages. One, to wit, "Is there to be dancing to-night?" being answered, "Now, if you please," provoked sarcastic cheering; and Laura ran up to say, "How kind of you! We appreciate it. Continue to dispense blessings on poor mortals."

"By the way, though" (Freshfield took his line from the calm closed lips of his mistress), "poor mortals are not in the habit of climbing Olympus to ask favours."

"I perceived no barrier," quoth Laura.

"Audacity never does."

"Pray, how am I to be punished?"

Freshfield paused for a potent stroke. "Not like Semele. She saw the God:—you never will!"

While Laura was hanging on the horrid edge between a false laugh and a starting blush, Arabella said: "That visual excommunication has been pronounced years ago, Freshfield."

"Ah! then he hasn't changed his name in heaven?" Laura touched her thus for the familiar use of the gentle-man's Christian name.

"You must not imagine that very great changes are demanded of those who can be admitted."

"I really find it hotter than below," said Laura, flying.

Arabella's sharp eyes discerned a movement in Lady Gosstre's circle; and she at once went over to her, and entreated the great lady, who set her off so well, not to go. The sunset fronted Besworth Lawn; the last light of day was danced down to inspiriting music: and now Arabella sent word for Besworth hall-doors and windows to be opened; and on the company beginning to disperse, there beckoned promise of a brilliant supper-table.

"Admirable!" said Lady Gosstre, and the encomium was general among the crowd surrounding Arabella; for up to this point the feasting had been delicate, and something like plain hunger prevailed. Indeed, Arabella had heard remarks of a bad nature, which she traced to the Tinley set, and bore with, to meet her present reward. Making light of her triumph, she encouraged Freshfield to start a wit-contest, and took part in it herself, with the gaiety of an unoccupied mind. Her sisters had aforetime more than once challenged her supremacy, but they bowed to it now; and Adela especially did when, after a ringing hit to Freshfield (which the Tinleys might also take to their own bosoms), she said in an undertone, "What is there between C. and—?" Surprised by this astonishing vigilance and power of thinking below the surface while she performed above it, Adela incautiously turned her face toward the meditative baronet, and was humiliated by Arabella's mute Indication of contempt for her coming answer. This march across the lawn to the lighted windows of Besworth was the culmination of Brookfield's joy, and the crown for which it had striven; though for how short a term it was to be worn was little known. Was it not a very queenly sphere of Fine Shades and Nice Feelings that Brookfield had realized?

In Arabella's conscience lay a certain reproach of herself for permitting the "vice of a lower circle" to cling to her—viz., she had still betrayed a stupid hostility to the Tinleys: she had rejoiced to see them incapable of mixing with any but their own set, and thus be stamped publicly for what they were. She had struggled to repress it, and yet, continually, her wits were in revolt against her judgement. Perhaps one reason was that Albert Tinley had haunted her steps at an early part of the day; and Albert—a sickening City young man, "full of insolence, and half eyeglass," according to Freshfield—had once ventured to propose for her.

The idea that the Tinleys strove to catch at her skirts made Arabella spiteful. Up to the threshold of Besworth, Freshfield, Mr. Powys, Tracy, and Arabella kept the wheel of a dazzling run of small-talk, throwing intermittent sparks. Laura Tinley would press up, apparently to hear, but in reality (as all who knew her could see) with the object of being a rival representative of her sex in this illustrious rare encounter of divine intelligences. "You are anxious to know?" said Arabella, hesitatingly.

"To know, dear?" echoed Laura.

"There was, I presumed, something you did not hear." Arabella was half ashamed of the rudeness to which her antagonism to Laura's vulgarity forced her.

"Oh! I hear everything," Laura assured her.

"Indeed!" said Arabella. "By the way, who conducts you?" (Laura was on Edward Burley's arm.) "Oh! will you go to"—such and such an end of the table. "And if, Lady Gosstre, I may beg of you to do me the service to go there also," was added aloud; and lower, but quite audibly, "Mr. Pericles will have music, so there can be no talking." This, with the soupcon of a demi-shrug; "You will not suffer much" being implied. Laura said to herself, "I am not a fool." A moment after, Arabella was admitting in her own mind, as well as Fine Shades could interpret it, that she was. On entering the dining-hall, she beheld two figures seated at the point whither Laura was led by her partner. These were Mrs. Chump and Mr. Pole, with champagne glasses in their hands. Arabella was pushed on by the inexorable crowd of hungry people behind.

CHAPTER XXXII

THE SUPPER

Despite the pouring in of the flood of guests about the tables, Mrs. Chump and Mr. Pole sat apparently unconcerned in their places, and, as if to show their absolute indifference to observation and opinion, went through the ceremony of drinking to one another, upon which they nodded and chuckled: a suspicious eye had the option of divining that they used the shelter of the table cloth for an interchange of squeezes. This would have been further strengthened by Mrs. Chump's arresting exclamation, "Pole! Company!" Mr. Pole looked up. He recognized Lady Gosstre, and made an attempt, in his usual brisk style, to salute her. Mrs. Chump drew him back. "Nothin' but his legs, my lady," she whispered. "There's nothin' sets 'm up like champagne, my dears!" she called out to the Three of Brookfield.

Those ladies were now in the hall, gazing, as mildly as humanity would allow, at their common destiny, thus startlingly displayed. There was no doubt in the bosom of either one of them that exposure was to follow this prelude. Mental resignation was not even demanded of them—merely physical. They did not seek comfort in an interchange of glances, but dropped their eyes, and masked their sight as they best could. Caesar assassinated did a similar thing.

"My dears!" pursued Mrs. Chump, in Irish exaggerated by wine, "I've found 'm for ye! And if ye'd seen 'm this afternoon—the little peaky, shaky fellow that he was! and a doctor, too, feelin' his pulse. 'Is ut slow,' says I, 'doctor?' and draws a bottle of champagne. He could hardly stand before his first glass. 'Pon my hon'r, my lady, ye naver saw s'ch a change in a mortal bein.—Pole, didn't ye go 'ha, ha!' now, and seem to be nut-cracking with your fingers? He did; and if ye aver saw an astonished doctor! 'Why,' says I, 'doctor, ye think ut's maguc! Why, where's the secret? drink with 'm, to be sure! And you go and do that, my lord doctor, my dear Mr. Doctor! Do ut all round, and your patients 'll bless your feet." Why, isn't cheerful society and champagne the vary best of medicines, if onnly the blood 'll go of itself a little? The fault's in his legs; he's all right at top!—if he'd smooth his hair a bit.

Checking her tongue, Mrs. Chump performed this service lightly for him, in the midst of his muttered comments on her Irish.

The fact was manifest to the whole assembly, that they had indeed been drinking champagne to some purpose.

Wilfrid stepped up to two of his sisters, warning them hurriedly not to go to their father: Adela he arrested with a look, but she burst the restraint to fulfil a child's duty. She ran up gracefully, and taking her father's hand, murmured a caressing "Dear papa!"

"There—all right—quite right—quite well," Mr. Pole repeated. "Glad to see you all: go away."

He tried to look kindly out of the nervous fit into which a word, in a significant tone, from one of his daughters had instantly plunged him. Mrs. Chump admonished her: "Will ye undo all that I've been doin' this blessed day?"

"Glad you haven't missed the day altogether, sir," Wilfrid greeted his father in an offhand way.

"Ah, my boy!" went the old man, returning him what was meant for a bluff nod.

Lady Charlotte gave Wilfrid an open look. It meant: "If you can act like that, and know as much as I know, you are worth more than I reckoned." He talked evenly and simply, and appeared on the surface as composed as any of the guests present. Nor was he visibly disturbed when Mrs. Chump, catching his eye, addressed him aloud:—

"Ye'd have been more grateful to me to have brought little Belloni as well now, I know, Mr. Wilfrid. But I was just obliged to leave her at the hotel; for Pole can't endure her. He 'bomunates the sight of 'r. If ye aver saw a dog burnt by the fire, Pole's second to 'm, if onnly ye speak that garl's name."

The head of a strange musician, belonging to the band stationed outside, was thrust through one of the window apertures. Mr. Pericles beckoned him imperiously to retire, and perform. He objected, and an altercation in bad English diverted the company. It was changed to Italian. "Mia figlia," seized Wilfrid's ear. Mr. Pericles bellowed, "Allegro." Two minutes after Braintop felt a touch on his shoulder; and Wilfrid, speaking in a tone of friend to friend, begged him to go to town by the last train and remove Miss Belloni to an hotel, which he named. "Certainly," said Braintop; "but if I meet her father...?" Wilfrid summoned champagne for him; whereupon Mrs. Chump cried out, "Ye're kind to wait upon the young man, Mr. Wilfrid; and that Mr. Braintop's an invalu'ble young man. And what do ye want with the hotel, when we've left it, Mr. Paricles?"

The Greek raised his head from Mr. Pole, shrugging at her openly. He and Wilfrid then measured eyes a moment. "Some champagne togezer?" said Mr. Pericles. "With all my heart," was the reply; and their glasses were filled, and they bowed, and drank. Wilfrid took his seat, drew forth his pocket-book; and while talking affably to Lady Charlotte beside him, and affecting once or twice to ponder over her remarks, or to meditate a fitting answer, wrote on a slip of paper under the table:—

"Mine! my angel! You will see me to-morrow.

"YOUR LOVER."

This, being inserted in an envelope, with zig-zag letters of address to form Emilia's name, he contrived to pass to Braintop's hands, and resumed his conversation with Lady Charlotte, who said, when there was nothing left to discover, "But what is it you concoct down there?" "I!" cried Wilfrid, lifting his hands, and so betraying himself after the fashion of the very innocent. She despised any reading of acts not on the surface, and nodded to the explanation he gave—to wit: "By the way, do you mean—have you noticed my habit of touching my fingers' ends as I talk? I count them backwards and forwards."

"Shows nervousness," said Lady Charlotte; "you are a boy!"

"Exceedingly a boy."

"Now I put a finger on his vanity," said she; and thought indeed that she had played on him.

"Mr. Pole," (Lady Gosstre addressed that gentleman,) "I must hope that you will leave this dining-hall as it is; there is nothing in the neighbourhood to match it!"

"Delightful!" interposed Laura Tinley; "but is it settled?"

Mr. Pole leaned forward to her ladyship; and suddenly catching the sense of her words, "Ah, why not?" he said, and reached his hand to some champagne, which he raised to his mouth, but drank nothing of. Reflection appeared to tell him that his safety lay in drinking, and he drained the glass at a gulp. Mrs. Chump had it filled immediately, and explained to a wondering neighbour, "It's that that keeps 'm on his legs."

"We shall envy you immensely," said Laura Tinley to Arabella; who replied, "I assure you that no decision has been come to."

"Ah, you want to surprise us with cards on a sudden from Besworth!"

"That is not the surprise I have in store," returned Arabella sedately.

"Then you have a surprise? Do tell me."

"How true to her sex is the lady who seeks to turn 'what it is' into 'what it isn't!'" said Freshfield, trusty lieutenant.

"I think a little peeping makes surprises sweeter; I'm weak enough to think that," Lady Charlotte threw in.

"That is so true!" exclaimed Laura.

"Well; and a secret shared is a fact uncommonly well aired—that is also true. But, remember, you do not desire the surprise; you are a destroying force to it;" and Freshfield bowed.

"Curiosity!" sighed some one, relieving Freshfield from a sense of the guilt of heaviness.

"I am a Pandora," Laura smilingly said.

"To whom?" Tracy Runningbrook's shout was heard.

"With champagne in the heads of the men, and classics in the heads of the women, we shall come; to something," remarked Lady Gosstre half to herself and Georgiana near her.

An observer of Mr. Pole might have seen that he was fretting at a restriction on his tongue. Occasionally he would sit forward erect in his chair, shake his coat-collar, frown, and sound a preparatory 'hem; but it ended in his rubbing his hair away on the back of his head. Mrs. Chump, who was herself perceiving new virtues in champagne with every glass, took the movements as indicative of a companion exploration of the spiritual resources of this vintage. She no longer called for it, but lifted a majestic finger (a Siddons or tenth-Muse finger, as Freshfield named it) behind the row of heads; upon which champagne speedily bubbled in the glasses. Laughter at the performance had fairly set in. Arabella glanced nervously round for Mr. Pericles, who looked at his watch and spread the fingers of one hand open thrice—an act that telegraphed fifteen minutes. In fifteen minutes an opera troupe, with three famous chiefs and a renowned prima-donna were to arrive. The fact was known solely to Arabella and Mr. Pericles. It was the Surprise of the evening. But within fifteen minutes, what might not happen, with heads going at champagne-pace?

Arabella proposed to Freshfield to rise. "Don't the ladies go first?" the wit turned sensualist stammered; and incurred that worse than frown, a cold look of half-comprehension, which reduces indefinitely the proportions of the object gazed at. There were probably a dozen very young men in the room waiting to rise with their partners at a signal for dancing; and these could not be calculated upon to take an initiative, or follow one—as ladies, poor slaves! will do when the electric hostess rustles. The men present were non-conductors. Arabella knew that she could carry off the women, but such a proceeding would leave her father at the mercy of the wine; and, moreover, the probability was that Mrs. Chump would remain by him, and, sole in a company of males, explode her sex with ridicule, Brookfield in the bargain. So Arabella, under a prophetic sense of evil, waited; and this came of it. Mr. Pole patted Mrs. Chump's hand publicly. In spite of the steady hum of small-talk—in spite of Freshfield Sumner's circulation of a crisp anecdote—in spite of Lady Gosstre's kind effort to stop him by engaging him in conversation, Mr. Pole forced on for a speech. He said that he had not been the thing lately. It might be his legs, as his dear friend Martha, on his right, insisted; but he had felt it in his head, though as strong as any man present.

"Harrk at 'm!" cried Mrs. Chump, letting her eyes roll fondly away from him into her glass.

"Business, my lady!" Mr. Pole resumed. "Ah, you don't know what that is. We've got to work hard to keep our heads up equal with you. We don't swim with corks. And my old friend, Ralph Tinley—he sells iron, and has got a mine. That's simple. But, my God, ma'am, when a man has his eye on the Indian Ocean, and the Atlantic, and the Baltic, and the Black Sea, and half-a-dozen colonies at once, he—you—"

"Well, it's a precious big eye he's got, Pole," Mrs. Chump came to his relief.

"—he don't know whether he's a ruined dog, or a man to hold up his head in any company."

"Oh, Lord, Pole, if ye're going to talk of beggary!" Mrs. Chump threw up her hands. "My lady, I naver could abide the name of 't. I'm a kind heart, ye know, but I can't bear a ragged friend. I hate 'm! He seems to give me a pinch."

Having uttered this, it struck her that it was of a kind to convulse Mrs. Lupin, for whose seizures she could never accurately account; and looking round, she perceived, sure enough, that little forlorn body agitated, with a handkerchief to her mouth.

"As to Besworth," Mr. Pole had continued, "I might buy twenty Besworths. If—if the cut shows the right card. If—" Sweat started on his forehead, and he lifted his eyebrows, blinking. "But none!" (he smote the table) "none can say I haven't been a good father! I've educated my girls to marry the best the land can show. I bought a house to marry them out of; it was their own idea." He caught Arabella's eyes. "I thought so, at all events; for why should I have paid the money if I hadn't thought so? when then—yes, that sum..." (was he choking!) "saved me!—saved me!"

A piteous desperate outburst marked the last words, that seemed to struggle from a tightened cord.

"Not that there's anything the matter," he resumed, with a very brisk wink. "I'm quite sound: heart's sound, lungs sound, stomach regular. I can see, and smell, and hear. Sense of touch is rather lumpy at times, I know; but the doctor says it's nothing—nothing at all; and I should be all right, if I didn't feel that I was always wearing a great leaden hat."

"My gracious, Pole, if ye're not talkin' pos'tuv nonsense!" exclaimed Mrs. Chump.

"Well, my dear Martha" (Mr. Pole turned to her argumentatively), "how do you account for my legs? I feel it at top. I declare I've felt the edge of the brim half a yard out. Now, my lady, a man in that state—sound and strong as the youngest—but I mean a vexed man—worried man bothered man, he doesn't want a woman to look after him;—I mean, he does—he does! And why won't young girls—oh! they might, they might—see that? And when she's no extra expense, but brings him—helps him to face—and no one has said the world's a jolly world so often as I have. It's jolly!" He groaned.

Lady Charlotte saw Wilfrid gazing at one spot on the table without a change of countenance. She murmured to him, "What hits you hits me."

Mr. Pole had recommenced, on the evident instigation of Laura Tinley, though Lady Gosstre and Freshfield Sumner had both sought to check the current. In Chump's lifetime, it appeared, he (Mr. Pole) had thought of Mrs. Chump with a respectful ardour; and albeit she was no longer what she was when Chump brought her over, a blooming Irish girl—"her hair exactly as now, the black curl half over the cheek, and a bright laugh, and a white neck, fat round arms, and—"

A shout of "Oh, Pole! ye seem to be undressin' of me before them all," diverted the neighbours of the Beauty.

"Who would not like such praise?" Laura Tinley, to keep alive the subject, laid herself open to Freshfield by a remark.

"At the same personal peril?" he inquired smoothly.

Mr. Pericles stood up, crying "Enfin!" as the doors were flung open, and a great Signora of operatic fame entered the hall, supported on one side by a charming gentleman (a tenore), who shared her fame and more with her. In the rear were two working baritones; and behind them, outside, Italian heads might be discerned.

The names of the Queen of Song and Prince of Singers flew round the room; and Laura uttered words of real gratitude, for the delightful surprise, to Arabella, as the latter turned from her welcome of them. "She is exactly like Emilia—young," was uttered. The thought went with a pang through Wilfrid's breast. When the Signora was asked if she would sup or take champagne, and she replied that she would sup by-and-by, and drink porter now, the likeness to Emilia was established among the Poles.

Meantime the unhappy Braintop received an indication that he must depart. As he left the hall he brushed past the chief-clerk of his office, who soon appeared bowing and elbowing among the guests. "What a substitute for me!" thought Braintop bitterly; and in the belief that this old clerk would certainly go back that night, and might undertake his commission, he lingered near the band on the verge of the lawn. A touch at his elbow startled him. In the half-light he discerned Emilia. "Don't say you have seen me," were her first words. But when he gave her the letter, she drew him aside, and read it by the aid of lighted matches held in Braintop's hat drawing in her fervent breath to a "Yes! yes!" at the close, while she pressed the letter to her throat. Presently the singing began in an upper room, that had shortly before flashed with sudden light. Braintop entreated Emilia to go in, and then rejoiced that she had refused. They stood in a clear night-air, under a yellowing crescent, listening to the voice of an imperial woman. Impressed as he was, Braintop had, nevertheless, leisure to look out of his vinous mist and notice, with some misgiving, a parading light at a certain distance—apparently the light of cigarettes being freshly kindled. He was too much elated to feel alarm: but "If her father were to catch me again," he thought. And with Emilia on his arm!

Mr. Pole's chief-clerk had brought discomposing news. He was received by an outburst of "No business, Payne; I won't have business!"

Turning to Mr. Pericles, the old clerk said. "I came rather for you, sir, not expecting to find Mr. Pole." He was told by Mr. Pericles to speak what he had to say: and then the guests, who had fallen slightly back, heard a cavernous murmur; and some, whose eyes where on Mr. Pole, observed a sharp conflict of white and red in his face.

"There, there, there, there!" went Mr. Pole. "'Hem, Pericles!" His handkerchief was drawn out; and he became engaged, as it were, in wiping a moisture from the palm of his hand. "Pericles, have you got pluck now? Eh?"

Mr. Pericles had leaned down his ear for the whole of the news.

"Ten sossand," he said, smoothing his waistbands, and then inserting his thumbs into the pits of his waistcoat. "Also a chance of forty. Let us not lose time for ze music."

He walked away.

"I don't believe in that d—d coolness, ma'am," said Mr. Pole, wheeling round on Freshfield Sumner. "It's put on. That wears a mask; he's one of those confounded humbugs who wear a mask. Ten-forty! and all for a shrug; it's not human. I tell you, he does that just out of a sort of jealousy to rival me as an Englishman. Because I'm cool, he must be. Do you think a mother doesn't feel the loss of her children?"

"I fear that I must grow petticoats before I can answer purely feminine questions," said Freshfield.

"Of course—of course," assented Mr. Pole; "and a man feels like a mother to his money. For the moment, he does—for the moment. What are those fellows—Spartans—women who cut off their breasts—?"

Freshfield suggested, "Amazons."

"No; they were women," Mr. Pole corrected him; "and if anything hurt them, they never cried out. That's what—ha!—our friend Pericles is trying at. He's a fool. He won't sleep to-night. He'll lie till he gets cold in the feet, and then tuck them up like a Dutch doll, and perspire cold till his heart gives a bound, and he'll jump up and think his last hour's come. Wind on the stomach, do ye call it? I say it's wearing a mask!"

The bird's-eye of the little merchant shot decisive meaning.

Two young ladies had run from his neighbourhood, making as if to lift hands to ears. The sight of them brought Mrs. Chump to his side. "Pole! Pole!" she said, "is there annything wrong?"

"Wrong, Martha?" He bent to her, attempting Irish—"Arrah, now! and mustn't all be right if you're here?"

She smote his cheek fondly. "Ye're not a bit of an Irish-man, ye deer little fella."

"Come along and dance," cried he imperiously.

"A pretty spectacle—two fandangoes, when there's singing, ye silly!" Mrs. Chump led him upstairs, chafing one of his hands, and remarking loudly on the wonder it was to see his knees constantly 'give' as he walked.

On the dark lawn, pressing Wilfrid's written words for fiery nourishment to her heart, Emilia listened to the singing.

"Why do people make a noise, and not be satisfied to feel?" she said angrily to Braintop, as a great clapping of hands followed a divine aria. Her ideas on this point would have been different in the room.

By degrees a tender delirium took hold of her sense; and then a subtle emotion—which was partly prompted by dim rivalry with the voice that seemed to be speaking so richly to the man she loved—set her bosom rising and falling. She translated it to herself thus: "What a joy it will be to him to hear me now!" And in a pause she sang clear out—

"Prima d'Italia amica;"

and hung on the last note, to be sure that she would be heard by him.

Braintop saw the cigarette dash into sparks on the grass. At the same moment a snarl of critical vituperation told Emilia that she had offended taste and her father. He shouted her name, and, striding up to her, stumbled over Braintop, whom he caught with one hand, while the other fell firmly on Emilia.

"'Amica—amica-a-a,'" he burlesqued her stress of the luckless note—lowing it at her, and telling her in triumphant Italian that she was found at last. Braintop, after a short struggle, and an effort at speech, which was loosely shaken in his mouth, heard that he stood a prisoner. "Eh! you have not lost your cheeks," insulted his better acquaintance with English slang.

Alternately in this queer tongue and in Italian the pair of victims were addressed.

Emilia knew her father's temper. He had a habit of dallying with an evil passion till it boiled over and possessed him. Believing Braintop to be in danger of harm, she beckoned to some of the faces crowding the windows; but the movement was not seen, as none of the circumstances were at all understood. Wilfrid, however, knew well who had sung those three bars, concerning which the 'Prima donna' questioned Mr. Pericles, and would not be put off by hearing that it was a startled jackdaw, or an owl, and an ole nightingale. The Greek rubbed his hands. "Now to recommence," he said; "and we shall not notice a jackdaw again." His eye went sideways watchfully at Wilfrid. "You like zat piece of opera?"

"Immensely," said Wilfrid, half bowing to the Signora—to whom, as to Majesty, Mr. Pericles introduced him, and fixed him.

"Now! To seats!"

Mr. Pericles' mandates was being obeyed, when a cry of "Wilfrid!" from Emilia below, raised a flutter.

Mr. Pole had been dozing in his chair. He rose at the cry, looking hard, with a mechanical jerk of the neck, at two or three successive faces, and calling, "Somebody—somebody" to take his outstretched hand trembling in a paroxysm of nervous terror.

Hearing his son's name again, but more faintly, he raised his voice for Martha. "Don't let that girl come near me! I—I can't get on with foreign girls!"

His eyes went among the curious faces surrounding him. "Wilfrid!" he shouted. To the second summons, "Sir" was replied, in the silence. Neither saw the other as they spoke.

"Are you going out to her, Wilfrid?"

"Someone called me, sir."

"He's got the cunning of hell," said Mr. Pole, baffled by his own agitation.

"Oh! don't talk o' that place," moaned Mrs. Chump.

"Stop!" cried the old man. "Are you going? Stop! you shan't do mischief. I mean—there—stop! Don't go. You're not to go. I say you're not to go out."

Emphasis and gesticulations gave their weight to the plain words.

But rage at the upset of all sentiments and dignity that day made Wilfrid reckless, and he now felt his love to be all he had. He heard his Emilia being dragged away to misery—perhaps to be sold to shame. Maddened, he was incapable of understanding his father's state, or caring for what the world thought. His sisters gathered near him, but were voiceless.

"Is he gone?" Mr. Pole burst forward. "You're gone, sir? Wilfrid, have you gone to that girl? I ask you whether...(there's one shot at my heart," he added in a swift undertone to one of the heads near him, while he caught at his breast with both hands). "Wilfrid, will you stay here?"

"For God's sake, go to him, Wilfrid," murmured Adela. "I can't."

"Because if you do—if you don't—I mean, if you go..." The old man gasped at the undertone. "Now I have got it in my throat."

A quick physical fear caught hold of him. In a moment his voice changed to entreaty. "I beg you won't go, my dear boy. Wilfrid, I tell you, don't go. Because, you wouldn't act like a d—d—I'm not angry; but it is like acting like a—Here's company, Wilfrid; come to me, my boy; do come here. You mayn't ha—have your poor old father long, now he's got you u—up in the world. I mean accidents, for I'm sound enough; only a little nervous from brain—Is he gone?"

Wilfrid was then leaving the room.

Lady Gosstre had been speaking to Mr. Powys. She was about to say a word to Lady Charlotte, when the latter walked to the doorway, and. In a manner that smote his heart with a spasm of gratitude, said; "Don't heed these people. He will bring on a fit if you don't stop. His nerves are out, and the wine they have given him... Go to him: I will go to Emilia, and do as much for her as you could."

Wilfrid reached his father in time to see him stagger back into the arms of Mrs. Chump, whose supplication was for the female stimulant known as 'something.'

CHAPTER XXXIII

DEFEAT AND FLIGHT OF MRS. CHUMP

On reaching home that night, Arabella surprised herself thinking, in the midst of her anguish: "Whatever is said of us, it cannot be said that there is a house where the servants have been better cared for." And this reflection continued to burn with an astounding brilliancy through all the revolutions of a mind contemplating the dread of a fallen fortune, the fact of a public exposure, and what was to her an ambition destroyed. Adela had no such thoughts. "I have been walking on a plank," she gasped from time to time, as she gave startled glances into the abyss of poverty, and hurried to her bedchamber—a faint whisper of self-condemnation in her ears at the 'I' being foremost. The sisters were too proud to touch upon one another's misery in complaints, or to be common by holding debate on it. They had not once let their eyes meet at Besworth, as the Tinleys wonderingly noticed. They said good night to their papa, who was well enough to reply, adding peremptorily, "Downstairs at half-past eight,"—an intimation that he would be at the break-fast table and read prayers as usual. Inexperienced in nervous disease, they were now filled with the idea that he was possibly acting—a notion that had never been kindled in them before; or, otherwise, how came these rapid, almost instantaneous, recoveries?

Cornelia alone sounded near the keynote. Since the night that she had met him in the passage, and the next morning when Mrs. Chump had raised the hubbub about her loss, Cornelia's thoughts had been troubled by some haunting spectral relationship with money. It had helped to make her reckless in granting interviews to Purcell Barrett. "If we are poor, I am free;" and that she might then give herself to whomever she pleased, was her logical deduction. The exposure at Besworth, and the partial confirmation of her suspicions, were not without their secret comfort to her. In the carriage, coming home, Wilfrid had touched her hand by chance, and pressed it with good heart. She went to the library, imagining that if he wished to see her he would appear, and by exposing his own weakness learn to excuse hers. She was right in her guess; Wilfrid came. He came sauntering into the room with "Ah! you here?" Cornelia consented to play into his hypocrisy. "Yes, I generally think better here," she replied.

"And what has this pretty head got to do with thinking?"

"Not much, I suppose, my lord," she replied, affecting nobly to acknowledge the weakness of the female creature.

Wilfrid kissed her with an unaccustomed fervour. This delicate mumming was to his taste. It was yet more so when she spoke playfully to him of his going soon to be a married man. He could answer to that in a smiling negative, playing round the question, until she perceived that he really desired to have his feeling for the odd dark girl who had recently shot across their horizon touched, if only it were led to by the muffled ways of innuendo.

As a dog, that cannot ask you verbally to scratch his head, but wishes it, will again and again thrust his head into your hand, petitioning mutely that affection may divine him, so:—but we deal with a sentimentalist, and the simile is too gross to be exact. For no sooner was Wilfrid's head scratched, than the operation stuck him as humiliating; in other words, the moment he felt his sisters fingers in the ticklish part, he flew to another theme, then returned, and so backward and forward—mystifying her not slightly, and making her think, "Then he has no heart." She by no means intended to encourage love for Emilia, but she hoped for his sake, that the sentiment he had indulged was sincere. By-and-by he said, that though he had no particular affection for Lady Charlotte, he should probably marry her.

"Without loving her, Wilfrid? It is unfair to her; it is unfair to yourself."

Wilfrid understood perfectly who it was for whom she pleaded thus vehemently. He let her continue: and when she had dwelt on the horrors of marriages without love, and the supreme duty of espousing one who has our 'heart's loyalty,' he said, "You may be right. A man must not play with a girl. He must consider that he owes a duty to one who is more dependent;"—implying that a woman s duty was distinct and different in such a case.

Cornelia could not rise and plead for her sex. Had she pushed forth the 'woman,' she must have stood for her.

This is the game of Fine Shades and Nice Feelings, under whose empire you see this family, and from which they are to emerge considerably shorn, but purified—examples of One present passage of our civilization.

"At least, dear, if" (Cornelia desperately breathed the name) "—if Emilia were forced to give her hand...loving...you...we should be right in pitying her?"

The snare was almost too palpable. Wilfrid fell into it, from the simple passion that the name inspired; and now his hand tightened. "Poor child!" he moaned.

She praised his kind heart: "You cannot be unjust and harsh, I know that. You could not see her—me— any of us miserable. Women feel, dear. Ah! I need not tell you that. Their tears are not the witnesses. When they do not weep, but the hot drops stream inwardly:—and, oh! Wilfrid, let this never happen to me. I shall not disgrace you, because I intend to see you happy with...with her, whoever she is; and I would leave you happy. But I should not survive it. I can look on Death. A marriage without love is dishonour."

Sentiment enjoys its splendid moods. Wilfrid having had the figure of his beloved given to him under nuptial benediction, cloaked, even as he wished it to be, could afford now to commiserate his sister, and he admired her at the same time. "I'll take care you are not made a sacrifice of when the event is fixed," he said—as if it had never been in contemplation.

"Oh! I have not known happiness for years, till this hour," Cornelia whispered to him bashfully; and set him wondering why she should be happy when she had nothing but his sanction to reject a man.

On the other hand, her problem was to gain lost ground by letting him know that, of the pair, it was not she who would marry beneath her station. She tried it mentally in various ways. In the end she thought it best to give him this positive assurance. "No," he rejoined, "a woman never should." There was no admission of equality to be got out of him, so she kissed him. Of their father's health a few words were said—of Emilia nothing further. She saw that Wilfrid's mind was resolved upon some part to play, but shrank from asking his confidence, lest facts should be laid bare.

At the breakfast-table Mr. Pole was a little late. He wore some of his false air of briskness on a hazy face, and read prayers—drawing breath between each sentence and rubbing his forehead; but the work was done by a man in ordinary health, if you chose to think so, as Mrs. Chump did. She made favourable remarks on his appearance, begging the ladies to corroborate her. They were silent.

"Now take a chop, Pole, and show your appetite," she said. "'A Chump-chop, my love?' my little man used to invite me of a mornin'; and that was the onnly joke he had, so it's worth rememberin'."

A chop was placed before Mr. Pole. He turned it in his plate, and wonderingly called to mind that he had once enjoyed chops. At a loss to account for the distressing change, he exclaimed to himself, "Chump! I wish the woman wouldn't thrust her husband between one's teeth. An egg!"

The chop was displaced for an egg, which he tapped until Mrs. Chump cried out, "Oh! if ye're not like a postman, Pole; and d'ye think ye've got a letter for a chick inside there?"

This allusion scared Mr. Pole from the egg. He quitted the table, muttering, "Business! business!" and went to the library.

When he was gone Mrs. Chump gave a cry to know where Braintop was, but, forgetting him immediately, turned to the ladies and ejaculated, "Broth'm. It's just brothin' he wants. Broth, I say, for anny man that won't eat his chop or his egg. And, my dears, now, what do ye say to me for bringing him home to ye? I expect to be thanked, I do; and then we'll broth Pole together, till he's lusty as a prize-ox, and capers like a monkey."

Wretched woman! that could not see the ruin she had inflicted—that could not imagine how her bitter breath cut against those sensitive skins! During a short pause little Mrs. Lupin trotted to the door, and shot through it, in a paroxysm.

Then Wilfrid's voice was heard. He leaned against a corner of the window, and spoke without directly looking at Mrs. Chump; so that she was some time in getting to understand the preliminary, "Madam, you must leave this house." But presently her chin dropped; and after feeble efforts to interpose an exclamation, she sat quiet—overcome by the deliberate gravity of his manner, and motioning despairingly with her head, to relieve the swarm of unborn figure-less ideas suggested by his passing speech. The ladies were ranged like tribunal shapes. It could not be said of souls so afflicted that they felt pleasure in the scene; but to assist in the administration of a rigorous justice is sweet to them that are smarting. They scarcely approved his naked statement of things when he came to Mrs. Chump's particular aspiration in the household—viz., to take a station and the dignity of their name. The effect he produced satisfied them that the measure was correct. Her back gave a sharp bend, as if an eternal support had snapped. "Oh! ye hit hard," she moaned.

"I tell you kindly that we (who, you will acknowledge, must count for something here) do not sanction any change that revolutionizes our domestic relations," said Wilfrid; while Mrs. Chump heaved and rolled on the swell of the big words like an overladen boat. "You have only to understand so much, and this—that if we resist it, as we do, you, by continuing to contemplate it, are provoking a contest which will probably injure neither you nor me, but will be death to ham in his present condition."

Mrs. Chump was heard to mumble that she alone knew the secret of restoring him to health, and that he was rendered peaky and poky only by people supposing him so.

"An astonishin' thing!" she burst out. "If I kiss 'm and say 'Poor Pole!' he's poor Pole on the spot. And, if onnly I—"

But Wilfrid's stern voice flowed over her. "Listen, madam, and let this be finished between us. You know well that when a man has children, he may wish to call another woman wife—a woman not their mother; but the main question is, will his children consent to let her take that place? We are of one mind, and will allow no one—no one—to assume that position. And now, there's an end. We'll talk like friends. I have only spoken in that tone that you might clearly comprehend me on an important point. I know you entertain a true regard for my father, and it is that belief which makes me—"

"Friends!" cried Mrs. Chump, getting courage from the savour of cajolery in these words. "Friends! Oh, ye fox! ye fox!"

And now commenced a curious duett. Wilfrid merely wished to terminate his sentence; Mrs. Chump wantonly sought to prevent him. Each was burdened with serious matter; but they might have struck hands here, had not this petty accidental opposition interposed. —"Makes me feel confident..." Wilfrid resumed.

"And Pole's promos, Mr. Wilfrud; ye're forgettin' that."

"Confident, ma'am."

"He was the first to be soft."

"I say, ma'am, for his sake—"

"An' it's for his sake. And weak as he is on 's legs, poor fells; which marr'ge 'll cure, bein' a certain rem'dy."

"Mrs. Chump! I beg you to listen."

"Mr. Wilfrud! and I can see too, and it's three weeks and ye kissed little Belloni in the passage, outside this vary door, and out in the garden."

The blow was entirely unexpected, and took Wilfrid's breath, so that he was not ready for his turn in this singular piece of harmony.

"Ye did!" Mrs. Chump rejoiced to behold how her chance spark kindled flame in his cheeks. "It's pos'tuv ye did. And ye're the best blusher of the two, my dear; and no shame to ye, though it is a garl's business. That little Belloni takes to 't like milk; but you—"

Wilfrid strode up to her, saying imperiously, "I tell you to listen!"

She succumbed at once to a show of physical ascendency, murmuring, "It's sure he was seen kissin' of her twice, and mayhap more; and hearty smacks of the lips, too—likin' it."

The ladies rewarded Wilfrid for his service to their cause by absolutely hearing nothing—a feat women can be capable of.

Wilfrid, however, was angered by the absurdity of the charge and the scene, and also by the profane touch on Emilia's name.

"I must tell you, ma'am, that for my father's sake I must desire you to quit this—you will see the advisability of quitting this house for a time."

"Pole's promus! Pole's promus!" Mrs. Chump wailed again.

"Will you give me your assurance now that you will go, to be our guest again subsequently?"

"In writin' and in words, Mr. Wilfrud!"

"Answer me, ma'am."

"I will, Mr. Wilfrud; and Mr. Braintop's a witness, knowin' the nature of an oath. There naver was a more sacrud promus. Says Pole, 'Martha—'"

Wilfrid changed his tactics. Sitting down by her side, he said: "I am sure you have an affection for my father."

"I'm the most lovin' woman, my dear! If it wasn't for my vartue I don't know what'd become o' me. Ye could ask Chump, if he wasn't in his grave, poor fella! I'll be cryin' like a squeezed orr'nge presently. What with Chump and Pole, two's too many for a melanch'ly woman."

"You have an affection for my father I know, ma'am. Now, see! he's ill. If you press him to do what we certainly resist, you endanger his life."

Mrs. Chump started back from the man who bewildered her brain without stifling her sense of justice. She knew that there was another way of putting the case, whereby she was not stuck in the criminal box; but the knowledge groped about blindly, and finding herself there, Mrs. Chump lost all idea of a counter-accusation, and resorted to wriggling and cajolery. "Ah! ye look sweeter when ye're kissin' us, Mr. Wilfrud; and I wonder where the little Belloni has got to!"

"Tell me, that there maybe no misunderstanding." Wilfrid again tried to fix her.

"A rosy rosy fresh bit of a mouth she's got! and pouts ut!"

Wilfrid took her hand. "Answer me."

"'Deed, and I'm modust, Mr. Wilfrud."

"You do him the honour to be very fond of him. I am to believe that? Then you must consent to leave us at the end of a week. You abandon any idea of an impossible ceremony, and of us you make friends and not enemies."

At the concluding word, Mrs. Chump was no longer sustained by her excursive fancy. She broke down, and wrung her hands, crying, "En'mies! Pole's children my en'mies! Oh, Lord! that I should live to hear ut! and Pole, that knew me a bride first blushin'!"

She wailed and wept so that the ladies exchanged compassionate looks, and Arabella rose to press her hand and diminish her distress. Wilfrid saw that his work would be undone in a moment, and waved her to her seat. The action was perceived by Mrs. Chump.

"Oh, Mr. Wilfrud! my dear! and a soldier! and you that was my favourut! If half my 'ffection for Pole wasn't the seein' of you so big and handsome! And all my ideas to get ye marrud, avery one so snug in a corner, with a neat little lawful ring on your fingers! And you that go to keep me a lone woman, frightened of the darrk! I'm an awful coward, that's the truth. And ye know that marr'ge is a holy thing! and it's such a beaut'ful cer'mony! Oh, Mr. Wilfrud!—Lieuten't y' are! and I'd have bought ye a captain, and made the hearts o' your sisters jump with bonnuts and gowns and jools. Oh, Pole! Pole! why did you keep me so short o' cash? It's been the roon of me! What did I care for your brooches and your gifts? I wanted the good will of your daughters, sir—your son, Pole!"

Mrs. Chump stopped her flow of tears. "Dear hearts!" she addressed her silent judges, in mysterious guttural tones, "is it becas ye think there's a bit of a fear of...?"

The ladies repressed a violent inclination to huddle together, like cattle from the blowing East.

"I assure ye, 'taint poss'ble," pursued Mrs. Chump. "Why do I 'gree to marry Pole? Just this, now. We sit chirpin' and chatterin' of times that's gone, and live twice over, Pole and myself; and I'm used to 'm; and I was soft to 'm when he was a merry buck, and you cradle lumber in ideas, mind! for my vartue was always un'mpeach'ble. That's just the reason. So, come, and let's all be friends, with money in our pockuts; yell find me as much of a garl as army of ye. And, there! my weak time's after my Porrt, my dears. So, now ye know when I can't be refusin' a thing to ye. Are we friends?—say! are we?"

Even if the ladies had been disposed to pardon her vulgarity, they could not by any effort summon a charitable sentiment toward one of their sex who degraded it by a public petition for a husband. This was not to be excused; and, moreover, they entertained the sentimentalist's abhorrence of the second marriage of a woman; regarding the act as simply execrable; being treason to the ideal of the sex—treason to Woman's purity—treason to the mysterious sentiment which places Woman so high, that when a woman slips there is no help for it but she must be smashed.

Seeing that each looked as implacable as the other, Mrs. Chump called plaintively, "Arr'bella!"

The lady spoke:—

"We are willing to be your friends, Mrs. Chump, and we request that you will consider us in that light. We simply do not consent to give you a name...."

"But, we'll do without the name, my dear," interposed Mrs. Chump. "Ye'll call me plain Martha, which is almost mother, and not a bit of 't. There—Cornelia, my love! what do ye say?"

"I can only reiterate my sister's words, which demand no elucidation," replied Cornelia.

The forlorn woman turned her lap towards the youngest.

"Ad'la! ye sweet little cajoler! And don't use great cartwheels o' words that leave a body crushed."

Adela was suffering from a tendency to levity, which she knew to be unbefitting the occasion, and likely to defeat its significance. She said: "I am sure, Mrs. Chump, we are very much attached to you as Mrs. Chump; but after a certain period of life, marriage does make people ridiculous, and, as much for your sake as our own, we would advise you to discard a notion that cannot benefit anybody. Believe in our attachment; and we shall see you here now and then, and correspond with you when you are away. And...."

"Oh, ye puss! such an eel as y' are!" Mrs. Chump cried out. "What are ye doin' but sugarin' the same dose, miss! Be qu't! It's a traitor that makes what's nasty taste agree'ble. D'ye think my stomach's a fool? Ye may wheedle the mouth, but not the stomach."

At this offence there fell a dead silence. Wilfrid gazed on them all indifferently, waiting for the moment to strike a final blow.

When she had grasped the fact that Pity did not sit in the assembly, Mrs. Chump rose.

"Oh! if I haven't been sitting among three owls and a raven," she exclaimed. Then she fussed at her gown. "I wish ye good day, young ladus, and mayhap ye'd like to be interduced to No. 2 yourselves, some fine mornin'? Prov'dence can wait. There's a patient hen on the eggs of all of ye! I wouldn't marry Pole now—not if he was to fall flat and howl for me. Mr. Wilfrud, I wish ye good-bye. Ye've done your work. I'll be out of this house in half-an-hour."

This was not quite what Wilfrid had meant to effect. He proposed to her that she should come to the yacht, and indeed leave Brookfield to go on board. But Mrs. Chump was in that frame of mind when, shamefully wounded by others, we find our comfort in wilfully wounding ourselves. "No," she said (betraying a meagre mollification at every offer), "I'll not stop. I won't go to the yacht—unless I think better of ut. But I won't stop. Ye've hurrt me, and I'll say good-bye. I hope ye'll none of ye be widows. It's a crool thing. And when ye've got no children of your own, and feel, all your inside risin' to another person's, and they hate ye—hate ye! Oh! Oh!—There, Mr. Wilfrud, ye needn't touch me elbow. Oh, dear! look at me in the glass! and my hair! Annybody'd swear I'd been drinkin'. I won't let Pole look at me. That'd cure 'm. And he must let me have money, because I don't care for 'cumulations. Not now, when there's no young—no garls and a precious boy, who'd say, when I'm gone, 'Bless her' Oh! 'Poor thing! Bless—' Oh! Augh!" A note of Sorrow's own was fetched; and the next instant, with a figure of dignity, the afflicted woman observed: "There's seven bottles of my Porrt, and there's eleven of champagne, and some comut clar't I shall write where ut's to be sent. And, if you please, look to the packing; for bits o' glass and a red stain's not like your precious hope when you're undoin a hamper. And that's just myself now, and I'm a broken woman; but naver mind, nobody!"

A very formal and stiff "Good-bye," succeeding a wheezy lamentation, concluded the speech. Casting a look at the glass, Mrs. Chump retired, with her fingers on the ornamental piece of hair.

The door having closed on her, Wilfrid said to his sisters: "I want one of you to come with me to town immediately. Decide which will go."

His eyes questioned Cornelia. Hers were dropped.

"I have work to do," pleaded Adela.

"An appointment? You will break it."

"No, dear, not—"

"Not exactly an appointment. Then there's nothing to break. Put on your bonnet."

Adela slipped from the room in a spirit of miserable obedience.

"I could not possibly leave papa," said Arabella, and Wilfrid nodded his head. His sisters knew quite well what was his business in town, but they felt that they were at his mercy, and dared not remonstrate. Cornelia ventured to say, "I think she should not come back to us till papa is in a better state."

"Perhaps not," replied Wilfrid, careless how much he betrayed by his apprehension of the person indicated.

The two returned late that night, and were met by Arabella at the gate.

"Papa has been—don't be alarmed," she began. "He is better now. But when he heard that she was not in the house, the blood left his hands and feet. I have had to use a falsehood. I said, 'She left word that she was coming back to-night or to-morrow.' Then he became simply angry. Who could have believed that the sight of him so would ever have rejoiced me!"

Adela, worn with fatigue, sobbed, "Oh! Oh!"

"By the way, Sir Twickenham called, and wished to see you," said Arabella curiously.

"Oh! so weary!" the fair girl ejaculated, half-dreaming that she saw herself as she threw back her head and gazed at stars and clouds. "We met Captain Gambier in town." Here she pinched Arabella's arm.

The latter said, "Where?"

"In a miserable street, where he looked like a peacock in a quagmire."

Arabella entreated Wilfrid to be careful in his management of their father. "Pray, do not thwart him. He has been anxious to know where you have gone. He—he thinks you have conducted Mrs. Chump, and will bring her back. I did not say it—I merely let him think so."

She added presently, "He has spoken of money."

"Yes?" went Adela, in a low breath.

"Cornelia imagines that—that we—he is perhaps in—in want of it. Merchants are, sometimes."

"Did Sir Twickenham say he would call to-morrow?" asked Adela.

"He said that most probably he would."

Wilfrid had been silent. As he entered the house, Mr. Pole's bedroom-bell rang, and word came that he was to go to his father. As soon as the sisters were alone, Adela groaned: "We have been hunting that girl all day in vile neighbourhoods. Wilfrid has not spoken more than a dozen sentences. I have had to dine on buns and hideous soup. I am half-dead with the smell of cabs. Oh! if ever I am poor it will kill me. That damp hay and close musty life are too intolerable! Yes! You see I care for what I eat. I seem to be growing an animal. And Wilfrid is going to drag me over the same course to-morrow, if you don't prevent him. I would not mind, only it is absolutely necessary that I should see Sir Twickenham."

She gave a reason why, which appeared to Arabella so cogent that she said at once: "If Cornelia does not take your place I will."

The kiss of thanks given by Adela was accompanied by a request for tea. Arabella regretted that she had sent the servants to bed.

"To bed!" cried her sister. "But they are the masters, not we! Really, if life were a round of sensual pleasure, I think our servants might congratulate themselves."

Arabella affected to show that they had their troubles; but her statement made it clear that the servants of Brookfield were peculiarly favoured servants, as it was their mistress's pride to make them. Eventually Adela consented to drink some sparkling light wine; and being thirsty she drank eagerly, and her tongue was loosed, insomuch that she talked of things as one who had never been a blessed inhabitant of the kingdom of Fine Shades. She spoke of 'Cornelia's chances;' of 'Wilfrid's headstrong infatuation—or worse;' and of 'Papa's position,' remarking that she could both laugh and cry.

Arabella, glad to see her refreshed, was pained by her rampant tone; and when Adela, who had fallen into one of her reflective 'long-shot' moods, chanced to say, "What a number of different beings there are in the world!" her reply was, "I was just then thinking we are all less unlike than we suppose."

"Oh, my goodness!" cried Adela. "What! am I at all—at all—in the remotest degree—like that creature we have got rid of?"

The negative was not decisively enunciated or immediate; that is, it did not come with the vehemence and volume that could alone have satisfied Adela's expectation.

The "We are all of one family" was an offensive truism, of which Adela might justly complain.

That night the ladies received their orders from Wilfrid—they were to express no alarm before their father as to the state of his health, or to treat him ostensibly as an invalid; they were to marvel publicly at Mrs. Chump's continued absence, and a letter requesting her to return was to be written. At the sign of an expostulation, Wilfrid smote them down by saying that the old man's life hung on a thread, and it was for them to cut it or not.

BOOK V

CHAPTER XXXIV

INDICATES THE DEGRADATION OF BROOKFIELD, TOGETHER WITH CERTAIN PROCEEDINGS OF THE YACHT

Lady Charlotte was too late for Emilia, when she went forth to her to speak for Wilfrid. She found the youth Braintop resting heavily against a tree, muttering to himself that he had no notion where he was, as an excuse for his stationary posture, while the person he presumed he should have detained was being borne away. Near him a scrap of paper lay on the ground, struck out of darkness by long slips of light from the upper windows. Thinking this might be something purposely dropped, she took possession of it; but a glance subsequently showed her that the writing was too fervid for a female hand. "Or does the girl write in that way?" she thought. She soon decided that it was Wilfrid who had undone her work in the line of thirsty love-speech. "How can a little fool read them and not believe any lie that he may tell!" she cried to herself. She chose to say contemptuously: "It's like a child proclaiming he is hungry." That it was couched in bad taste she positively conceived—taking the paper up again and again to correct her memory. The termination, "Your lover," appeared to her, if not laughable, revolting. She was uncertain in her sentiments at this point.

Was it amusing? or simply execrable? Some charity for the unhappy document Lady Charlotte found when she could say: "I suppose this is the general run of the kind of again." "Was it?" she reflected; and drank at the words again. "No," she came to think; "men don't commonly write as he does, whoever wrote this." She had no doubt that it was Wilfrid. By fits her wrath was directed against him. "It's villany," she said. But more and more frequently a crouching abject longing to call the words her own—to have them poured into her heart and brain—desire for the intoxication of the naked speech of love usurped her spirit of pride, until she read with envious tears, half loathing herself, but fascinated and subdued: "Mine! my angel! You will see me to-morrow.—Your Lover."

Of jealousy she felt very little—her chief thought coming like a wave over her: "Here is a man that can love!"

She was a woman of chaste blood, which spoke to her as shyly as a girl's, now that it was in tumult: so indeed that, pressing her heart, she thought youth to have come back, and feasted on the exultation we have when, at an odd hour, we fancy we have cheated time. The sensation of youth and strength seemed to set a seal of lawfulness and naturalness, hitherto wanting, on her feeling for Wilfrid. "I can help him," she thought. "I know where he fails, and what he can do. I can give him position, and be worth as much as any woman can be to a man." Thus she justified the direction taken by the new force in her.

Two days later Wilfrid received a letter from Lady Charlotte, saying that she, with a chaperon, had started to join her brother at the yacht-station, according to appointment. Amazed and utterly discomfited, he looked about for an escape; but his father, whose plea of sickness had kept him from pursuing Emilia, petulantly insisted that he should go down to Lady Charlotte. Adela was ready to go. There were numbers either going or now on the spot, and the net was around him. Cornelia held back, declaring that her place was by her father's side. Fine Shades were still too dominant at Brookfield for anyone to tell her why she stayed.

With anguish so deep that he could not act indifference, Wilfrid went on his miserable expedition—first setting a watch over Mr. Pericles, the which, in connection with the electric telegraph, was to enable him to join that gentleman speedily, whithersoever he might journey. He was not one to be deceived by the Greek's mask in running down daily to Brookfield. A manoeuvre like that was poor; and besides, he had seen the sallow eyes give a twinkle more than once.

Now, on the Besworth night, Georgiana Ford had studied her brother Merthyr's face when Emilia's voice called for Wilfrid. Her heart was touched; and, in the midst of some little invidious wonder at the power of a girl to throw her attraction upon such a man, she thought, as she hoped, that probably it was due to the girl's Italian blood. Merthyr was not unwilling to speak of her, and say what he feared and desired for Emilia's sake; and Georgiana read, by this mark of confidence, how sincerely she was loved and trusted by him. "One never can have more than half of a man's heart," she thought—adding, "It's our duty to deserve that, nevertheless."

She was mystified. Say that Merthyr loved a girl, whom he certainly distinguished with some visible affection, what sort of man must he be that was preferred to Merthyr? And this set Georgiana at work thinking of Wilfrid. "He has at times the air of a student. He is one who trusts his own light too exclusively. Is he godless?" She concluded: "He is a soldier, and an officer with brains—a good class:" Rare also. Altogether, though Emilia did not elevate herself in this lady's mind by choosing Wilfrid when she might have had Merthyr, the rivalry of the two men helped to dignify the one of whom she thought least. Might she have had Merthyr? Georgiana would not believe it—that is to say, she shut the doors and shot the bolts, the knocking outside went on.

Her brother had told her the whole circumstances of Emilia's life and position. When he said, "Do what you can for her," she knew that it was not the common empty phrase. Young as she was, simple in habits, clear in mind, open in all practices of daily life, she was no sooner brought into an active course than astuteness and impetuosity combined wonderfully in her. She did not tell Merthyr that she had done anything to discover Emilia, and only betrayed that she was moving at all in a little conversation they had about a meeting at the house of his friend Marini, an Italian exile.

"Possibly Belloni goes there," said Merthyr. "I wonder whether Marini knows anything of him. They have a meeting every other night."

Georgiana replied: "He went there and took his daughter the night after we were at Besworth. He took her to be sworn in."

"Still that old folly of Marini's!" cried Merthyr, almost wrathfully. He had some of the English objection to the mixing-up of women in political matters.

Georgiana instantly addressed herself to it: "He thinks that the country must be saved by its women as well as its men; and if they have not brains and steadfast devotion, he concludes that the country will not be saved. But he gives them their share of the work; and, dearest, has he had reason to repent it?"

"No," Merthyr was forced to admit—taking shelter in his antipathy to the administration of an oath to women. "And consider that this is a girl!"

"The oaths of girls are sometimes more binding on them than the oaths of women."

"True, it affects their imaginations vividly; but it seems childish. Does she have to kiss a sword and a book?"

Merthyr made a gesture like a shrug, with a desponding grimace.

"You know," answered Georgiana, smiling, "that I was excused any formula, by special exemption. I have no idea of what is done. Water, salt, white thorns, and other Carbonaro mysteries may be in use or not: I think no worse of the cause, whatever is done."

"I love the cause," said Merthyr. "I dislike this sort of conspiratorial masque Marini and his Chief indulge in. I believe it sustains them, and there's its only use."

"I," said Georgiana, "love the cause only from association with it; but in my opinion Marini is right. He deals with young and fervent minds, that require a ceremony to keep them fast—yes, dear, and women more than others do. After that, they cease to have to rely upon themselves—a reliance their good instinct teaches them is frail. There, now; have I put my sex low enough?"

She slid her head against her brother's shoulder. If he had ever met a man worthy of her, Merthyr would have sighed to feel that all her precious love was his own.

"Is there any likelihood that Belloni will be there tonight?" he asked.

She shook her head. "He has not been there since. He went for that purpose."

"Perhaps Marini is right, after all," said Merthyr, smiling.

Georgiana knew what he meant, and looked at him fondly.

"But I have never bound you to an oath," he resumed, in the same tone.

"I dare say you consider me a little different from most," said Georgiana. She had as small reserve with her brother as vanity, and could even tell him what she thought of her own worth without depreciating it after the fashion of chartered hypocrites.

Mr. Powys wrote to Marini to procure him an interview with Belloni as early as possible, and then he and Georgiana went down to Lady Charlotte.

Letters from Adela kept the Brookfield public informed of the doings on board the yacht. Before leaving home, Wilfrid with Arabella's concurrence certainly—at her instigation, as he thought—had led his father to imagine, on tolerably good grounds, that Mrs. Chump had quitted Brookfield to make purchases for her excursion on lively waters, and was then awaiting him at the appointed station. One of the old man's intermittent nervous fits had frightened them into the quasi-fabrication of this little innocent tale. The doctor's words were that Mr. Pole was to be crossed in nothing—"Not even if it should appear to be of imminent necessity that I should see him, and he refuses." The man of science stated that the malady originated in some long continued pressure of secret apprehension. Both Wilfrid and Arabella conceived that persuasion alone was wanted to send Mrs. Chump flying to the yacht; so they had less compunction in saying, "She is there."

And here began a terrible trial for the children of Nine Shades. To save a father they had to lie grievously—to continue the lie from day to day—to turn it from a lie extensive and inappreciable to the lie minute and absolute. Then, to get a particle of truth out of this monstrous lie, they had to petition in utter humiliation the woman they had scorned, that she would return among them and consider their house her own. No answer came from Mrs. Chump; and as each day passed, the querulous invalid, still painfully acting the man in health, had to be fed with fresh lies; until at last, writing of one of the scenes in Brookfield, Arabella put down the word in all its unblessed aboriginal bluntness, and did not ask herself whether she shrank from it. "Lies!" she wrote. "What has happened to Bella?" thought Adela, in pure wonder. Salt-air and dazzling society kept all idea of penance from this vivacious young person. It was queer that Sit Twickenham should be at the seaside, instead of at Brookfield, wooing; but a man's physical condition should be an excuse for any intermission of attentions. "Now that I know him better," wrote Adela, "I think him the pink of chivalry; and of this I am sure I can convince you, Bella, C. will be blessed indeed; for a delicate nature in a man of the world is a treasure. He has a beautiful little vessel of his own sailing beside us."

Arabella was critic enough to smile at this last. On the whole she was passably content for the moment, in a severe fashion, save to feel herself the dreadful lying engine and fruitlessly abject person that she had become.

We imagine that when souls have had a fall, they immediately look up and contrast their present with their preceding position. This does not occur. The lower their fall, the less, generally, their despair, for despair is a business of the Will, and when they come heavily upon their humanity, they get something of the practical seriousness of nature. If they fall very low, the shock and the sense that they are still on their feet make them singularly earnest to set about the plain plan of existence—getting air for their lungs and elbow-room. Contrast, that mother of melancholy, comes when they are some way advanced upon the upward scale. The Poles did not look up to their lost height, but merely exerted their faculties to go forward; and great as their ambition had been in them, now that it was suddenly blown to pieces, they did not sit and weep, but strove in a stunned way to work ahead. The truth is, that we rarely indulge in melancholy until we can take it as a luxury: little people never do, and they, when we have not put them on their guard, are humankind naked.

The yachting excursions were depicted vividly by Adela, and were addressed as a sort of reproach to the lugubrious letters of her sister. She said pointedly once: "Really, if we are to be miserable, I turn Catholic and go into a convent." The strange thing was that Arabella imagined her letters to be rather of a cheerful character. She related the daily events at Brookfield:—the change in her father's soups, and his remarks on them, and which he preferred; his fight with his medicine, and declaration that he was as sound as any man on shore; the health of the servants; Mr. Marter the curate's call with a Gregorian chant; doubts of his orthodoxy; Cornelia's lonely walks and singular appetite; the bills, and so forth—ending, "What is to be said further of her?"

In return, Adela's delight was to date each day from a different port, to which, catching the wind, the party had sailed, and there slept. The ladies were under the protecting wing of the Hon. Mrs. Bayruffle, a smooth woman of the world. "You think she must have sinned in her time, but are certain it will never be known," wrote Adela. "I do confess, kind as she is, she does me much harm; for when she is near me I begin to think that Society is everything. Her tact is prodigious; it is never seen—only felt. I cannot describe her influence; yet it leads to nothing. I cannot absolutely respect her; but I know I shall miss her acutely when we part. What charm does she possess? I call her the Hon. Mrs. Heathen—Captain G., the Hon. Mrs. Balm. I know you hate nicknames. Be merciful to people yachting. What are we to do? I would look through a telescope all day and calculate the number of gulls and gannets we see; but I am not so old as Sir T., and that occupation could not absorb me. I begin to understand Lady Charlotte and her liking for Mr. Powys better. He is ready to play or be serious, as you please; but in either case 'Merthyr is never a buffoon nor a parson'—Lady C. remarked this morning; and that describes him, if it were not for the detestable fling at the clergy, which she never misses. It seems in her blood to think that all priests are hypocrites. What a little boat to be in on a stormy sea, Bella! She appears to have no concern about it. Whether she adores Wilfrid or not I do not pretend to guess. She snubs him—a thing he would bear from nobody but her. I do believe he feels flattered by it. He is chiefly attentive to Miss Ford, whom I like and do not like, and like and do not like—but do like. She is utterly cold, and has not an affection on earth. Sir T.—I have not a dictionary—calls her a fair clictic, I think. (Let even Cornelia read hard, or woe to her in their hours of privacy!—his vocabulary grows distressingly rich the more you know him. I am not uneducated, but he introduces me to words that seem monsters; I must pretend to know them intimately.) Well, whether a clictic or not—and pray, burn this letter, lest I should not have the word correct—she has the air of a pale young princess above any creature I have seen in the world. I know it has struck Wilfred also; my darling and I are ever twins in sentiment. He converses with Miss Ford a great deal. Lady C. is peculiarly civil to Captain G. We scud along, and are becalmed. 'Having no will of our own, we have no knowledge of contrary winds,' as Mr. Powys says.—The word is 'eclictic,' I find. I ventured on it, and it was repeated; and I heard that I had missed a syllable. Ask C. to look it out—I mean, to tell me they mining on a little slip of paper in your next. I would buy a pocket-dictionary at one of the ports, but you are never alone. "Aesthetic," we know. Mr. Barrett used to be of service for this sort of thing. I admit I am inferior to Mrs. Bayruffle, who, if men talk difficult words in her presence, holds her chin above the conversation, and seems to shame them. I love to learn—I love the humility of learning. And there is something divine in the idea of a teacher. I listen to Sir T. on Parliament and parties, and chide myself if my interest flags. His algebra-puzzles, or Euclid-puzzles in figures—sometimes about sheep-boys and sheep, and hurdles or geese, oxen or anything—are delicious: he quite masters the conversation with them. I disagree with Mrs. Bayruffle when she complains that they are posts in the way of speech. There is a use in all men; and though she is an acknowledged tactician materially, she cannot see she has in Sir T. a quality necessary to intellectual conversation, if she knew how to employ it."

Remarks of this nature read very oddly to Arabella, insomuch that she would question herself at times, in forced seriousness, whether she had dreamed that an evil had befallen Brookfield, or whether Adela were forgetting that it had, in a dream. One day she enclosed a letter from her father to Mrs. Chump. Adela did not forge a reply; but she had the audacity to give the words of a message from the woman (in which Mrs. Chump was supposed to say that she could not write while she was being tossed about.) "We must carry it on," Adela told her sister, with horrible bluntness. The message savoured strongly of Mrs. Chump. It was wickedly clever. Arabella resolved to put it by; but morning after morning she saw her father's anxiety for the reply mounting to a pitch of fever. She consulted with Cornelia, who said, "No; never do such a thing!" and subsequently, with a fainter firmness, repeated the negative monosyllable. Arabella, in her wretchedness, became endued with remorseless discernment. "It means that Cornelia would never do it herself," she thought; and, comforted haply by reflecting that for their common good she could do it, she did it. She repeated an Irish message. Her father calmed immediately, making her speak it over twice. He smiled, and blinked his bird's-eyes pleasurably: "Ah! that's Martha," he said, and fell into a state of comparative repose. For some hours a sensation of bubbling hot-water remained about the sera of Arabella. Happily Mrs. Chump in person did not write.

A correspondence now commenced between the fictitious Mrs. Chump on sea and Mr. Pole, dyspeptic, in his armchair. Arabella took the doctor aside to ask him, if in a hypothetical instance, it would really be dangerous to thwart or irritate her father. She asked the curate if he deemed it wicked to speak falsely to an invalid for the invalid's benefit. The spiritual and bodily doctors agreed that occasion altered and necessity justified certain acts. So far there was comfort. But the task of assisting in this correspondence, and yet more, the contemplation of Adela's growing delight in it (she would now use Irish words, vulgar words, words expressive of physical facts; airing her natural wit in Irish as if she had found a new weapon), became a bitter strain on Arabella's mind, and she was compelled to make Cornelia take her share of the burden. "But I cannot conceal—I cannot feign," said Cornelia. Arabella looked at her, whom she knew to be feigning, thinking, "Must I lose my high esteem of both my sisters? Action alone saved her from denuding herself of this garment."

"That night!" was now the allusion to the scene at Besworth. It stood for all the misery they suffered; nor could they see that they had since made any of their own.

A letter with the Dover postmark brought exciting news.

A debate had been held on board the yacht. Wilfrid and Lady Charlotte gave their votes for the Devon coast. All were ready to be off, when Miss Ford received a telegram from shore, and said, "No; it must be Dover." Now, Mrs. Chump's villa was on the Devon coast. Lady Charlotte had talked to Wilfrid about her, and in the simplest language had said that she must be got on board. This was the reason of their deciding for Devon. But Georgiana stood for Dover; thither Merthyr said that he must go, whether be sailed or went on land. By a simultaneous reading of Georgiana's eyes, both Wilfrid and Lady Charlotte saw what was meant by her decision. Wilfrid at once affected to give way, half-protestingly. "And this," wrote Adela, "taught me that he was well pleased to abandon the West for the East. Lady C. favoured him with a look such as I could not have believed I should ever behold off the stage. There was a perfect dagger in her eyes. She fought against Dover: do men feel such compliments as these? They are the only true ones! She called the captain to witness that the wind was not for Dover she called the mate: she was really eloquent—yes, and handsome. I think Wilfrid thought so; or the reason far the opposition to Dover impressed my brother. I like him to be made to look foolish, for then he retrieves his character so dashingly—always. His face was red, and he seemed undecided—was—until one taunt (it must have been a taunt), roused him up. They exchanged about six sentences—these two. I cannot remember them, unhappily; but for neatness and irony, never was anything so delicious heard. They came sharp as fencing-thrusts; and you could really believe, if you liked, that they were merely stating grounds for diverse opinions. Of course we sailed East, reaching Dover at ten; and the story is this—I knew Emilia was in it:—Tracy Runningbrook had been stationed at Dover ten days by Miss Ford, to intercept Emilia's father, if he should be found taking her to the Continent by that route. He waited, and met them at last on the Esplanade. He telegraphed to Miss Ford and a Signor Marini (we were wrong in not adding illustrious exiles to our list), while he invited them to dine, and detained them till the steamboat was starting; and Signor Marini came down by rail in a great hurry, and would not let Emilia be taken away. There was a quarrel; but, by some mysterious power that he possesses, this Signor Marini actually prevented the father from taking his child. Mysterious? But is anything more mysterious than Emilia's influence? I cannot forget what she was ere we trained her; and when I think that we seem to be all—all who come near her—connected with her fortunes! Explain it if you can. I know it is not her singing; I know it is not her looks. Captivations she does not deal in. Is it the magic of indifference? No; for then some one whom you know and who longs to kiss her bella Bella now would be dangerous! She is very little so, believe me!

"Emilia is (am I chronicling a princess?)—she is in London with Signor Marini; and Wilfrid has not seen her. Lady Charlotte managed to get the first boat full, and pushed off as he was about to descend. I pitied his poor trembling hand I went on shore in the second boat with him. We did not find the others for an hour, when we heard that Emilia had gone with Signor M. The next day, whom should we sea but Mr. Pericles. He (I have never seen him so civil)—he shook Wilfrid by the hand almost like an Englishman; and Wilfrid too, though he detests him, was civil to him, and even laughed when he said: 'Here it is dull; ze Continent for a week. I follow Philomela—ze nightingales.' I was just going to say, 'Well then, you are running away from one.' Wilfrid pressed my fingers, and taught me to be still; and I did not know why till I reflected. Poor Mr. Pericles, seeing him friendly for the first time, rubbed his hands and it was most painful to me to see him shake hands with Wilfrid again and again, till he was on board the vessel chuckling. Wilfrid suddenly laughed with all his might—a cruel laugh; and Mr. Pericles tried to be as loud, but commenced coughing and tapping his chest, to explain that his intention was good. Bella! the passion of love must be judged by the person who inspires it; and I cannot even go so far as to feel pity for Wilfrid if he has stooped to the humiliation of—there is another way of regarding it, know. Let him be sincere and noble; but not his own victim. He scarcely holds up his head. We are now for Devon. Tracy is with us; and we never did a wiser thing than when we decided to patronize poets. If kept in order—under—they are the aristocracy of light conversationalists. Adieu! We speed for beautiful Devon. 'Me love to Pole, and I'm just,' etc. That will do this time; next, she will speak herself. That I should wish it! But the world is full of change, as I begin to learn. What will ensue?"

CHAPTER XXXV

MRS. CHUMP'S EPISTLE

When Mrs. Chump had turned her back on Brookfield, the feelings of the outcast woman were too deep for much distinctly acrimonious sensation toward the ladies; but their letters soon lifted and revived her, until, being in a proper condition of prickly wrath, she sat down to compose a reply that should bury them under a mountain of shame. The point, however, was to transfer this mountain from her bosom, which laboured heavily beneath it, to their heads. Nothing could appear simpler. Here is the mountain; the heads are yonder. Accordingly, she prepared to commence. In a moment the difficulty yawned monstrous. For the mountain she felt was not a mountain of shame; yet that was the character of mountain she wished to cast. If she crushed them, her reputation as a forgiving soul might suffer: she could not pardon without seeing them abased. Thus shaken at starting, she found herself writing: "I know that your father has been hearing tales told of me, or he would have written, and he has not; so you shall never see me, not if you cried to me from the next world—the hot part."

Perusing this, it was too tremendous. "Oh, that's awful!" she said, getting her body a little away from the manuscript. "Ye couldn't curse much louder."

A fresh trial found her again rounding the fact that Mr. Pole had not written to her, and again flying into consequent angers. She had some dim conception of the sculpture of an offended Goddess. "I look so," she said before the glass "I'm above ye, and ye can't hurt me, and don't come anigh me: but here's a cheque—and may ye be haunted in your dreams!—but here's a cheque."

There was pain in her heart, for she had felt faith in Mr. Pole's affection for her. "And he said," she cried out in her lonely room—"he said, 'Martha, ye've onnly to come and be known to 'm, and then they'll take to the ideea.' And wasn't I a patient creature! And it's Pole that's turned—Pole!"

Varied with the frequent 'Oh!' and 'Augh!' these dramatic monologues occupied her time while the yacht was sailing for her Devon bay.

At last the thought struck her that she would send for Braintop—telegraphing that expenses would be paid, and that he must come with a good quill. "It goes faster," she whispered, suggesting the pent-up torrent, as it were, of blackest ink in her breast that there was to pour forth. A very cunning postscript to the telegram brought Braintop almost as quick to her as a return message. It was merely 'Little Belloni.'

She had forgotten this piece of artifice: but when she saw him start at the opening of the door, keeping a sheepish watch in that direction, "By'n-by," she said, with a nod; and shortly afterward unfolded her object in summoning him from his London labours: "A widde-woman ought to get marrud, Mr. Braintop, if onnly to have a husband to write letters for 'rr. Now, that's a task! But sup to-night, and mind ye say yer prayers before gettin' into bed; and no tryin' to flatter your Maker with your knees cuddled up to your chin under the counterpane. I do 't myself sometimes, and I know one prayer out of bed's worrth ten of 'm in. Then I'll pray too; and mayhap we'll get permission and help to write our letter to-morrow, though Sunday, as ye say."

On the morrow Braintop's spirits were low, he having perceived that the 'Little Belloni' postscript had been but an Irish chuckle and nudge in his ribs, by way of sly insinuation or reminder. He looked out on the sea, and sighed to be under certain white sails visible in the offing. Mrs. Chump had received by the morning's post another letter from Arabella, enclosing one for Wilfrid. A dim sense of approaching mastery, and that she might soon be melted, combined with the continued silence of Mr. Pole to make her feel yet more spiteful. She displayed no commendable cunning when, to sharpen and fortify Braintop's wits, she plumped him at breakfast with all things tempting to the appetite of man. "I'll help ye to 'rr," she said from time to time, finding that no encouragement made him potent in speech.

Fronting the sea a desk was laid open. On it were the quills faithfully brought down by Braintop.

"Pole's own quills," she said, having fixed Braintop in this official seat, while she took hers at a station half-commanding the young clerk's face. The mighty breakfast had given Braintop intolerable desire to stretch his limbs by the sounding shore, and enjoy life in semi-oblivion. He cheered himself with the reflection that there was only one letter to write, so he remarked politely that he was at his hostess's disposal. Thereat Mrs. Chump questioned him closely whether Mr. Pole had spoken her name aloud; and whether he did it somehow, now and then by accident, and whether he had looked worse of late. Braintop answered the latter question first, assuring her that Mr. Pole was improving.

"Then there's no marcy from me," said Mrs. Chump; and immediately discharged an exclamatory narrative of her recent troubles, and the breach between herself and Brookfield, at Braintop's ears. This done, she told him that he was there to write the reply to the letters of the ladies, in her name. "Begin," she said. "Ye've got head enough to guess my feelin's. I'm invited, and I won't go—till I'm fetched. But don't say that. That's their guess ye know. 'And I don't care for ye enough to be angry at all, but it's pity I feel at a parcel of fine garls'—so on, Mr. Braintop."

The perplexities of epistolary correspondence were assuming the like proportions to the recruited secretary that they had worn to Mrs. Chump. Steadily watching his countenance; she jogged him thus: "As if ye couldn't help ut, ye know, ye begin. Jest like wakin' in the mornin' after dancin' all night. Ye make the garls seem to hear me seemin' to say—Oooo! I was so comfortable before your disturbin' me with your horrud voices. Ye understand, Mr. Braintop? 'I'm in bed, and you're a cold bath.' Begin like that, ye know. 'Here's clover, and you're nettles.' D'ye see? Here from my glass o' good Porrt to your tumbler of horrud acud vin'gar.' Bless the boy! he don't begin."

She stamped her foot. Braintop, in desperation, made a plunge at the paper. Looking over his shoulder in a delighted eagerness, she suddenly gave it a scornful push. "'Dear!'" she exclaimed. "You're dearin' them, absurd young man I'm not the woman to l dear 'em—not at the starrt! I'm indignant—I'm hurrt. I come round to the 'dear' by-and-by, after I have whipped each of the proud sluts, and their brother Mr. Wilfrid, just as if by accident. Ye'll promus to forget avery secret I tell ye; but our way is always to pretend to believe the men can't help themselves. So the men look like fools, ye sly laughin' fella! and the women horrud scheming spiders. Now, away, with ye, and no dearin'."

The Sunday-bells sounded mockingly in Braintop's ears, appearing to ask him how he liked his holiday; and the white sails on the horizon line have seldom taunted prisoner more. He spread out another sheet of notepaper and wrote "My," and there he stopped.

Mrs. Chump was again at his elbow. "But, they aren't 'my,'" she remonstrated, "when I've nothin' to do with 'm. And a 'my' has a 'dear' to 't always. Ye're not awake, Mr. Braintop; try again."

"Shall I begin formally, 'Mrs. Chump presents her compliments,' ma'am?" said Braintop stiffly.

"And I stick myself up on a post, and talk like a parrot, sir! Don't you see, I'm familiar, and I'm woundud? Go along; try again."

Braintop's next effort was, "Ladies."

"But they don't behave to me like ladus; and it's against my conscience to call 'em!" said Mrs. Chump, with resolution.

Braintop wrote down "Women," in the very irony of disgust.

"And avery one of 'em unmarred garls!" exclaimed Mrs. Chump, throwing up her hands. "Mr. Braintop! Mr. Braintop! ye're next to an ejut!"

Braintop threw dawn the pen. "I really do not know what to say," he remarked, rising in distress.

"I naver had such a desire to shake anny man in all my life," said Mrs. Chump, dropping to her chair.

The posture of affairs was chimed to by the monotonous bell. After listening to it for some minutes, Mrs. Chump was struck with a notion that Braintop's sinfulness in working on a Sunday, or else the shortness of the prayer he had put up to gain absolution, was the cause of his lack of ready wit. Hearing that he had gloves, she told him to go to church, listen devoutly, and return to luncheon. Braintop departed, with a sensation of relief in the anticipation of a sermon, quite new to him. When he next made his bow to his hostess, he was greeted by a pleasant sparkle of refreshments. Mrs. Chump herself primed him with Sherry, thinking in the cunning of her heart that it might haply help the inspiration derived from his devotional exercise. After this, pen and paper were again produced.

"Well, now, Mr. Braintop, and what have ye thought of?" said Mrs. Chump, encouragingly.

Braintop thought rapidly over what he might possibly have been thinking of; and having put a file of ideas into the past, said, with the air of a man who delicately suggests a subtlety: "It has struck me, ma'am, that perhaps 'Girls' might begin very well. To be sure 'Dear girls' is the best, if you would consent to it."

"Take another glass of wine, Mr. Braintop," Mrs. Chump nodded. "Ye're nearer to ut now. 'Garls' is what they are, at all events. But don't you see, my dear your man, it isn't the real thing we want so much as a sort of a proud beginnin', shorrt of slappin' their faces. Think of dinner. Furrst soup; that prepares ye for what's comin'. Then fish, which is on the road to meat, dye see?—we pepper 'em. Then joint, Mr. Braintop—out we burrst: (Oh, and what ins'lent hussies ye've been to me, and yell naver see annything of me but my back!) Then the sweets,—But I'm a forgivin' woman, and a Christian in the bargain, ye ungrateful minxes; and if ye really are sorrowful! And there, Mr. Braintop, ye've got it all laid out as flat as a pancake."

Mrs. Chump gave the motion of a lightning scrawl of the pen. Braintop looked at the paper, which now appeared to recede from his eyes, and flourish like a descending kite. The nature of the task he had undertaken became mountainous in his imagination, till at last he fixed his forehead in his thumbs and fingers, and resolutely counted a number of meaningless words one hundred times. As this was the attitude of a severe student, Mrs. Chump remained in expectation. Aware of the fearful confidence he had excited in her, Braintop fell upon a fresh hundred, with variations.

"The truth is, I think better in church," he said, disclosing at last as ingenuous a face as he could assume. He scarcely ventured to hope for a second dismissal.

To his joy, Mrs. Chump responded with a sigh: "There, go again; and the Lord forgive ye for directin' your mind to temporal matters when ye're there! It's none of my doin', remember that; and don't be tryin' to make me a partic'pator in your wickudness."

"This is so difficult, ma'am, because you won't begin with Dear," he observed snappishly, as he was retiring.

"Of coorse it's difficult if it bothers me," retorted Mrs. Chump, divided between that view of the case and contempt of Braintop for being on her own level.

"Do you see, we are not to say 'Dear' anything, or 'Ladies,' or—in short, really, if you come to think, ma'am!"

"Is that a woman's business, Mr. Braintop?" said Mrs. Chump, as from a height; and the youth retired in humiliation.

Braintop was not destitute of the ambition of his time of life, and yearned to be what he believed himself—something better than a clerk. If he had put forth no effort to compose Mrs. Chump's letter, he would not have felt that he was the partner of her stupidity; but he had thoughtlessly attempted the impossible thing, and now, contemplating his utter failure, he was in so low a state of mind that he would have taken pen and written himself down, with ordinary honesty, good-for-nothing. He returned to his task, and found the dinner spread. Mrs. Chump gave him champagne, and drank to him, requesting him to challenge her. "We won't be beaten," she said; and at least they dined.

The 'we' smote Braintop's swelling vanity. It signified an alliance, and that they were yoked to a common difficulty.

"Oh! let's finish it and have it over," he remarked, with a complacent roll in his chair.

"Naver stop a good impulse," said Mrs. Chump, herself removing the lamp to light him.

Braintop sat in the chair of torture, and wrote flowingly, while his taskmistress looked over him, "Ladies of Brookfield." He read it out: "Ladies of Brookfield."

"I'll be vary happy to represent ye at the forthcomin' 'lection," Mrs. Chump gave a continuation in his tone.

"Why, won't that do, ma'am?" Braintop asked in wonderment.

"Cap'tal for a circular, Mr. Braintop. And ye'll allow me to say that I don't think ye've been to church at all."

This accusation containing a partial truth (that is, true if it referred to the afternoon, but not as to the morning), it was necessary for Braintop's self-vindication that he should feel angry. The two were very soon recriminating, much in the manner of boy and girl shut up on a sunny afternoon; after which they, in like manner, made it up—the fact of both having a habit of consulting the glass, and the accident of their doing it at the same time, causing an encounter of glances there that could hardly fail to be succeeded by some affability. For a last effort, Mrs. Chump laid before Braintop a prospect of advancement in his office, if he so contrived as to write a letter that should land her in Brookfield among a scourged, repentant, and forgiven people. That he might understand the position, she went far modestly to reveal her weakness for Mr. Pole. She even consented to let 'Ladies' be the opening apostrophe, provided the word 'Young' went before it: "They'll feel that sting," she said. Braintop stipulated that she should not look till the letter was done; and, observing his pen travelling the lines in quick succession, Mrs. Chump became inspired by a great but uneasy hope. She was only to be restrained from peeping, by Braintop's petulant "Pray, ma'am!" which sent her bouncing back to her chair, with a face upon one occasion too solemn for Braintop's gravity. He had written himself into excellent spirits; and happening to look up as Mrs. Chump retreated from his shoulder, the woman's comic reverence for his occupation—the prim movement of her lips while she repeated mutely the words she supposed he might be penning—touched him to laughter. At once Mrs. Chump seized on the paper. "Young ladus," she read aloud, "yours of the 2nd, the 14th, and 21st ulto. The 'ffection I bear to your onnly remaining parent."

Her enunciation waxed slower and significantly staccato toward a pause. The composition might undoubtedly have issued from a merchant's office, and would have done no discredit to the establishment. When the pause came, Braintop, half for an opinion, and to encourage progress, said, "Yes, ma'am;" and with "There, sir!" Mrs. Chump crumpled up the paper and flung it at him. "And there, sir!" she tossed a pen. Hearing Braintop mutter, "Lady-like behaviour," Mrs. Chump came out in a fiery bloom. "Ye detestable young fella! Oh, ye young deceiver! Ye cann't do the work of a man! Oh! and here's another woman dis'pointed, and when she thought she'd got a man to write her letters!"

Braintop rose and retorted.

"Ye're false, Mr. Braintop—ye're offensuv, sir!" said Mrs. Chump; and Braintop instantly retired upon an expressive bow. When he was out of the room, Mrs. Chump appealed spitefully to an audience of chairs; but when she heard the front-door shut with a report, she jumped up in terror, crying incredulously, "Is the young man pos'tively one? Oh! and me alone in a rage!—" the contemplated horrors of which position set her shouting vociferously. "Mr. Braintop!" sounded over the stairs, and "Mr. Braintop!" into the street. The maid brought Mrs. Chump her bonnet. Night had fallen; and nothing but the greatest anxiety to recover Braintop would have tempted her from her house. She made half-a-dozen steps, and then stopped to mutter, "Oh! if ye'd onnly come, I'd forgive ye—indeed I would!"

"Well, here I am," was instantaneously answered; her waist was clasped, and her forehead was kissed.

The madness of Braintop's libertinism petrified her.

"Ye've taken such a liberty, sir 'deed ye've forgotten yourself!"

While she was speaking; she grew confused with the thought that Braintop had mightily altered both his voice and shape. When on the doorstep he said; "Come out of the darkness or, upon my honour, I shall behave worse," she recognized Wilfrid, and understood by his yachting costume in what manner he had come. He gave her no time to think of her dignity or her wrath. "Lady Charlotte is with me. I sleep at the hotel; but you have no objection to receive her, have you?" This set her mind upon her best bedroom, her linen, and the fitness of her roof to receive a title. Then, in a partial fit of gratitude for the honour, and immense thankfulness at being spared the task of the letter, she fell on Wilfrid's shoulder, beginning to sob—till he, in alarm at his absurd position, suggested that Lady Charlotte awaited a welcome. Mrs. Chump immediately flew to her drawing-room and rang bells, appearing presently with a lamp, which she set on a garden-pillar. Together they stood by the lamp, a spectacle to ocean: but no Lady Charlotte drew near.

CHAPTER XXXVI

ANOTHER PITFALL OF SENTIMENT

Though Mrs. Chump and Wilfrid, as they stood by the light of the lamp, saw no one, they themselves were seen. Lady Charlotte had arranged to give him a moment in advance to make his peace. She had settled it with that air of practical sense which her title made graceful to him. "I will follow; and I dare say I can complete what you leave unfinished," she said. Her humorous sense of the aristocratic prestige was conveyed to him in a very taking smile. He scarcely understood why she should have planned so decisively to bring about a reconciliation between Mrs. Chump and his family; still, as it now chimed perfectly with his own views and wishes, he acquiesced in her scheme, giving her at the same time credit for more than common wisdom.

While Lady Charlotte lingered on the beach, she became aware of a figure that hung about her; as she was moving away, a voice of one she knew well enough asked to be directed to the house inhabited by Mrs. Chump. The lady was more startled than it pleased her to admit to herself.

"Don't you know me?" she said, bluntly.

"You!" went Emilia's voice.

"Why on earth are you here? What brings you here? Are you alone?" returned the lady.

Emilia did not answer.

"What extraordinary expedition are you making? But, tell me one thing: are you here of your own accord, or at somebody else's bidding?"

Impatient at the prospect of a continuation of silences, Lady Charlotte added, "Come with me."

Emilia seemed to be refusing.

"The appointment was made at that house, I know," said the lady; "but if you come with me, you will see him just as readily."

At this instant, the lamp was placed on the pillar, showing Wilfrid, in his sailor's hat and overcoat, beside the fluttering Irishwoman.

"Come, I must speak to you first," said Lady Charlotte hurriedly, thinking that she saw Emilia's hands stretch out. "Pray, don't go into attitudes. There he is, as you perceive; and I don't use witchcraft. Come with me; I will send for him. Haven't you learnt by this time that there's nothing he detests so much as a public display of the kind you're trying to provoke?"

Emilia half comprehended her.

"He changes when he's away from me," she said, low toneless voice.

"Less than I fancied," the lady thought.

Then she told Emilia that there was really no necessity for her to whine and be miserable; she was among friends, and so forth. The simplicity of her manner of speech found its way to Emilia's reason quicker than her arguments; and, in the belief that Wilfrid was speaking to Mrs. Chump on urgent private matters (she had great awe of the word 'business'), Emilia suffered herself to be led away. She uttered twice a little exclamation, as she looked back, that sounded exceedingly comical to Lady Charlotte's ears. They were the repressions of a poignant outcry. "Doggies make that noise," thought the lady, and succeeded in feeling contemptuous.

Wilfrid, when he found that Lady Charlotte was not coming, bestowed a remark upon her sex, and went indoors for his letter. He considered it politic not to read it there, Mrs. Chump having grown so friendly, and even motherly, that she might desire, out of pure affection, to share the contents. He put it by and talked gaily, till Mrs. Chump, partly to account for the defection of the lady, observed that she knew they had a quarrel. She was confirmed in this idea on a note being brought in to him, over which, before opening it, he frowned and flushed. Aware of the treachery of his countenance, he continued doing so after his eyes had taken in the words, though there was no special ground furnished by them for any such exhibition. Mrs. Chump immediately, with a gaze of mightiest tribulation, burst out: "I'll help ye; 'pon my honour, I'll help ye. Oh! the arr'stocracy! Oh, their pride! But if I say, my dear, when I die (which it's so horrud to think of), you'll have a share, and the biggest—this vary cottage, and a good parrt o' the Bank property—she'll come down at that. And if ye marry a lady of title, I'll be 's good as my word, I will."

Wilfrid pressed her fingers. "Can you ever believe that, I have called you a 'simmering pot of Emerald broth'?"

"My dear! annything that's lots o' words, Ye may call me," returned Mrs. Chump, "as long as it's no name. Ye won't call me a name, will ye? Lots o' words—it's onnly as if ye peppered me, and I sneeze, and that's all; but a name sticks to yer back like a bit o' pinned paper. Don't call me a name," and she wriggled pathetically.

"Yes," said Wilfrid, "I shall call you Pole."

"Oh! ye sweetest of young fellas!"

Mrs. Chump threw out her arms. She was on the point of kissing him, but he fenced with the open letter; and learning that she might read it, she gave a cry of joy.

"Dear W.!" she begins; and it's twice dear from a lady of title. She's just a multiplication-table for annything she says and touches. "Dear W.!" and the shorter time a single you the better. I'll have my joke, Mr. Wilfrud. "Dear W.!" Bless her heart now! I seem to like her next best to the Queen already.—"I have another plan. Ye'd better keep to the old; but it's two paths, I suppose, to one point.—Another plan. Come to me at the Dolphin, where I am alone. Oh, Lord! 'Alone,' with a line under it, Mr. Wilfrud! But there—the arr'stocracy needn't matter a bit."

"It's a very singular proceeding not the less," said Wilfrid. "Why didn't she go to the hotel where the others are, if she wouldn't come here?"

"But the arr'stocracy, Mr. Wilfrud! And alone—alone! d'ye see? which couldn't be among the others; becas of sweet whisperin'. 'Alone,'" Mrs. Chump read on; "'and to-morrow I'll pay my respects to what you call your simmering pot of Emerald broth.' Oh ye hussy! I'd say, if ye weren't a borrn lady. And signs ut all, 'Your faithful Charlotte.' Mr. Wilfrud, I'd give five pounds for this letter if I didn't know ye wouldn't part with it under fifty. And 'deed I am a simmerin' pot; for she'll be a relation, my dear! Go to 'r. I'll have your bed ready for ye here at the end of an hour; and to-morrrow perhaps, if Lady Charlotte can spare me, I'll condescend to see Ad'la."

Wilfrid fanned her cheek with the note, and then dropped it on her neck and left the room. He was soon hurrying on his way to the Dolphin: midway he stopped. "There may be a bad shot in Bella's letter," he thought. Shop-lights were ahead: a very luminous chemist sent a green ray into the darkness. Wilfrid fixed himself under it. "Confoundedly appropriate for a man reading that his wife has run away from him!" he muttered, and hard quickly plunged into matter quite as absorbing. When he had finished it he shivered. Thus it ran:

"My beloved brother,

"I bring myself to plain words. Happy those who can trifle with human language! Papa has at last taken us into his confidence. He has not spoken distinctly; he did us the credit to see that it was not necessary. If in our abyss of grief we loss delicacy, what is left?—what!

"The step he desired to take, Which We Opposed, he has anticipated, And Must Consummate.

"Oh, Wilfrid! you see it, do you not? You comprehend me I am surf! I should have said 'had anticipated.' How to convey to you! (but it would be unjust to him—to ourselves—were I to say emphatically what I have not yet a right to think). What I have hinted above is, after all; nothing but Cornelia's conjecture, I wish I could not say confirmed by mine. We sat with Papa two hours before any idea of his meaning dawned upon us. He first scolded us. We both saw from this that more was to come.

"I hope there are not many in this world to whom the thought of honour being tied to money ever appears possible. If it is so there is wide suffering—deep, for it, must be silent. Cornelia suggests one comfort for them that they will think less of poverty.

"Why was Brookfield ever bought? Our old peaceful City-life—the vacant Sundays!—my ears are haunted by their bells for Evening Service. I said 'There they go, the dowdy population of heaven!' I remember it now. It should be almost punishment enough to be certain that of all those people going to church, there cannot be one more miserable than we who stood at the old window ridiculing them. They at least do not feel that everything they hope for in human life is dependent upon one human will—the will of a mortal weather-vane! It is the case, and it must be conciliated. There is no half-measure—no choice. Feel that nothing you have ever dreamed of can be a disgrace if it is undergone to forestall what positively impends, and act immediately. I shall expect to see you in three days. She is to have the South-west bedroom (mine), for which she expressed a preference. Prepare every mind for the ceremony:—an old man's infatuation—money—we submit. It will take place in town. To have the Tinleys in the church! But this is certainly my experience, that misfortune makes me feel more and more superior to those whom I despise. I have even asked myself—was I so once? And, Apropos of Laura! We hear that their evenings are occupied in performing the scene at Besworth. They are still as distant as ever from Richford. Let me add that Albert Tinley requested my hand in marriage yesterday. I agree with Cornelia that this is the first palpable sign that we have sunk. Consequent upon the natural consequences came the interview with Papa.

"Dearest, dearest Wilfrid! can you, can I, can any one of us settle—that is, involve another life in doubt while doubt exists? Papa insists; his argument is, 'Now, now, and no delay.' I accuse nothing but his love. Excessive love is perilous for principle!

"You have understood me, I know, and forgiven me for writing so nakedly. I dare not reperuse it. You must satisfy him that Lady C. has fixed a date. Adela is incomprehensible. One day she sees a friend in Lady C., and again it is an enemy. Papa's immediate state of health is not alarming. Above all things, do not let the girl come near him. Papa will send the cheque you required."

"When?" Wilfrid burst out upon Arabella's affectionate signature. "When will he send it? He doesn't do me the honour to mention the time. And this is his reply to a third application!"

The truth was that Wilfrid was in dire want of tangible cash simply to provision his yacht. The light kindled in him by this unsatisfied need made him keen to comprehend all that Arabella's attempt at plain writing designed to unfold.

"Good God, my father's the woman's trustee!" shaped itself in Wilfrid's brain.

And next: "If he marries her we may all be as poor as before." That is to say, "Honour may be saved without ruin being averted."

His immediate pressing necessity struck like a pulse through all the chords of dismal conjecture. His heart flying about for comfort, dropped at Emilia's feet.

"Bella's right," he said, reverting to the green page in his hand; "we can't involve others in our scrape, whatever it may be."

He ceased on the spot to be at war with himself, as he had been for many a day; by which he was taught to imagine that he had achieved a mental indifference to misfortune. This lightened his spirit considerably. "So there's an end of that," he emphasized, as the resolve took form to tell Lady Charlotte flatly that his father was ruined, and that the son, therefore, renounced his particular hope and aspiration.

"She will say, in the most matter-of-fact way in the world, 'Oh, very well, that quite alters the case,'" said Wilfrid aloud, with the smallest infusion of bitterness. Then he murmured, "Poor old governor!" and wondered whether Emilia would come to this place according to his desire. Love, that had lain crushed in him for the few recent days, sprang up and gave him the thought, "She may be here now;" but, his eyes not being satiated instantly with a sight of her, the possibility of such happiness faded out.

"Blessed little woman!" he cried openly, ashamed to translate in tenderer terms the soft fresh blossom of love that his fancy conjured forth at the recollection of her. He pictured to himself hopefully, moreover, that she would be shy when they met. A contradictory vision of her eyes lifted hungry for his first words, or the pressure of his arm displeased him slightly. It occurred to him that they would be characterized as a singular couple. To combat this he drew around him all the mysteries of sentiment that had issued from her voice and her eyes. She had made Earth lovely to him and heaven human. She—what a grief for ever that her origin should be what it was! For this reason:—lovers must live like ordinary people outwardly; and say, ye Fates, how had she been educated to direct a gentlemen's household?

"I can't exist on potatoes," he pronounced humorously.

But when his thoughts began to dwell with fitting seriousness on the woman-of-the-world tone to be expected from Lady Charlotte, he folded the mental image of Emilia closely to his breast, and framed a misty idea of a little lighted cottage wherein she sat singing to herself while he was campaigning. "Two or three fellows—Lumley and Fredericks—shall see her," he thought. The rest of his brother officers were not even to know that he was married.

His yacht was lying in a strip of moonlight near Sir Twickenham's companion yawl. He gave one glance at it as at a history finished, and sent up his name to Lady Charlotte.

"Ah! you haven't brought the good old dame with you?" she said, rising to meet him. "I thought it better not to see her to-night."

He acquiesced, mentioning the lateness of the hour, and adding, "You are alone?"

She stared, and let fall "Certainly," and then laughed. "I had forgotten your regard for the proprieties. I have just sent my maid for Georgiana; she will sleep here. I preferred to come here, because those people at the hotel tire me; and, besides, I said I should sleep at the villa, and I never go back to people who don't expect me."

Wilfrid looked about the room perplexed, and almost suspicious because of his unexplained perplexity. Her (as he deemed it—not much above the level of Mrs. Chump in that respect) aristocratic indifference to opinion and conventional social observances would have pleased him by daylight, but it fretted him now.

Lady Charlotte's maid came in to say that Miss Ford would join her. The maid was dismissed to her bed. "There's nothing to do there," said her mistress, as she was moving to the folding-doors. The window facing seaward was open. He went straight to it and closed it. Next, in an apparent distraction, he went to the folding-doors. He was about to press the handle, when Lady Charlotte's quiet remark, "My bedroom," brought him back to his seat, crying pardon.

"Have you had news?" she inquired. "You thought that a letter might be there. Bad, is it?"

"It is not good," he replied, briefly.

"I am sorry."

"That is—it tells me—" (Wilfrid disciplined his tongue) "that I—we are—a lieutenant on half-pay may say that he is ruined, I suppose, when his other supplies are cut off!..."

"I can excuse him for thinking it," said Lady Charlotte. She exhibited no sign of eagerness for his statement of facts.

Her outward composure and a hard animation of countenance (which, having ceased the talking within himself, he had now leisure to notice) humiliated him. The sting helped him to progress.

"I may try to doubt it as much as I please, to avoid seeing what must follow.... I may shut my eyes in the dark, but when the light stares me in the face...I give you my word that I have not been justified even in imagining such a catastrophe."

"The preamble is awful," said Lady Charlotte, rising from her recumbent posture.

"Pardon me; I have no right to intrude my feelings. I learn to-day, for the first time, that we are—are ruined."

She did not lift her eyebrows, or look fixedly; but without any change at all, said, "Is there no doubt about it?"

"None whatever." This was given emphatically. Resentment at the perfect realization of her anticipated worldly indifference lent him force.

"Ruined?" she said.

"Yes."

"You I'll be more so than you were a month ago. I mean, you tell me nothing new, I have known it."

Amid the crush and hurry in his brain, caused by this strange communication, pressed the necessity to vindicate his honour.

"I give you the word of a gentleman, Lady Charlotte, that I came to you the first moment it has been made known to me. I never suspected it before this day."

"Nothing would prompt me to disbelieve that." She reached him her hand.

"You have known it!" he broke from a short silence.

"Yes—never mind how. I could not allude to it. Of course I had to wait till you took the initiative."

The impulse to think the best of what we are on the point of renouncing is spontaneous. If at the same time this object shall exhibit itself in altogether new, undreamt-of, glorious colours, others besides a sentimentalist might waver, and be in some danger of clutching it a little tenderly ere it is cast off.

"My duty was to tell you the very instant it came to my knowledge," he said, fascinated in his heart by the display of greatness of mind which he now half divined to be approaching, and wished to avoid.

"Well, I suppose that is a duty between friends?" said she.

"Between friends! Shall we still—always be friends?"

"I think I have said more than once that it won't be my fault if we are not."

"Because, the greater and happier ambition to which I aspired..." This was what he designed to say, sentimentally propelled, by way of graceful exit, and what was almost printed on a scroll in his head for the tongue to read off fluently. He stopped at 'the greater,' beginning to stumble—to flounder; and fearing that he said less than was due as a compliment to the occasion, he said more.

By no means a quick reader of character, Lady Charlotte nevertheless perceived that the man who spoke in this fashion, after what she had confessed, must be sentimentally, if not actually, playing double.

Thus she came to his assistance: "Are you begging permission to break our engagement?"

"At least, whatever I do get I must beg for now!" He took refuge adroitly in a foolish reply, and it served him. That he had in all probability lost his chance by the method he had adopted, and by sentimentalizing at the wrong moment, was becoming evident, notwithstanding. In a sort of despair he attempted comfort by critically examining her features, and trying to suit them to one or other of the numerous models of Love that a young man carries about with him. Her eyes met his, and even as he was deciding against her on almost every point, the force of their frankness held his judgement in suspense.

"The world is rather harsh upon women in these cases," she said, turning her head a lithe, with a conscious droop of the eyelids. "I will act as if we had an equal burden between us. On my side, what you have to tell me does not alter me. I have known it.... You see that I am just the same to you. For your part, you are free, if you please. That is fair dealing, is it not?"

The gentleman's mechanical assent provoked the lady's smile.

But Wilfrid was torn between a profound admiration of her and the galling reflection that until she had named the engagement, none had virtually existed which diplomacy, aided by time and accident, might not have stopped.

"You must be aware that I am portionless," she continued. "I have—let me name the sum—a thousand pounds. It is some credit to me that I have had it five years and not spent it. Some men would think that a quality worth double the amount. Well, you will make up your mind to my bringing you no money;—I have a few jewels. En revanche, my habits are not expensive. I like a horse, but I can do without one. I like a large house, and can live in a small one. I like a French cook, and can dine comfortably off a single dish. Society is very much to my taste; I shall indulge it when I am whipped at home."

Wilfrid took her hand and pressed his lips to the fingers, keeping his face ponderingly down. He was again so divided that the effort to find himself absorbed all his thinking faculties.

At last he muttered: "A lieutenant's pay!"—expecting her to reply, "We can wait," as girls do that find it pleasant to be adored by curates, Then might follow a meditative pause—a short gaze at her, from which she could have the option of reflecting that to wait is not the privilege of those who have lived to acquire patience. The track he marked out was clever in a poor way; perhaps it was not positively unkind to instigate her to look at her age: but though he read character shrewdly, and knew hers pretty accurately, he was himself too much of a straw at the moment to be capable of leading-moves.

"We can make up our minds, without great difficulty, to regard the lieutenant's pay as nothing at all," was Lady Charlotte's answer. "You will enter the Diplomatic Service. My interest alone could do that. If we are married, there would be plenty to see the necessity for pushing us. I don't know whether you could keep the lieutenancy; you might. I should not like you to quit the Army: an opening might come in it. There's the Indian Staff—the Persian Mission: they like soldiers for those Eastern posts. But we must take what we can get. We should, anyhow, live abroad, where in the matter of money society is more sensible. We should be able to choose our own, and advertize tea, brioche, and conversation in return for the delicacies of the season."

"But you, Charlotte—you could never live that life!" Wilfrid broke in, the contemplation of her plain sincerity diminishing him to himself. "It would drag you down too horribly!"

"Remorse at giving tea in return for dinners and balls?"

"Ah! there are other things to consider."

She blushed unwontedly.

Something, lighted by the blush, struck him as very feminine and noble.

"Then I may flatter myself that you love me?" he whispered.

"Do you not see?" she rejoined. "My project is nothing but a whim—a whim."

The divided man saw himself whole, if not happy in the ranks of Diplomacy, with a resolute, frank, faithful woman (a lady of title) loving him, to back him. Fortune shone ahead, and on the road he saw where his deficiencies would be filled up by her. She was firm and open—he irresolute and self-involved. Animal courage both possessed. Their differences were so extreme that they met where they differed. It struck him specially now that she would be like Day to his spirit in continued intercourse. Young as he was he had wisdom to know the right meaning of the word "helpmate." It was as if the head had dealt the heart a blow, saying, "See here the lady thou art to serve." But the heart was a surly rebel. Lady Charlotte was fully justified in retorting upon his last question: "I think I also should ask, do you love me? It is not absolutely imperative for the occasion or for the catastrophe, I merely ask for what is called information."

And yet, despite her flippancy, which was partly designed to relieve his embarrassment, her hand was moist and her eyes were singularly watchful.

"You who sneer at love!" He gave a musical murmur.

"Not at all. I think it a very useful part of the capital to begin the married business upon."

"You unsay your own words."

"Not 'absolutely imperative,' I think I said, if I remember rightly."

"But I take the other view, Charlotte."

"You imagine that there must be a little bit of love."

"There should be no marriage without it."

"On both sides?"

"At least, if not on both sides, one should bring such a love."

"Enough for two! So, then, we are not to examine your basket?"

Touched by the pretty thing herein implied, he squeezed her hand.

"This is the answer?" said she.

"Can you doubt me?"

She rose from her seat. "Oh! if you talk in that style, I really am tempted to say that I do. Are there men—women and women—men? My dear Wilfrid, have we changed parts to-night?"

His quickness in retrieving a false position, outwardly, came to his aid. He rose likewise, and, while perfecting the minor details of an easy attitude against the mantelpiece, said: "I am so constituted, Charlotte, that I can't talk of my feelings in a business tone; and I avoid that subject unless... You spoke of a basket just now. Well, I confess I can't bring mine into the market and bawl out that I have so many pounds' weight of the required material. Would a man go to the market at all if he had nothing to dispose of? In plain words—since my fault appears to be, according to your reading, in the opposite direction—should I be here if my sentiments could not reply eloquently to your question?"

This very common masterpiece of cunning from a man in a corner, which suggests with so persuasive an air that he has ruled his actions up to the very moment when he faces you, and had almost preconceived the present occasion, rather won Lady Charlotte; or it seemed to, or the scene had been too long for her vigilance.

"In the affirmative?" she whispered, coming nearer to him.

She knew that she had only to let her right shoulder slip under his left arm, and he would very soon proclaim himself her lover as ardently as might be wished. Why did she hesitate to touch the blood of the man? It was her fate never to have her great heart read aright. Wilfrid could not know that generosity rather than iciness restrained her from yielding that one unknown kiss which would have given the final spring to passion in his breast. He wanted the justification of his senses, and to run headlong blindly. Had she nothing of a woman's instinct?

"In the affirmative!" was his serene reply.

"That means 'Yes.'" Her tone had become pleasantly soft.

"Yes, that means 'Yes,'" said he.

She shut her eyes, murmuring, "How happy are those who hear that they are loved!" and opening them, all her face being red, "Say it!" she pleaded. Her fingers fell upon his wrist. "I have this weakness, Wilfrid; I wish to hear you say it."

The flush of her face, and tremour of her fingers, told of an unimagined agitation hardly to be believed, though seen and felt. Yet, still some sign, some shade of a repulsion in her figure, kept him as far from her as any rigid rival might have stipulated for.

The interrogation to the attentive heavens was partially framed in his mind, "How can I tell this woman I love her, without..." without putting his arm about her waist, and demonstrating it satisfactorily to himself as well as to her? In other words, not so framed, "How, without that frenzy which shall make me forget whether it be so or not?"

He remained in his attitude, incapable of moving or speaking, but fancying, that possibly he was again to catch a glimpse of the vanished mountain nymph, sweet Liberty. Her woman's instinct warmed more and more, until, if she did not quite apprehend his condition, she at least understood that the pause was one preliminary to a man's feeling himself a fool.

"Dear Wilfrid," she whispered, "you think you are doubted. I want to be certain that you think you have met the right woman to help you, in me."

He passed through the loophole here indicated, and breathed.

"Yes, Charlotte, I am sure of that. If I could be only half as worthy! You are full of courage and unselfishness, and, I could swear, faithful as steel."

"Thank you—not dogs," she laughed. "I like steel. I hope to be a good sword in your hand, my knight—or shield, or whatever purpose you put me to."

She went on smiling, and seeming to draw closer to him and throw down defences.

"After all, Wilfrid, the task of loving your good piece of steel won't be less thoroughly accomplished because you find it difficult. Sir, I do not admit any protestation. Handsome faces, musical voices, sly manners, and methods that I choose not to employ, make the business easy to men."

"Who discover that the lady is not steel," said Wilfrid. "Need she, in any case, wear so much there?"

He pointed, flittingly as it were, with his little finger to the slope of her neck.

She turned her wrist, touching the spot: "Here? You have seen, then, that it is something worn?"

There followed a delicious interplay of eyes. Who would have thought that hers could be sweet and mean so much?

"It is something worn, then? And thrown aside for me only, Charlotte?"

"For him who loves me," she said.

"For me!"

"For him who loves me," she repeated.

"Then it is for me!"

She had moved back, showing a harder figure, or the "I love you, love you!" would have sounded with force. It came, though not so vehemently as might have been, to the appeal of a soft fixed look.

"Yes, I love you, Charlotte; you know that I do."

"You love me?"

"Yes."

"Say it."

"I love you! Dead, inanimate Charlotte, I love you!"

She threw out her hand as one would throw a bone to a dog.

"My living, breathing, noble Charlotte," he cried, a little bewitched, "I love you with all my heart!"

It surprised him that her features should be gradually expressing less delight.

"With all your heart?"

"Could I give you a part?"

"It is done, sometimes," she said, mock-sadly. Then, in her original voice: "Good. I never credited that story of you and the girl Emilia. I suppose what people say is a lie?"

Her eyes, in perfect accordance with the tone she had adopted, set a quiet watch on him.

"Who says it?" he thundered, just as she anticipated.

"It's not true?"

"Not true!—how can it be true?"

"You never loved Emilia Belloni?—don't love her now?—do not love her now? If you have ever said that you love Emilia Belloni, recant, and you are forgiven; and then go, for I think I hear Georgiana below. Quick! I am not acting. It's earnest. The word, if you please, as you are a gentleman. Tell me, because I have heard tales. I have been perplexed about you. I am sure you're a manly fellow, who would never have played tricks with a girl you were bound to protect; but you might have—pardon the slang—spooned,—who knows? You might have been in love with her downright. No harm, even if a trifle foolish; but in the present case, set my mind at rest. Quick! There are both my hands. Take them, press them, and speak."

The two hands were taken, but his voice was not so much at command. No image of Emilia rose in his mind to reproach him with the casting over of his heart's dear mistress, but a blind struggle went on. It seemed that he could do what he dared not utter. The folly of lips more loyal than the spirit touched his lively perception; and as the hot inward struggle, masked behind his softly-playing eyes, had reduced his personal consciousness so that if he spoke from his feeling there was a chance of his figuring feebly, he put on his ever-ready other self:—

"Categorically I reply: Have I loved Miss Emilia Belloni?—No. Do I?—No. Do I love Charlotte Chillingworth?—Yes, ten thousand times! And now let Britomart disarm."

He sought to get his reward by gentle muscular persuasion. Her arms alone yielded: and he judged from the angle of the neck, ultra-sharp though it was, that her averted face might be her form of exhibiting maidenly reluctance, feminine modesty. Suddenly the fingers in his grasp twisted, and not being at once released, she turned round to him.

"For God's sake, spare the girl!"

Emilia stood in the doorway.

CHAPTER XXXVII

EMILIA'S FLIGHT

A knock at Merthyr's chamber called him out while he sat writing to Marini on the national business. He heard Georgiana's voice begging him to come to her quickly. When he saw her face the stain of tears was there.

"Anything the matter with Charlotte?" was his first question.

"No. But, come: I will tell you on the way. Do not look at me."

"No personal matter of any kind?"

"Oh, no! I can have none;" and she took his hand for a moment.

They passed into the dark windy street smelling of the sea.

"Emilia is here," said Georgiana. "I want you to persuade her—you will have influence with her. Oh, Merthyr! my darling brother! I thank God I love my brother with all my love! What a dreadful thing it is for a woman to love a man:"

"I suppose it is, while she has nothing else to do," said Merthyr. "How did she come?—why?"

"If you had seen Emilia to-night, you would have felt that the difference is absolute." Georgiana dealt first with the general case, "she came, I think, by some appointment."

"Also just as absolute between her and her sex," he rejoined, controlling himself, not to be less cool. "What has happened?"

Georgiana pointed to the hotel whither their steps were bent. "That is where Charlotte sleeps. Her going there was not a freak; she had an object. She wished to cure Emilia of her love for Mr. Wilfrid Pole. Emilia had come down to see him. Charlotte put her in an adjoining room to hear him say—what I presume they do say when the fit is on them! Was it not singular folly?"

It was a folly that Merthyr could not understand in his friend Charlotte. He said so, and then he gave a kindly sad exclamation of Emilia's name.

"You do pity her still!" cried Georgiana, her heart leaping to hear it expressed so simply.

"Why, what other feeling can I have?" said he unsuspiciously.

"No, dear Merthyr," she replied; and only by her tone he read the guilty little rejoicing in her heart, marvelling at jealousy that could twist so straight a stem as his sister's spirit. This had taught her, who knew nothing of love, that a man loving does not pity in such a case.

"I hope you will find her here:" Georgiana hurried her steps. "Say anything to comfort her. I will have her with me, and try and teach her what self-control means, and how it is to be won. If ever she can act on the stage as she spoke to-night, she will be a great dramatic genius. She was transformed. She uses strange forcible expressions that one does not hear in every-day life. She crushed Charlotte as if she had taken her up in one hand, and without any display at all: no gesture, or spasm. I noticed, as they stood together, that there is such a contrast between animal courage and imaginative fire."

"Charlotte could meet a great occasion, I should think," said Merthyr; and, taking his sister by the elbow: "You speak as if you had observed very coolly. Did Emilia leave you so cold? Did she seem to speak from head, not from heart?"

"No; she moved me—poor child! Only, how humiliating to hear her beg for love!—before us."

Merthyr smiled: "I thought it must be the woman's feeling that would interfere to stop a natural emotion. Is it true—or did I not see that certain eyes were red just now?"

"That was for him," said Georgiana, hastily. "I am sure that no man has stood in such a position as he did. To see a man made publicly ashamed, and bearing it. I have never had to endure so painful a sight."

"To stand between two women, claimed by both, like Solomon's babe! A man might as well at once have Solomon's judgement put into execution upon him. You wept for him! Do you know, Georgey, that charity of your sex, which makes you cry at any 'affecting situation,' must have been designed to compensate to us for the severities of Providence."

"No, Merthyr;" she arrested his raillery. "Do I ever cry? But I thought—if it had been my brother! and almost at the thought I felt the tears rush at my eyelids, as if the shame had been mine."

"The probability of its not being your brother seemed distant at the moment," said Merthyr, with his half-melancholy smile. "Tell me—I can conjure up the scene: but tell me whether you saw more passions than one in her face?"

"Emilia's? No. Her face reminded me of the sombre—that dull glow of a fire that you leave burning in the grate late on winter nights. Was that natural? It struck me that her dramatic instinct was as much alive as her passion."

"Had she been clumsy, would you not have been less suspicious of her? And if she had only shown the accustomed northern retenue, and merely looked all that she had to say 'preserved her dignity'—our womanly critic would have been completely satisfied."

"But, Merthyr, to parade her feelings, and then to go on appealing!"

"On the principle that she ought to be ashamed of them, she was wrong."

"If you had heard her utter abandonment!"

"I can believe that she did not blush."

"It seems to me to belong to those excesses that prompt—that are in themselves a species of suicide."

"Love is said to be the death of self."

"No; but I must use cant words, Merthyr; I do wish to see modesty. Yes, I know I must be right."

"There is very little of it to be had in a tropical storm."

"You admit, then, that this sort of love is a storm that passes?"

"It passes, I hope."

"But where is your defence of her now?"

"Have I defended her? I need not try. A man has deceived her, and she doesn't think it possible; and has said so, I presume. When she sees it, she will be quieter than most. She will not reproach him subsequently. Here is the hotel, and that must be Charlotte's room, if I may judge by the lights. What pranks will she always be playing! We seem to have brought new elements into the little town. Do you remember Bergamo the rainy night the Austrian trooped out of Milan?—one light that was a thousand in the twinkling of an eye!"

Having arrived, he ran hastily up to the room, expecting to find the three; but Lady Charlotte was alone, sitting in her chair with knotted arms. "Ah, Merthyr!" she said, "I'm sorry you should have been disturbed. I perceive what Georgey's leaving the room meant. I suppose the hotel people are used to yachting-parties." And then, not seeing any friendly demonstration on his part, she folded her arms in another knot. Georgiana asked where Emilia was. Lady Charlotte replied that Emilia had gone, and then Wilfrid had followed her, one minute later, to get her into shelter somewhere. Or put penknives out of her way. "I am rather fatigued with a scene, Merthyr. I never had an idea before of what your Southern women were. One plays decidedly second to them while the fit lasts. Of course, you have a notion that I planned the whole of the absurd business. This is the case:—I found the girl on the beach: she follows him everywhere, which is bad for her reputation, because in this climate people suspect, positive reasons for that kind of female devotedness. So, to put an end to it—really for her own sake, quite as much as anything else—am I a monster of insensibility, Merthyr?—I made her swear an oath: one must be a point above wild animals to feel that to be binding, however! I made her swear to listen and remain there silent till I opened the door to set her at liberty. She consented—gave her word solemnly. I calculated that she might faint, and fixed her in an arm-chair. Was that cruel? Merthyr, you have called me Austrian more than once; but, upon my honour, I wanted her to get over her delusion comfortably. I thought she would have kept the oath, I confess; she looked up like a child when she was making it. You have heard the rest from Georgey. I must say the situation was rather hard on Wilfrid. If he blames me it will be excuseable, though what I did plan was to save him from a situation somewhat worse. So now you know the whole, Merthyr. Commence your lecture. Make me a martyr to the sorrows of Italy once more."

Merthyr took her wrist, feeling the quick pulse, and dropped it. She was effectually humbled by this direct method of dealing with her secret heart. After some commonplace remarks had passed, she herself urged him to send out men in search for Emilia. Before he went, she murmured a soft "Forgive me." The pressure of her fingers was replied to, but the words were not spoken.

"There," she cried to Georgiana, "I have offended the only man for whose esteem I care one particle! Devote yourself to your friends!"

"How? 'devote yourself!'" murmured Georgiana, astonished.

"Do you think I should have got into this hobble if I hadn't wished to serve some one else? You must have seen that Merthyr has a sentimental sort of fondness—call it passion—for this girl. She's his Italy in the flesh. Is there a more civilized man in the world than Merthyr? So he becomes fascinated by a savage. We all play the game of opposites—or like to, and no woman in his class will ever catch him. I couldn't have believed that he was touched by a girl, but for two or three recent indications. You must have noticed that he has given up reading others, and he objected the other day to a responsible office which would have thrown him into her neighbourhood alone. These are unmistakeable signs in Merthyr, though he has never been in love, and doesn't understand his case a bit. Tell me, do you think it impossible?"

Georgiana answered dryly, "You have fallen into a fresh mistake."

Exactly. Then let me rescue you from a similar fatality, Georgey. If your eyes are bandaged now..."

"Are you going to be devoted to me also, Charlotte?"

"I believe I'm a miracle of devotion," said the lady, retiring into indifferent topics upon that phrase. She had at any rate partially covered the figure of ridicule presented to her feminine imagination by the aspect of her fair self exposed in public contention with one of her sex—and for a man. It was enough to make her pulse and her brain lively. On second thoughts, too, it had struck her that she might be serving Merthyr in disengaging Emilia; and undoubtedly she served Georgiana by giving her a warning. Through this silliness went the current of a clear mind, nevertheless. The lady's heart was justified in crying out: "What would I not abandon for my friend in his need?" Meantime her battle in her own behalf looked less pleasing by the light of new advantages. The question recurred: "Shall I care to win at all?" She had to force the idea of a violent love to excuse her proceedings. To get up any flame whatsoever, an occasional blast of jealousy had to be called for. Jealousy was a quality she could not admit as possible to her. So she acted on herself by an agent she repudiated, and there was no help for it. Had Wilfrid loved her the woman's heart was ready. It was ready with a trembling tenderness, softer and deeper than a girl's. For Charlotte would have felt: "With this love that I have craved for, you give me life." And she would have thanked him for both, exultingly, to feel: "I can repay you as no girl could do;" though she had none of the rage of love to give; as it was, she thought conscientiously that she could help him. She liked him: his peculiar suppleness of a growing mind, his shrouded sensibility, in conjunction with his reputation for an evidently quite reliable prompt courage, and the mask he wore, which was to her transparent, pleased her and touched her fancy.

Nor was he so vain of his person as to make him seem like a boy to her. He affected maturity. He could pass a mirror on his right or his left without an abstracted look over either shoulder;—a poor example, but worth something to a judge of young men. Indeed, had she chosen from a crowd, the choice would have been one of his age. She was too set for an older man; but a youth aspiring to be older than he was; whose faults she saw and forgave; whose merits supplied two or three of her own deficiencies; whom her station might help to elevate; to whom she might come as a benefactress; feeling so while she accomplished her own desire;—such a youth was everything to her, as she awoke to discover after having played with him a season. If she lost him, what became of her? Even if she had rejoiced in a mother to plot and play,—to bait and snare for her, her time was slipping, and the choosers among her class were wary. Her spirit, besides, was high and elective. It was gradually stooping to nature, but would never have bowed to a fool, or, save under protest, to one who gave all. On Wilfrid she had fixed her mind: so, therefore, she bore the remembrance of the recent scene without much fretting at her burdens;—the more, that Wilfrid had in no way shamed her; and the more, that the heat of Emilia's love played round him and illumined him. This borrowing of the passion of another is not uncommon.

At daybreak Mrs. Chump was abroad. She had sat up for Wilfrid almost through the night. "Oh! the arr'stocracy!" she breathed exclamations, as she swept along the esplanade. "I'll be killed and murdered if I tell a word." Meeting Captain Gambier, she fell into a great agitation, and explained it as an anxiety she entertained for Wilfrid; when, becoming entangled in the mesh of questions, she told all she knew, and nearly as much as she suspected: which fatal step to retrieve, she entreated his secresy. Adela was now seen fluttering hastily up the walk, fresh as a creature of the sea-wave. Before Mrs. Chump could summon her old wrath of yesterday, she was kissed, and to the arch interrogation as to what she had done with this young lady's brother, replied by telling the tale of the night again. Mrs. Chump was ostentatiously caressed into a more comfortable opinion of the world's morality, for the nonce. Invited by them to breakfast at the hotel, she hurried back to her villa for a flounced dress and a lace cap of some pretensions, while they paced the shore.

"See what may be said!" Adela's countenance changed as she muttered it. "Thought, would be enough," she added, shuddering.

"Yes; if one is off guard—careless," the captain assented, flowingly.

"Can one in earnest be other than careless? I shall walk on that line up to the end. Who makes me deviate is my enemy!"

The playful little person balanced herself to make one foot follow the other along a piece of washed grey rope on the shingle. Soon she had to stretch out her hand for help, and the captain at full arm's length conducted her to the final knot.

"Arrived safe!" she said, smiling.

"But not disengaged," he rejoined, in similar style.

"Please!" She doubled her elbow to give a little tug for her fingers.

"No." He pressed them tighter.

"Pray?"

"No."

"Must I speak to somebody else to get me released?"

"Would you?"

"Must I?"

"Thank heaven, he is not yet in existence!"

'Husband' being implied. Games of this sweet sort are warranted to carry little people as far as they may go swifter than any other invention of lively Satan.

The yachting party, including Mrs. Chump, were at the breakfast-table, and that dumb guest had done all the blushing for Lady Charlotte, when Wilfrid entered, neat, carefully brushed, and with ready answers, though his face could put on no fresh colours. To Mrs. Chump he bent, passing, and was pushed away and drawn back. "Your eyes!" she whispered.

"My—yeyes!" went Wilfrid, in schoolboy style; and she, who rarely laughed, was struck by his humorous skill, saying to Sir Twickenham, beside her: "He's as cunnin' as a lord!"

Sir Twickenham expressed his ignorance of lords having usurped priority in that department. Frightened by his portentous parliamentary phraseology, she remained tolerably demure till the sitting was over: now sidling in her heart to the sins of the great, whom anon she angrily reproached. Her principal idea was, that as the world was discovered to be so wicked, they were all in a boat going to perdition, and it would be as well to jump out immediately: but while so resolving, she hung upon Lady Charlotte's looks and little speeches, altogether seduced by so fresh and frank a sinner. If safe from temptation, here was the soul of a woman in great danger of corruption.

"Among the aristocracy," thought Mrs. Chump, "it's just the male that hangs his head, and the female struts and is sprightly." The contrast between Lady Charlotte and Wilfrid (who when he ceased to set outrageously, sat like a man stricken by a bolt), produced this reflection: and in spite of her disastrous vision of the fate of the boat they were in, Mrs. Chump owned to the intoxication of gliding smoothly—gliding on the rapids.

The breakfast was coming to an end, when Braintop's name was sent in to Mrs. Chump. She gave a cry of motherly compassion for Braintop, and began to relate the little deficiencies of his temper, while, as it were, simmering on her seat to go to him. Wilfrid sent out word for him to appear, which he did, unluckily for himself, even as Mrs. Chump wound up the public description of his character by remarking: "He's just the opposite of a lord, now, in everything." Braintop stood bowing like the most faithful confirmation of an opinion ever seen. He looked the victim of fatigue, in the bargain. A light broke on Mrs. Chump.

"I'll never forgive myself, ye poor gentle heart, to throw pens and pen-wipers at ye, that did your best, poor boy! What have ye been doin'? and why didn't ye return, and not go hoppin' about about all night like a young kangaroo, as they say they do? Have ye read the 'Arcana of Nature and Science,' ma'am?"

The Hon. Mrs. Bayruffle, thus abruptly addressed, observed that she had not, and was it an amusing book?

"Becas it'll open your mind," pursued Mrs. Chump; "and there, he's eatin'! and when a man takes to eatin', ye'll never have any fear about his abouts. And if ye read the 'Arcana of Nature and Science,' ma'am, ye'll first feel that ye've gone half mad. For it contains averything in the world; and ye'll read ut ten times all through, and not remember five lines runnin'! Oh, it's a dreadful book: and that's the book to read to your husband when he's got a fit o' the gout. He's got nothin' to do but swallow knolludge then. Now, Mr. Braintop, don't stop, but tell me as ye go on what ye did with yourself all night."

A slight hesitation in Braintop caused her to cross-examine him rigidly, suggesting that he might not dare to tell, and he, exercising some self-command, adopted narrative as the less ignominious form of confession. No one save Mrs. Chump listened to him until he mentioned the name Miss Belloni; and then it was curious to see the steadiness with which certain eyes, feigning abstraction, fixed in his direction. He had met Emilia on the outskirts of the town, and unable to persuade her to take shelter anywhere, had walked on with her in dead silence through the night, to the third station of the railway for London.

"Is this a mad person?" asked the Hon. Mrs. Bayruffle.

Adela shrugged. "A genius."

"Don't eat with the tips of your teeth, like a bird, Mr. Braintop, for no company minds your eatin'," cried Mrs. Chump, angrily and encouragingly; "and this little Belloni—my belief is that she came after you; and what have ye done with her?"

It was queerly worried out of Braintop, who was trying his best all the time to be obedient to Wilfrid's direct eye, that the two wanderers by night had lost themselves in lanes, refreshed themselves with purloined apples from the tree at dawn, obtained a draught of morning milk, with a handful of damsons apiece, and that nothing would persuade Emilia to turn back from the route to London. Braintop bit daintily at his toast, unwilling to proceed under the discouraging expression of Wilfrid's face, and the meditative silence of two or three others. The discovery was forcibly extracted that Emilia had no money;—that all she had in her possession was sevenpence and a thimble; and that he, Braintop, had but a few shillings, which she would not accept.

"And what has become of her?" was asked.

Braintop stated that she had returned to London, and, blushing, confessed that he had given her his return ticket.

Georgiana here interposed to save him from the awful encomiums of Mrs. Chump, by desiring to know whether Emilia seemed unhappy or distressed. Braintop's spirited reply, "Not at all," was corrected to: "She did not cry;" and further modified: "That is, she called out sharply when I whistled an opera tune."

Lady Charlotte put a stop to the subject by rising pointedly. Watch in hand, she questioned the ladies as to their occupations, and told them what time they had to dispose of. Then Baynes, captain of the yacht, heard to be outside, was summoned in. He pronounced doubtfully about the weather, but admitted that there was plenty of wind, and if the ladies did not mind it a little fresh, he was sure he did not. Wind was favourable for the island head-quarters of the yacht. "We'll see who gets there first," she said to Wilfrid, and the company learnt that Wilfrid was going to other head-quarters on special business, whereupon there followed chatter and exclamations. Wilfrid quickly explained that his father's condition called him away imperiously. To Adela and Mrs. Chump, demanding peculiar personal explanations, he gave reassuring reasons separately, aside. Mrs. Chump understood that this was merely his excuse to get away, that he might see her safe to Brookfield. Adela only required a look and a gesture. Merthyr and Georgiana likewise spoke expected adieux, as did Sir Twickenham, who parted company in his own little yawl. Lady Charlotte, with her head over a map, and one hand arranging an eye-glass, hastily nodded them off, scarcely looking at them. She allowed herself to be diverted from this study for an instant by the unbefitting noise made by Adela for the loss of her brother; not that she objected to the noise particularly (it was modulated and delicate in tone), but that she could not understand it. Seeing Sir Twickenham, however, in a leave-taking attitude, she uttered an easy "Oh!" to herself, and diligently recommenced spying at ports and harbours, and following the walnut thumb of Baynes on the map. All seemed to be perfectly correct in the arrangements. To go to London was Wilfrid's thought; and the rest were almost as much occupied with their own ideas. Captain Gambier received their semi-ironical congratulations and condolences incident to the man who is left alone in the charge of sweet ladies; and the Hon. Mrs. Bayruffle remarked, that she supposed ten hours not a long period of time, though her responsibility was onerous.

"Lady Gosstre is at the island," said Lady Charlotte, to show where it might end, if she pleased. Within an hour the yacht was flying for the island with a full Western breeze: and Mrs. Chump and Wilfrid were speeding to Brookfield, as the latter permitted her to imagine. Braintop realized the fruits of the sacrifice of his return ticket by facing Mrs. Chump in the train. Merthyr had telegraphed to Marini to meet Emilia at the station in London, and instructed Braintop to deliver a letter for her at Marini's house. To Marini he wrote: "Let Giulia guard her as no one but a woman can in such a case. By this time Giulia will know her value. There is dangerous stuff in her now, and my anxiety is very great. Have you seen what a nature it is? You have not alluded to her beyond answers to instructions, but her character cannot have escaped you. I am never mistaken in my estimates of Italian and Cymric blood. Singularly, too, she is part Welsh on the mother's side, to judge by the name. Leave her mind entirely free till it craves openly for some counteraction. Her Italy and her music will not do. Let them be. My fear is that you have seen too clearly what a daughter of Italy I have found for you. But whatever you put up now to distract her, you sacrifice. My good Marini! bear that in mind. It will be a disgust in her memory, and I wish her to love her country and her Art when she recovers. So we treat the disease, dear friend. Let your Italy have no sorrows for her ears till the storm within is tranquil. I am with you speedily."

Marini's reply said: "Among all the things we have to thank our Merthyr for, this treasure, if it is not the greatest he has given to us, makes us grateful the most. We met her at the station. Ah! there was an elbow when she gave her hand. She thought to be alone, and started, and hated, till Giulia smothered her face. And there was dead fire in the eyes, which is powder when you spring it. We go with her to her new lodging, and the track is lost. This is your wish? It is pitching new camps to avoid the enemy. But so! a man takes this disease and his common work at once of a woman—she is all the disease, till it is extinct, or she! What is this disease but a silly, a senseless waste? Giulia—woman that she is!—will not call it so. See her eyes doze and her voice go a soft buzz when she speaks it! As a dove of the woods! That it almost makes it sweet to me! Yes, a daughter of Italy! So Giulia has been:—will be? I know not! So will this your Emilia be in the time that comes to the young people, she has this, as you say, malady very strong—ma, ogni male ha la sua ricetta; I can say it of persons. Of nations to think my heart is as an infidel—very heavy. Ah! till I turn to you—who revive to the thought, as you were an army of deliverance. For you are Hope. You know not Despair. You are Hope. And you love as myself a mother whose son you are not! 'Oh!' is Giulia's cry, 'will our Italy reward him with a daughter?'—the noblest that we have. Yes, for she would be Italian always through you. We pray that you may not get old too soon, before she grows for you and is found, only that you may know in her our love. See! I am brought to talk this language. The woman is in me."

Merthyr said, as he read this, "I could wish no better." His feeling for Emilia waxed toward a self-avowal as she advanced to womanhood; and the last stage of it had struck among trembling strings in the inmost chambers of his heart. That last stage of it—her passionate claiming of Wilfrid before two women, one her rival—slept like a covered furnace within him. "Can you remember none of her words?" he said more than once to Georgiana, who replied: "I would try to give you an idea of what she said, but I might as well try to paint lightning."

"'My lover'?" suggested Merthyr.

"Oh, yes; that she said."

"It sounded oddly to your ears?"

"Very, indeed."

"What more?"

"—did she say, do you mean?"

"Is my poor sister ashamed to repeat it?"

"I would repeat anything that would give you pleasure to hear."

"Sometimes pain, you know, is sweet."

Little by little, and with a contest at each step, Georgiana coasted the conviction that her undivided reign was over. Then she judged Emilia by human nature's hardest standard: the measure of the qualities brought as usurper and successor. Unconsciously she placed herself in the seat of one who had fulfilled all the great things demanded of a woman for Merthyr, and it seemed to her that Emilia exercised some fatal fascination, girl though she was, to hurl her from that happy sovereignty.

But Emilia's worst crime before the arraigning lady was that Wilfrid had cast her off. Female justice, therefore, said: "You must be unworthy of my brother;" and female delicacy thought: "You have been soiled by a previous history." She had pitied Wilfrid: now she held him partially blameless: and while love was throbbing in many pulses all round her. The man she had seen besieged by passionate love, touched her cold imagination with a hue of fire, as Winter dawn lies on a frosty field. She almost conceived what this other, not sisterly, love might be; though not as its victim, by any means. She became, as she had never before been, spiritually tormented and restless. The thought framed itself that Charlotte and Wilfrid were not, by any law of selection, to match. What mattered it? Simply that it in some way seemed to increase the merits of one of the two. The task, moreover, of avoiding to tease her brother was made easier to her by flying to this new refuge of mysterious reflection. At times she poured back the whole flood of her heart upon Merthyr, and then in alarm at the host of little passions that grew cravingly alive in her, she turned her thoughts to Wilfrid again; and so, till they turned wittingly to him. That this host of little passions will invariably surround a false great one, she learnt by degrees, by having to quell them and rise out of them. She knew that now she occasionally forced her passion for Merthyr; but what nothing could teach her was, that she did so to eject another's image. On the contrary, her confession would have been: "Voluntarily I dwell upon that other, that my love for Merthyr may avoid excess." To such a state of clearness much self-questioning brought her: but her blood was as yet unwarmed; and that is a condition fostering self-deception as much as when it rages.

Madame Marini wrote to ask whether Emilia might receive the visits of a Sir Purcell Barrett, whom they had met, and whom Emilia called her friend; adding: "The other gentleman has called at our old lodgings three times. The last time our landlady says, he wept. Is it an Englishman, really?"

Merthyr laughed at this, remarking: "Charlotte is not so vigilant, after all."

"He wept." Georgiana thought and remembered the cold self-command that his face had shown when Emilia claimed him, and his sole reply was, "I am engaged to this lady," designating Lady Charlotte. Now, too, some of Emilia's phrases took life in her memory. She studied them, thinking over them, as if a voice of nature had spoken. Less and less it seemed to her that a woman need feel shame to utter them. She interpreted this as her growth of charity for a girl so violently stricken with love. "In such a case, the more she says the more is she to be excused; for nothing but a frenzy of passion could move her to speak so," thought Georgiana. Accepting the words, and sanctioning the passion, the person of him who had inspired it stood magnified in its light. She believed that if he had played with the girl, he repented, and the idea of a man shedding tears burnt to her heart.

Merthyr and Georgiana remained in Devonshire till a letter from Madame Marini one morning told them that Emilia had disappeared.

"You delayed too long to go to her, Merthyr," said his sister, astonishing him. "I understand why; but you may trust to time and scorn chance too much. Let us go now and find her, if it is not too late."

Marini met them at the station in London, and they heard that Wilfrid had discovered Marini's new abode, and had called there that morning. "I had my eye on him. It was not a piece of love-play," said Marini: "and today she should have seen my Chief, which would have cured her of sis pestilence of a love, to give her sublime thoughts. Do you love her, Miss Ford? Aha! it will be Christian names in Italy again."

"I like her very much," said Georgiana; "but I confess it mystifies me to see you all so excited about her. It must be some attraction possessed by her—what, I cannot say. I like her, certainly."

"Figlia mia! she is an element—she is fire!" said Marini. "My sought, when our Mertyr brought her, was, it is Italy he sees in her face—her voice—name—anysing! And a day passed, and I could not lose her for my own sake, and felt a somesing, too! She is half man."

"A singular reason for an attraction." Georgiana smiled.

"She is not," Marini put out his fingers like claws to explain, while his eyelashes met over his eyes—"she is not what man has made of your sex; and she is brave of heart."

"Can you possibly tell what such a child can be?" questioned Georgiana, almost irritably.

Marini did not reply to her.

"A face to find a home in!—eh, Mertyr?"

"Let's discover where that face has found a home," said Merthyr. "She is a very plain and unpretending person, if people will not insist upon her being more. This morbid admiration of heroines puts a trifle too much weight upon their shoulders, does it not?"

Georgiana knew that to call Emilia 'child' was to wound the most sensitive nerve in Merthyr's system, if he loved her, and she had determined to try harshly whether he did. Nevertheless, though the expression succeeded, and was designedly cruel, she could not forgive the insincerity of his last speech; craving in truth for confidence as her smallest claim on him now. So, at all the consultations, she acquiesced in any scheme that was proposed; the advertizings and the use of detectives; the communication with Emilia's mother and father; and the callings at suburban concert-rooms. Sir Purcell Barrett frequently called to assist in the discovery. At first he led them to suspect Mr. Pericles; but a trusty Italian playing spy upon that gentleman soon cleared him, and they were more in the dark than ever. It was only when at last Georgiana heard Merthyr, the picture of polished self-possession, giving way to a burst of disappointment in the room before them all: "Are we sure that she lives?" he cried:— then Georgiana, looking at the firelight over her joined fingers, said:—

"But, have you forgotten the serviceable brigade you have in your organ-boys, Marini? If Emilia sees one, be sure she will speak to him."

"Have I not said she is a General?" Marini pointed at Georgiana with a gleam of his dark eyes, and Merthyr squeezed his sister's hand, thanking her; by which he gave her one whole night of remorse, because she had not spoken earlier.

CHAPTER XXXVIII

SHE CLINGS TO HER VOICE

"My voice! I have my voice!"

Emilia had cried it out to herself almost aloud, on the journey from Devon to London. The landscape slipping under her eyes, with flashing grey pools and light silver freshets, little glades, little copses, farms, and meadows rounding away to spires of village churches under blue hills, would not let her sink, heavy as was the spirit within her, and dead to everything as she desired to be. Here, a great strange old oak spread out its arms and seemed to hold the hurrying train a minute. When gone by, Emilia thought of it as a friend, and that there, there, was the shelter and thick darkness she had hoped she might be flying to. Or the reach of a stream was seen, and in the middle of it one fair group of clouds, showing distance beyond distance in colour. Emilia shut her sight, and tried painfully to believe that there were no distances for her. This was an easy task when the train stopped. It was surprising to her then why the people moved. The whistle of the engine and rush of the scenery set her imagination anew upon the horror of being motionless.

"My voice! I have my voice!" The exclamation recurred at intervals, as a quick fear, that bubbled up from blind sensation, of her being utterly abandoned, and a stray thing carrying no light, startled her. Darkness she still had her desire for; but not to be dark in the darkness. She looked back on the recent night as a lake of fire, through which she had plunged; and of all the faculties about her, memory had suffered most, so that it could recall no images of what had happened, but lay against its black corner a shuddering bundle of nerves. The varying fields and woods and waters offering themselves to her in the swiftness, were as wine dashed to her lips, which could not be dead to it. The wish to be of some worth began a painful quickening movement. At first she could have sobbed with the keen anguish that instantaneously beset her. For—"If I am of worth, who looks on me?" was her outcry, and the darkness she had previously coveted fell with the strength of a mace on her forehead; but the creature's heart struggled further, and by-and-by in despite of her the pulses sprang a clear outlook on hope. It struck through her like the first throb of a sword-cut. She tried to blind herself to it; the face of hope was hateful.

This conflict of the baffled spirit of youth with its forceful flood of being continued until it seemed that Emilia was lifted through the fiery circles into daylight; her last cry being as her first: "I have my voice!"

Of that which her voice was to achieve for her she never thought. She had no thought of value, but only an eagerness to feel herself possessor of something. Wilfrid had appeared to her to have taken all from her, until the recollection of her voice made her breathe suddenly quick and deep, as one recovering the taste of life.

Despair, I have said before, is a wilful business, common to corrupt blood, and to weak woeful minds: native to the sentimentalist of the better order. The only touch of it that came to Emilia was when she attempted to penetrate to Wilfrid's reason for calling her down to Devon that he might renounce and abandon her. She wanted a reason to make him in harmony with his acts, and she could get none. This made the world look black to her. But, "I have my voice!" she said, exhausted by the passion of the night, tearless, and only sensible to pain when the keen swift wind, and the flying squares of field and meadow prompted her nature mysteriously to press for healthy action.

A man opposite to her ventured a remark: "We're going at a pretty good pace now, miss."

She turned her eyes to him, and the sense of speed was reduced in her at once, she could not comprehend how. Remembering presently that she had not answered him, she said: "It is because you are going home, perhaps, that you think it fast."

"No, miss," he replied, "I'm going to market. They can't put on steam too stiff for me when I'm bound on business."

Emilia found it impossible to fathom the sensations of the man, and their common desire for speed bewildered her more. She was relieved when the train was lightened of him. Soon the skirts of red vapour were visible, and when the guard took poor Braintop's return-ticket from her petulant hand, all of the journey that she bore in mind was the sight of a butcher-boy in blue, with a red cap, mounted on a white horse, who rode gallantly along a broad highroad, and for whom she had struck out some tune to suit the measure of his gallop.

She accepted her capture by the Marinis more calmly than Merthyr had been led to suppose. The butcher-boy's gallop kept her senses in motion for many hours, and that reckless equestrian embodied the idea of the vivifying pace from which she had dropped. He went slower and slower. By degrees the tune grew dull, and jarred; and then Emilia looked out on the cold grey skies of our autumn, the rain and the fogs, and roaring London filled her ears. So had ended a dream, she thought. She would stand at the window listening to street-organs, whose hideous discord and clippings and drawls did not madden her, and whose suggestion of a lovely tune rolled out no golden land to her. That treasure of her voice, to which no one in the house made allusion, became indeed a buried treasure.

In the South-western suburb where the Marinis lived, plots of foliage were to be seen, and there were lanes not so black but that they showed the hues of the season. These led to the parks and to noble gardens. Emilia daily went out to keep the dying colours of the year in view, and walked to get among the trees, where, with Madame attendant on her, she sat counting the leaves as each one curved, and slid, and spun to earth, or on a gust of air hosts went aloft; but it always ended in their coming down; Emilia verified that fact repeatedly. However high they flew, the ground awaited them. Madame entertained her with talk of Italy, and Tuscan wine, and Lombard bread, and Turin chocolate. Marini never alluded to his sufferings for the loss of these cruelly interdicted dainties, never! But Madame knew how his exile affected him. And in England the sums one paid for everything! "One fancies one pays for breath," said Madame, shivering.

One day the ex-organist of Hillford Church passed before them. Emilia let him go. The day following he passed again, but turned at the end of the alley and simulated astonishment at the appearance of Emilia, as he neared her. They shook hands and talked, while Madame zealously eyed any chance person promenading the neighbourhood. She wrote for instructions concerning this gentleman calling himself Sir Purcell Barrett, and receiving them, she permitted Emilia to invite him to their house. "He is an Englishman under a rope, ready for heaven," Madame described him to her husband, who, though more at heart with Englishmen, could not but admit that this one wore a look that appeared as a prognostication of sadness.

Sir Purcell informed Emilia of his accession to title; and in reply to her "Are you not glad?" smiled and said that a mockery could scarcely make him glad; indicating nevertheless how feeble the note of poverty was in his grand scale of sorrow. He came to the house and met them in the gardens frequently. With some perversity he would analyze to herself Emilia's spirit of hope, partly perhaps for the sake of probing to what sort of thing it might be in its nature and defences; and, as against an accomplished disputant she made but a poor battle, he injured what was precious to her without himself gaining any good whatever.

"Why, what do you look forward to?" she said wondering, at the end of one of their arguments, as he courteously termed this play of logical foils with a baby.

"Death," answered the grave gentleman, striding on.

Emilia pitied him, thinking: "I might feel as he does, if I had not my voice." Seeing that calamity very remote, she added: "I should!"

She knew of his position toward Cornelia: that is, she knew as much as he did: for the want of a woman's heart over which to simmer his troubles was urgent within him and Emilia's, though it lacked experience, was a woman's regarding love. And moreover, she did not weep, but practically suggested his favourable chances, which it was a sad satisfaction to him to prove baseless, and to knock utterly over. The grief in which the soul of a human creature is persistently seeking (since it cannot be thrown off) to clothe itself comfortably, finds in tears an irritating expression of sympathy. Hints of a brighter future are its nourishment. Such embryos are not tenacious of existence, and when destroyed they are succulent food for a space to the moody grief I am describing.

The melancholy gentleman did Emilia this good, that, never appearing to imagine others to know misery save himself, he gave her full occupation apart from the workings of her own mind. As to her case, he might have offered the excuse that she really had nothing of the aspect of a lovesick young lady, and was not a bit sea-green to view, or lamentable in tone. He was sufficiently humane to have felt for anyone suffering, and the proof of it is, that the only creature he saw under such an influence he pitied so deplorably, as to make melancholy a habit with him. He fretted her because he would do nothing, and this spectacle of a lover beloved, but consenting to be mystified, consentingly paralyzed:—of a lover beloved—!

"Does she love you?" said Emilia, beseechingly.

"If the truth is in her, she does," he returned.

"She has told you she loves you?—that she loves no one else?"

"Of this I am certain."

"Then, why are you downcast? my goodness! I would take her by the hand 'Woman; do you know yourself? you belong to me!'—I would say that; and never let go her hand. That would decide everything. She must come to you then, or you know what it is that means to separate you. My goodness! I see it so plain!"

But he declined to look thus low, and stood pitifully smiling:—This spectacle, together with some subtle spur from the talk of love, roused Emilia from her lethargy. The warmth of a new desire struck around her heart. The old belief in her power over Wilfrid joined to a distinct admission that she had for the moment lost him; and she said, "Yes; now, as I am now, he can abandon me:" but how if he should see her and hear her in that hushed hour when she was to stand as a star before men? Emilia flushed and trembled. She lived vividly though her far-projected sensations, until truly pity for Wilfrid was active in her bosom, she feeling how he would yearn for her. The vengeance seemed to her so keen that pity could not fail to come. Thus, to her contemplation, their positions became reversed: it was Wilfrid now who stood in the darkness, unselected. Her fiery fancy, unchained from the despotic heart, illumined her under the golden future.

"Come to us this evening, I will sing to you," she said, and the 'Englishman under a rope' bowed assentingly.

"Sad songs, if you like," she added.

"I have always thought sadness more musical than mirth," said he. "Surely there is more grace in sadness!"

Poetry, sculpture, and songs, and all the Arts, were brought forward in mournful array to demonstrate the truth of his theory.

When Emilia understood him, she cited dogs and cats, and birds, and all things of nature that rejoiced and revelled, in support of the opposite view.

"Nay, if animals are to be your illustration!" he protested. He had been perhaps half under the delusion that he spoke with Cornelia, and with a sense of infinite misery, he compressed the apt distinction that he had in his mind; which was to show where humanity and simple nature drew a line, and wherein humanity claimed the loftier seat.

"But such talk must be uttered to a soul," he phrased internally, and Emilia was denied what belonged to Cornelia.

Hitherto Emilia had refused to sing, and Madame Marini, faithful to her instructions, had never allowed her to be pressed to sing. Emilia would brood over notes, thinking: "I can take that; and that; and dwell on such and such a note for any length of time;" but she would not call up her voice; she would not look at her treasure. It seemed more to her, untouched; and went on doubling its worth, until doubtless her idea of capacity greatly relieved her of the burden on her breast, and the reflection that she held a charm for all, and held it from all, flattered one who had been cruelly robbed.

On their way homeward, among the chrysanthemums in the long garden-walk, they met Tracy Runningbrook, between whose shouts of delight and Emilia's reserve there was so marked a contrast that one would have deemed Tracy an offender in her sight. She had said to him entreatingly, "Do not come," when he volunteered to call on the Marinis in the evening; and she got away from him as quickly as she could, promising to be pleased if he called the day following. Tracy flew leaping to one of the great houses where he was tame cat. When Sir Purcell as they passed on spoke a contemptuous word of his soft habits and idleness, Emilia said: "He is one of my true friends."

"And why is he interdicted the visit this evening?"

"Because," she answered, and grew pale, "he—he does not care for music. I wish I had not met him."

She recollected how Tracy's flaming head had sprung up before her—he who had always prophesied that she would be famous for arts unknown to her, and not for song just when she was having a vision of triumph and caressing the idea of her imprisoned voice bursting its captivity, and soaring into its old heavens.

"He does not care for music!" interjected Sir Purcell, with something like a frown. "I have nothing in common with him. But that I might have known. I can have nothing in common with a man who is not to be impressed by music."

"I love him quite as well," said Emilia. "He is a quick friend. I am always certain of him."

"And I imagine also that you are quits with your quick friend," added Sir Purcell. "You do not care for verse, or he for voices!"

"Poetry?" said Emilia; "no, not much. It seems like talking on tiptoe; like animals in cages, always going to one end and back again...."

"And making the same noise when they get at the end—like the bears!" Sir Purcell slightly laughed. "You don't approve of the rhymes?"

"Yes, I like the rhymes; but when you use words—I mean, if you are in earnest—how can you count and have stops, and—no, I do not care anything for poetry."

Sir Purcell's opinion of Emilia, though he liked her, was, that if a genius, she was an incomplete one; and his positive judgement (which I set down in phrase that would have startled him) ranked both her and Tracy as a pair of partial humbugs, entertaining enough. They were both too real for him.

Haply at that moment the girl was intensely susceptible, for she chilled by his side; and when he left her she begged Madame to walk fast. "I wonder whether I have a cold!" she said.

Madame explained all the signs of it with tragic minuteness, deciding that Emilia was free at present, and by miracle, from this English scourge; but Emilia kept her hands at her mouth. Over the hornbeam hedge of the lane that ran through the market-gardens, she could see a murky sunset spreading its deep-coloured lines, that seemed to her really like a great sorrowing over earth. It had never seemed so till now; and, entering the house, the roar of vehicles in a neighbouring road sounded like something implacable in the order of things among us, and clung about her ears pitilessly. Running upstairs, she tried a scale of notes that broke on a cough. "Did I cough purposely?" she asked herself; but she had not the courage to try the notes again. While dressing she hummed a passage, and sought stealthily to pass the barrier of her own watchfulness by dwelling on a deep note, from which she was to rise bursting with full bravura energy, and so forth on a tide of song. But her breath failed. She stared into the glass and forced the note. A panic caught at her heart when she heard the sound that issued. "Am I ill? I must be hungry!" she exclaimed. "It is a cough! But I don't cough! What is the matter with me?"

Under these auspices she forced her voice again, and subsequently loosened her dress, complaining of the dressmaker's affection for tightness. "Now," she said, having fallen upon an attempt at simple "do, re, me, fa," and laughed at herself. Was it the laugh, that stopping her at "si," made that "si" so husky, asthmatic, like the wheezing of a crooked old witch? "I am unlucky, to-night," said Emilia. Or, rather, so said her surface-self. The submerged self—self in the depths—rarely speaks to the occasions, but lies under calamity quietly apprehending all; willing that the talker overhead should deceive others, and herself likewise, if possible. Emilia found her hands acting daintily and critically in the attirement of her person; and then surprised herself murmuring: "I forgot that Tracy won't be here to-night." By which she betrayed that she had divined those arts she was to shine in, according to Tracy; and betrayed that she had a terrible fear of a loss of all else. It pained her now that Tracy should not be coming. "Can I send for him?" she thought, as she looked winningly into the glass, trying to feel what sort of a feeling it was to be in love with a face like that one fronting her, so familiar in its aspects, so strange when scrutinized studiously! She drew a chair, and laying her elbow on the toilet-table, gazed hard, until the thought: "What face did Wilfrid see last?" (meaning, "when he saw me last") drove her away.

Not only did she know herself now a face of many faces; but the life within her likewise as a soul of many souls. The one Emilia, so unquestioning, so sure, lay dead; and a dozen new spirits, with but a dim likeness to her, were fighting for possession of her frame, now occupying it alone, now in couples; and each casting grim reflections on the other. Which is only a way of telling you that the great result of mortal suffering—consciousness—had fully set in; to ripen; perhaps to debase; at any rate, to prove her.

To be of worth was still her fixed idea—all that was clear in the thickening mist. "I cannot be ugly," she said, and reproved herself for simulating a childish tone. "Why do I talk in that way? I know I am not ugly. But if a fire scorched my face? There is nothing that seems safe!" The love of friends was suggested to her as something to rely on; and the loving them. "But if I have nothing to give!" said Emilia, and opened both her empty hands. She had diverted her mind from the pressure upon it, by this colloquy with a looking-glass, and gave herself a great rapture by running up notes to this theme:—

"No, no, no, no, no!—nothing! nothing!"

Clear, full, sonant notes; the notes of her true voice. She did not attempt them a second time; nor, when Sir Purcell requested her to sing in the course of the evening, did she comply. "The Signora thinks I have a cold," she said. Madame Marini protested that she hoped not, she even thought not, though none could avoid it at this season in this climate, and she turned to Sir Purcell to petition for any receipts he might have in his possession, specifics for warding off the frightful affliction of households in England.

"I have now twenty," said Madame, and throwing up her eyes; "I have tried all! oh! so many lozenge!"

Marini and Emilia laughed. While Sir Purcell was maintaining the fact of his total ignorance of the subject against Madame's incredulity, Emilia left the room. When she came back Madame was pressing her visitor to be explicit with regard to a certain process of cure conducted by an application of cold water. The Neapolitan gave several shudders as she marked him attentively. "Water cold!" she murmured with the deepest pathos, and dropped her face in her hands with narrowed shoulders. Emilia held a letter over to Sir Purcell. He took it, first assuring himself that Marini was in complicity with them. To Marini Emilia addressed a Momus forefinger, and Marini shrugged, smiling. "Water cold!" ejaculated Madame, showing her countenance again. "In winter! Luigi, they are mad!" Marini poked the fire briskly, for his sensations entirely sided with his wife.

The letter Sir Purcell held contained these words:

"Be kind, and meet me to-morrow at ten in the morning, at that place where you first saw me sitting. I want you to take me to one who will help me. I cannot lose time any more. I must work. I have been dead for I cannot say how long. I know you will come.

"I am, for ever,

"Your thankful friend,

"Emilia."

CHAPTER XXXIX

HER VOICE FAILS

The pride of punctuality brought Sir Purcell to that appointed seat in the gardens about a minute in advance of Emilia. She came hurrying up to him with three fingers over her lips. The morning was cold; frost edged the flat brown chestnut and beech leaves lying about on rimy grass; so at first he made no remark on her evident unwillingness to open her mouth, but a feverish look of her eyes touched him with some kindly alarm for her.

"You should not have come out, if you think you are in any danger," he said.

"Not if we walk fast," she replied, in a visibly-controlled excitement. "It will he over in an hour. This way."

She led the marvelling gentleman toward the row, and across it under the big black elms, begging him to walk faster. To accommodate her, he suggested, that if they had any distance to go, they might ride, and after a short calculating hesitation, she consented, letting him know that she would tell him on what expedition she was bound whilst they were riding. The accompaniment of the wheels, however, necessitated a higher pitch of her voice, which apparently caused her to suffer from a contraction of the throat, for she remained silent, with a discouraged aspect, her full brown eyes showing as in a sombre meditation beneath the thick brows. The direction had been given to the City. On they went with the torrent, and were presently engulfed in fog. The roar grew muffled, phantoms poured along the pavement, yellow beamless lights were in the shop-windows, all the vehicles went at a slow march.

"It looks as if Business were attending its own obsequies," said Sir Purcell, whose spirits were enlivened by an atmosphere that confirmed his impression of things.

Emilia cried twice: "Oh! what cruel weather!" Her eyelids blinked, either with anger or in misery.

They were set down a little beyond the Bank, and when they turned from the cabman, Sir Purcell was warm in his offer of his arm to her, for he had seen her wistfully touching what money she had in her pocket, and approved her natural good breeding in allowing it to pass unmentioned.

"Now," he said, "I must know what you want to do."

"A quiet place! there is no quiet place in this City," said Emilia fretfully.

A gentleman passing took off his hat, saying, with City politeness, "Pardon me: you are close to a quiet place. Through that door, and the hall, you will find a garden, where you will hear London as if it sounded fifty miles off."

He bowed and retired, and the two (Emilia thankful, Sir Purcell tending to anger), following his indication, soon found themselves in a most perfect retreat, the solitude of which they had the misfortune, however, of destroying for another, and a scared, couple.

Here Emilia said: "I have determined to go to Italy at once. Mr. Pericles has offered to pay for me. It's my father's wish. And—and I cannot wait and feel like a beggar. I must go. I shall always love England— don't fear that!"

Sir Purcell smiled at the simplicity of her pleading look.

"Now, I want to know where to find Mr. Pericles," she pursued. "And if you will come to him with me! He is sure to be very angry—I thought you might protect me from that. But when he hears that I am really going at last—at once!—he can laugh sometimes! you will see him rub his hands."

"I must enquire where his chambers are to be found," said Sir Purcell.

"Oh! anybody in the City must know him, because he is so rich." Emilia coughed. "This fog kills me. Pray make haste. Dear friend, I trouble you very much, but I want to get away from this. I can hardly breathe. I shall have no heart for my task, if I don't see him soon."

"Wait for me, then," said Sir Purcell; "you cannot wait in a better place. And I must entreat you to be careful." He half alluded to the adjustment of her shawl, and to anything else, as far as she might choose to apprehend him. Her dexterity in tossing him the letter, unseen by Madame Marini, might have frightened him and given him a dread, that albeit woman, there was germ of wickedness in her.

This pained him acutely, for he never forgot that she had been the means of his introduction to Cornelia, from whom he could not wholly dissociate her: and the idea that any prospective shred of impurity hung about one who had even looked on his beloved, was utter anguish to the keen sentimentalist. "Be very careful," he would have repeated, but that he had a warning sense of the ludicrous, and Emilia's large eyes when they fixed calmly on a face were not of a flighty east She stood, too, with the "dignity of sadness," as he was pleased to phrase it.

"She must be safe here," he said to himself. And yet, upon reflection, he decided not to leave her, peremptorily informing her to that effect. Emilia took his arm, and as they were passing through the hall of entrance they met the same gentleman who had directed them to the spot of quiet. Both she and Sir

Purcell heard him say to a companion: "There she is." A deep glow covered Emilia's face. "Do they know you?" asked Sir Purcell. "No," she said: and then he turned, but the couple had gone on.

"That deserves chastisement," he muttered. Briefly telling her to wait, he pursued them. Emilia was standing in the gateway, not at all comprehending why she was alone. "Sandra Belloni!" struck her ear. Looking forward she perceived a hand and a head gesticulating from a cab-window. She sprang out into the street, and instantly the hand clenched and the head glared savagely. It was Mr. Pericles himself, in travelling costume.

"I am your fool?" he began, overbearing Emilia's most irritating "How are you?" and "Are you quite well?

"I am your fool? hein? You send me to Paris! to Geneve! I go over Lago Maggiore, and aha! it is your joke, meess! I juste return. Oh capital! At Milano I wait—I enquire—till a letter from old Belloni, and I learn I am your fool—of you all! Jomp in."

"A gentleman is coming," said Emilia, by no means intimidated, though the forehead of Mr. Pericles looked portentous. "He was bringing me to you."

"Zen, jomp in!" cried Mr. Pericles.

Here Sir Purcell came up.

Emilia said softly: "Mr. Pericles."

There was the form of a bow of moderate recognition between them, but other hats were off to Emilia. The two gentlemen who had offended Sir Purcell had insisted, on learning the nature of their offence, that they had a right to present their regrets to the lady in person, and beg an excuse from her lips. Sir Purcell stood white with a futile effort at self-control, as one of them, preluding "Pardon me," said: "I had the misfortune to remark to my friend, as I passed you, 'There she is.' May I, indeed, ask your pardon? My friend is an artist. I met him after I had first seen you. He, at least, does not think foolish my recommendation to him that he should look on you at all hazards. Let me petition you to overlook the impertinence."

"I think, gentlemen, you have now made the most of the advantage my folly, in supposing you would regret or apologize fittingly for an impropriety, has given you," interposed Sir Purcell.

His new and superior tone (for he had previously lost his temper and spoken with a silly vehemence) caused them to hesitate. One begged the word of pardon from Emilia to cover his retreat. She gave it with an air of thorough-bred repose, saying, "I willingly pardon you," and looking at them no more, whereupon they vanished. Ten minutes later, Emilia and Sir Purcell were in the chambers of Mr. Pericles.

The Greek had done nothing but grin obnoxiously to every word spoken on the way, drawing his hand down across his jaw, to efface the hard pale wrinkles, and eyeing Emilia's cavalier with his shrewdest suspicious look.

"You will excuse,"—he pointed to the confusion of the room they were in, and the heap of unopened letters,—"I am from ze Continent; I do not expect ze pleasure. A seat?"

Mr. Pericles handed chairs to his visitors.

"It is a climate, is it not," he resumed.

Emilia said a word, and he snapped at her, immediately adding, "Hein? Ah! so!" with a charming urbanity.

"How lucky that we should meet you," exclaimed Emilia. "We were just coming to you—to find out, I mean, where you were, and call on you."

"Ough! do not tell me lies," said Mr. Pericles, clasping the hollow of his cheeks between thumb and forefinger.

"Allow me to assure you that what Miss Belloni has said is perfectly correct," Sir Purcell remarked.

Mr. Pericles gave a short bow. "It is ze same; I am much obliged."

"And you have just come from Italy?" said Emilia.

"Where you did me ze favour to send me, it is true. Sanks!"

"Oh, what a difference between Italy and this!" Emilia turned her face to the mottled yellow windows.

"Many sanks," repeated Mr. Pericles, after which the three continued silent for a time.

At last Emilia said, bluntly, "I have come to ask you to take me to Italy."

Mr. Pericles made no sign, but Sir Purcell leaned forward to her with a gaze of astonishment, almost of horror.

"Will you take me?" persisted Emilia.

Still the sullen Greek refused either to look at her or to answer.

"Because I am ready to go," she went on. "I want to go at once; to-day, if you like. I am getting too old to waste an hour."

Mr. Pericles uncrossed his legs, ejaculating, "What a fog! Ah!" and that was all. He rose, and went to a cupboard.

Sir Purcell murmured hurriedly in Emilia's ear, "Have you considered what you've been saying?"

"Yes, yes. It is only a journey," Emilia replied, in a like tone.

"A journey!"

"My father wishes it."

"Your mother?"

"Hush! I intend to make him take the Madre with me."

She designated Mr. Pericles, who had poured into a small liqueur glass some green Chartreuse, smelling strong of pines. His visitors declined to eject the London fog by this aid of the mountain monks, and Mr. Pericles warmed himself alone.

"You are wiz old Belloni," he called out.

"I am not staying with my father," said Emilia.

"Where?" Mr. Pericles shed a baleful glance on Sir Purcell.

"I am staying with Signor Marini."

"Servente!" Mr. Pericles ducked his head quite low, while his hand swept the floor with an imaginary cap. Malice had lighted up his features, and finding, after the first burst of sarcasm, that it was vain to indulge it toward an absent person, he altered his style. "Look," he cried to Emilia, "it is Marini stops you and old Belloni—a conspirator, aha! Is it for an artist to conspire, and be carbonaro, and kiss books, and, mon Dieu! bon! it is Marini plays me zis trick. I mark him. I mark him, I say! He is paid by young Pole. I hold zat family in my hand, I say! So I go to be met by you, and on I go to Italy. I get a letter at Milano,— 'Marini stop me at Dover,' signed 'Giuseppe Belloni.' Ze letter have been spied into by ze Austrians. I am watched—I am dogged—I am imprisoned—I am examined. 'You know zis Giuseppe Belloni?' 'Meine Herrn! he was to come. I leave word at Paris for him, at Geneve, at Stresa, to bring his daughter to ze Conservatoire, for which I pay. She has a voice—or she had.'"

"Has!" exclaimed Emilia.

"Had!" Mr. Pericles repeated.

"She has!"

"Zen sing!" with which thunder of command, Mr. Pericles gave up his vindictive narration of the points of his injuries sustained, and, pitching into a chair, pressed his fingers to his temples, frowning attention. His eyes were on the floor. Presently he glanced up, and saw Emilia's chest rising quickly. No voice issued.

"It is to commence," cried Mr. Pericles. "Hein! now sing."

Emilia laid her hand under her throat. "Not now! Oh, not now! When you have told me what those Austrians did to you. I want to hear; I am very anxious to hear. And what they said of my father. How could he have come to Milan without a passport? He had only a passport to Paris."

"And at Paris I leave instructions for ze procuration of a passport over Lombardy. Am I not Antonio Pericles Agriolopoulos? Sing, I say!"

"Ah, but what voices you must have heard in Italy," said Emilia softly. "I am afraid to sing after them. Si: I dare not."

She panted, little in keeping with the cajolery of her tones, but she had got Mr. Pericles upon a theme serious to his mind.

"Not a voice! not one!" he cried, stamping his foot. "All is French. I go twice wizin six monz, and if I go to a goose-yard I hear better. Oh, yes! it is tune—'ta-ta-ta—ti-ti-ti—to!' and of ze heart—where is zat? Mon Dieu! I despair. I see music go dead. Let me hear you, Sandra."

His enthusiasm had always affected Emilia, and painfully since her love had given her a consciousness of infidelity to her Art, but now the pathetic appeal to her took away her strength, and tears rose in her eyes at the thought of his faith in her. His repetition of her name—the 'Sandra' being uttered with unwonted softness—plunged her into a fit of weeping.

"Ah!" Mr. Pericles shouted. "See what she has come to!" and he walked two or three paces off to turn upon her spitefully, "she will be vapeurs, nerfs, I know not! when it wants a physique of a saint! Sandra Belloni," he added, gravely, "lift up ze head! Sing, 'Sempre al tuo santo nome.'"

Emilia checked her tears. His hand being raised to beat time, she could not withstand the signal. "Sempre;"—there came two struggling notes, to which another clung, shuddering like two creatures on the deeps.

She stopped; herself oddly calling out "Stop."

"Stop who, donc?" Mr. Pericles postured an indignant interrogation.

"I mean, I must stop," Emilia faltered. "It's the fog. I cannot sing in this fog. It chokes me."

Apparently Mr. Pericles was about to say something frightfully savage, which was restrained by the presence of Sir Purcell. He went to the door in answer to a knock, while Emilia drew breath as calmly as she might; her head moving a little backward with her breathing, in a sad mechanical way painful to witness. Sir Purcell stretched his hand out to her, but she did not take it. She was listening to voices at the door. Was it really Mr. Pole who was there? Quite unaware of the effect the sight of her would produce on him, Emilia rose and walked to the doorway. She heard Mr. Pole abusing Mr. Pericles half banteringly for his absence while business was urgent, saying that they must lay their heads together and consult, otherwise—a significant indication appeared to close the sentence.

"But if you've just come off your journey, and have got a lady in there, we must postpone, I suppose. Say, this afternoon. I'll keep up to the mark, if nothing happens...."

Emilia pushed the door from the hand of Mr. Pericles, and was advancing toward the old man on the landing; but no sooner did the latter verify to his startled understanding that he had seen her, than with an exclamation of "All right! good-bye!" he began a rapid descent, of the stairs. A distance below, he bade Mr. Pericles take care of her, and as an excuse for his abrupt retreat, the word "busy" sounded up.

"Does my face frighten him?" Emilia thought. It made her look on herself with a foreign eye. This is a dreadful but instructive piece of contemplation; acting as if the rich warm blood of self should have ceased to hug about us, and we stand forth to be dissected unresistingly. All Emilia's vital strength now seemed to vanish. At the renewal of Mr. Pericles' peremptory mandate for her to sing, she could neither appeal to him, nor resist; but, raising her chest, she made her best effort, and then covered her face. This was done less for concealment of her shame-stricken features than to avoid sight of the stupefaction imprinted upon Mr. Pericles.

"Again, zat A flat!" he called sternly.

She tried it.

"Again!"

Again she did her utmost to accomplish the task. If you have seen a girl in a fit of sobs elevate her head, with hard-shut eyelids, while her nostrils convulsively take in a long breath, as if for speech, but it is expended in one quick vacant sigh, you know how Emilia looked. And it requires a humane nature to pardon such an aspect in a person from whom we have expected triumphing glances and strong thrilling tones.

"What is zis?" Mr. Pericles came nearer to her.

He would listen to no charges against the atmosphere. Commanding her to give one simple run of notes, a contralto octave, he stood over her with keenly watchful eyes. Sir Purcell bade him observe her distress.

"I am much obliged," Mr. Pericles bowed, "she is ruined. I have suspected. Ha! But I ask for a note! One!"

This imperious signal drew her to another attempt. The deplorable sound that came sent Emilia sinking down with a groan.

"Basta, basta! So, it is zis tale," said Mr. Pericles, after an observation of her huddled shape. "Did I not say—"

His voice was so menacingly loud and harsh that Sir Purcell remarked: "This is not the time to repeat it—pardon me—whatever you said."

"Ze fool—she play ze fool! Sir, I forget ze Christian—ah! Purcell!—I say she play ze fool, and look at her! Why is it she comes to me now? A dozen times I warn her. To Italy! to Italy! all is ready: you will have a place at ze Conservatorio. No: she refuse. I say 'Go, and you are a queen. You are a Prima at twenty, and Europe is beneas you.' No: she refuse, and she is ruined. 'What,' I say, 'what zat dam silly smile mean?' Oh, no! I am not lazy!' 'But you area fool!' 'Oh, no!' 'And what are you, zen? And what shall you do?' Nussing! nussing! nussing! And, dam! zere is an end."

Emilia had caught blindly at Sir Purcell's hand, by which she raised herself, and then uncovering her face, looked furtively at the malign furnace-white face of Mr. Pericles.

"It cannot have gone,"—she spoke, as if mentally balancing the possibility.

"It has gone, I say; and you know why, Mademoiselle ze Fool!" Mr. Pericles retorted.

"No, no; it can't be gone. Gone? voices never go!"

The reiteration of the "You know why," from Mr. Pericles, and all the wretchedness of loss it suggested, robbed her of the little spark of nervous fire by which she felt half-reviving in courage and confidence.

"Let me try once more," she appealed to him, in a frenzy.

Mr. Pericles, though fully believing in his heart that it might only be a temporary deprivation of voice, affected to scout the notion of another trial, but finally extended his forefinger: "Well, now; start! 'Sempre al tuo Santo!' Commence: Sem—" and Mr. Pericles hummed the opening bar, not as an unhopeful man would do. The next moment he was laughing horribly. Emilia, to make sure of the thing she dreaded, forced the note, and would not be denied. What voice there was in her came to the summons. It issued, if I may so express it, ragged, as if it had torn through a briar-hedge: then there was a whimper of tones, and the effect was like the lamentation of a hardly-used urchin, lacking a certain music that there is in his undoubted heartfelt earnestness. No single note poised firmly for the instant, but swayed, trembling on its neighbour to right and to left when pressed for articulate sound, it went into a ghastly whisper. The laughter of Mr. Pericles was pleasing discord in comparison.

Emilia stretched out her hand and said, "Good-bye." Seeing that the hardened girl, with her dead eyelids, did not appear to feel herself at his mercy, and also that Sir Purcell's forehead looked threatening, Mr. Pericles stopped his sardonic noise. He went straight to the door, which he opened with alacrity, and mimicking very wretchedly her words of adieu, stood prepared to bow her out. She astonished him by passing without another word. Before he could point a phrase bitter enough for expression, Sir Purcell had likewise passed, and in going had given him a quietly admonishing look.

"Zose Poles are beggars!" Mr. Pericles roared after them over the stairs, and slammed his door for emphasis. Almost immediately there was a knock at it. Mr. Pericles stood bent and cat-like as Sir Purcell reappeared. The latter, avoiding all preliminaries, demanded of the Greek that he should promise not to use the names of his friends publicly in such a manner again.

"I require a promise for the future. An apology will be needless from you."

"I shall not give it," said Mr. Pericles, with a sharp lift of his upper lip.

"But you will give me the promise I have returned for."

In answer Mr. Pericles announced that he had spoken what was simply true: that the prosperity of the Poles was fictitious: that he, or any unfavourable chance, could ruin them: and that their friends might do better to protect their interests than by menacing one who had them in his power.

Sir Purcell merely reiterated his demand for the promise, which was ultimately snarled to him; whereupon he retired, joy on his features. For, Cornelia poor, she might be claimed by him fearlessly: that is to say, without the fear of people whispering that the penniless baronet had sued for gold, and without the fear of her father rejecting his suit. At least he might, with this knowledge that he had gained, appoint to meet her now! All the morning Sir Purcell had been combative, owing to that subordinate or secondary post he occupied in a situation of some excitement;—which combativeness is one method whereby men thus placed, imagining that they are acting devotedly for their friends, contrive still to assert themselves. He descended to the foot of the stairs, where he had told Emilia to wait for him, full of kind feelings and ready cheerful counsels; as thus: "Nothing that we possess belongs to us;—All will come round rightly in the end; Be patient, look about for amusement, and improve your mind." And more of this copper coinage of wisdom in the way of proverbs. But Emilia was nowhere visible to receive the administration of comfort. Outside the house the fog appeared to have swallowed her. With some chagrin on her behalf (partly a sense of duty unfulfilled) Sir Purcell made his way to the residence of the Marinis, to report of her there, if she should not have arrived. The punishment he inflicted on himself in keeping his hand an hour from that letter to be written to Cornelia, was almost pleasing; and he was rewarded by it, for the projected sentences grew mellow and rich, condensed and throbbed eloquently. What wonder, that with such a mental occupation, he should pass Emilia and not notice her? She let him go.

But when he was out of sight, all seemed gone. The dismally-lighted city wore a look of Judgement terrible to see. Her brain was slave to her senses: she fancied she had dropped into an underground kingdom, among a mysterious people. The anguish through which action had just hurried her, now fell with a conscious weight upon her heart. She stood a moment, seeing her desolation stretch outwardly into endless labyrinths; and then it narrowed and took hold of her as a force within: changing thus, almost with each breathing of her body.

The fog had thickened. Up and down the groping city went muffled men, few women. Emilia looked for one of her sex who might have a tender face. Desire to be kissed and loved by a creature strange to her, and to lay her head upon a woman's bosom, moved her to gaze around with a longing once or twice; but no eyes met hers, and the fancy recurred vividly that she was not in the world she had known. Otherwise, what had robbed her of her voice? She played with her fancy for comfort, long after any real vitality in it had oozed out. Her having strength to play at fancies showed that a spark of hope was alive. In truth, firm of flesh as she was, to believe that all worth had departed from her was impossible, and when she reposed simply on her sensations, very little trouble beset her: only when she looked abroad did the aspect of numerous indifferent faces, and the harsh flowing of the world its own way, tell her she had lost her power. Could it be lost? The prospect of her desolation grew so wide to her that she shut her eyes, abandoning herself to feeling; and this by degrees moved her to turn back and throw herself at the feet of Mr. Pericles. For, if he said, "Wait, my child, and all will come round well," she was prepared blindly to think so. The projection of the words in her mind made her ready to weep: but as she neared the house of his office the wish to hear him speak that, became passionate; she counted all that depended on it, and discovered the size of the fabric she had built on so thin a plank. After a while, her steps were mechanically swift. Before she reached the chambers of Mr. Pericles she had walked, she knew not why, once round the little quiet enclosed city-garden, and a cold memory of those men who had looked at her face gave her some wonder, to be quickly kindled into fuller comprehension.

Beholding Emilia once more, Mr. Pericles enjoyed a revival of his taste for vengeance; but, unhappily for her, he found it languid, and when he had rubbed his hands, stared, and by sundry sharp utterances brought her to his feet, his satisfaction was less poignant than he had expected. As a consequence, instead of speaking outrageously, according to his habit, in wrath, he was now frigidly considerate, informing Emilia that it would be good for her if she were dead, seeing that she was of no use whatever; but, as she was alive, she had better go to her father and mother, and learn knitting, or some such industrial employment. "Unless zat man for whom you play fool!—" Mr. Pericles shrugged the rest of his meaning.

"But my voice may not be gone," urged Emilia. "I may sing to you to-morrow—this evening. It must be the fog. Why do you think it lost? It can't be—"

"Cracked!" cried Mr. Pericles.

"It is not! No; do not think it. I may stay here. Don't tell me to go yet. The streets make me wish to die. And I feel I may, perhaps, sing presently. Wait. Will you wait?"

A hideous imitation of her lamentable tones burst from Mr. Pericles. "Cracked!" he cried again.

Emilia lifted her eyes, and looked at him steadily. She saw the idea grow in the eyes fronting her that she had a pleasant face, and she at once staked this little bit of newly-conceived worth on an immediate chance. Remember; that she was as near despair as a creature constituted so healthily could go. Speaking no longer in a girlish style, but with the grave pleading manner of a woman, she begged Mr. Pericles to take her to Italy, and have faith in the recovery of her voice. He, however, far from being softened, as he grew aware of her sweetness of feature, waxed violent and insulting.

"Take me," she said. "My voice will reward you. I feel that you can cure it."

"For zat man! to go to him again!" Mr. Pericles sneered.

"I never shall do that." There sprang a glitter as of steel in Emilia's eyes. "I will make myself yours for life, if you like. Take my hand, and let me swear. I do not break my word. I will swear, that if I recover my voice to become what you expected,—I will marry you whenever you ask me, and then—"

More she was saying, but Mr. Pericles, sputtering a laugh of "Sanks!" presented a postured supplication for silence.

"I am not a man who marries."

He plainly stated the relations that the woman whom he had distinguished by the honours of selection must hold toward him.

Emilia's cheeks did not redden; but, without any notion of shame at the words she listened to, she felt herself falling lower and lower the more her spirit clung to Mr. Pericles: yet he alone was her visible personification of hope, and she could not turn from him. If he cast her off, it seemed to her that her voice was condemned. She stood there still, and the cold-eyed Greek formed his opinion.

He was evidently undecided as regards his own course of proceeding, for his chin was pressed by thumb and forefinger hard into his throat, while his eyebrows were wrinkled up to their highest elevation. From this attitude, expressive of the accurate balancing of the claims of an internal debate, he emerged into the posture of a cock crowing, and Emilia heard again his bitter mimicry of her miserable broken tones, followed by, "Ha! dam! Basta! basta!"

"Sit here," cried Mr. Pericles. He had thrown himself into a chair, and pointed to his knee.

Emilia remained where she was standing.

He caught at her hand, but she plucked that from him. Mr. Pericles rose, sounding a cynical "Hein!"

"Don't touch me," said Emilia.

Nothing exasperates certain natures so much as the effort of the visibly weak to intimidate them.

"I shall not touch you?" Mr. Pericles sneered. "Zen, why are you here?"

"I came to my friend," was Emilia's reply.

"Your friend! He is not ze friend of a couac-couac. Once, if you please: but now" (Mr. Pericles shrugged), "now you are like ze rest of women. You are game. Come to me."

He caught once more at her hand, which she lifted; then at her elbow.

"Will you touch me when I tell you not to?"

There was the soft line of an involuntary frown over her white face, and as he held her arm from the doubled elbow, with her clenched hand aloft, she appeared ready to strike a tragic blow.

Anger and every other sentiment vanished from Mr. Pericles in the rapturous contemplation of her admirable artistic pose.

"Mon Dieu! and wiz a voice!" he exclaimed, dashing his fist in a delirium of forgetfulness against the one plastered lock of hair on his shining head. "Little fool! little dam fool!—zat might have been"—(Mr. Pericles figured in air with his fingers to signify the exaltation she was to have attained)—"Mon Dieu! and look at you! Did I not warn you? non a vero? Did I not say 'Ruin, ruin, if you go so? For a man!—a voice! You will not come to me? Zen, hear! you shall go to old Belloni. I do not want you, my pretty dear. Woman is a trouble, a drug. You shall go to old Belloni; and, crack! if ze voice will come back to a whip,—bravo, old Belloni!"

Mr. Pericles turned to reach down his hat from a peg. At the same instant Emilia quitted the room.

Dusk was deepening the yellow atmosphere, and the crowd was now steadily flowing in one direction. The bereaved creature went with the stream, glad to be surrounded and unseen, till it struck her, at last, that she was moving homeward. She stopped with a pang of grief, turned, and met all those people to whom the fireside was a beacon. For some time she bore against the pressure, but her loneliness overwhelmed her. None seemed to go her way. For a refuge, she turned into one of the city side streets, where she was quite alone. Unhappily, the street was of no length, and she soon came to the end of it. There was the choice of retracing her steps, or entering a strange street; and while she hesitated a troop of sheep went by, that made a piteous noise. She followed them, thinking curiously of the something broken that appeared to be in their throats. By-and-by, the thought flashed in her that they were going to be slaughtered. She held her step, looking at them, but without any tender movement of the heart. They came to a butcher's yard, and went in.

When she had passed along a certain distance, a shiver seized her, and her instinct pushed her toward the lighted shops, where there were pictures. In one she saw the portrait of that Queen of Song whom she had heard at Besworth. Two young men, glancing as they walked by arm in arm, pronounced the name of the great enchantress, and hummed one of her triumphant airs. The features expressed health, humour, power, every fine animal faculty. Genius was on the forehead and the plastic mouth; the forehead being well projected, fair, and very shapely, showing clear balance, as well as capacity to grasp flame, and fling it. The line reaching to a dimple from the upper lip was saved from scornfulness by the lovely gleam, half-challenging, half-consoling, regal, roguish—what you would—that sat between her dark eyelashes, like white sunlight on the fringed smooth roll of water by a weir. Such a dimple, and such a gleam of eyes, would have been keys to the face of a weakling, and it was the more fascinating from the disregard of any minor charm notable upon this grand visage, which could not suffer a betrayal. You saw, and there was no effort to conceal, that the spirit animating it was intensely human; but it was human of the highest chords of humanity, indifferent to finesse and despising subtleties; gifted to speak, to inspire, and to command all great emotions. In fact, it was the masque of a dramatic artist in repose. Tempered by beauty, the robust frame showed that she possessed a royal nature, and could, as a foremost qualification for Art, feel harmoniously. She might have many of the littlenesses of which women are accused; for Art she promised unspotted excellence; and, adorable as she was by attraction of her sex, she was artist over all.

Emilia found herself on one of the bridges, thinking of this aspect. Beneath her was the stealing river, with its red intervals, and the fog had got a wider circle. She could not disengage that face from her mind. It seemed to say to her, boldly, "I live because success is mine;" and to hint, as with a paler voice, "Death the fruit of failure." Could she, Emilia, ever be looked on again by her friends? The dread of it gave her shudders. Then, death was certainly easy! But death took no form in her imagination, as it does to one seeking it. She desired to forget and to hide her intolerable losses; to have the impostor she felt herself to be buried. As she walked along she held out her hands, murmuring, "Helpless! useless!" It came upon her as a surprise that one like herself should be allowed to live. "I don't want to," she said; and the neat moment, "I wonder what a drowned woman is like?" She hurried back to the streets and the shops. The shops failed now to give her distraction, for a stiff and dripping image floated across all the windows, and she was glad to see the shutters being closed; though, when the streets were dark, some friendliness seemed to have gone. When the streets were quits dark, save for the row of lamps, she walked fast, fearing she knew not what.

A little Italian boy sat doubled over his organ on a doorstep, while a yet smaller girl at his elbow plied him with questions in English. Emilia stopped before them, and the girl complained to her that the perverse little foreigner would not answer. Two or three words in his native tongue soon brought his face to view. Emilia sat down between them, and listened to the prattle of two languages. The girl said that she never had supper, which was also the case with the boy; so Emilia felt for her purse, and sent the girl with sixpence in search of a shop that sold cafes. The girl came back with her apron full. As they were all about to eat, a policeman commanded them to quit the spot, informing them that he knew both them and their dodges. Emilia stood up, and was taking her little people away, when the policeman, having suddenly changed his accurate opinion of her, said, "You're giving 'em some supper, miss? Oh, they must sit down to their suppers, you know!" and walked away, not to be a witness of this infraction of the law. So, they sat down and ate, and the boy and girl tried to say intelligible things to one another, and laughed. Emilia could not help joining in their laughter. The girl was very anxious to know whether the boy was ever beaten, and hearing that he was, she appeared better satisfied, remarking that she was also, but curious still as to the different forms of chastisement they received. This being partially explained, she wished to know whether he would be beaten that night, Emilia interpreting. A grin, and a rapid whistle and 'cluck,' significant of the application of whips, told the state of his expectations; at which the girl clapped her hands, adding, lamentably, "So shall I, 'cause I am always." Emilia gathered them under each shoulder, when, to her delight and half perplexity, they closed their eyes, leaning against her.

The policeman passed, and for an hour endured this spectacle. At last he felt compelled to explain to Emilia what were the sentiments of gentlefolks with regard to their doorsteps, apart from the law of the matter. He put it to her human nature whether she would like her doorsteps to be blocked, so that no one could enter, and anyone emerging stood a chance of being precipitated, nose foremost, upon the pavement. Then, again, as gentle-folks had good experience of, the young ones in London were twice as cunning as the old. Emilia pleaded for her sleeping pair, that they might not be disturbed. Her voice gave the keeper of the peace notions of her being one of the eccentric young ladies who are occasionally 'missing,' and have advertizing friends. He uttered a stern ahem! preliminary to assent; but the noise wakened the children, who stared, and readily obeyed his gesture, which said, "Be off!" while his words were those of remonstrance. Emilia accompanied them a little way. Both promised eagerly that they would be at the same place the night following and departed—the boy with laughing nods and waving of hands, which the girl imitated. Emilia's feeling of security went with them. She at once feigned a destination in the distance, and set forward to reach it, but the continued exposure of this delusion made it difficult to renew. She fell to counting the hours that were to elapse before she would meet those children, saying to herself, that whatever she did she must keep her engagement to be at the appointed steps. This restriction set her darkly fancying that she wished for her end.

Remembering those men who had looked at her admiringly, "Am I worth looking at?" she said; and it gave her some pleasure to think that she had it still in her power to destroy a thing of value. She was savagely ashamed of going to death empty-handed. By-and-by, great fatigue stiffened her limbs, and she sat down from pure want of rest. The luxury of rest and soothing languor kept hard thoughts away. She felt as if floating, for a space. The fear of the streets left her. But when necessity for rest had gone, she clung to the luxury still, and sitting bent forward, with her hands about her knees, she began to brood over tumbled images of a wrong done to her. She had two distinct visions of herself, constantly alternating and acting like the temptation of two devils. One represented her despicable in feature, and bade her die; the other showed a fair face, feeling which to be her own, Emilia had fits of intolerable rage. This vision prevailed; and this wicked side of her humanity saved her. Active despair is a passion that must be superseded by a passion. Passive despair comes later; it has nothing to do with mental action, and is mainly a corruption or degradation of our blood. The rage in Emilia was blind at first, but it rose like a hawk, and singled its enemy. She fixed her mind to conceive the foolishness of putting out a face that her rival might envy, and of destroying anything that had value. The flattery of beauty came on her like a warm garment. When she opened her eyes, seeing what she was and where, she almost smiled at the silly picture that had given her comfort. Those men had looked on her admiringly, it was true, but would Wilfrid have ceased to love her if she had been beautiful? An extraordinary intuition of Wilfrid's sentiment tormented her now. She saw herself in the light that he would have seen her by, till she stood with the sensations of an exposed criminal in the dark length of the street, and hurried down it, back, as well as she could find her way, to the friendly policeman.

Her question on reaching him, "Are you married?" was prodigiously astonishing, and he administered the rebuff of an affirmative with severity. "Then," said Emilia, "when you go home, let me go with you to your wife. Perhaps she will consent to take care of me for this night." The policeman coughed mildly and replied, "It's plain you know nothing of women—begging your pardon, miss,—for I can see you're a lady." Emilia repeated her petition, and the policeman explained the nature of women. Not to be baffled, Emilia said, "I think your wife must be a good woman." Hereat the policeman laughed, arming "that the best of them knew what bad suspicions was." Ultimately, he consented to take her to his wife, when he was relieved, after the term of so many minutes. Emilia stood at a distance, speculating on the possible choice he would make of a tune to accompany his monotonous walk to and fro, and on the certainty of his wearing any tune to nothing.

She was in a bed, sleeping heavily, a little before dawn.

The day that followed was her day of misery. The blow that had stunned her had become as a loud intrusive pulse in her head. By this new daylight she fathomed the depth, and reckoned the value, of her loss. And her senses had no pleasure in the light, though there was sunshine. The woman who was her hostess was kind, but full of her first surprise at the strange visit, and too openly ready for any information the young lady might be willing to give with regard to her condition, prospects, and wishes. Emilia gave none. She took the woman's hand, asking permission to remain under her protection. The woman by-and-by named a sum of money as a sum for weekly payment, and Emilia transferred all to her that she had. The policeman and his wife thought her, though reasonable, a trifle insane. She sat at a window for hours watching a 'last man' of the fly species walking up and plunging down a pane of glass. On this transparent solitary field for the most objectless enterprise ever undertaken, he buzzed angrily at times, as if he had another meaning in him, which was being wilfully misinterpreted. Then he mounted again at his leisure, to pitch backward as before. Emilia found herself thinking with great seriousness that it was not wonderful for boys to be always teasing and killing flies, whose thin necks and bobbing heads themselves suggested the idea of decapitation. She said to her hostess: "I don't like flies. They seem never to sing but when they are bothered." The woman replied: "Ah, indeed?" very smoothly, and thought: "If you was to bust out now, which of us two would be strongest?" Emilia grew distantly aware that the policeman and his wife talked of her and watched her with combined observation.

When it was night she went to keep her appointment. The girl was there, but the boy came late. He said he had earned only a few pence that day, and would be beaten. He spoke in a whimpering tone which caused the girl to desire a translation of his words. Emilia told her how things were with him, and the girl expressed a wish that she had an organ, as in that case she would be sure to earn more than sixpence a day; such being the amount that procured her nightly a comfortable reception in the arms of her parents. "Do you like music?" said Emilia. The girl replied that she liked organs; but, as if to avoid committing an injustice, cited parrots as foremost in her affections. Holding them both to her breast, Emilia thought that she would rescue them from this beating by giving them the money they had to offer for kindness: but the restlessness of the children suddenly made her a third party to the thought of cakes. She had no money. Her heart bled for the poor little hungry, apprehensive creatures. For a moment she half fancied she had her voice, and looked up at the windows of the pitiless houses with a bold look; but there was a speedy mockery of her thought "You shall listen: you shall open!" She coughed hoarsely, and then fell into fits of crying. Her friend the policeman came by and took her arm with a force that he meant to be persuasive; so lifting her and handing her some steps beyond the limit of his beat, with stern directions for her to proceed home immediately. She obeyed. Next day she asked her hostess to lend her half-a-crown. The woman snapped shortly in answer: "No; the less you have the better." Emilia was obliged to abandon her little people.

She was to this extent the creature of mania: that she could not conceive of a way being open by which she might return to her father and mother, or any of her friends. It was to her not a matter for her will to decide upon, but simply a black door shut that nothing could displace. When the week, for which term of shelter she had paid, was ended, her hostess spoke upon this point, saying, more to convince Emilia of the necessity for seeking her friends than from any unkindness: "Me and my husband can't go on keepin' you, you know, my dear, however well's our meaning." Emilia drew the woman toward her with both her lands, softly shaking her head. She left the house about noon.

It was now her belief that she had probably no more than another day to live, for she was destitute of money. The thought relieved her from that dreadful fear of the street, and she walked at her own pace, even after dark. The rumble and the rattle of wheels; the cries and grinding noises; the hum of motion and talk; all under the lingering smoky red of a London Winter sunset, were not discord to her animated blood. Her unhunted spirit made a music of them. It was not like the music of other days, nor was the exultation it created at all like happiness: but she at least forgot herself. Voices came in her ear, and hung unheard until long after the speaker had passed. Hunger did not assail her. She was not beset by an animal weakness; and having in her mind no image of death, and with her ties to life cut away;—thus devoid of apprehension or regret, she was what her quick blood made her, for the time. She recognized that, for one near extinction, it was useless to love or to hate: so Wilfrid and Lady Charlotte were spared. Emilia thought of them both with a sort of equanimity; not that any clear thought filled her brain through that delirious night. The intoxicating music raged there at one level depression, never rising any scale, never undulating ever so little, scarcely changing its barbarous monotony of notes. She had no power over it. Her critical judgement would at another moment have shrieked at it. She was moved by it as by a mechanical force.

The South-west wind blew, and the hours of the night were not evil to outcasts. Emilia saw many lying about, getting rest where they might. She hurried her eye pityingly over little children, but the devil that had seized her sprang contempt for the others—older beggars, who appeared to succumb to their fate when they should have lifted their heads up bravely. On she passed from square to market, market to park; and presently her mind shot an arrow of desire for morning, which was nothing less than hunger beginning to stir. "When will the shops open?" She tried to cheat herself by replying that she did not care when, but pangs of torment became too rapid for the counterfeit. Her imagination raised the roof from those great rich houses, and laid bare a brilliancy of dish-covers; and if any sharp gust of air touched the nerve in her nostril, it seemed instantaneously charged with the smell of old dinners. "No," cried Emilia, "I dislike anything but plain food." She quickly gave way, and admitted a craving for dainty morsels. "One lump of sugar!" she subsequently sighed. But neither sugar nor meat approached her.

Her seat was under trees, between a man and a woman who slanted from her with hidden chins. The chilly dry leaves began to waken, and the sky showed its grey. Hunger had become as a leaden ball in Emilia's chest. She could have eaten eagerly still, but she had no ravenous images of food. Nevertheless, she determined to beg for bread at a baker's shop. Coming into the empty streets again, the dread of exposing her solitary wretchedness and the stains of night upon her, kept her back. When she did venture near the baker's shop, her sensation of weariness, want of washing, and general misery, made her feel a contrast to all other women she saw, that robbed her of the necessary effrontery. She preferred to hide her head.

The morning hours went in this conflict. She was between-whiles hungry and desperate, or stricken with shame. Fatigue, bringing the imperious necessity for rest, intervened as a relief. Emilia moaned at the weary length of the light, but when dusk fell and she beheld flame in the lamps, it seemed to be too sudden and she was alarmed. Passive despair had set in. She felt sick, though not weak, and the thought of asking help had gone.

A street urchin, of the true London species, in whom excess of woollen comforter made up for any marked scantiness in the rest of his attire, came trotting the pavement, pouring one of the favourite tunes of his native metropolis through the tube of a penny-whistle, from which it did not issue so disguised but that attentive ears might pronounce it the royal march of the Cannibal Islands. A placarded post beside a lamp met this musician's eye; and, still piping, he bent his knees and read the notification. Emilia thought of the Hillford and Ipley clubmen, the big drum, the speeches, the cheers, and all the wild strength that lay in her that happy morning. She watched the boy piping as if he were reading from a score, and her sense of humour was touched. "You foolish boy!" she said to herself softly. But when, having evidently come to the last printed line, the boy rose and pocketed his penny-whistle, Emilia was nearly laughing. "That's because he cannot turn over the leaf," she said, and stood by the post till long after the boy had disappeared. The slight emotion of fun had restored to her some of her lost human sensations, and she looked about for a place where to indulge them undisturbed. One of the bridges was in sight She yearned for the solitude of the wharf beside it, and hurried to the steps. To descend she had to pass a street-organ and a small figure bent over it. "Sei buon' Italiano?" she said. The answer was a surly "Si." Emilia cried convulsively "Addio!" Her brain had become on a sudden vacant of a thought, and all she knew was that she descended.

CHAPTER XLI

SHE IS FOUND

"Sei buon' Italiana?"

Across what chasm did the words come to her?

It seemed but a minutes and again many hours back, that she had asked that question of a little fellow, who, if he had looked up and nodded would have given her great joy, but who kept his face dark from her and with a sullen "Si" extinguished her last feeling of a desire for companionship with life.

"Si," she replied, quite as sullenly, and without looking up.

But when her hand was taken and other words were uttered, she that had crouched there so long between death and life immovable, loving neither, rose possessed of a passion for the darkness and the void, and struggling bitterly with the detaining hand, crying for instant death. No strength was in her to support the fury.

"Merthyr Powys is with you," said her friend, "and will never leave you."

"Will never take me up there?" Emilia pointed to the noisy level above them.

"Listen, and I will tell you how I have found you," replied Merthyr.

"Don't force me to go up."

She spoke from the end of her breath. Merthyr feared that it was more than misery, even madness, afflicting her. He sat on the wharf-bench silent till she was reassured. But at his first words, the eager question came: "You will not force me to go up there?"

"No; we can stay and talk here," said Merthyr. "And this is how I have found you. Do you suppose you have been hidden from us all this time? Perhaps you fancy you do not belong to your friends? Well, I spoke to all of your 'children,' as you used to call them. Do you remember? The day before yesterday two had seen you. You said to one, 'From Savoy or Piedmont?' He said, 'From Savoy;' and you shook your head: 'Not looking on Italy!' you said. This night I roused one of them, and he stretched his finger down the steps, saying that you had gone down there. 'Sei buon' Italiano?" you said. "And that is how I have found you. Sei buon' Italiana?"

Emilia let her hand rest in Merthyr's, wondering to think that there should be no absolute darkness for a creature to escape into while living. A trembling came on her. "Let me look over at the water," she said; and Merthyr, who trusted her even in that extremity, allowed her to lean forward, and felt her grasp grow moist in his, till she turned back with shudders, giving him both her hands. "A drowned woman looks so dreadful!" Her speech was faint as she begged to be taken away from that place. Merthyr put his hand to her arm-pit, sustaining her steps. As they neared the level where men were, she looked behind her and realized the black terrors she had just been blindly handling. Fright sped her limbs for a second or two, and then her whole weight hung upon Merthyr. He held her in both arms, thinking that she had swooned, but she murmured: "Have you heard that my voice has gone?"

"If you have suffered, I do not wonder," he said.

"I am useless. My voice is dead."

"Useless to your friends? Tush, my little Emilia! Sandra mia! Don't you know that while you love your friends that's all they want of you?"

"Oh!" she moaned; "the gas-lamp hurts me. What a noise there is!"

"We shall soon get away from the noise."

"No; I like it; but not the light. Oh, my feet!—why are you walking still? What friends?"

"For instance, myself."

"You knew of my wandering about London! It makes me believe in heaven. I can't bear to think of being unseen."

"This morning," said Merthyr, "I saw the policeman in whose house you have been staying."

Emilia bowed her head to the mystery by which this friend was endowed to be cognizant of her actions. "I feel that I have not seen the streets for years. If it were not for you I should fall down.—Oh! do you understand that my voice has quite gone?"

Merthyr perceived her anxiety to be that she might not betaken on doubtful terms. "Your hand hasn't," he said, pressing it, and so gratified her with a concrete image of something that she could still bestow upon a friend. To this she clung while the noisy wheels bore her through London, till her weak body failed to keep courage in her breast, and she wept and came closer to Merthyr. He who supposed that her recent despair and present tears were for the loss of her lover, gave happily more comfort than he took. "When old gentlemen choose to interest themselves about very young ladies," he called upon his humorous philosophy to observe internally, as men do to forestall the possible cynic external;—and the rest of the sentence was acted under his eyes by the figures of three persons. But, there she was, lying within his arm, rescued, the creature whom he had found filling his heart, when lost, and whom he thought one of the most hopeful of the women of earth! He thanked God for bare facts. She lay against him with her eyelids softly joined, and as he felt the breathing of her body, he marvelled to think how matter-of-fact they had both been on the brink of a tragedy, and how naturally she had, as it were, argued herself up to the gates of death. For want of what? "My sister may supply it," thought Merthyr.

"Oh! that river is like a great black snake with a sick eye, and will come round me!" said Emilia, talking as from sleep; then started, with fright in her face: "Oh! my hunger again!"

"Hunger!" said he, horrified.

"It comes worse than ever," she moaned. "I was half dead just now, and didn't feel it. There's—there's no pain in death. But this—it's like fire and frost! I feel being eaten up. Give me something."

Merthyr set his teeth and enveloped her in a tight hug that relieved her from the sharper pangs; and so held her, the tears bursting through his shut eyelids, till at the first hotel they reached he managed to get food for her. She gave a little gasping cry when he put bread through the window of the cab. Bit by bit he handed her the morsels. It was impossible to procure broth. When they drove on, she did not complain of suffering, but her chest rose and fell many times heavily. She threw him out in the reading of her character, after a space, by excusing herself for having eaten with such eagerness; and it was long before he learnt what Wilfrid's tyrannous sentiment had done to this simple nature. He understood better the fear she expressed of meeting Georgiana. Nevertheless, she exhibited none on entering the house, and returned Georgiana's embrace with what strength was left to her.

CHAPTER XLII

DEFECTION OF MR. PERICLES FROM THE BROOKFIELD CIRCLE

Up the centre aisle of Hillford Church, the Tinleys (late as usual) were seen trooping for morning service in midwinter. There was a man in the rear known to be a man by the sound of his boots and measure of his stride, for the ladies of Brookfield, having rejected the absurd pretensions of Albert Tinley, could not permit curiosity to encounter the risk of meeting his gaze by turning their heads. So, with charitable condescension they returned the slight church nod of prim Miss Tinley passing, of the detestable Laura

Tinley, of affected Rose Tinley (whose complexion was that of a dust-bin), and of Madeline Tinley (too young for a character beyond what the name bestowed), and then they arranged their prayer-books, and apparently speculated as to the possible text that morning to be given forth from the pulpit. But it seemed to them all that an exceedingly bulky object had passed as guardian of the light-footed damsels preceding him. Though none of the ladies had looked up as he passed, they were conscious of a stature and a circumference which they had deemed to be entirely beyond the reach of the Tinleys, and a scornful notion of the Tinleys having hired a guardsman, made Arabella smile at the stretch of her contempt, that could help her to conceive the ironic possibility. Relieved on the suspicion that Albert was in attendance of his sisters, they let their eyes fall calmly on the Tinley pew. Could two men upon this earthly sphere possess such a bearskin? There towered the shoulders of Mr. Pericles; his head looking diminished by the hugeous collar. Arabella felt a seizure of her hand from Adela's side. She placed her book open before her, and stared at the pulpit. From neither of the three of Brookfield could Laura's observation extract a sign of the utter astonishment she knew they must be experiencing; and had it not been for the ingenuous broad whisper of Mrs. Chump, which sounded toward the verge even of her conception of possibilities, the Tinleys would not have been gratified by the first public display of the prize they had wrested from the Poles.

"Mr. Paricles—oh!" went Mrs. Chump, and a great many pews were set in commotion.

Forthwith she bent over Cornelia's lap, and Cornelia, surveying her placidly, had to murmur, "By-and-by; by-and-by."

"But, did ye see 'm, my dear? and a forr'ner in a Protestant Church! And such a forr'ner as he is, to be sure! And, ye know, ye said he'd naver come with you, and it's them creatures ye don't like. Corrnelia!"

"The service commences," remarked that lady, standing up.

Many eyes were on Mr. Pericles, who occasionally inspected the cornices and corbels and stained glass to right and left, or detected a young lady staring at him, or anticipated her going to stare, and put her to confusion by a sharp turn of his head, and then a sniff and smoothing down of his moustache. But he did not once look at the Brookfield pew. By hazard his eye ranged over it, and after the first performance of this trick he would have found the ladies a match for him, even if he had sought to challenge their eyes. They were constrained to admit that Laura Tinley managed him cleverly. She made him hold a book and appear respectably devout. She got him down in good time when seats were taken, and up again, without much transparent persuasion. The first notes of the organ were seen to agitate the bearskin. Laura had difficulty to induce the man to rise for the hymn, and when he had listened to the intoning of a verse, Mr. Pericles suddenly bent, as if he had snapped in two: nor could Laura persuade him to rejoin the present posture of the congregation. Then only did Laura, to cover her failure, turn the subdued light of a merry smile upon the Brookfield pew.

The smile was noticed by Apprehension sitting in the corner of one eye, and it was likewise known that Laura's chagrin at finding that she was not being watched affected her visibly. At the termination of the sermon, the ladies bowed their heads a short space, and placing Mrs. Chump in front drove her out, so that her exclamations of wonderment, and affectedly ostentatious gaspings of sympathy for Brookfield, were heard by few. On they hurried, straight and fast to Brookfield. Mr. Pole was talking to Tracy Runningbrook at the gate. The ladies cut short his needless apology to the young man for not being found in church that day, by asking questions of Tracy. The first related to their brother's whereabouts; the second to Emilia's condition. Tracy had no time to reply. Mrs. Chump had identified herself with

Brookfield so warmly that the defection of Mr. Pericles was a fine legitimate excitement to her. "I hate 'm!" she cried. "I pos'tively hate the man! And he to go to church! A pretty figure for an angel—he, now! But, my dears, we cann't let annybody else have 'm. Shorrt of his bein' drowned or killed, we must intrigue to keep the wretch to ourselves."

"Oh, dear!" said Adela impatiently.

"Well, and I didn't say to myself, ye little jealous thing!" retorted Mrs. Chump.

"Indeed, ma'am, you are welcome to him."

"And indeed, miss, I don't want 'm. And, perhaps, ye were flirtin' all the fun out of him on board the yacht, and got tired of 'm; and that's why."

Adela said: "Thank you," with exasperating sedateness, which provoked an intemperate outburst from Mrs. Chump. "Sunday! Sunday!" cried Mr. Pole.

"Ain't I the first to remember ut, Pole? And didn't I get up airly so as to go to church and have my conscience qui't, and 'stead of that I come out full of evil passions, all for the sake o' these ungrateful garls that's always where ye cann't find 'em. Why, if they was to be married at the altar, they'd stare and be 'ffendud if ye asked them if they was thinking of their husbands, they would! 'Oh, dear, no! and ye're mistaken, and we're thinkin' o' the coal-scuttle in the back parlour,'—or somethin' about souls, if not coals. There's their answer. What did ye do with Mr. Paricles on board the yacht? Aha!"

"What's this about Pericles?" said Mr. Pole.

"Oh, nothing, Papa," returned Adela.

"Nothing, do ye call ut!" said Mrs. Chump. "And, mayhap, good cause too. Didn't ye tease 'm, now, on board the yacht? Now, did he go on board the yacht at all?"

"I should think you ought to know that as well as Adela," said Mr. Pole.

Adela interposed, hurriedly: "All this, my dear Papa, is because Mr. Pericles has thought proper to visit the Tinleys' pew. Who would complain how or where he does it, so long as the duty is fulfilled?"

Mr. Pole stared, muttering: "The Tinleys!"

"She's botherin' of ye, Pole, the puss!" said Mrs. Chump, certain that she had hit a weak point in that mention of the yacht. "Ask her what sorrt of behaviour—"

"And he didn't speak to any of you?" said Mr. Pole.

"No, Papa."

"He looked the other way?"

"He did us that honour."

"Ask her, Pole, how she behaved to 'm on board the yacht," cried Mrs. Chump. "Oh! there was flirtin', flirtin'! And go and see what the noble poet says of tying up in sacks and plumpin' of poor bodies of women into forty fathoms by them Turks and Greeks, all because of jeal'sy. So, they make a woman in earnest there, the wretches, 'cause she cann't have onny of her jokes. Didn't ye tease Mr. Paricles on board the yacht, Ad'la? Now, was he there?"

"Martha! you're a fool!" said Mr. Pole, looking the victim of one of his fits of agitation. "Who knows whether he was there better than you? You'll be forgetting soon that we've ever dined together. I hate to see a woman so absurd! There—never mind! Go in: take off bonnet something—anything! only I can't bear folly! Eh, Mr. Runningbrook?"

"'Deed, Pole, and ye're mad." Mrs. Chump crossed her hands to reply with full repose. "I'd like to know how I'm to know what I never said."

The scene was growing critical. Adela consulted the eyes of her sisters, which plainly said that this was her peculiar scrape. Adela ended it by going up to Mrs. Chump, taking her by the shoulders, and putting a kiss upon her forehead. "Now you will see better," she said. "Don't you know Mr. Pericles was not with us? As surely as he was with the Tinleys this morning!"

"And a nice morning it is!" ejaculated Mr. Pole, trotting off hurriedly.

"Does Pole think—" Mrs. Chump murmured, with reference to her voyaging on the yacht. The kiss had bewildered her sequent sensations.

"He does think, and will think, and must think," Adela prattled some persuasive infantine nonsense: her soul all the while in revolt against her sisters, who left her the work to do, and took the position of spectators and critics, condemning an effort they had not courage to attempt.

"By the way, I have to congratulate a friend of mine," said Tracy, selecting Adela for an ironical bow.

"Then it is Captain Gambier," cried Mrs. Chump, as if a whole revelation had burst on her. Adela blushed. "Oh! and what was that I heard?" continued the aggravating woman.

Adela flashed her eyes round on her sisters. Even then they left her without aid, their feeling being that she had debased the house by her familiarity with this woman before Tracy.

"Stay! didn't ye both—" Mrs. Chump was saying.

"Yes?"—Adela passed by her—"only in your ears alone, you know!" At which hint Mrs. Chump gleefully turned and followed her. A rumour was prevalent of some misadventure to Adela and the captain on board the yacht. Arabella saw her depart, thinking, "How singular is her propensity to imitate me!" for the affirmative uttered in the tone of interrogation was quite Arabella's own; as also occasionally the negative,—the negative, however, suiting the musical indifference of the sound, and its implied calm breast.

"As for Pericles," said Tracy, "you need not wonder that the fellow prays in other pews than yours. By heaven! he may pray and pray: I'd send him to Hades with an epigram in his heart!"

From Tracy the ladies learnt that Wilfrid had inflicted public chastisement upon Mr. Pericles for saying a false thing of Emilia. He danced the prettiest pas seul that was ever footed by debutant on the hot iron plates of Purgatory. They dared not ask what it was that Mr. Pericles had said, but Tracy was so vehement on the subject of his having met his deserts, that they partly guessed it to bear some relation to their sex's defencelessness, and they approved their brother's work.

Sir Twickenham and Captain Gambier dined at Brookfield that day. However astonishing it might be to one who knew his character and triumphs, the captain was a butterfly netted, and was on the highroad to an exhibition of himself pinned, with his wings outspread. During the service of the table Tracy relieved Adela from Mrs. Chump's inadvertencies and little bits of feminine malice, but he could not help the captain, who blundered like a schoolboy in her rough hands. It was noted that Sir Twickenham reserved the tolerating smile he once had for her. Mr. Pole's nervous fretfulness had increased. He complained in occasional underbreaths, correcting himself immediately with a "No, no!" and blinking briskly.

But after dinner came the time when the painfullest scene was daily enacted. Mrs. Chump drank Port freely. To drink it fondly, it was necessary that she should have another rosy wineglass to nod to, and Mr. Pole, whose taste for wine had been weakened, took this post as his duty. The watchful, pinched features of the poor pale little man bloomed unnaturally, and his unintelligible eyes sparkled as he emptied his glass. His daughters knew that he drank, not for his pleasure, but for their benefit; that he might sustain Martha Chump in the delusion that he was a fitting bridegroom, and with her money save them from ruin. Each evening, with remorse that blotted all perception of the tragic comicality of the show, they saw him, in his false strength and his anxiety concerning his pulse's play, act this part. The recurring words, "Now, Martha, here's the Port," sent a cold wave through their blood. They knew what the doctor remarked on the effect of that Port. "Ill!" Mrs. Chump would cry, when she saw him wink after sipping; "you, Pole! what do they say of ye, ye deer!" and she returned the wink, the ladies looking on. Not to drink a proper quantum of Port, when Port was on the table, was, in Mrs. Chump's eyes, mean for a man. Even Chump, she would say, was master of his bottle, and thought nothing of it. "Who does?" cried her present suitor, and the Port ebbed, and his cheeks grew crimson.

This frightful rivalry with the ghost of Alderman Chump continued night after night. The rapturous Martha was incapable of observing that if she drank with a ghost in memory, in reality she drank with nothing better than an animated puppet. The nights ended with Mr. Pole either sleeping in his arm-chair (upon which occasions one daughter watched him and told dreadful tales of his waking), or staggering to bed, debating on the stairs between tea and brandy, complaining of a loss of sensation at his knee-cap, or elbow, or else rubbing his head and laughing hysterically. His bride was not at such moments observant. No wonder Wilfrid kept out of the way, if he had not better occupation elsewhere. The ladies, in their utter anguish, after inveighing against the baneful Port, had begged their father to delay no more to marry the woman. "Why?" said Mr. Pole, sharply; "what do you want me to marry her for?" They were obliged to keep up the delusion, and said, "Because she seems suited to you as a companion." That satisfied him. "Oh! we won't be in a hurry," he said, and named a day within a month; and not liking their unready faces, laughed, and dismissed the idea aloud, as if he had not earnestly been entertaining it.

The ladies of Brookfield held no more their happy, energetic midnight consultations. They had begun to crave for sleep and a snatch of forgetfulness, the scourge being daily on their flesh: and they had now no plans to discuss; they had no distant horizon of low vague lights that used ever to be beyond their morrow. They kissed at the bedroom door of one, and separated. Silence was their only protection to the Nice Feelings, now that Fine Shades had become impossible. Adela had almost made herself distinct from her sisters since the yachting expedition. She had grown severely careful of the keys of her writing-desk, and would sometimes slip the bolt of her bedroom door, and answer "Eh?" dubiously in tone, when her sisters had knocked twice, and had said "Open" once. The house of Brookfield showed those divisional rents which an admonitory quaking of the earth will create. Neither sister was satisfied with the other. Cornelia's treatment of Sir Twickenham was almost openly condemned, but at the same time it seemed to Arabella that the baronet was receiving more than the necessary amount of consolation from the bride of Captain Gambier, and that yacht habits and moralities had been recently imported to Brookfield. Adela, for her part, looked sadly on Arabella, and longed to tell her, as she told Cornelia, that if she continued to play Freshfield Sumner purposely against Edward Buxley, she might lose both. Cornelia quietly measured accusations and judged impartially; her mind being too full to bring any personal observations to bear. She said, perhaps, less than she would have said, had she not known that hourly her own Nice Feelings had to put up a petition for Fine Shades: had she not known, indeed, that her conduct would soon demand from her sisters an absolutely merciful interpretation. For she was now simply attracting Sir Twickenham to Brookfield as a necessary medicine to her Papa. Since Mrs. Chump's return, however, Mr. Pole had spoken cheerfully of himself, and, by innuendo emphasized, had imparted that his mercantile prospects were brighter. In fact, Cornelia half thought that he must have been pretending bankruptcy to gain his end in getting the consent of his daughters to receive the woman. She, and Adela likewise, began to suspect that the parental transparency was a little mysterious, and that there is, after all, more than we see in something that we see through. They were now in danger of supposing that because the old man had possibly deceived them to some extent, he had deceived them altogether. But was not the after-dinner scene too horribly true? Were not his hands moist and cold while the forehead was crimson? And could a human creature feel at his own pulse, and look into vacancy with that intense apprehensive look, and be but an actor? They could not think so. But his conditions being dependent upon them, the ladies felt in their hearts a spring of absolute rebellion when the call for fresh sacrifices came. Though they did not grasp the image, they had a feeling that he was nourished bit by bit by everything they held dear; and though they loved him, and were generous, they had begun to ask, "What next?"

The ladies were at a dead-lock, and that the heart is the father of our histories, I am led to think when I look abroad on families stagnant because of so weak a motion of the heart. There are those who have none at all; the mass of us are moved from the propulsion of the toes of the Fates. But the ladies of Brookfield had hearts lively enough to get them into scrapes. The getting out of them, or getting on at all, was left to Providence. They were at a dead-lock, for Arabella, flattered as she was by Freshfield Sumner's wooing, could not openly throw Edward over, whom indeed she thought that she liked the better of the two, though his letters had not so wide an intellectual range. Her father was irritably anxious that she should close with Edward. Adela could not move: at least, not openly. Cornelia might have taken an initiative; but tenderness for her father's health had hitherto restrained her, and she temporized with Sir Twickenham on the noblest of principles. She was, by the devotion of her conduct, enabled to excuse herself so far that she could even fish up an excuse in the shape of the effort she had made to find him entertaining: as if the said effort should really be re-payment enough to him for his assiduous and most futile suit. One deep grief sat on Cornelia's mind. She had heard from Lady Gosstre that there was something like madness in the Barrett family. She had consented to meet Sir Purcell clandestinely (after debate on his claim to such a sacrifice on her part), and if, on those occasions, her lover's tone was raised, it gave her a tremour. And he had of late appeared to lose his noble calm; he had spoken (it might almost be interpreted) as if he doubted her. Once, when she had mentioned her care for her father, he had cried out upon the name of father with violence, looking unlike himself.

His condemnation of the world, too, was not so Christian as it had been; it betrayed what the vulgar would call spite, and was not all compassed in his peculiar smooth shrug—expressive of a sort of border-land between contempt and charity: which had made him wear in her sight all the superiority which the former implies, with a considerable share of the benign complacency of the latter. This had gone. He had been sarcastic even to her; saying once, and harshly: "Have you a will?" Personally she liked the poor organist better than the poor baronet, though he had less merit. It was unpleasant in her present mood to be told "that we have come into this life to fashion for ourselves souls;" and that "whosoever cannot decide is a soulless wretch fit but to pass into vapour." He appeared to have ceased to make his generous allowances for difficult situations. A senseless notion struck Cornelia, that with the baronetcy he had perhaps inherited some of the madness of his father.

The two were in a dramatic tangle of the Nice Feelings worth a glance as we pass on. She wished to say to him, "You are unjust to my perplexities;" and he to her, "You fail in your dilemma through cowardice." Instead of uttering which, they chid themselves severally for entertaining such coarse ideas of their idol. Doubtless they were silent from consideration for one another: but I must add, out of extreme tenderness for themselves likewise. There are people who can keep the facts that front them absent from their contemplation by not framing them in speech; and much benevolence of the passive order may be traced to a disinclination to inflict pain upon oneself. "My duty to my father," being cited by Cornelia, Sir Purcell had to contend with it.

"True love excludes no natural duty," she said.

And he: "Love discerns unerringly what is and what is not duty."

"In the case of a father, can there be any doubt?" she asked, the answer shining in her confident aspect.

"There are many things that fathers may demand of us!" he interjected bitterly.

She had a fatal glimpse here of the false light in which his resentment coloured the relations between fathers and children; and, deeming him incapable of conducting this argument, she felt quite safe in her opposition, up to a point where feeling stopped her.

"Devotedness to a father I must conceive to be a child's first duty," she said.

Sir Purcell nodded: "Yes; a child's!"

"Does not history give the higher praise to children who sacrifice themselves for their parents?" asked Cornelia.

And he replied: "So, you seek to be fortified in such matters by history!"

Courteous sneers silenced her. Feeling told her she was in the wrong; but the beauty of her sentiment was not to be contested, and therefore she thought that she might distrust feeling: and she went against it somewhat; at first very tentatively, for it caused pain. She marked a line where the light of duty should not encroach on the light of our human desires. "But love for a parent is not merely duty," thought Cornelia. "It is also love;—and is it not the least selfish love?"

Step by step Sir Purcell watched the clouding of her mind with false conceits, and knew it to be owing to the heart's want of vigour. Again and again he was tempted to lay an irreverent hand on the veil his lady walked in, and make her bare to herself. Partly in simple bitterness, he refrained: but the chief reason was that he had no comfort in giving a shock to his own state of deception. He would have had to open a dark closet; to disentangle and bring to light what lay in an undistinguishable heap; to disfigure her to herself, and share in her changed eyesight; possibly to be, or seem, coarse: so he kept the door of it locked, admitting sadly in his meditation that there was such a place, and saying all the while: "If I were not poor!" He saw her running into the shelter of egregious sophisms, till it became an effort to him to preserve his reverence for her and the sex she represented. Finally he imagined that he perceived an idea coming to growth in her, no other than this: "That in duty to her father she might sacrifice herself, though still loving him to whom she had given her heart; thus ennobling her love for father and for lover." With a wicked ingenuity he tracked her forming notions, encouraged them on, and provoked her enthusiasm by putting an ironical question: "Whether the character of the soul was subdued and shaped by the endurance and the destiny of the perishable?"

"Oh! no, no!" she exclaimed. "It cannot be, or what comfort should we have?"

Few men knew better that when lovers' sentiments stray away from feeling, they are to be suspected of a disloyalty. Yet he admired the tone she took. He had got an 'ideal' of her which it was pleasanter to magnify than to distort. An 'ideal' is so arbitrary, that if you only doubt of its being perfection, it will vanish and never come again. Sir Purcell refused to doubt. He blamed himself for having thought it possible to doubt, and this, when all the time he knew.

Through endless labyrinths of delusion these two unhappy creatures might be traced, were it profitable. Down what a vale of little intricate follies should we be going, lighted by one ghastly conclusion! At times, struggling from the midst of her sophisms, Cornelia prayed her lover would claim her openly, and so nerve her to a pitch of energy that would clinch the ruinous debate. Forgetting that she was an 'ideal'—the accredited mistress of pure wisdom and of the power of deciding rightly—she prayed to be dealt with as a thoughtless person, and one of the herd of women. She felt that Sir Purcell threw too much on her. He expected her to go calmly to her father, and to Sir Twickenham, and tell them individually that her heart was engaged; then with a stately figure to turn, quit the house, and lay her hand in his. He made no allowance for the weakness of her sex, for the difficulties surrounding her, for the consideration due to Sir Twickenham's pride, and to her father's ill-health. She half-protested to herself that he expected from her the mechanical correctness of a machine, and overlooked the fact that she was human. It was a grave comment on her ambition to be an 'ideal.'

So let us leave them, till we come upon the ashy fruit of which this blooming sentimentalism is the seed.

It was past midnight when Mrs. Chump rushed to Arabella's room, and her knock was heard vociferous at the door. The ladies, who were at work upon diaries and letters, allowed her to thump and wonder whether she had come to the wrong door, for a certain period; after which, Arabella placidly unbolted her chamber, and Adela presented herself in the passage to know the meaning of the noise.

"Oh! ye poor darlin's, I've heard ut all, I have."

This commencement took the colour from their cheeks. Arabella invited her inside, and sent Adela for Cornelia.

"Oh, and ye poor deers!" cried Mrs. Chump to Arabella, who remarked: "Pray wait till my sisters come;" causing the woman to stare and observe: "If ye're not as cold as the bottom of a pot that naver felt fire." She repeated this to Cornelia and Adela as an accusation, and then burst on "My heart's just breakin' for ye, and ye shall naver want bread, eh! and roast beef, and my last bottle of Port ye'll share, though ye've no ideea what a lot o' thoughts o' poor Chump's under that cork, and it'll be a waste on you. Oh! and that monster of a Mr. Paricles that's got ye in his power and's goin' to be the rroon of ye—shame to 'm! Your father's told me; and, oh! my darlin' garls, don't think ut my fault. For, Pole—Pole—"

Mrs. Chump was choked by her grief. The ladies, unbending to some curiosity, eliminated from her gasps and sobs that Mr. Pole had, in the solitude of his library below, accused her of causing the defection of Mr. Pericles, and traced his possible ruin to it, confessing, that in the way of business, he was at Mr. Pericles' mercy.

"And in such a passion with me!" Mrs. Chump wrung her hands. "What could I do to Mr. Paricles? He isn't one o' the men that I can kiss; and Pole shouldn't wish me. And Pole settin' down his rroon to me! What'll I do? My dears! I do feel for ye, for I feel I'd feel myself such a beast, without money, d'ye see? It's the most horrible thing in the world. It's like no candle in the darrk. And I, ye know, I know I'd naver forgive annybody that took my money; and what'll Pole think of me? For oh! ye may call riches temptation, but poverty's punishment; and I heard a young curate say that from the pulpit, and he was lean enough to know, poor fella!"

Both Cornelia and Arabella breathed more freely when they had heard Mrs. Chump's tale to an end. They knew perfectly well that she was blameless for the defection of Mr. Pericles, and understood from her exclamatory narrative that their father had reason to feel some grave alarm at the Greek's absence from their house, and had possibly reasons of his own for accusing Mrs. Chump, as he had done. The ladies administered consolation to her, telling her that for their part they would never blame her; even consenting to be kissed by her, hugged by her, playfully patted, complimented, and again wept over. They little knew what a fervour of secret devotion they created in Mrs. Chump's bosom by this astounding magnanimity displayed to her, who laboured under the charge of being the source of their ruin; nor could they guess that the little hypocrisy they were practising would lead to any singular and pregnant resolution in the mind of the woman, fraught with explosion to their house, and that quick movement which they awaited.

Mrs. Chump, during the patient strain of a tender hug of Arabella, had mutely resolved in a great heat of gratitude that she would go to Mr. Pericles, and, since he was necessary to the well-being of Brookfield, bring him back, if she had to bring him back in her arms.

CHAPTER XLIII

IN WHICH WE SEE WILFRID KINDLING

[Georgiana Ford to Wilfrid:]

"I have omitted replying to your first letter, not because of the nature of its contents: nor do I write now in answer to your second because of the permission you give me to lay it before my brother. I cannot think that concealment is good, save for very base persons; and since you take the initiative in writing very openly, I will do so likewise.

"It is true that Emilia is with me. Her voice is lost, and she has fallen as low in spirit as one can fall and still give us hope of her recovery. But that hope I have, and I am confident that you will not destroy it. In the summer she goes with us to Italy. We have consulted one doctor, who did not prescribe medicine for her. In the morning she reads with my brother. She seems to forget whatever she reads: the occupation is everything necessary just now. Our sharp Monmouth air provokes her to walk briskly when she is out, and the exercise has once or twice given colour to her cheeks. Yesterday being a day of clear frost, we drove to a point from which we could mount the Buckstone, and here, my brother says, the view appeared to give her something of her lost animation. It was a look that I had never seen, and it soon went: but in the evening she asked me whether I prayed before sleeping, and when she retired to her bedroom, I remained there with her for a time.

"You will pardon me for refusing to let her know that you have written to your relative in the Austrian service to obtain a commission for you. But, on the other hand, I have thought it right to tell her incidentally that you will be married in the Summer of this year. I can only say that she listened quite calmly.

"I beg that you will not blame yourself so vehemently. By what you do, her friends may learn to know that you regret the strange effect produced by certain careless words, or conduct: but I cannot find that self-accusation is ever good at all. In answer to your question, I may add that she has repeated nothing of what she said when we were together in Devon.

"Our chief desire (for, as we love her, we may be directed by our instinct), in the attempt to restore her, is to make her understand that she is anything but worthless. She has recently followed my brother's lead, and spoken of herself, but with a touch of scorn. This morning, while the clear frosty sky continues, we were to have started for an old castle lying toward Wales; and I think the idea of a castle must have struck her imagination, and forced some internal contrast on her mind. I am repeating my brother's suggestion—she seemed more than usually impressed with an idea that she was of no value to anybody. She asked why she should go anywhere, and dropped into a chair, begging to be allowed to stay in a darkened room. My brother has some strange intuition of her state of mind. She has lost any power she may have had of grasping abstract ideas. In what I conceived to be play, he told her that many would buy her even now. She appeared to be speculating on this, and then wished to know how much those persons would consider her to be worth, and who they were. Nor did it raise a smile on her face to hear my brother mention Jews, and name an absolute sum of money; but, on the contrary, after evidently thinking over it, she rose up, and said that she was ready to go. I write fully to you, telling you these things, that you may see she is at any rate eager not to despair, and is learning, much as a child might learn it, that it need not be.

"Believe me, that I will in every way help to dispossess your mind of the remorse now weighing upon you, as far as it shall be within my power to do so.

"Mr. Runningbrook has been invited by my brother to come and be her companion. They have a strong affection for one another. He is a true poet, full of reverence for a true woman."

[Wilfrid to Georgiana Ford:]

"I cannot thank you enough. When I think of her I am unmanned; and if I let my thoughts fall back upon myself, I am such as you saw me that night in Devon—helpless, and no very presentable figure. But you do not picture her to me. I cannot imagine whether her face has changed; and, pardon me, were I writing to you alone, I could have faith that the delicate insight and angelic nature of a woman would not condemn my desire to realize before my eyes the state she has fallen to. I see her now under a black shroud. Have her features changed? I cannot remember one—only at an interval her eyes. Does she look into the faces of people as she used? Or does she stare carelessly away? Softly between the eyes, is what I meant. I mean—but my reason for this particularity is very simple. I would state it to you, and to no other. I cannot have peace till she is restored; and my prayer is, that I may not haunt her to defeat your labour. Does her face appear to show that I am quite absent from her thoughts? Oh! you will understand me. You have seen me stand and betray no suffering when a shot at my forehead would have been mercy. To you I will dare to open my heart. I wish to be certain that I have not injured her—that is all. Perhaps I am more guilty than you think: more even than I can call to mind. If I may fudge by the punishment, my guilt is immeasurable. Tell me—if you will but tell me that the sacrifice of my life to her will restore her, it is hers. Write, and say this, and I will come: Do not delay or spare me. Her dumb voice is like a ghost in my ears. It cries to me that I have killed it. Be actuated by no charitable considerations in refraining to write. Could a miniature of her be sent? You will think the request strange; but I want to be sure she is not haggard—not the hospital face I fancy now, which accuses me of murder. Does she preserve the glorious freshness she used to wear? She had a look—or did you see her before the change? I only want to know that she is well."

[Tracy Runningbrook to Wilfrid:]

"You had my promise that I would write and give your conscience a nightcap. I have a splendid one for you. Put it on without any hesitation. I find her quite comfortable. Powys reads Italian with her in the morning. His sister (who might be a woman if she liked, but has an insane preference for celestial neutrality) does the moral inculcation. The effect is comical. I should like you to see Cold Steel leading Tame Fire about, and imagining the taming to be her work! You deserve well of your generation. You just did enough to set this darling girl alight. Knights and squires numberless will thank you. The idea of your reproaching yourself is monstrous. Why, there's no one thanks you more than she does. You stole her voice, which some may think a pity, but I don't, seeing that I would rather have her in a salon than before the footlights. Imagine my glory in her!—she has become half cat! She moves softly, as if she loved everything she touched; making you throb to feel the little ball of her foot. Her eyes look steadily, like green jewels before the veil of an Egyptian temple. Positively, her eyes have grown green—or greenish! They were darkish hazel formerly, and talked more of milkmaids and chattering pastorals than a discerning master would have wished. Take credit for the change; and at least I don't blame you for the tender hollows under the eyes, sloping outward, just hinted... Love's mark on her, so that men's hearts may faint to know that love is known to her, and burn to read her history. When she is about to speak, the upper lids droop a very little; or else the under lids quiver upward—I know not which. Take further credit for her manner. She has now a manner of her own. Some of her naturalness has gone, but she has skipped clean over the 'young lady' stage; from raw girl she has really got as much of the great manner as a woman can have who is not an ostensibly retired dowager, or a matron on a pedestal shuffling the naked virtues and the decorous vices together. She looks at you with an immense, marvellous gravity, before she replies to you—enveloping you in a velvet light. This, is fact, not fine stuff, my dear fellow. The light of her eyes does absolutely cling about you. Adieu! You are a great master, and know exactly when to make your bow and retire. A little more, and you would have spoilt her. Now she is perfect."

[Wilfrid to Tracy Runningbrook:]

"I have just come across a review of your last book, and send it, thinking you may wish to see it. I have put a query to one of the passages, which I think misquoted: and there will be no necessity to call your attention to the critic's English. You can afford to laugh at it, but I confess it puts your friends in a rage. Here are a set of fellows who arm themselves with whips and stand in the public thoroughfare to make any man of real genius run the gauntlet down their ranks till he comes out flayed at the other extremity! What constitutes their right to be there?—By the way, I met Sir Purcell Barrett (the fellow who was at Hillford), and he would like to write an article on you that should act as a sort of rejoinder. You won't mind, of course—it's bread to him, poor devil! I doubt whether I shall see you when you comeback, so write a jolly lot of letters. Colonel Pierson, of the Austrian army, my uncle (did you meet him at Brookfield?), advises me to sell out immediately. He is getting me an Imperial commission—cavalry. I shall give up the English service. And if they want my medal, they can have it, and I'll begin again. I'm sick of everything except a cigar and a good volume of poems. Here's to light one, and now for the other!

"'Large eyes lit up by some imperial sin,'" etc.
(Ten lines from Tracy's book are here copied neatly.)

[Tracy Runningbrook to Wilfrid:]

"Why the deuce do you write me such infernal trash about the opinions of a villanous dog who can't even en a decent sentence? I've been damning you for a white-livered Austrian up and down the house. Let the fellow bark till he froths at the mouth, and scatters the virus of the beast among his filthy friends. I am mad-dog proof. The lines you quote were written in an awful hurry, coming up in the train from Richford one morning. You have hit upon my worst with commendable sagacity. If it will put money in Barren's pocket, let him write. I should prefer to have nothing said. The chances are all in favour of his writing like a fool. If you're going to be an Austrian, we may have a chance of shooting one another some day, so here's my hand before you go and sell your soul; and anything I can do in the meantime command me."

[Georgiana Ford to Wilfrid:]

"I do not dare to charge you with a breach of your pledged word. Let me tell you simply that Emilia has become aware of your project to enter the Austrian service, and it has had the effect on her which I foresaw. She could bear to hear of your marriage, but this is too much for her, and it breaks my heart to see her. It is too cruel. She does not betray any emotion, but I can see that every principle she had gained is gone, and that her bosom holds the shadows of a real despair. I foresaw it, and sought to guard her against it. That you, whom she had once called (to me) her lover, should enlist himself as an enemy, of her country!—it comes to her as a fact striking her brain dumb while she questions it, and the poor body has nothing to do but to ache. Surely you could have no object in doing this? I will not suspect it. Mr. Runningbrook is acquainted with your plans, I believe; but he has no remembrance of having mentioned this one to Emilia. He distinctly assures me that he has not done so, and I trust him to speak truth. How can it have happened? But here is the evil done. I see no remedy. I am not skilled in sketching the portraits you desire of her, and yet, if you have ever wished her to know this miserable thing, it would be as well that you should see the different face that has come among us within twenty hours."

[Wilfrid to Georgiana Ford:]

"I will confine my reply to a simple denial of having caused this fatal intelligence to reach her ears; for the truth of which, I pledge my honour as a gentleman. A second's thought would have told me—indeed I at once acquiesced in your view—that she should not know it. How it has happened it is vain to attempt to guess. Can you suppose that I desired her to hate me? Yet this is what the knowledge of the step I am taking will make her do! If I could see—if I might see her for five minutes, I should be able to explain everything, and, I sincerely think (painful as it would be to me), give her something like peace. It is too late even to wish to justify myself; but her I can persuade that she—Do you not see that her mind is still unconvinced of my—I will call it baseness! Is this the self-accusing you despise? A little of it must be heard. If I may see her I will not fail to make her understand my position. She shall see that it is I who am worthless—not she! You know the circumstances under which I last beheld her—when I saw pang upon pang smiting her breast from my silence! But now I may speak. Do not be prepossessed against my proposal! It shall be only for five minutes—no more. Not that it is my desire to come. In truth, it could not be. I have felt that I alone can cure her—I who did the harm. Mark me: she will fret secretly—, but dear and kindest lady, do not smile too critically at the tone I adopt. I cannot tell how I am writing or what saying. Believe me that I am deeply and constantly sensible of your generosity. In case you hesitate, I beg you to consult Mr. Powys."

[Georgiana Ford to Wilfrid:]

"I had no occasion to consult my brother to be certain that an interview between yourself and Emilia should not take place. There can be no object, even if the five minutes of the meeting gave her happiness, why the wound of the long parting should be again opened. She is wretched enough now, though her tenderness for us conceals it as far as possible. When some heavenly light shall have penetrated her, she will have a chance of peace. The evil is not of a nature to be driven out by your hands. If you are not going into the Austrian service, she shall know as much immediately. Otherwise, be as dead to her as you may, and your noblest feelings cannot be shown under any form but that."

[Wilfrid to Tracy Runningbrook:]

"Some fellows whom I know want you to write a prologue to a play they are going to get up. It's about Shakespeare—at least, the proceeds go to something of that sort. Do, like a good fellow, toss us off twenty lines. Why don't you write? By the way, I hope there's no truth in a report that has somehow reached me, that they have the news down in Monmouth of my deserting to the black-yellow squadrons? Of course, such a thing as that should have been kept from them. I hear, too, that your—I suppose I must call her now your—pupil is falling into bad health. Think me as cold and 'British' as you like; but the thought of this does really affect me painfully. Upon my honour, it does! 'And now he yawns!' you're saying. You're wrong. We Army men feel just as you poets do, and for a longer time, I think, though perhaps not so acutely. I send you the 'Venus' cameo which you admired. Pray accept it from an old friend. I mayn't see you again."

[Tracy Runningbrook to Wilfrid:] (enclosing lines)

"Here they are. It will require a man who knows something about metre to speak them. Had Shakespeare's grandmother three Christian names? and did she anticipate feminine posterity in her rank of life by saying habitually, 'Drat it?' There is as yet no Society to pursue this investigation, but it should be started. Enormous thanks for the Venus. I wore it this morning at breakfast. Just as we were rising, I leaned forward to her, and she jumped up with her eyes under my chin. 'Isn't she a beauty?' I said. 'It was his,' she answered, changing eyes of eagle for eyes of dove, and then put out the lights. I had half a mind to offer it, on the spot. May I? That is to say, if the impulse seizes me I take nobody's advice, and fair Venus certainly is not under my chin at this moment. As to ill health, great mother Nature has given a house of iron to this soul of fire. The windows may blaze, or the windows may be extinguished, but the house stands firm. When you are lightning or earthquake, you may have something to reproach yourself for; as it is, be under no alarm. Do not put words in my mouth that I have not uttered. 'And now he yawns,' is what I shall say of you only when I am sure you have just heard a good thing. You really are the best fellow of your set that I have come across, and the only one pretending to brains. Your modesty in estimating your value as a leader of Pandours will be pleasing to them who like that modesty. Good-bye. This little Emilia is a marvel of flying moods. Yesterday she went about as if she said, 'I've promised Apollo not to speak till to-morrow.' To-day, she's in a feverish gabble—or began the day with a burst of it; and now she's soft and sensible. If you fancy a girl at her age being able to see, that it's a woman's duty to herself and the world to be artistic—to perfect the thing of beauty she is meant to be by nature!—and, seeing, too, that Love is an instrument like any other thing, and that we must play on it with considerate gentleness, and that tearing at it or dashing it to earth, making it howl and quiver, is madness, and not love!—I assure you she begins to see it! She does see it. She is going to wear a wreath of black briony (preserved and set by Miss Ford, a person cunning in these matters). She's going to the ball at Penarvon Castle, and will look—supply your favourite slang word. A little more experience, and she will have malice. She wants nothing but that to make her consummate. Malice is the barb of beauty. She's just at present a trifle blunt. She will knock over, but not transfix. I am anxious to watch the effect she produces at Penarvon. Poor little woman! I paid a compliment to her eyes. 'I've got nothing else,' said she. Dine as well as you can while you are in England. German cookery is an education for the sentiment of hogs. The play of sour and sweet, and crowning of the whole with fat, shows a people determined to go down in civilization, and try the business backwards. Adieu, curst Croat! On the Wallachian border mayst thou gather philosophy from meditation."

CHAPTER XLIV

ON THE HIPPOGRIFF IN AIR: IN WHICH THE PHILOSOPHER HAS A SHORT SPELL

Dexterously as Wilfrid has turned Tracy to his uses by means of the foregoing correspondence, in doing so he had exposed himself to the retributive poison administered by that cunning youth. And now the Hippogriff seized him, and mounted with him into mid-air; not as when the idle boy Ganymede was caught up to act as cup-bearer in celestial Courts, but to plunge about on yielding vapours, with nothing near him save the voice of his desire.

The Philosopher here peremptorily demands the pulpit. We are subject, he says, to fantastic moods, and shall dry ready-minted phrases picture them forth? As, for example, can the words 'delirium,' or 'frenzy,' convey an image of Wilfrid's state, when his heart began to covet Emilia again, and his sentiment not only interposed no obstacle, but trumpeted her charms and fawned for her, and he thought her lost, remembered that she had been his own, and was ready to do any madness to obtain her? 'Madness' is the word that hits the mark, but it does not fully embrace the meaning. To be in this state, says the Philosopher, is to be 'On The Hippogriff;' and to this, as he explains, the persons who travel to Love by the road of sentiment will come, if they have any stuff in them, and if the one who kindles them is mighty. He distinguishes being on the Hippogriff from being possessed by passion. Passion, he says, is noble strength on fire, and points to Emilia as a representation of passion. She asks for what she thinks she may have; she claims what she imagines to be her own. She has no shame, and thus, believing in, she never violates, nature, and offends no law, wild as she may seem. Passion does not turn on her and rend her when it is thwarted. She was never carried out of the limit of her own intelligent force, seeing that it directed her always, with the simple mandate to seek that which belonged to her. She was perfectly sane, and constantly just to herself, until the failure of her voice, telling her that she was a beggar in the world, came as a second blow, and partly scared her reason. Constantly just to herself, mind! This is the quality of true passion. Those who make a noise, and are not thus distinguishable, are on Hippogriff. —By which it is clear to me that my fantastic Philosopher means to indicate the lover mounted in this wise, as a creature bestriding an extraneous power. "The sentimentalist," he says, "goes on accumulating images and hiving sensations, till such time as (if the stuff be in him) they assume a form of vitality, and hurry him headlong. This is not passion, though it amazes men, and does the madder thing."

In fine, it is Hippogriff. And right loath am I to continue my partnership with a fellow who will not see things on the surface, and is, as a necessary consequence, blind to the fact that the public detest him. I mean, this garrulous, super-subtle, so-called Philosopher, who first set me upon the building of 'The Three Volumes,' it is true, but whose stipulation that he should occupy so large a portion of them has made them rock top-heavy, to the forfeit of their stability. He maintains that a story should not always flow, or, at least, not to a given measure. When we are knapsack on back, he says, we come to eminences where a survey of our journey past and in advance is desireable, as is a distinct pause in any business, here and there. He points proudly to the fact that our people in this comedy move themselves,—are moved from their own impulsion,—and that no arbitrary hand has posted them to bring about any event and heap the catastrophe. In vain I tell him that he is meantime making tatters of the puppets' golden robe illusion: that he is sucking the blood of their warm humanity out of them. He promises that when Emilia is in Italy he will retire altogether; for there is a field of action, of battles and conspiracies, nerve and muscle, where life fights for plain issues, and he can but sum results. Let us, he entreats, be true to time and place. In our fat England, the gardener Time is playing all sorts of delicate freaks in the lines and traceries of the flower of life, and shall we not note them? If we are to understand our species, and mark the progress of civilization at all, we must. Thus the Philosopher. Our partner is our master, and I submit, hopefully looking for release with my Emilia, in the day when Italy reddens the sky with the banners of a land revived.

I hear Wilfrid singing out that he is aloft, burning to rush ahead, while his beast capers in one spot, abominably ludicrous. This trick of Hippogriff is peculiar, viz., that when he loses all faith in himself, he sinks—in other words, goes to excesses of absurd humility to regain it. Passion has likewise its panting intervals, but does nothing so preposterous. The wreath of black briony, spoken of by Tracy as the crown of Emilia's forehead, had begun to glow with a furnace-colour in Wilfrid's fancy. It worked a Satanic distraction in him. The girl sat before him swathed in a darkness, with the edges of the briony leaves shining deadly—radiant above—young Hecate! The next instant he was bleeding with pity for her, aching with remorse, and again stung to intense jealousy of all who might behold her (amid a reserve of angry sensations at her present happiness).

Why had she not made allowance for his miserable situation that night in Devon? Why did she not comprehend his difficulties in relation to his father's affairs? Why did she not know that he could not fail to love her for ever?

Interrogations such as these were so many switches of the whip in the flanks of Hippogriff.

Another peculiarity of the animal gifted with wings is, that around the height he soars to he can see no barriers nor any of the fences raised by men. And here again he differs from Passion, which may tug against common sense but is never, in a great nature, divorced from it: In air on Hippogriff, desires wax boundless, obstacles are hidden. It seemed nothing to Wilfrid (after several tremendous descents of humility) that he should hurry for Monmouth away, to gaze on Emilia under her fair, infernal, bewitching wreath; nothing that he should put an arm round her; nothing that he should forthwith carry her off, though he died for it. Forming no design beyond that of setting his eyes on her, he turned the head of Hippogriff due Westward.

Penarvon castle lay over the borders of Monmouthshire. Thither, on a night of frosty moonlight, troops of carriages were hurrying with the usual freightage for a country ball:—the squire who will not make himself happy by seeing that his duty to the softer side of his family must be performed during the comfortable hours when bachelors snooze in arm-chairs, and his nobler dame who, not caring for Port or tobacco, cheerfully accepts the order of things as bequeathed to her: the everlastingly half-satisfied young man, who looks forward to the hour when his cigar-light will shine; and the damsel thrice demure as a cover for her eagerness. Within a certain distance of one of the carriages, a man rode on horseback. The court of the castle was reached, and he turned aside, lingering to see whether he could get a view of the lighted steps. To effect his object, he dismounted and led his horse through the gates, turning from gravel to sward, to keep in the dusk. A very agile middle-aged gentleman was the first to appear under the portico-lamps, and he gave his hand to a girl of fifteen, and then to a most portly lady in a scarlet mantle. The carriage-door slammed and drove off, while a groan issued from the silent spectator. "Good heavens! have I followed these horrible people for five-and-twenty miles!" Carriage after carriage rattled up to the steps, was disburdened of still more 'horrible people' to him, and went the way of the others. "I shan't see her, after all," he cried hoarsely, and mounting, said to the beast that bore him, "Now go sharp."

Whether you recognize the rider of Hippogriff or not, this is he; and the poor livery-stable screw stretched madly till wind failed, when he was allowed to choose his pace. Wilfrid had come from London to have sight of Emilia in the black-briony wreath: to see her, himself unseen, and go. But he had not seen her; so he had the full excuse to continue the adventure. He rode into a Welsh town, and engaged a fresh horse for the night.

"She won't sing, at all events," thought Wilfrid, to comfort himself, before the memory that she could not, in any case, touched springs of weakness and pitying tenderness. From an eminence to which he walked outside the town, Penarvon was plainly visible with all its lighted windows.

"But I will pluck her from you!" he muttered, in a spasm of jealousy; the image of himself as an outcast against the world that held her, striking him with great force at that moment.

"I must give up the Austrian commission, if she takes me."

And be what? For he had sold out of the English service, and was to receive the money in a couple of days. How long would the money support him? It would not pay half his debts! What, then, did this pursuit of Emilia mean? To blink this question, he had to give the spur to Hippogriff. It meant (upon Hippogriff at a brisk gallop), that he intended to live for her, die for her, if need be, and carve out of the world all that she would require. Everything appears possible, on Hippogriff, when he is going; but it is a bad business to put the spur on so willing a beast. When he does not go of his own will;—when he sees that there are obstructions, it is best to jump off his back. And we should abandon him then, save that having once tasted what he can do for us, we become enamoured of the habit of going keenly, and defying obstacles. Thus do we begin to corrupt the uses of the gallant beast (for he is a gallant beast, though not of the first order); we spoil his instincts and train him to hurry us to perdition.

"If my sisters could see me now!" thought Wilfrid, half-smitten with a distant notion of a singularity in his position there, the mark for a frosty breeze, while his eyes kept undeviating watch over Penarvon.

After a time he went back to the inn, and got among coachmen and footmen, all battling lustily against the frost with weapons scientifically selected at the bar. They thronged the passages, and lunged hearty punches at one another, drank and talked, and only noticed that a gentleman was in their midst when he moved to get a light. One complained that he had to drive into Monmouth that night, by a road that sent him five miles out of his way, owing to a block—a great stone that had fallen from the hill. "You can't ask 'em to get out and walk ten steps," he said; "or there! I'd lead the horses and just tip up the off wheels, and round the place in a twinkle, pop 'm in again, and nobody hurt; but you can't ask ladies to risk catchin' colds for the sake of the poor horses."

Several coachmen spoke upon this, and the shame and marvel it was that the stone had not been moved; and between them the name of Mr. Powys was mentioned, with the remark that he would spare his beasts if he could.

"What's that block you're speaking of, just out of Monmouth?" enquired Wilfrid; and it being described to him, together with the exact bearings of the road and situation of the mass of stone, he at once repeated a part of what he had heard in the form of the emphatic interrogation, "What! there?" and flatly told the coachman that the stone had been moved.

"It wasn't moved this morning, then, sir," said the latter.

"No; but a great deal can be done in a couple of hours," said Wilfrid.

"Did you see 'em at work, sir?"

"No; but I came that way, and the road was clear."

"The deuce it was!" ejaculated the coachman, willingly convinced.

"And that's the way I shall return," added Wilfrid.

He tossed some money on the bar to aid in warming the assemblage, and received numerous salutes as he passed out. His heart was beating fast. "I shall see her, in the teeth of my curst luck," he thought, picturing to himself the blessed spot where the mass of stone would lie; and to that point he galloped, concentrating all the light in his mind on this maddest of chances, till it looked sound, and finally certain.

"It's certain, if that's not a hired coachman," he calculated. "If he is, he won't risk his fee. If he isn't, he'll feel on the safe side anyhow. At any rate, it's my only chance." And away he flew between glimmering slopes of frost to where a white curtain of mist hung across the wooded hills of the Wye.

CHAPTER XLVI

RAPE OF THE BLACK-BRIONY WREATH

Emilia was in skilful hands, and against anything less powerful than a lover mounted upon Hippogriff, might have been shielded. What is poison to most girls, Merthyr prescribed for her as medicine. He nourished her fainting spirit upon vanity. In silent astonishment Georgiana heard him address speeches to her such as dowagers who have seen their day can alone of womankind complacently swallow. He encouraged Tracy Runningbrook to praise the face of which she had hitherto thought shyly. Jewels were placed at her disposal, and dresses laid out cunningly suited to her complexion. She had a maid to wait on her, who gabbled at the momentous hours of robing and unrobing: "Oh, miss! of all the dark young ladies I ever see!"—Emilia was the most bewitching. By-and-by, Emilia was led to think of herself; but with a struggle and under protest. How could it be possible that she was so very nice to the eye, and Wilfrid had abandoned her? The healthy spin of young new blood turned the wheels of her brain, and then she thought: "Perhaps I am really growing handsome?" The maid said artfully of her hair: "If gentlemen could only see it down, miss! It's the longest, and thickest, and blackest, I ever touched!" And so saying, slid her fingers softly through it after the comb, and thrilled the owner of that hair till soft thoughts made her bosom heave, and then self-love began to be sensibly awakened, followed by self-pity, and some further form of what we understand as consciousness. If partially a degradation of her nature, this saved her mind from true despair when it began to stir after the vital shock that had brought her to earth. "To what purpose should I be fair?" was a question that did not yet come to her; but it was sweet to see Merthyr's eyes gather pleasure from the light of her own. Sweet, though nothing more than coldly sweet. She compared herself to her father's old broken violin, that might be mended to please the sight; but would never give the tones again. Sometimes, if hope tormented her, she would strangle it by trying her voice: and such a little piece of self-inflicted anguish speedily undid all Merthyr's work. He was patient as one who tends a flower in the Spring. Georgiana marvelled that the most sensitive and proud of men should be striving to uproot an image from the heart of a simple girl, that he might place his own there. His methods almost led her to think that his estimate of human nature was falling low. Nevertheless, she was constrained to admit that there was no diminution of his love for her, and it chastened her to think so. "Would it be the same with me, if I—?" she half framed the sentence, blushing remorsefully while she denied that anything could change her great love for her brother. She had caught a glimpse of Wilfrid's suppleness and selfishness. Contrasting him with Merthyr, she was singularly smitten with shame, she knew not why.

The anticipation of the ball at Penarvon Castle had kindled very little curiosity in Emilia's bosom. She seemed to herself a machine; "one of the rest;" and looked more to see that she was still coveted by Merthyr's eyes than at the glitter of the humming saloons. A touch of her old gladness made her smile when Captain Gambier unexpectedly appeared and walked across the dancers to sit beside her. She asked him why he had come from London: to which he replied, with a most expressive gaze under her eyelids, that he had come for one object. "To see me?" thought Emilia, wondering, and reddening as she ceased to wonder. She had thought as a child, and the neat instant felt as a woman. He finished

Merthyr's work for him. Emilia now thought: "Then I must be worth something." And with "I am," she ended her meditation, glowing. He might have said that she had all beauty ever showered upon woman: she would have been led to believe him at that moment of her revival.

Now, Lady Charlotte had written to Georgiana, telling her that Captain Gambier was soon to be expected in her neighbourhood, and adding that it would be as well if she looked closely after her charge. When Georgiana saw him go over to Emilia she did not remember this warning: but when she perceived the sudden brilliancy and softness in Emilia's face after the first words had fallen on her ears, she grew alarmed, knowing his reputation, and executed some diversions, which separated them. The captain made no effort to perplex her tactics, merely saying that he should call in a day or two. Merthyr took to himself all the credit of the visible bloom that had come upon Emilia, and pacing with her between the dances, said: "Now you will come to Italy, I think."

She paused before answering, "Now?" and feverishly continued: "Yes; at once. I will go. I have almost felt my voice again to-night."

"That's well. I shall write to Marini to-morrow. You will soon find your voice if you will not fret for it. Touch Italy!"

"Yes; but you must be near me," said Emilia.

Georgiana heard this, and could not conceive other than that Emilia was growing to be one of those cormorant creatures who feed alike on the homage of noble and ignoble. She was critical, too, of that very assured pose of Emilia's head and firm planting of her feet as the girl paraded the room after the dances in which she could not join. Previous to this evening, Georgiana had seen nothing of the sort in her; but, on the contrary, a doubtful droop of the shoulders and an unwilling gaze, as of a soul submerged in internal hesitations. "I earnestly trust that this is a romantic folly of Merthyr's, and no more," thought Georgiana, who would have had that view concerning his love for Italy likewise, if recollection of her own share of adventure there had not softly interposed.

Tracy, Georgiana, Merthyr, and Emilia were in the carriage, well muffled up, with one window open to the white mist. Emilia was eager to thank her friend, if only for the physical relief from weariness and sluggishness which she was experiencing. She knew certainly that the dim light of a recovering confidence in herself was owing, all, to him, and burned to thank him. Once on the way their hands touched, and he felt a shy pressure from her fingers as they parted. Presently the carriage stopped abruptly, and listening they heard the coachman indulge his companion outside with the remark that they were a couple of fools, and were now regularly 'dished.'

"I don't see why that observation can't go on wheels," said Tracy.

Merthyr put out his head, and saw the obstruction of the mass of stone across the road. He alighted, and together with the footman, examined the place to see what the chance was of their getting the carriage past. After a space of waiting, Georgiana clutched the wraps about her throat and head, and impetuously followed her brother, as her habit had always been. Emilia sat upright, saying, "I must go too." Tracy moaned a petition to her to rest and be comfortable while the Gods were propitious. He checked her with his arm, and tried to pacify her by giving a description of the scene. The coachman remained on his seat. Merthyr, Georgiana, and the footman were on the other side of the rock, measuring the place to see whether, by a partial ascent of the sloping rubble down which it had bowled, the carriage might be got along.

"Go; they have gone round; see whether we can give any help," said Emilia to Tracy, who cried: "My goodness! what help can we give? This is an express situation where the Fates always appear in person and move us on. We're sure to be moved, if we show proper faith in them. This is my attitude of invocation." He curled his legs up on the seat, resting his head on an arm; but seeing Emilia preparing for a jump he started up, and immediately preceded her. Emilia looked out after him. She perceived a figure coming stealthily from the bank. It stopped, and again advanced, and now ran swiftly down. She drew back her head as it approached the open door of the carriage; but the next moment trembled forward, and was caught with a cat-like clutch upon Wilfrid's breast.

"Emilia! my own for ever! I swore to die this night it I did not see you!"

"You love me, Wilfrid? love me?"

"Come with me now!"

"Now?"

"Away! with me! your lover!"

"Then you love me!

"I love you! Come!"

"Now? I cannot move."

"I am out in the night without you."

"Oh, my lover! Oh, Wilfrid!"

"Come to me!"

"My feet are dead!"

"It's too late!"

A sturdy hulloa! sounding from the coachman made Merthyr's ears alive. When he returned he found Emilia huddled up on the seat, alone, her face in her hands, and the touch of her hands like fire. He had to entreat her to descend, and in helping her to alight bore her whole weight, and supported her in a sad wonder, while the horses were led across the rubble, and the carriage was with difficulty, and some confusions, guided to clear its wheels of the obstructing mass. Emilia persisted in saying that nothing ailed her; and to the coachman, who could have told him something, and was willing to have done so (notwithstanding a gold fee for silence that stuck in his palm), Merthyr put no question.

As they were taking their seats in the carriage again, Georgiana said, "Where is your wreath, Sandra?"

The black-briony wreath was no longer on her head.

"Then, it wasn't a dream!" gasped Emilia, feeling at her temples.

Georgiana at once fell into a scrutinizing coldness, and when Merthyr, who fancied the wreath might have fallen as he was lifting Emilia from the carriage, proposed to go and search the place for it, his sister laid her fingers on his arm, remarking, "You will not find it, dear;" and Emilia cried "Oh! no, no! it is not there;" and, with her hands pressed hard against her bosom, sat fixed and silent.

Out of this mood she issued with looks of such tenderness that one who watched her, speculating on her character as Merthyr did, could see that in some mysterious way she had been, during the few minutes that separated them, illumined upon the matter nearest her heart. Was it her own strength, inspired by some sublime force, that had sprung up suddenly to eject a worthless love? So he hoped in despite of whispering reason, till Georgiana spoke to him.

CHAPTER XLVII

THE CALL TO ACTION

When the force of Wilfrid's embrace had died out from her body, Emilia conceived wilfully that she had seen an apparition, so strange, sudden, and wild had been his coming and going: but her whole body was a song to her. "He is not false: he is true." So dimly, however, was the 'he' now fashioned in her brain, and so like a thing of the air had he descended on her, that she almost conceived the abstract idea, 'Love is true,' and possibly, though her senses did not touch on it to shape it, she had the reflection in her: "After all, power is mine to bring him to my side." Almost it seemed to her that she had brought him from the grave. She sat hugging herself in the carriage, hating to hear words, and seeing a ball of fire away in the white mist. Georgiana looked at her no more; and when Tracy remarked that he had fancied having seen a fellow running up the bank, she said quietly, "Did you?"

"Robert must have seen him, too," added Merthyr, and so the interloper was dismissed.

On reaching home, no sooner were they in the hall than Emilia called for her bedroom candle in a thin, querulous voice that made Tracy shout with laughter and love of her quaintness.

Emilia gave him her hand, and held up her mouth to kiss Georgiana, but no cheek was bent forward for the salute. The girl passed from among them, and then Merthyr said to his sister: "What is the matter?"

"Surely, Merthyr, you should not be at a loss," she answered, in a somewhat unusual tone, that was half irony.

Merthyr studied her face. Alone with her, he said: "I could almost suppose that she has seen this man."

Georgiana smiled sadly. "I have not seen him, dear; and she has not told me so."

"You think it was so?"

"I can imagine it just possible."

"What! while we were out and had left her! He must be mad!"

"Not necessarily mad, unless to be without principle is to be mad."

"Mad, or graduating for a Spanish comedie d'intrigue," said Merthyr. "What on earth can he mean by it? If he must see her, let him come here. But to dog a carriage at midnight, and to prefer to act startling surprises!—one can't help thinking that he delights in being a stage-hero."

Georgiana's: "If he looks on her as a stage-heroine?" was unheeded, and he pursued: "She must leave England at once," and stated certain arrangements that were immediately to be made.

"You will not give up this task you have imposed on yourself?" she said.

"To do what?"

She could have answered: "To make this unsatisfactory creature love you;" but her words were, "To civilize this little savage."

Merthyr was bright in a moment: "I don't give up till I see failure."

"Is it not possible, dear, to be dangerously blind?" urged Georgiana.

"Keep to the particular case," he returned; "and don't tempt me into your woman's snare of a generalization. It's possible, of course, to be one-ideaed and obstinate. But I have not yet seen your savage guilty of a deceit. Her heart has been stirred, and her heart, as you may judge, has force enough to be constant, though none can deny that it has been roughly proved."

"For which you like her better?" said Georgiana, herself brightening.

"For which I like her better," he replied, and smiled, perfectly armed.

"Oh! is it because I am a woman that I do not understand this sort of friendship?" cried Georgiana. "And from you, Merthyr, to a girl such as she is! Me she satisfies less and less. You speak of force of heart, as if it were manifested in an abandonment of personal will."

"No, my darling, but in the strong conception of a passion."

"Yes; if she had discriminated, and fixed upon a worthy object!"

"That," rejoined Merthyr, "is akin to the doctrine of justification by success."

"You seek to foil me with sophisms," said Georgiana, warming. "A woman—even a girl—should remember what is due to herself. You are attracted by a passionate nature—I mean, men are."

"The general instance," assented Merthyr.

"Then, do you never reflect," pursued Georgiana, "on the composition and the elements of that sort of nature? I have tried to think the best of it. It seems to me still no, not contemptible at all—but selfishness is the groundwork of it; a brilliant selfishness, I admit. I see that it shows its best feature, but is it the nobler for that? I think, and I must think, that excellence is a point to be reached only by unselfishness, and that usefulness is the test of excellence."

"Before there has been any trial of her?" asked Merthyr. "Have you not been a little too eager to put the test to her?"

Georgiana reluctantly consented to have her argument attached to a single person. "She is not a child, Merthyr."

"Ay; but she should bethought one."

"I confess I am utterly at sea," Georgiana sighed. "Will you at least allow that sordid selfishness does less mischief than this 'passion' you admire so much?"

"I will allow that she may do herself more mischief than if she had the opposite vice of avarice— anything you will, of that complexion."

"And why should she be regarded as a child?" asked Georgiana piteously.

"Because, if she has outnumbered the years of a child, she is no further advanced than a child, owing to what she has to get rid of. She is overburdened with sensations that set her head on fire. Her solid, firm, and gentle heart keeps her balanced, so long as there is no one playing on it. That a fool should be doing so, is scarcely her fault."

Georgiana murmured to herself, "He is not a fool." She said, "I do see a certain truth in what you say, dear Merthyr. But I have been disappointed in her. I have taken her among my poor. She listens to their tales, without sympathy. I took her into a sick-room. She stood by a dying bed like a statue. Her remark when we came into the air was, 'Death seems easy, if it were not so stifling!' Herself always! herself the centre of what she sees and feels! And again, she has no active desire to do good to any mortal thing. A passive wish that everybody should be happy, I know she has. Few have not. She would give money if she had it. But this is among the mysteries of Providence to me, that one no indifferent to others should be gifted with so inexplicable a power of attraction."

Merthyr put this case to her: "Suppose you saw any of the poor souls you wait on lying sick with fever, would it be just to describe the character of one so situated as fretful, ungrateful, of rambling tongue, poor in health, and generally of loose condition of mind?"

"There, again, is that foreign doctrine which exults in the meanest triumphs by getting the thesis granted that we are animal—only animals!" Georgiana burst out. "You argue that at this season and at that season she is helpless. If she is a human creature, must she not have a mind to cover those conditions?"

"And a mind," Merthyr took her up, "specially experienced, armed, and alert to be a safeguard to her at the most critical period of her life! Oh, yes! Whether she 'must' have it is one thing; but no one can content the value of such a jewel to any young person."

Georgiana stood silenced; and knew later that she had been silenced by a fallacy. For, is youth the most critical period of life? Neither brother nor sister, however, were talking absolutely for the argument. Beneath this dialogue, the current in her mind pressed to elicit some avowal of his personal feeling for the girl, toward whom Georgiana's disposition was kindlier than her words might lead one to think. He, on the other hand, talked with the distinct object of disguising his feelings under a tone of moderate friendship for Emilia, that was capable of excusing her. A sensitive man of thirty odd years does not loudly proclaim his appreciation of a girl under twenty: moreover, Merthyr wished to spare his sister.

He thought of questioning Robert, the coachman, whether anyone had visited the carriage during his five minutes' absence from it: but Merthyr's peculiar Welsh delicacy kept him from doing that, hard as it was to remain in doubt and endure the little poisoned shafts of a suspicion.

In the morning there was a letter from Marini on the breakfast-table. Merthyr glanced down the contents. His countenance flashed with a marvellous light. "Where is she?" he said, looking keenly for Emilia.

Emilia came in from the garden.

"Now, my Sandra!" cried Merthyr, waving the letter to her; "can you pack up, to start in an hour? There's work coming on for us, and I shall be a boy again, and not the drumstick I am in this country. I have a letter from Marini. All Lombardy is prepared to rise, and this time the business will be done. Marini is off for Genoa. Under the orange-trees, my Sandra! and looking on the bay, singing of Italy free!"

Emilia fell back a step, eyeing him with a grave expression of wonder, as if she beheld another being from the one she had hitherto known. The calm Englishman had given place to a volcanic spirit.

"Isn't that the sketch we made?" he resumed. "The plot's perfect. I detest conspiracies, but we must use what weapons we can, and be Old Mole, if they trample us in the earth. Once up, we have Turin to back us. This I know. We shall have nothing but the Tedeschi to manage: and if they beat us in cavalry, it's certain that they can't rely on their light horse. The Magyars would break in a charge. We know that they will. As for the rest:—

'Soldati settentrionali,
Come sarebbe Boemi a Croati,'

we are a match for them! Artillery we shall get. The Piedmontese are mad for the signal. Come; sit and eat. The air seems dead down in this quiet country; we're out of the stream. I must rush up to London to breathe and then we won't lose a moment. We shall be in Italy in four days. Four days, my Sandra! And Italy going to be free; Georgey, I'm fasting. And you will see all your old friends. All? Good God! No!— not all! Their blood shall nerve us. The Austrian thinks he wastes us by slaughter. With every dead man he doubles the life of the living! Am I talking like a foreigner, Sandra mia? My child, you don't eat! And I, who dreamed last night that I looked out over Novara from the height of the Col di Colma, and saw the plain under a red shadow from a huge eagle!"

Merthyr laughed, swinging round his arm. Emilia continued staring at him as at a man transformed, while Georgiana asked: "May Marini's letter be seen?" Her visage had become firm and set in proportion as her brother's excitement increased.

"Eat, my Sandra! eat!" called Merthyr, who was himself eating with a campaigning appetite.

Georgiana laid down the letter folded under Merthyr's fingers, keeping her hand on it till he grew alive to her meaning, that it should be put away.

"Marini is vague about artillery," she murmured.

"Vague!" echoed Merthyr. "Say prudent. If he said we could lay hands on fifty pieces, then distrust him!"

"God grant that this be not another pit for further fruitless bloodshed!" was the interjection standing in Georgiana's eyes, and then she dropped them pensively, while Merthyr recounted the patient schemes that had led to this hour, the unuttered anxieties and the bursting hopes.

Still Emilia kept her distressfully unenthusiastic looks turned from one to the other, though her Italy was the theme. She did not eat, but had dropped one hand flat on her plate, looking almost idiotic. She heard of Italy as of a distant place, known to her in ancient years. Merthyr's transformation, too, helped some form of illusion in her brain that she was cut off from any kindred feeling with other people.

As soon as he had finished, Merthyr jumped up; and coming round to Emilia, touched her shoulder affectionately, saying: "Now! There won't be much packing to do. We shall be in London to-night in time for your mother to pass the evening with you."

Emilia rose straightway, and her eyes fell vacantly on Georgiana for help, as far as they could express anything.

Georgiana gave no response, save a look well nigh as vacant in the interchange.

"But you haven't eaten at all!" said Merthyr.

Emilia shook her head. "No."

"Eat, my Sandra! to please me! You will need all your strength if you would be a match for Georgey anywhere where there's action."

"Yes!" Emilia traversed his words with a sudden outcry. "Yes, I will go to London. I am ready to go to London now."

It was clear that a new light had fallen on her intelligence.

Merthyr was satisfied to see her sit down to the table, and he at once went out to issue directions for the first step in the new and momentous expedition.

Emilia put the bread to her mouth, and crumbled it on a dry lip: but it was evident to Georgiana, hostile witness as she was, that Emilia's mind was gradually warming to what Merthyr had said, and that a picture was passing before the girl. She perceived also a thing that no misery of her own had yet drawn from Emilia. It was a tear that fell heavily on the back of her hand. Soon the tears came in quick succession, while the girl tried to eat, and bit at salted morsels. It was a strange sight for Georgiana, this statuesque weeping, that got human bit by bit, till the bosom heaved long sobs: and yet no turn of the head for sympathy; nothing but passionless shedding of big tear-drops!

She went to the girl, and put her hand upon her; kissed her, and then said: "We have no time to lose. My brother never delays when he has come to a resolve."

Emilia tried to articulate: "I am ready."

"But you have not eaten!"

Emilia made a mechanical effort to eat.

"Remember," said Georgiana, "we have a long distance to go. You will want your strength. You would not be a burden to him? Eat, while I get your things ready." And Georgiana left her, secretly elated to feel that in this expedition it was she, and she alone, who was Merthyr's mate. What storm it was, and what conflict, agitated the girl and stupefied her, she cared not to guess, now that she had the suitable designation, 'savage,' confirmed in all her acts, to apply to her.

When Tracy Runningbrook came down at his ordinary hour of noon to breakfast, he found a twisted note from Georgiana, telling him that important matters had summoned Merthyr to London, and that they were all to be seen at Lady Gosstre's town-house.

"I believe, by Jove! Powys manoeuvres to get her away from me," he shouted, and sat down to his breakfast and his book with a comforted mind. It was not Georgiana to whom he alluded; but the appearance of Captain Gambier, and the pronounced discomposure visible in the handsome face of the captain on his hearing of the departure, led Tracy to think that Georgiana's was properly deplored by another, though that other was said to be engaged. 'On revient toujours,' he hummed.

CHAPTER XLVIII

CONTAINS A FURTHER VIEW OF SENTIMENT

Three days passed as a running dream to Emilia. During that period she might have been hurried off to Italy without uttering a remonstrance. Merthyr's spirited talk of the country she called her own; of its heroic youth banded to rise, and sworn to liberate it or die; of good historic names borne by men, his comrades, in old campaigning adventures; and stories and incidents of those past days—all given with his changed face, and changed ringing voice, almost moved her to plunge forgetfully into this new tumultuous stream while the picture of the beloved land, lying shrouded beneath the perilous star it was about to follow grew in her mind.

"Shall I go with the Army?" she asked Georgiana.

"No, my child; you will simply go to school," was the cold reply.

"To school!" Emilia throbbed, "while they are fighting!"

"To the Academy. My brother's first thought is to further your progress in Art. When your artistic education is complete, you will choose your own course."

"He knows, he knows that I have no voice!" Emilia struck her lap with twisted fingers. "My voice is thick in my throat. If I am not to march with him, I can't go; I will not go. I want to see the fight. You have. Why should I keep away? Could I run up notes, even if I had any voice, while he is in the cannon-smoke?"

"While he is in the cannon-smoke!" Georgiana revolved the line thoughtfully. "You are aware that my brother looks forward to the recovery of your voice," she said.

"My voice is like a dead serpent in my throat," rejoined Emilia. "My voice! I have forgotten music. I lived for that, once; now I live for nothing, only to take my chance everywhere with my friend. I want to smell powder. My father says it is like salt, the taste of blood, and is like wine when you smell it. I have heard him shout for it. I will go to Italy, if I may go where my friend Merthyr goes; but nothing can keep me shut up now. My head's a wilderness when I'm in houses. I can scarcely bear to hear this London noise, without going out and walking till I drop."

Coming to a knot in her meditation, Georgiana concluded that Emilia's heart was warming to Merthyr. She was speedily doubtful again.

These two delicate Welsh natures, as exacting as they were delicate, were little pleased with Emilia's silence concerning her intercourse with Wilfrid. Merthyr, who had expressed in her defence what could be said for her, was unwittingly cherishing what could be thought in her disfavour. Neither of them hit on the true cause, which lay in Georgiana's coldness to her. One little pressure of her hand, carelessly given, made Merthyr better aware of the nature he was dealing with. He was telling her that a further delay might keep them in London for a week; and that he had sent for her mother to come to her.

"I must see my mother," she had said, excitedly. The extension of the period named for quitting England made it more imminent m her imagination than when it was a matter of hours. "I must see her."

"I have sent for her," said Merthyr, and then pressed Emilia's hand. But she who, without having brooded on complaints of its absence, thirsted for demonstrative kindness, clung to the hand, drawing it, doubled, against her chin.

"That is not the reason," she said, raising her full eyes up at him over the unrelinquished hand. "I love the poor Madre; let her come; but I have no heart for her just now. I have seen Wilfrid."

She took a tighter hold of his fingers, as fearing he might shrink from her. Merthyr hated mysteries, so he said, "I supposed it must have been so—that night of our return from Penarvon?"

"Yes," she murmured, while she read his face for a shadow of a repulsion; "and, my friend, I cannot go to Italy now!"

Merthyr immediately drew a seat beside her. He perceived that there would be no access to her reason, even as he was on the point of addressing it.

"Then all my care and trouble are to be thrown away?" he said, taking the short road to her feelings.

She put the hand that was disengaged softly on his shoulder. "No; not thrown away. Let me be what Merthyr wishes me to be! That is my chief prayer."

"Why, then, will you not do what Merthyr wishes you to do?"

Emilia's eyelids shut, while her face still fronted him.

"Oh! I will speak all out to you," she cried. "Merthyr, my friend, he came to kiss me once, before I have only just understood it! He is going to Austria. He came to touch me for the last time before his hand is red with my blood. Stop him from going! I am ready to follow you:—I can hear of his marrying that woman:—Oh! I cannot live and think of him in that Austrian white coat. Poor thing!—my dear! my dear!" And she turned away her head.

It is not unnatural that Merthyr hearing these soft epithets, should disbelieve in the implied self-conquest of her preceding words. He had no clue to make him guess that these were simply old exclamations of hers brought to her lips by the sorrowful contrast in her mind.

"It will be better that you should see him," he said, with less of his natural sincerity; so soon are we corrupted by any suspicion that our egoism prompts.

"Here?" And she hung close to him, open-lipped, open-eyed, open-eared, as if (Georgiana would think it, thought Merthyr) her savage senses had laid the trap for this proposal, and now sprung up keen for their prey. "Here, Merthyr? Yes! let me see him. You will! Let me see him, for he cannot resist me. He tries. He thinks he does: but he cannot. I can stretch out my finger—I can put it on the day when, if he has galloped one way he will gallop another. Let him come."

She held up both her hands in petition, half dropping her eyelids, with a shadowy beauty.

In Merthyr's present view, the idea of Wilfrid being in ranks opposed to him was so little provocative of intense dissatisfaction, that it was out of his power to believe that Emilia craved to see him simply to dissuade the man from the obnoxious step. "Ah, well! See him; see him, if you must," he said. "Arrange it with my sister."

He quitted the room, shrinking from the sound of her thanks, and still more from the consciousness of his torment.

The business that detained him was to get money for Marini. Georgiana placed her fortune at his disposal a second time. There was his own, which he deemed it no excess of chivalry to fling into the gulf. The two sat together, arranging what property should be sold, and how they would share the sacrifice in common. Georgiana pressed him to dispose of a little estate belonging to her, that money might immediately be raised. They talked as they sat over the fire toward the dusk of the winter evening.

"You would not have refused me once, Merthyr!"

"When you were a child, and I hardly better than a boy. Now it's different. Let mine go first, Georgey. You may have a husband, who will not look on these things as we do."

"How can I love a husband!" was all she said; and Merthyr took her in his arms. His gaiety had gone.

"We can't go dancing into a pit of this sort," he sighed, partly to baffle the scrutiny he apprehended in her silence. "The garrison at Milan is doubled, and I hear they are marching troops through Tyrol. Some alerte has been given, and probably some traitors exist. One wouldn't like to be shot like a dog! You haven't forgotten poor Tarani? I heard yesterday of the girl who calls herself his widow."

"They were betrothed, and she is!" exclaimed Georgiana.

"Well, there's a case of a man who had two loves—a woman and his country; and both true to him!"

"And is he so singular, Merthyr?"

"No, my best! my sweetest! my heart's rest! no!"

They exchanged tender smiles.

"Tarani's bride—beloved! you can listen to such matters—she has undertaken her task. Who imposed it? I confess I faint at the thought of things so sad and shameful. But I dare not sit in judgement on a people suffering as they are. Outrage upon outrage they have endured, and that deadens—or rather makes their heroism unscrupulous. Tarani's bride is one of the few fair girls of Italy. We have a lock of her hair. She shore it close the morning her lover was shot, and wore the thin white skull-cap you remember, until it was whispered to her that her beauty must serve."

"I have the lock now in my desk," said Georgiana, beginning to tremble. "Do you wish to look at it?"

"Yes; fetch it, my darling."

He sat eyeing the firelight till she returned, and then taking the long golden lock in his handy he squeezed it, full of bitter memories and sorrowfulness.

"Giulietta?" breathed his sister.

"I would put my life on the truth of that woman's love. Well!"

"Yes?"

"She abandons herself to the commandant of the citadel."

A low outcry burst from Georgiana. She fell at Merthyr's knees sobbing violently. He let her sob. In the end she struggled to speak.

"Oh! can it be permitted? Oh! can we not save her? Oh, poor soul! my sister! Is she blind to her lover in heaven?"

Georgiana's face was dyed with shame.

"We must put these things by," said Merthyr. "Go to Emilia presently, and tell her—settle with her as you think fitting, how she shall see this Wilfrid Pole. I have promised her she shall have her wish."

Coloured by the emotion she was burning from, these words smote Georgiana with a mournful compassion for Merthyr.

He had risen, and by that she knew that nothing could be said to alter his will.

A sentimental pair likewise, if you please; but these were sentimentalists who served an active deity; and not that arbitrary protection of a subtle selfishness which rules the fairer portion of our fat England.

CHAPTER XLIX

BETWEEN EMILIA AND GEORGIANA

"My brother tells me it is your wish to see Mr. Wilfrid Pole."

Emilia's "Yes" came faintly in answer to Georgiana's cold accents.

"Have you considered what you are doing in expressing such a desire?"

Another "Yes" was heard from under an uplifted head:—a culprit affirmative, whereat the just take fire.

"Be honest, Emilia. Seek counsel and guidance to-night, as you have done before with me, and profited, I think. If I write to bid him come, what will it mean?"

"Nothing more," breathed Emilia.

"To him—for in his way he seems to care for you fitfully—it will mean—stop! hear me. The words you speak will have no part of the meaning, even if you restrain your tongue. To him it will imply that his power over you is unaltered. I suppose that the task of making you perceive the effect it really will have on you is hopeless."

"I have seen him, and I know," said Emilia, in a corresponding tone.

"You saw him that night of our return from Penarvon? Judge of him by that. He would not spare you. To gratify I know not what wildness in his nature, he did not hesitate to open your old wound. And to what purpose? A freak of passion!"

"He could not help it. I told him he would come, and he came."

"This, possibly, you call love; do you not?"

Emilia was about to utter a plain affirmative, but it was checked. The novelty of the idea of its not being love arrested her imagination.

"If he comes to you here," resumed Georgiana—

"He must come!" cried Emilia.

"My brother has sanctioned it, so his coming or not will rest with him. If he comes, let me know the good that you think will result from an interview? Ah! you have not weighed that question. Do so;—or you give no heed to it? In any ease, try to look into your own breast. You were not born to live unworthily. You can be, or will be, if you follow your better star, self-denying and noble. Do you not love your country? Judge of this love by that. Your love, if you have this power over him, is merely a madness to him; and his—what has it done for you? If he comes, and this begins again, there will be a similar if not the same destiny for you."

Emilia panted in her reply. "No; it will not begin again." She threw out both arms, shaking her head. "It cannot, I know. What am I now? It is what I was that he loves. He will not know what I am till he sees me. And I know that I have done things that he cannot forgive. You have forgiven it, and Merthyr, because he is my friend; but I am sure Wilfrid will not. He might pardon the poor 'me,' but not his Emilia! I shall have to tell him what I did; so" (and she came closer to Georgiana) "there is some pain for me in seeing him."

Georgiana was not proof against this simplicity of speech, backed by a little dying dimple, which seemed a continuation of the plain sadness of Emilia's tone.

She said, "My poor child!" almost fondly, and then Emilia looked in her face, murmuring, "You sometimes doubt me."

"Not your truth, but the accuracy of your perceptions and your knowledge of your real designs. You are certainly deceiving yourself at this instant. In the first place, the relation of that madness—no, poor child, not wickedness—but if you tell it to him, it is a wilful and unnecessary self-abasement. If he is to be your husband, unburden your heart at once. Otherwise, why? why? You are but working up a scene, provoking needless excesses: you are storing misery in retrospect, or wretchedness to be endured. Had you the habit of prayer! By degrees it will give you the thirst for purity, and that makes you a fountain of prayer, in whom these blind deceits cannot hide."

Georgiana paused emphatically; as when, by our unrolling out of our ideas, we have more thoroughly convinced ourselves.

"You pray to heaven," said Emilia, and then faltered, and blushed. "I must be loved!" she cried. "Will you not put your arms round me?"

Georgiana drew her to her bosom, bidding her continue. Emilia lay whispering under her chin. "You pray, and you wish to be seen as you are, do you not? You do. Well, if you knew what love is, you would see it is the same. You wish him to see and know you: you wish to be sure that he loves nothing but exactly you; it must be yourself. You are jealous of his loving an idea of you that is not you. You think,

'He will wake up and find his mistake;' or you think, 'That kiss was not intended for me; not for me as I am.' Those are tortures!"

Her discipline had transformed her, when she could utter such sentiments as these!

Feeling her shudder, and not knowing how imagination forestalls experience in passionate blood, Georgiana said, "You speak like one who has undergone them. But now at least you have thrown off the mask. You love him still, this man! And with as little strength of will! Do you not see impiety in the comparison you have made?"

"Oh! what I see is, that I wish I could say to him, 'Look on me, for I need not be ashamed—I am like Miss Ford!'"

The young lady's cheeks took fire, and the clear path of speech becoming confused in her head she said, "Miss Ford?"

"Georgiana," said Emilia, and feeling that her friend's cold manner had melted; "Georgey! my beloved! my darling in Italy, where will we go! I envy no woman but you who have seen my dear ones fight. You and I, and Merthyr! Nothing but Austrian shot shall part us."

"And so we make up a pretty dream!" interjected Georgiana. "The Austrian shot, I think, will be fired by one who is now in the Austrian service, or who will soon be."

"Wilfrid?" Emilia called out. "No; that is what I am going to stop. Why did I not tell you so at first? But I never know what I say or do when I am with you, and everything seems chance. I want to see him to prevent him from doing that. I can."

"Why should you?" asked Georgiana; and one to whom the faces of the two had been displayed at that moment would have pronounced them a hostile couple.

"Why should I prevent him?" Emilia doled out the question slowly, and gave herself no further thought of replying to it.

Apparently Georgiana understood the significance of this odd silence: she was perhaps touched by it. She said, "You feel that you have a power over him. You wish to exercise it. Never mind wherefore. If you do—if you try, and succeed—if, by the aid of this love presupposed to exist, you win him to what you require of him—do you honestly think the love is then immediately to be dropped?"

Emilia meditated. She caught up her voice hastily. "I think so. Yes. I hope so. I mean it to be."

"With a noble lover, Emilia. Not with a selfish one. In showing him the belief you have in your power over him, you betray that he has power over you. And it is to no object. His family, his position, his prospects—all tell you that he cannot marry you if he would. And he is, besides, engaged—"

"Let her suffer!" Emilia's eyes flashed.

"Ah!" and Georgiana thought, "Have I come upon your nature at last?"

However it might be, Emilia was determined to show it.

"She took my lover from me, and I say, let her suffer! I would not hurt her myself—I would not lay my finger on her: but she has eyes like blue stones, and such a mouth!—I think the Austrian executioner has one like it. If she suffers, and goes all dark as I did, she will show a better face. Let her keep my lover. He is not mine, but he was; and she took him from me. That woman cannot feed on him as I did. I know she has no hunger for love. He will look at those blue bits of ice, and think of me. I told him so. Did I not tell him that in Devon? I saw her eyelids move as fast as I spoke. I think I look on Winter when I see her lips. Poor, wretched Wilfrid!"

Emilia half-sobbed this exclamation out. "I don't wish to hurt either of them," she added, with a smile of such abrupt opposition to her words that Georgiana was in perplexity. A lady who has assumed the office of lecturer, will, in such a frame of mind, lecture on, if merely to vindicate to herself her own preconceptions. Georgiana laid her finger severely upon Wilfrid's manifest faults; and, in fine, she spoke a great deal of the common sense that the situation demanded. Nevertheless, Emilia held to her scheme. But, in the meantime, Georgiana had seen more clearly into the girl's heart; and she had been won, also, by a natural gracefulness that she now perceived in her, and which led her to think, "Is Merthyr again to show me that he never errs in his judgement?" An unaccountable movement of tenderness to Emilia made her drop a few kisses on her forehead. Emilia shut her eyes, waiting for more. Then she looked up, and said, "Have you felt this love for me very long?" at which the puny flame, scarce visible, sprang up, and warmed to a great heat.

"My own Emilia! Sandra! listen to me: promise me not to seek this interview."

"Will you always love me as much?" Emilia bargained.

"Yes, yes; I never vary. It is my love for you that begs you."

Emilia fell into a chair and propped her head behind both hands, tapping the floor briskly with her feet. Georgiana watched the conflict going on. To decide it promptly, she said: "And not only shall I love you thrice as well, but my brother Merthyr, whom you call your friend—he will—he cannot love you better; but he will feel you to be worthy the best love he can give. There is a heart, you simple girl! He loves you, and has never shown any of the pain your conduct has given him. When I say he loves you, I tell you his one weakness—the only one I have discovered. And judge whether, he has shown want of self-control while you were dying for another. Did he attempt to thwart you? No; to strengthen you; and never once to turn your attention to himself. That is love. Now, think of what anguish you have made him pass through: and think whether you have ever witnessed an alteration of kindness in his face toward you. Even now, when he had the hope that you were cured of your foolish fruitless affection for a man who merely played with you, and cannot give up the habit, even now he hides what he feels—"

So far Emilia let her speak without interruption; but gradually awakening to the meaning of the words:—

"For me?" she cried.

"Yes; for you."

"The same sort of love as Wilfrid feels?"

"By no means the same sort; but the love of man for woman."

"And he saw me when I was that wretched heap? And he knows everything! and loves me. He has never kissed me."

"Does that miserable test—?" Georgiana was asking.

"Pardon, pardon," said Emilia penitently; "I know that is almost nothing, now. I am not a child. I spoke from a sudden feeling. For if he loves me, how—! Oh, Merthyr! what a little creature I seem. I cannot understand it. I lose a brother. And he was such a certainty to me. What did he love—what did he love, that night he found me on the pier? I looked like a creature picked off a mud-bank. I felt like a worm, and miserably abandoned, I was a shameful sight. Oh! how can I look on Merthyr's face again?"

In these interjections Georgiana did not observe the proper humility and abject gratitude of a young person who had heard that she was selected by a prince of the earth. A sort of 'Eastern handmaid' prostration, with joined hands, and, above all things, a closed mouth, the lady desired. She half regretted the revelation she had made; and to be sure at once that she had reaped some practical good, she said: "I need scarce ask you whether you have come to a right decision upon that other question."

"To see Wilfrid?" said Emilia. She appeared to pause musingly, and then turned to Georgiana, showing happy features; "Yes: I shall see him. I must see him. Let him know he is to come immediately."

"That is your decision."

"Yes."

"After what I have told you?"

"Oh, yes; yes! Write the letter."

Georgiana chid at an internal wrath that struggled to win her lips. "Promise me simply that what I have told you of my brother, you will consider yourself bound to keep secret. You will not speak of it to others, nor to him."

Emilia gave the promise, but with the thought; "To him?—will not he speak of it?"

"So, then, I am to write this letter?" said Georgiana.

"Do, do; at once!" Emilia put on her sweetest look to plead for it.

"Decidedly the wisest of men are fools in this matter," Georgiana's reflection swam upon her anger.

"And dearest! my Georgey!" Emilia insisted on being blunt to the outward indications to which she was commonly so sensitive and reflective; "my Georgey! let me be alone this evening in my bedroom. The little Madre comes, and—and I haven't the habit of being respectful to her. And, I must be alone! Do not send up for me, whoever wishes it."

Georgiana could not stop her tongue: "Not if Mr. Wilfrid Pole—?"

"Oh, he! I will see him," said Emilia; and Georgiana went from her straightway.

Emilia remained locked up with her mother all that evening. The good little shrill woman, tender-eyed and slatternly, had to help try on dresses, and run about for pins, and express her critical taste in undertones, believing all the while that her daughter had given up music to go mad with vanity. The reflection struck her, notwithstanding, that it was a wiser thing for one of her sex to make friends among rich people than to marry a foreign husband.

The girl looked a brilliant woman in a superb Venetian dress of purple velvet, which she called 'the Branciani dress,' and once attired in it, and the rich purges and swelling creases over the shoulders puffed out to her satisfaction, and the run of yellow braid about it properly inspected and flattened, she would not return to her more homely wear, though very soon her mother began to whimper and say that she had lost her so long, and now that she had found her it hardly seemed the same child. Emilia would listen to no entreaties to put away her sumptuous robe. She silenced her mother with a stamp of her foot, and then sighed: "Ah! Why do I always feel such a tyrant with you?" kissing her.

"This dress," she said, and held up her mother's chin fondlingly between her two hands, "this dress was designed by my friend Merthyr—that is, Mr. Powys—from what he remembered of a dress worn by Countess Branciani, of Venice. He had it made to give to me. It came from Paris. Countess Branciani was one of his dearest friends. I feel that I am twice as much his friend with this on me. Mother, it seems like a deep blush all over me. I feel as if I looked out of a rose."

She spread her hands to express the flower magnified.

"Oh! what silly talk," said her mother: "it does turn your head, this dress does!"

"I wish it would give me my voice, mother. My father has no hope. I wish he would send me news to make me happy about him; or come and run his finger up the strings for hours, as he used to. I have fancied I heard him at times, and I had a longing to follow the notes, and felt sure of my semi-tones. He won't see me! Mother! he would think something of me if he saw me now!"

Her mother's lamentations reached that vocal pitch at last which Emilia could not endure, and the little lady was despatched to her home under charge of a servant.

Emilia feasted on the looking-glass when alone. Had Merthyr, in restoring her to health, given her an overdose of the poison?

"Countess Branciani made the Austrian Governor her slave," she uttered, planting one foot upon a stool to lend herself height. "He told her who were suspected, and who would be imprisoned, and gave her all the State secrets. Beauty can do more than music. I wonder whether Merthyr loved her? He loves me!"

Emilia was smitten with a fear that he would speak of it when she next saw him. "Oh! I hope he will be just the same as he has been," she sighed; and with much melancholy shook her head at her fair reflection, and began to undress. It had not struck her with surprise that two men should be loving her, until, standing away from the purple folds, she seemed to grow smaller and smaller, as a fire-log robbed of its flame, and felt insufficient and weak. This was a new sensation. She depended no more on her own vital sincerity. It was in her nature, doubtless, to crave constantly for approval, but in the service of personal beauty instead of divine Art, she found herself utterly unwound without it: victim of a sense of most uncomfortable hollowness. She was glad to extinguish the candle and be covered up dark in the circle of her warmth. Then her young blood sang to her again.

An hour before breakfast every morning she read with Merthyr. Now, this morning how was she to appear to him? There would be no reading, of course. How could he think of teaching one to whom he trembled. Emilia trusted that she might see no change in him, and, above all, that he would not speak of his love for her. Nevertheless, she put on her robe of conquest, having first rejected with distaste a plainer garb. She went down the stairs slowly. Merthyr was in the library awaiting her. "You are late," he said, eyeing the dress as a thing apart from her, and remarking that it was hardly suited for morning wear. "Yellow, if you must have a strong colour, and you wouldn't exhibit the schwartz-gelb of the Tedeschi willingly. But now!"

This was the signal for the reading to commence.

"Wilfrid would not have been so cold to me," thought Emilia, turning the leaves of Ariosto as a book of ashes. Not a word of love appeared to be in his mind. This she did not regret; but she thirsted for the assuring look. His eyes were quietly friendly. So friendly was he, that he blamed her for inattention, and took her once to task about a melodious accent in which she vulgarized the vowels. All the flattery of the Branciani dress could not keep Emilia from her feeling of smallness. Was it possible that he loved her? She watched him as eagerly as her shyness would permit. Any shadow of a change was spied for. Getting no softness from him, or superadded kindness, no shadow of a change in that direction, she stumbled in her reading purposely, to draw down rebuke; her construing was villanously bad. He told her so, and she replied: "I don't like poetry." But seeing him exchange Ariosto for Roman History, she murmured, "I like Dante." Merthyr plunged her remorselessly into the second Punic war.

But there was worse to follow. She was informed that after breakfast she would be called upon to repeat the principal facts she had been reading of. Emilia groaned audibly.

"Take the book," said Merthyr.

"It's so heavy," she complained.

"Heavy?"

"I mean, to carry about."

"If you want to 'carry it about,' the boy shall follow you with it."

She understood that she was being laughed at. Languor, coupled with the consciousness of ridicule, overwhelmed her.

"I feel I can't learn," she said.

"Feel, that you must," was replied to her.

"No; don't take any more trouble with me!"

"Yes; I expect you to distinguish Scipio from Cicero, and not make the mistake of the other evening, when you were talking to Mrs. Cameron."

Emilia left him, abashed, to dread shrewdly their meeting within five minutes at the breakfast-table; to dread eating under his eyes, with doubts of the character of her acts generally. She was, indeed, his humble scholar, though she seemed so full of weariness and revolt. He, however, when alone, looked fixedly at the door through which she had passed, and said, "She loves that man still. Similar ages, similar tastes, I suppose! She is dressed to be ready for him. She can't learn: she can do nothing. My work mayn't be lost, but it's lost for me."

Merthyr did not know that Georgiana had betrayed him, but in no case would he have given Emilia the signs she expected: in the first place, because he had self-command; and, secondly, because of those years he counted in advance of her. So she had the full mystery of his loving her to think over, without a spot of the weakness to fasten on.

Georgiana's first sight of Emilia in her Branciani dress shut her heart against the girl with iron clasps. She took occasion to remark, "We need not expect visitors so very early;" but the offender was impervious. Breakfast finished, the reading with Merthyr recommenced, when Emilia, having got over her surprise at the sameness of things this day, acquitted herself better, and even declaimed the verses musically. Seeing him look pleased, she spoke them out sonorously. Merthyr applauded. Upon which Emilia said, with odd abruptness and solemnity, "Will he come to-day?" It was beyond Merthyr's power of self-control to consent to be taken into a consultation on this matter, and he attempted to put it aside. "He may or he may not—probably to-morrow."

"No; to-day, in the afternoon," said Emilia, "be near me."

"I have engagements."

"Some word, say, that will seem to be you with me."

"Some flattery, or you won't remember it."

"Yes, I like flattery."

"Well, you look like Countess Branciani when, after thinking her husband the basest of men, she discovered him to be the noblest."

Emilia blushed. "That's not easily forgotten! But she must have looked braver, bolder, not so under a burden as I feel."

"The comparison was meant to suit the moment of your reciting."

"Yes," said Emilia, half-mournfully, "then 'myself' doesn't sit on my shoulders: I don't even care what I am."

"That is what Art does for you."

"Only by fits and starts now. Once I never thought of myself."

There was a knock at the street-door, and she changed countenance. Presently there came a gentle tap at their own door.

"It is that woman," said Emilia.

"I fancy it must be Lady Charlotte. You will not see her?"

Merthyr was anticipating a negative, but Emilia said, "Let her come in."

She gave her hand to the lady, and was the less concerned of the two. Lady Charlotte turned away from her briskly.

"Georgey didn't say anything of you in her letter, Merthyr; I am going up to her, but I wished to satisfy myself that you were in town, first:—to save half-a-minute, you see I anticipate the philosophic manly sneer. Is it really true that you are going to mix yourself up in this mad Italian business again? Now that you're a man, my dear Merthyr, it seems almost inexcuseable—for a sensible Englishman!"

Lady Charlotte laughed, giving him her hand at the same time.

"Don't you know I swore an oath?" Merthyr caught up her tone.

"Yes, but you never succeed. I complain that you never succeed. Of what use on earth are all your efforts if you never succeed?"

Emilia's voice burst out:—

"'Piacemi almen che i miei sospir sien quali
Spera 'l Tevero e 'l Arno,
E 'l Po,—'"

Merthyr continued the ode, acting a similar fervour:—

"'Ben provvide Natura al nostro stato
Quando dell' Alpi schermo
Pose fra noi e la tedesca rabbis."

"We are merely bondsmen to the re-establishment of the provisions of nature."

"And we know we shall succeed!" said Emilia, permitting her antagonism to pass forth in irritable emphasis.

Lady Charlotte quickly left them, to run up to Georgiana. She was not long in the house. Emilia hung near Merthyr all day, and she was near him when the knock was heard which she could suppose to be Wilfrid's, as it proved. Wilfrid was ushered in to Georgiana. Delicacy had prevented Merthyr from taking special notice to Emilia of Lady Charlotte's visit, and he treated Wilfrid's similarly, saying, "Georgey will send down word."

"Only, don't leave me till she does," Emilia rejoined.

Her agitation laid her open to be misinterpreted. It was increased when she saw him take a book and sit in the armchair between two lighted candles, calmly careless of her. She did not actually define to herself that he should feel jealously, but his indifference was one extreme which provoked her instinct to imagine a necessity for the other. Word came from Georgiana, and Emilia moved to the door. "Remember, we dine half-an-hour earlier to-day, on account of the Cameron party," was all that he uttered. Emilia made an effort to go. She felt herself as a ship sailing into perilous waters, without compass. Why did he not speak tenderly? Before Georgiana had revealed his love for her, she had been strong to see Wilfrid. Now, the idea smote her softened heart that Wilfrid's passion might engulf her if she had no word of sustainment from Merthyr. She turned and flung herself at his feet, murmuring, "Say something to me." Merthyr divined this emotion to be a sort of foresight of remorse on her part: he clasped the interwoven fingers of her hands, letting his eyes dwell upon hers. The marvel of their not wavering or softening meaningly kept her speechless. She rose with a strength not her own: not comforted, and no longer speculating. It was as if she had been eyeing a golden door shut fast, that might some day open, but was in itself precious to behold. She arose with deep humbleness, which awakened new ideas of the nature of worth in her bosom. She felt herself so low before this man who would not be played upon as an obsequious instrument—who would not leap into ardour for her beauty! Before that man upstairs how would she feel? The question did not come to her. She entered the room where he was, without a blush. Her step was firm, and her face expressed a quiet gladness. Georgiana stayed through the first commonplaces: then they were alone.

CHAPTER LI

A CHAPTER INTERRUPTED BY THE PHILOSOPHER

Commonplaces continued to be Wilfrid's refuge, for sentiment was surging mightily within him. The commonplaces concerning father, sisters, health, weather, sickened him when uttered, so much that for a time he was unobservant of Emilia's ready exchange of them. To a compliment on her appearance, she said: "You like this dress? I will tell you the history of it. I call it the Branciani dress. Mr. Powys designed it for me. The Countess Branciani was his friend. She used always to dress in this colour; just in this style. She also was dark. And she imagined that her husband favoured the Austrians. She believed he was an Austrian spy. It was impossible for her not to hate him—"

"Her husband!" quoth Wilfrid. The unexpected richness that had come upon her beauty and the coolness of her prattle at such an interview amazed and mortified him.

"She supposed him to be an Austrian spy!"

"Still he was her husband!"

Emilia gave her features a moment's play, but she had not full command of them, and the spark of scorn they emitted was very slight.

"Ah!" his tone had fallen into a depth, "how I thank you for the honour you have done me in desiring to see me once before you leave England! I know that I have not merited it."

More he said on this theme, blaming himself emphatically, until, startled by the commonplaces he was uttering, he stopped short; and the stopping was effective, if the speech was not. Where was the tongue of his passion? He almost asked it of himself. Where was Hippogriff? He who had burned to see her, he saw her now, fair as a vision, and yet in the flesh! Why was he as good as tongue-tied in her presence when he had such fires to pour forth?

(Presuming that he has not previously explained it, the philosopher here observes that Hippogriff, the foal of Fiery Circumstance out of Sentiment, must be subject to strong sentimental friction before he is capable of a flight: his appetites must fast long in the very eye of provocation ere he shall be eloquent. Let him, the Philosopher, repeat at the same time that souls harmonious to Nature, of whom there are few, do not mount this animal. Those who have true passion are not at the mercy of Hippogriff— otherwise Sur-excited Sentiment. You will mark in them constantly a reverence for the laws of their being, and a natural obedience to common sense. They are subject to storm, as in everything earthly, and they need no lesson of devotion; but they never move to an object in a madness.)

Now this is good teaching: it is indeed my Philosopher's object—his purpose—to work out this distinction; and all I wish is that it were good for my market. What the Philosopher means, is to plant in the reader's path a staring contrast between my pet Emilia and his puppet Wilfrid. It would be very commendable and serviceable if a novel were what he thinks it: but all attestation favours the critical dictum, that a novel is to give us copious sugar and no cane. I, myself, as a reader, consider concomitant cane an adulteration of the qualities of sugar. My Philosopher's error is to deem the sugar, born of the cane, inseparable from it. The which is naturally resented, and away flies my book back at the heads of the librarians, hitting me behind them a far more grievous blow.

Such is the construction of my story, however, that to entirely deny the Philosopher the privilege he stipulated for when with his assistance I conceived it, would render our performance unintelligible to that acute and honourable minority which consents to be thwacked with aphorisms and sentences and a fantastic delivery of the verities. While my Play goes on, I must permit him to come forward occasionally. We are indeed in a sort of partnership, and it is useless for me to tell him that he is not popular and destroys my chance.

CHAPTER LII

A FRESH DUETT BETWEEN WILFRID AND EMILIA

"Don't blame yourself, my Wilfrid."

Emilia spoke thus, full of pity for him, and in her adorable, deep-fluted tones, after the effective stop he had come to.

The 'my Wilfrid' made the owner of the name quiver with satisfaction. He breathed: "You have forgiven me?"

"That I have. And there was indeed no blame. My voice has gone. Yes, but I do not think it your fault."

"It was! it is!" groaned Wilfrid. "But, has your voice gone?" He leaned nearer to her, drawing largely on the claim his incredulity had to inspect her sweet features accurately. "You speak just as—more deliciously than ever! I can't think you have lost it. Ah! forgive me! forgive me!"

Emilia was about to put her hand over to him, but the prompt impulse was checked by a simultaneous feminine warning within. She smiled, saying: "'I forgive' seems such a strange thing for me to say;" and to convey any further meaning that might comfort him, better than words could do, she held on her smile. The smile was of the acceptedly feigned, conventional character; a polished Surface: belonging to the passage of the discourse, and not to the emotions. Wilfrid's swelling passion slipped on it. Sensitively he discerned an ease in its formation and disappearance that shot a first doubt through him, whether he really maintained his empire in her heart. If he did not reign there, why had she sent for him? He attributed the unheated smile to a defect in her manner, that was always chargeable with something, as he remembered. He began systematically to account for his acts: but the man was so constituted that as he laid them out for pardon, he himself condemned them most; and looking back at his weakness and double play, he broke through his phrases to cry without premeditation: "Can you have loved me then?"

Emilia's cheeks tingled: "Don't speak of that night in Devon," she replied.

"Ah!" sighed he. "I did not mean then. Then you must have hated me."

"No; for, what did I say? I said that you would come to me—nothing more. I hated that woman. You? Oh, no!"

"You loved me, then?"

"Did I not offer to work for you, if you were poor? And—I can't remember what I said. Please, do not speak of that night."

"Emilia! as a man of honour, I was bound—"

She lifted her hands: "Oh! be silent, and let that night die."

"I may speak of that night when you drove home from Penarvon Castle, and a robber? You have forgotten him, perhaps! What did he steal? not what he came for, but something dearer to him than anything he possesses. How can I say—? Dear to me? If it were dipped in my heart's blood!—"

Emilia was far from being carried away by the recollection of the scene; but remembering what her emotion had then been, she wondered at her coolness now.

"I may speak of Wilming Weir?" he insinuated.

Her bosom rose softly and heavily. As if throwing off some cloak of enchantment that clogged her spirit! "I was telling you of this dress," she said: "I mean, of Countess Branciani. She thought her husband was the Austrian spy who had betrayed them, and she said, 'He is not worthy to live.' Everybody knew that she had loved him. I have seen his portrait and hers. I never saw faces that looked so fond of life. She had that Italian beauty which is to any other like the difference between velvet and silk."

"Oh! do I require to be told the difference?" Wilfrid's heart throbbed.

"She," pursued Emilia, "she loved him still, I believe, but her country was her religion. There was known to be a great conspiracy, and no one knew the leader of it. All true Italians trusted Countess Branciani, though she visited the Austrian Governor's house—a General with some name on the teeth. One night she said to him, 'You have a spy who betrays you.' The General never suspected Countess Branciani. Women are devils of cleverness sometimes.

"But he did suspect it must be her husband—thinking, I suppose, 'How otherwise would she have known he was my spy?' He gave Count Branciani secret work and high pay. Then he set a watch on him. Count Branciani was to find out who was this unknown leader. He said to the Austrian Governor, 'You shall know him in ten days.' This was repeated to Countess Branciani, and she said to herself, 'My husband! you shall perish, though I should have to stab you myself.'"

Emilia's sympathetic hand twitched. Wilfrid's seized it, but it proved no soft melting prize. She begged to be allowed to continue. He entreated her to. Thereat she pulled gently for her hand, and persisting, it was grudgingly let go.

"One night Countess Branciani put the Austrians on her husband's track. He knew that she was true to her country, and had no fear of her, whether she touched the Black-yellow gold or not. But he did not confide any, of his projects to her. And his reason was, that as she went to the Governor's, she might accidentally, by a word or a sign, show that she was an accomplice in the conspiracy. He wished to save her from a suspicion. Brave Branciani!"

Emilia had a little shudder of excitement.

"Only," she added, "why will men always think women are so weak? The Count worked with conspirators who were not dreaming they would do anything, but were plotting to do it. The Countess belonged to the other party—men who never thought they were strong enough to see their ideas acting—I mean, not bold enough to take their chance. As if we die more than one death, and the blood we spill for Italy is ever wasted! That night the Austrian spy followed the Count to the meeting-house of the conspirators. It was thought quite natural that the Count should go there. But the spy, not having the password, crouched outside, and heard from two that came out muttering, the next appointment for a meeting. This was told to Countess Branciani, and in the meantime she heard from the Austrian Governor that her husband had given in names of the conspirators. She determined at once. 'Now may Christ and the Virgin help me!'"

Emilia struck her knees, while tears started through her shut eyelids. The exclamation must have been caught from her father, who liked not the priests of his native land well enough to interfere between his English wife and their child in such a matter as religious training.

"What happened?" said Wilfrid, vainly seeking for personal application in this narrative.

"Listen!—Ah!" she fought with her tears, and said, as they rolled down her face: "For a miserable thing one can not help, I find I must cry. This is what she did. She told him she knew of the conspiracy, and asked permission to join it, swearing that she was true to Italy. He said he believed her.—Oh, heaven!— And for some time she had to beg and beg; but to spare her he would not let her join. I cannot tell why—he gave her the password for the neat meeting, and said that an old gold coin must be shown. She must have coaxed it, though he was a strong man, who could resist women. I suppose he felt that he had been unkind.—Were I Queen of Italy he should stand for ever in a statue of gold!—The next appointed night a spy entered among the conspirators, with the password and the coin. Did I tell you the Countess had one child—a girl! She lives now, and I am to know her. She is like her mother. That little girl was playing down the stairs with her nurse when a band of Austrian soldiers entered the hall underneath, and an officer, with his sword drawn, and some men, came marching up in their stiff way— the machines! This officer stooped to her, and before the nurse could stop her, made her say where her father was. Those Austrians make children betray their parents! They don't think how we grow up to detest them. Do I? Hate is not the word: it burns so hot and steady with me. The Countess came out on the first landing; she saw what was happening. When her husband was led out, she asked permission to embrace him. The officer consented, but she had to say to him, 'Move back,' and then, with her lips to her husband's cheek, 'Betray no more of them!' she whispered. Count Branciani started. Now he understood what she had done, and why she had done it. 'Ask for the charge that makes me a prisoner,' he said. Her husband's noble face gave her a chill of alarm. The Austrian spoke. 'He is accused of being the chief of the Sequin Club.' And then the Countess looked at her husband; she sank at his feet. My heart breaks. Wilfrid! Wilfrid! You will not wear that uniform? Say 'Never, never!' You will not go to the Austrian army—Wilfrid? Would you be my enemy? Brutes, knee-deep in blood! with bloody fingers! Ogres! Would you be one of them? To see me turn my head shivering with loathing as you pass? This is why I sent for you, because I loved you, to entreat you, Wilfrid, from my soul, not to blacken the dear happy days when I knew you! Will you hear me? That woman is changeing you—doing all this. Resist her! Think of me in this one thing! Promise it, and I will go at once, and want no more. I will swear never to trouble you. Oh, Wilfrid it's not so much our being enemies, but what you become, I think of. If I say to myself, 'He also, who was once my lover—Oh! paid murderer of my dear people!'"

Emilia threw up both hands to her eyes: but Wilfrid, all on fire with a word, made one of her hands his own, repeating eagerly: "Once? once?"

"Once?" she echoed him.

"'Once my love?'" said he. "Not now?—does it mean, 'not now?' My darling!—pardon me, I must say it. My beloved! you said: 'He who was once my lover:'—you said that. What does it mean? Not that— not—? does it mean, all's over? Why did you bring me here? You know I must love you forever. Speak! 'Once?'"

"'Once?'" Emilia was breathing quick, but her voice was well contained: "Yes, I said 'once.' You were then."

"Till that night in Devon?

"Let it be."

"But you love me still?"

"We won't speak of it."

"I see! You cannot forgive. Good heavens! I think I remember your saying so once—Once! Yes, then: you said it then, during our 'Once;' when I little thought you would be merciless to me—who loved you from the first! the very first! I love you now! I wake up in the night, thinking I hear your voice. You haunt me. Cruel! cold!—who guards you and watches over you but the man you now hate? You sit there as if you could make yourself stone when you pleased. Did I not chastise that man Pericles publicly because he spoke a single lie of you? And by that act I have made an enemy to our house who may crush us in ruin. Do I regret it? No. I would do any madness, waste all my blood for you, die for you!"

Emilia's fingers received a final twist, and were dropped loose. She let them hang, looking sadly downward. Melancholy is the most irritating reply to passion, and Wilfrid's heart waged fierce at the sight of her, grown beautiful!—grown elegant!—and to reject him! When, after a silence which his pride would not suffer him to break, she spoke to ask what Mr. Pericles had said of her, he was enraged, forgot himself, and answered: "Something disgraceful."

Deep colour came on Emilia. "You struck him, Wilfrid?"

"It was a small punishment for his infamous lie, and, whatever might be the consequences, I would do it again."

"Wilfrid, I have heard what he has said. Madame Marini has told me. I wish you had not struck him. I cannot think of him apart from the days when I had my voice. I cannot bear to think of your having hurt him. He was not to blame. That is, he did not say: it was not untrue."

She took a breath to make this last statement, and continued with the same peculiar implicity of distinctness, which a terrific thunder of "What?" from Wilfrid did not overbear: "I was quite mad that day I went to him. I think, in my despair I spoke things that may have led him to fancy the truth of what he has said. On my honour, I do not know. And I cannot remember what happened after for the week I wandered alone about London. Mr. Powys found me on a wharf by the river at night."

A groan burst from Wilfrid. Emilia's instinct had divined the antidote that this would be to the poison of revived love in him, and she felt secure, though he had again taken her hand; but it was she who nursed a mere sentiment now, while passion sprang in him, and she was not prepared for the delirium with which he enveloped her. She listened to his raving senselessly, beginning to think herself lost. Her tortured hands were kissed; her eyes gazed into. He interpreted her stupefaction as contrition, her silence as delicacy, her changeing of colour as flying hues of shame: the partial coldness at their meeting he attributed to the burden on her mind, and muttering in a magnanimous sublimity that he forgave her, he claimed her mouth with force.

"Don't touch me!" cried Emilia, showing terror.

"Are you not mine?"

"You must not kiss me."

Wilfrid loosened her waist, and became in a minute outwardly most cool and courteous.

"My successor may object. I am bound to consider him. Pardon me. Once!—"

The wretched insult and silly emphasis passed harmlessly from her: but a word had led her thoughts to Merthyr's face, and what is meant by the phrase 'keeping oneself pure,' stood clearly in Emilia's mind. She had not winced; and therefore Wilfrid judged that his shot had missed because there was no mark. With his eye upon her sideways, showing its circle wide as a parrot's, he asked her one of those questions that lovers sometimes permit between themselves. "Has another—?" It is here as it was uttered. Eye-speech finished the sentence.

Rapidly a train of thought was started in Emilia, and she came to this conclusion, aloud: "Then I love nobody!" For she had never kissed Merthyr, or wished for his kiss.

"You do not?" said Wilfrid, after a silence. "You are generous in being candid."

A pressure of intensest sorrow bowed his head. The real feeling in him stole to Emilia like a subtle flame.

"Oh! what can I do for you?" she cried.

"Nothing, if you do not love me," he was replying mournfully, when, "Yes! yes!" rushed to his lips; "marry me: marry me to-morrow. You have loved me. 'I am never to leave you!' Can you forget the night when you said it? Emilia! Marry me and you will love me again. You must. This man, whoever he is—Ah! why am I such a brute! Come! be mine! Let me call you my own darling! Emilia!—or say quietly 'you have nothing to hope for:' I shall not reproach you, believe me."

He looked resigned. The abrupt transition had drawn her eyes to his. She faltered: "I cannot be married." And then: "How could I guess that you felt in this way?"

"Who told me that I should?" said he. "Your words have come true. You predicted that I should fly from 'that woman,' as you called her, and come to you. See! here it is exactly as you willed it. You—you are changed. You throw your magic on me, and then you are satisfied, and turn elsewhere."

Emilia's conscience smote her with a verification of this charge, and she trembled, half-intoxicated for the moment, by the aspect of her power. This filled her likewise with a dangerous pity for its victim; and now, putting out both hands to him, her chin and shoulders raised entreatingly, she begged the victim to spare her any word of marriage.

"But you go, you run away from me—I don't know where you are or what you are doing," said Wilfrid. "And you leave me to that woman. She loves the Austrians, as you know. There! I will ask nothing—only this: I will promise, if I quit the Queen's service for good, not to wear the white uniform—"

"Oh!" Emilia breathed inward deeply, scarce noticing the 'if' that followed; nodding quick assent to the stipulation before she heard the nature of it. It was, that she should continue in England.

"Your word," said Wilfrid; and she pledged it, and did not think she was granting much in the prospect of what she gained.

"You will, then?" said he.

"Yes, I will."

"On your honour?"

These reiterated questions were simply pretexts for steps nearer to the answering lips.

"And I may see you?" he went on.

"Yes."

"Wherever you are staying? And sometimes alone? Alone!—"

"Not if you do not know that I am to be respected," said Emilia, huddled in the passionate fold of his arms. He released her instantly, and was departing, wounded; but his heart counselled wiser proceedings.

"To know that you are in England, breathing the same air with me, near me! is enough. Since we are to meet on those terms, let it be so. Let me only see you till some lucky shot puts me out of your way."

This 'some lucky shot,' which is commonly pointed at themselves by the sentimental lovers, with the object of hitting the very centre of the hearts of obdurate damsels, glanced off Emilia's, which was beginning to throb with a comprehension of all that was involved in the word she had given.

"I have your promise?" he repeated: and she bent her head.

"Not," he resumed, taking jealousy to counsel, now that he had advanced a step: "Not that I would detain you against your will! I can't expect to make such a figure at the end of the piece as your Count Branciani—who, by the way, served his friends oddly, however well he may have served his country."

"His friends?" She frowned.

"Did he not betray the conspirators? He handed in names, now and then."

"Oh!" she cried, "you understand us no better than an Austrian. He handed in names—yes he was obliged to lull suspicion. Two or three of the least implicated volunteered to be betrayed by him; they went and confessed, and put the Government on a wrong track. Count Branciani made a dish of traitors—not true men—to satisfy the Austrian ogre. No one knew the head of the plot till that night of the spy. Do you not see?—he weeded the conspiracy!"

"Poor fellow!" Wilfrid answered, with a contracted mouth: "I pity him for being cut off from his handsome wife."

"I pity her for having to live," said Emilia.

And so their duett dropped to a finish. He liked her phrase better than his own, and being denied any privileges, and feeling stupefied by a position which both enticed and stung him, he remarked that he presumed he must not detain her any longer; whereupon she gave him her hand. He clutched the ready hand reproachfully.

"Good-bye," said she.

"You are the first to say it," he complained.

"Will you write to that Austrian colonel, your cousin, to say 'Never! never!' to-morrow, Wilfrid?"

"While you are in England, I shall stay, be sure of that."

She bade him give her love to all Brookfield.

"Once you had none to give but what I let you take back for the purpose!" he said. "Farewell! I shall see the harp to-night. It stands in the old place. I will not have it moved or touched till you—"

"Ah! how kind you were, Wilfrid!"

"And how lovely you are!"

There was no struggle to preserve the backs of her fingers from his lips, and, as this time his phrase was not palpably obscured by the one it countered, artistic sentiment permitted him to go.

CHAPTER LIII

ALDERMAN'S BOUQUET

A minute after his parting with Emilia, Wilfrid swung round in the street and walked back at great strides. "What a fool I was not to see that she was acting indifference!" he cried. "Let me have two seconds with her!" But how that was to be contrived his diplomatic brain refused to say. "And what a stiff, formal fellow I was all the time!" He considered that he had not uttered a sentence in any way pointed to touch her heart. "She must think I am still determined to marry that woman."

Wilfrid had taken his stand on the opposite side of the street, and beheld a male figure in the dusk, that went up to the house and then stood back scanning the windows. Wounded by his audacious irreverence toward the walls behind which his beloved was sheltered, Wilfrid crossed and stared at the intruder. It proved to be Braintop.

"How do you do, sir!—no! that can't be the house," stammered Braintop, with a very earnest scrutiny.

"What house? what do you want?" enquired Wilfrid.

"Jenkinson," was the name that won the honour of rescuing Braintop from this dilemma.

"No; it is Lady Gosstre's house: Miss Belloni is living there; and stop: you know her. Just wait, and take in two or three words from me, and notice particularly how she is looking, and the dress she wears. You can say—say that Mrs. Chump sent you to enquire after Miss Belloni's health."

Wilfrid tore a leaf from his pocket-book, and wrote:

"I can be free to-morrow. One word! I shall expect it, with your name in full."

But even in the red heat of passion his born diplomacy withheld his own signature. It was not difficult to override Braintop's scruples about presenting himself, and Wilfrid paced a sentinel measure awaiting the reply. "Free to-morrow," he repeated, with a glance at his watch under a lamp: and thus he soliloquized: "What a time that fellow is! Yes, I can be free to-morrow if I will. I wonder what the deuce Gambier had to do in Monmouthshire. If he has been playing with my sister's reputation, he shall have short shrift. That fellow Braintop sees her now—my little Emilia! my bird! She won't have changed her dress till she has dined. If she changes it before she goes out—by Jove, if she wears it to-night before all those people, that'll mean 'Good-bye' to me: 'Addio, caro,' as those olive women say, with their damned cold languor, when they have given you up. She's not one of them! Good God! she came into the room looking like a little Empress. I'll swear her hand trembled when I went, though! My sisters shall see her in that dress. She must have a clever lady's maid to have done that knot to her back hair. She's getting as full of art as any of them—Oh! lovely little darling! And when she smiles and holds out her hand! What is it—what is it about her? Her upper lip isn't perfectly cut, there's some fault with her nose, but I never saw such a mouth, or such a face. 'Free to-morrow?' Good God! she'll think I mean I'm free to take a walk!"

At this view of the ghastly shortcoming of his letter as regards distinctness, and the prosaic misinterpretation it was open to, Wilfrid called his inventive wits to aid, and ran swiftly to the end of the street. He had become—as like unto a lunatic as resemblance can approach identity. Commanding the length of the pavement for an instant, to be sure that no Braintop was in sight, he ran down a lateral street, but the stationer's shop he was in search of beamed nowhere visible for him, and he returned at the same pace to experience despair at the thought that he might have missed Braintop issuing forth, for whom he scoured the immediate neighbourhood, and overhauled not a few quiet gentlemen of all ages. "An envelope!" That was the object of his desire, and for that he wooed a damsel passing jauntily with a jug in her hand, first telling her that he knew her name was Mary, at which singular piece of divination she betrayed much natural astonishment. But a fine round silver coin and an urgent request for an envelope, told her as plainly as a blank confession that this was a lover. She informed him that she lived three streets off, where there were shops. "Well, then," said Wilfrid, "bring me the envelope here, and you'll have another opportunity of looking down the area."

"Think of yourself," replied she, saucily; but proved a diligent messenger. Then Wilfrid wrote on a fresh slip:

"When I said 'Free,' I meant free in heart and without a single chain to keep me from you. From any moment that you please, I am free. This is written in the dark."

He closed the envelope, and wrote Emilia's name and the address as black as his pencil could achieve it, and with a smart double-knock he deposited the missive in the box. From his station opposite he guessed the instant when it was taken out, and from that judged when she would be reading it. Or perhaps she would not read it till she was alone? "That must be her bedroom," he said, looking for a light in one of the upper windows; but the voice of a fellow who went by with: "I should keep that to myself, if I was you," warned him to be more discreet.

"Well, here I am. I can't leave the street," quoth Wilfrid, to the stock of philosophy at his disposal. He burned with rage to think of how he might be exhibiting himself before Powys and his sister.

It was half-past nine when a carriage drove up to the door. Into this Mr. Powys presently handed Georgiana and Emilia. Braintop followed the ladies, and then the coachman received his instructions and drove away. Forthwith Wilfrid started in pursuit. He calculated that if his wind held till he could jump into a light cab, his legitimate prey Braintop might be caught. For, "they can't be taking him to any party with them!" he chose to think, and it was a fair calculation that they were simply conducting Braintop part of his way home. The run was pretty swift. Wilfrid's blood was fired by the pace, until, forgetting the traitor Braintop, up rose Truth from the bottom of the well in him, and he felt that his sole desire was to see Emilia once more—but once! that night. Running hard, in the midst of obstacles, and with eye and mind fined on one object, disasters befell him. He knocked apples off a stall, and heard vehement hallooing behind: he came into collision with a gentleman of middle age courting digestion as he walked from his trusty dinner at home to his rubber at the Club: finally he rushed full tilt against a pot-boy who was bringing all his pots broadside to the flow of the street. "By Jove! is this what they drink?" he gasped, and dabbed with his handkerchief at the beer-splashes, breathlessly hailing the looked-for cab, and, with hot brow and straightened-out forefinger, telling the driver to keep that carriage in sight. The pot-boy had to be satisfied on his master's account, and then on his own, and away shot Wilfrid, wet with beer from throat to knee—to his chief protesting sense, nothing but an exhalation of beer! "Is this what they drink?" he groaned, thinking lamentably of the tastes of the populace. All idea of going near Emilia was now abandoned. An outward application of beer quenched his frenzy. She seemed as an unattainable star seen from the depths of foul pits. "Stop!" he cried from the window.

"Here we are, sir," said the cabman.

The carriage had drawn up, and a footman's alarum awakened one of the houses. The wretched cabman had likewise drawn up right under the windows of the carriage. Wilfrid could have pulled the trigger of a pistol at his forehead that moment. He saw that Miss Ford had recognized him, and he at once bowed elegantly. She dropped the window, and said, "You are in evening dress, I think; we will take you in with us."

Wilfrid hoped eagerly he might be allowed to hand them to the door, and made three skips across the mire. Emilia had her hands gathered away from the chances of seizure. In wild rage he began protesting that he could not possibly enter, when Georgiana said, "I wish to speak to you," and put feminine pressure upon him. He was almost on the verge of the word "beer," by way of despairing explanation, when the door closed behind him.

"Permit me to say a word to your recent companion. He is my father's clerk. I had to see him on urgent business; that is why I took this liberty," he said, and retreated.

Braintop was still there, quietly posted, performing upon his head with a pocket hair-brush.

Wilfrid put Braintop's back to the light, and said, "Is my shirt soiled?"

After a short inspection, Braintop pronounced that it was, "just a little."

"Do you smell anything?" said Wilfrid, and hung with frightful suspense on the verdict. "A fellow upset beer on me."

"It is beer!" sniffed Braintop.

"What on earth shall I do?" was the rejoinder; and Wilfrid tried to remember whether he had felt any sacred joy in touching Emilia's dress as they went up the steps to the door.

Braintop fumbled in the breast-pocket of his coat. "I happen to have," he said, rather shamefacedly.

"What is it?"

"Mrs. Chump gave it to me to-day. She always makes me accept something: I can't refuse. It's this:—the remains of some scent she insisted on my taking, in a bottle."

Wilfrid plucked at the stopper with a reckless desperation, saturated his handkerchief, and worked at his breast as if he were driving a lusty dagger into it.

"What scent is it?" he asked hurriedly.

"Alderman's Bouquet, sir."

"Of all the detestable!—" Wilfrid had no time for more, owing to fresh arrivals. He hastened in, with his smiling, wary face, half trusting that there might after all be purification in Alderman's Bouquet, and promising heaven due gratitude if Emilia's senses discerned not the curse on him. In the hall a gust from the great opening contention between Alderman's Bouquet and bad beer, stifled his sickly hope. Frantic, but under perfect self-command outwardly, he glanced to right and left, for the suggestion of a means of escape. They were seven steps up the stairs before his wits prompted him to say to Georgiana, "I have just heard very serious news from home. I fear—"

"What?—or, pardon me: does it call you away?" she asked, and Emilia gave him a steady look.

"I fear I cannot remain here. Will you excuse me?"

His face spoke plainly now of mental torture repressed. Georgiana put her hand out in full sympathy, and Emilia said, in her deep whisper, "Let me hear to-morrow." Then they bowed. Wilfrid was in the street again.

"Thank God, I've seen her!" was his first thought, overhearing "What did she think of me?" as he sighed with relief at his escape. For, lo! the Branciani dress was not on her shoulders, and therefore he might imagine what he pleased:—that she had arrayed herself so during the day to delight his eyes; or that, he having seen her in it, she had determined none others should. Though feeling utterly humiliated, he was yet happy. Driving to the station, he perceived starlight overhead, and blessed it; while his hand waved busily to conduct a current of fresh, oblivious air to his nostrils. The quiet heavens seemed all crowding to look down on the quiet circle of the firs, where Emilia's harp had first been heard by him, and they took her music, charming his blood with imagined harmonies, as he looked up to them. Thus all the way to Brookfield his fancy soared, plucked at from below by Alderman's Bouquet.

The Philosopher, up to this point rigidly excluded, rushes forward to the footlights to explain in a note, that Wilfrid, thus setting a perfume to contend with a stench, instead of wasting for time, change of raiment, and the broad lusty airs of heaven to blow him fresh again, symbolizes the vice of Sentimentalism, and what it is always doing. Enough!

CHAPTER LIV

THE EXPLOSION AT BROOKFIELD

"Let me hear to-morrow." Wilfrid repeated Emilia's petition in the tone she had used, and sent a delight through his veins even with that clumsy effort of imitation. He walked from the railway to Brookfield through the circle of firs, thinking of some serious tale of home to invent for her ears to-morrow. Whatever it was, he was able to conclude it—"But all's right now." He noticed that the dwarf pine, under whose spreading head his darling sat when he saw her first, had been cut down. Its absence gave him an ominous chill.

The first sight that saluted him as the door opened, was a pile of Mrs. Chump's boxes: he listened, and her voice resounded from the library. Gainsford's eye expressed a discretion significant that there had been an explosion in the house.

"I sha'nt have to invent much," said Wilfrid to himself, bitterly.

There was a momentary appearance of Adela at the library-door; and over her shoulder came an outcry from Mrs. Chump. Arabella then spoke: Mr. Pole and Cornelia following with a word, to which Mrs. Chump responded shrilly: "Ye shan't talk to 'm, none of ye, till I've had the bloom of his ear, now!" A confused hubbub of English and Irish ensued. The ladies drew their brother into the library.

Doubtless you have seen a favourite sketch of the imaginative youthful artist, who delights to portray scenes on a raft amid the tossing waters, where sweet and satiny ladies, in a pardonable abandonment to the exigencies of the occasion, are exhibiting the full energy and activity of creatures that existed before sentiment was born. The ladies of Brookfield had almost as utterly cast off their garb of lofty reserve and inscrutable superiority. They were begging Mrs. Chump to be, for pity's sake, silent. They were arguing with the woman. They were remonstrating—to such an extent as this, in reply to an infamous outburst: "No, no: indeed, Mrs. Chump, indeed!" They rose, as she rose, and stood about her, motioning a beseeching emphasis with their hands. Not visible for one second was the intense indignation at their fate which Wilfrid, spying keenly into them, perceived. This taught him that the occasion was as grave as could be. In spite of the oily words his father threw from time to time abruptly on the tumult, he guessed what had happened.

Briefly, Mrs. Chump, aided by Braintop, her squire, had at last hunted Mr. Pericles down, and the wrathful Greek had called her a beggar. With devilish malice he had reproached her for speculating in such and such Bonds, and sending ventures to this and that hemisphere, laughing infernally as he watched her growing amazement. "Ye're jokin', Mr. Paricles," she tried to say and think; but the very naming of poverty had given her shivers. She told him how she had come to him because of Mr. Pole's reproach, which accused her of causing the rupture. Mr. Pericles twisted the waxy points of his moustache. "I shall advise you, go home," he said; "go to a lawyer: say, 'I will see my affairs, how zey stand.' Ze man will find Pole is ruined. It may be—I do not know—Pole has left a little of your money; yes, ma'am, it may be."

The end of the interview saw Mrs. Chump flying past Mr. Pericles to where Braintop stood awaiting her with a meditative speculation on that official promotion which in his attention to the lady he anticipated. It need scarcely be remarked that he was astonished to receive a scent-bottle on the spot, as the only reward his meritorious service was probably destined ever to meet with. Breathless in her panic, Mrs. Chump assured him she was a howling beggar, and the smell of a scent was like a crool blow to her; above all, the smell of Alderman's Bouquet, which Chump—"tell'n a lie, ye know, Mr. Braintop, said was after him. And I, smell'n at 't over 'n Ireland—a raw garl I was—I just thought 'm a prince, the little sly fella! And oh! I'm a beggar, I am!" With which, she shouted in the street, and put Braintop to such confusion that he hailed a cab recklessly, declaring to her she had no time to lose, if she wished to catch the train. Mrs. Chump requested the cabman that as a man possessed of a feeling heart for the interests of a helpless woman, he would drive fast; and, at the station, disputed his charge on the ground of the knowledge already imparted to him of her precarious financial state. In this frame of mind she fell upon Brookfield, and there was clamour in the house. Wilfrid arrived two hours after Mrs. Chump. For that space the ladies had been saying over and over again empty words to pacify her. The task now devolved on their brother. Mr. Pole, though he had betrayed nothing under the excitement of the sudden shock, had lost the proper control of his mask. Wilfrid commenced by fixedly listening to Mrs. Chump until for the third time her breath had gone. Then, taking on a smile, he said: "Perhaps you are aware that Mr. Pericles has a particular reason for animosity tome. We've disagreed together, that's all. I suppose it's the habit of those fellows to attack a whole family where one member of it offends them." As soon as the meaning of this was made clear to Mrs. Chump, she caught it to her bosom for comfort; and finding it gave less than at the moment she required, she flung it away altogether; and then moaned, a suppliant, for it once more. "The only thing, if you are in a state of alarm about my father's affairs, is for him to show you by his books that his house is firm," said Wilfrid, now that he had so far helped to eject suspicion from her mind.

"Will Pole do ut?" ejaculated Mrs. Chump, half off her seat.

"Of course I will—of course! of course! Haven't I told you so?" said Mr. Pole, blinking mightily from his armchair over the fire. "Sit down, Martha."

"Oh! but how'll I understand ye, Pole?" she cried.

"I'll do my best to assist in explaining," Wilfrid condescended to say.

The ladies were touched when Mrs. Chump replied, with something of a curtsey, "I'll thank ye vary much, sir." She added immediately, "Mr. Wilfrud," as if correcting the 'sir,' for sounding cold.

It was so trustful and simple, that it threw alight on the woman under which they had not yet beheld her. Compassion began to stir in their bosoms, and with it an inexplicable sense of shame, which soon threw any power of compassion into the background. They dared not ask themselves whether it was true that their father had risked the poor thing's money in some desperate stake. What hopeful force was left to them they devoted to her property, and Adela determined to pray that night for its safe preservation. The secret feeling in the hearts of the ladies was, that in putting them on their trial with poverty, Celestial Powers would never at the same time think it necessary to add disgrace.

Consequently, and as a defence against the darker dread, they now, for the first time, fully believed that monetary ruin had befallen their father. They were civil to Mrs. Chump, and forgiving toward her brogue, and her naked outcries of complaint and suddenly—suggested panic; but their pity, save when some odd turn in her conduct moved them, was reserved dutifully for their father. His wretched sensations at the pouring of a storm of tears from the exhausted creature, caused Arabella to rise and say to Mrs. Chump kindly, "Now let me take you to bed."

But such a novel mark of tender civility caused the woman to exclaim: "Oh, dear! if ye don't sound like wheedlin' to keep me blind."

Even this was borne with. "Come; it will do you good to rest," said Arabella.

"And how'll I sleep?"

"By shutting my eye—'peeps,'—as I used to tell my old nurse," said Adela; and Mrs. Chump, accustomed to an occasional (though not public) bit of wheedling from her, was partially reassured.

"I'll sit with you till you do sleep," said Arabella.

"Suppose," Mrs. Chump moaned, "suppose I'm too poor aver to repay ye? If I'm a bankrup'?—oh!"

Arabella smiled. "Whatever I may do is certainly not done for a remuneration, and such a service as this, at least, you need not speak of."

Mrs. Chump's evident surprise, and doubt of the honesty of the change in her manner, caused Arabella very acutely to feel its dishonesty. She looked at Cornelia with envy. The latter lady was leaning meditatively, her arm on a side of her chair, like a pensive queen, with a ready, mild, embracing look for the company. 'Posture' seemed always to triumph over action.

Before quitting the room, Mrs. Chump asked Mr. Pole whether he would be up early the next morning.

"Very early,—you beat me, if you can," said he, aware that the question was put as a test to his sincerity.

"Oh, dear! Suppose it's onnly a false alarrm of the 'bomunable Mr. Paricles—which annybody'd have listened to—ye know that!" said Mrs. Chump, going forth.

She stopped in the doorway, and turned her head round, sniffing, in a very pronounced way. "Oh, it's you," she flashed on Wilfrid; "it's you, my dear, that smell so like poor Chump. Oh! if we're not rooned, won't we dine together! Just give me a kiss, please. The smell of ye's comfortin'."

Wilfrid bent his cheek forward, affecting to laugh, though the subject was tragic to him.

"Oh! perhaps I'll sleep, and not look in the mornin' like that beastly tallow, Mr. Paricles says I spent such a lot of money on, speculator—whew, I hate ut!—and hemp too! Me!—Martha Chump! Do I want to hang myself, and burn forty thousand pounds worth o' candles round my corpse danglin' there? Now, there, now! Is that sense? And what'd Pole want to buy me all that grease for? And where'd I keep ut,

I'll ask ye? And sure they wouldn't make me a bankrup' on such a pretence as that. For, where's the Judge that's got the heart?"

Having apparently satisfied her reason with these interrogations, Mrs. Chump departed, shaking her head at Wilfrid: "Ye smile so nice, ye do!" by the way. Cornelia and Adela then rose, and Wilfrid was left alone with his father.

It was natural that he should expect the moment for entire confidence between them to have come. He crossed his legs, leaning over the fireplace, and waited. The old man perceived him, and made certain humming sounds, as of preparation. Wilfrid was half tempted to think he wanted assistance, and signified attention; upon which Mr. Pole became immediately absorbed in profound thought.

"Singular it is, you know," he said at last, with a candid air, "people who know nothing about business have the oddest ideas—no common sense in 'em!"

After that he fell dead silent.

Wilfrid knew that it would be hard for him to speak. To encourage him, he said: "You mean Mrs. Chump, sir?"

"Oh! silly woman—absurd! No, I mean all of you; every man Jack, as Martha'd say. You seem to think—but, well! there! let's go to bed."

"To bed?" cried Wilfrid, frowning.

"Why, when it's two or three o'clock in the morning, what's an old fellow to do? My feet are cold, and I'm queer in the back—can't talk! Light my candle, young gentleman—my candle there, don't you see it? And you look none of the freshest. A nap on your pillow'll do you no harm."

"I wanted to talk to you a little, sir," said Wilfrid, about as much perplexed as he was irritated.

"Now, no talk of bankers' books to-night!" rejoined his father. "I can't and won't. No cheques written 'tween night and morning. That's positive. There! there's two fingers. Shall have three to-morrow morning—a pen in 'em, perhaps."

With which wretched pleasantry the little merchant nodded to his son, and snatching up his candle, trotted to the door.

"By the way, give a look round my room upstairs, to see all right when you're going to turn in yourself," he said, before disappearing.

The two fingers given him by his father to shake at parting, had told Wilfrid more than the words. And yet how small were these troubles around him compared with what he himself was suffering! He looked forward to the bittersweet hour verging upon dawn, when he should be writing to Emilia things to melt the vilest obduracy. The excitement which had greeted him on his arrival at Brookfield was to be thanked for its having made him partially forget his humiliation. He had, of course, sufficient rational feeling to be chagrined by calamity, but his dominant passion sucked sustaining juices from every passing event.

In obedience to his father's request, Wilfrid went presently into the old man's bedroom, to see that all was right. The curtains of the bed were drawn close, and the fire in the grate burnt steadily. Calm sleep seemed to fill the chamber. Wilfrid was retiring, with a revived anger at his father's want of natural confidence in him, or cowardly secresy. His name was called, and he stopped short.

"Yes, sir?" he said.

"Door's shut?"

"Shut fast."

The voice, buried in curtains, came after a struggle.

"You've done this, Wilfrid. Now, don't answer:—I can't stand talk. And you must undo it. Pericles can if he likes. That's enough for you to know. He can. He won't see me. You know why. If he breaks with me—it's a common case in any business—I'm... we're involved together." Then followed a deep sigh. The usual crisp brisk way of his speaking was resumed in hollow tones: "You must stop it. Now, don't answer. Go to Pericles to-morrow. You must. Nothing wrong, if you go at once."

"But, Sir! Good heaven!" interposed Wilfrid, horrified by the thought of the penance here indicated.

The bed shook violently.

"If not," was uttered with a sort of muted vehemence, "there's another thing you can do. Go to the undertaker's, and order coffins for us all. There—good night!"

The bed shook again. Wilfrid stood eyeing the mysterious hangings, as if some dark oracle had spoken from behind them. In fear of irritating the old man, and almost as much in fear of bringing on himself a revelation of the frightful crisis that could only be averted by his apologizing personally to the man he had struck, Wilfrid stole from the room.

CHAPTER LV

THE TRAGEDY OF SENTIMENT

There is a man among our actors here who may not be known to you. It had become the habit of Sir Purcell Barren's mind to behold himself as under a peculiarly malign shadow. Very young men do the same, if they are much afflicted: but this is because they are still boys enough to have the natural sense to be ashamed of ill-luck, even when they lack courage to struggle against it. The reproaching of Providence by a man of full growth, comes to some extent from his meanness, and chiefly from his pride. He remembers that the old Gods selected great heroes whom to persecute, and it is his compensation for material losses to conceive himself a distinguished mark for the Powers of air. One who wraps himself in this delusion may have great qualities; he cannot be of a very contemptible nature; and in this place we will discriminate more closely than to call him fool. Had Sir Purcell sunk or bent under the thong that pursued him, he might, after a little healthy moaning, have gone along as others do. Who knows?—though a much persecuted man, he might have become so degraded as to have looked forward with cheerfulness to his daily dinner; still despising, if he pleased, the soul that would invent a sauce. I mean to say, he would, like the larger body of our sentimentalists, have acquiesced in our simple humanity, but without sacrificing a scruple to its grossness, or going arm-in-arm with it by any means. Sir Purcell, however, never sank, and never bent. He was invariably erect before men, and he did not console himself with a murmur in secret. He had lived much alone; eating alone; thinking alone. To complain of a father is, to a delicate mind, a delicate matter, and Sir Purcell was a gentleman to all about him. His chief affliction in his youth, therefore, kept him dumb. A gentleman to all about him, he unhappily forgot what was due to his own nature. Must we not speak under pressure of a grief? Little people should know that they must: but then the primary task is to teach them that they are little people. For, if they repress the outcry of a constant irritation, and the complaint against injustice, they lock up a feeding devil in their hearts, and they must have vast strength to crush him there. Strength they must have to kill him, and freshness of spirit to live without him, after he has once entertained them with his most comforting discourses. Have you listened to him, ever? He does this:—he plays to you your music (it is he who first teaches thousands that they have any music at all, so guess what a dear devil he is!); and when he has played this ravishing melody, he falls to upon a burlesque contrast of hurdy-gurdy and bag-pipe squeal and bellow and drone, which is meant for the music of the world. How far sweeter was yours! This charming devil Sir Purcell had nursed from childhood.

As a child, between a flighty mother and a father verging to insanity from caprice, he had grown up with ideas of filial duty perplexed, and with a fitful love for either, that was not attachment: a baffled natural love, that in teaching us to brood on the hardness of our lot, lays the foundation for a perniciously mystical self-love. He had waged precociously philosophic, when still a junior. His father had kept him by his side, giving him no profession beyond that of the obedient expectant son and heir. His first allusion to the youth's dependency had provoked their first breach, which had been widened by many an ostentatious forgiveness on the one hand, and a dumbly-protesting submission on the other. His mother died away from her husband's roof. The old man then sought to obliterate her utterly. She left her boy a little money, and the injunction of his father was, that he was never to touch it. He inherited his taste for music from her, and his father vowed, that if ever he laid hand upon a musical instrument again, he would be disinherited. All these signs of a vehement spiteful antagonism to reason, the young man might have treated more as his father's misfortune than his own, if he could only have brought himself to acknowledge that such a thing as madness stigmatized his family. But the sentimental mind conceived it as 'monstrous impiety' to bring this accusation against a parent who did not break windows, or grin to deformity. He behaved toward him as to a reasonable person, and felt the rebellious rancour instead of the pity. Thus sentiment came in the way of pity. By degrees, Sir Purcell transferred all his father's madness to the Fates by whom he was persecuted. There was evidently madness somewhere, as his shuddering human nature told him. It did not offend his sentiment to charge this upon the order of the universe.

Against such a wild-hitting madness, or concentrated ire of the superior Powers, Sir Purcell stood up, taking blow upon blow. As organist of Hillford Church, he brushed his garments, and put a polish on his apparel, with an energetic humility that looked like unconquerable patience; as though he had said: "While life is left in me, I will be seen for what I am." We will vary it—"For what I think myself." In reality, he fought no battle. He had been dead-beaten from his boyhood. Like the old Spanish Governor, the walls of whose fortress had been thrown down by an earthquake, and who painted streets to deceive the enemy, he was rendered safe enough by his astuteness, except against a traitor from within.

One who goes on doggedly enduring, doggedly doing his best, must subsist on comfort of a kind that is likely to be black comfort. The mere piping of the musical devil shall not suffice. In Sir Purcell's case, it had long seemed a magnanimity to him that he should hold to a life so vindictively scourged, and his comfort was that he had it at his own disposal. To know so much, to suffer, and still to refrain, flattered his pride. "The term of my misery is in my hand," he said, softened by the reflection. It is our lowest philosophy.

But, when the heart of a man so fashioned is stirred to love a woman, it has a new vital force, new health, and cannot play these solemn pranks. The flesh, and all its fatality, claims him. When Sir Purcell became acquainted with Cornelia, he found the very woman his heart desired, or certainly a most admirable picture of her. It was, perhaps, still more to the lady's credit, if she was only striving to be what he was learning to worship. The beneficial change wrought in him, made him enamoured of healthy thinking and doing. Had this, as a result of sharp mental overhauling, sprung from himself, there would have been hope for him. Unhappily, it was dependent on her who inspired it. He resolved that life should be put on a fresh trial in her person; and expecting that naturally to fail, of which he had always entertained a base conception, he was perforce brought to endow her with unexampled virtues, in order to keep any degree of confidence tolerably steadfast in his mind. The lady accepted the decorations thus bestowed on her, with much grace and willingness. She consented, little aware of her heroism, to shine forth as an 'ideal;' and to this he wantonly pinned his faith. Alas! in our world, where all things must move, it becomes, by-and-by, manifest that an 'ideal,' or idol, which you will, has not been gifted with two legs. What is, then, the duty of the worshipper? To make, as I should say, some compromise between his superstitious reverence and his recognition of facts. Cornelia, on her pedestal, could not prefer such a request plainly; but it would have afforded her exceeding gratification, if the man who adored her had quietly taken her up and fixed her in a fresh post, of his own choosing entirely, in the new circles of changeing events. Far from doing that, he appeared to be unaware that they went, with the varying days, through circles, forming and reforming. He walked rather as a man down a lengthened corridor, whose light to which he turns is in one favourite corner, visible till he reaches the end. What Cornelia was, in the first flaming of his imagination around her, she was always, unaffected by circumstance, to remain. It was very hard. The 'ideal' did feel the want—if not of legs—of a certain tolerant allowance for human laws on the part of her worshipper; but he was remorselessly reverential, both by instinct and of necessity. Women are never quite so mad in sentimentalism as men.

We have now looked into the hazy interior of their systems—our last halt, I believe, and last examination of machinery, before Emilia quits England.

About the time of the pairing of the birds, and subsequent to the Brookfield explosion, Cornelia received a letter from her lover, bearing the tone of a summons. She was to meet him by the decayed sallow—the 'fruitless tree,' as he termed it. Startled by this abruptness, her difficulties made her take counsel of her dignity. "He knows that these clandestine meetings degrade me. He is wanting in faith, to require constant assurances. He will not understand my position!" She remembered the day at Besworth, of which Adela (somewhat needlessly, perhaps) had told her; that it had revealed two of the family, in situations censurable before a gossiping world, however intrinsically blameless. That day had been to the ladies a lesson of deference to opinion. It was true that Cornelia had met her lover since, but she was then unembarrassed. She had now to share in the duties of the household—duties abnormal, hideous, incredible. Her incomprehensible father was absent in town. Daily Wilfrid conducted Adela thither on mysterious business, and then Mrs. Chump was left to Arabella and herself in the lonely house. Numberless things had to be said for the quieting of this creature, who every morning came downstairs with the exclamation that she could no longer endure her state of uncertainty, and was "off to a lawyer." It was useless to attempt the posture of a reply. Words, and energetic words, the woman demanded, not expostulations—petitions that she would be respectful to the house before the household. Yes, occasionally (so gross was she!) she had to be fed with lies. Arabella and Cornelia heard one another mouthing these dreadful things, with a wretched feeling of contemptuous compassion. The trial was renewed daily, and it was a task, almost a physical task, to hold the woman back from London, till the hour of lunch came. If they kept her away from her bonnet till then they were safe.

At this meal they had to drink champagne with her. Diplomatic Wilfrid had issued the order, with the object, first, of dazzling her vision; and secondly, to set the wheels of her brain in swift motion. The effect was marvellous; and, had it not been for her determination never to drink alone, the miserable ladies might have applauded it. Adela, on the rare days when she was fortunate enough to reach Brookfield in time for dinner, was surprised to hear her sisters exclaim, "Oh, the hatefulness of that champagne!" She enjoyed it extremely. She, poor thing, had again to go through a round of cabs and confectioners' shops in London. "If they had said, 'Oh, the hatefulness of those buns and cold chickens!'" she thought to herself. Not objecting to champagne at lunch with any particular vehemence, she was the less unwilling to tell her sisters what she had to do for Wilfrid daily.

"Three times a week I go to see Emilia at Lady Gosstre's town-house. Mr. Powys has gone to Italy, and Miss Ford remains, looking, if I can read her, such a temper. On the other days I am taken by Wilfrid to the arcades, or we hire a brougham to drive round the park,—for nothing but the chance of seeing that girl an instant. Don't tell me it's to meet Lady Charlotte! That lovely and obliging person it is certainly not my duty to undeceive. She's now at Stornley, and speaks of our affairs to everybody, I dare say. Twice a week Wilfrid—oh! quite casually!—calls on Miss Ford, and is gratified, I suppose; for this is the picture:—There sits Emilia, one finger in her cheek, and the thumb under her chin, and she keeps looking down so. Opposite is Miss Ford, doing some work—making lint for patriots, probably. Then Wilfrid, addressing commonplaces to her; and then Emilia's father—a personage, I assure you! up against the window, with a violin. I feel a bitter edge on my teeth still! What do you think he does to please his daughter for one whole hour! He draws his fingers—does nothing else; she won't let him; she won't hear a tune-up the strings in the most horrible caterwaul, up and down. It is really like a thousand lunatics questioning and answering, and is enough to make you mad, but there that girl sits, listening. Exactly in this attitude—so. She scarcely ever looks up. My brother talks, and occasionally steals a glance that way. We passed one whole hour as I have described. In the middle of it, I happened to look at Wilfrid's face, while the violin was wailing down. I fancied I heard the despair of one of those huge masks in a pantomime. I was almost choked."

When Adela had related thus much, she had to prevent downright revolt, and spoil her own game, by stating that Wilfrid did not leave the house for his special pleasure, and a word, as to the efforts he was making to see Mr. Pericles, convinced the ladies that his situation was as pitiable as their own.

Cornelia refused to obey her lover's mandate, and wrote briefly. She would not condescend to allude to the unutterable wretchedness afflicting her, but spoke of her duty to her father being foremost in her prayers for strength. Sir Purcell interpreted this as indicating the beginning of their alienation. He chided her gravely in an otherwise pleasant letter. She was wrong to base her whole reply upon the little sentence of reproach, but self-justification was necessary to her spirit. Indeed, an involuntary comparison of her two suitors was forced on her, and, dry as was Sir Twickenham's mind, she could not but acknowledge that he had behaved with an extraordinary courtesy, amounting to chivalry, in his suit. On two occasions he had declined to let her be pressed to decide. He came to the house, and went, like an ordinary visitor. She was indebted to him for that splendid luxury of indecision, which so few of the maids of earth enjoy for a lengthened term. The rude shakings given her by Sir Purcell, at a time when she needed all her power of dreaming, to support the horror of accumulated facts, was almost resented. "He as much as says he doubts me, when this is what I endure!" she cried to herself, as Mrs. Chump ordered her champagne-glass to be filled, with "Now, Cornelia, my dear; if it's bad luck we're in for, there's nothin' cheats ut like champagne," and she had to put the (to her) nauseous bubbles to her lips. Sir Purcell had not been told of her tribulations, and he had not expressed any doubt of her truth; but sentimentalists can read one another with peculiar accuracy through their bewitching gauzes. She read his unwritten doubt, and therefore expected her unwritten misery to be read.

So it is when you play at Life! When you will not go straight, you get into this twisting maze. Now he wrote coldly, and she had to repress a feeling of resentment at that also. She ascribed the changes of his tone fundamentally to want of faith in her, and absolutely, during the struggle she underwent, she by this means somehow strengthened her idea of her own faithfulness. She would have phrased her projected line of conduct thus: "I owe every appearance of assent to my poor father's scheme, that will spare his health. I owe him everything, save the positive sacrifice of my hand." In fact, she meant to do her duty to her father up to the last moment, and then, on the extreme verge, to remember her duty to her lover. But she could not write it down, and tell her lover as much. She knew instinctively that, facing the eyes, it would not look well. Perhaps, at another season, she would have acted and thought with less folly; but the dull pain of her great uncertainty, and the little stinging whips daily applied to her, exaggerated her tendency to self-deception. "Who has ever had to bear so much?—what slave?" she would exclaim, as a refuge from the edge of his veiled irony. For a slave has, if not selection of what he will eat and drink, the option of rejecting what is distasteful. Cornelia had not. She had to act a part every day with Mrs. Chump, while all those she loved, and respected, and clung to, were in the same conspiracy. The consolation of hating, or of despising, her tormentress was denied. The thought that the poor helpless creature had been possibly ruined by them, chastened Cornelia's reflections mightily, and taught her to walk very humbly through the duties of the day. Her powers of endurance were stretched to their utmost. A sublime affliction would, as she felt bitterly, have enlarged her soul. This sordid misery narrowed it. Why did not her lover, if his love was passionate, himself cut the knot claim her, and put her to a quick decision? She conceived that were he to bring on a supreme crisis, her heart would declare itself. But he appeared to be wanting in that form of courage. Does it become a beggar to act such valiant parts? perhaps he was even then replying from his stuffy lodgings.

The Spring was putting out primroses,—the first handwriting of the year,—as Sir Purcell wrote to er prettily. Deire for fresh air, and the neighbourhood of his beloved, sent him on a journey down to Hillford. Near the gates of the Hillford station, he passed Wilfrid and Adela, hurrying to catch the up-train, and received no recognition. His face scarcely changed colour, but the birds on a sudden seemed to pipe far away from him. He asked himself, presently, what were those black circular spots which flew chasing along the meadows and the lighted walks. It was with an effort that he got the landscape close about his eyes, and remembered familiar places. He walked all day, making occupation by directing his steps to divers eminences that gave a view of the Brookfield chimneys. After night-fall he found himself in the firwood, approaching the 'fruitless tree.' He had leaned against it musingly, for a time, when he heard voices, as of a couple confident in their privacy.

The footman, Gainsford, was courting a maid of the Tinley's, and here, being midway between the two houses, they met. He had to obtain pardon for tardiness, by saying that dinner at Brookfield had been delayed for the return of Mr. Pole. The damsel's questions showed her far advanced in knowledge of affairs at Brookfield and may account for Laura Tinley's gatherings of latest intelligence concerning those 'odd girls,' as she impudently called the three.

"Oh! don't you listen!" was the comment pronounced on Gainsford's stock of information. But, he told nothing signally new. She wished to hear something new and striking, "because," she said, "when I unpin Miss Laura at night, I'm as likely as not to get a silk dress that ain't been worn more than half-a-dozen times—if I manage. When I told her that Mr. Albert, her brother, had dined at your place last Thursday—demeaning of himself, I do think—there!—I got a pair of silk stockings,—not letting her see I knew what it was for, of coursed and about Mrs. Dump,—Stump;—I can't recollect the woman's name; and her calling of your master a bankrupt, right out, and wanting her money of him,—there! if Miss Laura didn't give me a pair of lavender kid-gloves out of her box!—and I wish you would leave my hands alone, when you know I shouldn't be so silly as to wear them in the dark; and for you, indeed!"

But Gainsford persisted, upon which there was fooling. All this was too childish for Sir Purcell to think it necessary to give warning of his presence. They passed, and when they had gone a short way the damsel cried, "Well, that is something," and stopped. "Married in a month!" she exclaimed. "And you don't know which one?"

"No," returned Gainsford; "master said 'one of you' as they was at dinner, just as I come into the room. He was in jolly spirits, and kept going so: 'What's a month! champagne, Gainsford,' and you should have sees Mrs.—not Stump, but Chump. She'll be tipsy to-night, and I shall bust if I have to carry of her upstairs. Well, she is fun!—she don't mind handin' you a five-shilling piece when she's done tender: but I have nearly lost my place two or three time along of that woman. She'd split logs with laughing:—no need of beetle and wedges! 'Och!' she sings out, 'by the piper!'—and Miss Cornelia sitting there—and, 'Arrah!'—bother the woman's Irish," (thus Gainsford gave up the effort at imitation, with a spirited Briton's mild contempt for what he could not do) "she pointed out Miss Cornelia and said she was like the tinker's dog:—there's the bone he wants himself, and the bone he don't want anybody else to have. Aha! ain't it good?"

"Oh! the tinker's dog! won't I remember that!" said the damsel, "she can't be such a fool."

"Well, I don't know," Gainsford meditated critically. "She is; and yet she ain't, if you understand me. What I feel about her is—hang it! she makes ye laugh."

Sir Purcell moved from the shadow of the tree as noiselessly as he could, so that this enamoured couple might not be disturbed. He had already heard more than he quite excused himself for hearing in such a manner, and having decided not to arrest the man and make him relate exactly what Mr. Pole had spoken that evening at the Brookfield dinner-table, he hurried on his return to town.

It was not till he had sight of his poor home; the solitary company of chairs; the sofa looking bony and comfortless as an old female house drudge; the table with his desk on it; and, through folding-doors, his cold and narrow bed; not till then did the fact of his great loss stand before him, and accuse him of living. He seated himself methodically and wrote to Cornelia. His fancy pictured her now as sharp to every turn of language and fall of periods: and to satisfy his imagined, rigorous critic, he wrote much in the style of a newspaper leading article. No one would have thought that tragic meaning underlay those choice and sounding phrases. On reperusing the composition, he rejected it, but only to produce one of a similar cast. He could not get to nature in his tone. He spoke aloud a little sentence now and then, that had the ring of a despairing tenderness. Nothing of the sort inhabited his written words, wherein a strained philosophy and ironic resignation went on stilts. "I should desire to see you once before I take a step that some have not considered more than commonly serious," came toward the conclusion; and the idea was toyed with till he signed his name. "A plunge into the deep is of little moment to one who has been stripped of all clothing. Is he not a wretch who stands and shivers still?" This letter, ending with a short and not imperious, or even urgent, request for an interview, on the morrow by the 'fruitless tree,' he sealed for delivery into Cornelia's hands some hours before the time appointed. He then wrote a clear business letter to his lawyer, and one of studied ambiguity to a cousin on his mother's side. His father's brother, Percival Barrett, to whom the estates had gone, had offered him an annuity of five hundred pounds: "though he had, as his nephew was aware, a large family." Sir Purcell had replied: "Let me be the first to consider your family," rejecting the benevolence. He now addressed his cousin, saying: "What would you think of one who accepts such a gift?—of me, were you to hear that I had bowed my head and extended my hand? Think this, if ever you hear of it: that I have acceded for the sake of winning the highest prize humanity can bestow: that I certainly would not have done it for aught less than the highest." After that he went to his narrow bed. His determination was to write to his uncle, swallowing bitter pride, and to live a pensioner, if only Cornelia came to her tryst, "the last he would ask of her," as he told her. Once face to face with his beloved, he had no doubt of his power; and this feeling which he knew her to share, made her reluctance to meet him more darkly suspicious.

As he lay in the little black room, he thought of how she would look when a bride, and of the peerless beauty towering over any shades of earthliness which she would present. His heated fancy conjured up every device and charm of sacredness and adoring rapture about that white veiled shape, until her march to the altar assumed the character of a religious procession—a sight to awe mankind! And where, when she stood before the minister in her saintly humility, grave and white, and tall—where was the man whose heart was now racing for that goal at her right hand? He felt at the troubled heart and touched two fingers on the rib, mock-quietly, and smiled. Then with great deliberation he rose, lit a candle, unlocked a case of pocket-pistols, and loaded them: but a second idea coming into his head, he drew the bullet out of one, and lay down again with a luxurious speculation on the choice any hand might possibly make of the life-sparing or death-giving of those two weapons. In his neat half-slumber he was twice startled by a report of fire-arms in a church, when a crowd of veiled women and masked men rushed to the opening, and a woman throwing up the veil from her face knelt to a corpse that she lifted without effort, and weeping, laid it in a grave, where it rested and was at peace, though multitudes hurried over it, and new stars came and went, and the winds were strange with new tongues. The sleeper saw the morning upon that corpse when light struck his eyelids, and he awoke like a man who knew no care.

His landlady's little female scrubber was working at the grate in his sitting-room. He had endured many a struggle to prevent service of this nature being done for him by one of the sex—at least, to prevent it within his hearing and sight. He called to her to desist; but she replied that she had her mistress's orders. Thereupon he maintained that the grate did not want scrubbing. The girl took this to be a matter of opinion, not a challenge to controversy, and continued her work in silence. Irritated by the noise, but anxious not to seem harsh, he said: "What on earth are you about, when there was no fire there yesterday?"

"There ain't no stuff for afire now, sir," said she.

"I tell you I did not light it."

"It's been and lit itself then," she mumbled.

"Do you mean to say you found the fire burnt out, when you entered the room this morning?"

She answered that she had found it so, and lots of burnt paper lying about.

The symbolism of this fire burnt out, that had warmed and cheered none, oppressed his fancy, and he left the small maid-of-all-work to triumph with black-lead and brushes.

She sang out, when she had done: "If you please, sir, missus have had a hamper up from the country, and would you like a country aig, which is quite fresh, and new lay. And missus say, she can't trust the bloaters about here bein' Yarmouth, but there's a soft roe in one she've squeezed; and am I to stop a water-cress woman, when the last one sold you them, and all the leaves jellied behind 'em, so as no washin' could save you from swallowin' some, missus say?"

Sir Purcell rolled over on his side. "Is this going to be my epitaph?" he groaned; for he was not a man particular in his diet, or exacting in choice of roes, or panting for freshness in an egg. He wondered what his landlady could mean by sending up to him, that morning of all others, to tempt his appetite after her fashion. "I thought I remembered eating nothing but toast in this place;" he observed to himself. A grunting answer had to be given to the little maid, "Toast as usual." She appeared satisfied, but returned again, when he was in his bath, to ask whether he had said "No toast to-day?"

"Toast till the day of my death—tell your mistress that!" he replied; and partly from shame at his unaccountable vehemence, he paused in his sponging, meditated, and chilled. An association of toast with spectral things grew in his mind, when presently the girl's voice was heard: "Please, sir, did say you'd have toast, or not, this morning?" It cost him an effort to answer simply, "Yes."

That she should continue, "Not sir?" appeared like perversity. "No aig?" was maddening.

"Well, no; never mind it this morning," said he.

"Not this morning," she repeated.

"Then it will not be till the day of your death, as you said," she is thinking that, was the idea running in his brain, and he was half ready to cry out "Stop," and renew his order for toast, that he might seem consecutive. The childishness of the wish made him ask himself what it mattered. "I said 'Not till the day;' so, none to-day would mean that I have reached the day." Shivering with the wet on his pallid skin, he thought this over.

His landlady had used her discretion, and there was toast on the table. A beam of Spring's morning sunlight illuminated the toast-rack. He sat, and ate, and munched the doubt whether "not till" included the final day, or stopped short of it. By this the state of his brain may be conceived. A longing for beauty, and a dark sense of an incapacity to thoroughly enjoy it, tormented him. He sent for his landlady's canary, and the ready shrill song of the bird persuaded him that much of the charm of music is wilfully swelled by ourselves, and can be by ourselves withdrawn: that is to say, the great chasm and spell of sweet sounds is assisted by the force of our imaginations. What is that force?—the heat and torrent of the blood. When that exists no more—to one without hope, for instance—what is music or beauty? Intrinsically, they are next to nothing. He argued it out so, and convinced himself of his own delusions, till his hand, being in the sunlight, gave him a pleasant warmth. "That's something we all love," he said, glancing at the blue sky above the roofs. "But there's little enough of it in this climate," he thought, with an eye upon the darker corners of his room. When he had eaten, he sent word to his landlady to make up his week's bill. The week was not at an end, and that good woman appeased before him, astonished, saying: "To be sure, your habits is regular, but there's little items one I'll guess at, and how make out a bill, Sir Purcy, and no items?"

He nodded his head.

"The country again?" she asked smilingly.

"I am going down there," he said.

"And beautiful at this time of the year, it is! though, for market gardening, London beats any country I ever knew; and if you like creature comforts, I always say, stop in London! And then the policemen! who really are the greatest comfort of all to us poor women, and seem sent from above especially to protect our weakness. I do assure you, Sir Purcy, I feel it, and never knew a right-minded woman that did not. And how on earth our grandmothers contrived to get about without them! But there! people who lived before us do seem like the most uncomfortable! When—my goodness! we come to think there was some lived before tea! Why, as I say over almost every cup I drink, it ain't to be realized. It seems almost wicked to say it, Sir Purcy; but it's my opinion there ain't a Christian woman who's not made more of a Christian through her tea. And a man who beats his wife my first question is, 'Do he take his tea regular?' For, depend upon it, that man is not a tea-drinker at all."

He let her talk away, feeling oddly pleased by this mundane chatter, as was she to pour forth her inmost sentiments to a baronet.

When she said: "Your fire shall be lighted to-night to welcome you," the man looked up, and was going to request that the trouble might be spared, but he nodded. His ghost saw the burning fire awaiting him. Or how if it sparkled merrily, and he beheld it with his human eyes that night? His beloved would then have touched him with her hand—yea, brought the dead to life! He jumped to his feet, and dismissed the worthy dame. On both sides of him, 'Yes,' and 'No,' seemed pressing like two hostile powers that battled for his body. They shrieked in his ears, plucked at his fingers. He heard them hushing deeply as he went to his pistol-case, and drew forth one—he knew not which.

CHAPTER LVI

AN ADVANCE AND A CHECK

On a wild April morning, Emilia rose from her bed and called to mind a day of the last year's Spring when she had watched the cloud streaming up, and felt that it was the curtain of an unknown glory. But now it wore the aspect of her life itself, with nothing hidden behind those stormy folds, save peace. South-westward she gazed, eyeing eagerly the struggle of twisting vapour; long flying edges of silver went by, and mounds of faint crimson, and here and there a closing space of blue, swift as a thought of home to a soldier in action. The heavens were like a battle-field. Emilia shut her lips hard, to check an impulse of prayer for Merthyr fighting in Italy: for he was in Italy, and she once more among the Monmouth hills: he was in Italy fighting, and she chained here to her miserable promise! Three days after she had given the promise to Wilfrid, Merthyr left, shaking her hand like any common friend. Georgiana remained, by his desire, to protect her. Emilia had written to Wilfrid for release, but being no apt letter-writer, and hating the task, she was soon involved by him in a complication of bewildering sentiments, some of which she supposed she was bound to feel, while perhaps one or two she did feel, at the summons. The effect was that she lost the true wording of her blunt petition for release: she could no longer put it bluntly. But her heart revolted the more, and gave her sharp eyes to see into his selfishness. The purgatory of her days with Georgiana, when the latter was kept back from her brother in his peril, spurred Emilia to renew her appeal; but she found that all she said drew her into unexpected traps and pitfalls. There was only one thing she could say plainly: "I want to go." If she repeated this, Wilfrid was ready with citations from her letters, wherein she had said 'this,' and 'that,' and many other phrases. His epistolary power and skill in arguing his own case were creditable to him. Affected as Emilia was by other sensations, she could not combat the idea strenuously suggested by him, that he had reason to complain of her behaviour. He admitted his special faults, but, by distinctly tracing them to their origin, he complacently hinted the excuse for them. Moreover, and with artistic ability, he painted such a sentimental halo round the 'sacredness of her pledged word,' that Emilia could not resist a superstitious notion about it, and about what the breaking of it would imply. Georgiana had removed her down to Monmouth to be out of his way. A constant flight of letters pursued them both, for Wilfrid was far too clever to allow letters in his hand-writing to come for one alone of two women shut up in a country-house together. He saw how the letterless one would sit speculating shrewdly and spitefully; so he was careful to amuse his mystified Dragon, while he drew nearer and nearer to his gold apple. Another object was, that by getting Georgiana to consent to become in part his confidante, he made it almost a point of honour for her to be secret with Lady Charlotte.

At last a morning came with no Brookfield letter for either of them. The letters stopped from that time. It was almost as if a great buzzing had ceased in Emilia's ears, and she now heard her own sensations clearly. To Georgiana's surprise, she manifested no apprehension or regret. "Or else," the lady thought, "she wears a mask to me;" and certainly it was a pale face that Emilia was beginning to wear. At last came April and its wild morning. No little female hypocrisies passed between them when they met; they shook hands at arm's length by the breakfast-table. Then Emilia said: "I am ready to go to Italy: I will go at once."

Georgiana looked straight at her, thinking: "This is a fit of indignation with Wilfrid." She answered: "Italy! I fancied you had forgotten there was such a country."

"I don't forget my country and my friends," said Emilia.

"At least, I must ask the ground of so unexpected a resolution," was rejoined.

"Do you remember what Merthyr wrote in his letter from Arona? How long it takes to understand the meaning of some, words! He says that I should not follow an impulse that is not the impulse of all my nature—myself altogether. Yes! I know what that means now. And he tells me that my life is worth more than to be bound to the pledge of a silly moment. It is! He, Georgey, unkind that you are!—he does not distrust me; but always advises and helps me: Merthyr waits for me. I cannot be instantly ready for every meaning in the world. What I want to do, is to see Wilfrid: if not, I will write to him. I will tell him that I intend to break my promise."

A light of unaffected pride shone from the girl's face, as she threw down this gauntlet to sentimentalism.

"And if he objects?" said Georgiana.

"If he objects, what can happen? If he objects by letter, I am gone. I shall not write for permission. I shall write what my will is. If I see him, and he objects, I can look into his eyes and say what I think right. Why, I have lived like a frozen thing ever since I gave him my word. I have felt at times like a snake hissing at my folly. I think I have felt something like men when they swear."

Georgiana's features expressed a slight but perceptible disgust. Emilia continued humbly: "Forgive me. I wish you to know how I hate the word I gave that separates me from Merthyr in my Italy, and makes you dislike your poor Emilia. You do. I have pardoned it, though it was twenty stabs a day."

"But, why, if this promise was so hateful to you, did you not break it before?" asked Georgiana.

"I had not the courage," Emilia stooped her head to confess; "and besides," she added, curiously half-closing her eyelids, as one does to look on a minute object, "I could not see through it before."

"If," suggested Georgiana, "you break your word, you release him from his."

"No! if he cannot see the difference," cried Emilia, wildly, "then let him keep away from me for ever, and he shall not have the name of friend! Is there no difference—I wish you would let me cry out as they do in Shakespeare, Georgey!" Emilia laughed to cover her vehemence. "I want something more than our way of talking, to witness that there is such a difference between us. Am I to live here till all my feelings are burnt out, and my very soul is only a spark in a log of old wood? and to keep him from murdering my countrymen, or flogging the women of Italy! God knows what those Austrians would make him do. He changes. He would easily become an Austrian. I have heard him once or twice, and if I had shut my eyes, I might have declared an Austrian spoke. I wanted to keep him here, but it is not right that I—I should be caged till I scarcely feel my finger-ends, or know that I breathe sensibly as you and others do. I am with Merthyr. That is what I intend to tell him."

She smiled softly up to Georgiana's cold eyes, to get a look of forgiveness for her fiery speaking.

"So, then, you love my brother?" said Georgiana.

Emilia could have retorted, "Cruel that you are!" The pain of having an unripe feeling plucked at without warning, was bitter; but she repressed any exclamation, in her desire to maintain simple and unsensational relations always with those surrounding her.

"He is my friend," she said. "I think of something better than that other word. Oh, that I were a man, to call him my brother-in-arms! What's a girl's love in return for his giving his money, his heart, and offering his life every day for Italy?"

As soon as Georgiana could put faith in her intention to depart, she gave her a friendly hand and embrace.

Two days later they were at Richford, with Lady Gosstre. The journals were full of the Italian uprising. There had been a collision between the Imperial and patriotic forces, near Brescia, from which the former had retired in some confusion. Great things were expected of Piedmont, though many, who had reason to know him, distrusted her king. All Lombardy awaited the signal from Piedmont. Meanwhile blood was flowing.

In the excitement of her sudden rush from dead monotony to active life, Emilia let some time pass before she wrote to Wilfrid. Her letter was in her hand, when one was brought in to her from him. It ran thus:—

"I have just returned home, and what is this I hear? Are you utterly faithless? Can I not rely on you to keep the word you have solemnly pledged! Meet me at once. Name a place. I am surrounded by misery and distraction. I will tell you all when we meet. I have trusted that you were firm. Write instantly. I cannot ask you to come here. The house is broken up. There is no putting to paper what has happened. My father lies helpless. Everything rests on me. I thought that I could rely on you."

Emilia tore up her first letter, and replied:—

"Come here at once. Or, if you would wish to meet me elsewhere, it shall be where you please: but immediately. If you have heard that I am going to Italy, it is true. I break my promise. I shall hope to have your forgiveness. My heart bleeds for my dear Cornelia, and I am eager to see my sisters, and embrace them, and share their sorrow. If I must not come, tell them I kiss them. Adieu!"

Wilfrid replied:—

"I will be by Richford Park gates to-morrow at a quarter to nine. You speak of your heart. I suppose it is a habit. Be careful to put on a cloak or thick shawl; we have touches of frost. If I cannot amuse you, perhaps the nightingales will. Do you remember those of last year? I wonder whether we shall hear the same?—we shall never hear the same."

This iteration, whether cunningly devised or not, had a charm for Emilia's ear. She thought: "I had forgotten all about them." When she was in her bedroom at night, she threw up her window. April was leaning close upon May, and she had not to wait long before a dusky flutter of low notes, appearing to issue from the great rhododendron bank across the lawn, surprised her. She listened, and another little beginning was heard, timorous, shy, and full of mystery for her. The moon hung over branches, some that showed young buds, some still bare. Presently the long, rich, single notes cut the air, and melted to their glad delicious chuckle. The singer was answered from a farther bough, and again from one. It grew to be a circle of melody round Emilia at the open window. Was it the same as last year's? The last year's lay in her memory faint and well-nigh unawakened. There was likewise a momentary sense of unreality in this still piping peacefulness, while Merthyr stood in a bloody-streaked field, fronting death. And yet the song was sweet. Emilia clasped her arms, shut her eyes, and drank it in. Not to think at all, or even to brood on her sensations, but to rest half animate and let those divine sounds find a way through her blood, was medicine to her.

Next day there were numerous visits to the house. Emilia was reserved, and might have been thought sad, but she welcomed Tracy Runningbrook gladly, with "Oh! my old friend!" and a tender squeeze of his hand.

"True, if you like; hot, if you like; but I old?" cried Tracy.

"Yes, because I seem to have got to the other side of you; I mean, I know you, and am always sure of you," said Emilia. "You don't care for music; I don't care for poetry, but we're friends, and I am quite certain of you, and think you 'old friend' always."

"And I," said Tracy, better up to the mark by this time, "I think of you, you dear little woman, that I ought to be grateful to you, for, by heaven! you give me, every time I see you, the greatest temptation to be a fool and let me prove that I'm not. Altro! altro!"

"A fool!" said Emilia caressingly; showing that his smart insinuation had slipped by her.

The tale of Brookfield was told over again by Tracy, and Emilia shuddered, though Merthyr and her country held her heart and imagination active and in suspense, from moment to moment. It helped mainly to discolour the young world to her eyes. She was under the spell of an excitement too keen and quick to be subdued, by the sombre terrors of a tragedy enacted in a house that she had known. Brookfield was in the talk of all who came to Richford. Emilia got the vision of the wretched family seated in the library as usual, when upon midnight they were about to part, and a knock came at the outer door, and two men entered the hall, bearing a lifeless body with a red spot above the heart. She saw Cornelia fall to it. She saw the pale-faced family that had given her shelter, and moaned for lack of a way of helping them and comforting them. She reproached herself for feeling her own full physical life so warmly, while others whom she had loved were weeping. It was useless to resist the tide of fresh vitality in her veins, and when her thoughts turned to their main attraction, she was rejoicing at the great strength she felt coming to her gradually. Her face was smooth and impassive: this new joy of strength came on her like the flowing of a sea to a land-locked water. "Poor souls!" she sighed for her friends, while irrepressible exultation filled her spirit.

That afternoon, in the midst of packing and preparations for the journey, at all of which Lady Gosstre smiled with a complacent bewilderment, a card, bearing the name of Miss Laura Tinley, was sent up to Emilia. She had forgotten this person, and asked Lady Gosstre who it was. Arabella's rival presented herself most winningly. For some time, Emilia listened to her, with wonder that a tongue should be so glib on matters of no earthly interest. At last, Laura said in an undertone: "I am the bearer of a message from Mr. Pericles; do you walk at all in the garden?"

Emilia read her look, and rose. Her thoughts struck back on the creature that she was when she had last seen Mr. Pericles, and again, by contrast, on what she was now. Eager to hear of him, or rather to divine the mystery in her bosom aroused by the unexpected mention of his name, she was soon alone with Laura in the garden.

"Oh, those poor Poles!" Laura began.

"You were going to say something of Mr. Pericles," said Emilia.

"Yes, indeed, my dear; but, of course, you have heard all the details of that dreadful night? It cannot be called a comfort to us that it enables my brother Albert to come forward in the most disinterested—I might venture to say, generous—manner, and prove the chivalry of his soul; still, as things are, we are glad, after such misunderstandings, to prove to that sorely-tried family who are their friends. I—you would little think so from their treatment of me—I was at school with them. I knew them before they became unintelligible, though they always had a turn for it. To dress well, to be refined, to marry well—I understand all that perfectly; but who could understand them? Not they themselves, I am certain! And now penniless! and not only that, but lawyers! You know that Mrs. Chump has commenced an action?—no? Oh, yes! but I shall have to tell you the whole story."

"What is it?—they want money?" said Emilia.

"I will tell you. Our poor gentlemanly organist, whom you knew, was really a baronet's son, and inherited the title."

Emilia interrupted her: "Oh, do let me hear about them!"

"Well, my dear, this unfortunate—I may call him 'lover,' for if a man does not stamp the truth of his affection with a pistol, what other means has he? And just a word as to romance. I have been sighing for it—no one would think so—all my life. And who would have thought that these poor Poles should have lived to convince me of the folly! Oh, delicious humdrum!—there is nothing like it. But you are anxious, naturally. Poor Sir Purcell Barren—he may or may not have been mad, but when he was brought to the house at Brookfield—quite by chance—I mean, his body—two labouring men found him by a tree—I don't know whether you remembered a pollard-willow that stood all white and rotten by the water in the fir-wood:—well, as I said, mad or not, no sooner did poor Cornelia see him than she shrieked that she was the cause of his death. He was laid in the hall—which I have so often trod! and there Cornelia sat by his poor dead body, and accused Wilfrid and her father of every unkindness. They say that the scene was terrible. Wilfrid—but I need not tell you his character. He flutters from flower to flower, but he has feeling Now comes the worst of all—in one sense; that is, looking on it as people of the world; and being in the world, we must take a worldly view occasionally. Mr. Pole—you remember how he behaved once at Besworth: or, no; you were not there, but he used your name. His mania was, as everybody could see, to marry his children grandly. I don't blame him in any way. Still, he was not justified in living beyond his means to that end, speculating rashly, and concealing his actual circumstances. Well, Mr. Pericles and he were involved together; that is, Mr. Pericles—"

"Is Mr. Pericles near us now?" said Emilia quickly.

"We will come to him," Laura resumed, with the complacency of one who saw a goodly portion of the festival she was enjoying still before her. "I was going to say, Mr. Pericles had poor Mr. Pole in his power; has him, would be the correcter tense. And Wilfrid, as you may have heard, had really grossly insulted him, even to the extent of maltreating him—a poor foreigner—rich foreigner, if you like! but not capable of standing against a strong young man in wrath. However, now there can be little doubt that Wilfrid repents. He had been trying ever since to see Mr. Pericles; and the very morning of that day, I believe, he saw him and humbled himself to make an apology. This had put Mr. Pole in good spirits, and in the evening—he and Mrs. Chump were very fond of their wine after dinner—he was heard that very evening to name a day for his union with her; for that had been quite understood, and he had asked his daughters and got their consent. The sight of Sir Purcell's corpse, and the cries of Cornelia, must have turned him childish. I cannot conceive a situation so harrowing as that of those poor children hearing their father declare himself an impostor! a beggar! a peculator! He cried, poor unhappy man, real tears! The truth was that his nerves suddenly gave way. For, just before—only just before, he was smiling and talking largely. He wished to go on his knees to every one of them, and kept telling them of his love—the servants all awake and listening! and more gossiping servants than the Poles always, by the most extraordinary inadvertence, managed to get, you never heard of! Nothing would stop him from humiliating himself! No one paid any attention to Mrs. Chump until she started from her chair. They say that some of the servants who were crying outside, positively were compelled to laugh when they heard her first outbursts. And poor Mr. Pole confessed that he had touched her money. He could not tell her how much. Fancy such a scene, with a dead man in the house! Imagination almost refuses to conjure it up! Not to dwell on it too long—for, I have never endured such a shock as it has given me—Mrs. Chump left the house, and the next thing received from her was a lawyer's letter. Business men say she is not to blame: women may cherish their own opinion. But, oh, Miss Belloni! is it not terrible? You are pale."

Emilia behind what she felt for her friends, had a dim comprehension of the meaning of their old disgust at Laura, during this narration. But, hearing the word of pity, she did not stop to be critical. "Can you do nothing for them?" she said abruptly.

The thought in Laura's shocked grey eyes was, "They have done little enough for you," i.e., toward making you a lady. "Oh!" she cried; "I can you teach me what to do? I must be extremely delicate, and calculate upon what they would accept from me. For—so I hear—they used to—and may still—nourish a—what I called—silly—though not in unkindness—hostility to our family—me. And perhaps now natural delicacy may render it difficult for them to..."

In short, to accept an alms from Laura Tinley; so said her pleading look for an interpretation.

"You know Mr. Pericles," said Emilia, "he can do the mischief—can he not? Stop him."

Laura laughed. "One might almost say that you do not know him, Miss Belloni. What is my influence? I have neither a voice, nor can I play on any instrument. I would—indeed I will—do my best my utmost; only, how even to introduce the subject to him? Are not you the person? He speaks of you constantly. He has consulted doctors with regard to your voice, and the only excuse, dear Miss Belloni, for my visit to you to-day, is my desire that any misunderstanding between you may be cleared. Because, I have just heard—Miss Belloni will forgive me!—the origin of it; and tidings coming that you were in the neighbourhood, I thought—hoped that I might be the means of re-uniting two evidently destined to be of essential service to one another. And really, life means that, does it not?"

Emilia was becoming more critical of this tone the more she listened. She declared, her immediate willingness to meet Mr. Pericles. With which, and Emilia's assurance that she would write, and herself make the appointment, Laura retired, in high glee at the prospect of winning the gratitude of the inscrutable millionaire. It was true that the absence of any rivalry for the possession of the man took much of his sweetness from him. She seemed to be plucking him from the hands of the dead, and half recognized that victory over uncontesting rivals claps the laurel-wreath rather rudely upon our heads.

Emilia lost no time in running straight to Georgiana, who was busy at her writing-desk. She related what she had just heard, ending breathlessly: "Georgey! my dear! will you help them?"

"In what possible way can I do so?" said Georgiana. "To-morrow night we shall have left England."

"But to-day we are here." Emilia pressed a hand to her bosom: "my heart feels hollow, and my friends cry out in it. I cannot let him suffer." She looked into Georgiana's eyes. "Will you not help them?—they want money."

The lady reddened. "Is it not preposterous to suppose that I can offer them assistance of such a kind?"

"Not you," returned Emilia, sighing; and in an under-breath, "me—will you lend it to me? Merthyr would. I shall repay it. I cannot tell what fills me with this delight, but I know I am able to repay any sum. Two thousand pounds would help them. I think—I think my voice has come back."

"Have you tried it?" said Georgiana, to produce a diversion from the other topic.

"No; but believe me when I tell you, it must be. I scarcely feel the floor; no misery touches me. I am only sorry for my friends, not down on the ground with them. Believe me! And I have been studying all this while. I have not lost an hour. I would accept a part, and step on the boards within a week, and be certain to succeed. I am just as willing to go to the Conservatorio and submit to discipline. Only, dear friend, believe me, that I ask for money now, because I am sure I can repay it. I want to send it immediately, and then, good-bye to England."

Georgiana closed her desk. She had been suspicious at first of another sentiment in the background, but was now quite convinced of the simplicity of Emilia's design. She said: "I will tell you exactly how I am placed. I do not know, that under any circumstances, I could have given into your hands so large a sum as this that you ask for. My brother has a fortune; and I have also a little property. When I say my brother has a fortune, he has the remains of one. All that has gone has been devoted to relieve your countrymen, and further the interests he has nearest at heart. What is left to him, I believe, he has now thrown into the gulf. You have heard Lady Charlotte call him a fanatic."

Emilia's lip quivered.

"You must not blame her for that," Georgiana continued. "Lady Gosstre thinks much the same. The world thinks with them. I love him, and prove my love by trusting him, and wish to prove my love by aiding him, and being always at hand to succour, as I should be now, but that I obeyed his dearest wish in resting here to watch over you. I am his other self. I have taught him to feel that; so that in his devotion to this cause he may follow every impulse he has, and still there is his sister to fall back on. My child! see what I have been doing. I have been calculating here." Georgiana took a scroll from her desk, and laid it under Emilia's eyes. "I have reckoned our expenses as far as Turin, and have only consented to take Lady Gosstre's valet for courier, just to please her. I know that he will make the cost double, and I feel like a miser about money. If Merthyr is ruined, he will require every farthing that I have for our common subsistence. Now do you understand? I can hardly put the case more plainly. It is out of my power to do what you ask me to do."

Emilia sighed lightly, and seemed not much cast down by the refusal. She perceived that it was necessarily positive, and like all minds framed to resolve to action, there was an instantaneous change of the current of her thoughts in another direction.

"Then, my darling, my one prayer!" she said. "Postpone our going for a week. I will try to get help for them elsewhere."

Georgiana was pleased by Emilia's manner of taking the rebuff; but it required an altercation before she consented to this postponement; she nodded her head finally in anger.

CHAPTER LVII

CONTAINS A FURTHER ANATOMY OF WILFRID

By the park-gates that evening, Wilfrid received a letter from the hands of Tracy Runningbrook. It said: "I am not able to see you now. When I tell you that I will see you before I leave England, I insist upon your believing me. I have no head for seeing anybody now. Emilia"—was the simple signature, perused over and over again by this maddened lover, under the flitting gate-lamp, after Tracy had left him. The coldness of Emilia's name so briefly given, concentrated every fire in his heart. What was it but miserable cowardice, he thought, that prevented him from getting the peace poor Barrett had found? Intolerable anguish weakened his limbs. He flung himself on a wayside bank, grovelling, to rise again calm and quite ready for society, upon the proper application of the clothes-brush. Indeed; he patted his shoulder and elbow to remove the soil of his short contact with earth, and tried a cigar: but the first taste of the smoke sickened his lips. Then he stood for a moment as a man in a new world. This strange sensation of disgust with familiar comforting habits, fixed him in perplexity, till a rushing of wild thoughts and hopes from brain to heart, heart to brain, gave him insight, and he perceived his state, and that for all he held to in our life he was dependent upon another; which is virtually the curse of love.

"And he passed along the road," adds the Philosopher, "a weaker man, a stronger lover. Not that love should diminish manliness or gains by so doing; but travelling to love by the ways of Sentiment, attaining to the passion bit by bit, does full surely take from us the strength of our nature, as if (which is probable) at every step we paid fee to move forward. Wilfrid had just enough of the coin to pay his footing. He was verily fining himself down. You are tempted to ask what the value of him will be by the time that he turns out pure metal? I reply, something considerable, if by great sacrifice he gets to truth—gets to that oneness of feeling which is the truthful impulse. At last, he will stand high above them that have not suffered. The rejection of his cigar."

This wages too absurd. At the risk of breaking our partnership for ever, I intervene. My Philosopher's meaning is plain, and, as usual, good; but not even I, who have less reason to laugh at him than anybody, can gravely accept the juxtaposition of suffering and cigars. And, moreover, there is a little piece of action in store.

Wilfrid had walked half way to Brookfield, when the longing to look upon the Richford chamber-windows stirred so hotly within him that he returned to the gates. He saw Captain Gambier issuing on horseback from under the lamp. The captain remarked that it was a fine night, and prepared to ride off, but Wilfrid requested him to dismount, and his voice had the unmistakeable ring in it by which a man knows that there must be no trifling. The captain leaned forward to look at him before he obeyed the summons, All self-control had abandoned Wilfrid in the rage he felt at Gambier's having seen Emilia, and the jealous suspicion that she had failed to keep her appointment for the like reason.

"Why do you come here?" he said, hoarsely.

"By Jove! that's an odd question," said the captain, at once taking his ground.

"Am I to understand that you've been playing with my sister, as you do with every other woman?"

Captain Gambier murmured quietly, "Every other woman?" and smoothed his horse's neck. "They're not so easily played with, my dear fellow. You speak like a youngster."

"I am the only protector of my sister's reputation," said Wilfrid, "and, by heaven! if you have cast her over to be the common talk, you shall meet me."

The captain turned to his horse, saying, "Oh! Well!" Being mounted, he observed: "My dear Pole, you might have sung out all you had to say. Go to your sister, and if she complains of my behaviour, I'll meet you. Oh, yes! I'll meet you; I have no objection to excitement. You're in the hands of an infernally clever woman, who does me the honour to wish to see my blood on the carpet, I believe; but if this is her scheme, it's not worthy of her ability. She began pretty well. She arranged the preliminaries capitally. Why, look here," he relinquished his ordinary drawl; "I'll tell you something, which you may put down in my favour or not—just as you like. That woman did her best to compromise your sister with me on board the yacht. I can't tell you how, and won't. Of course, I wouldn't if I could; but I have sense enough to admire a very charming person, and I did the only honourable thing in my power. It's your sister, my good fellow, who gave me my dismissal. We had a little common sense conversation—in which she shines. I envy the man that marries her, but she denies me such luck. There! if you want to shoot me for my share in that transaction, I'll give you your chance: and if you do, my dear Pole, either you must be a tremendous fool, or that woman's ten times cleverer than I thought. You know where to find me. Good night."

The captain gave heel to his horse, hearing no more.

Adela confirmed to Wilfrid what Gambier had spoken; and that it was she who had given him his dismissal. She called him by his name, "Augustus," in a kindly tone, remarking, that Lady Charlotte had persecuted him dreadfully. "Poor Augustus! his entire reputation for evil is owing to her black paint-brush. There is no man so easily 'hooked,' as Mrs. Bayruffle would say, as he, though he has but eight hundred a year: barely enough to live on. It would have been cruel of me to keep him, for if he is in love, it's with Emilia."

Wilfrid here took upon himself to reproach her for a certain negligence of worldly interests. She laughed and blushed with humorous satisfaction; and, on second thoughts, he changed his opinion, telling her that he wished he could win his freedom as she had done.

"Wilfrid," she said suddenly, "will you persuade Cornelia not to wear black?"

"Yes, if you wish it," he replied.

"You will, positively? Then listen, dear. I don't like the prospect of your alliance with Lady Charlotte."

Wilfrid could not repress a despondent shrug.

"But you can get released," she cried; and ultimately counselled him: "Mention the name of Lord Eltham before her once, when you are alone. Watch the result. Only, don't be clumsy. But I need not tell you that."

For hours he cudgelled his brains to know why she desired Cornelia not to wear black, and when the light broke in on him he laughed like a jolly youth for an instant. The reason why was in a web so complicated, that, to have divined what hung on Cornelia's wearing of black, showed a rare sagacity and perception of character on the little lady's part. As thus:—Sir Twickenham Pryme is the most sensitive of men to ridicule and vulgar tattle: he has continued to visit the house, learning by degrees to prefer me, but still too chivalrous to withdraw his claim to Cornelia, notwithstanding that he has seen indications of her not too absolute devotion towards him:—I have let him become aware that I have broken with Captain Gambier (whose income is eight hundred a year merely), for the sake of a higher attachment:

now, since the catastrophe, he can with ease make it appear to the world that I was his choice from the first, seeing that Cornelia will assuredly make no manner of objection:—but, if she, with foolish sentimental persistence, assumes the garb of sorrow, then Sir Twickenham's ears will tingle; he will retire altogether; he will not dare to place himself in a position which will lend a colour to the gossip, that jilted by one sister, he flew for consolation to the other; jilted, too, for the mere memory of a dead man! an additional insult!

Exquisite intricacy! Wilfrid worked through all the intervolutions, and nearly forgot his wretchedness in admiration of his sister's mental endowments. He was the more willing to magnify them, inasmuch as he thereby strengthened his hope that liberty would follow the speaking of the talismanic name of Eltham to Lady Charlotte, alone. He had come to look upon her as the real barrier between himself and Emilia.

"I think we have brains," he said softly, on his pillow, upon a review of the beggared aspect of his family; and he went to sleep with a smile on his face.

CHAPTER LVIII

FROST ON THE MAY NIGHT

A sharp breath of air had passed along the dews, and all the young green of the fresh season shone in white jewels. The sky, set with very dim distant stars, was in grey light round a small brilliant moon. Every space of earth lifted clear to her; the woodland listened; and in the bright silence the nightingales sang loud.

Emilia and Tracy Runningbrook were threading their way toward a lane over which great oak branches intervolved; thence under larches all with glittering sleeves, and among spiky brambles, with the purple leaf and the crimson frosted. The frost on the edges of the brown-leaved bracken gave a faint colour. Here and there, intense silver dazzled their eyes. As they advanced amid the icy hush, so hard and instant was the ring of the earth under them, their steps sounded as if expected.

"This night seems made for me!" said Emilia.

Tracy had no knowledge of the object of the expedition. He was her squire simply; had pitched on a sudden into an enamoured condition, and walked beside her, caring little whither he was led, so that she left him not.

They came upon a clearing in the wood where a tournament of knights might have been held. Ranged on two sides were rows of larches, and forward, fit to plume a dais, a clump of tall firs stood with a flowing silver fir to right and left, and the white stems of the birch-tree shining from among them. This fair woodland court had three broad oaks, as for gateways; and the moon was above it. Moss and the frosted brown fern were its flooring.

Emilia said eagerly, "This way," and ran under one of the oaks. She turned to Tracy following: "There is no doubt of it." Her hand was lying softly on her throat.

"Your voice?" Tracy divined her.

She nodded, but frowned lovingly at the shout he raised, and he understood that there was haply some plot to be worked out. The open space was quite luminous in the middle of those three deep walls of shadow. Emilia enjoined him to rest where he was, and wait for her on that spot like a faithful sentinel, whatsoever ensued. Coaxing his promise, she entered the square of white light alone. Presently she stood upon a low mound, so that her whole figure was distinct, while the moon made her features visible.

Expectancy sharpened the stillness to Tracy's ears. A nightingale began the charm. He was answered by another. Many were soon in song, till even the pauses were sweet with them. Tracy had the thought that they were calling for Emilia to commence; that it was nature preluding the divine human voice, weaving her spell for it. He was seized by a thirst to hear the adorable girl, who stood there patiently, with her face lifted soft in moonlight. And then the blood thrilled along his veins, as if one more than mortal had touched him. It seemed to him long before he knew that Emilia's voice was in the air.

In such a place, at such a time, there is no wizardry like a woman's voice. Emilia had gained in force and fulness. She sang with a stately fervour, letting the notes flow from her breast, while both her arms hung loose, and not a gesture escaped her. Tracy's fiery imagination set him throbbing, as to the voice of the verified spirit of the place. He heard nothing but Emilia, and scarce felt that it was she, or that tears were on his eyelids, till her voice sank richly, deep into the bosom of the woods. Then the stillness, like one folding up a precious jewel, seemed to pant audibly.

"She's not alone!" This was human speech at his elbow, uttered in some stupefied amazement. In an extremity of wrath, Tracy turned about to curse the intruder, and discerned Wilfrid, eagerly bent forward on the other side of the oak by which he leaned. Advancing toward Emilia, two figures were seen. Mr. Pericles in his bearskin was easily to be distinguished. His companion was Laura Tinley. The Greek moved at rapid strides, and coming near upon Emilia, raised his hands as in exclamation. At once he disencumbered his shoulders of the enormous wrapper, held it aloft imperiously, and by main force extinguished Emilia. Laura's shrill laugh resounded.

"Oh! beastly bathos!" Tracy groaned in his heart. "Here we are down in Avernus in a twinkling!"

There was evidently quick talk going on among the three, after which Emilia, heavily weighted, walked a little apart with Mr. Pericles, who looked lean and lank beside her, and gesticulated in his wildest manner. Tracy glanced about for Wilfrid. The latter was not visible, but, stepping up the bank of sand and moss, appeared a lady in shawl and hat, in whom he recognized Lady Charlotte. He went up to her and saluted.

"Ah! Tracy," she said. "I saw you leave the drawing room, and expected to find you here. So, the little woman has got her voice again; but why on earth couldn't she make the display at Richford? It's very pretty, and I dare say you highly approve of this kind of romantic interlude, Signor Poet, but it strikes me as being rather senseless."

"But, are you alone? What on earth brings you here?" asked Tracy.

"Oh!" the lady shrugged. "I've a guard to the rear. I told her I would come. She said I should hear something to-night, if I did. I fancied naturally the appointment had to do with her voice, and wished to please her. It's only five minutes from the west-postern of the park. Is she going to sing any more? There's company apparently. Shall we go and declare ourselves?"

"I'm on duty, and can't," replied Tracy, and twisting his body in an ecstasy, added: "Did you hear her?"

Lady Charlotte laughed softly. "You speak as if you had taken a hurt, my dear boy. This sort of scene is dangerous to poets. But, I thought you slighted music."

"I don't know whether I'm breathing yet," Tracy rejoined. "She's a Goddess to me from this moment. Not like music? Am I a dolt? She would raise me from the dead, if she sang over me. Put me in a boat, and let her sing on, and all may end! I could die into colour, hearing her! That's the voice they hear in heaven."

"When they are good, I suppose," the irreverent lady appended. "What's that?" And she held her head to listen.

Emilia's mortal tones were calling Wilfrid's name. The lady became grave, as with keen eyes she watched the open space, and to a second call Wilfrid presented himself in a leisurely way from under cover of the trees; stepping into the square towards the three, as one equal to all occasions, and specially prepared for this. He was observed to bow to Mr. Pericles, and the two men extended hands, Laura Tinley standing decently away from them.

Lady Charlotte could not contain her mystification. "What does it mean?" she said. "Wilfrid was to be in town at the Ambassador's to-night! He wrote to me at five o'clock from his Club! Is he insane? Has he lost every sense of self-interest? He can't have made up his mind to miss his opportunity, when all the introductions are there! Run, like a good creature, Tracy, and see if that is Wilfrid, and come back and tell me; but don't say I am here."

"Desert my post?" Tracy hugged his arms tight together. "Not if I freeze here!"

The doubt in Lady Charlotte's eyes was transient. She dropped her glass. Visible adieux were being waved between Mr. Pericles and Laura Tinley on the one hand, and Wilfrid and Emilia, on the other. After which, and at a quick pace, manifestly shivering, Mr. Pericles drew Laura into the shadows, and Emilia, clad in the immense bearskin, as with a trailing black barbaric robe, walked toward the oaks. Wilfrid's head was stooped to a level with Emilia's, into whose face he was looking obliviously, while the hot words sprang from his lips. They neared the oak, and Emilia slanted her direction, so as to avoid the neighbourhood of the tree. Tracy felt a sudden grasp of his arm. It was momentary, coming simultaneously with a burst of Wilfrid's voice.

"Do I know what I love, you ask? I love your footprints! Everything you have touched is like fire to me. Emilia! Emilia!"

"Then," came the clear reply, "you do not love Lady Charlotte?"

"Love her!" he shouted scornfully, and subdued his voice to add: "she has a good heart, and whatever scandal is talked of her and Lord Eltham, she is a well-meaning friend. But, love her! You, you I love!"

"Theatrical business," Lady Charlotte murmured, and imagined she had expected it when she promised Emilia she would step out into the night air, as possibly she had.

The lady walked straight up to them.

"Well, little one!" she addressed Emilia; "I am glad you have recovered your voice. You play the game of tit-for-tat remarkably well. We will now sheath our battledores. There is my hand."

The unconquerable aplomb in Lady Charlotte, which Wilfrid always artistically admired, and which always mastered him; the sight of her pale face and courageous eyes; and her choice of the moment to come forward and declare her presence;—all fell upon the furnace of Wilfrid's heart like a quenching flood. In a stupefaction, he confessed to himself that he could say actually nothing. He could hardly look up.

Emilia turned her eyes from the outstretched hand, to the lady's face.

"What will it mean?" she said.

"That we are quits, I presume; and that we bear no malice. At any rate, that I relinquish the field. I like a hand that can deal a good stroke. I conceived you to be a mere little romantic person, and correct my mistake. You win the prize, you see."

"You would have made him an Austrian, and he is now safe from that. I win nothing more," said Emilia.

When Tracy and Emilia stood alone, he cried out in a rapture of praise, "Now I know what a power you have. You may bid me live or die."

The recent scene concerned chiefly the actors who had moved onward: it had touched Emilia but lightly, and him not at all. But, while he magnified the glory of her singing, the imperishable note she had sounded this night, and the power and the triumph that would be hers, Emilia's bosom began to heave, and she checked him with a storm of tears. "Triumph! yes! what is this I have done? Oh, Merthyr, my true hero! He praises me and knows nothing of how false I have been to you. I am a slave! I have sold myself—sold myself!" She dropped her face in her hands, broken with grief. "He fights," she pursued; "he fights for my country. I feel his blood—it seems to run from my body as it runs from his. Not if he is dying—I dare not go to him if he is dying! I am in chains. I have sworn it for money. See what a different man Merthyr is from any on earth! Would he shoot himself for a woman? Would he grow meaner the more he loved her? My hero! my hero! and Tracy, my friend! what is my grief now? Merthyr is my hero, but I hear him—I hear him speaking it into my ears with his own lips, that I do not love him. And it is true. I never should have sold myself for three weary years away from him, if I had loved him. I know it now it is done. I thought more of my poor friends and Wilfrid, than of Merthyr, who bleeds for my country! And he will not spurn me when we meet. Yes, if he lives, he will come to me gentle as a ghost that has seen God!"

She abandoned herself to weeping. Tracy, in a tender reverence for one who could speak such solemn matter spontaneously, supported her, and felt her tears as a rain of flame on his heart.

The nightingales were mute. Not a sound was heard from bough or brake.

CHAPTER LIX

EMILIA'S GOOD-BYE

A wreck from the last Lombard revolt landed upon our shores in June. His right arm was in a sling, and his Italian servant following him, kept close by his side, with a ready hand, as if fearing that at any moment the wounded gentleman's steps might fail. There was no public war going on just then: for which reason he was eyed suspiciously by the rest of the passengers making their way up the beach; who seemed to entertain an impression that he had no business at such a moment to be crippled, and might be put down as one of those foreign fools who stand out for a trifle as targets to fools a little luckier than themselves. Here, within our salt girdle, flourishes common sense. We cherish life; we abhor bloodshed; we have no sympathy with your juvenile points of honour: we are, in short, a civilized people; and seeing that Success has made us what we are, we advise other nations to succeed, or be quiet. Of all of which the gravely-smiling gentleman appeared well aware; for, with an eye that courted none, and a perfectly calm face, he passed through the crowd, only once availing himself of his brown-faced Beppo's spontaneously depressed shoulder when a twinge of pain shooting from his torn foot took his strength away. While he remained in sight, some speculation as to his nationality continued: he had been heard to speak nothing but Italian, and yet the flower of English cultivation was signally manifest in his style and bearing. The purchase of that day's journal, giving information that the Lombard revolt was fully, it was thought finally, crushed out, and the insurgents scattered, hanged, or shot, suggested to a young lady in a group melancholy with luggage, that the wounded gentleman was one who had escaped from the Austrians.

"Only, he is English."

"If he is, he deserves what he's got."

A stout Briton delivered this sentence, and gave in addition a sermon on meddling, short, emphatic, and not uncheerful apparently, if estimated by the hearty laugh that closed it; though a lady remarked, "Oh, dear me! You are very sweeping."

"By George! ma'am," cried the Briton, holding out his newspaper, "here's a leader on the identical subject, with all my views in it! Yes! those Italians are absurd: they never were a people: never agreed. Egad! the only place they're fit for is the stage. Art! if you like. They know all about colouring canvas, and sculpturing. I don't deny 'em their merits, and I don't mind listening to their squalling, now and then: though, I'll tell you what: have you ever noticed the calves of those singers?—I mean, the men. Perhaps not—for they' ve got none. They're sticks, not legs. Who can think much of fellows with such legs? Now, the next time you go to the Italian Opera, notice 'em. Ha! ha!—well, that would sound queer, told at secondhand; but, just look at their legs, ma'am, and ask yourself whether there's much chance for a country that stands on legs like those! Let them paint, and carve blocks, and sing. They're not fit for much else, as far as I can see."

Thus, in the pride of his manliness, the male Briton. A shrill cry drew the attention of this group once more to the person who had just kindly furnished a topic. He had been met on his way by a lady unmistakeably foreign in her appearance. "Marini!" was the word of the cry; and the lady stood with her head bent and her hands stiffened rigidly.

"Lost her husband, I dare say!" the Briton murmured. "Perhaps he's one of the 'hanged, or shot,' in the list here Hanged! shot! Ask those Austrians to be merciful, and that's their reply. Why, good God! it's like the grunt of a savage beast! Hanged! shot!—count how many for one day's work! Ten at Verona; fifteen at Mantua; five—there, stop! If we enter into another alliance with those infernal ruffians!—if they're not branded in the face of Europe as inhuman butchers! if I—by George! if I were an Italian I'd handle a musket myself, and think great guns the finest music going. Mind, if there's a subscription for the widows of these poor fellows, I put down my name; so shall my wife, so shall my daughters, so we will all, down to the baby!"

Merthyr's name was shouted first on his return to England by Mrs. Chump. He was waiting on the platform of the London station for the train to take him to Richford, when, "Oh! Mr. Pow's, Mr. Pow's!" resounded, and Mrs. Chump fluttered before him. She was on her way to Brookfield, she said; and it was, she added, her firm belief that heaven had sent him to her sad, not deeming "that poor creature, Mr. Braintop, there, sufficient for the purpose. For what I've got to go through, among them at Brookfield, Mr. Pow's, it's perf'ctly awful. Mr. Braintop," she turned to the youth, "you may go now. And don't go takin' ship and sailin' for Italy after the little Belloni, for ye haven't a chance—poor fella! though he combs 's hair so careful, Mr. Pow's, and ye might almost laugh and cry together to see how humble he is, and audacious too—all in a lump. For, when little Belloni was in the ship, ye know, and she thinkin', 'not one of my friends near to wave a handkerchief!' behold, there's that boy Braintop just as by maguc, and he wavin' his best, which is a cambric, and a present from myself, and precious wet that night, ye might swear; for the quiet lovers, Mr. Pow's, they cry, they do, buckutsful!"

"And is Miss Belloni gone?" said Merthyr, looking steadily for answer.

"To be sure, sir, she has; but have ye got a squeak of pain? Oh, dear! it makes my blood creep to see a man who's been where there's been firing of shots in a temper. Ye're vary pale, sir."

"She went—on what day?" asked Merthyr.

"Oh! I can't poss'bly tell ye that, Mr. Pow's, havin' affairs of my own most urrgent. But, Mr. Paricles has got her at last. That's certain. Gall'ns of tears has poor Mr. Braintop cried over it, bein' one of the mew-in-a-corner sort of young men, ye know, what never win the garl, but cry enough to float her and the lucky fella too, and off they go, and he left on the shore."

Merthyr looked impatiently out of the window. His wounds throbbed and his forehead was moist.

"With Mr. Pericles?" he queried, while Mrs. Chump was giving him the reasons for the immediate visit to Brookfield.

"They're cap'tal friends again, ye know, Mr. Pow's, Mr. Paricles and Pole; and Pole's quite set up, and yesterday mornin' sends me two thousand pounds—not a penny less! and ye'll believe me, I was in a stiff gape for five minutes when Mr. Braintop shows the money. What a temptation for the young man! But Pole didn't know his love for little Belloni."

"Has she no one with her?" Merthyr seized the opportunity of her name being pronounced to get clear tidings of her, if possible.

"Oh, dear, yes, Mr. Paricles is with her," returned Mrs. Chump. "And, as I was sayin', sir, two thousand pounds! I ran off to my lawyer; for, it'll seem odd to ye, now, Mr. Pow's, that know my 'ffection for the Poles, poor dears, I'd an action against 'em. 'Stop ut,' I cries out to the man: if he'd been one o' them that wears a wig, I couldn't ha' spoken so—'Stop ut,' I cries, not a bit afraid of 'm. I wouldn't let the man go on, for all I want to know is, that I'm not rrooned. And now I've got money, I must have friends; for when I hadn't, ye know, my friends seemed against me, and now I have, it's the world that does, where'll I hide it? Oh, dear! now I'm with you, I don't mind, though this brown-faced forr'ner servant of yours, he gives me shivers. Can he understand English?—becas I've got ut all in my pockut!"

Merthyr sighed wearily for release. At last the train slackened speed, and the well-known fir-country appeared in sight. Mrs. Chump caught him by the arm as he prepared to alight. "Oh! and are ye goin' to let me face the Poles without anyone to lean on in that awful moment, and no one to bear witness how kind I've spoken of 'em. Mr. Pow's! will ye prove that you're a blessed angel, sir, and come, just for five minutes—which is a short time to do a thing for a woman she'll never forget."

"Pray spare me, madam," Merthyr pleaded. "I have much to learn at Richford."

"I cann't spare ye, sir," cried Mrs. Chump. "I cann't go before that fam'ly quite alone. They're a tarr'ble fam'ly. Oh! I'll be goin' on my knees to ye, Mr. Pow's. Weren't ye sent by heaven now? And you to run away! And if you're woundud, won't I have a carr'ge from the station, which'll be grander to go in, and impose on 'em, ye know. Pray, sir! I entreat ye!"

The tears burst from her eyes, and her hot hand clung to his imploringly.

Merthyr was a witness of the return of Mrs. Chump to Brookfield. In that erewhile abode of Fine Shades, the Nice Feelings had foundered. The circle of a year, beginning so fairly for them, enfolded the ladies and their first great scheme of life. Emilia had been a touchstone to this family. They could not know it in their deep affliction, but in manger they had much improved. Their welcome of Mrs. Chump was an admirable seasoning of stateliness with kindness. Cornelia and Arabella took her hand, listening with an incomparable soft smile to her first protestations, which they quieted, and then led her to Mr. Pole; of whom it may be said, that an accomplished coquette could not in his situation have behaved with a finer skill; so that, albeit received back into the house, Mrs. Chump had yet to discover what her footing there was to be, and trembled like the meanest of culprits. Mr. Pole shook her hand warmly, tenderly, almost tearfully, and said to the melted woman: "You're right, Martha; it's much better for us to examine accounts in a friendly way, than to have strangers and lawyers, and what not—people who can't possibly know the whole history, don't you see—meddling and making a scandal; and I'm much obliged to you for coming."

Vainly Mrs. Chump employed alternately innuendo and outcry to make him perceive that her coming involved a softer business, and that to money, she having it now, she gave not a thought. He assured her that in future she must; that such was his express desire; that it was her duty to herself and others. And while saying this, which seemed to indicate that widowhood would be her state as far as he was concerned, he pressed her hand with extreme sweetness, and his bird's-eyes twinkled obligingly. It is to be feared that Mr. Pole had passed the age of improvement, save in his peculiar art. After a time Nature stops, and says to us 'thou art now what thou wilt be.'

Cornelia was in black from neck to foot. She joined the conversation as the others did, and indeed more flowingly than Adela, whose visage was soured. It was Cornelia to whom Merthyr explained his temporary subjection to the piteous appeals of Mrs. Chump. She smiled humorously to reassure him of her perfect comprehension of the apology for his visit, and of his welcome: and they talked, argued a little, differed, until the terrible thought that he talked, and even looked like some one else, drew the blood from her lips, and robbed her pulses of their play. She spoke of Emilia, saying plainly and humbly: "All we have is owing to her." Arabella spoke of Emilia likewise, but with a shade of the foregone tone of patronage. "She will always be our dear little sister." Adela continued silent, as with ears awake for the opening of a door. Was it in ever-thwarted anticipation of the coming of Sir Twickenham?

Merthyr's inquiry after Wilfrid produced a momentary hesitation on Cornelia's Part—"He has gone to Verona. We have an uncle in the Austrian service," she said; and Merthyr bowed.

What was this tale of Emilia, that grew more and more perplexing as he heard it bit by bit? The explanation awaited him at Richford. There, when Georgiana had clasped her brother in one last jealous embrace, she gave him the following letter straightway, to save him, haply, from the false shame of that eager demand for one, which she saw ready to leap to words in his eyes. He read it, sitting in the Richford library alone, while the great rhododendron bloomed outside, above the shaven sunny sward, looking like a monstrous tropic bird alighted to brood an hour in full sunlight.

"My Friend!"

"I would say my Beloved! I will not write it, for it would be false. I have read of the defeat. Why was a battle risked at that cruel place! Here are we to be again for so many years before we can win God to be on our side! And I—do you not know? we used to talk of it!—I never can think it the Devil who has got the upper hand. What succeeds, I always think should succeed—was meant to, because the sky looks clear over it. This knocks a blow at my heart and keeps it silent and only just beating. I feel that you are safe. That, I am thankful for. If you were not, God would warn me, and not let me mock him with thanks when I pray. I pray till my eyelids burn, on purpose to get a warning if there is any black messenger to be sent to me. I do not believe it.

"For three years I am a prisoner. I go to the Conservatorio in Milan with Mr. Pericles, and my poor little mother, who cries, asking me where she will be among such a people, until I wonder she should be my mother. My voice has returned. Oh, Merthyr! my dear, calm friend! to keep calling you friend, and friend, puts me to sleep softly!—Yes, I have my voice. I felt I had it, like some one in a room with us when we will not open our eyes. There was misery everywhere, and yet I was glad. I kept it secret. I began to feel myself above the world. I dreamed of what I would do for everybody. I thought of you least! I tell you so, and take a scourge and scourge myself, for it is true that in her new joy this miserable creature that I am thought of you least. Now I have the punishment!

"My friend! the Poles were at the mercy of Mr. Pericles: Wilfrid had struck him: Mr. Pericles was angry and full of mischief. Those dear people had been kind to me, and I heard they were poor. I felt money in my breast, in my throat, that only wanted coining. I went to Georgiana, and oh! how truly she proved to me that she loves you better than I do. She refused to part with money that you might soon want. I laid a scheme for Mr. Pericles to hear me sing. He heard me, and my scheme succeeded. If Italy knew as well as I, she would never let her voice be heard till she is sure of it:—Yes! from foot to head, I knew it was impossible to fail. If a country means to be free, the fire must run through it and make it feel that certainty. Then—away the whitecoat! I sang, and the man twisted, as if I had bent him in my hand. He rushed to me, and offered me any terms I pleased, if for three years I would go to the Conservatorio at Milan, and learn submissively. It is a little grief to me that I think this man loves music more deeply than

I do. In the two things I love best, the love of others exceeds mine. I named a sum of money—immense! and I desired that Mr. Pericles should assist Mr. Pole in his business. He consented at once to everything. The next day he gave me the money, and I signed my name and pledged my honour to an engagement. My friends were relieved.

"It was then I began to think of you. I had not to study the matter long to learn that I did not love you: and I will not trust my own feelings as they come to me now. I judge myself by my acts, or, Merthyr! I should sink to the ground like a dead body when I think of separation from you for three years. But, what am I? I am a raw girl. I command nothing but raw and flighty hearts of men. Are they worth anything? Let me study three years, without any talk of hearts at all. It commenced too early, and has left nothing to me but a dreadful knowledge of the weakness in most people:—not in you!

"If I might call you my Beloved! and so chain myself to you, I think I should have all your firmness and double my strength. I will not; for I will not have what I do not deserve. I think of you reading this, till I try to get to you; my heart is like a bird caught in the hands of a cruel boy. By what I have done I know I do not love you. Must we half-despise a man to love him? May no dear woman that I know ever marry the man she first loves! My misery now is gladness, is like rain-drops on rising wings, if I say to myself 'Free! free, Emilia!' I am bound for three years, but I smile at such a bondage to my body. Evviva! my soul is free! Three years of freedom, and no sounding of myself—three years of growing, and studying; three years of idle heart!—Merthyr! I throb to think that those three years—true man! my hero, I may call you!—those three years may make me worthy of you. And if you have given all to Italy, that a daughter of Italy should help to return it, seems, my friend, so tenderly sweet—here is the first drop from my eyes!

"I would break what you call a Sentiment: I broke my word to Wilfrid. But this sight of money has a meaning that I cannot conquer. I know you would not wish me to for your own pleasure; and therefore I go. I hope to be growing; I fly like a seed to Italy. Let me drill, and take sharp words, and fret at trifles! I lift my face to that prospect as if I smelt new air. I am changeing—I have no dreams of Italy, no longings, but go to see her like a machine ready to do my work. Whoever speaks to me, I feel that I look at them and know them. I see the faults of my country—Oh, beloved Breseians! not yours, Florentines! nor yours, dear Venice! We will be silent when they speak of the Milanese, till Italy can say to them, 'That conduct is not Italian, my children.' I see the faults. Nothing vexes me.

"Addio! My friend, we will speak English in dear England! Tell all that I shall never forget England! My English Merthyr! the blood you have shed is not for a woman. The blood that you have shed, laurels spring from it! For a woman, the blood spilt is sickly and poor, and nourishes nothing. I shudder at the thought of one we knew. He makes Love seem like a yellow light over a plague-spotted city, like a painting I have seen. Goodbye to the name of Love for three years! My engagement to Mr. Pericles is that I am not to write, not to receive letters. To you I say now, trust me for three years! Merthyr's answer is already in my bosom. Beloved!—let me say it once—when the answer to any noble thing I might ask of you is in my bosom instantly, is not that as much as marriage? But be under no deception. See me as I am. Oh, good-bye! good-bye! Good-bye to you! Good-bye to England!

"I am,

"Most humbly and affectionately,

"Your friend,

"And her daughter by the mother's side,

"Emilia Alessandra Belloni."

George Meredith – A Concise Bibliography

Novels
The Shaving of Shagpat (1856)
Farina (1857)
The Ordeal of Richard Feverel (1859)
Evan Harrington (1861)
Emilia in England (1864), republished as Sandra Belloni in 1887
Rhoda Fleming (1865)
Vittoria (1867)
The Adventures of Harry Richmond (1871)
Beauchamp's Career (1875)
The House on the Beach (1877)
The Case of General Ople and Lady Camper (1877)
The Tale of Chloe (1879)
The Egoist (1879)
The Tragic Comedians (1880)
Diana of the Crossways (1885)
One of our Conquerors (1891)
Lord Ormont and his Aminta (1894)
The Amazing Marriage (1895)
Celt and Saxon (1910)

Poetry
Poems (1851)
Modern Love (1862)
The Lark Ascending (1881)
Poems and Lyrics of the Joy of Earth (1883)
The Woods of Westermain (1883)
A Faith on Trial (1885)
Ballads and Poems of Tragic Life (1887)
A Reading of Earth (1888)
The Empty Purse (1892)
Odes in Contribution to the Song of French History (1898)
A Reading of Life (1901)
Selected Poems of George Meredith (1903, author's supervision)
Last Poems (1909)

Essays
Essay on Comedy (1877)

www.ingramcontent.com/pod-product-compliance
Lightning Source LLC
Chambersburg PA
CBHW051528280626
47161CB00021B/426